The Babes in the Wood

Live Flesh

Ruth Rendell

arrow books

Published by Arrow Books in 2006

2 4 6 8 10 9 7 5 3 1

Babes in the Wood first published in the United Kingdom by Hutchinson
Live Flesh first published in the United Kingdom by Hutchinson

Arrow Books Limited
The Random House Group Limited
20 Vauxhall Bridge Road, London, SW1V 2SA

Random House Australia (Pty) Limited
20 Alfred Street, Milsons Point, Sydney,
New South Wales 2061, Australia

Random House New Zealand Limited
18 Poland Road, Glenfield
Auckland 10, New Zealand

Random House (Pty) Limited
Isle of Houghton, Corner of Boundary Road & Carse O'Gowrie,
Houghton 2198, South Africa

The Random House Group Limited Reg. No. 954009

www.randomhouse.co.uk

A CIP catalogue record for this book
is available from the British Library

Papers used by Random House are natural, recyclable products made from wood grown in sustainable forests. The manufacturing processes conform to the environmental regulations of the country of origin

ISBN 0 09 191531 7

Printed and bound in Great Britain by
Bookmarque Ltd, Croydon, Surrey

The Babes in the Wood

For Karl and Lilian Fredriksson
with love

Beforehand

It was warm enough to be outdoors at ten and not feel a chill. The sky was all covered with stars and the moon had come up among them, a reddish harvest moon. Where they were was a wood with a clearing in it broad enough for a thousand people to dance on, but its springiness came from the dense green turf and its walls were a ring of tall forest trees, beech and ash and chestnut. Because the leaves hadn't yet begun to fall the house, which wasn't far away, couldn't be seen. Nor could its outbuildings and its gardens.

In the centre of the open space the people, a hundred or so, had formed a circle. Most of them had no idea the house was there. They had come in mini-buses and vans and some in their own cars, down a lane which debouched from another lane, which led from a rather narrow road. Nothing at the entrance to the lane indicated whether this was private land or not and nothing gave a clue to the presence of the house. Some of the people wore the ordinary clothes favoured by the young and middle-aged alike and both sexes, jeans, a shirt, a sweater or jacket, but others were enveloped in robes, black or brown. They held hands and waited, expectant, perhaps excited.

A man dressed in white – open-necked white shirt, white trousers, white shoes – strode into the middle of the ring. When he reached the centre the people began to sing. It was a rousing tune which might have been a hymn or a chorus from an opera or musical. When it was done they clapped their hands rhythmically. The clapping ceased when the man in white spoke.

He called out in ringing tones, 'Are there any evil spirits tormenting you? Is there anyone here possessed by a bad spirit?'

The silence was deep. No one stirred. A little breeze rose and flitted across the circle, lifting long hair and making draperies flutter. It fell again as someone appeared within the ring. None of those holding hands, the singers, those who had clapped, could have told where the newcomer came from. No observer, even from close to, could have told if this was a man or a woman and no living person could be seen immediately behind it, yet it stumbled a little as if given a push. It was draped from neck to feet in a black robe and its head covered by a black veil. A cry went up from the man who had asked about evil spirits.

'Send your fire down, Lord, burn the evil spirits!'

'Burn, burn, burn!' cried the ring.

The man in white and the figure in black met. From a distance they looked like a pair of lovers in disguise, masked and cloaked figures from the Venice Carnival perhaps. It was growing darker now, thin cloud passing across the face of the moon. The priest and supplicant, if that is what they were, were close enough to touch but no one could see if they touched or not. Seeing was less important than hearing and suddenly there was much to hear as the black figure let out a long low wail, a keening moan, but louder than a moan, and followed by a series of such cries. They sounded real, not staged, they sounded as if they came from a distressed and anguished heart, a soul in torment, and now they rose and fell, rose and fell.

The white figure kept quite still. The ring of people began to shiver and sway from side to side and soon they too were moaning while some beat at their bodies with their hands or, in several cases, with twigs they picked up from the ground. They swayed and wailed and the cloud passed so that the moon came out once more and blazed on this ritual, bathing it in white fire. Then the figure in black also began to move. Not slowly as the people did but with swift movements that became frenzied as it beat with its hands not on its own body but on the chest and arms of the man in white. Its moans became growls and you could hear its teeth chattering as it growled.

Apparently oblivious of the violent assault made on him, the man in white raised his arms above his head. In the voice of some ancient priest he called, 'Confess your sins and wickedness!'

Then it came, a catalogue of errors, of commission and omission, some of it murmured, some of it uttered so that all could hear, the voice rising to a shout of desperation. The people were quiet, listening avidly. The confession went on but in less impassioned tones, dwindling until the creature in black was stammering, growing limp and cringing. Then there was silence broken only by a soft, almost sensual, sigh which rose from the crowd.

The priest spoke. He laid one hand on the black-cloaked shoulder and said in a ringing voice, 'Now come out of him!' There was no absolution, only that assured command: 'Come out of him!'

A cloud drifted across the moon, an event which evoked another sigh from the people, more perhaps a gasp of wonderment. A shudder passed through them as if a gust of wind had ruffled a field of corn.

'See the evil spirits, my children! See them in the

air flying across the moon! See Ashtaroth, the demon, she who dwells in the moon!'

'I see! I see!' came the cry from the ring of people. 'We see the demon Ashtaroth!'

'The creature that was their home has confessed to great sins of the flesh but she, the demon, the embodiment of fleshly sin, has come out, and with her those lesser spirits. See them high above us in the air now!'

'I see! I see!'

And at last the supplicant in black spoke. It was in a broken voice, weak and sexless. 'I see, I see . . .'

'Thanks be to the Lord God of Hosts!' cried the man in white. 'Thanks be to the Blessed Trinity and all angels!'

'Thanks be to the Lord!'

'Thanks be to the Lord and all angels,' said the figure in black.

Within moments it was in black no longer. Two women broke through the ring and came into the centre, bearing armfuls of white clothing. Then they dressed the black figure, covering it from head to foot until there were two in white.

The one who had been black called aloud but in misery no longer, 'Thanks be to the Lord who has delivered his servant from sin and restored purity once more.'

The words were scarcely uttered when the dance began. The two white figures were swallowed up in the crowd as someone made music, a tune coming from somewhere, a melody like a Scottish reel that at the same time, strangely, was a hymn. They danced and clapped. A woman had a tambourine and another a zither. The figure who had sinned and been redeemed and purified stood in the midst of them, laughing a merry laugh like someone enjoying himself at a children's party. There was nothing to eat, nothing to smoke and nothing to drink, but they were drunk on fervour, on excitement, on the hysteria which comes when many are gathered together in a single belief, a single passion. And the one who was absolved continued to laugh peal after peal, merry and joyful as a child.

The dance lasted for half an hour but ceased when the music was withdrawn. It was a signal for departure and everyone, suddenly subdued once more, moved back to the lane where vehicles were parked on the grass verge.

The priest figure, who had come alone, waited until the people had gone before stripping off his robes and emerging as an ordinary man in jeans and combat jacket. The robes he put into the boot of his car. Then he walked down the drive to the house. It was large by present-day standards, early Victorian, with two shallow flights of stairs mounting to a front door inside a modestly pillared portico, and a balustrade bordering its slate roof, a house that was pleasing to look at if rather dull. There are hundreds, if not thousands, like it all over England. Plainly, no one was at home, but no one would be on a week night. He mounted the steps on the left-hand side, took an envelope from his pocket and slipped it through the letter box. He lived in straitened circumstances like most of his flock and wanted to save the cost of postage.

The owner of the house and grounds had asked for a fee. Naturally, though he was a rich man. But the priest, if priest he was, had jibbed at two hundred pounds and they had finally agreed on a hundred. The envelope also held a note of thanks. The people might want to make use of the open space again, as they had done several times in the past. The priest always referred to it as 'the open space', though he had heard it called the dancing floor, a name he thought had an idolatrous ring to it.

He went back to his car.

Chapter 1

The Kingsbrook was not usually visible from his window. Not its course, nor its twisty meanders, nor the willows which made a double fringe along its banks. But he could see it now, or rather see what it had become, a river as wide as the Thames but flat and still, a broad lake that filled its own valley, submerging its water meadows in a smooth silver sheet. Of the few houses that stood in that valley, along a lane which had disappeared leading from a bridge which had disappeared, only their roofs and upper storeys showed above the waters. He thought of his own house, on the other side of that gently rising lake, as yet clear of the floods, only the end of his garden lapped by an encroaching tide.

It was raining. But as he had remarked to Burden some four hours before, rain was no longer news, it was tedious to remark on it. The exciting thing worthy of comment was when it wasn't raining. He picked up the phone and called his wife.

'Much the same as when you went out,' she said. 'The end of the garden's under water but it hasn't reached the mulberry tree. I don't think it's moved. That's what I'm measuring by, the mulberry tree.'

'Good thing we don't breed silkworms,' said Wexford, leaving his wife to decipher this cryptic remark.

There hadn't been anything like it in this part of Sussex in living memory – not, at least, in his memory. In spite of a double wall of sandbags the Kingsbrook had inundated the road at the High Street bridge, flooded the Job Centre and Sainsbury's but miraculously – so far – spared the Olive and Dove Hotel. It was a hilly place and most of the dwellings on higher ground had escaped. Not so the High Street, Glebe Road, Queen and York Streets with their ancient shopfronts and overhanging eaves. Here the water lay a foot, two feet, in places three feet, deep. In St Peter's churchyard the tops of tombstones pierced a grey, rain-punctured lake like rocks showing above the surface of the sea. And still it rained.

According to the Environment Agency, the land in the flood plains of England and Wales was saturated, was waterlogged, so that none of this latest onslaught could drain away. There were houses in Kingsmarkham, and even more in flatter low-lying Pomfret, which had been flooded in October and were flooded again now at the end of November. Newspapers helpfully informed their readers that such 'properties' would be unsaleable, worth nothing. Their owners had left them weeks ago, gone to stay with relatives or in temporarily rented flats. The local authority had used up all the ten thousand sandbags it had ordered, scoffing at the possibility of half of them being used. Now they were all under the waters and more had been sent for but not arrived.

Wexford tried not to think about what would happen if another inch of rain fell before nightfall and the water reached and passed Dora's gauge, the mulberry. On the house side of the tree, from that point, the land sloped very gradually downwards until it came to a low wall, quite useless as a flood defence, that separated lawn from terrace and french windows. He tried not to think about it but still he pictured the water reaching and then pouring over that wall . . . Once more he reached for the phone but this time he only touched the receiver and withdrew his hand as the door opened and Burden came in.

'Still raining,' he said.

Wexford just looked at him, the kind of look you'd give something you'd found at the back of the fridge with a sell-by date of three months before.

'I've just heard a crazy thing, thought it might amuse you. You look as if you need cheering up.' He seated himself on the corner of the desk, a favourite perch. Wexford thought he was thinner than ever and looked rather as if he'd just had a facelift, total body massage and three weeks at a health farm. 'Woman phoned to say she and her husband went to Paris for the weekend, leaving their children with a – well, a teen-sitter, I suppose, got back late last night to find the lot gone and naturally she assumes they've all drowned.'

'That's amusing?'

'It's pretty bizarre, isn't it? The teenagers are fifteen and thirteen, the sitter's in her thirties, they can all swim and the house is miles above the floods.'

'Where is it?'

'Lyndhurst Drive.'

'Not far from me then. But miles above the floods. The water's slowly creeping up my garden.'

Burden put one leg across the other and swung his elegantly shod foot in negligent fashion. 'Cheer up. It's worse in the Brede Valley. Not a single house has escaped.' Wexford had a vision of buildings growing legs and running, pursued by an angry tide. 'Jim Pemberton has gone up there. Lyndhurst Drive, I mean. And he's alerted the Subaqua Task Force.'

'The *what*?'

'You must have heard of it.' Burden just avoided saying 'even you'. 'It's the joint enterprise of Kingsmarkham Council and the Fire Brigade. Mostly volunteers in wetsuits.'

'If it's amusing,' said Wexford, 'that is to say, if we aren't taking it seriously, why such extreme measures?'

'No harm in being on the safe side,' said Burden comfortably.

'All right, let me get this straight. These children – what are they, by the way? Boy and girl? And what's their name?'

'Dade. They're called Giles and Sophie Dade. I don't know the sitter's name. They can both swim. In fact, the boy's got some sort of silver medal for life-saving and the girl just missed getting into the county junior swimming team. God knows why the mother thinks they've drowned. They'd no reason to go near the floods as far as I know. Jim'll get it sorted.'

Wexford said no more. The rain had begun beating against the glass. He got up and went to the window but by the time he got there it was raining so hard that there was nothing to see, just a white fog and, near at hand, raindrops exploding on the sill. 'Where are you going to eat?' he said to Burden.

'Canteen, I suppose. I'm not going out in this.'

Pemberton came back at three to say that a couple of volunteer frogmen had begun searching for Giles and Sophie Dade but it was more a formality, an allaying of Mrs Dade's fears, than a genuine anxiety. None of the water lying in the Kingsmarkham area had reached a depth of four feet. It was over in the Brede Valley that things were more serious. A woman who couldn't swim had been drowned there a month before when she fell from the temporary walkway that had been built from one of her upper windows to the higher ground. She had tried to cling to the walkway struts but the floods came over her head and the rain and wind swept her away. Nothing like that could have happened to the Dade children, competent swimmers to whom twice the present depth of water would have presented no problems.

More a cause for concern in everyone's view was the looting currently going on from shops in the flooded High Street. A good many shopkeepers had removed their goods, clothes, books, magazines and stationery, china and glass, kitchen equipment to an upper floor and then removed themselves. Looters waded through the water by night – some of them carrying ladders – smashed upper windows and helped themselves to what they fancied. One thief, arrested by Detective Sergeant Vine, protested that the iron and microwave oven he had stolen were his by right. In his view, the goods were compensation for his ground-floor flat being inundated, he was sure he would get no other. Vine suspected that a bunch of teenagers, still at school, were responsible for stealing the entire CD and cassette stock from the York Audio Centre.

Wexford would have liked to check with his wife every half-hour but he controlled himself and didn't phone again until half past four. By then the heavy rain had given place to a thin relentless drizzle. The phone rang and rang, and he had almost decided she must be out when she picked up the receiver.

'I was outside. I heard it ringing but I had to get my boots off and try not to make too much mess. Rain and mud make the simplest outdoor tasks take twice as long.'

'How's the mulberry tree?'

'The water's reached it, Reg. It's sort of lapping against the trunk. Well, it was bound to, the way it's been raining. I was wondering if there was anything we could do to stop it, the water coming up, I mean, not the rain. They haven't found a way to stop that yet. I was thinking about sandbags, only the council haven't any, I phoned them and this woman said they're waiting for them to come in. Like a shop assistant, I thought.'

He laughed, though not very cheerfully. 'We can't stop the water but we can start thinking about moving our furniture upstairs.' Get Neil over to help, he nearly said, and then he remembered his son-in-law was gone out of their lives since he and Sylvia split up. Instead he told Dora he'd be home by six.

That morning he hadn't brought the car. Lately he'd been walking a lot more. The almost endless downpours stimulated his need to walk – there was human nature for you! – because the chance to do so in comfort and in the dry came so seldom. At first light no rain had been falling and the sky was a wet pearly blue. It was still dry at eight thirty and he'd begun to walk. Huge heavy clouds were gathering, covering up the blue and the pale, milky sun. By the time he reached the station the first drops were falling. Now he thought he would have to make it home through this wet mist that intermittently became drizzle, but when he came out of the newly installed automatic doors the rain had lifted and for the first time for a long while he felt a marked chill in the air. It *smelt* drier. It smelt like a change in the weather. Better not be too optimistic, he told himself.

It was dark. Already dark as midnight. From this level, on foot, he could see nothing of the floods, only that the pavements and roadways were wet and puddles lay deep in the gutters. He crossed the High Street and began the slightly uphill walk to home. The Dades he had forgotten and wouldn't have recalled them even then but for passing the end of Kingston Gardens and reading the street name in the yellow light from a lamp. Lyndhurst Drive met it at its highest point and those living there could have looked down from their windows on to his roof and his garden. They were safe.

Someone had told him that for the floods to reach such a height they would have had first to rise above the cupola on Kingsmarkham Town Hall.

Yes, the Dades were safe up there. And the chance of their children being drowned practically nil. Before he left, a message had come through from the Subaqua Task Force to say that no living people or bodies had been found. Wexford stared up the hill, wondering exactly where they lived. And then he stopped dead. What was the matter with him? Was he losing his grip on things? Those children might not have drowned but they were missing, weren't they? Their parents had come home from a weekend away and found them gone. Last night. All this nonsense about floods and drowning had obscured for him the central issue. Two children, aged fifteen and thirteen, were *missing*.

He walked on fast, thinking fast. Of course, the chances were that they were back by now. They had been, according to Burden, in the care of an older person, and they were all three missing. That surely meant that the sitter, presumably a woman, had taken them somewhere. Probably she had told the mother on the previous Friday or whenever it was the parents went away, that she intended to take them on some outing and the mother had forgotten. A woman who would assume that her children had drowned, just because they weren't there and part of the town was flooded, had to be – well, to put it charitably, somewhat scatterbrained.

Dora wasn't in the house. He found her down the garden, directing the beam from a torch on to the roots of the mulberry tree. 'I don't think it's come up any more since I spoke to you at four thirty,' she said. 'Do we really have to move the furniture?'

They went indoors. 'We could shift some of the stuff we value most. Books. Favourite pictures. That console table that was your mother's. We could make a start with that and listen to the weather forecast at ten.'

He gave her a drink and poured one for himself. With the much-diluted whisky on the table beside him, he phoned Burden. The inspector said, 'I was about to call you. It just struck me. The Dade kids, they must be missing.'

'I had the same thought. Still, correction: they *may* be missing. Who knows but that their sitter's just brought them back from an educational trip to Leeds Castle?'

'Which started yesterday, Reg?'

'No, you're right. Look, we have to find out. The last thing they'd do is let us know if they've turned up safe. We're strictly reserved for disasters. If these children still haven't turned up the parents, or one of them, will have to come down to the station and fill in a missing persons form and give us a bit more information. No need for you to do it. Get Karen on to it, she hasn't been exactly crushed with toil lately.'

'I'd like to call the Dades before I do anything,' Burden said.

'And ring me back, would you?'

He sat at the table and he and Dora had their dinner. The letter box flapped as the evening paper, the *Kingsmarkham Evening Courier*, arrived.

'It's too bad,' Dora said. 'It's nearly eight o'clock, two hours late.'

'Understandable in the circumstances, don't you think?'

'Oh, I suppose so. I shouldn't complain. I expect the poor newsagent had to bring it himself. Surely he wouldn't let that girl go out in this.'

'Girl?'

'It's his daughter delivers the papers. Didn't you

know? I suppose she does look rather like a boy in those jeans and that woolly cap.'

They kept the curtains at the french windows drawn back so that they could see if the rain started again and see too the tide of flood which had crept perhaps six feet across the lawn since last night. One of the neighbours, his garden elevated a few inches above the Wexfords', but enough, enough, had an Edwardian street lamp at the bottom of his lawn and tonight the light was on, a powerful white radiance that revealed the water lying gleaming and still. It was a shining grey colour, like a sheet of slate and the little river, somewhere down there, was lost in the broad shallow lake. It was weeks since Wexford had seen the stars and he couldn't see them now, only the bright but hazy lamplight below and a scurrying clotted mass across the sky where the rising wind agitated the clouds. Black leafless tree branches bowed and swayed. One swept the surface of the water, sending up spray like a car driving through a puddle.

'Do you want to start moving stuff now?' Dora asked when they had finished their coffee. 'Or do you want to see this?'

He shook his head, rejecting the paper which seemed to hold nothing but photographs of floods. 'We'll move the books and that cabinet. No more till we've seen the weather forecast.'

The phone rang as he was carrying the sixth and last cardboard box of books upstairs. Luckily, most of his books were already on the upper floor, in the little room they had once called his study and now was more like a mini-library. Dora took the call while he set the box down on the top stair.

'It's Mike.'

Wexford took the receiver from her. 'I've a feeling they haven't turned up.'

'No. The Subaqua Task Force want to resume the search tomorrow. They've got some idea of going under the deep water in the Brede Valley. They've not much to do and I think they like the excitement.'

'And Mr and Mrs Dade?'

'I didn't phone, Reg, I went up there,' said Burden. 'They're a funny pair. She cries.'

'She what?'

'She cries all the time. It's weird. It's pathological.'

'Is that right, doctor? And what does he do?'

'He's just rude. Oh, and he seems to be a workaholic, never an idle moment. He said he was going back to work while I was there. The kids are definitely missing. Their dad says it's all rubbish about them drowning. Why would they go near floodwater in the depths of winter? Who got hold of this ridiculous idea? His wife said she did and started crying. Jim Pemberton suggested maybe they went in the water to rescue someone else but in that case, who? The only other person to go missing is this Joanna Troy . . .'

'Who?'

'She's the friend of Mrs Dade who was spending the weekend in their house to keep an eye on the two kids. Dade's doing the missing persons forms now.' Burden's voice took on a hesitant tone. Perhaps he was remembering the heartfelt note in Wexford's voice when he expressed a wish not to get involved. 'As it happens, things are a bit more serious than they seemed at first. The Dades got home from Paris – they came in through Gatwick – a little while after midnight. The house was in darkness, the children's bedroom doors were shut, and the parents just went to bed without checking. Well, I suppose they wouldn't check. After all, Giles is fifteen and Sophie is thirteen. It wasn't till mid-morning that Mrs Dade found the kids weren't there. And that means not only that they've been missing since Sunday midnight but possibly since Friday evening when the parents left.'

'And this Joanna Whatever?'

'Troy. Mrs Dade's been phoning her home number all day without getting a reply and Dade went round there this afternoon but no one was there.'

'It doesn't seem to matter whether I sincerely hope or don't bother,' said Wexford wearily. 'But we'll leave it all till tomorrow.'

Burden, who could be sententious, said cheerfully that tomorrow was another day.

'You're right there, Scarlett. Tomorrow will be another day, always providing Dora and I haven't been drowned during the night. But I dare say we'll be able to get out of the bedroom windows.'

He had been watching for more rain as he was speaking and the first drops had splashed against the glass midway through his last sentence. He put the receiver back and opened the front door. It was milder out there than he could ever remember for the time of year. Even the wind was warm. It had brought with it the next downpour and the rain increased in intensity as he watched, straight-down rain like glass or steel rods crashing on to the stone flags and splashing into the waterlogged gullies between them. The down-flow pipe from the roof gutters began to pour out water like a tap turned full on and the drain, unable to cope with so great a volume, was soon lost under an eddying flood of its own.

Dora was watching the news. It ended as he came in and the weather forecast began with its typical irritating preamble: a kind of improbably glamorous creature in the guise of a water sprite and a silver lamé designer gown, sitting on top of a fountain while a concealed fan blew her hair and draperies about. The meteorologist, an altogether more normal sort of woman, pointing with a ferrule at her map, told them of flood warnings out on four new rivers and an area of low pressure rushing across the Atlantic in pursuit of the one presently affecting the United Kingdom. By morning, she said, as if this wasn't true already, heavy rain would be falling across southern England.

Wexford turned it off. He and Dora stood at the french windows looking at the water which now, as in the front garden, filled the paved area immediately outside. The rain made little waves on its surface where a twig bobbed about like a boat on a choppy sea. The trunk of the mulberry tree was half submerged and it was now a lilac bush which had become the criterion. The rising water lapped its roots. A few yards of dry land remained before the incoming tide would reach the wall. As he watched, the light at the end of the garden next door went out and the whole scene was plunged into darkness.

He went up the stairs to bed. The possibility of two young proficient swimmers being drowned no longer seemed to him so absurd. You didn't need too much imagination to fancy the whole country sinking and vanishing under this vast superfluity of water. Everyone overcome by it like shipwrecked men, their raft inadequate, their strength gone, the young and the old alike, the strong and the weak.

Chapter 2

So much for not getting involved. He was on his way there now, heading up Kingston Gardens towards Lyndhurst Drive, with Vine who was driving. Vine seemed to think drowning in the Brede Valley, particularly in the very deep water now filling Savesbury Deeps, where the frogmen had begun searching again, a real possibility. The night before he had thought so himself. Now, with the sun shining on wet pavements and glittering dripping branches, he wasn't so sure.

Three hours earlier, when he got up, the rain had apparently just stopped. It was still dark but light enough to see what had happened during the night. He didn't look out of the window. Not then. He was afraid of what he might see, and even more afraid, when he went down to make Dora's tea, of the water waiting for him at the foot of the stairs or lying, still and placid, across the kitchen floor. But the house was dry and when he had put the kettle on and at last made himself pull back the curtains and look out of the french windows, he saw that the silvery grey lake still stopped some ten feet from the little wall that divided lawn from paving.

Since then there had been no more rain. The weather forecast had been right as far as the coming of a further downpour but wrong in its timing. There was still the second approaching area of low pressure to look forward to. As he got out of the car at the point where Kingston Gardens met Lyndhurst Drive, a large drop of water fell on to his head, on to his bald spot, from a hollybush by the gate.

The house on the corner was called 'Antrim', a name neither pretentious nor apparently appropriate. Unlike any other in Lyndhurst Drive, where neo-Georgian sat side by side with nineteen thirties art deco, nineteen sixties functional, eighteen nineties Gothic and late-twentieth-century 'Victorian', the Dades' house was Tudor, so well done that the undiscerning might have mistaken it for the real thing. Beams of stripped oak criss-crossed slightly darker plaster, the windows were diamond-paned and the front door heavily studded. The knocker was the ubiquitous lion's head and the bellpull a twisty wrought-iron rod. Wexford pulled it.

The woman who came to the door was very obviously the anxious mother, her face tear-stained. She was thin, wispy and breathless. Early forties, he thought. Rather pretty, her face unpainted, her hair a mass of untidy brown curls. But it was one of those faces on which years of stress and yielding to that stress show in its lines and tensions. As she led them into a living room a man came out. He was very tall, a couple of inches taller than Wexford, which would make him six feet five, his head too small for his body.

'Roger Dade,' he said brusquely and in a public school accent which sounded as if he purposely exaggerated it. 'My wife.'

Wexford introduced himself and Vine. The Tudor style was sustained inside the house where there was a great deal of carved woodwork, gargoyles on the stone fireplace (containing a modern, unlit gas fire), paisley pattern wallpaper and lamps of wrought iron and parchment painted with indecipherable ancient glyphs. The top of the coffee table round which they sat held, under glass, a map of the world as it was known in, say, fifteen fifty, with dragons and tossing galleons. Its choppy seas reminded Wexford of his back garden. He asked the Dades to tell him about the weekend and to begin at the beginning.

The children's mother began, making much use of her hands. 'We hadn't been away on our own, my husband and I, since our honeymoon. Can you believe that? We were desperate just to get away without the children. When I think of that now, I feel just so guilty I can't tell you. A hundred times since then I've bitterly regretted even thinking like that.'

Her husband, looking as if going away with her was the last thing he had been desperate to do, sighed and cast up his eyes. 'You've nothing to be guilty about, Katrina. Give it a rest, for God's sake.'

At this the tears had come into her eyes and she made no effort to restrain them. Like the water outside, they welled and burst their banks, trickling down her cheeks as she gulped and swallowed. As if it were a gesture which he was more than accustomed to perform, as automatic as turning off a tap or closing a door, Roger Dade pulled a handful of tissues from a box on the table and passed them to her. The box was contained in another of polished wood with brass fittings, evidently as essential a part of the furnishings as a magazine or CD rack might be in another household. Katrina Dade wore a blue crossover garment. A skimpy dressing gown or something a fashionable woman would wear in the daytime? To his amusement, he could see Vine doing his best to avert his eyes from the bare expanse of thigh she showed when the front of the blue thing parted.

'But what's the use?' The tears roughened her voice and half choked it. 'We can't put the clock back, can we? What time did we leave on Friday,

Roger? You know how hopeless I am about things like that.'

Roger Dade indeed looked as if, with varying degrees of impatience and exasperation, he had borne years of unpunctuality, forgetfulness and a sublime indifference to time. 'About half past two,' he said. 'Our flight was four thirty from Gatwick.'

'You went by car?' Vine asked.

'Oh, yes, I drove.'

'Where were the children at this time?' Wexford had directed his eyes on to Dade and hoped he would answer but he was to be disappointed.

'At school, of course. Where else? They're quite used to letting themselves into the house. They wouldn't have to be on their own for long. Joanna was coming over at five.'

'Yes. Joanna. Who exactly is she?'

'My absolutely dearest closest friend. That's what makes all this so awful, that she's missing too. And I don't even know if she can swim. I've never had any reason to know. Perhaps she never learned. Suppose she couldn't and she fell into the water, and Giles and Sophie plunged into the water to save her and they all . . .'

'Don't get in a state,' said Dade as the tears bubbled up afresh. 'You're not helping with all this blubbing.' Wexford had never actually heard the word used before, only seen it in print years before in boys' school stories, old-fashioned even when he read them. Dade looked from one police officer to the other. 'I'll take over,' he said. 'I'd better if we're to get anywhere.'

She shouted at him, 'I want to do the talking! I can't help crying. Isn't it natural for a woman whose children have drowned to be crying? What do you expect?'

'Your children haven't drowned, Katrina. You're

being hysterical as usual. If you want to tell them what happened, just do it. Get on with it.'

'Where was I? Oh, yes, in Paris.' Her voice had steadied a little. She pulled down the blue garment and sat up straight. 'We phoned them from Paris, from the hotel. It was eight thirty. I mean, it was eight thirty French time, seven thirty for them. I just don't understand why Europe has to be a whole hour ahead of us. Why do they have to be different?' No one supplied her with an answer. 'I mean we're all in the Common Market or the Union or whatever they call it, the name's always changing. We're supposed to be all the same.' She caught her husband's eye. 'Yes, all right, all right. We phoned them, like I said, and Giles answered. He said everything was fine, he and Sophie had been doing their homework. Joanna was there and they were going to have their supper and watch TV. I wasn't worried – why should I be?'

This too was obviously a rhetorical question. To Wexford, although he had been in her company only half an hour, it seemed inconceivable that she would ever be free from worry. She was one of those people who manufacture anxieties if none naturally occur. Her face puckered once more and he was afraid she was going to begin crying but she went on with her account.

'I phoned again next day at the same sort of time but nobody answered. I mean not a real person. The answering machine did. I thought maybe they were all watching something on television or that Giles had gone out and Joanna and Sophie weren't expecting me to call. I hadn't *said* I'd call. I left the number of the hotel – not that they didn't have that already – and I thought they might have called me back but they never did.'

Vine intervened. 'You said you thought your son might have gone out, Mrs Dade. Where would he go?

Somewhere with his mates? Cinema? Too young for clubbing, I expect.'

A glance passed between husband and wife. Wexford couldn't interpret it. Katrina Dade said, as if she were skirting round the subject, avoiding a direct reply, 'He wouldn't go to the cinema or a club. He isn't that sort of boy. Besides, my husband wouldn't allow it. Absolutely not.'

Dade put in swiftly, 'Children have too much freedom these days. They've had too much for years now. I did myself and I know it had an adverse effect on me for a long time. Until I dealt with it, that is, until I disciplined myself. If Giles went out he'd have gone to church. They sometimes have a service on Saturday evening. But in fact, last weekend it was on the Sunday morning. I checked before we left.'

Most parents in these degenerate times, thought Wexford, who was an atheist, would be gratified to know that their fifteen-year-old son had been to a church service rather than to some kind of popular entertainment. Never mind the religious aspect. No drugs in church, no AIDS, no predatory girls. But Dade was looking unhappy, his expression at best resigned.

'What church would that be?' Wexford asked. 'St Peter's? The Roman Catholics?'

'They call themselves the Church of the Good Gospel,' said Dade. 'They use the old hall in York Street, the one the Catholics used to have before their new church was built. God knows, I'd rather he went to the C of E but any church is better than none.' He hesitated, said almost aggressively, 'Why do you want to know?'

Vine spoke in an equable calming tone. 'It might be a good idea to find out if Giles did actually go there on Sunday, don't you think?'

'Oh, possibly.' Dade was a man who liked to

provide ideas, not receive them from some other source. He glanced at his watch, frowning. 'All this is making me late,' he said.

'Shall we hear about the rest of the weekend?' Wexford glanced from Dade to his wife and back again.

This time, Katrina Dade was silent, making only a petulant gesture and sniffing. Roger said, 'We didn't phone on the Sunday because we were going back in the evening.'

'That night, rather,' said Vine. 'You were very late.' He probably didn't mean to sound severe.

'Are you trying to insinuate something? Because if you are I'd like to know what it is. May I remind you that you're to *find my missing children*, not find fault with my conduct.'

Soothingly, Wexford said, 'No one is insinuating anything, Mr Dade. Will you go on, please?'

Dade looked at him, curling his lip. 'The flight was delayed nearly three hours. Something to do with water on the runways at Gatwick. And then they took half an hour getting the bags off. It was just after midnight when we got home.'

'And you took it for granted everyone was in bed and asleep?'

'Not everyone,' said Katrina. 'Joanna wasn't staying that night. She was due to go home on Sunday evening. They could be alone for a little while. Giles is nearly sixteen. We all thought – everyone thought – we'd be home by nine.'

'But you didn't phone home from the airport?'

'I'd have told you if we had,' snapped Dade. 'It would have been after ten thirty and I like my children to be in bed at a reasonable hour. They need their sleep if they're to do their school work.'

'What difference would it have made if we had phoned?' This was Katrina, sniffling. 'The answerphone was still on. Roger checked yesterday morning.'

'You went straight to bed?'

'We were exhausted. The children's bedroom doors were shut. We didn't look inside if that's what you mean. They're not babies to be checked up on every moment. In the morning I had a lie-in. My husband went off to the office at the crack of dawn, of course. I woke up and it was gone nine. It was unbelievable, I haven't overslept like that for years, not since I was a teenager myself, it was incredible.' Katrina's speech quickened in pace, the words tumbling over one another. 'Of course, my first thought was that the children had to go to school. I hadn't heard them, I'd been so deeply asleep. I thought, they'll have got up, they'll have gone, but as soon as I got up myself I knew they hadn't. You could tell no one had used the bathroom, their beds were made, something they never do, and it looked as if someone who knew what she was doing had made them. Joanna, obviously. There was no mess, everything was tidy – I mean, it was *unknown*.'

'You must have tried to find out where they were,' Wexford said. 'Phoned round friends and relatives? Did you phone the school?'

'I phoned my husband and he did, though we knew they weren't there. And they weren't. Of course they weren't. Then he phoned his mother. God knows why. For some unaccountable reason that's quite beyond me the children seem fond of her. But he drew a complete blank. The same with the children's friends' parents – those we could get hold of, that is. So many mothers aren't content to be homemakers, are they? They must have careers as well. Anyway, none of them knew a thing.'

Vine said, 'Did you try to get in touch with Ms Troy?'

Katrina Dade stared at him as if he'd uttered some extreme obscenity. 'Well, of course we did. *Of course.* That was the first thing we did. Before we even phoned the school. There was no answer – well, her answerphone was on.'

'I was obliged to come home,' Dade said, implying it was the last place he wanted to be. 'I went over to her house. No one was there. I went next door and the woman there said she hadn't seen Joanna since Friday.'

That meant very little. A neighbour isn't always aware of the comings and goings of the people next door. Wexford said, 'And then?'

Katrina had assumed the vacant look and glazed eyes of a member of the local drama group playing Lady Macbeth in the sleepwalking scene. 'It was while my husband was out that I looked out of the window. I hadn't looked out before. I saw a devastating sight. You can see all the floods from here, like a great sea, an *ocean.* I could hardly believe my eyes but I had to, I had to. That was when I knew my children must be out there somewhere.'

In the calmest, steadiest voice he could muster, Wexford said, 'The frogmen have resumed their search, Mrs Dade, but what you suggest is very unlikely. The floods are quite a distance from here and nowhere in Kingsmarkham are they more than four feet deep. The search has moved to the Brede Valley, three miles away at the nearest point. Unless Giles and Sophie are great walkers or Ms Troy is, I find it hard to see why they should go near the Brede.'

'None of them would walk anywhere if they could help it,' said Dade.

Katrina looked as if he had betrayed her and she withdrew her hand. 'Then where are they?' she appealed to the two policemen. 'What has become of them?' Then came the question Wexford had been anticipating, the question that always came from a parent in this sort of situation, and came early, 'What are you doing about it?'

'First we'll need some help from you, Mrs Dade,' said Vine. 'Photographs of Giles and Sophie for a start. And a description. Some background – what sort of people they are.' He glanced at Wexford.

'A photograph of Ms Troy as well, if possible,' the Chief Inspector said. 'And we have a few more questions. How did Ms Troy get here on Friday evening? By car?'

'Of course.' Dade was looking at him as if he'd questioned Joanna Troy's possession of legs or as if every normal person knew human beings were born with motor vehicles attached, as it might be hair or noses. 'Naturally, she came by car. Look, is this going to go on much longer? I'm late as it is.'

'Where is her car now? Has she a garage at home?'

'No. She leaves it parked on a kind of drive or pad in front of the house.'

'And was it there?'

'No, it wasn't.' Dade began to look a little ashamed of his recent scorn. 'Would you like her address? I don't know if we have a photograph?'

'Of course we have a photograph.' His wife was shaking her head in apparent wonder. 'Not have a photograph of my very dearest friend? Darling, how could you think that?'

How he could Dade didn't explain. He went into another room and came back with two photographs which he removed from their silver frames. They were of the children, not their sitter. The girl looked like neither parent. Her features were classical, almost sharp, her nose Roman, her eyes very dark, her hair nearly black. The boy was better-looking than Roger Dade, his features more nearly corresponding to a classical ideal, but he looked as if he also might be tall.

'Just topping six feet,' said Dade proudly as if reading Wexford's thoughts. Katrina had fallen silent. Her husband glanced at her, went on, 'You can see they've both got dark eyes. Giles has fairer hair. I don't know what else I can tell you.'

Some time, thought Wexford, you can explain what makes a good-looking, tall and far from deprived fifteen-year-old join something called the Good Gospel Church. But perhaps you won't have to, perhaps we'll have found them before that's necessary. 'Do you know', he said to Katrina Dade, 'the names of any close relatives of Ms Troy?'

She was speaking dully now, though still far from naturally. 'Her father. Her mother's dead and he's married again.' She got up, moving like a woman recovering from a long and serious illness. She opened a drawer in a desk designed to look as if made for a contemporary of Shakespeare, lifted out a thick leather-bound album and extracted from one of its grey, gilt-ornamented pages a photograph of a young woman. Still slow and somnambulant, she handed it to Wexford. 'Her father lives at 28 Forest Road, if you know where that is.'

The last street in the district to bear the postal address Kingsmarkham. It turned directly off the Pomfret road and the houses in it would very likely have a pleasant view of Cheriton Forest. Katrina Dade was sitting down again but on a buttoned and swagged sofa, beside her husband, who was making an exasperated face. Wexford concentrated on the picture of Joanna Troy. The first thing that struck him was her youth. He had assumed she would be the same sort of age as Katrina but this woman looked years younger, a girl still.

'When was this taken?'

'Last year.'

Well. Of course it was true that many people had friends a lot older or a lot younger than themselves. He wondered how these women had met. Joanna Troy looked confident and in control rather than handsome. Her short straight hair was fair, her eyes perhaps grey, it was hard to tell. Her skin was the fresh pink and white that used to be called a 'real English complexion'. Somehow he could tell she would never be very clothes-conscious, but rather a jeans and sweater woman when she could get away with it, though the photograph showed nothing of her below the shoulders. He was asking himself if there were any more questions he need put to the Dades at this stage when a shattering scream brought him to his feet. Vine also leapt up. Katrina Dade, her head back and her neck stretched, her fists pumping the air, was shrieking and yelling at the top of her lungs.

Dade tried to put his arms round her. She fought him off and continued to make some of the loudest screams Wexford had ever heard, as loud as children in supermarket aisles, as loud as his granddaughter Amulet at her most wilful. Seldom at a loss as to what to do, he was almost flummoxed. Perhaps the woman's face should be slapped – that used to be the sovereign remedy – but if so, if that wasn't about as politically incorrect as could be, he wasn't going to be the one to do it. He beckoned to Vine and they moved as far from the screaming Katrina and her ineffectual husband as they could get, standing by a pair of french windows that gave on to a terraced garden and then to the floods below.

Katrina having subsided into sobs, Dade said, 'Would you get me a glass of water, please?'

Vine shrugged but went to fetch it. He watched Katrina choke over the water, dodged out of the way before she hurled the remaining contents in his direction. This action seemed to relieve her feelings and she laid her head back against a cushion. Wexford took advantage of the silence to tell Dade they would like to have a look at the children's rooms.

'I can't leave her, can I? You'll have to find them yourselves. Look, as soon as she shuts up I have to get off to work. All right with you, is it? I have your permission?'

'Rude bugger, isn't he?' Vine said when they were on the stairs.

'He's got a lot to put up with.' Wexford grinned. 'You have to make allowances. I can't really believe anything much has happened to these kids. Maybe I should, maybe it's their mother's behaviour making me think none of this is quite real. I could be entirely wrong and we have to act as if I am.'

'Isn't it because there are three of them, sir? It's harder to believe in three people disappearing. Unless they're hostages, of course.' Vine was remembering that Wexford's wife had been one of the hostages in the Kingsmarkham bypass affair. 'But these three aren't, are they?'

'I doubt it.'

It was probably mention of the bypass abductions which reminded Wexford that sooner or later the media were going to have to know about this. He remembered last time with a shudder, the intrusion into his own privacy, the continued onslaughts of Brian St George, editor of the *Kingsmarkham Courier*, the embargoes he could barely enforce. Then there had been the furore over that one-time paedophile and poor Hennessy's death . . .

'This is the boy's room, sir,' Vine was saying. 'Someone certainly tidied it and it wasn't a fifteen-year-old, not even a religious maniac.'

'I'm not sure we should brand him like that, Barry.

Not at this stage. You might feel like going along to the old Catholic Church after we've left here and get some background on these Good Gospel people, not to mention whether the boy went to church on Sunday or not.'

If there are any two features which distinguish a teenager's bedroom from anyone else's, it must be the presence of posters on the walls and a means of playing music. These days, too, a computer with Internet access and a printer, and these last Giles Dade had, though the posters and player were absent. Almost absent. Instead of a recommendation for a pop group, endangered species rescue or soccer star, the wall facing Giles's bed had tacked to it an unframed life-size reproduction Wexford recognised as Constable's painting of *Christ Blessing the Bread and Wine.*

Perhaps it was only because he didn't, couldn't, believe that he found this distasteful. Not because of what it was, though Constable's genius found its best expression in landscape, but *where* it was and who had put it there. He wondered what Dora, a church-goer, would say. He'd ask her. Vine was looking inside a clothes cupboard at what both of them would have expected to find there, jeans, shirts, T-shirts, a pea jacket and a school blazer, dark-brown, bordered in gold braid. One of the T-shirts, on a hanger and probably valued, was red and printed in black and white with a photograph of Giles Dade's face, 'Giles' lettered underneath it.

'You see he had some elements of normal adolescence,' said Wexford.

They must ask Dade, or if it had to be, his wife, which particular clothes were missing from the children's wardrobes. Football boots were there, trainers, a single pair of black leather shoes. For going to church in, no doubt.

A shelf of books held a Bible, *Chambers Dictionary*, Orwell's *Animal Farm* – a GCSE set book? – some Zola in French – surprisingly – Daudet's *Lettres de mon Moulin*, Maupassant's short stories, Bunyan's *Grace Abounding to the Chief of Sinners* and something called *Purity as a Life Goal* by Parker T. Ziegler. Wexford took it down and looked inside. It had been published in the United States by a company named the Creationist Foundation and sold there for the hefty sum of $35. On the shelf below, plugged in for recharging, was a mobile phone.

Drawers below held underpants, shorts, T-shirts – or one did. In the middle drawer was a mêlée of papers, some of them apparently a homework essay Giles was writing, a paperback on trees and another on the early church, ballpoints, a comb, a used light bulb, shoelaces, a ball of string. The top one was much the same but out of the confusion Vine extracted the small dark-red booklet that is a British passport. It had been issued three years before to Giles Benedict Dade.

'At least we know he hasn't left the country,' said Wexford.

The girl's room had far more books and posters enough. Just what you'd expect, including one of David Beckham, Posh Spice and their child, apparently off on a shopping spree. In the bookcase were the works of J. K. Rowling and Philip Pullman, the two *Alice* volumes, a lot of poetry, some of it just what you would not expect, notably the *Complete Works* of T. S. Eliot and a selection from Gerard Manley Hopkins. The girl, after all, was only thirteen. A photograph of a handsome but very old woman and one she resembled stood on top of the bookcase but the one of her brother, identical to that which they had been given, was on the bedside cabinet. A rack of CDs held hip-hop and Britney Spears, showing Sophie to be more normal than her brother. Her clothes contributed nothing in the way of enlightenment except that things to wear didn't much interest her. From the brown-and-gold blazer and brown pleated skirt, they saw that she went to the same school as her brother. There was a hockey stick and a tennis racquet in the wardrobe as well. Sophie's computer was a humbler version of Giles's with Internet access but no printer. No doubt, she shared his. She also had a combined radio and cassette player, and a CD Walkman.

Wexford and Vine went downstairs and put a few more questions to the parents. Katrina Dade was lying down. Her husband was on his knees picking up broken glass, having made her a cup of coffee. None was offered to the two police officers. Wexford asked about clothes and Dade said they had looked, this had seemed important to his wife, but they had been unable to say what had gone. So many of the clothes their children wore looked just the same, blue jeans and black jeans, plain T-shirts and T-shirts with logos, black, grey and white trainers.

'How about coats?' Vine asked. 'Where do you keep coats? When they went out they must have worn something more than a sweater at this time of the year.'

Wexford wasn't so sure. It had become a sign of a kind of macho strength and youthful stamina not to wear a coat outdoors, not even in snow, not even when the temperature fell below freezing. And it hadn't been cold for the time of year. But was Giles Dade that sort of boy? The boastful swaggering sort who would strut about in a sleeveless vest while others wore padded jackets? He followed Vine and Giles's father out into the hall, and the inside of a large and rather ornate clothes cupboard was examined.

A fur coat hung there, mink probably, very likely Roger Dade's gift to his wife in happier days before disillusionment set in, but very politically incorrect just the same. Wexford wondered when and where she dared wear it. In Italy, on a winter holiday? There were two other winter coats, both belonging to the parents, a man's raincoat, a padded jacket, a fleece, a reinforced red garment that looked as if designed for ski-ing in and a striped cagoule with hood.

'Giles has got an army surplus greatcoat,' said Dade. 'It's hideous but he likes it. It should be here but it's not. And Sophie has a brown padded jacket like that one but that's not hers. That's Giles's.'

Then it looks likely they at least went of their own volition, Wexford thought. Roger Dade took his own raincoat out of the cupboard, hung it over his arm, said, 'I'm going. I just hope this will all have blown over before I get back tonight.'

Wexford didn't answer. 'You say you phoned parents of the children's friends. We'd like names and addresses, please. As soon as possible. Have you cleared the messages from your answerphone?'

'We've listened to them, not cleared them.'

'Good. We'll take the tape.'

He walked back into the living room to say goodbye to Katrina. They would keep in touch. They would want to see her and her husband very soon. Lying on her back, she kept her eyes closed and her breathing steady. He knew she was awake.

'Mrs Dade?' Vine said. She didn't stir. 'We're leaving.'

'I suppose it's understandable,' said Wexford in the car. 'All the many times I've talked to parents whose children are missing I've never been able to understand why they don't scream the place down with rage and fear. And when I come across one who does I pass judgement on her.'

'It's because we don't believe anything serious has happened to them, sir.'

'Don't we? It's far too soon to make up our minds.'

Chapter 3

Kingsmarkham's new Roman Catholic church of Christ the King was a handsome modern building designed by Alexander Dix and built with donations from the town's growing Catholic population, including Dix himself. Foreign tourists might not immediately have recognised it as a sacred building, it looked more like a villa on some Mediterranean promontory, but there was nothing secular about its interior, white and gold and precious hardwoods, a stained-glass window depicting a contemporary version of the Stations of the Cross and, above the black marble altar, a huge crucifix in ivory and gold. A far cry, as members of the congregation often remarked, from 'the hut' where they had heard mass from 1911 till two years ago.

It was this humble building which Barry Vine was approaching now. Its appearance aroused no curiosity in him and not much interest. He had seen several like it in every country town he had ever visited in the United Kingdom, was so accustomed to these single-storey century-old (or more) brick edifices with double wooden doors and windows high up in the walls that he had scarcely noticed this one before. Nevertheless, it was instantly recognisable. What else could it be but a church hall or a church itself, most likely in use by an obscure sect?

No fence or gate protected it. The small area of broken paving which separated it from the York

Street pavement held pools of water that seemed to have no means of escape. Someone signing himself Fang had decorated the brickwork on either side of the doors with incomprehensible graffiti, black and red. For some reason, perhaps a taboo born of superstition, he hadn't touched the oblong plaque attached to the left side on which was printed in large letters: CHURCH OF THE GOOD GOSPEL, and in small ones, THE LORD LOVES PURITY OF LIFE. There followed a list of the times of services and various weekly meetings. Underneath this: *Pastor, the Rev. Jashub Wright, 42 Carlyle Villas, Forest Road, Kingsmarkham.*

Jashub, thought Vine, just where do you get a name like that? I bet he was christened John. Then he noticed the coincidence, if coincidence it was, that this pastor lived in the same street as Joanna Troy's father. He tried the church door and found to his surprise that it was unlocked. This, he saw as soon as he was inside, was plainly because there was nothing inside worth stealing. It was almost empty, rather dark and very cold. Decades must have passed since the walls had been painted. The congregation was expected to sit on wooden benches without backs, and these were bolted to the wooden floor. On a dais at the far end stood a desk, such a desk as Vine hadn't seen since he left his primary school thirty years before. Even then parents had pronounced the school furniture a disgrace. This one, he saw as he bent over it, had been operated on with penknives by several generations of children, and when cutting and carving palled, scribbled over, initialled and generally decorated with ink, crayon and paint. There was a cavity for an inkwell but the inkwell was missing and someone had cut a hole of corresponding size in the middle of the lid. A stool, presumably for the officiating priest to sit on, looked so uncomfortable that Vine supposed Mr Wright preferred to stand.

Jashub . . . 'Where do you reckon it comes from, sir?' Vine said to Wexford when he got back.

'God knows. You could try the Book of Numbers. "Take ye the sum of all the congregation of the children of Israel after their families, by the house of their fathers . . ." You know the sort of thing.'

Vine didn't look as though he knew.

'Or you could ask the man himself. Mike Burden wants to see this Troy chap and since they live practically next door to each other you might as well go together.'

Wexford himself was off to Savesbury Deeps, or as near as he could get, to see how the Subaqua frogmen were getting on. But as soon as Pemberton had driven half a mile out of Myfleet it was clear that the only way to get an overview was to take a circular route round what had become a lake. Lakes, of course, usually have a road encircling them and this had nothing but soggy meadows and a few houses whose owners, like himself, watched the lapping waters with apprehension.

'Go back the way we've come,' he said, 'and try approaching it from Framhurst.' He noticed for the first time that the windscreen wipers weren't on.

Once they were returning, splashing through a ford where no ford had been before, he dialled his own number on the car phone. Dora answered after the second ring.

'It's just the same as it was when you left. It may even have gone down a bit. I thought I might bring some of those books down.'

'I wouldn't,' he said, remembering how he'd humped the boxes up those stairs.

Framhurst looked as on a summer's day, apart from the puddles. The clouds had gone while Wexford was on the phone, the sky was blue and everything glittered in the sun. Pemberton took the Kingsmarkham road until he could see ahead of him something very like the seashore with the tide coming in. Reversing for a dozen yards, he took a right-hand turn along what was usually a country lane but which now skirted the lake. The sun on the water was so bright, turning the surface to blazing silver, that at first they could see nothing. The River Brede had disappeared under the waters. A little way ahead on the road, Wexford spotted a van, a fire engine and a private car parked as near to the water's edge as was safe. A motor boat could be seen slowly circling. They drove up and parked. As Wexford got out he saw a black gleaming amphibian break the surface, rise a little into the brightness and then begin the swim to shore. He waded the last part.

'Ah, the Loch Brede Monster,' he said.

The frogman peeled himself out of some of his gear. 'There's nothing down there. You can be positive about that. My mate's yet to come up but he'll tell you the same.'

'Anyway, thanks for your help.'

'My pleasure. We do enjoy it, you know. Though, if I may say so, it was a pretty crazy idea in the first place, thinking anyone might be down there. I mean, why would they go in?'

'You may say so. I feel the same,' said Wexford. 'The mother got it into her head they'd been drowned.'

'It's not as if there'd been ice on it and they'd been skating, is it?' the frogman persisted, creating unlikely options. 'It's not as if it's hot and they'd felt like swimming. Or that anyone could fall in and need rescuing, it's as shallow as a kids' paddling pool round the edges. Ah, here's my mate, getting in the boat. He'll tell you the same.'

He did. Wexford wondered whether to return to

Lyndhurst Drive and 'Antrim' but, recalling details of Katrina Dade's hysteria, decided to phone instead.

George Troy lived in the only house of any architectural interest in Forest Road. It had once been the lodge of a mansion, demolished at the start of the previous century, whose parkland filled the area bounded by Kingsmarkham, Pomfret, Cheriton Forest and the Pomfret road. All this was since changed out of recognition but the lodge still stood, an awkwardly shaped small Gothic house with a pinnacle and two castellated turrets, separated from the road by an incongruously suburban garden of lawn and flowerbeds bounded by a white wooden fence and gate.

A lot of explaining and production of warrant cards was needed before the woman who came to the door would let them in. The second Mrs Troy seemed unwilling to understand that two police officers could actually come to her house, wish to enter it and talk to her husband about the whereabouts of his daughter. She said, 'She's at home. In her own home. She doesn't live here.'

Burden repeated that at home Joanna Troy was not, that he and Vine had checked and checked thoroughly before coming here. 'May we come in, Mrs Troy?'

She remained suspicious. 'I must ask my husband. Please wait there . . .'

A voice from the staircase cut her short. 'Who is it, Effie?'

Burden answered for her. 'Detective Inspector Burden and Detective Sergeant Vine, Kingsmarkham Crime Management, sir.'

'*Crime* management?' The voice had become incredulous and Burden thought, not for the first time, what an unfortunate effect this new title had on the law-abiding. 'Crime? I don't believe it. What's this about?'

'If we could come in, sir . . .'

The owner of the voice appeared, Effie Troy whispered to him and stepped aside. He was a stout, upright man who had had the good fortune to keep his hair and its fair sandy colour into, Burden guessed, his sixties. Vine, who had seen Joanna Troy's photograph, thought how very like her father she must be. Here were the same high forehead, longish nose, blue eyes and fresh-coloured skin, in George Troy's case rather reddened especially about the high cheekbones.

Burden had to repeat his request and now Troy nodded and exclaimed, 'Of course, of course, I can't think what we were doing, keeping you out there. On the doorstep in the wet. Come in, come in. Welcome to our humble abode. What was it you wanted Joanna for?'

Before answering that, they waited until they were in a small rather dark sitting room. At the best of times, not much light would have penetrated the two narrow arched windows, and this was far from the best of times, the sun fast disappearing and rain-clouds gathering once more. Effie Troy switched on a table lamp and sat down, looking inscrutable. 'When did you last speak to your daughter, Mr Troy?'

'Well, I . . .' Anxiety was beginning to show in the drawing together of George Troy's eyebrows. 'She's all right, isn't she? I mean, she's all *right*?'

'As far as we know, sir. Would you mind telling me when you last spoke to her?'

'It would have been – let me see – last Friday afternoon. Or was it Thursday? No, Friday, I'm almost positive. In the afternoon. About four. Or maybe four thirty, was it, Effie?'

'About that,' said his wife in a guarded tone.

'You phoned her?'

'She phoned me. Yes, Joanna made the call. She phoned me – us –' here a reassuring smile at his wife '– somewhere between four and four thirty.' This was going to be slow work, Burden thought, largely due to George Troy's habit of saying everything two or three times over. 'I'm retired, you see,' he went on. 'Yes, I've given up gainful employment, a bit of an old has-been, that's me. No longer the breadwinner. I'm always at home. She could be sure of getting me any old time. She *is* all right?'

'As far as we know. What did she say, Mr Troy?'

'Now let me see. I wonder what she actually *did* say. Nothing much, I'm sure it didn't amount to much. Not that I'm saying she wasn't a well-informed, highly educated young woman with plenty to say for herself, oh, yes, but on that particular occasion . . .'

To general surprise except perhaps on her husband's part, Effie Troy suddenly butted in, a cool and crisp contrast to him, 'She said she was going to her friend Katrina Dade for the weekend. She was going to keep the children company while their parents were away. Paris, I think. She'd be back home on Sunday night. Another thing was that she'd come round on Wednesday, that's tomorrow, and drive George and me over to Tonbridge to see my sister who's not been well. The car's George's but he lets her use it because he's given up driving.'

Troy smiled, proud of his wife. Burden spoke to her. 'What kind of car, Mrs Troy? Would you know the index number?'

'I would,' she said. 'But first I'd like you to tell Joanna's father what's brought all this on.'

Vine glanced from one to the other, the man who looked young for his age and acted old, and the woman whose initial suspiciousness had changed to a thoughtful alertness. She was good-looking in a strange way, perhaps ten years her husband's junior, as thin as he was fat and as dark as he was fair, with a mass of black hair, grey-threaded, and thick black eyebrows, the swarthy effect heightened by the glasses she wore in heavy black frames.

His eyes on Troy, he said, 'Ms Troy appears to be missing, sir. She and the Dade children were not in the house when Mr and Mrs Dade returned and their present whereabouts aren't known. The car – *your* car – also appears to be gone.'

Troy sat, shaking his head. But he was plainly an optimist, one to take as cheerful a view as possible. 'Surely she's only taken them on some trip, hasn't she? Some outing somewhere? She's done that before. That's all it is, isn't it?'

'Hardly, Mr Troy. The children should have gone to school yesterday morning. And wouldn't your daughter have to go to work? What does she do for a living?'

Possibly fearing a ten-minute-long disquisition from her husband on work, jobs, retirement and employment in general, Effie Dade said in her practised way, 'Joanna used to be a teacher. She trained as a teacher and taught at Haldon Finch School. But now she's self-employed and works as a translator and editor. She has a degree in modern languages and a Master's Degree, and she teaches a French course on the Internet.' She glanced at Burden. 'I don't know if it's relevant –' irrelevance was something she must know plenty about, he thought '– but that's how she and Katrina met. She taught at the school and Katrina was the head teacher's secretary. I'll find the car number for you.'

'My wife is a marvel,' said Troy while she was away. 'I'm a bit of a dreamer myself, a bit vague they tell me, find it hard to stick to the point. But she –

well, she has such grasp, she has such ability to *manage* things, organise, you know, get everything straight – well, shipshape and Bristol fashion. She'll find that number,' he said, as if his wife would be obliged to use differential calculus to do so, 'nothing's beyond her. Don't know why she married me, never have understood, thank God every day of my life, of course, but the "why" of it's a mystery. She says I'm a nice man, how about that? She says I'm kind. Funny old reason for marrying someone, eh? Funny old thing to . . .'

'The number's LC02 YMY,' said Effie Troy as she came back into the room. 'The car is a VW Golf, dark-blue with four doors.'

Only a couple of years old then, Burden thought, with a L registration. What had happened to George Troy just after buying a new car to make him decide to give up driving? At the moment it wasn't important. 'I would like to enter your daughter's house, Mr Troy. Do you by any chance have a key?'

He addressed the father but hoped the reply would come from the stepmother. It did but only after Troy had bumbled on for a couple of minutes about types of keys, Yale and Banham locks, the danger of losing keys and the paramount need to lock all one's doors at night.

'We have a key,' said Effie Troy. Suspicion returned. 'I'm not at all sure she'd like the idea of your having it.'

'That's all right, my darling. That's quite OK. They're police officers, they're OK. They won't do anything they shouldn't. Let them have it, it'll be all right.'

'Very well.' The wife had evidently decided long ago that, notwithstanding her superior intellect and grasp, her husband must make the decisions. She fetched the key but not before Troy had told them what a marvel she was and how there was no doubt she would run that key to earth.

'In Ms Troy's absence you personally would have no objection to our taking a look inside the house?'

The fact that his daughter had disappeared and had been gone for two days, and possibly more, at last seemed to penetrate the father's cheerful bonhomie. Repetition, apparently for the sake of it, was abruptly forgotten. He said with slow deliberation, 'Joanna is actually missing, then? No one knows where she is?'

'We've only just begun our enquiries, sir. We've no reason to think any harm has come to her.'

Hadn't they? The very fact that she had vanished without leaving a note or a message for the Dades was close to a reason. But his reply seemed to have gone some way to allaying Troy's fears.

'One more question, Mrs Troy. Did your stepdaughter have a good relationship with Giles and Sophie Dade? Did they get on?' God, he was doing it himself now . . .

'Oh, yes. She was a great favourite with both of them. She'd known them since they were nine and seven, that was when Katrina started working at the school.'

'Anything you want to ask, Barry?' he said to Vine.

'Just one thing. Can she swim?'

'Joanna?' For the first time Effie Troy smiled. The smile transformed her almost into a beauty. 'She's a top-class swimmer. When the woman who taught PE was off sick for a whole term Joanna took the students to swimming and gave lessons to the first and second years. That was a year before she gave up.' She hesitated, then said, 'If you're thinking of the floods – that is, that there could have been an accident, don't. Joanna was always saying how terrible the last lot we had were, the damage they'd do, she wished she could hibernate till all this was over. She had quite a thing about it. And the upshot was that in October she never went out except in the car. When she talked to us on Friday she said to me that once she got to the Dades she wasn't going to set foot outside till she drove home on Sunday evening.'

No outings then, no trips. And the rain had come down more heavily on Friday night and most of Saturday than it had on any single two days in the October floods. Joanna Troy wouldn't have gone near Savesbury Deeps. She wouldn't have taken Giles and Sophie for a nice Sunday afternoon walk in macs and wellies to see the water rising over the top of the Kingsbrook Bridge. When she went out, as she must have done, she went by car and the children with her. Because, Burden thought suddenly, she had to. Something happened to make it paramount for them all to leave the house at some time during the weekend . . .

'You mentioned a course she teaches on the Internet. Would you happen to know . . .?' He was certain she wouldn't. Neither of them would.

George Troy didn't but that didn't stop him beginning a lecture on the intricacies and obscurity of cyberspace, his own total inability to understand any of it and his position as an 'absolute fool when it comes to things like that'. Effie waited for him to finish his sentence before saying quietly, 'www.langlearn.com.'

'By the way, the media have been told,' Wexford said. At the look on Burden's face he added, 'Yes, I know. But it was a directive from Freeborn.' Mention of the Assistant Chief Constable's name evoked a groan. 'He says it's the best way to find them and maybe he's right.'

'The best way to get calls and no doubt e-mails from all the nuts.'

'I quite agree. We know in advance they'll have been seen in Rio and Jakarta, and going over Niagara Falls in a barrel. But they may be in a hotel somewhere. She may be renting a flat for the three of them.'

'Why would she?'

'I'm not saying she is, Mike. It's a possibility. We know so little about her. For instance, you say she has a good relationship with the Dade kids. Suppose it's more than that, suppose she's so fond of them she wants them for herself.'

'Adopt them, you mean? They're not exactly the babes in the wood. The boy's *fifteen*. She'd have to be mad.'

'So? The very fact that she's disappeared and with two children makes her a bit out of the ordinary, doesn't it? Did you get to see the shepherd of the gospel flock?'

Burden had. He and Barry Vine had walked up the road a hundred yards or so to a house very different from the Troys', a semi-detached bungalow, plain and unprepossessing. The Rev. Mr Wright had been a surprise. Burden had a preconceived idea of what he would be like, an image which derived from television drama and newspaper stories of American fundamentalists. He would be a fanatic with burning eyes, a fixed stare and an orator's voice, a tall, thin ascetic in a shabby suit and constricting collar. The reality was different. Jashub Wright was thin certainly but rather small, no more than thirty, quiet-voiced and with a pleasant manner. He invited the two officers in without hesitation and introduced them to a fair-haired young girl with a baby in her arms. 'My wife, Thekla.'

Seated in an armchair and given a cup of strong hot

tea, Burden had asked the most important question. 'Did Giles Dade attend church last Sunday morning?'

'No, he didn't,' the pastor answered promptly. No beating about the bush, no wanting to know why Burden wanted to know. 'Nor the service in the afternoon. We have a young people's service on a Sunday afternoon once a month. I remarked to my wife that his not coming was odd and I hoped he wasn't unwell.'

'That's right.' Thekla Wright was now holding the baby in the crook of her left arm while passing the sugar basin to Vine with her right hand. Vine helped himself freely. 'It was so unusual that I rang up to ask if he was all right,' she said. 'We were both anxious.'

Burden leant forward in his chair. 'Would you tell me what time you phoned, Mrs Wright?'

She sat down, placing the baby, now fast asleep, on her lap. 'It was after afternoon service. I didn't go in the morning, I can't go to every service because of the baby, but I did go in the afternoon and when I got home – it was about five – I phoned the Dades' house.'

'Did you get a reply?'

'Only the answerphone. It just said no one was available, the usual thing.' Thekla Wright said very politely, 'Would you mind telling us why you want to know all this?'

Vine explained. Both Wrights looked deeply concerned. 'I *am* sorry,' Jashub Wright said. 'That must be deeply distressing for Mr and Mrs Dade. Is there anything we can do?'

'I doubt if there's anything you could do for them personally, sir, but it would help if you'd answer one more question.'

'Of course.'

Burden had found himself in a fix. These people

were so *nice*, so helpful, so unlike what he had expected. And now he had to ask a question which, unless he phrased it with the greatest care, must sound insulting. He made the attempt. 'I've been wondering, Mr Wright, what attracts a teenager to your church. Forgive me if that sounds rude, I don't mean it to. But your, er, slogan, "The Lord loves purity of life" sounds – again, forgive me – sounds something more likely to arouse – well, derision in a boy of fifteen than a desire to belong to it.'

In spite of his apologies, Wright looked rather offended. His voice had stiffened. 'We practise a simple faith, Inspector. Love your neighbour, be kind, tell the truth and keep your sexual activities for within marriage. I won't go into our ritual and liturgy, you don't want that and anyway it too is simple. Giles was a confirmed member of the Church of England, he'd sung in the choir at St Peter's. Apparently, he decided one day that it was all too complicated and confused for him. All these different prayer books in use, all these Bibles. You couldn't be sure if you were getting the RC mass or matins of 1928 or happy-clappy or the Alternative Service Book. It might be smells and bells or it might be tambourines and soul. So he came over to us.'

'His parents aren't members of your church? Are any of his friends or relatives?'

'Not so far as I know.'

Thekla Wright cut in, 'We're simple, you see. That's what people like. We're direct and we don't compromise. That's the – well, the essence of us. The rules don't change and the principles don't, they haven't changed much in a hundred and forty years.'

This intervention provoked a glance from her husband. Burden couldn't interpret it until she said, rather humbly, 'I'm sorry, dear. I know it's not for me to talk about matters of doctrine.'

A smile from Wright brought a little flush to her pretty face. What did it mean? That she mustn't intervene because she was a *woman*? 'We welcome new people, Inspector, though we don't make a song and dance about it. Youngsters, as I'm sure you know, often have much more enthusiasm than older people. They put their hearts and souls into worship.'

To this neither Burden nor Vine had any response to make.

Thekla Wright nodded. 'Would you like another cup of tea?'

The experience he had related to Wexford. 'He wasn't particularly fanatical. Seems quite a decent chap and his church is simple and straightforward, nothing suspicious about it.'

'Sounds as if you'll be their next convert,' said the Chief Inspector. 'You'll be popping along there next Sunday morning.'

'Of course I won't. For one thing, I don't like their attitude to women. They're as bad as the Taleban.'

'Anyway, the main thing is that Giles Dade didn't go to church on Sunday morning and it seems that if he was at home he would have gone, come what might. Nor did he go in the afternoon. On Friday evening when Mrs Dade phoned from Paris the answerphone was not on but it was on Saturday evening and again on Sunday evening. All this makes it look as if the three of them left the house some time on Saturday. On the other hand, the answerphone may have been on on Saturday evening for no better reason than that they all wanted to watch something on television without being disturbed.

'Now on Saturday evening, as the whole country knows, the last ever episode of *Jacob's Ladder*, in which Inspector Martin Jacob dies, was shown on ITV. It's said to have had twelve million viewers and it may well be that Giles and Sophie Dade and Joanna Troy were among them. To put the answerphone on would be the obvious way of assuring peace and quiet. Giles's failure to go to church next day is much more indicative of when they left the house.'

'Early on Sunday morning,' said Burden, 'or possibly around lunchtime. But why did they leave? What for?'

Chapter 4

The water had advanced during the morning and was now within inches of the wall. Dora had been taking photographs of it, first when it was approaching but not touching the mulberry tree, later of the point it had reached by four o'clock. Dusk had come and now darkness, a merciful veiling of that sight. The camera had been put away until the morning.

'I couldn't do it,' said Wexford, half horrified, half admiring.

'No, Reg, but you've never been much of a photographer, have you?'

'You know I don't mean that. We're about to be engulfed and you're taking *pictures.*'

'Like Nero fiddling while Rome burned?'

'More like Sheridan sitting in a coffee house opposite the burning Drury Lane Theatre and saying that surely a man could have a drink by his own fireside.'

That made Sylvia laugh. Not so her new man whom she had brought round for a drink. It wasn't the first time Wexford had met him and he was no more impressed than on the last occasion. Callum Chapman was good-looking but neither clever nor a conversationalist. Did good looks in a man really mean so much to a woman? He had always supposed not but unless his daughter was the exception he must be wrong. Charm too was lacking. The man seldom smiled. Wexford had never heard him laugh.

Perhaps he was like Diane de Poitiers whose good looks meant so much to her that she never smiled lest the movement wrinkle her face.

Now Chapman was looking puzzled by Wexford's anecdote. He said in his nasal Birmingham tones, 'I don't see the point of that. What does it mean?'

Wexford tried to tell him. He explained how the theatre was virtually the playwright's own, that his plays had all been performed there, he had put his heart and soul into it and now, before his eyes, it was being destroyed.

'Is that supposed to be funny?'

'It's an example of panache, light-hearted bravado in the face of tragedy.'

'I just don't see it.'

Sylvia laughed again, quite unfazed. 'Maybe by tomorrow Dad'll be having a drink beside his own pond. Let's go, Cal. The sitter will be fidgeting.'

'Cal,' said Wexford when they had gone. 'Cal.'

'She calls him "darling" too,' said Dora mischievously. 'Oh, don't look so gloomy. I don't suppose she'll marry him. They're not even living together, not really.'

'What does "not really" mean?'

She didn't deign to answer. He knew she wouldn't. 'She says he's kind. When he stays the night he makes her morning tea and gets the breakfast.'

'That won't last,' said Wexford. 'That New Men stuff never does. He reminds me of that Augustine Casey Sheila once brought here. The Booker shortlist bloke. Oh, I know he's not in the least like him. I admit he's not so obnoxious and he's got a pretty face. But he's not clever either or entertaining or . . .'

'Or rude,' said Dora.

'No, it's not that he's like Casey, it's just that I don't understand why my daughters take up with these sorts of men. Ghastly men. Sheila's Paul's not ghastly, I'll grant you that. He's just so handsome and charming I can't believe he won't be off chasing some other woman. It's not natural to look like him and be neither gay nor unfaithful to your wife or partner or whatever. I can't help suspecting him of having a secret life.'

'You're impossible.'

She sounded cross, not teasing or indulgent any more. He went to the window to look at the water, illuminated now by his neighbour's lamp, and at the steadily falling insistent rain. Not long now. Another half-inch or whatever that was in millimetres and it would be at the wall. Another inch . . .

'You said you wanted to see the news.'

'I'm coming.'

Just the bare facts coming after another rail crash, chaos on the railways, congestion on the roads, another child murdered in the north, another newborn baby left in a phone box. Just an announcement that the three were missing, then their photographs much magnified. A phone number was given for the public to call if they had information. Wexford sighed, thinking he knew well the kind of information they would have.

'Tell me something. Why would a bright, good-looking, middle-class teenage boy, a boy with a comfortable home who goes to a good school, why would he join a fundamentalist church? His parents don't go there. His friends don't.'

'Perhaps it provides him with answers, Reg. Teenagers want answers. Lots of them find modern life revolts them. They think that if everything became more simple and straightforward, more fundamentalist, in fact, the world would be a better place. Maybe it would. Mostly they don't care for ritual and facts that ought to be plain covered up in archaic words they can't understand. He'll grow out of it and I don't know if that's a shame or something to be thankful about.'

He woke up in the night. It was just after three and rain was still falling. He went downstairs, into the dining room and over to the french windows. The lamp was out but when he turned out the light behind him and his eyes grew used to the dark he could see out well enough. The water had moved up to lap the wall.

Two men were unloading sacks of something on to the police station forecourt. For a moment Wexford couldn't think what. Then he understood. He parked the car, went inside and asked Sergeant Camb at the desk, 'What do we want sandbags for? There's no possible chance of the floods reaching here.'

No one could answer him. The driver of the truck came in with a note acknowledging receipt of the sandbags and Sergeant Peach came out from the back to sign it. 'Though what we're to do with them I don't know.' He looked at Wexford. 'You're not far from the river, are you, sir?' He spoke in a wheedling tone, though half jokingly. 'I don't suppose you'd like a few. Take them off our hands?'

In the same style, Wexford said, 'I wouldn't mind helping you out, Sergeant.'

Ten minutes later four dozen had been loaded into a van Pemberton drove to Wexford's home. He phoned his wife. 'I can't get home to put up the fortifications till this evening.'

'Don't worry, darling. Cal and Sylvia are here and Cal's going to do it.'

Cal . . . He didn't know what to say and came up with an ineffectual, 'That's good.'

It was. Especially as it was once more pouring with rain. Wexford checked on the calls they had received as a result of the media publicity but there was nothing helpful, not even anything that seemed the suggestion of a sane person. Burden came in and told him the outcome of calls on the various friends and relatives of the missing children. In the main, negative. Giles's and Sophie's maternal grandparents lived at Berningham on the Suffolk coast, where in the seventies and eighties had been a large United States Air Force base. They seemed to get on well with their grandchildren but they hadn't seen either of them since September when they came to stay in Berningham for a week.

Roger Dade's mother, remarried since her divorce from his father, was apparently a favourite with the children. Her home was a village in the Cotswolds and she lived alone. The last time she had seen them was at their half-term in October when she had stayed for three nights with the Dades, leaving under some sort of cloud. A quarrel, Burden had gathered, though no details had been given. Katrina Dade was an only child.

'How about Joanna Troy?'

'No siblings,' said Burden. 'The present Mrs Troy has two children by a previous marriage. Joanna's been married and divorced. The marriage lasted less than a year. We haven't traced her ex-husband yet.'

Wexford said thoughtfully, 'The answer to all this is with Joanna Troy, don't you think? I don't see how it can be otherwise. A boy of fifteen isn't going to be able to persuade a woman of thirty-one to take him and his sister off somewhere without telling their parents or leaving any clue to where they were going. It has to be her plan and her decision. Nor can I see how she could have taken them away without criminal intent.'

'That's a bit sweeping.'

'Is it? All right, give me a scenario that covers everything and in which Joanna Troy is innocent.'

'Drowning would be.'

'They didn't drown, Mike. Even if it remained a possibility, what became of her car? Or, rather, her dad's car. Who fell in and who rescued whom? If by a huge stretch of the imagination you can get that far, isn't it a bit odd they all drowned? Wouldn't one have survived, especially in four feet of water?'

'You can make anything sound ridiculous,' Burden said peevishly. 'You're always doing it. I'm not sure it's a virtue.'

Wexford laughed. 'You and Barry went to her house. Where's your report on that?'

'On your desk. Under a mountain of stuff. You haven't penetrated to it yet. I'll tell you about it if you like.'

It was a very small house, a living room and kitchen on the ground floor, two bedrooms and a bathroom above, part of a row of eight called Kingsbridge Mews put up by a speculative builder in the eighties.

'As Dade said, the car was kept outside in the front,' said Burden. 'Needless to say, it's not there now.'

Inside the house it was cold. Joanna Troy had apparently switched off the central heating before she left on Friday. She was either naturally frugal or obliged to make economies. Vine found her passport too. It was inside a desk which held little else of interest. There were no letters, no vehicle registration document, no certificate of insurance, though these of course would have been with her father, nothing pertaining to a mortgage. Insurance policies for the house itself and for its contents were also in the drawer. A large envelope contained certificates acknowledging a degree in French from the University of Warwick, a Master's Degree in European Literature from the University of Birmingham and a diploma Burden said was the Postgraduate Certificate in Education. Upstairs one of the bedrooms had been turned into an office with computer and printer, a photocopier, a sophisticated recording device and two large filing cabinets. The walls were lined with books, in this room mostly French and German fiction and dictionaries.

'Vine says she has all those French books you found in Giles's bedroom. *Lettres de mon* something and Emile Zola and whatever the other one was. Mind you, she's got about a hundred others in French too.'

On the desk, to the left of the PC had lain a set of page proofs of a novel in French. To the right were pages in English, fresh from Joanna Troy's printer. She had apparently been engaged in the work of translation on the day she left for Lyndhurst Drive and her weekend with the Dade children. In the bedroom Burden had looked with interest at her clothes.

'You would,' said Wexford nastily, eyeing Burden's slate-blue suit, lighter blue shirt and deep-purple slub silk tie. Not for a moment would anyone have taken him for a policeman.

'To my mind,' Burden said in a distant tone, 'dressing decently is one of the markers of civilisation.'

'OK, OK, depends what you mean by "decently". You found something funny about her clothes, I can see it in your beady eye.'

'Well, yes, I did. I think so. Everything in her wardrobe was casual, *everything*. And I mean really casual. Not a single skirt or dress, for instance. Jeans, chinos, Dockers . . .'

'I haven't the faintest idea what these things are,' Wexford interrupted.

'Then leave it to me. I have. T-shirts, shirts, sweaters, jackets, pea coats, padded coats, a fleece . . .

All right, I know you don't know what that is either. Take it from me, it's not something a woman would wear to a party. The point is she'd nothing she could wear to a party, nothing dress-up, except possibly one pair of black trousers. What did she do if someone asked her out to dinner or a theatre?'

'I've been to theatres, even to the National when my daughter Sheila's been in something, and there've been women dressed as if about to muck out the pigpen. For all you being such a fashionista you don't seem to realise this isn't the nineteen thirties. But you'll say that's beside the point. I agree it's odd. It just adds to what I've been thinking already. We need to go back to the Dades, search the place, get a team in there if necessary. Those children have been missing four days by now, Mike.'

It was a short drive to the house called 'Antrim' but Wexford asked Donaldson the driver to make a detour and take in some of the flooded areas. Heavy rain was falling, the water was still rising and of the Kingsbrook Bridge only the parapet rails still showed above the water.

'It's a good deal more than four feet deep there,' said Burden.

'It is now. Wherever they are and whatever they've been doing, they haven't been hanging about waiting for the water to get deep enough to drown themselves in.'

Burden made an inarticulate noise indicative of finding a remark in bad taste, and DC Lynn Fancourt, who was sitting in front next to Donaldson, cleared her throat. There were mysteries about the Chief Inspector she hadn't yet solved in her two years attached to Kingsmarkham Crime Management. How was it possible, for instance, to find such irreconcilables bunched together in one man's character? How could one man be liberal, compassionate, sensitive, well-read and at the same time ribald, derisive, sardonic and flippant about serious things? Wexford had never been nasty to her, not the way he could be to some people, but she was afraid of him just the same. In awe of him, might be a better way to put it. Not that she'd have admitted it to a soul. Sitting there in the front of the car, trying to see out of the passenger window down which rain was streaming, she knew it was wisest for her to keep silent unless spoken to, and no one spoke to her. Donaldson made the detour required of all vehicles when they approached the bridge, splashing up York Street and then following the one-way system.

Wexford was a stickler for duty. And exacting obedience from his subordinates. Lynn had once been disobedient, it was during the investigation of the Devenish murder that somehow got mixed up with the paedophile demos, and Wexford had spoken to her in a way that made her shiver. It was only justice, not nastiness, she admitted that, and it had taught her something. About a police officer's duty, for one thing, and it was because of this that she was all the more astonished when Wexford told Donaldson to drive first up the road where his own house was and drop him off for two minutes.

Wexford let himself in with his key, called out but got no reply. He went through to the dining room. Outside the french window, in driving rain, Dora, Sylvia and Callum Chapman were raising the height of the two little walls with sandbags, evidently working as fast as they could, for the water was creeping up the walls. The sandbags had arrived just in time. Wexford tapped on the glass, then opened one of the side windows.

'Thanks for what you're doing,' he called to Callum.

'My pleasure.'

That it could hardly be. Sylvia, who had been much nicer and easier to get on with since her divorce, held on to her boyfriend's shoulder and, standing on one leg, took off her boot, pouring water out of it. 'Speak for yourself,' she said. 'I'm hating every minute of it and so is Mother.'

'It could be worse. Just think, if the ground floor floods we shall have to come and stay with you.'

He shut the window, went back to the car. He wondered if his daughter was still doing voluntary work for that women's refuge in addition to her job with the local authority. She must be or Dora would have told him, but he must ask. It would be a relief to know she wasn't, that she was removed from a situation where being assaulted by other women's rejected husbands or partners was always a risk. He got in next to Burden and within two minutes they were at 'Antrim'.

A creature of moods, Katrina Dade seemed quite different today, girlish but quiet, withdrawn, her eyes wide and staring. She was sensibly dressed too, wearing trousers and a jumper. Her husband, by contrast, was more expansive and more polite. What was he doing home from work at this hour? They looked as if neither of them had slept much.

'I suppose it's really come home to us. It wasn't real before, it was like a bad dream.' Katrina added wistfully, 'That drowning business, that was nonsense, wasn't it? I don't know what made me think they'd drowned.'

'Quite understandable, Mrs Dade,' said Burden, earning himself a frown from Wexford. 'Later on, we'd like to talk to you in greater depth.' He hoped no one noticed the unintentional pun. Wexford would have, of course. 'First we should take a look at the room where Ms Troy spent the night or the two nights.'

'She didn't leave anything behind,' said Katrina when they were on the stairs. 'She must have brought a bag but if she did she took it away with her.'

The room was under one of the steep-roofed gables of the house. Its ceiling was beamed and sharply sloping above the single bed. If you sat up unexpectedly during the night, thought Wexford, you could give your head a nasty bang. What Katrina had said appeared to be true and Joanna had indeed left nothing behind but he watched with approval as Lynn got down on her knees and scanned the floor. There was no en suite bathroom and the built-in clothes cupboard was empty. The drawers in a chest were also empty but for an earring in the top one on the left-hand side.

'That isn't hers,' Katrina said in her new little girl voice. 'Joanna *never* wore earrings.' Where anyone else might have talked of 'pierced' ears, she said, 'She didn't have holes in her ears for them to go through.' She held the single pearl in the palm of her hand, said mischievously as if she hadn't a care in the world, 'It must belong to my horrible old ma-in-law. She stayed here in October, the old bat. Shall I throw it away? I bet it's valuable.'

No one answered her. Lynn got up from the floor, plainly disappointed, and they all went down the stairs. There the old Katrina returned. She subsided on to a chair in the hall and began to cry. She sobbed that she was ashamed of herself. Why did she talk like that? Her children leaving her was a judgement on her for saying the things she did. Roger Dade came out from the living room with a handful of tissues and put a not very enthusiastic arm round her.

'She's in such a state,' he said, 'she doesn't know what she's saying.'

Wexford thought the opposite, that while *in vino*

veritas might be true, *in miseria veritas*, or 'in grief truth', certainly was. He didn't say so. He was watching Lynn who had once more got down on hands and knees, but not in mere speculation this time – she had spotted something. She knelt up and said, like the promising young officer she was, 'Could I have a new plastic bag, please, sir, and a pair of sterile tweezers?'

'Call Archbold,' said Wexford. 'That's the best way. He'll bring what's necessary. It'll be more efficient than anything we can do without him.'

'But what is it?' said Dade, gaping, when they were in the living room.

'Let's wait and see, shall we?' Burden had a pretty good idea but he wasn't going to say. Not yet. 'Now, Mrs Dade, do you feel able to tell us something about Ms Troy? We know she's a translator who's been a teacher, that she's thirty-one and been married and divorced. I believe you met her when you were a school secretary and she was teaching at Haldon Finch School?'

'I only did it for a year,' said Katrina. 'My husband didn't like me doing it. I got so tired.'

'You were exhausted, you know you were. Other women may be able to juggle a job and the home but you're not one of them. Regularly every Friday night you'd have a nervous collapse.'

He said it lightly but Wexford could imagine those nervous collapses. He very nearly shuddered. 'When was this, Mrs Dade?'

'Let me think. Sophie was six when I started. It must be seven years. Oh, my darling little Sophie! Where is she? What's happened to her?'

Everyone would have liked to answer that. Burden said, 'We're doing our best to find her and her brother, Mrs Dade. Telling us whatever you can about Ms Troy is the best way to help us find them.

So you met and became friends.' He added bluntly, 'She was a good deal your junior.'

Katrina Dade's expression was one of a woman who has just been not so much insulted as deeply wounded. If he had unjustly accused her of child cruelty, selling her country's secrets to a foreign power or breaking and entering her neighbour's property, she couldn't have looked more appalled. She countered it with a stammered-out, half-broken, 'Do you think it's fair to speak to me like that? Considering what I'm going through? Do you?'

'I'd no intention of upsetting you, Mrs Dade,' Burden said stiffly. 'We'll leave it.' I know there was a good thirteen years between them, anyway, he thought. 'Ms Troy gave up teaching some time after that – do you know when?'

It was a reply sulkily given. 'Three years ago.'

'Why was that? Why did she give up?'

Dade broke in. 'I'm surprised you have to ask. Isn't the way kids behave at these comprehensives reason enough? The noise, the foul language, the violence. The way no one can keep discipline. A teacher who dares to give a child a little tap gets up before the Human Rights Court. Isn't that reason enough?'

'I take it Giles and Sophie attend a private school?' Wexford said.

'You take it right. I believe in the best education for my children and I don't believe in letting them take it easy. They'll thank me one day. I'm a stickler for homework promptly done. Both of them have private tutors as well as school.'

'But Ms Troy isn't one of them?'

'Absolutely not.'

Before Dade could say any more there came a shrill ringing at the doorbell as if Archbold clutched the bell pull and hung on – as he probably had. Lynn went to let him in.

Burden resumed, 'Had Ms Troy come to look after your children on previous occasions?'

'I *told* you. Roger and I had never been away together all the time we were married. Not till last weekend. If you mean for an evening sometimes while we went out – it didn't happen often, mind – she'd done that. The last time would have been a month ago, something like that. Oh, and there was one night we went to a dinner-dance in London and she stayed then.'

'I'd hoped this weekend away would be the very last time they'd need a sitter. Giles would have been – *will* be – sixteen very shortly.' Roger Dade flushed deeply at what he had said, made it worse: 'I mean – what I meant to say was . . .'

'That you think he's dead!' Katrina's tears began afresh.

Her husband put his head in his hands, muttered from between his fingers, 'I don't know what I think. I can't think straight. This is driving me mad.' He looked up. 'How much time am I going to have to take off work over this?'

Wexford had almost decided he must give up for the day, try some other tack, when Archbold tapped on the door and came in. He had a small sterile pack in his hand, which he held up for Wexford's inspection. Peering through the transparent stuff of which the envelope was made, he saw something that looked like a small fragment of whitish porcelain, backed with a strip of gold.

'What is it?'

'It looks to me like the crown or cap off a tooth, sir.'

This fetched Dade out of his despair. He sat up. Katrina scrubbed at her eyes with a tissue. The sealed pack was passed to them, then to Burden and Lynn.

'Did either of your children have crowns in their mouths?' Burden asked.

Katrina shook her head. 'No, but Joanna did. She had two of her teeth crowned. It was years ago. She had a fall in the gym, something like that, and broke her teeth. Then one of the crowns came off when she was eating a caramel. The dentist put it back and Joanna told me he'd said she ought to have them both replaced. He said meantime not to chew gum but she did sometimes.'

Wexford had never heard her speak so lucidly. He wondered if it was because what they were discussing was something not so much physical and personal as pertaining to the appearance. She would probably talk as informatively on such subjects as diet and exercise, cosmetic surgery and minor ailments, subjects dear to her heart.

'Wouldn't she notice it had fallen out?'

'She might not,' Katrina said in the same earnest tone. 'Not at once. She mightn't until she sort of wiggled her tongue round her mouth and felt a rough bit.'

'We'd like to come back this afternoon,' Wexford said, 'and find out more about the children, their tastes and interests and their friends, and anything more you can tell us about Ms Troy.'

Dade said in his unpleasantly harsh and scathing voice, 'Have you never heard that actions speak louder than words?'

'We are acting, Mr Dade.' Wexford controlled his rising anger. 'We have all available resources working on the disappearance of your children.' He hated the terms he was obliged to use. For him they made things worse. What did this man expect? That he and Burden would help matters by personally digging up his back garden or poking into the lakes of water with sticks? 'You'd surely agree that the best way of discovering where Ms Troy and your children have gone is to find out what they are most likely to do and where they are most likely to go.'

Dade gave one of his shrugs, more an indication of contempt than helplessness. 'I shan't be here, anyway. You'll have to make do with her.'

Wexford and Burden got up to go. Archbold and Lynn Fancourt had already left. He meant to say something to Katrina but she had so profoundly retreated into herself that it was as if a shell sat there, the outer carapace of a woman with staring but sightless eyes. Her transformation into a rational being had not lasted long.

The inevitable house-to-house enquiries in Lyndhurst Drive elicited very little. Every householder questioned about the previous weekend spoke of the rain, the torrential, relentless rain. Water may be see-through but rain nevertheless, when descending heavily, creates a grey wall that is no longer transparent but like a thick ever-moving, constantly shifting veil. Moreover, human beings in our climate take a different attitude to weather from those who live in arid countries, being conditioned not to welcome rain but to dislike and turn away from it. That is what those neighbours of the Dades had done once the rain began on the Saturday afternoon. The more it fell, the more they retreated, closing their curtains. It was noisy too. When at its heaviest it made a continuous low roar that masked other sounds. So the Fowlers who lived on one side of the Dades and the Holloways next door to them had heard and seen nothing. Both families heard their letter boxes open and close when their evening paper, the *Evening Courier*, was delivered at about six, and both assumed a copy was delivered as usual to Antrim. The neighbours on the other side of the Dades, the first house, in fact, in Kingston Drive, were away for the weekend.

However, Rita Fowler had seen Giles leave the house on Saturday afternoon before the rain began.

'I can't remember the time. We'd had our lunch and cleared up. My husband was watching the rugby on TV. It wasn't raining then.'

Lynn Fancourt told her it had begun raining just before four but she knew she had seen Giles earlier than that. By four it would have started to get dark and it wasn't dark when she saw him. Maybe half past two? Or three? Giles had been on his own. She hadn't seen him return. She hadn't returned to the front of the house until she went to pick up the evening paper off the doormat.

'Did you see a dark-blue car parked on the Dades' driveway during the weekend?'

She had and was proud of her memory. 'I saw her come – she was the children's sitter – I saw her come on the Friday evening. And I can tell you that car was there when I saw Giles go out.'

But had it still been there when she picked up the evening paper? She hadn't noticed, it had been raining so hard. Was it still there next morning? She couldn't answer that but she knew it hadn't been there on Sunday afternoon.

If someone had entered the house in order to abduct Joanna Troy and Giles and Sophie Dade, or somehow to entice them away, it began to look as if this must have happened after the rain began. Or else they had all gone for a drive on Saturday evening, a very unlikely time to go out at all. The teeming rain had kept everyone who didn't have to leave his or her house firmly indoors. Wexford was turning all this over in his mind and noting how it made the drowning theory less and less probable when Vine came in and held out to him something soaking wet and mud-stained on a tray.

'What is it?'

'It's a T-shirt, sir. A woman found it in the water in her back garden and brought it in here. It's got a name printed on it, you see, and that's what alerted her.'

Wexford took the garment by the shoulders and lifted it an inch or two out of the muddy water in which it lay. The background was blue and it was smaller but otherwise it was the twin to the red one they had seen in Giles Dade's cupboard. Only the face was a girl's and the name on it was 'Sophie'.

Chapter 5

The river floods were at their widest here. The woman who had found the T-shirt said ruefully that when she and her partner had been looking for a home in the neighbourhood, they almost rejected this house because it was so far from the Kingsbrook. 'Not far enough, evidently.'

But a good deal further away than Wexford's. Still, it was also lower-lying and in spite of the rain which had been falling steadily since nine, the tide had reached only about a third of the way up the garden, bringing with it a scummy detritus of plastic bottles, a carrier bag, a Coke can, broken twigs, dead leaves, used condoms, a toothbrush . . .

'And that T-shirt.'

'You found it here?'

'That's right. Among all this lot. I saw the name and it rang a bell.'

Wexford went on home. He was meeting Burden for a 'quick' lunch but he wanted to see the new wall first. It wasn't necessary to go outside. No one would go outside today if he didn't have to. Four tiers of sandbags on each side raised the height of the walls by two feet but the swirling water hadn't yet quite reached the bottom of the lowest tier.

'It was very kind of Cal,' Dora said.

'Yes.'

'He's taking me out to lunch.'

'What, just you? Where's Sylvia?'

'Gone to work. It's her day off but she offered to do the helpline at The Hide. One of the other women is off sick.'

Wexford said no more. It struck him that a man doesn't take his girlfriend's mother out to a meal on her own unless he is very serious about that girlfriend, unless, in fact, he contemplates making her mother his mother-in-law or something very near it. Why did he mind so much? Callum Chapman was suitable enough. He had been married but his wife had died. There were no children. He had a reasonable job as an actuary (whatever that was), a flat of his own in Stowerton. At his last birthday he had become forty. According to Sylvia, her children liked him. Dora apparently liked him. He had been eager to do a good deed by volunteering as a sandbag shifter in the water crisis.

'He's dull,' Wexford said to himself as he drove down the hill through the rain to meet Burden at the Moonflower Takeaway's new restaurant. 'Abysmally dull and dreary.' But was that important? Wexford wasn't going to have to live with him, see his handsome face on the pillow beside him – he grinned at the thought of that – watch his deadpan look when anything amusing was said. But, wait a minute, maybe this last was more than a possibility if Sylvia got into some permanent arrangement with him . . . How much of a New Man was he? These days, he thought, women seemed to like best a man who'd do the housework and mind the kids and iron his own shirts, and never mind if he was boring as hell. In much the same way, men had once preferred and many still did, housewifely women with empty heads and pretty faces. It didn't say much for human discernment.

Burden was already seated at one of the Moonflower's twelve tables. Famous in the district for their

Chinese takeaway, this restaurant had been opened a year before by Mark Ling and his brother Pete. It was already popular and with visitors not only local but from further afield, not least because of its (self-styled) head waiter, Raffy Johnson, the Lings' nephew. Raffy was young, black, handsome and in Wexford's opinion the most courteous server of food in mid-Sussex. No one could spread a napkin over a customer's lap with a more graceful flourish than Raffy, no one be more prompt with the menu or more assiduous to check that the single red or purple anemone in its cut glass vase was placed on the table where it neither blocked diners' sight of each other nor got in the way of the dishes of lemon chicken and black bean squid. He was engaged now in pouring for Burden a glass of sparkling water. He set the bottle down, smiled and drew back Wexford's chair.

'Good morning, Mr Wexford. How are you? Not liking all this rain, I dare say.'

If ever there was a success story . . . Wexford remembered Raffy a few years back when he had been a hopeless seventeen-year-old layabout, a feckless boy whose only virtue seemed to be his love for his mother, and whom his aunt Mhonum Ling had called a hopeless case, one who would never find work his life long. But his mother Oni had had a win on the Lottery and much of the money had gone on Raffy's training. There had been hotel work in London, in Switzerland and Jordan, and now he was a partner with his uncles and aunt in this prosperous business.

'I comfort myself with thoughts of Raffy when I'm feeling low,' said Wexford.

'Good. I must try it. I reckon we're all feeling low at the moment. I'm going to have the dragon's eggs and cherry blossom noodles.'

'You're joking. You made that up.'

'I did not. It's on page four. Raffy recommended it. It's not real dragon's eggs.'

Wexford looked up from the menu. 'I don't suppose it is since there aren't any real dragons. I may as well have the same. We have the unenviable task of showing that T-shirt to the Dades this afternoon and the sooner we get it over with the better.'

Their order was taken and Raffy, agreeing that perhaps 'dragon's eggs' was an unfortunate name, assured them it was a delicious seafood concoction. He'd tell his uncle and they'd find something that sounded more suitable. Could Mr Wexford suggest somehing? Wexford said he'd think about it.

'What I'm thinking at the moment', he said to Burden, 'is that we ought to be sure just when these floods began. I mean, when the Kingsbrook first burst its banks, that sort of thing. When I got home last Friday it was raining, but not heavily and there weren't any floods. I didn't go out at all on Saturday and I didn't know about the flood warning till I saw the television news at five fifteen.'

'Yes, well, I heard the flood warning on Radio Four on Saturday morning early but I guessed we'd be OK, we're too high up and too far from the Brede or the Kingsbrook. But on Saturday afternoon – well, early evening – Jenny and I and Mark went round to her parents to see how it was affecting them. As you know they've got a river frontage, their house backs on to the Kingsbrook, and as it happens, they moved out and went to Jenny's sister Candy on Sunday afternoon. But to get to their place we crossed the Kingsbrook Bridge and you could do it at six with ease. The height of the river wasn't anywhere near the bridge and it wasn't at seven thirty when we came back.

'But it wasn't raining very heavily then. The really heavy rain didn't start until about ten or later, nearer eleven. You know I've got that skylight in my house? Well, I heard it starting to crash on there as I was going to bed. I thought for a bit the water would come in and Jenny found an old enamel bath to put underneath it in case. Skylights are a menace. Anyway, the water didn't come in but we both lay awake a long time listening to the rain. I don't know when I've heard it heavier. It woke Mark and we had to take him in with us. I did go to sleep at last but I woke up at five and the crashing was still going on. I can tell you, I was scared to look out of the window.'

The dragon's eggs came. It was a prettily coloured dish, mostly butterfly prawns and shrimps and lobster claws with beansprouts and shredded carrot in a primrose-coloured sauce. Wexford, who had forgotten to take the linen napkin printed with anemones and birds of paradise out of its silver clip, had it graciously spread across his knees by Raffy.

'And the water went on rising all day,' he said.

'Absolutely. The Dade kids and Joanna Troy could have gone out at any time on the Sunday to take a look and that's when they possibly all went in.'

'Impossible,' said Wexford.

As he spoke, the street door opened and Dora entered with Callum Chapman. At first they didn't see him and Burden. Raffy was showing them to a table when Dora looked round and spotted him. Both came over and Wexford was starting to thank Chapman for his morning's work when, glancing from one to the other of them, he smiled – at last he smiled – and interrupted in his slow monotone, 'Skiving off, eh? So this is how you fritter away our taxes.'

Wexford was suddenly so angry he couldn't speak. He turned his back while Dora attempted to laugh it off. There was no introducing Burden now and Sylvia's mother and Sylvia's lover went back to their table. Whether his wife had much appetite for her lunch Wexford couldn't tell but his had gone. Burden glanced over his shoulder.

'Who *was* that?'

'Obviously my daughters don't get their taste in men from their mother.' Wexford had tried a joke but it failed miserably. 'Sylvia's new bloke.'

'You're kidding.'

'If only I were.'

'It takes all sorts, I suppose.'

'Yes, but I wish it didn't, don't you? I wish it took two or three sorts. Funny people, kind and thoughtful, sensitive people with imagination, tolerant and forbearing with good conversation, those sorts. No room for pompous, mean-spirited bastards like him.'

They ate as much as they were going to and Burden paid the bill. 'What he said, it wasn't that bad, you know,' he said as they were leaving. 'Haven't you got it a bit out of proportion? People are always saying that sort of thing to us.'

'They aren't all sleeping with my daughter.'

Burden shrugged. 'You were going to tell me why you didn't think finding the T-shirt was evidence of those three being in the water.'

Wexford got into the car.

'I don't know about not being in the water. I mean not being drowned. If she'd been wearing the T-shirt, why would it come off? I looked at it quite carefully. It's got a fairly tight round neck – do they call that a crew neck?' Burden nodded. 'It might be dragged off if she'd gone over Niagara but not in the flooded Kingsbrook. Another thing is, wouldn't she have had a coat over it? At least something rainproof. And if so, where's that? You'll say it's still to come to light. Maybe. This afternoon we have to find out positively what topcoats are missing.'

'If it didn't come off Sophie Dade what was it doing there?'

'It was put there to make us think she drowned. A red herring. It was to distract us, at least for a while, from looking further.'

Katrina Dade identified the T-shirt, though there had never been any doubt about its ownership. Once again she became rational and calm when anything connected with outward appearance was involved. 'Sophie and Giles both had these done. It was when we were all on holiday in Florida last April. You can have a look at his, it's in his room.'

'We've seen it, thank you, Mrs Dade.'

'Now maybe you'll accept that they've drowned.' Once more she had changed her tack. They had drowned. From reproaching herself for even considering the possibility, she had returned to believing it. 'Oh, I wish my husband was here. I want him. Why is he always working when I need him?' No one could answer that. 'I want my children's bodies. I want to give them a dignified burial.'

'It hasn't come to that, Mrs Dade,' said Burden. He assured her truthfully that the frogmen had begun searching again as soon as the T-shirt had been found. 'But it's a precaution,' he said, denying his own private belief. 'We don't accept the drowning theory, we still don't. While we're here we want to establish positively what topcoats or jackets Giles and Sophie were wearing when they left this house. They must have been wearing coats.'

'I was quite surprised Sophie was wearing that brown anorak,' she said. 'I can't think why. Not when she had a brand-new jacket in canary yellow with a plaid lining. She chose it herself. She loved that jacket.'

I can think why, Wexford said to himself. So that she wouldn't be easily identified, so that she wouldn't stand out a mile. That, too, may be a better reason for getting rid of the T-shirt. Or someone else getting rid of it and someone else persuading her not to wear the bright yellow jacket . . .

'Did Ms Troy see much of her former husband, Mrs Dade?'

'She never saw him.'

'His name is Ralph Jennings, I believe, and he lives in Reading.'

'I don't know where he lives.' Katrina, for whom acting naturally was impossible, whose posturing was almost pathological, seemed uncertain how to proceed with regard to Joanna Troy. Was her former friend still her friend or had she become an enemy? 'I said to her once that she wouldn't know about something, I don't remember what it was, because she'd never been married, I said, and she said, oh, yes, she had. "Believe it or not," she said, "but I was once a Mrs Ralph Jennings," and she laughed. The name just stuck in my mind. She isn't suited to marriage, you can tell that.'

'Why would that be?' Burden asked.

'My husband says it's because she's a lesbian. He says you can see that with half an eye.' Her sudden coyness and eyelid-batting was an embarrassment. 'He knows a dyke when he sees one, he says.'

Wexford thought he had seldom come across a more unpleasant man. Chapman was a pussy cat beside him.

'I'm innocent, he says, and he's glad I didn't know because it proves she never tried anything on.' Katrina achieved a convincing shudder. Then she said, 'Joanna's done this, hasn't she? Whatever it is. Taken them where they shouldn't go, got them into trouble. Maybe it's her that's drowned them, is that it?'

Before Wexford could come up with an answer the front door closed with a slam and Dade came striding in. 'You wanted me home,' he said to his wife, 'and I've come. For ten minutes.' He gave Wexford an exasperated glare.

Wexford said, 'I'd like a list of names of Giles's and Sophie's friends. I expect they'd be school friends. Their names and addresses, please.'

Katrina got up and went to the french windows where she stood, holding on to the curtain with one hand and looking out. With a show of impatience her husband began writing, in a large backward-sloping hand, on the sheet of paper Wexford had given him. He crossed the room to fetch a telephone directory.

'What do you do for a living, Mr Dade?'

The ballpoint was flung down. 'What can my profession possibly have to do with this inquiry? Can you tell me that?'

'You never know. But probably nothing. Nevertheless, I would like to know.'

The writing was resumed. 'I'm a domestic property broker.'

'Is that what I'd call an estate agent?' asked Burden.

Dade didn't answer. He handed Wexford the list. Katrina turned round and said thrillingly, 'Look, the sun has come out!'

It had, in a watery blaze. The Dades' garden, trees, shrubs, the last of waterlogged autumn flowers, sparkled with a million water drops. Curving across slatey clouds and blue patches the arc of a rainbow had one foot in the flooded Brede Valley and the other in Forby.

'May I keep my little girl's T-shirt?'

'I'm afraid not, Mrs Dade. Not at present. It will be returned to you later, of course.'

Wexford disliked the way he had to put this but he couldn't think of a better phrasing. It smacked to him, inescapably, of post-mortems. Then, as he and Burden moved towards the door, she threw herself at his feet and clasped her arms round his knees. Such a thing had never happened to him before and, unusually for him, he felt deeply awkward.

'Find my children, Mr Wexford! You will find my darling children?'

Afterwards, as he told Dora, he didn't know how he and Burden managed to escape. They heard the domestic property broker snarling at his wife for 'making an exhibition of herself' as he strained to raise her from the carpet.

'I'd like to go down and see how Subaqua are getting on,' Wexford said when he had recovered from his embarrassment. 'Where are they now?'

'Back at the bridge. They were going to have another look in the weir pool. It's the deepest part. Apparently they've turned the weir off. Did you know they could do that?'

'No, but seeing they can turn off Niagara Falls I'm not surprised.'

'I supposed we've checked on the whereabouts of Joanna Troy's car? Or, rather, checked it's not parked anywhere around here?'

'That was done yesterday. No dark-blue Golf with that index number anywhere in the area. The, er, tooth's gone off to the lab at Stowerton for something or other, I'm not sure what. Maybe only to establish that it's what we think it is.'

Wearing rubber boots and raincapes, they were standing on the temporary wooden bridge which had been put up during a pause in Tuesday's downpour to carry river frontage dwellers up to the comparatively dry land of the High Street. Wednesday's lull was still going on and, as always, everyone was hoping it was less a lull than a cessation. But the clouds were too massy and dark for that, the wind too brisk and the temperature too mild. Upstream the frogmen were in the weir pool. It was always deep water there, a favourite place for the local children to swim in until a new council member created alarm about it in a national newspaper – 'there will be a fatality sooner rather than later . . .' The water was deeper now and widening into an inland sea, the furthest reaches of which were creeping up Wexford's garden. That this might be the fatality, happening in the here and now, was taking shape in everyone's mind but his.

A boat on this water was something he had thought he would never see. The frogman surfaced and hung on to the gunwale. Wexford didn't know if he was the one he'd talked to on the Brede or someone different. Everything was so wet, everything dripping and spraying, that he couldn't tell if the cold drop he felt on his cheek was renewed rain or a splash from a stone Burden had kicked into the water. But it was soon followed by another and another, a shower of splashes, and the rain began in earnest, threatening to drench them. They waded back to the car. Wexford's cellphone was ringing.

'Freeborn wants to see me.' Sir James Freeborn was the Assistant Chief Constable. 'He sounded thrilled to bits that we were down here "watching the operations", as he put it. I wonder why.'

He was soon told. Freeborn was waiting for him in Wexford's office. This was what he always did when he came to Kingsmarkham rather than summoning the Chief Inspector to Headquarters at Myringham. There was nothing private in the office and Wexford wasn't one of those men who keep photographs of his wife and children on his desk, yet Freeborn was always to be found seated in Wexford's chair, looking into Wexford's computer and once, when the Chief Inspector returned rather sooner than expected, with his nose and a hand in one of the desk drawers. This time he wasn't sitting down but standing at the window, contemplating in the dying light and through the fine misty rain, the sheets of water that lay this side of Cheriton Forest.

'Makes it look like Switzerland,' he remarked, still gazing.

Coniferous forest and a lake . . . Well, perhaps, a little. 'Does it, sir? What did you want to see me about?'

In order to see him, Freeborn was obliged to turn round, which he did ponderously. 'Sit,' he said, and took Wexford's own seat himself. The chair on this side wasn't quite big enough for Wexford's bulk but he had no choice and settled himself uneasily. 'Those children and that woman are somewhere under all that.' Freeborn waved impatiently at the window. 'Here or in the Brede Valley. They have to be. Finding that, er, garment, clinched things, didn't it?'

'I don't think so. That, I believe, is what Joanna Troy wants us to think.'

'Really? You've evidence to show that Miss Troy is an abductor of children, have you? Possibly a child murderer?'

'No, sir, I haven't. But there's absolutely no evidence of any of the three of them entering the water, still less drowning. And in any case, where's the car?'

'Under the water too,' said Freeborn. 'I've been to Framhurst myself, I've seen how the floods have engulfed the road there. There's a steep drop from that road into the valley – or there was. They were all out in the car, the water was rising and she tried to drive through it. The car went over and down the incline with them all in it. Straightforward.'

Then how did the T-shirt find its way into the water between the Kingsbrook Bridge and the weir, a distance of at least three miles? If it's a possibility the bodies are still there, that Subaqua haven't yet found them, they could hardly have failed to find a car. And the water didn't begin to rise until late Saturday night, so this trip in the car, presumably to view the floods, couldn't have taken place until Sunday morning, more probably Sunday afternoon. In that case why didn't Giles Dade go to church *as he always did*? Why did his sister wear a dark, anonymous-looking jacket when she had a new yellow one she loved?

Wexford knew it would be useless to say any of this. 'I still think there's some point in trying to trace these people, sir. I believe they all left the house on Saturday evening before the floods started.'

'On what grounds?'

He could imagine Freeborn's face if he said, 'Because Giles didn't go to church.' He wasn't going to say it but, anyway, Freeborn didn't give him a chance. 'I want you to call off the search, Reg. Call off this "tracing", as you put it. Leave it to Subaqua. They're highly competent and they've reinforcements coming in from Myringham. I'm assured by their boss – incidentally, a fellow Rotarian – that they won't rest until they've found them. If they're there – and they are – they'll find them.'

If they're there . . . Since they weren't, couldn't be, time was going by, anything could have happened. He went home, asked Dora, who had been taking and apparently excelled at a computer course, if she could get into a website on the Internet for him.

'I should think so.'

'It's called www.langlearn.com. And when you've found it perhaps you'd give me a call so I can look at it.'

'Darling,' she said indulgently, 'I don't have to do that. I can print it out.' She sought for language he would understand. 'It will be like a book or a newspaper. You'll see.'

It was. 'Page 1 of 2' it said at the top and, in Times New Roman type, thirty-six point: 'Fantastic French with Joanna Troy.' The portrait photograph was smudgy. It might have been almost any young woman. There was a page of text, most of it incomprehensible to Wexford, not because it was in French, it wasn't, but because of the cyber-speak which he couldn't follow. A column down the left-hand side, extending on to page 2, offered twenty or thirty options including All the Words You Want, Verbs Made Easy, Books You Need and Instant Chat. You highlighted the one you wanted. Dora had apparently highlighted All the Words You Want for him and downloaded page 1 (of 51). It held an eye-opening vocabulary but not a word he could ever imagine using. Here the student could learn the French for pop music, 'house' and 'garage', the kind of drinks teenagers like, types of cigarette and, he suspected, types of cannabis, the translation of 'miniskirt', 'tank top', 'distressed leather' and 'kitten heels', the when, where and how of buying condoms and how a French girl would ask for the morning-after pill.

Did it tell him anything about Joanna Troy? Maybe it did. That, for instance, she had a grasp of what people of the age of her former students required from the Internet, that she was uninhibited, unshocked by drug-taking and the free availability of contraceptive measures. That she was what, in his day, used to be called 'with it' and in his father's 'on the ball'. She might not be a fashionable dresser herself but she knew about teenagers' clothes. And it was hardly part of his self-imposed brief to enquire why she assumed that everyone who wanted to learn French must be under eighteen and conversant with a language far more obscure than that she was aiming to teach.

But how very different from Katrina Dade she must be showed in all the words of this text he could understand and perhaps even more in those he couldn't. Did it also show that, her own age more or less halfway between theirs and that of their children, she had common ground with those children? Far more in common than with Katrina who would have defined 'garage', he was sure, as somewhere you kept a car and 'spliff' as an expostulatory noise made by a character in a comic strip.

And why did he feel, now more than ever, that the answer to all this would lie in the reason for the friendship between Katrina Dade and Joanna Troy? Whatever that might be. Katrina's motives were obvious enough. She was flattered by the attentions of a woman younger and cleverer than herself. Besides, she was what the psychotherapists, what Wexford's Sylvia, would call 'needy'. But what about Joanna's purpose? Perhaps it will emerge, he thought, as he put the printout into his pocket.

Chapter 6

According to the Environment Agency, all the ground in mid-Sussex, all the south of England, come to that, was waterlogged. Even when the rain stopped there would be nowhere for the accumulated water to go. Sheila Wexford, flying into Gatwick from the west of the United States, came to stay a night with her parents and told them the aircraft's descent had felt like a seaplane landing, the floods spread across thousands of acres and the downs rising out of it like islands.

The days passed, damp days, wet days, but the rain lessening, downpours giving place to showers, torrents to drizzle. The weekend was cloudy, the sky threatening, but what the Met Office had once called 'precipitation', an absurd name they had dropped recently, that had stopped. Joanna Troy and Giles and Sophie Dade had been missing for a week. On Monday a feeble watery sun came out. Instead of churning it into billows, the wind merely ruffled the gleaming grey surface of the floods. And contrary to what had been gloomily foretold, the water began to recede.

Its level had never reached the topmost sandbags in Wexford's garden but had lapped the walls and lain there, a menacing stagnant pool, unchanging for days. As Monday passed it started to sink and by the evening the whole of the highest sandbags were exposed. That evening Wexford brought his books downstairs and Dora's favourite small items of furniture.

Subaqua, whose headquarters were in Myringham, had opened a temporary office in Kingsmarkham. Since they had found nothing, its only use, as far as Wexford could tell, was as somewhere to send Roger and Katrina Dade when their demands on him became peremptory. They were quite natural, these demands. More and more he was begining to feel deep sympathy for these parents. Katrina's tears and Dade's brusqueness were forgotten in an overwhelming pity for a couple whose children had disappeared and who must feel total impotence in the face of an investigating officer temporarily warned off investigating. She at least probably spent long hours in the Subaqua trailer parked on the dry side of Brook Road next to the Nationwide Building Society and waited for the news that never came. Roger Dade's snatching time off work was very likely an agony to him. Neither of them looked as if they had eaten for a week.

George and Effie Troy, as anxious now as those other parents, called to see him and them he sent to Subaqua too. Not that he had entirely obeyed Freeborn's injunction. Rather he had interpreted it as applying to activity on his part and that of his officers. Passivity was another matter. He couldn't (or wouldn't) stop people coming to *him* or even, if they phoned first, forbid them to air their fears in his presence. Of course, he could send them to Subaqua as well but surely that was no reason not to hear them out first?

The first of them arrived while he was reading the lab report on the little object Lynn Fancourt had found in the Dades' hall. A tooth it was, or rather, the crown of a tooth, constructed of porcelain and gold. There was no reason to suppose violence had contributed to its separation from the root and base of the natural tooth to which it had been attached. An interesting factor, in the opinion of the forensic examiner, was that a small amount of an adhesive was found on the crown and this was of the type which Joanna Troy might have bought over the counter in a pharmacy temporarily to reattach the crown if, say, she had been unable to visit her dentist. Wexford wasn't sure it was particularly interesting. While having no crowns on his own teeth, he felt that if he had and one came out he might, especially if pain resulted, buy and use such an adhesive. Surely anyone would as a temporary measure. Patch up your tooth and ring your dentist for an appointment.

But now she might be in pain. Would she seek a dentist wherever she was? And should he do something about this? Alert dentists nationwide . . . Only he couldn't because Freeborn had banned any further action. While he was thinking about this Vine came in and said there was a Mrs Carrish wanted to see him. Matilda Carrish.

'She said it as if I was expected to have heard of her. Perhaps you have.'

Wexford had. 'She's a photographer or used to be. Famous for taking pictures of eyesores, blots on the countryside, that sort of thing.' Wexford had been going to add that Matilda Carrish had also been much praised some five years back for her exhibition of street people's portraits in the National Portrait Gallery, but one look at Vine's expression of apprehensive distaste stopped him. 'She must be getting on a bit now. What does she want?'

'You, sir. She's the Dade kids' grandmother. Roger Dade's mum.'

'Really?' How unlikely, he thought. Could she be a hoaxer? Frauds and con-people turned up in hordes when they had cases like this. Yet she was called

Carrish, he recalled, and it was an unusual name. If he had had to conjecture the sort of woman Dade's mother would be, also taking into account the pearl earring and Katrina's crushing put-down of her as an 'old bat', he would have come up with a meretricious interfering creature, never a professional woman, but someone who had too little to occupy her or allay her chronic frustration. 'You'd better bring her up here,' he said, curious now to see what she was like, hoaxer or not.

That Matilda Carrish was indeed 'getting on a bit' showed in her lined face and her bright silver hair but not in her step, her carriage and her general agility. She was very thin and springy, though without the nervous energy that showed in so many of her daughter-in-law's movements. The hand she held out to him was dry and cool, ringless, the nails filed short. Sometimes he ignored extended hands but hers he took and was oddly surprised by the fragile bones. Remembering the photograph in Sophie Dade's bedroom told him at once she was who she said she was.

The black trouser suit she wore had been designed for a woman half her age, yet it was entirely suitable, it fitted as if it had been made for her, as perhaps it had. Aquiline though her face was, her lips thin and her cheekbones sharp, he could see Roger Dade in her and realised that only a little padding out and smoothing, a little lifting and plumping, would make mother and son as alike as twins.

She came straight to the point, no preamble, no excuses. 'What are you doing to find my missing grandchildren?'

This was the question Wexford dreaded. It was he who had to answer it, not Freeborn, and he was aware that by now any response he gave must sound feeble and as if the police simply weren't bothering.

But he tried. From the first Mrs Dade had believed her children had drowned and that was now the police belief. Today or at the latest tomorrow the waters would have receded sufficiently to put the matter beyond doubt.

'I understood that frogmen had been down and there had been a comprehensive search.'

'That is so and –' he could use these words to a grandparent, not a parent '– no bodies have been found.'

'Then – if I'm not being naïve – why haven't you widened the search? Have ports and airports been alerted? What of other police authorities? I understand we now have a national missing persons register. Are they on that register?'

She sounded more like an investigative journalist than a photographer. Her voice was crisp and direct, her turquoise-blue eyes piercing. When she started speaking they had fixed themselves on his face and never left it, never blinked. He wanted to tell her she wasn't being naïve. Instead he said lamely, 'The children's passports are here. Ms Troy can't, for instance, have taken them out of the country.'

She shrugged, the way her son did. For the first time she expressed an opinion. 'I was staying at my son's home in October. For three nights. I found those children exceptionally mature for their ages. Mature and particularly intelligent. I don't know if you're aware that Giles took a French GCSE last spring and got an A star.' I wonder if he managed to get the French for 'miniskirt' and 'garage' into his essay, Wexford thought. 'Sophie will be a scientist one day,' Matilda Carrish said. 'It is beyond me why they had to have a sitter at all. Sophie is a responsible thirteen and her brother is nearly sixteen. Let me correct that, he *is* sixteen. His birthday was two days ago.'

'Young to be left.'

'You think so? A boy or girl may marry at sixteen, Chief Inspector. If what I read in the newspapers is true, a large proportion of the female population of this country have babies at thirteen, fourteen and fifteen, and are set up in flats with their child by their local authority. No one babysits them, they are babysitters themselves.'

'It was Mr and Mrs Dade's decision,' Wexford said, thinking that whatever had been the guiding principle behind Roger Dade's choice of a wife, he hadn't married his mother. 'We have no reason –' he nearly said 'as yet' but suppressed it '– to associate Ms Troy with any criminal activity. Whatever has happened to these three people, she may be as much an innocent victim as the children.'

Matilda Carrish smiled. There was no humour in that smile, it was the stretching of the lips of someone who has superior knowledge and knows it, a facial expression of triumph. 'You think so? What you don't know, I can see, is the reason Joanna Troy gave up her teaching job at Haldon Finch. I will tell you. She was dismissed for stealing a twenty-pound note from one of her own students.'

Wexford nodded. There was nothing else he could do. He remembered this woman's son telling him Joanna Troy had left her job because she had been unable to put up with the behaviour of class members. 'If we need to widen our search,' he said, 'you may be sure Ms Troy's antecedents will be investigated. Now, if there is nothing else, Mrs Carrish . . .'

'Oh, but there is. I must tell you that first thing this morning, before I came down here – I live in Gloucestershire – I got in touch with a private investigation agency. Search and Find Limited of Bedford Square. I'll give you their telephone number.'

'Bedford Square, London?' Wexford asked.

'Is there another?'

Wexford sighed. She would make an excellent witness, he thought, as he showed her to the door and closed it behind her. A drift of her perfume had wafted past him as for a moment she stood close by him, perfume and some other scent as well. It was – it *couldn't* be – cannabis? It couldn't be. Not at her age, in her position. The cologne she used must have some pot-like ingredient in it and his sometimes too-acute sense of smell had picked it out.

He dismissed it from his mind. He hadn't asked her how well she got on with her grandchildren and it was too late now. It was hard to imagine small children liking her, but Sophie and Giles were of course small no longer. Yet he couldn't picture her being drawn to teenagers, making concessions to them, entering in any way into their interests. Would she, for instance, know what hip-hop was? Or gangsta rap? Or the identity and nature of Eminem? Would the availability of the morning-after pill mean anything to her and, if it did, would she censure it out of hand? She had, he thought, spoken of teenage mothers as of some alien species permitted to exist only by the dispensation of a merciful authority.

But what of this story of hers accounting for Joanna Troy's abandonment of her profession? If it were true, why hadn't the Dades revealed it? Why had Roger Dade been at some pains to cover it up? Wexford couldn't fit Matilda Carrish into the Dade ménage at all. She seemed to have nothing in common with Roger except a physical resemblance. It was possible, of course, that she was a fantasist, that she had invented her account of Joanna's stealing from a pupil. He knew better than to believe that because a woman or man seemed straightforward, direct, was articulate, avoided circumlocution and evasiveness, they must also be truthful and beyond deceit. One had only to think of successful conmen. He went to the window and looked out across the landscape. Waterlogged or not, the solid ground could still absorb more, was absorbing more. He could see the floods receding, the water sinking into somewhere still enough of a sponge to receive it, meadows reappearing, willows rising, their trunks free and their fine trailing branches swaying once more in the wind.

Suppose, when the Brede became a river again and not a lake, a mud-coated blue four-door saloon VW Golf was revealed lying in what had been the deepest part. And suppose three bodies had failed to come to the surface when gases inflated them because the three people had all this time been *inside* the car. Reason told him this was impossible, that there was no way the car could have got into the deepest part unless it had been parked on the river bank and everyone inside it unconscious for the time it took for the water to rise to its highest level. Suppose this was so and they had been overcome by carbon monoxide fumes . . . Impossible, though this must be something like what Freeborn and Burden had in mind. And if so, when had Joanna Troy parked there? On Sunday morning? In heavy rain with a flood warning out? In any case, Giles wouldn't have gone. He had to go to church . . .

All this went round and round in Wexford's head. He put on his raincoat from force of habit rather than because he needed it and went out to get himself a sandwich for his lunch. He could have sent someone but he wanted to look at the water levels at the same time. For the first time for nearly a fortnight the pavements were dry. He walked along the High Street and noted that St Peter's churchyard was no longer flooded. Gravestones looked like what they were, markers of burial sites. They had ceased to be rocks protruding from the sea. The parapet of the Kingsbrook Bridge was clear, its roadway awash with mud drifts. As stonework and walls, lamp standards, bollards, signposts emerged from the receding flood, everything had a sodden look, not washed clean but soiled with tidemarks, mud-stained and draped with dirty waterweed. What was it going to cost, putting all this to rights? And what of the flooded houses, some of them twice engulfed since September? Would insurance companies pay up and would their owners ever be able to sell them?

Going back, he made a detour up York Street to buy his sandwich. Kingsmarkham's finest were to be obtained at the Savoy Sandwich Bar where they made them for you while you waited. He chose brown bread and smoked salmon, no spread. Dr Akande had forbidden butter except in minuscule amounts, had forbidden so many kinds of substitutes that Wexford couldn't remember which. It was easier to do without but he asked for some watercress on the salmon, not because he liked it but because Akande did. The next customer, a small man wearing a clerical collar, asked for cheese and pickle, the cheapest kind they did. It was this which made Wexford linger, his suspicion confirmed when the man behind the counter called out to someone in the kitchen, 'The usual for Mr Wright!'

'You won't know me,' Wexford said when the sandwiches had been packaged and handed over. 'Two of my officers interviewed you. Chief Inspector Wexford, Kingsmarkham Crime Management.'

Wright gave him an uncertain look. Many people did when they first met him, Wexford was used to it. They wondered what it was they had done and what he wanted them for. Wright's wary expression gave way to a faint smile.

'Giles Dade and his sister are still missing, I believe?'

'Still missing.'

They left the shop. Because Jashub Wright turned right and began walking in the direction of 'the hut' Wexford went that way too. The pastor of the Church of the Good Gospel talked about the floods. Everyone in Kingsmarkham and the villages talked constantly about the floods and would for weeks, months, to come. As he was speaking a pale sun, a mere pool of light, appeared among the clouds.

'What sort of purity of life?' Wexford asked when they paused in front of the church and its signboard with the sub-title.

'All sorts really. Purity of mind and conduct. A sort of inward cleanness, if that doesn't sound too much like the fashionable vogue for clearing the body of toxins.' Wright laughed heartily at his joke. 'You might say our aim is actually to clear mind, body *and* spirit of toxins.'

Wexford had always had difficulty in establishing the difference between mind and spirit. Which was which and where were they? As for the soul . . . He said none of this but instead, very simply, 'How do you do it?'

'That's a pretty big question to ask at midday out on the pavement.' More hearty laughter.

'Briefly.'

'If new members want to join the congregation they must make confession before they can be accepted. We hold a cleansing for them and they undertake not to commit the sin again. We understand about temptation and if they are tempted they have only to come to us – that is, to me and the church elders – and we give them all the help we can to resist whatever it is. Now if you'll excuse me . . .'

Wexford watched him enter the church by a side

door. He wondered what on earth Burden had been thinking of to describe Wright as 'decent'. That creepy laugh had made him shiver. The cleansing sounded ominous – how could you get in and witness it? Only by applying to join, he supposed, and he wasn't as interested as that.

'I've been away,' the woman said. 'I've been away for a fortnight. When I got home yesterday someone down the street told me Joanna had disappeared.'

This was his second uninvited guest, a short dumpy woman of forty dressed in red. She had been waiting a long time and he had to bolt his sandwich to prevent her waiting any longer. Grumblings of heartburn troubled him. 'And you are?'

They had told him but only her Christian name, Yvonne, had stayed with him. 'Yvonne Moody. I live next door to Joanna. There's something I think you ought to know. I don't know what those Dades have told you and Joanna's father but if they've said she was fond of those kids and they were fond of her, they couldn't be more wrong.'

'What do you mean, Mrs Moody?'

'Miss,' she said. 'I'm not married. I'll tell you what I mean. First, you shouldn't run away with the idea she and Katrina were best friends. Joanna may have been Katrina's but Katrina wasn't hers. Far from it. They'd nothing in common. I don't know what brought them together in the first place, though I have my ideas. One day Joanna said she wasn't going to have any more to do with the family. But she did, though she'd come home and tell me that was the last time she'd babysit – well, not babysit but you know what I mean – she only did it for Katrina's sake, she was sorry for Katrina, and the next week there she was, up there again.'

'What did you mean, you have your ideas?'

'It's obvious, isn't it? She liked Roger Dade – liked him too well, I mean. The way no one should let herself think about a married man. I don't know him, I've only come across the son, but whatever he's like it was wrong what she was doing. She's said to me once or twice that if Katrina went on the way she did, all those scenes and tears and drama, she'd lose him. If that doesn't tell you she meant she'd step into her shoes I don't know what does. I told her she was heading for trouble besides behaving immorally. You can commit adultery in your heart just as much as in the flesh. I said that but she laughed and refused to discuss it.'

Wexford wasn't surprised. He certainly wouldn't have wanted to expose his private life to this woman. Just as Burden came into the room his phone rang and he was told the Assistant Chief Constable was on the line.

'You can go ahead now, Reg. Tomorrow we can be certain.' Freeborn sounded mildly embarrassed. 'There's, er, nothing down there.' Would he have preferred to find three corpses and a waterlogged car?

Burden had been over to Framhurst where the floods were disappearing fast. 'As if someone had pulled the plug out,' he said. 'By this time tomorrow you'll be able to see the fields again.'

Wexford thought this a bit over-optimistic. 'What do we make of the sanctimonious Yvonne Moody? If it's true what she says, why would abducting the Dade kids help Joanna? Surely it would be more likely to put the Dades against her for ever, both of them. Or is everything Ms Moody says a lie?'

'Who knows? You have to admit there are some funny aspects about this case. I mean, what on earth did Katrina have in common with a highly educated single woman fourteen or fifteen years younger than herself? Katrina may have admired her greatly, which one can imagine, but Joanna? What this Moody woman says does provide a reason for Joanna's friendship with Katrina, it would account for her going over there to look after the children. But there's so much about the lot of them we don't know. For instance, that weekend seems to have been the first time she'd stayed in the house . . .'

'No, I asked. Back last April or May, they couldn't remember which, she stayed overnight while the Dades went off to some estate agents' bunfight in London. Roger didn't want to drive back in case he was over the limit.'

Burden nodded. 'OK. The other occasions she'd only have been there for the evening, but there may have been times when she sat in so that Katrina could go out while Roger was working late. Only he got home earlier than he expected or earlier than he'd told Katrina. Other times she may have deliberately come without her car so that he had to drive her home.'

'I'd never have suspected you were such an expert on seduction, not to say adultery.'

The once-widowed, twice-married Burden said frankly, 'Well, as you know, I've committed what they used to call fornication but never adultery. Still, you pick up this stuff in our line of business.'

'True. Your solution is ingenious but it doesn't help with why she took the kids, if she did. Stealing a twenty-pound note is hardly a rehearsal for stealing two people. However, when your weather forecast comes true tomorrow or whenever and we know for sure the car and those three were never down there, we can proceed to find out more.'

'Better start by asking all the dentists in the United Kingdom to be on the watch for a young woman coming to them with a missing tooth crown. Or asking them if any young woman has already come to them.'

'We can try,' said Wexford, 'but if she's as intelligent as you say, and I dare say she is, though that website could have fooled me, she'd guess we'd check up on dentists and instead of getting the crown professionally fixed she'll have been back to the pharmacist and bought another pack of that adhesive stuff.'

Chapter 7

As the floods subsided, among the detritus left behind were a bicycle, two supermarket trolleys, an umbrella with spokes but no cover, the usual crisp packets, Coke cans, condoms, single trainers, miscellaneous clothes as well as a wicker chair, a prototype video recorder and a Turkey carpet.

Wexford expected a further directive from Freeborn but none came. He phoned headquarters and was told the Assistant Chief Constable had started on a week of his annual leave. 'We proceed, I think, don't you?' he said to Burden.

'Is there any point in checking on where all these sweatshirts and jeans come from? Some of them are barely recognisable, they're in shreds.'

'Get Lynn on it. It can't do any harm. Our priorities are the parents and a further investigation of Joanna Troy's background.'

Early that morning, as soon as it began to be light, he had carried out a survey of his garden. A depressing business. It wasn't that he was much of a gardener himself. He didn't know the names of many plants, knew nothing of their Latin or Linnaean names, had never understood what needs sunshine, what shade, what plenty of water, what very little. But he liked to look at it. He liked to sit in it of a summer evening, enjoying the scents and the quiet and the beauty as pale flowers closed their petals for the night.

Although Browning's poem itself revolted him, the awful adjectives like 'lovesome' – God walks in gardens indeed! – he agreed with the sentiment. His garden was the veriest seat of peace. Now it looked like a swamp and worse, the kind of marsh that has been irresponsibly drained and abandoned as a waste land. Things which had grown there and which he had known as 'that lovely red thing' or 'the one with the wonderful scent' had either disappeared entirely or survived as a bunch of wet sticks. It was Dora he felt sorrier for than himself. She had done it, chosen the plants and shrubs, tended them, loved the place. Only the lawn seemed to have come out of the water unscathed, a brilliant, yellowish, *evil* green.

He went indoors, took off his boots and searched for the shoes he'd left somewhere. Dora was on the phone. She said, 'That's for you to decide, isn't it?' and he knew it must be something unpleasant, something he wouldn't want to know.

She said goodbye and put the receiver down. Only one person apart from Burden ever phoned at eight in the morning, and she'd never speak in that crushing tone to Mike.

'You'd better tell me what Sylvia's up to now.'

'Cal's moving in with her. Apparently, it's been suggested before but Neil made a fuss. On account of the boys, I suppose.'

'I'm not surprised. So would I.'

'He seems to have withdrawn his objections now he's got someone of his own.'

He thought about these things now as he had himself driven to Forest Road. Had he and Dora been exceptionally lucky in that their marriage had endured? Or was it rather that in their day people worked harder at marriage, divorce if not actually disgraceful was a distant last resort, you married and you stayed married? If his first wife had lived would Burden's marriage have endured? He couldn't recall any child in his class at his own school whose natural mother and father weren't together. Among his parents' friends and neighbours no one was divorced. So were half those marriages deeply and secretly unhappy? Did their homes ring with frequent bitter quarrels conducted in the presence of their children, his classmates? No one would ever know. He disliked even thinking of the feelings of his son-in-law Neil, whom he was fond of and who loved his children. Now he would see these boys in the care of what amounted to a new father of whom they would perhaps grow fonder. Would he also give them a new stepmother? And all because he bored Sylvia and hadn't talked to her much. Maybe that was unfair but wasn't this Cal the most awful crashing bore? With time his looks would fade and his sexual prowess, if that was also part of the attraction, would wane . . .

Banish it from your mind, he told himself as he and Vine made their way to the last street in Kingsmarkham. This would be his first meeting with George and Effie Troy, though Vine had met and talked to them before. He noted the girth of George, fatter than he, Wexford, had been at the worst of his overeating, and a lot less tall. His wife had an interesting face and manner, a woman of character. These little Gothic houses, of which there were a number scattered around Kingsmarkham and Pomfret, looked quaint but were poky and dark, comfort, even when they were first built, sacrificed to some mistaken idea – the Oxford Movement and then Ruskin, he thought vaguely – that England would be a better place if mediaevalised. He seated himself in a chair far too small for him.

Already, after having only exchanged a few words

with the Troys, he knew that Effie would speak for them both. Effie would be the coherent one, the less emotional one, and the question he had to ask was highly emotive.

'I'm sorry I have to ask you about this and I wouldn't if I didn't think it necessary.' The dark-browed face, the dark eyes, were turned on him inscrutably. 'I've learned that your daughter gave up teaching because she was accused of stealing money from one of the students.'

'Who told you such a thing?' It was the father who asked, not the stepmother.

'That I'm not at liberty to tell you. Is it true?'

Effie Troy spoke slowly, in measured tones. Wexford suddenly thought that if you had to have a stepmother, the way his grandsons would, this might not be such a bad one to have. 'It's true that Joanna was accused by a boy of sixteen of taking a twenty-pound note out of his backpack. He later, er, recanted. This is some few years ago. You're right when you say she "gave up" teaching because of this. She did, of her own volition. She wasn't sacked or asked to resign. She was never charged with stealing.'

This last Wexford already knew. He was about to ask why she gave up when she had apparently been exonerated when the father, unable to contain himself any longer, burst into a harangue. Joanna was victimised, the boy was a psychopath, he accused her purely to make trouble and make himself the centre of attention, he hated her because she expected him to do too much homework. Effie listened to all this with an indulgent smile, finally patting her husband's hand and whispering to him as to a child, 'All right, darling. Don't get in a state.'

Obedient but still looking mutinous, George Troy

fell silent. Vine said, 'Do you know the boy's name?'

'Damian or Damon, one of those fashionable names. I don't remember the surname.'

'Mr Troy?'

'Don't ask me. All I wanted was to put it out of my head. The monstrous behaviour of the modern child is beyond my comprehension. I don't understand and I don't want to. Joanna may have told us his surname but I don't recall. I don't want to. No one has surnames any more, do they? She brought one of her pupils here once – I'm not calling them students, students are in colleges – I forget why, she called in and this pupil was with her. Called me George if you please. Because my wife did. No, they don't have surnames any more. They all of them called my daughter Joanna at that school. When I was a child we called our teachers "sir" or "miss", we were respectful . . .'

'Tell me about your daughter,' Wexford said. 'What sort of a person is she? What's she like.' He seemed to address both of them but he looked at Effie.

She said, to his astonishment, because he thought her husband about to ask this of her, 'Would you like to make us all a cup of coffee, darling?'

He went. He seemed not to suspect Effie wanted him briefly out of the way. But did she?

'Her mother died when she was sixteen,' Effie began. 'I married her father three years later. It wasn't difficult for me, being her stepmother, I'd known her all her life. She was never rebellious, she was never resentful. She's very bright, you know, won all the scholarships, went to Warwick University and Birmingham. I expect she worked hard but she managed to give the impression she never worked at all. This is the kind of thing you want to know?'

Wexford nodded. The old man was slow and he was thankful for it.

'I was surprised when she went in for teaching. That sort of teaching, anyway. But she loved it. It was her life, she said.'

'She got married?'

'She met her husband when they were both in graduate school in Birmingham and lived together for a while. Ralph's some sort of computer buff. His father died and left him quite a lot of money, enough to buy a house. Joanna wanted to live around here and Ralph bought quite a big house. She got her job at Haldon Finch School, a very good job for someone so young, but of course her qualifications were marvellous. She and Ralph seemed to be a case of two people who got on fine while they lived together but just couldn't handle being married. They split up after a year, he sold the place and she bought that little house of hers with her share.'

Effie smiled sweetly at her husband as he lumbered in with a tray on the surface of which coffee had slopped. Their drinks were in mugs, milk in whether desired or not, no spoons, no sugar. 'Thank you, George, darling.'

She hadn't said a word her husband might not hear, Wexford thought. Perhaps she would have if he had taken longer. Since he had heard her last words, George launched into criticism of the Kingbridge Mews house. It was too small, badly planned, the windows too narrow, the staircase perilous. A psychiatrist would call this projection, thought Wexford, who had noticed the stairs in this house, as steep and narrow as a ladder. He addressed the father.

'Your daughter uses your car, I understand.'

Wexford guessed this question might result in a long and intricate explanation from George as to why he bought a new car and passed it on to his daughter instead of driving it himself, so he wasn't surprised by the fresh flow of words. Effie interrupted smoothly when he paused to take a sip of coffee.

'My husband wasn't confident at the wheel any longer, I'm afraid. He'd suddenly become rather nervous of causing an accident.' Or *you* had, Wexford thought. 'His eyesight was letting him down. Of course, I ought to have taken over the driving but the fact is I can't drive. I never learned. Absurd, isn't it? Joanna said she was thinking of buying a car and George said, don't do that, you can have mine on permanent loan.'

Far from being offended at his wife's taking over the conversation, George Troy looked pleased and proud. He patted her hand in a congratulatory way. Effie went on, 'Joanna set up as a freelance translator and editor. And of course she did private teaching – coaching, I suppose you'd call it. French and German. The students, er, pupils mostly came to her house but sometimes she went to them. Then she landed this job writing French lessons for the Internet. I'm sure I haven't put that well but perhaps you know what I mean. The company had a website and she put these lessons on it, first of all an elementary course, now an intermediate one, and she's doing a third for advanced students. I don't really know what more I can tell you.'

What a pity the old man had come back! 'Boyfriends since the break-up of her marriage, Mrs Troy?'

'There haven't been any,' said George. 'She was too busy for that sort of thing. She had a new career to establish, didn't she? No room for men and any of that nonsense.'

The stepmother said, 'Joanna wasn't fond of children, she told me that. Not small children, that is.

Of course she liked them when they were old enough for her to teach them. She liked *bright* children. She wouldn't have wanted to marry again for the sake of having children.'

According to their grandmother, the Dade children were very bright indeed. 'Mr Troy, Mrs Troy, have you ever heard of the Church of the Good Gospel? Their slogan is "God loves purity of life".'

Both looked blank.

'Giles Dade is a member of it. Ms Troy never mentioned that to you?'

'Never,' Effie said. 'Joanna isn't religious herself. I don't think she was very interested in religion.'

'Lot of mumbo-jumbo,' said her husband. 'I feel the same.'

'Finally,' Wexford said, 'did Joanna have crowned teeth?'

'Crowned teeth?'

'We have found what we believe to be a crown off one of her teeth in the Dades' house. It looks as if it fell out and she had temporarily – and obviously not effectively – secured it with some kind of adhesive.'

Effie knew exactly what he was talking about. 'Oh, yes, she had two teeth that were crowned. She had them done years ago because they were discoloured. She said they aged her, which of course wasn't true. She can't have been more than twenty-one when they were done. The crown you're talking about came off two or three weeks back, it actually came off while she was eating a chocolate caramel in this house. She said she'd have to go to the dentist but she hadn't the time, she couldn't make it that week. I was just going to the shops and she said while I was out would I get her a tube of that stuff from the pharmacy. And I did.'

Of the other parents only the mother was at home. Roger Dade was, as usual, at work. Katrina had her own mother with her, a woman very unlike her and very different from Matilda Carrish, plump and sturdy, maternal, wearing what are usually called 'sensible' clothes, a skirt, blouse and cardigan, and lace-up walking shoes. The house looked as if she had taken charge. It had never been dirty, just rather too untidy for comfort, but Mrs Bruce had transformed it like the housewifely woman she was. All those diamond panes had been polished, ornaments washed and on a coffee table, as in the lounge of a country house hotel, magazines were stacked, their corners perfectly aligned with the angle of the table. A bowl that had looked as if it could serve no useful purpose had been filled with red and yellow chrysanthemums and a sleek black cat with a coat like satin, presumably owned by the Bruces, lay stretched out on the mantelpiece.

The only unkempt and wretched object (animate or inanimate) in the room was Katrina who sat huddled, a blanket round her shoulders, her once pretty brown hair hanging in rats' tails, her face gaunt. Wexford sensed there would be no more acting, no more posing, striking of attitudes, scene-setting. In the face of reality all that faded. She no longer cared how she looked or what impression she might make.

No tea or coffee or even water had ever been offered them in that house. Doreen Bruce now offered all three. Wexford was sure that if drinks had been accepted, they would have appeared in matching china on a lace cloth. He asked the children's grandmother when she had last seen Giles and Sophie or spoken to them on the phone.

She looked like a woman who would have a low, comfortable sort of voice but hers was high and rather shrill. 'I never spoke to them, dear. I'm not keen on phones, never know what to talk about. I can say what I've got to say or pass on a message but as to conversation, never have been able to and never shall.'

'They came to stay with you in the school holidays, I believe.'

'Oh, yes, dear, that's a different thing altogether. We like having them with us, that's quite different. They've always come to stay with us in the holidays, Easter as well as the summer sometimes. There's lots to do round where we live, you see. It's lovely country, quite isolated, plenty of things for young people.'

Not much, as far as Wexford could see. Nothing for the kind who used Joanna's website. Of course, he hadn't been there but he knew that parts of the Suffolk coast, though only seventy miles from London, had a remoteness scarcely felt here. What would there be to do? The seaside perhaps no more than ten miles away but no seaside resort, fields all strictly fenced in with barbed wire, fast traffic making the roads difficult to walk along. No facilities for young people, no youth club, no cinema, no shops, and probably one bus a day with luck.

'Where do you think Giles and Sophie are, Mrs Bruce?'

She glanced at her daughter. 'Well, I don't know, dear. They didn't come near us. I'm sure they were happy at home, they had everything they wanted, their parents couldn't do enough for them. They weren't one of those – what-d'you-call-it – dysfunctional families.'

He noticed the past tense. So, perhaps, did Katrina, for she turned to look at him and, still cowering under her blanket, shouted, 'When are you going to find them? When? Have you looked? Has anybody been looking?'

With perfect truth he said, 'Mrs Dade, every police force in the United Kingdom knows they are missing.

Everyone is looking for them. We have made a television appeal. The media know. We shall continue to do everything we can to find them. I assure you of that.'

It sounded impotent to him, it sounded feeble. Two teenagers and a woman of thirty-one had vanished off the face of the earth. The muffled face emerged and tears began to wash it so that it was as wet as if put under the tap.

Later that day he discussed it with Burden. 'It's almost two weeks now, Mike.'

'What do you think happened to them? You must have a theory, you always do.'

Wexford didn't say that it was Burden's theory of drowning, influencing Freeborn, which had delayed the investigation for eight days. 'Joanna Troy has no criminal record. That we know for sure. But what's the truth about that allegedly stolen note? And are there any more such incidents in her past?'

'Her ex-husband's been found. He doesn't live in Brighton any more. He's moved to Southampton, got himself a new girlfriend who comes from there. Anything like that he may be able to tell us.'

'I feel about her that she's a bit of mystery. She's a young woman who's been married but she's apparently had no boyfriends since. She's a teacher who loves teaching but dislikes children, yet she minds two children quite regularly while their parents go out. If she has friends apart from Katrina and up to a point the woman next door, we haven't found any. When she's challenged about a possible affair with Roger Dade she laughs but she doesn't deny it. We need to know more.'

'You haven't said what your theory is.'

'Mike, I suppose I think, on the slight evidence we've got, that Joanna has killed those children. I don't know her motive. I don't know where –

certainly not in the Dades' house. I don't know how she's disposed of the bodies or what she's done with her car. But if all this happened on Saturday evening, she had time to dispose of them and time to leave the country before anyone knew they were missing.'

'Only she didn't leave the country. Her passport's in her house.'

'Exactly,' said Wexford. 'And we don't believe in false passports, do we? Except for spies and gangsters and international crooks, especially fictional ones. Not unless the killing was carefully premeditated and I'm sure it wasn't. Improbable as it sounds, she took those children out somewhere and killed them on an impulse because she's a psychopath with a hatred of teenagers. And if you think that's rubbish, can you come up with anything better?'

Chapter 8

Toxborough lies north-east of Kingsmarkham, just over the Kentish border, but the Sussex side of the M20. Once a small town of great beauty and antiquity, its spoliation began in the 1970s with the coming of industry to its environs and its ruin was complete when an approach road was built from it to the motorway. But several villages in its vicinity, yet in remote countryside, have retained their isolation and unspoilt prettiness. One of these is Passingham St John (pronounced, for reasons unknown, 'Passam Sinjen') which, being no more than two miles from Passingham Park station, is a favourite with wealthier commuters. Such a one was Peter Buxton who, two years before, had bought Passingham Hall as a weekend retreat.

Originally intending to retreat there every Friday evening and return to London on Monday morning, Buxton soon found that escape to rural Kent was not so easy as it had at first appeared. For one thing the traffic on Fridays after four in the afternoon and before nine at night was appalling. Going back on Monday morning was just as bad. Moreover, most of the invitations he and his wife received to London functions it was prudent for an up-and-coming media tycoon like himself to accept were for Friday or Saturday evenings, while Sunday lunchtime parties were not unknown. Especially in the winter these invitations came thick and fast, and thus it was that the first weekend of December was the first he and his wife had been to Passingham Hall in more than a month.

The house stood on the side of a shallow hill, so Buxton knew there was little danger of its flooding. In any case Pauline, who came in two or three times a week and kept an eye on things, had reported to Sharonne Buxton that all was well. Her husband had also worked for the Buxtons as handyman and gardener but had given up in October, offering the excuse of a bad back. Urban Buxton, originally from Greenwich, was learning how common this disability is in the countryside. Unless you are prepared to pay extravagantly for basic services, bad backs explain why it is so hard to find anyone to work for you.

He and Sharonne arrived very late on the night of Friday, 1 December, drove along the gravel drive through the eight-acre wood and up to the front door. The exterior lights were on, the heating was on and the bed linen had been changed. Pauline, at any rate, hadn't a bad back. It was long past midnight and the Buxtons went straight to bed. The weather forecast had been good, no more rain was predicted, and Peter was awakened at eight thirty by sunshine streaming through his bedroom window. This was early by his weekend standards but mid-morning in rural Kent.

He thought of taking Sharonne a cup of tea but decided not to wake her. Instead, he put on the Barbour jacket he had recently acquired and a pair of green wellies, requisite wear for a country landowner, and went outdoors. The sun shone brightly and it wasn't particularly cold. Peter was intensely proud of owning his twenty acres of land but his pride he kept secret. Not even Sharonne knew of it. As far as she was concerned this garden, paddock, green slopes and wood were only what a woman like her could expect to possess. They were her due as a star of the catwalk and one of those few models to be known – and known nation- if not worldwide – by her (somewhat enhanced) given name alone. But Peter, secretly, gloried in his land. He intended adding to it and was already in negotiation with the farmer to buy an adjoining field. He dreamed of the huge garden party he planned for the following summer with a marquee on the lawn and picnic tables in the sunny flower-sprinkled clearing, the open space in the centre of the wood.

It was towards this clearing that he was walking now, along the lane to where a track wound its way through the hornbeam plantation. In the absence of Pauline's husband, the grass verge wasn't as overgrown as he expected – Peter still didn't know that grass grows hardly at all between November and March – but still he must find another gardener and woodsman, and soon. Sharonne hated untidiness, mess, neglect. She liked to make a good first impression on visitors. He turned on to the track and wondered why no birds were singing. The only sound he could hear was the buzz and rattle of a drill, which he assumed to be the farmer doing something to a fence. It was, in fact, a woodpecker whose presence would have thrilled him had he known what it was.

The track continued up to the old quarry, but a path branched off it to the left. Peter meant to take this path, for the quarry, an ancient and now overgrown chalk deposit, was of no interest to him, but at the turn-off he noticed something a more observant man would have seen as soon as he left the lane. The ruts a car's tyres make were deeply etched into the gravelly earth of the track. They were not new, these ruts. Water still lay in the bottom of them, though it hadn't rained for days. Peter looked back the way he had come and saw that they began at the lane. Someone had been in here since he was last at Passingham Hall. Pauline's husband, according to Pauline, had been forbidden to drive on account of his back and she had never learned. It wasn't them. The farmer might come into the wood but would certainly do so on foot. Some trespasser had been in here. Sharonne would be furious . . .

Peter followed the rutted track up to the edge of the quarry. It was plain to see that the vehicle, whatever it was, had gone over, taking part of the quarry's grassy lip with it as well as two young trees. Down there it was full of small trees and bushes, and among them was the car, a dark-blue car which lay on its side but hadn't fully turned over. Stouter trees had prevented its taking a somersault on to its roof. Then, in the dappled sunshine, the stillness and the silence but for the woodpecker's drilling, he smelt the smell. It must have been there from the first but the sight before him had temporarily dulled his other senses. He had smelt something like it before, when he was very young and poor, and had a Saturday job cleaning the kitchens in a restaurant. The restaurant had been closed down by the food hygiene people but before that happened he'd one night opened up a plastic bag leaning against the wall. He had a dustpan of floor sweepings to get rid of but as soon as the bag was open a dreadful smell wafted out and in the bottom he saw decaying offal running with white maggots.

Much the same smell was coming from the car in his quarry. He wasn't going to look inside, he didn't want to know. He didn't want to continue up to the clearing either. What he must do was go back to the house and call the police. If he had been carrying his mobile, as he always did when in London, he would have made that call on the spot. Dialled nine-nine-nine for want of knowing the local police number. But a country gentleman in a Barbour doesn't carry a mobile, he hardly knows what it is. Peter walked back the way he had come, feeling a bit weak at the knees. If he had eaten breakfast before he came out he would probably have been sick.

Sharonne had got up and was sitting at the kitchen table with a cup of instant coffee and a glass of orange juice in front of her. Though nothing could detract from the beauty of her figure and her facial structure, she was one of those women who look completely different, and hugely improved, by good dressing, make-up and a hairdo. Now, as usual in the mornings, she was in her natural state, wrapped in his old Jaeger dressing gown, her feet in feathery mules, her face pale, greasy and anaemic-looking, and her ash-blonde hair in uneven spikes. Such a style may be fashionable but not when the spikes stand out at right angles on the sides of the head and lie flat on the crown like a wind-ravaged cornfield. Sharonne was so confident of her good looks at all times that she bothered only when an impression was called for.

'What's the matter with you?' she said. 'You look like you've seen a corpse.'

Peter sat down at the table. 'I have. Well, I think I have. I need a drink.'

To Sharonne these last alarming words were triggers of danger, annulling the sentence which had preceded them. 'No, you don't. Not at nine in the morning, you don't. You'd better remember what Dr Klein said.'

'Sharonne,' said Peter, helping himself to her orange juice as a poor substitute, 'there's a car in the quarry. I think there's someone in it, someone dead. The smell's ghastly, like rotten meat.'

She stared at him. 'What are you talking about?'

'I said there's a dead person in a car in the quarry. In our quarry. Up in the wood.'

She stood up. She was twelve years younger but much tougher than he, he had always known it. If he was ever in danger of forgetting, she reminded him. 'This car, did you look inside?'

'I couldn't. I thought I'd throw up. I've got to call the police.'

'You didn't look inside, you just smelt a smell. How d'you know it was a body? How d'you know it wasn't rotten meat?'

'God, I could do with a drink. Why would a car have meat in it? It'd have a driver in it and maybe passengers. I have to get on to the police now.'

'Pete,' said Sharon in a voice more suited to an animal rights or anti-capitalism activist than a model, 'you can't do that. That's crazy. What business is it of yours? If you'd not gone up there – God knows why you did – you'd never have seen a car in there. You're probably imagining the smell – you do imagine things.'

'I didn't imagine it, Sharonne. And I know whose car it is. It's that blue VW Golf that's missing, the one that belongs to that woman who's kidnapped those kids. It's been on telly, it's been in the papers.'

'How d'you know that? Did you go down and look? No, you didn't. You couldn't tell it was a Golf, it was just a blue car.'

'I'm getting on to the police now.'

'No, you're not, Pete. We're lunching with the Warrens at one and this evening we've got the Gilberts' drinks party. I'm not missing out on those. You get the police here and we'll not be able to go anywhere. We'll be stuck here and all for something that's not our business. If there is a body in that car, which I doubt, they'll suspect you. They'll think you did it.

They always think the person who found the body did it. They'll have you down here next week talking to them and then they'll have you in court. Is that what you want, Pete?'

'We can't just leave it there.'

When her husband uttered those words, Sharonne knew the battle was won. 'If you mean leave the car there, why not? We needn't go near the place.' She never did, so this wouldn't be difficult. 'Come the spring there'll be leaves on the trees and everything overgrown, and you won't even be able to see it. I don't see why it shouldn't stay there for years.'

'Suppose someone else finds it?'

'Great. Let them. It won't affect us then, will it?'

Secure in her conviction that she had brought Peter round to her point of view, she went off upstairs to begin the two-hour-long process that would make her fit to attend the Warrens' lunch party. Peter took himself into the dining room where, safe from her hectoring, he helped himself to a generous tot of Bushmills. Very soon the stench was dispelled from his nostrils. It was several hours later before the subject was again raised. They were returning from Trollfield Farm where they had lunched and Sharonne, who never touched anything stronger than sparkling water, was driving, Peter being rather the worse for wear.

'I'll have to call the police tomorrow,' he said, slurring his words. 'I'll tell them I've only just found it.'

'You won't call them, Pete.'

'It's probably against the law to consheal – I mean conceal – a body.'

'There's no body. You imagined it.'

In spite of overdoing it at lunchtime, Peter overdid it again at the Gilberts'. In normal circumstances, he more or less kept within the limits laid down by Dr

Klein because he wanted to keep his liver for a few more years, but normal circumstances didn't include his finding abandoned cars which stank of rotting flesh. Next day he felt as if he were rotting himself and he didn't call the police, only heaving his racked body out of bed at three in the afternoon to drive them back to London.

'Out of sight, out of mind' is a truism of remarkable soundness. Once back in the South Kensington mews house where the only cars were his own and those on the residents' parking in the street, and the only trees those planted in the pavement, the memory of his discovery became hazy and dreamlike. Perhaps he *had* imagined the smell. Perhaps it wasn't from a decaying body, or not a human body, but a dead deer or badger lying concealed in the undergrowth. What did he know of such country matters? Sharonne was right when she said he couldn't have said from where he stood if the car was a VW Golf or some other make of small saloon. He hadn't seen its grid or read the name on its boot lid.

He was a busy man, he always was. There was a possible takeover to avert, a new merger to accelerate. Such things become very real in a mirror-façaded tower just off Trafalgar Square while events in rural Kent take on a peculiar remoteness. But Friday always comes. Unless you die or the world ends, Friday will come.

His way of continuing to avoid the issue would be not to go to Passingham St John until – well, after Christmas. But something strange had happened, displacing his detachment. The blue car began to prey on his mind. He knew it was there and he knew the smell came from inside it. Sharonne was right when she said he imagined things. He was gifted, or burdened, with a powerful imagination, and now it magnified the car to twice its size, clearing away the bushes and trees which partly concealed it, while it strengthened and worsened the smell, spreading it from its source in the quarry up into the wood, along the track and all the way up to the house. He began to fancy that next time he drove to his country home, whenever that might be, the smell would meet him as he turned into the lane. Inexorably, Friday came. He both wanted to go to Kent and he didn't, and now he was beginning to fear that the presence of that car in the quarry would alienate him from his beautiful house and grounds, and make them repulsive to him. Suppose he never wanted to go there again?

Sharonne had no intention of going to Passingham Hall two weekends in succession. Owning a country place was great so long as you seldom went there. It was useful for mentioning idly to people you sat next to at dining tables. She had a new dress which she meant to wear at a charity gala dinner at the Dorchester on Saturday night, and on Sunday she'd got her mother and her sister and four other people coming to lunch and caterers were booked. None of that was going to be put off so that they could go to Passingham. Peter dared not go without her. Such a thing had never happened. He must study to banish that car from his mind and restore himself to what now seemed the carefree state he was in before he went walking in the wood last Saturday morning.

Chapter 9

Once he had cleared it with the Hampshire police, Wexford phoned Ralph Jennings for an appointment. As soon as possible, please. He had to leave this message with an answering service. On the desk in front of him was a stack of reports and messages from other police authorities, and as he went through them he soon saw that most were negative. The same with the collated list, the huge protracted list, of sightings of the three by members of the public. To fail to follow them up would be negligent even though he knew the idea that Joanna Troy had advertised both children for sale on the Internet and that she and Giles Dade had been married at Gretna Green was gross nonsense. Barry Vine, Karen Malahyde, Lynn Fancourt and the rest of them would get on with the weary work.

Several hours passed, during which he had dialled the Southampton number twice more, before Ralph Jennings called him back. The voice was cautious, almost fearful. What was it about? What could Kingsmarkham Crime Management have to do with him? He hadn't lived in the neighbourhood for six years.

'You've read the newspapers, Mr Jennings? You've seen television? Your former wife is missing and has been now for a fortnight.'

'Maybe but it's got nothing to do with me. She's my *ex*-wife.'

He made the term sound not as if it referred to a no longer extant relationship but rather as if Joanna Troy were X-rated.

'Nevertheless I would like to see you. There are questions it's important I ask you. When would it be convenient for me and another officer to call on you?'

'At my *home*?'

'Where else, Mr Jennings? I'm not asking you to come here. The interview wouldn't take long, probably an hour at most.' The silence was long. Wexford thought they had been cut off. 'Mr Jennings, are you there?'

In an abstracted, not to say *dis*tracted, voice, Jennings muttered, 'Yes, yes . . .' Then, as if making a decision that would radically change the whole course of his life, 'Look, you can't come to my home. It won't do. It's not on. Too much – explanation would be involved and then . . . You really do need to see me?'

'I thought I'd made that clear, sir,' said Wexford patiently.

'We can fix something. We could, er, meet outside. In a pub – no. In a – a restaurant and have a coffee. How's that?'

He couldn't exactly insist on visiting the man's home, though his curiosity had been aroused. Probably Jennings was capable of not answering the door or being out at the crucial time or answering the door and refusing them entry. It wasn't a situation in which he could get a warrant. 'Very well,' he said, much as it went against the grain.

Jennings named a time on the following day and the meeting place as a café. There was plenty of parking 'around there', he said, speaking now in a helpful, even cheerful, voice. And the coffee was very good, you could get ninety-nine different varieties. That was their gimmick, that was why the place was called the Ninety-Nine Café. Wexford thanked him and rang off.

What could be the reason behind Jennings's refusal to let them call on him? The sinister possibility was that Joanna Troy was there. Even more sinister that the bodies of Giles and Sophie Dade were concealed there. Wexford didn't believe either was true. Jennings would have got Joanna out of the way during the interview. As for the bodies, if they were, say, buried in his garden, far from refusing the visit he would have put on a show of welcoming the police with open arms. So what was it? He intended to find out.

When his phone rang again almost immediately he thought it was Jennings calling back with some fresh excuse or change of venue. But it was his daughter Sylvia at The Hide, the women's refuge where she currently worked two evenings and one morning a week.

'You may know already, Dad, but a guy's just been arrested outside this building for attacking his wife with a hammer. I saw it. From this window. It's shaken me up a bit.'

'I'm not surprised. You don't mean she was killed, do you?'

'Not as bad as that. He's shorter than her. He aimed at her head but he got her in the shoulder and the back. She fell down screaming and then – then she stopped screaming. Someone phoned for the police and they came. He was sitting beside his wife on the path by then, crying and still holding the hammer. There was blood everywhere.'

'D'you want me to come?'

'No, it's all right. I think I just wanted to talk about it. Cal's got the car today, he's said he'll come over and fetch me. I'll be OK.'

Wexford ground his teeth, but not until after she'd

put the phone down. Did she mean that on the days she was at The Hide she let Chapman have her car and went to work on the bus? Perhaps only some days, but that was bad enough. Hadn't he a car of his own? He'd done pretty well for himself, thought the father, a fine big house, the Old Rectory that Neil had refurbished, a ready-made family, the use of a car, and all because he'd made himself pleasant – or something – to a lonely woman.

He looked out of the window. It was raining again, the fine light rain that once it had started seemed to find no reason to stop. A car came in from the High Street, windscreen wipers on to the fast speed, parked close up to the doors and Vine and Lynn Fancourt got out of it, hustling into the station a man who had his head covered with a coat. The wielder of the hammer, that would very likely be.

And what of Sylvia? Perhaps he and Dora should go over to what everyone had got into the habit of called 'the Old Rectory' and see how she was. He was always pleased to see his grandsons. Chapman would be there, though. Wexford was cursed with a too-volatile imagination and now the horrid thought came to him that Sylvia *might have another child*. Why not? It was what women wanted to do when they embarked on a new and presumably intended to be a steady – and what was the current politically correct word? Ah, yes, *stable* – relationship. The nauseating phrase was 'I want to have his child'. No reasonable person could want to have Chapman's child. He might be good-looking but he was stupid too and lack of brains was as likely to be inherited as beauty – perhaps more likely, but Sylvia's father had often thought Sylvia very unreasonable.

Still, they would go. She was his daughter, whomsoever she took up with, and she had had a bad shock. Not for the first time he wished she would work for a less worthy cause.

'I picture a handsome wimp,' said Wexford when he and Burden were being driven down the M3, his mind still on Callum Chapman. 'And yet I don't know why. Joanna Troy doesn't seem to have been very conscious of appearance.'

'Those clothes.' Burden uttered the two words in a monotone that expressed more of his feelings than an impassioned outburst would have done. He himself was wearing the slate-blue suit once more with a white shirt this time and a blue, emerald and white patterned tie. Wexford fancied he had been reluctant to cover all this with his raincoat, but he conceded that this aspersion might be unfounded. 'If you want to know how I picture him, I see a skinny little pipsqueak with big teeth.'

'Nice word, pipsqueak,' said Wexford. 'Old-fashioned now. In the First World War it's what they called a shell distinguished for the sound it made in flight.'

'I don't see why that should apply to an insignificant sort of person.'

'Nor do I.'

'Anyway, it's useless speculating about what someone's going to be like. People never are the way we expect. The law of averages ought to make us right sometimes but we never are.'

'I don't believe in the law of averages,' said Wexford.

The café was indistinguishable from thousands like it all over the country. Vaguely hi-tech with a lot of chrome, red vinyl floor and black leather seating, it had booths for hiding or taking refuge in, circular tables for sitting round and circular tables at chest height for standing at. They were early and Jennings wasn't. There were no men on their own in the Ninety-Nine Café.

'Why would anyone want coffee with walnuts?' Wexford asked after he and Burden had seated themselves in a booth and ordered respectively a large filter and a cappuccino.

'Or almonds or cinnamon, come to that? God knows. It's a gimmick.'

Their coffee came. Wexford faced the door to spot Jennings when he came in. He wondered if it was obvious to the man behind the counter and the woman who served them that they were police officers. Probably in his case, if not in sartorially elegant Burden's. It couldn't be helped. Jennings had chosen to meet them here and not at his home. 'Where is he, anyway?' Wexford said, looking at his watch. 'It's ten past and he was due here at eleven.'

'Time doesn't mean as much to people as it used. Haven't you noticed? Especially the young. They put a sort of mental "about" in front of an appointment time, so it's "about ten" or "about eleven" and that can easily be half past, though you notice it's never a quarter to.'

Wexford nodded. 'The trouble is we can't stalk off in high dudgeon. We need him a good deal more than he needs us. "Dudgeon", by the way, is a dagger hilt, so why it should mean resentment is something else I don't know.' He finished his coffee, sighed and said, 'You remember that pain in the arse Callum Chapman? Well, he's . . . But here's our reluctant witness, unless I'm much mistaken.'

As Burden had forecast, he was very different from the way either of them had imagined him. Wexford had been right, though, in his belief that they were easily recognisable as policemen, for Jennings homed in on them immediately. It was a tallish thin man who sat down next to Burden and opposite Wexford.

Joanna's father had told them Jennings was thirty-two. Apart from a bald patch he had tried to conceal by combing his hair over it, he looked much younger than that age. His was one of those puckish or Peter Pan faces, almost babyish, large-eyed, the nose small and tip-tilted, the mouth not quite but nearly a rosebud. Fair hair, slightly wavy and copious in front, clustered round his temples and grew in little fringes above his ears.

'What kept you, Mr Jennings?' Wexford's tone was pleasanter than his words.

'I'm sorry I'm late. I couldn't get away.' The voice by contrast was rather deep and, though Jennings looked as if no razor had ever passed across those rosy cheeks, unmistakeably masculine. 'I had a bit of a tussle, actually. My, er, story wasn't believed.'

'Your story?' said Burden.

'Yes, that's what I said.' The waitress came. 'I'll have one of your lattes with cinnamon, please. Look, I've decided I have to explain to you. I know it looks odd. The fact is – Oh God, this is so embarrassing – the fact is my partner – she's called Virginia – she's madly jealous. I mean, pathologically jealous, though maybe it's unkind to say so.'

'We shan't tell her,' said Wexford gravely.

'No. No, I'm sure not. The fact is she can't bear it that I've been married. I mean, if my wife had died I don't suppose it would be so bad. But I was divorced, as you know, and I've been forbidden even to mention, er, Joanna's name. Just to show you how bad it is, she can't bear it if she reads the name Joanna in some other context and if she meets a Joanna . . . I suppose it's flattering in a way – well, it is. I'm very lucky to be – well, loved like that.'

'I was adored once,' mumured Wexford. 'What you're saying, if I understand you, Mr Jennings, is that you stopped us coming to your home because your girlfriend would be there and would take exception to the subject of our conversation?'

Jennings said admiringly, 'You *do* put it well.'

'And in order to come at all, you had to construct a cast-iron excuse for, er, going out on your own for an hour at eleven in the morning? Yes? Well, no doubt you know your own business best, Mr Jennings.' A sensible man would run a mile from this Virginia, Wexford thought to himself. 'And now perhaps we can get down to the purpose of our meeting. Tell us about your ex-wife, would you? What kind of a person she is, her interests, pursuits, her habits.' He added in the same grave tone, 'Don't worry. There is no one to overhear you.'

Jennings wasn't a sensible man. His prevarications and failure to stand up to tyranny proved that. But he didn't make a bad job of character analysis, even though he sometimes looked over his shoulder while he talked, presumably fearing Virginia might materialise from the street door. Wexford, who had anticipated a 'Well, she's just like anyone else' approach, was pleasantly surprised.

'We met at university. She was doing a post-graduate modern languages degree and I was doing one in business studies. I guess a lot of people would say we were too young to settle down together but that's what we did. We were both twenty-three. She was after a job at a school in Kingsmarkham. Her father lives there. Her mother was dead.

'Joanna's very bright. She wouldn't have got that job before she was twenty-four if she hadn't been. Very, er, positive. I mean she's got strong opinions about almost everything. Impulsive too, I'd say. If she wants something she's got to have it and she's got to have it *now.* I suppose I was in love, whatever that may mean – Aren't I quoting some famous person?'

'The Prince of Wales,' said Burden.

'Oh, was it? Well, I must have been in love with Joanna because she's not . . . What I'm trying to say is, I never actually liked her, she's not very *likeable*. She can make herself pleasant if she wants something but alone with the person she'd chosen – well, presumably to spend her life with, she can be a bit of a pain. Nasty, if you know what I mean. When I first met her I noticed she hadn't any friends. No, that's not quite true. She had one or two but after we split up I realised they were both very weak types of people, they'd be the sort to let Joanna push them around. It's like she can't have an equal relationship.'

Now he had embarked on his ex-wife's nature and proclivities, Jennings was in full swing. He had even stopped starting each time anyone came into the Ninety-Nine Café. Wexford let him talk. Any questions could come later.

'We decided to get married. I don't know why. Looking back, I can't imagine. I mean, I knew by then I'd be in serious trouble if I disagreed with her over anything. Her views were right and everyone else had to have them too, especially me. I suppose I thought, I'll never find anyone else as clever and as dynamic as Joanna. I'd never find anyone with so much energy and – well, drive. She's on the go all day and she's an early riser, I mean like six thirty a.m., weekends and all, showered, dressed, but – well, you don't want to hear all this. The upshot was I thought that no one else would do for me after her. Well, I was wrong but I thought I was right.' That would make a good epitaph for a lot of people, Wexford thought, maybe most people. He was wrong but he thought he was right. 'My dad bought us a house in Pomfret. He was dying but he said I might as well have it then and there while he was still alive. He died about two months after we were married. Joanna had a job at a school in Kingsmarkham – Haldon Finch it was – and I was with a London firm. I used to commute.

'D'you want some more coffee? I think I will.' Wexford and Burden both nodded. Each was afraid that if they didn't choose this way to prolong things, Jennings might notice the time and be off. He waved to the waitress. 'Where was I? Yes, right. I've heard people say you can get on perfectly well with someone you're living with but as soon as you get married it starts to go wrong. Maybe, but Joanna and I only really got on if I was a yes-man and she called the tune. Then there was the sex.' He broke off as the waitress came to take their order, glanced at his watch, said, 'I told Virginia I'd not be more than an hour and a half, so I've still got a bit of time. Yes, the sex. You do want to hear this?' Wexford nodded. 'Right. It had been quite good at first, I mean when we first met but it went off long before we got married. By the time we'd been married six months it was almost non-existent. Don't think I just took this lying down.' An unfortunate phrase in the circumstances, Wexford thought, but Jennings didn't seem aware of what he had said. 'No, I tried to tell her what I thought. I did tell her. I mean, I was twenty-six years old, a normal healthy man. I will say for Joanna she didn't pretend. She never did. She came straight out with it. "I don't fancy you any more," she said. "You're going bald." I said she must be mad. I mean, premature baldness runs in my family. So what? Apparently, my father was bald before he even met my mother and he was only thirty. They still had three kids.'

Their coffee came. Jennings sniffed his, presumably to detect if it contained the appropriate amount of cinnamon. 'To resume,' he said. 'I thought there must be someone else. She'd just met this Katrina, the mother of those missing kids. They were always together. Now don't get any ideas Joanna's a lesbian. For one thing, I noticed she'd never let any woman touch her, she wouldn't even let her stepmother kiss her and there's nothing repulsive about Effie, far from it. Once or twice Katrina would put her hand on her arm or something but Joanna always retreated or actually took it off. Besides, I wasn't the first man in her life, far from it. She'd had a lot of relationships before me, started at school. But they were all of the male sex. I did wonder if she was so keen on Katrina because she fancied her husband. He's nothing to look at and a bit of a shit but you never know with women, do you? I couldn't think of any other reason for her going about with Katrina – well, yes, I suppose I could. She just agreed with everything Joanna said and did, and she was always telling her how clever and gifted she was. Joanna liked that, she *basked* in it. I still don't know the answer. Anyway, soon after the arrival of the Dades on the scene she said she'd decided there'd be no more sex. Our marriage was to be a partnership, I quote, "for convenience and companionship".'

'It was you who left, Mr Jennings?'

'You bet it was and don't let anyone tell you different. I sold the house and gave her half the proceeds. Anything to get clear of all that. I haven't seen her since.'

Burden said, 'Was Ms Troy ever violent towards you? In these arguments you had, if you disagreed with her, would she have struck you? And do you know of any incidents of violence in her past, perhaps before you met her but that she told you about?'

'There was nothing like that. It was all verbal. Joanna's very verbal. There's only one . . .'

'Yes, Mr Jennings?'

'I was going to say one incident of – well, what you

mean. Not to me. It was long before we met. She didn't tell me, someone else did, someone I knew at university. I don't know whether I ought to tell you, though I can't say this chap told me in confidence, not really.'

'I think you had better tell us, Mr Jennings,' Wexford said firmly.

'Well, yes. I will. When this chap heard I was going about with Joanna he said she'd been at school – Kingsmarkham Comprehensive, that was – with his cousin. They were both in their teens but she was older, three years older, I think. She beat this kid up, blacked both his eyes, actually knocked a tooth out. He was bruised all over but nothing was actually broken. It was all hushed up because his cousin recovered and no harm done but also because Joanna's mother had just died and some counsellor said that accounted for it. Of course, I asked Joanna about it and she said the same, her mum had died and she was in shock, she didn't know what she was doing. The cousin denied it, by the way, but she said he'd said something rude about her mother. That's what she told me, that he'd insulted her mother's memory.

'But there was a funny thing. Not really funny but you know what I mean. The kid died. Years later, leukaemia, I think it was. He must have been twenty-one or twenty-two. It was Joanna who told me. It was before we were married, we were still doing our MAs. She said, "You know that Ludovic Brown –" funny I remember the name but it's a peculiar one, isn't it? "– you know that Ludovic Brown," she said. "He's dead. Some sort of cancer." And then she said, "Some people do get what they deserve, don't they?" That was typical of her. The poor kid maybe said something rude and for that he deserved to die of leukaemia. But that was Joanna. That's what I meant when I said she wasn't very likeable.'

Ludovic Brown, thought Wexford. Kingsmarkham, I suppose, or environs. He went to Kingsmarkham Comprehensive, died young, his family shouldn't be hard to find. 'You've been very helpful, Mr Jennings. Thank you.'

'Better not say my pleasure, had I?' Again the watch was glanced at, to alarming effect. 'My God, I've got five minutes to get back in. A cab, I think, if I can get one.'

He ran. The waitress watched him go, a faint smile on her lips. Did he come in here with Virginia and she give public examples of her possessiveness?

'Some people', said Burden, when Wexford had paid the bill, 'don't seem to have a clue about self-preservation. Talk about out of the frying pan into the fire.'

'He's weak and he's attracted by strong women. Unfortunately, he's so far picked two with the kind of strength that's malevolent. You could persuade him into anything, sell his grandmother into slavery, swallow cyanide, I dare say. Still, from our point of view he's an improvement on everyone else we've questioned in this case, isn't he? He's given us some good stuff.'

Chapter 10

Burden fell asleep in the car and Donaldson never spoke unless he was spoken to or felt obliged to intervene, so Wexford retreated into his own thoughts, mainly concentrated on Sylvia and their encounter the evening before. He and Dora had gone over to the Old Rectory after supper, ostensibly to check on their daughter's condition after what she had witnessed at The Hide that morning. Chapman came to the door and seemed less than pleased to see them.

'Sylvia didn't say she was expecting you.'

Dora had cautioned him to watch his tongue so Wexford remained silent. She asked how Sylvia was.

'She's OK. Why shouldn't she be?'

They found the boys occupied with their homework in what was known as the family room where the television was on, albeit turned very low, and where by the look of the half-full wineglass on the side table, the dent in the seat cushion of an armchair and the *Radio Times* on its arm, Chapman had been relaxing before their arrival. Wexford, who had put his head round the door and quickly absorbed all this, said hello to Robin and Ben, and followed Dora to the kitchen. There they found Sylvia cooking the evening meal, pasta boiling in a saucepan, mushrooms, tomatoes and herbs in another pan, the materials for a salad spread on the counter.

'I've only just got home,' she said, as if self-defence or excuse was necessary. 'Cal was going to do it but there was this programme on TV it was important for him to watch and now he's helping the boys with their homework.'

Again Wexford was silent – on that subject, at least. 'How are you?'

'I'm fine. I ought to be used to that kind of thing by now. I've seen enough of it. Only usually I've not witnessed the actual attack, just heard about it afterwards. But I'm fine, had to be. Life goes on.'

Any sort of man who called himself a man – Wexford was amazed at himself, using such an expression even in his thoughts – any decent sort of man would have sat her down with a drink, moved the kids elsewhere, got her to talk while he listened and sympathised.

'It's terribly late to eat but I couldn't get away. D'you want anything? Drink?'

'We only came in for a minute,' Dora said soothingly. 'We'll go.'

In the car, driving home, he'd said, 'Wasn't he supposed to be the New Man? I thought that was the point. What other point is there to him?'

And Dora, who usually put a curb on his excesses, had agreed with him. He'd often heard it said that it wasn't a man's appearance or character that kept a woman with him but his sexual performance, but he'd never believed it. Surely the sex was fine if you loved the other person or were powerfully attracted to them. Otherwise it made men and women into machines with buttons to press and switches to turn on. He'd ask Burden's view if the man weren't so prudish about things like this. Besides, he was asleep. Pondering on Sylvia and Chapman and Sylvia's jobs and Neil, he let Burden sleep for another ten minutes and then woke him up.

'I wasn't asleep,' said Burden like an old fogey in a club armchair.

'No, you were in a cataleptic trance. What's the name of the head teacher of Kingsmarkham Comprehensive?'

'Don't ask me. Jenny would know.'

'Yes, but Jenny's not here. No doubt she's at work in that very school.'

Donaldson, though he hadn't been addressed, said, 'Dame Flora Gregg, sir.'

'*Dame*?'

'That's right,' said Burden. 'She got it in the Birthday Honours.'

'For rescuing the school from the mess it was in. My fourteen-year-old's a student there, sir.'

'Then she must be relatively new,' said Wexford. 'This business with Joanna Troy happened – when? Fifteen years ago. Who came before Dame Flora?'

Donaldson didn't know. 'A man,' Burden said. 'Let me think. He was there when I first met Jenny and she was teaching there. She used to say he was lazy, I particularly remember that, lazy and fussy about the wrong things. It's coming back to me – Lockhart, that was his name. Brendon Lockhart.'

'I don't suppose you know where we can find him.'

'You don't suppose right, as Roger Dade would say. Wait a minute, though. It's going to be five or six years since he retired and Flora Gregg took over. He'd have been sixty-five then. He may be dead.'

'Any of us might be dead at any old time. Where did he retire *to*?'

'He stayed in the district, that I do know.'

Wexford considered. 'So who do we see first? Lockhart or the parents of poor Ludovic Brown?'

'First we've got to find them.'

Tracing Lockhart was the easier and done through the phone book. Wexford left Lynn Fancourt with the unenviable task of phoning every one of the fifty-eight Browns in the local directory and asking as gently and tactfully as she could which one of them had lost a son to leukaemia at the age of twenty-one. He reflected, as he and Barry Vine were driven to Camelford Road, Pomfret, that the two possibly criminal incidents in Joanna Troy's life were both school-related. First there was the assault on the fourteen-year-old, then the alleged theft. Was the school aspect significant? Or was it merely coincidence?

Brendon Lockhart was a widower. He told Wexford this within two minutes of the policemen entering the house. Perhaps it was only to account for his living alone, yet in almost chilling order and neatness. It was a cottage he had, Victorian, detached, surrounded by what would very likely be a calendar candidate garden in the summer. He showed them into a living room entirely free of clutter, a characterless place rather like the kind of photograph seen in Sunday supplements advertising loose covers. Instinctively, Wexford knew no tea would be offered. He sat down gingerly on pristine floral chintz. Vine perched on the edge of an upright chair, its arms polished like glass.

'The school, yes,' said Lockhart. 'A woman took over from me, you know. I don't usually care for new importations into our vocabulary but I make an exception for "pushy". A very good word "pushy". It perfectly describes *Dame* Flora Gregg. What a farce, wasn't it, giving a woman like that a title? I only met her once but I found her overbearing, didactic, distressingly left-wing and *pushy*. But women rule the world now, don't they? How they have taken over our schools! Haldon Finch also have a woman head now, I hear. In an amazingly short time women have completely taken over, they have *pushed* themselves into every sphere once prohibited to them. I am very glad to see two police*men* calling on me.'

'In that case, Mr Lockhart,' said Wexford, 'perhaps you won't mind answering some questions about two former pupils of yours, Joanna Troy and Ludovic Brown.'

Lockhart was a small man, thin and spry, his face pink and smooth for his age, his white hair more evenly distributed than Ralph Jennings's. But as he spoke that face contorted and stretched, taking on a skull-like look. 'So glad to hear you use that word. "Pupil", I mean. "Student" would be favoured by the good *Dame*, no doubt.'

How very much Wexford would have liked to ask him if he'd thought of seeing someone about his paranoia. Of course he couldn't. 'Joanna Troy, sir. And Ludovic Brown.'

'That was the young lady who mounted a savage attack on the boy, wasn't it? Yes. In the cloakroom, if I remember rightly. After the Drama Group, as I was expected to call the Dramatic Society. I believe she alleged afterwards that he'd done something to annoy her while they were rehearsing some play. Yes, I recall. *Androcles and the Lion*, it was. A choice much favoured by school dramatic societies, largely, I believe, because it has such a large cast.'

'He was quite badly injured, wasn't he, though no bones were broken?'

'He had two black eyes. He had a lot of bruises.'

'But the police weren't called, nor an ambulance? I've been told it was hushed up.'

Lockhart looked a little uncomfortable. He twisted up his face into a gargoyle mask before answering. 'The boy wanted it that way. We sent for the parents – well, the mother. I believe there was a divorce in the offing. There usually is these days, isn't there? She agreed with her son. Let's not have any fuss, she said.'

The boy had been only fourteen. Wexford tried to remember something about *Androcles and the Lion* but could only recall Ancient Rome and Christians thrown to wild beasts. 'Ludovic would have been an extra, would he? A slave or minor Christian?'

'Oh, yes, something like that. I believe she said he tripped her up or made a face at her or something. I do know it was totally trivial. By the by, it wasn't leukaemia he died of. I think you said leukaemia?'

Wexford nodded.

'No, no, no. He *had* leukaemia, that part is true, but it was controlled by some drug or other. My dear late wife knew the boy's grandmother. She was charwoman or some kind of servant to a friend. My wife told me what this woman told her. No, what happened was that he fell to his death off a cliff.'

Vine said, 'Where was this, sir?'

'I'm coming to that. Let me finish. His mother and – well, stepfather, I suppose. He may have been Mrs Brown's paramour, I know nothing of these things. They took him on a holiday to somewhere on the south coast, not all that far. He went out alone one afternoon and fell off a cliff. It was really a very tragic business. There was an inquest but no suspicious circumstances, as you would put it. He was weak, he wasn't able to walk far, and the suggestion was that he was too near the edge and he collapsed.'

Wexford got up. 'Thank you, Mr Lockhart. You've been very helpful.'

'I heard Joanna Troy had become a teacher. Can that be right? She was a most unsuitable woman to be in charge of children.'

*

'So where was Joanna while Ludovic Brown was in Eastbourne or Hastings or whatever?'

Wexford asked this rhetorical question of Burden while they shared a pot of tea in his office. 'And how are we going to find that out?' said Burden. 'It must have been – let's see – eight years ago. I suppose she was teaching at Haldon Finch. Shacked up with Jennings, though not yet married to him. No reason why she shouldn't have popped down to the south coast for a couple of hours. It wouldn't be much of a drive.'

'There seems to be some doubt as to what Brown did to annoy her. Insulted her mother, says Jennings. Tripped her up or made a face, says Lockhart. Which is it? Or is it both? Did she still know Ludovic Brown? Had she ever really known him beyond being somehow insulted or affronted by him at a play rehearsal? When they were both teenagers?'

'There's a possible yes to all that if she's a criminal psychopath.'

'We've no evidence that she is. If you don't want another cup we'll make our way *chez* Brown. Lynn found her in a flat at Stowerton and she's still called Brown in spite of the paramour.'

'The *what*?'

'It's what that old dinosaur Lockhart called him.'

It looked as if Jacqueline Brown had done far less well out of her divorce than Joanna Troy had from hers. Her home was half a house in Rhombus Road, Stowerton, and the house had been small to start with. The front window overlooked the one-way traffic system. Thumps, a heavy beat and the voice of Eminem penetrated the wall that divided this flat from next door. Jacqueline Brown thumped on it with her fist and the volume was very slightly reduced.

'I don't know why she attacked Ludo.' Her voice

was weary, greyish, like her appearance. Life had drained her of colour and joy and energy, and it showed. 'Silly name, isn't it? It was his father's choice. That girl Joanna, he didn't even know her, she was a lot older than him. Well, it's a lot older when you're in your teens. She'd never done it before to anyone, or so they said. And all he'd done was make a face at her when she was acting that part. He put out his tongue, that's all.'

'I'm sorry to have to ask you these questions, Mrs Brown,' said Wexford. 'I will try to make them as painless as possible. You took your son on holiday in 1993 – to where exactly?'

'Me and my partner it was. He's called Mr Wilkins. It was his idea, he's always kind. We went to Eastbourne, stayed with his sister.'

Burden intervened. 'Neither you nor your son had ever encountered Ms Troy since her assault on Ludovic?'

'No, never. Why would we? Ludo went for a walk most afternoons. The doctor said it was good for him. Mr Wilkins usually went too but that day he'd got a bad foot, couldn't hardly put it to the ground, we don't know what it was, never did know, but the upshot was he couldn't walk so Ludo went alone. Most times he was only out twenty minutes at the most. This time he never came back.'

Foosteps sounded on the stairs, the door opened and a man came in. He was short and round, and he had several chins. He was introduced as 'Mr Wilkins'. Wexford wished Lockhart could see him. That might stop him describing this unromantic man as a 'paramour'. 'We were discussing Ludovic's unfortunate death.'

'Oh, yes?'

At the arrival of her partner, Jacqueline Brown had brightened. Now she repeated what she had said earlier but in a far more cheerful voice. 'Silly name, isn't it? It was my husband's choice.'

'You want to know where he got it from?' Wilkins sat down and took Jacqueline's hand. 'He'd been reading a book.' He spoke as if this was an esoteric activity, comparable perhaps to collecting sigmodonts or studying metaplasm. 'A book called *Ten Rillington Place* by Ludovic Kennedy – see? Funny thing, that, calling your only child after the author of a book about a serial killer.'

Jacqueline achieved a tiny smile, shaking her head. 'Poor Ludo. But it may have been all for the best. He wouldn't have lasted long anyway, never have made old bones.'

'People don't cease to amaze me,' said Wexford as they went down the steep dark staircase.

'Me too. I mean, me neither. There's another set of parents to see and maybe the boy too. The one she may or may not have stolen the twenty-pound note from.'

'Not today. He'll keep. I have to pay my usual visit to the Dades. You can come if you want. And while I'm there I want to look in on those Holloways. There's been something niggling at the back of my mind for days, something the boy's mother said and he denied.'

Roger Dade was at home. He answered the door, saying nothing but looking at them the way one might look at a couple of teenagers come to ask for their ball back for the fifth time. Katrina was lying down, her face buried in cushions.

'How are you?'

'How d'you expect?' said Dade. 'Bloody miserable and out of our minds with worry.'

'I'm not worried,' came the muffled voice of Katrina. 'I'm past that. I'm *mourning*.'

'Oh, shut up,' said Dade.

'Mr Dade,' said Wexford. 'We have been trying to reconstruct the events of that Saturday. Your son appears to have gone out in the afternoon on his own. Do you know where he might have gone?'

'How should I know? Shopping, probably. Taking advantage of my absence. These kids are always shopping when they get the chance. They don't get much chance when I'm home, I can tell you. I can hardly think of a more time-wasting empty occupation.'

Wexford nodded. He fancied Burden looked a little awkward, shopping being a pastime he rather enjoyed. If Giles Dade had been to the shops, what had he bought? This was almost impossible to say. One didn't know which of the objects in his room were old, newish or brand-new and he was sure Dade wouldn't.

'One of his friends, Scott Holloway, your neighbours' son, left a message on your phone and phoned several times after that without getting a reply. He intended to come round and take Giles back to hear some new CDs. Was he a frequent visitor?'

Dade looked exasperated. 'I thought I'd made it clear my children don't have frequent visitors or go to other people's houses. They don't have time.'

Suddenly Katrina sat up. She seemed to have forgotten that she had recently called her 'best and dearest friend' a murderer. 'I was able to do Joanna a good turn there. I recommended her when Peter wanted someone to tutor Scott in French.'

'Peter?' said Burden.

'Holloway,' said Dade. 'Giles, needless to say, didn't need help with his French.'

'And she did tutor him?'

'For a while.' Katrina put on a *schadenfreude* face. 'I

felt so sorry for those poor Holloways. Joanna said Scott was hopeless.'

Dade's insults, on the lines of how ineffectual and unprofessional they were, accompanied them to the door.

'Funny, really,' said Wexford as they walked the fifty yards to the Holloways, 'I don't mind what he says nearly as much as a milder jibe from Callum Chapman. It seems an inseparable part of his character, I suppose, the way', he added mischievously, 'shopping and natty dressing is of yours.'

'Thanks very much.'

The Holloways' doorbell was virtually unreachable owing to the garland of red poinsettias, green leaves and gold ribbon hanging in front of it. They were well in advance of others in the street with their Christmas decorations. A wreath of holly hung over the cast-iron door knocker but Burden managed to insert his fingers under it and give it a double bang.

'Goodness,' Mrs Holloway looked severe. 'What a noise that makes!' As if they were responsible for the poinsettias. 'Did you want Scott again?'

The boy was coming down the stairs, ducking his head under a bunch of mistletoe, hung there no doubt to catch kissable callers. They all went into a living room as glittery and bauble-hung as the Christmas section of a department store.

'Doesn't it look lovely?' said Mrs Holloway. 'Scott and his sisters did it all themselves.'

'Very nice,' said Wexford. It surely wasn't his imagination that the boy appeared terrified. His hands were actually shaking and, to control them, he pressed the palms into his knees. 'Now, Scott, there's no need to be nervous. You only have to tell us the simple truth.'

Scott's mother interrupted. 'What on earth do you

mean? Of course he'll tell the truth. He always does. All my children are truthful.'

What a paragon he must be, thought Wexford, more than that, a superhuman being. Did anyone *always* tell the truth? 'Did you call at Giles's house that Saturday afternoon, Scott?' Scott shook his head and Mrs Holloway fired up. 'If he said he didn't go he didn't and that's all there is to it.'

'I didn't,' whispered Scott and, rather more loudly, 'I didn't.'

Burden nodded. He said in a gentle tone, 'It is only that we are trying to reconstruct what happened that day at the Dades' house, who called, who came and went and so on. If you had been there you might have been able to help us but since you say you didn't . . .'

'I didn't.'

'I expect you know that Miss Troy, Joanna Troy, is also missing. She gave you private coaching –' did they use that term any more? '– in French?'

'Scott and my daughter Kerry.' Mrs Holloway had evidently decided, with some justification, that Scott was unfit to answer any more questions. 'Scott only had three sessions with her, he couldn't get on with her. Kerry didn't like her – no one seemed to like her – but she got something from what she was taught. At any rate, she passed her exam.'

There was no more to be done. 'I know the boy is lying,' Wexford said as they got back into the car. 'I just wonder why. And what's he so afraid of? We'll go home now. What I want to do tonight is think about it all and see if I can come up with some reasonable idea of where that car can be. It's been our stumbling block all the way. And yet, apart from every force in the country looking for it, we haven't done much to construct a workable theory for its whereabouts.'

'We've heard about a boy falling off a cliff into the

sea. Maybe she pushed him and later on maybe she pushed her car over.'

'Not on the south coast she didn't,' said Wexford. 'It's not like the west coast of Scotland where you might drive a car right up to the edge. Can you imagine doing that somewhere around Eastbourne? I'll think about it. I'm going to go home and think about it. Drop me off, will you, Jim?'

It is, in fact, very difficult to sit down in a chair, even if it's quiet and you're alone, and concentrate on one particular subject. As men and women trying to pray or meditate have found, there is much to distract your thoughts, a human voice from outside the room or in the street, traffic noise, 'the buzzing of a fly', as John Donne said. Wexford wasn't trying to pray, only to find the solution to a problem, but after he had sat for half an hour, had once dozed off, once forced himself to stay awake, and twice felt his thoughts drift off towards Sylvia and the possibility of more flooding, he acknowledged his failure. Concentration is more easily achieved while going for a long walk. But it was raining, sometimes only lightly and sometimes lashing down, and the vagaries of the rain had been another factor in disrupting his train of thought. He had no more idea of what had happened to George Troy's dark-blue VW Golf four-door saloon, index number LC02 YMY, than when he first sat down.

In the night he dreamed of it, one of those mad chaotic dreams in which bizarre metamorphosis is the rule. The car, driven by a vaguely male driver, was ahead of him on some arterial road but when it moved into a lay-by and parked it changed into an elephant which stood placidly chomping the leaves of an apple tree. The driver had disappeared. He had some idea of climbing on to the elephant's back but again it had changed, wriggling its outlines into a

Trojan Horse of dark-blue shiny coachwork, and as he stared, one of the four doors in its side opened and a woman and two children climbed out. Before he could see their faces he woke up.

It wasn't the kind of wakefulness you know will soon give place to sleep once more. He would lie there sleepless for at least an hour. So he got up, found the *Complete Plays* of George Bernard Shaw and turned to *Androcles and the Lion*. More whimsical than he remembered – it was thirty-five years since he had read it – deeply dated and the sentiments, which may have seemed new when it was written, now stale. There were only two women's parts, Megaera, Androcles's wife, and Lavinia, the beautiful Christian. This latter must have been played by Joanna Troy. What then of Ludovic Brown? The only young boy's part was that of the Call Boy who had six or seven lines to speak. That surely would have been Ludovic's.

At some point, perhaps when Lavinia was flirting with the Captain, a scene likely to make fourteen-year-old boys snigger, he had made a face and stuck out his tongue. Or he had done so on one of the occasions when he had to come on to call a gladiator or lion's victim into the arena. And for this Joanna had beaten him mercilessly? Where did the story of insulting Joanna's mother come from? It was pretty obvious this was just the version Joanna had given her husband. It made the attack on Ludovic more justifiable. All he had really done was stick out his tongue at her.

Wexford went back to bed, slept, woke at seven. The first words that came into his mind were: the car is somewhere on private land. It is on an estate, the parkland of a great house, the wild untended grounds of some neglected demesne. Somewhere no one goes for long months in the winter. She drove it there and abandoned it. Because there were ineradicable things inside, stains, damage, incriminating evidence – or the children's bodies.

Chapter 11

George Troy tried to supply an answer and failed, diverting from the central enquiry into all kinds of irrelevant by-paths. These threaded their way through properties he had visited owned by the National Trust, great houses such as Chatsworth and Blenheim he had always wanted to see but never had the time for and a stretch of Scottish moorland where a distant cousin, long-dead, had been shot in the leg while injudiciously walking there during a shoot. His wife, not Vine, finally cut him short with a, 'That's very interesting, darling, but not quite what the sergeant wants just at present.'

'This moorland,' said Vine, 'where your cousin was, was it family-owned? I mean, did someone he knew or was related to own it?'

'Good heavens, no,' said Effie Troy, who had evidently heard the story before, perhaps many times before. 'The Troys aren't in that sort of league. This cousin came from Morecambe and, anyway, it was in nineteen twenty-six.'

Vine wasn't surprised. 'So Joanna –' he had graduated to calling her Joanna since no one seemed to object '– didn't know anyone who owned a large country property?'

'Not to say "know". The nearest she ever came to anyone like that was when she was giving GCSE candidates extra coaching for their exams. There was a girl, I can't remember what she was called –' Mrs

Troy looked as if she would like to have asked her husband for help but knew what the result would be '– Julia something, Judith something. Joanna didn't care for her, said she was rude. Her parents owned Saltram House, probably still do. You know that big house that was completely refurbished ten or fifteen years back in about twenty acres? It's on the Forby road. What was their name?'

'Greenwell,' said Vine. As part of a general search of estates in the neighbourhood, Saltram House and grounds had already been visited and the Greenwells interviewed. 'There's nowhere Joanna herself liked to go to? She wouldn't necessarily have to know the owners and it wouldn't have to be around here. A place where she went walking where there were public footpaths?'

'She isn't much for walking,' said George Troy, no longer suppressible. 'She'd go running, or jogging as they call it nowadays, or race-walking I think some would say. Not that she or anyone else would go a distance to a footpath on private land to do that. No, you can't imagine anyone doing that, not if they had ample jogging or running space at home. When she wanted exercise she'd go to the gym, as they call it, short for "gymnasium" of course. She told me it comes from a Greek word meaning "to strip naked". Not that she did strip naked, of course not. Joanna is always decently dressed, isn't she, Effie? We've seen her in shorts, in hot weather that is, and possibly she wears shorts for this gym. Whatever she does wear, there's no doubt that's where she gets her exercise, at the gym.'

He paused to draw breath and Effie cut in swiftly, 'We really can't help you, I'm afraid. Joanna was born in the country and most of her life she'd lived in it but I wouldn't call her a country person, not really. The environment, farming, wildlife, that sort of thing didn't much interest her.'

'You'll let us know when you find her, won't you?' George Troy, who seemed to have abandoned worrying about his daughter, spoke as if Kingsmarkham Police and forces all over the country were looking for an umbrella he had mislaid on a bus. 'When she turns up, wherever she is? We'd like to know.'

'You may be sure of that, sir,' said Vine, trying to keep the grimness out of his voice.

'That's good to know, isn't it, Effie? It's good to know they'll keep us informed. I was worried at first, we were both worried. My wife was as worried as I was. She's not your typical stepmother, you know, no, not at all. She was a family friend while my poor dear first wife was alive, she was in fact Joanna's godmother. Godmother and stepmother, that can't be a very usual combination, what do you think? Effie's both, you see, godmother and stepmother. Poor Joanna was only sixteen when her mother died, terrible thing for a young girl, she was disturbed by it, very badly disturbed, and there was nothing I could do. Effie did everything. Along came Effie like an angel, completely saved Joanna, she was mother as well as godmother and stepmother, all three she was, and I'm not exaggerating when I say she saved Joanna's sanity . . .'

But at this point Barry Vine, feeling as if he had been hit over the head with something large and heavy, shut off his hearing. He sat, as Wexford might have paraphrased it, like patience on a monument smiling at these streams of pointless drivel, until Effie released him by springing to her feet and repeating her last words, 'We really can't help you, I'm afraid.'

She accompanied him to the door, paused before opening it and said, 'I'm still worried. Should I be?'

Vine said truthfully, 'I don't know, Mrs Troy. I really don't know.'

Not a single dentist had come forward to report a young woman coming to him or her with a missing tooth crown. Wexford was sure some would have claimed to have seen her and worked on her mouth, even if these patients had obviously been incorrectly identified. But there had been none at all. Because it was so unusual he even had a call put through to a police headquarters, selected at random in a remote part of Scotland, and checked with the Detective Superintendent in charge there that his officers actually had alerted dentists. No doubt about it, every dentist in the large sprawling area had been told and every one had been anxious to help.

If a crown fell off your tooth wouldn't you be in pain? He didn't know. He phoned his own dentist and was told that it depended what the crown was attached to. If the nerve in the tooth whose root was still there was dead or if the crown were attached to an implant there would be no pain. From a cosmetic point of view, the broken tooth wouldn't show if it were a molar as it very likely was. But when he rang off Wexford remembered what Effie Troy had said, that Joanna had her teeth crowned because she thought them unsightly and they aged her . . .

The tooth would be even more unsightly now. If she hadn't been to a dentist, why hadn't she? Because she no longer cared about this aspect of her appearance and wasn't in pain? Because she guessed dentists would be alerted and didn't want to attract attention to herself? Or for a more sinister reason?

While the searches went on at Savesbury House and Mynford New Hall, both properties with extensive grounds easily accessible from the road, he walked to his appointment at Haldon Finch School.

This too was a large comprehensive but generally considered – at least before the coming of Philippa Sikorski – as far more upmarket than the former Kingsmarkham County High School. It was where you sent your children if you could. Education-conscious parents had been known to move into the Haldon Finch catchment area with this purpose in mind. Joanna Troy must have obtained very good degrees and made an unusual impression to have got a job there at so young an age.

It was the last day of term. Haldon Finch would break up at lunchtime and go home for the Christmas holiday. After today, no one would be there to look at the Chrismas tree, decorated in austere white and silver, which stood on a shallow plinth in the entrance hall. A man came out of the lift who looked neither like a teacher, a parent nor a schools inspector, but might have been any of these. He was small, thin and sandy-haired, dressed in jeans and a brown leather jacket. Wexford was escorted upstairs to the head teacher's room. She was not at all his idea of what he had to stop himself calling a 'headmistress'. She had dark-red fingernails and dark-red lipstick, and if her skirt wasn't quite a mini it reached only to her kneecaps. Pale-blonde hair curled closely round her well-shaped head. She looked about forty, was tall and willowy, and smelt of a scent Wexford – who was good on perfumes – recognised as Laura Biagiotti's Roma. Like many successful women in the newly turned century, Philippa Sikorski's appearance, manner and way of speaking were quite different from her stereotype.

'Naturally, I've read about Joanna's disappearance, Chief Inspector. I imagine you want to ask me about the circumstances that led up to her resignation.' The voice he expected to be patrician held a strong intonation of Lancashire. Another surprise.

'By the way, you may care to know that a man called Colman has just been here. He said he was a private investigator. Of course I couldn't see him, I had my appointment with you.'

'I think I saw him downstairs. His firm has been engaged by the missing children's grandmother.'

'I see. But you'll want me to get back to Joanna Troy now. I had only been here six months at the time she resigned and though it's five years ago I still haven't got over the shock.'

'Why is that, Miss Sikorski?'

'It was so *unnecessary*,' she said. 'She hadn't done anything. The silly boy imagined it or invented or whatever. I don't know why. Some counsellor said he was on the verge of a breakdown. Nonsense, I said, I don't believe in these breakdowns.' Wexford heartily agreed but didn't say so. 'You'll want to know what happened. Have you heard the Wimbornes' side of the story?'

'The Wimbornes?'

'Oh, I'm sorry. They're Damon's parents. He's called Damon Wimborne. Obviously, you haven't heard it. It's briefly like this. Joanna had been substituting for the PE teacher who was ill. She'd been out with the students on the courts where the girls were playing netball and the boys, about eight of them, tennis. It was a double period in the afternoon. She came back with them into the cloakroom but she didn't stay more than a couple of minutes. Next day Mr and Mrs Wimborne turned up here in a fine old rage and told me Damon said Joanna had stolen a twenty-pound note out of his backpack. It was hanging on his peg and when he came into the cloakroom with the other boys – all the girls were already there – and Miss Troy was doing something to his bag. She had her hand inside it, he said.

'Well, it was all very awkward. I questioned

Damon and he stuck to his story. He hadn't realised till he got home, he said. Then he looked for his money and it was gone. I asked him what on earth he thought he was doing leaving a twenty-pound note in a bag hanging up in the cloakroom, but of course that wasn't really the point. I questioned the girls who were there but none of them had seen a thing. The next thing was that I had to ask Joanna.'

'Not a pleasant task,' said Wexford.

'No. But it was rather odd. I'd anticipated outrage, disbelief, shock. But she didn't seem all that surprised. No, that's the wrong way to put it. She seemed to accept it the way – well, the way you'd accept hearing something bad had happened when there was a strong probability of its happening. You'll wonder how I can remember after so long.' She smiled as Wexford shook his head. 'I just can. I remember everything about those interviews, they made such an impression on me. Joanna said something very strange. I could hardly believe what I was hearing. She said, "I didn't steal his money but I'll give him twenty pounds if that will make him feel better." She spoke absolutely steadily, in a very cool and calm voice. Then she said, "I shall resign anyway. You'll get my resignation this afternoon." She didn't say anything about the police, didn't ask me not to call the police in. I said, "I can't stop Mr and Mrs Wimborne calling in the police if they want to," and she said, "Of course you can't. I know that."'

'What happened?'

'The Wimbornes didn't call the police, as I expect you know. I don't know why not but my guess is they knew more about their precious boy than they were letting on. Perhaps he'd made unfounded accusations of this sort before. But as I say, I don't know. Joanna was adamant, there was no turning her. I was very sorry. She was an excellent teacher and I can't help feeling it's rather a waste when you can teach and you're as good at it as she was, it's a pity to waste that talent on translations and lessons on the Net or whatever it is she does now.'

Philippa Sikorski had become very animated. A faint flush had mounted into her face. Here was someone else who appeared to be or have been fond of Joanna Troy, the woman her ex-husband had described as not likeable. 'Have you kept in touch with her?' Wexford asked.

'It's strange you should ask in the circumstances. I tried to but she didn't seem keen. I had the impression she wanted to cut all connection with Haldon Finch School, put it behind her and try to forget. Damon, by the way, left school with just two GCSEs and the last I heard of him he was wandering about the world doing odd jobs to pay his way.' She smiled. 'The incident in the cloakroom, whatever that really was, evidently hasn't put him off backpacks.'

Thanking her and leaving, Wexford wondered if it would be much good talking to the Wimborne family if Damon, now aged twenty-two, was away in some distant place. On the other hand, the parents might know as much or more about it than he did. Why would a boy of sixteen accuse a teacher of stealing from him? Perhaps because he really had seen, or thought he had seen, her searching through his bag. So what happened to make him change his mind? Or he hadn't seen her and knew he hadn't but wished for some reason to get her into trouble and so injure her. Again, why later change his mind? Mrs Wimborne or her husband might be able to enlighten him. Their home wasn't far from the school. As he walked along the street where their house was, he thought about the protective and defensive mechanisms that were usually switched on when a parent was called upon to listen to accusations against his or her child. Especially *her* child. Women could be tigerish when they perceived their offspring as threatened. Even the most reasonable were unlikely to agree with anyone that their child had behaved badly.

Rosemary Wimborne wasn't among the most reasonable. As soon as he had told her what he wanted, seated opposite her in her very small and untidy living room, she broke into shrill denials that Damon's conduct had been anything less than exemplary. All he'd done was make a genuine mistake. Anyone could make a mistake, couldn't they? He thought he'd seen 'that woman' stealing his money. He was so upset he didn't know what he was saying. But when he found his twenty-pound note was missing . . . Twenty pounds was a lot of money to poor Damon, a small fortune. They weren't wealthy people, they had enough to get by on but that was all. Damon had earned that money working for the greengrocer on his stall on Saturdays.

'But Miss Troy hadn't stolen it, had she, Mrs Wimborne?'

'No one had stolen it, like I said. Anyone can make a mistake, though, can't they?' She was a virago of a woman, sharp-featured, her face prematurely furrowed. 'There was no call for her to leave like that. Damon admitted he'd made a mistake. She was proud of herself, that was what it was, she thought such a lot of herself that she couldn't take it when an innocent boy made a genuine mistake. She just went off in a huff.'

'Did Damon like Miss Troy?'

'Like her? What's that got to do with it? She was just a teacher to him. I'm not saying he didn't prefer the real PE teacher. That was a man anyway, he didn't need a woman supervising him, he said.'

Wexford said mildly, 'Where did Damon eventually find the note?'

'It was in his bag all the time, folded up and stuck inside his book to keep the place.'

A pointless exercise, a fruitless enquiry, Wexford thought as he walked back. It was quite a long way to the police station and now he couldn't understand what had possessed him to make the journey on foot. Good for him it might be but he hadn't at the time faced the fact that he would have to walk back again. The rain had begun once more, was now falling steadily.

Stocking up for Christmas? said the bad pun on a winking neon sign spanning the Kingsbrook Bridge. Once it would have said *Five Shopping Days to Christmas* but all days were shopping days now. Had the sign been there earlier and he hadn't noticed? Probably he hadn't noticed the decorations in the High Street either, the customary symbols, angels, fir trees, bells, old men with beards in funny hats. This lot, executed in red, green and white lights, seemed more than usually tasteless. What hadn't been there earlier was the poster headed 'Missing from Home' with two colour photographs of Giles and Sophie under it. He didn't recognise the phone number. It wasn't a local one but probably belonged to a dedicated line opened by Search and Find Limited. For some reason it made him cross, exacerbating his anger with himself for so far failing to buy any presents. Would he and Dora be expected to buy something for Callum Chapman? The usual Christmas panic seized him. But, really, it was only for Dora he had to buy. All the rest she would have seen to, had probably bought them already and wrapped them as exquisitely as usual. He felt a pang of guilt, hoping she *liked* doing this, hadn't been only pretending to like it all these years.

The film showing at the cinema was too appropriate: *What Women Want*. They never seemed to want anything he bought them. He went into the Kingsbrook Centre, walking slowly, catching sight of more 'Missing from Home' posters, then staring bemusedly at displays of clothes, handbags, small ridiculous bric-a-brac 'for the woman who has everything', at bottles of perfume, tights, absurd, mind-boggling underwear. Into this boutique he went. Burden was standing at the counter, making what looked like a knowledgeable choice.

'Snap,' said Wexford, but he felt better. Mike would *know*. He would probably know more than Wexford himself what other men's wives liked or wore. He might even know what size other men's wives were. With a sigh of relief he gave himself into the inspector's keeping.

Chapter 12

Peter Buxton's idea of marriage had never been that the two people in question should live in one another's pockets. He had been married before. His first wife and he hadn't exactly lived separate lives but they had individually had their own interests and pursuits, and often went out without the other. That was where the rot started, Sharonne said, that was what went wrong. Her beliefs were quite different.

Her husband needed her support and counsel, an ever-present voice in his ear uttering words of wisdom and prudence. Without her he would be lost. She didn't even care to have him sit next to someone else at a dinner party lest his indiscreet behaviour and unwise words landed him in trouble. It wasn't that she was jealous or even particularly possessive. Her absolute confidence in her appearance, sexual attractions and personality saw to that. In her own eyes, she was there to look after him every minute of the day except when he was in Trafalgar Square, and then she phoned frequently. Her power over him consisted in a need for her which she had largely manufactured herself. She had set out to mould him into the pattern of the man she wanted and all she had failed to do was stop him drinking.

Almost all. Such is human nature that few people are willing prisoners for long. Peter didn't want to escape from his marriage. He was pleased with his marriage and proud of his wife. When she had two or three babies she would transfer her bossiness and need to be needed to them. He didn't want permanent escape, only the chance to get away for a few hours. To be by himself, an individual, not one of a pair, half of the entity that is marriage, and he only wanted it for a little while.

Another weekend had gone by and another. Sharonne shopped for Christmas and he shopped for Sharonne. As well as her 'big' present she liked him to prepare a stocking full of goodies: perfume, expensive little make-up gimmicks, an eighteen-carat gold key ring, pearl ear studs. She appeared to have forgotten all about the blue car in the quarry, what was inside it and the smell. They never discussed it, not a word had been said about it by either of them since they left Passingham Hall that Sunday afternoon. Sharonne no doubt believed he had taken her advice to heart and, as she had, decided to forget the car, let it remain where it was until branches and brambles and ferns grew over it, rust corroded its bodywork, and the things inside decayed and dissolved until bones only remained. Until time aborbed and neutralised that terrible smell.

He hadn't forgotten it. By now he was thinking about the car almost all the time. He thought about it at meetings, at conferences, while Christmas shopping, while viewing new productions, when he was on-line and when he was signing contracts. The only way to rid himself of the monstrous fantasy that the car was the size of a bus, filling the quarry, and that the smell was wafting across the countryside like poison gas, was to go down there, see for himself and maybe – maybe – do something about it. But how, without Sharonne knowing?

He was, after all, the boss. If he didn't want to go to the midweek conference, no one could reproach him. Certainly – unless the threatened takeover happened – no one could fire him. He had only to say he had another, more important, engagement. But Sharonne would phone. His assistant wouldn't disturb him in conference unless the message was urgent but he *wouldn't be in conference,* he'd be on the way to the M2. If Sharonne asked where the other engagement was, the assistant could say she didn't know, she *wouldn't* know because it didn't exist, but Sharonne would play merry hell. In the event, things turned out quite differently from what he expected. They usually do. He told his wife he had a meeting with an important investor in Basingstoke and he'd be out of London most of the morning and over lunchtime. She didn't even ask who it was or for a phone number. She was having her hair done at ten and afterwards going to a fashion show.

The company, or those he bothered to tell, got a different story. A funeral in Surrey. His driver got quite pushy and insistent when Peter said he wouldn't be needing him or the Bentley but would drive himself. Such a thing was unheard of. When Peter said his own car needed the run, it hadn't been out of the garage for three weeks, Antonio offered to drive it down to Godalming. His employer, forced into a corner, was obliged to say weakly that he wanted to be alone to think.

He hadn't been alone in the Mercedes since he bought it eighteen months before. At first, being alone and at the wheel was quite pleasant but after a time, when there were queues and hold-ups and roadworks, he began to miss someone to talk to about the traffic, someone to tell him how much worse it was than last year and that she blamed the government. But at last he had a clear run ahead of him, he left the main road, entered the lane and just before midday the narrower one that was the approach to Passingham Hall. Although it was a chilly day, he lowered the car window and sniffed the air. No smell, nothing. Had he really thought there would be? Up here? Of course he had, his fears had troubled his days and horribly haunted his nights. Now, because there was no smell and none as he ascended the lane towards the house, hope seized him, a hope he knew was absurd and irrational, that the car had gone, had sunk into the wet ground or been towed away into the field. He even half convinced himself that he had imagined it all. After all, no one else had seen it, this whole terror depended on something that might be a hallucination . . .

Although he could have parked at the point where the track turned off, he went on all the way down to the house. Now he was here he felt a craven need to put off investigating the quarry. For of course it hadn't been a hallucination, nor had he imagined it. He got slowly out of the car, sniffed the air. If he didn't do something about that car he would spend his time down here sniffing the air, it would become an indispensable part of life at Passingham Hall. Arrive, park, sniff. Get up in the morning, go outside, sniff. . . . He changed his shoes for rubber boots and began to walk along the lane. And then a very awkward thing happened. He had forgotten all about the farmer's shed in the field but there the farmer was, standing on its roof, lopping off overhanging tree branches with a chainsaw. Avoiding him was impossible. Rick Mitchell saw Peter, raised one hand and called out, 'Long time no see. You OK, then?' Peter nodded, waved vaguely. At the turn-off to the track, out of the farmer's sight, he once more lifted his head, breathed in through his nose, and again. Nothing. If it really wasn't there he would have to see a psychiatrist, for this was serious stuff. Behind him, the chainsaw began to rattle and whine.

Of course it was there. A small, dark-blue car lying on its side, emitting through its open window that terrible stench. He could smell it here all right and he was twenty feet above it. Should he go down a bit, go nearer, *take a look inside*?

The sides of the quarry were a cliff of small landslides, tree roots, brambles, dead bracken and loose broken sticks. Treacherous sticks you might mistake for a root, step on and be sent flying. Peter began to climb down gingerly. The timber was slippery with wet, blackened moss. Once he made a mistake and grabbed on to what looked like a root but turned out to be a lopped-off branch. He slid, let out a sound halfway between a cry and a curse, but seized on to a growing root this time and came to a halt. From there he looked down once more. Inside the car he could see something blue which might have been a denim garment and he could see a hand, a pale, long-fingered hand.

That was it. He wasn't going any nearer. That was one of those children. He began to climb back. Going up was easier than getting down. He was more aware of the pitfalls and dangers now. At the top he tried to wipe his muddy hands on damp grass, withdrew them sharply when his finger came into contact with a three-inch-long slug. Standing up, looking up, he saw something which made him catch his breath. Rick Mitchell was coming towards him along the path from the lane.

'You OK?' called Mitchell when he was within earshot. It was a favourite phrase of his. 'I heard you shout out. You're all over mud.'

Peter cursed that involuntary cry. He knew it was all up now. He could no longer pretend there was nothing down there. Mitchell was sniffing now, approaching the quarry edge. 'What's that stink?'

Coming clean at last, Peter said, 'You see that car? There's a body in it – well, two, I think.'

'It's those missing kids.' Mitchell was awe-stricken. He took a step backwards, then two steps. 'What made you look? You haven't been down here for weeks, have you?' He answered his own question. 'The smell, I suppose. Good thing you came down. Piece of luck.'

Peter turned and began to walk back along the path. Mitchell beside him asked if he was OK and began offering helpful advice. Phone the police. Get on to them now. Did he have a mobile on him? If not he, Mitchell, did. He'd stay with him, give him some support. Peter said he'd prefer to make the phone call from the house. 'Don't let me keep you,' he said. 'I can handle it. There's no need for you to get involved.'

Mitchell shook his head. 'My pleasure. I wouldn't leave you to handle this alone.' He was evidently dying to play a part in the unfolding drama. It would beat messing about with a chainsaw any day. Incredibly, as they came into the lane, he said chattily, 'What you doing for Christmas? You and Mrs Buxton coming down for a day or two or have you got plans for living it up in London?'

Resisting the temptation to say that he felt like never setting foot in Passingham St John again, Peter said they'd be in London. He stared at the house. It looked unkempt, untended, even neglected, the way a place will when no one goes near it for weeks on end but a cleaner longing to get the job done and go home. No Christmas tree in the drawing room window, no lights, though it was a gloomy day.

Followed by Mitchell, he went up the shallow flight of steps on the right-hand side, unlocked the front door on its three locks and let them in.

Cold inside. Very cold. What had happened to the efficient central heating, set to come on daily at 9 a.m. and go off at 9 p.m.

'I'd have thought you'd keep the heating on,' said Mitchell.

'We do. It must have gone wrong.'

Ostentatiously, to set an example to Mitchell, he took off his boots on the doormat, but the farmer who wore trainers by now caked with mud, kept them on. He tramped across the hall floor. Peter tried not to look at the footmarks. Trapped as he was, he knew the best thing was to do it and get it over. Sharonne's Christmas would be ruined and therefore his. Why hadn't he thought more carefully before coming down today? But he had thought, he had done nothing but think about that bloody car for weeks, he had thought to the exclusion of everything that should more usefully and profitably have occupied his mind. He picked up the phone receiver, realised he had no idea of the number of the local police and he turned to his helper.

'Zero-one-eight-nine-two . . .' Mitchell began. He knew it off by heart. He would.

They came, two uniformed officers, both men, and they asked Peter to show them where the car was. The sergeant knew Rick Mitchell and was very matey with him, asking after his family and what he was going to do for Christmas. Neither officer seemed to find the farmer's presence irksome. When the car had been pointed out to them they suggested that Peter go back to the house to 'avoid a repetition of your unpleasant experience, sir'.

Peter felt he had no choice. He sat at the table in the

icy kitchen and asked himself what he would have done if Mitchell hadn't turned up. Nothing, he thought now, nothing. He'd have left the car where it was and gone home. After a moment or two he got up, switched on the oven to its fullest heat and opened its door. This reminded him of his early days when he'd lived in a bedsitter with 'kitchen area' and putting on the oven had sometimes been the only way to heat the place. Sitting down again, he tried to phone Pauline and then the central-heating engineer. Both had switched their phones on to an answering service. Conveniently forgetting his own roots, Peter thought things had come to a pretty pass in this country when cleaning women had cars and answerphones.

Half an hour had passed before the police – and Mitchell – came back. All three commented on the cold and the fact that his oven was on, but neither officer seemed to see this as a reason for Peter not to hold himself in readiness indefinitely at Passingham Hall for phone calls and for more police to come.

'I have to go back to London.'

'I'm sure there's no reason why you shouldn't go back this evening, sir,' said the sergeant.

His subordinate suggested it would give Peter the chance, 'hopefully', to get his heating seen to. 'I want to go back now,' said Peter.

'Afraid not. This is a case for the CID. Very likely the pathologist will want to see the, er, on the site. Then equipment will have to be brought in to remove the vehicle.'

'What's in it?' Peter asked.

'That I'm not at liberty to tell you at this stage,' said the sergeant.

He asked Mitchell the same question when the police had gone. It struck him as ludicrous that this busybody of a neighbour might know more about a car with bodies in it *on his land* than he did. 'Better leave that to the police, don't you think?' said Mitchell officiously, a smug look on his face. 'It's down to them to tell you when they think fit.' This made Peter believe they hadn't let Mitchell get near the car. 'Perishing in here, isn't it? I'll get off home for my dinner. Now can I get the wife to bring you down something? Maybe a pizza or a slice of her quiche?'

'I shall be fine.' Peter spoke through clenched teeth. Like cleaners with answerphones, the world was turned upside down when peasants like this one were eating pizza and quiche. 'Please don't bother.'

'Thanks for all your help, Rick,' said Mitchell, taking his leave. 'Have to say it yourself when no one else will, don't you?'

Muddy footprints were all over the kitchen floor. Like most householders today who employ a limited staff, Peter was always afraid of losing Pauline. She wouldn't like cleaning up mud two days before Christmas. He almost got down on his hands and knees to wipe it up. He would have done but for hearing a mechanical tune tinkling out. Such was his nervous state that for a moment he didn't know why someone was playing 'Sur le pont d'Avignon' in his kitchen at ten past noon. Then he realised and took the mobile out of his jacket pocket. It was Sharonne.

'Where have you been, Peter? I've been trying all over, the office, some place where they thought you'd be. They said you'd gone to a funeral. Where are you?'

He didn't answer. 'Is it important, er, darling?'

'That depends on whether you want the pipes at Passingham to freeze if we get a cold snap. Pauline's been on to say the heating's gone off and she can't start it. Where *are* you?'

It was a let-out. He could say . . . Ideas for what he could say came thronging. 'I'm in Guildford. Look, why don't I get over to the Hall and see what I can do? I've got an hour or two to spare.' He'd say the smell was so bad he'd had to tell the police . . . 'I may be able to fix the heating myself.'

'Promise to call me back, Peter.'

'Of course I will.'

He had recourse to the drinks cupboard and, indulging in something he knew was a step down the road to ruin, gulped down quite a lot of neat whisky out of the bottle. Then he went upstairs and opened the cupboard where the boiler lived. The front cover lifted off, a switch pressed, a flame struck and maintained and the heating was on again. This is the kind of thing that cheers one up, going a long way to show that one merits a degree in gas engineering. The radiators chugged and bubbled, and the place began to warm up. He wouldn't phone Sharonne back yet. Better let her think he'd had to work on the system for an hour or two. The front doorbell and the phone rang simultaneously as he was coming downstairs. Phone first. It was a man called Vine from Kingsmarkham Crime Management.

'Hold on a minute,' said Peter.

At the front door were two uniformed police officers. In their car, on the forecourt, sat a silver-haired man in a camel coat.

'Lord Tremlett is here, sir.'

Harassed, Peter said, 'Who the hell is Lord Tremlett?'

'The pathologist. He's here to examine the body *in situ.*'

'You mean the *bodies*, don't you?'

'That I can't say, sir.'

Perhaps the chap on the phone could. Peter asked him, but he didn't answer. 'We'd like to see you, Mr Buxton. As soon as possible.'

Chapter 13

By the time Burden and Barry Vine got to Passingham Hall the pathologist had gone but the car was still where Peter Buxton said he had first seen it. Scene-of-crime officers had been busy measuring and taking samples, and the fingerprint people were still there. A truck with a crane on it followed them down the drive, prepared to haul the VW Golf and its contents out of the quarry, and behind the truck a car driven by Pauline Pearson's husband Ted, his back and the doctor's injunction forgotten. It was half past five and dark but powerful lamps had been brought to the scene and these could be seen between the trees, lighting up the wood. Two cars and a van were parked on the grass verge that bordered the lane.

A single exterior light showed Burden the façade of the hall, the two flights of steps leading up to the portico and front door, and the two cars on the forecourt, a staid-looking Mercedes and a dashing Porsche. Lights appeared to be on in several rooms. Vine rang the bell and the door was answered by a spectacularly beautiful woman of about twenty-seven. She looked less than pleased to see them. Yet, thought Burden, the expert on all things sartorial and cosmetic, the effect of casual carelessness – apparently no make-up, pale-blonde hair spikily untidy, blue jeans, white sweater, no jewellery – must have been achieved for their benefit or that of the scenes-of-crime men.

'My husband's in the drawing room,' were the only words she was to utter for some time. She opened double doors and walked in ahead of them.

Peter Buxton was thirty-nine and looked fifteen years older. The skin of his face was a dull greyish red. He was one of those men who are very thin with narrow shoulders and spindly legs but wear their belly as if it were a cushion hung on them in a bag. They have the problem too of arranging it to bulge above the trouser belt or below it. Buxton had opted for the former. He was sitting in an armchair with a drink that looked like whisky and water on a small table beside him. The room contained a great many such small tables, piecrust-edged and with lamps on them, consoles and a couple of chaise longues, bunchy flounced curtains at the windows. It had the air of having been put together by an interior decorator recovering from a nervous breakdown.

'When can I go back to London?' said Peter Buxton.

Burden knew a little about him, where he lived and what he did for a living. 'Chief Inspector Wexford will want to see you tomorrow, Mr Buxton . . .'

'Here?'

'You can come to the police station in Kingsmarkham if you prefer that.'

'Of course I don't. I want to go back to London. It's Christmas. Sharonne – my wife, that is – and I have to get ready for Christmas. She kindly came down here this afternoon to support me but now we want to go home.'

'Why don't you tell me about your discovery of this car on your property, sir? You drove down here this morning, I believe. You came because your central heating wasn't functioning, is that right?'

Before Peter Buxton could answer, the door opened and a woman walked in, followed by a rather stout man who, as soon as he saw the company, pressed his hand into the small of his back. The woman was solid, upright, middle-aged and, from her newly set hair to her lace-up ankle boots, might have been an actress playing a farmer's wife in some rustic soap opera. A flood of words poured out of her. 'Sorry to come bursting in like this, Mrs Buxton, but having a key I thought I wouldn't trouble you to answer the door. I heard about your spot of bother in the village, you know what village gossip is, and I thought you might be in need of some help. I see the heating's on again. I feel it, rather. Nice and warm, isn't it? And it's turning quite cold out, I wouldn't be surprised if we had a white Christmas. Oh, whoops, I'm sorry, I didn't realise you'd got company.'

'They are police officers,' said Buxton in a voice as cold as the weather.

'In that case, I'll sit down a minute if you've no objection. I might be able to contribute. You sit on that hard chair, Ted, you have to think of your back.'

Apparently, Buxton baulked at actually telling them to go. He tried to catch his wife's eye but she kept her head averted, determined not to be caught.

'You were saying, Mr Buxton,' said Burden, 'about coming down to see to your central heating.' Something in Buxton's face told him all was not well. The man was more uneasy than he should have been. 'What time was that?'

It was the right question to ask. 'I don't know. I don't remember.'

Sharonne Buxton spoke at last. 'Yes, you do, Peter. Let me jog your memory. The first time I tried to get hold of you at the office was just after ten. That was on my mobile at the hairdresser's and you'd already left. They said you'd gone on your own instead of having Antonio drive you. I wanted to tell you Jason's asked us to dine at the Ivy the day after

Boxing Day. Then I'd planned on going to Amerigo's new collection but I went home first and that was when Pauline phoned to tell me about the heating.'

Quick on the uptake, Vine said, 'But you already knew about the heating, Mr Buxton, because that was the reason for your coming down here.'

'No, he didn't.' Pauline Pearson seized her opportunity. 'He couldn't have known. I didn't know till I came in to have a tidy up and dust round. That was at half past ten. I kept trying to phone Mrs Buxton to tell her and I thought she must be out. I thought she'd be home for lunch so I kept on trying and I finally got hold of her just after eleven.'

'You'd left long before that, darling. Don't you remember? And when I got hold of you at last you weren't here. You were in Guildford. You said so.'

Interesting, thought Vine. Very interesting. Peter Buxton had driven himself to Passingham Hall, had unusually dispensed with his driver and had used the central-heating failure as an excuse for his visit. So what was his true purpose? Something to do with a woman? Possible but, according to Vine's information, the man had been married less than three years and Sharonne Buxton was very beautiful. Moreover, he spoke of her and looked at her with admiration bordering on idolatry. And what was he doing in Guildford? Leave it for now, Vine thought. Think about it. And who the devil was Amerigo and what did he collect?

'You went up into the wood,' Burden said. 'Why was that?' He glanced at the notes he'd made earlier. 'A Mr Mitchell who farms nearby told the local police he encountered you at about eleven by the quarry. You told him about the car and the, er, smell was very strong. He went back to the house with you and gave you the number of the nearest police station. Is that right? But what made you go into the wood?'

'You couldn't have smelt it from down here,' said Vine.

Pauline Pearson intervened. 'You certainly could not. I've got a very good sense of smell, haven't I, Ted? I was here earlier and I couldn't smell it. Thank God. Makes you feel sick to your stomach, doesn't it?'

'Nasty,' said Ted. 'Very nasty.'

'If it wasn't that made you go into the wood, what did?'

'Look, I found the bloody car and told you people. What does it matter why or how?'

'This is a suspicious death, sir,' said Burden. 'All the circumstances may be very important.'

'Not to me. Nobody has told me anything. I don't even know how many people were in the car. I don't know if it was those kids and that woman who was with them. I'm told nothing.'

'There's very little to tell, sir,' said Vine. 'The body in the car hasn't yet been identified.'

'What else do you want to know?' Peter Buxton reached for his glass, realised it was empty and looked longingly at his wife.

Her reaction amused Burden. 'No, darling,' she said firmly, 'no more. Not yet. I'll make you a nice cup of tea in a minute.' She turned her head, as exquisite as a flower on a stalk, towards the policemen. 'I hope you won't be long. My husband should go to bed early. He's had a shock.'

It was ten past six. 'I'll make the tea, Mrs Buxton,' said Pauline, 'when they've gone.'

'When did you last come down to Passingham Hall?' Burden addressed the wife this time.

It was a question, he inferred from her suddenly wavering manner, that she wasn't entirely happy to answer. 'I can't say offhand. Some weeks ago. When was it, darling? Maybe the last weekend in

November or the first in December. Something like that. It's not exactly a fun place in winter, you know.'

This piqued Pauline Pearson, the native, who showed her displeasure in a tightening of the lips and a stiffening of the shoulders. Ted gave a loud sniff. The Buxtons would be lucky if they got their tea, Burden thought, reflecting how he'd have liked a cup himself.

'Did you go to Guildford *after* you found the car in the quarry, Mr Buxton?' Vine looked at his notes. 'I don't quite understand the time sequence here. You found the car at about eleven, phoned the local police station at about a quarter past, they got here just before twelve, talked to you and went up into the wood with Mr Mitchell. At ten past twelve Mrs Buxton phoned you on your mobile and you were in Guildford. But *I* phoned you on your home number here at twelve twenty and you answered.'

Burden's lips twitched. He put on a serious expression. 'How do you manage to be in two places at once, sir? It must be a useful accomplishment.'

Peter Buxton looked at his wife and this time their eyes met. 'My wife made a mistake. I never said I was in Guildford. I'd no reason to go there.'

'But you'd a reason to come here? Did you make a mistake, Mrs Buxton?'

She said sulkily, 'I must have.'

'All right.' Burden got up. 'I think we'll leave it there. Chief Inspector Wexford will want to interview you in the morning. Will ten a.m. be convenient?'

'I want to go home,' said Peter Buxton like a child on his first day at primary school.

'No doubt you may – after the Chief Inspector has talked to you.'

Outside in the car Burden started laughing. Vine joined in. They were still laughing when the Pearsons came down the steps and got into their car. Pauline gave them a glare and muttered something to her husband. 'I shouldn't laugh,' Burden said. 'God knows what he's been up to. Now they're alone the showdown will start.'

'The divine Sharonne is very easy on the eye,' said Vine.

'True. I dare say he'll forgive her for spilling the beans or whatever she did. Funny they didn't arrange things better before we got there, wasn't it?'

'I reckon she'd only just arrived. He didn't have the chance.'

The lamps were gone, the truck with the crane was gone and all that showed it had ever been there were double lines of ruts in the soft soil revealed by their car headlights.

'Who'll identify the body?' Vine asked.

'God knows. It'll be a grim task, whoever it is. His *Lordship* seemed to think she'd been there getting on for a month. It's probable she's been there since that weekend the Dades were in Paris. She won't be a pleasant sight.'

Too unpleasant a sight for a father to see, Wexford had decided. For this must be Joanna Troy. They had marked her down as perpetrator, quite a reasonable assumption, but she was the victim and quite possibly the missing children were victims too. The grounds of Passingham Hall and the whole area of open countryside surrounding it would have to be searched for their bodies. Meanwhile, this morning, Tremlett would begin on the post-mortem. Her dentist, whoever that was, to identify her? To match the broken-off piece of crown to her dentition? Then, if they could do some sort of make-over on her face, restore it to a semblance of the human, ask the stepmother to look at it? Wexford shuddered.

A nice Christmas present, to be shown the decaying face of your husband's only child. Perhaps they could avoid it. How had she died? It wasn't immediately apparent, according to Tremlett. No obvious wounds. Taking Vine with him – 'They won't be over the moon seeing me again.' The sergeant grinned – Wexford had himself driven to Passingham Hall for ten o'clock and arrived as Peter Buxton was carrying a suitcase out to the open boot of the Porsche.

'Anticipating an early departure, Mr Buxton?' said Vine.

'You said I could go home once I've talked to whoever it is.'

'Chief Inspector Wexford. And we'll have to see about that.' Being, like God, no respector of persons, Wexford looked at him reflectively. 'Can we go inside?'

Buxton shrugged, then nodded. They followed him in. 'The divine Sharonne', as Barry Vine had called her, was nowhere to be seen. Too early in the morning for a high-maintenance woman, Wexford decided. They went into a smallish room with leather chairs, a desk and a few books, the kind that, while they have handsomely tooled spines, look hollow and as if no pages are behind those morocco and gilt façades. A window afforded a view of Passingham Hall woods. Peter Buxton jumped, starting violently when a pheasant rose out of the undergrowth, flapping and squawking.

'So when did you *first* see this car in the quarry, Mr Buxton?' Wexford was acting on intuition and what Burden and Vine had told him. He was rewarded by the dark flush that mounted into Buxton's face.

'Yesterday morning. Haven't they told you that?'

'*They* have told me what you said. What they haven't told me, because they don't know, is why you came down here yesterday. Not because there was something wrong with your heating, you didn't know that. At your London office you told Mr Antonio Bellini you were going to a funeral in Godalming. Your wife seems to think you were in Guildford when she phoned you.'

'She's already said she made a mistake about that.'

'Did Mr Bellini make a mistake too? When Inspector Burden spoke to him on his home phone at nine last evening, he seemed very sure of what you'd told him.'

Peter Buxton affected to sigh impatiently. 'What does all this matter? I came down here. To my own house. Is there something unusual in that? I wasn't trespassing, I wasn't breaking and entering. *This is my house.* I've a perfect right to be here. I found a car in the woods and told the police. What's wrong with that?'

'On the face of it, nothing. It sounds very public-spirited. But when did you *first* see the car in the quarry? Was it the last time you came here? Was it the weekend of Saturday, December the second, just under three weeks ago?'

'I don't know what you're insinuating.' Buxton jumped to his feet and pointed out of the window. 'What are all those people doing on my land? Who are they? What are they looking for?'

'First of all, they are not on your land. They are on Mr Mitchell's land. They are police officers and conscientious members of the public helping them in the search for two missing children. We should like to search your land also. I've no doubt there'll be no objection on your part.'

'I don't know about that,' said Buxton. 'I don't know at all. Here's my wife. We're of one mind on this. We resent being kept here, we want to go home.'

Sharonne Buxton was of a type Wexford had never

found attractive, belonging as he did to the class of men who admire sweeter-faced, darker, livelier women with hour-glass figures, but he acknowledged her beauty. A less sullen and contemptuous expression would have improved her. Instead of a 'Good morning', 'hello' or even 'hi', she said in a voice and with an accent that required but hadn't received the same honing and polishing as her face and body, 'You don't need us here. We've engagements in London. It's Christmas or hadn't you noticed?'

Wexford ignored her. He said to her husband, 'Thank you for your permission. The search is very important and the searchers will be as careful of your property as possible'

'I didn't give permission. And I shan't. Not unless you let us go. That's a fair exchange, isn't it? Let us return to London and you can search the place until the New Year for all I care.'

Wexford, who had been looking at his notes, snapped the book shut. He felt like paraphrasing *Through the Looking Glass* with a, 'Police officers don't make bargains.' Instead he said, 'In that case I shall apply for a warrant. I have no powers to force you to stay here but I think I should remind you that obstructing the police in the course of their enquiries is an offence.'

'We'll stay,' said Sharonne Buxton, 'But we'd like it to go on record that we didn't want the place searched or any of you here.'

It was Burden who attended the post-mortem. For a man of such fastidious tastes and sleek appearance, he was surprisingly unmoved by the sight of an autopsy. He watched it impassively with much the same attitude as anyone else viewing a hospital sitcom on television. Wexford, who felt differently, but was accustomed by now to hiding those feelings, arrived when it was nearly over. Hilary, Lord Tremlett, whose macabre sense of humour had increased with his elevation to the peerage, was at the stage of talking about bagging up the dead mutton and doing a 'quickie facelift' for the benefit of the relatives. He seemed to find it hugely amusing that the dentist who had looked in to check the dentition against his chart and to match the crown, unused to such sights, had retched and required a glass of water before he could look inside the cadaver's mouth.

'It's her, though,' said Burden, as callous as Tremlett in his attitude to the poor dentist. 'It's Joanna Troy.'

'I shall get Effie Troy to look just the same,' Wexford said, remembering certain mis-identifications in the past. 'She's a sensible woman and Lord Tremlett's tidied up the face. So what did she die of?'

Tremlett began stripping off his gloves. 'A blow to the head. Death would have been instantaneous. Could have been inflicted with that dear old standby, the blunt instrument, but I think not. I favour a fall and a striking of her head against something hard, possibly the ground, but not soft ground. Not that famous wood of yours, that wouldn't have killed her, more likely sucked her in, like the quagmire in *The Hound of the Baskervilles*.'

'Could it have been the car itself?' Wexford asked. 'I mean, when the car went over the quarry could she have struck her head on the windscreen with sufficient force to kill her?'

'Your people can tell you more about that. Marks on the screen and whatever. But I doubt it. I doubt if she was driving the car. I doubt it very much. It's a crying shame I didn't get to see her sooner, she's been dead a month.'

'You would have done if I'd had a say in it,' said Wexford. But thanks to that clown . . . 'Did the fall or the blow knock the crown off her tooth?'

'How do I know? I'm not an orthodontist. A common butcher, that's me. It might have. I can't say. There was nothing else wrong with her and she wasn't pregnant. You'll get it all in appropriate language you won't understand a word of when I've done my report.'

'I can't stand that man,' said Burden when they were back in Wexford's office. 'Give me the other one – what's he called? Mavrikiev – any time.'

'You're not alone in that. What was she doing in Passingham Hall woods, Mike, why was she there? I had a look around after that fool Buxton had tried to make a bargain with me. I went up to the quarry and walked about in the wood. There's a great rather beautiful – well, it'd be beautiful in the spring – kind of open space in the middle, all ringed by trees, but there's nothing else except the quarry and more trees. If she wasn't driving, who was? And where are Giles and Sophie Dade?'

'The search is well under way. And we'll have that warrant by this afternoon to search Buxton's grounds.'

'By which time it'll be getting dark. I'm glad I kept Buxton there, I'll keep him over Christmas, I'll keep him till the New Year if I can. I'm not usually vindictive but I'd like to lock him up.'

'The divine Sharonne will have to drive to the nearest supermarket and buy herself a frozen turkey,' said Burden, 'and a Christmas pud in a packet *and* cook it all herself.'

'If I were a religious man I'd say God is not mocked.'

That afternoon it began to snow. This was the first snow to fall on Kingsmarkham and points eastward for seven years. The search of Rick Mitchell's land was called off at three thirty and the searchers, Kent police, mid-Sussex police and Passingham St John villagers, all adjourned to the Mitchells' large farmhouse kitchen. There Rick regaled them with mugs of tea (whisky-laced), newly baked scones and Dundee cake, and a spiteful account of his treatment at the hands of Peter Buxton the previous morning. It was a tale of ingratitude, snobbery and the contempt of the town dweller for honest country yeomen. If Buxton thought he, Rick, was going to sell him even half an acre of his land he had another think coming. As for Sharonne, according to Mrs Mitchell, a large woman in leggings and shocking-pink sweatshirt, she was 'common as dirt' and only in it for the money. She'd give that marriage another year at most.

It was still snowing when they left, the world was glowing white in the dusk, any bodies or newly dug graves obscured. During the evening, according to the meteorologist doing the weather forecast after the ten o'clock news, 12.7 centimetres of snow fell. This was a figure understood by only that segment of the population under sixteen. Wexford looked it up and found it was five inches. He waited until Dora had gone to bed and then he wrapped up the scent he'd bought her, the silver-framed photograph of her four grandchildren, the two boys and the two girls, and the pink silk jacket Burden had promised him would fit her. Gift-wrapping wasn't his forte and he didn't make much of a job of it. Dora was asleep when he got upstairs. He hid the presents in the back of his wardrobe and went to bed, lying there sleepless for a while, wondering if there would be more floods when the thaw came.

George Troy's car yielded a harvest of information. Fingerprints were all over its interior, most of them

Joanna's. But if you had relied on prints to show you who had been driving it you would have concluded no one had, for the steering wheel, automatic shift rod and windscreen showed nothing. All had been carefully wiped. The car was untidy, books on the back seat, books and papers on the floor, chocolate papers, a half-drunk bottle of water in one of the rear door pockets, screwed-up credit card chits from petrol sales. The glove compartment held sunglasses, two ballpoint pens, a notepad, a comb and two paper-wrapped barley sugar sweets. Hairs from those back seats belonged to Joanna, the rest possibly to George Troy and his wife. A hair on the floor in the front was dark brown, a fine *young* hair, that could have come from the head of Sophie Dade. It had gone to the lab with hairs from her own hairbrush for comparison.

In the boot was an overnight bag, small, dark-blue in colour, with the intials 'JRT' in white on one side. Inside it were a pair of clean black jeans, a clean white T-shirt, a clean white bra and pants, a pair of grey socks, a grey wool cardigan, and two used bras with two used pairs of pants and two used pairs of socks in a Marks and Spencer's carrier bag. The sponge bag in the bottom held a toothbrush, a tin of baby powder, a sachet of shampoo and a spray bottle of very expensive perfumed cologne, Dior's Forever and Ever. That cologne surprised Wexford. Unless the bag had contained a couture evening gown, it was the last thing he had expected to find there.

The clothing of the body itself had puzzled him. A pair of black trainers were on the feet but only a barely knee-length pale-blue T-shirt covered it and this was of the kind made for a very large man. Nothing else, no underwear, no socks. If she had sprayed herself with Forever and Ever, no trace of its scent remained.

Effie Troy went to the mortuary two days before Christmas and identified the body as that of her stepdaughter, Joanna Rachel Troy. She did it calmly, without flinching, but when she turned away and the face was covered once more, she was very pale. Wexford accompanied her home to Forest Road and spent half an hour with the bereaved father. Apparently, it hadn't occurred to George Troy that something as seriously terrible as this, the worst thing, might have happened to his daughter. He had never contemplated it. She'd be all right, she was a sensible girl, she knew what she was doing. At first he was disbelieving, then shocked beyond words, literally beyond them for the founts and streams of speech so characteristic of him were dried up by horror. He could only stare at Wexford, his mouth open, his head shaking. His wife had tried to prepare him but he had taken her caution and her warning as referring to her being in some sort of trouble with the law or having left the country for some suspect reason. That she might be dead, and dead by violence, he had refused to confront, and the news had blasted him.

Wexford saw him as being in the best hands and he left, telling Effie Troy of the counselling available to her and her husband, and of other sources of help, though he had little faith in this himself. Next to the Dades, up to Lyndhurst Drive, past houses with cypress trees in front gardens hung with fairy lights, Christmas trees in windows, paper chains, angels and cribs just visible in interiors. Nothing in the windows of Antrim, not a light showing on this gloomy overcast morning. He had to tell the Dades there was still nothing known of the whereabouts of their son and daughter, though the body of Joanna Troy had been found. But no news is good news and this was better than what he had had to tell Joanna's father.

They bombarded him with queries, Katrina pleadingly, Roger rudely. His question as to why the police had made the effort to find Joanna but not his children was one Wexford had never been asked before in comparable circumstances. He didn't want to stress that the search at Passingham St John was continuing because it sounded as if it was bodies they searched for, as indeed it was, but he had to say it, reducing Katrina to weeping. Her departure from the room in tears was a cue he couldn't afford to miss but he braced himself for the storm which must inevitably follow. He came out with it bluntly.

'Have you ever had reason to believe Joanna Troy was in love with you?'

'*What*?'

'What' is easy to say, Wexford thought. 'You heard me, Mr Dade. Have you? Did you have any interest in her yourself? Were you attracted?'

Dade began roaring like a lion, his actual words indecipherable, his articulation entirely lost. Katrina could be heard, sobbing in the kitchen.

'Good morning,' Wexford said, and added more gently, 'I shall want to talk to you again soon.'

On Christmas Eve more snow fell and the hunt for the children was temporarily suspended. As yet there was no sign of them, nothing of theirs that might have given a clue as to where they were.

Late that day Wexford was told from the lab that the hair was not Sophie Dade's but had come from the head of some unknown child. He wondered why the perpetrator had brought Joanna's bag in the car but nothing for the children.

Chapter 14

It was less the enjoyment of their own festivities in peace that kept Wexford and his officers from pursuing their enquiries on Christmas Day than a sense of the wrongness of such action, the outrage of intruding even on the Troys and the Dades at that time. To him Christmas had never afforded much pleasure and he took no joy in a white one. But Dora did and the sight of their garden blanketed and gleaming seemed to inspire her in all those inescapable tasks of cooking and table setting and finding places to put things.

'I hate the way it covers everything up,' said Wexford. 'You talk about a blanket of snow and that's what I dislike. As if it's all been put to bed for the – the duration.'

'The duration of what? What are you talking about?'

'Oh, I don't know. I don't like hibernation, suspension, everyone having to stop doing things.'

'You don't have to stop doing things,' said Dora. 'You should be doing things now like opening the red wine to let it breathe and seeing we've got enough ice – oh, and you might check on the liqueur glasses in case anyone wants apricot brandy or Cointreau after dinner.'

The 'anyone' who might want liqueurs were Sylvia and Callum and Sheila and Paul. All would be accompanied by children – 'Check the orange juice and Coke, would you, darling,' said Dora – Sylvia's Ben and Robin, and Sheila's Amulet and the new one, Annoushka, Amy and Annie to most people.

'Have you got a present for Chapman?'

'Cal, Reg. You'll have to get used to it. Yes, of course I have.'

Pauline Pearson had treated as ludicrous the suggestion that she should cook the Buxtons' Christmas dinner. 'You won't find a soul who'll do that, Mrs Buxton. Not on Christmas Day. They'll all be cooking their own, won't they? It was different in my grandma's time but them days are gone when they put everything on the back burner to wait on the gentry. Not that there's any gentry left, not in our classless society, and thank God for it. You want to get that bird you've bought thoroughly defrosted, at least twenty-four hours, and that you haven't got. You leave a bit of ice inside there and you'll get salmonella or worse. A lady my auntie knew went down with that stuff women stick in their faces – what's it called? Bot-something – from a half-defrosted turkey.'

It was something of a revelation to Peter that Sharonne couldn't cook. He hadn't left his roots as far behind as he thought and he still took it for granted that all women could cook a straightforward dinner, it was part of them, in their genes. Sharonne couldn't. Hopelessly, she watched the frost slowly slipping off the turkey and asked Peter why they couldn't go out to lunch.

'Because every place you'd set foot in and a lot you wouldn't have been booked up for Christmas dinner for months.'

'Don't say dinner when you mean lunch, Peter, it's common.'

'Everybody says Christmas *dinner*. Never mind what time of day it is, it's *dinner*.'

Peter cooked the turkey. He smothered it with butter, stuck it in the oven and left it for six hours. He could have done worse. There were tinned potatoes and frozen peas and Bisto gravy and he was rather proud of what he'd achieved. His cooking had been helped on by liberal tots of single malt and by the time the meal was ready he was unsteady on his feet and glad to sit down.

Drink helped him forget about past police visits and, worse, possible future police visits. But along with the dry mouth, raging thirst and banging head which ensued during the evening came the suspicion that they knew he had found the car weeks before he said he had. Now he couldn't understand his own behaviour. Why hadn't he told the police then? Surely it wasn't because if he had done so he would have had to cancel two local engagements that, in any case, held no particular charm for him. Surely it couldn't have been that. No, it was Sharonne. She had stopped him.

He looked at her through bleary eyes that intermittently afforded him double vision. She was curled up in an armchair, her shoes kicked off, her face calm, serene, unsmiling, watching a Christmas comedy show on television. The inevitable glass of sparkling water was beside her. Why had he let her stop him do what was manifestly his duty as a good citizen? The events of the first weekend in December had become inexplicable. He, a sensible man who would be forty next birthday, had let his wife, twelve years his junior, a model but by no means a *super*-model, a woman who had never done a thing beyond walk up and down catwalks in that third-class designer Amerigo's clothes, *tell him what to do.* And now God knew what would happen to him. He hadn't liked that jibe about obstructing the police being an offence. If he appeared in court it would get into the papers.

'Sharonne?' he said.

She didn't turn her head. 'What? I'm watching this.'

'Is there a bed made up in one of the spare rooms?'

'I suppose so. Why? Are you feeling ill?' Now she did turn, perhaps remembering her role as his carer. 'You've only yourself to blame, Peter. I'm sure I don't know what's the attraction of all that hard liquor. Stay where you are and I'll get you a big glass of water and some Nurofen.'

Why didn't she know if a bed was made up? It was her job to know if not do it herself. He couldn't see why she didn't do it herself, she did nothing else. She hadn't even supported him when he tried to explain why he'd come down here. Nobody asked her to intervene when that detective inspector was questioning him. She'd done it off her own bat, almost spitefully. There was no call for her to tell the *whole* truth. She could have kept quiet. As for that ridiculous Pauline, she wouldn't have said all that about the heating if Sharonne hadn't set her an example.

He drank the water and swallowed the painkiller. Sharonne returned to her television programme and this time a smile disturbed her flawless features. Peter looked at her with something bordering on dislike. Then, without a word, he got up and went off to find himself a bed with blankets on it if not sheets as far from the master bedroom as possible.

Callum Chapman played with the two boys and the two-year-old girl, thus vindicating his reputation as a man who was 'good with children'. He was rather rough with them, though, Wexford thought, disliking the manhandling of little Amy. It mattered less with the boys who were big and could take care of themselves. But it was for Amy's parents to intervene, not a grandfather.

A woman living with the lover of her choice ought to be serene and revitalised but Sylvia looked unhappy. Of course they were all on edge, all trying too hard to enjoy this 'family' Christmas, Sheila worn out with breastfeeding and rehearsing for a new play, and Paul worried about her. Dora was piqued with him because he'd forgotten her injunction about the ice and he couldn't relax, his thoughts turning to the missing Dade children, the discovery of Joanna Troy's body and the inexplicable behaviour of Peter Buxton.

Whoever had driven the blue VW into the Passingham Hall woods must have known the place, at least known the woods were there and there was a way in for a vehicle. But not known it well enough to avoid driving it over the edge of the quarry? Or known it well and driven the car into the quarry on purpose? No, not driven it. Got out of it and pushed it over. With Joanna passively agreeing to sit in the driving seat? That wasn't possible. She must have been dead or at least unconscious before the car went over. Dead most probably. And what of the children? Were they dead at the time or hidden somewhere? If he, whoever he was, had killed the children and buried them why not kill and bury Joanna too? He saw no purpose in putting her body in the car. The blue VW could just as well have been pushed over the quarry edge empty. Whoever it was must have known the Hall and its grounds were seldom visited, so was he known to Peter Buxton? The perpetrator could have *been* Peter Buxton. Wexford was convinced he would never have reported finding that car if Rick Mitchell hadn't come into the wood at that moment . . .

'Reg,' said Dora, 'wake up. I've made tea.'

Sylvia set cup and saucer in front of him. 'Do you want anything to eat, Dad?'

'Good God, no. Not after that dinner.'

He looked up and as she drew back her arm saw a mark like a burn, a dark-red abrasion, encircling her wrist. Later on, he was to wonder why he had failed to ask her what it was.

On Boxing Day they resumed the search. They weren't looking for living people but for graves. Teaching himself the metric system, Wexford calculated there were now about 7.6 centimetres of snow on the ground. Whatever it was – and three inches meant much more to him and always would – it made searching pointless, confirming his opinion that snow was a nuisance, covering everything up. His thoughts returned to the day before, Callum Chapman throwing Amy up into the air and feigning not to catch her, Sheila falling asleep the moment she sat down in a chair, Dora edgy, and all the time the spectre at the feast, the one who wasn't there and never would be again, Neil Fairfax, Sylvia's ex-husband.

Grandparents – who would be one? You couldn't interfere, you couldn't even advise. You had to shut up and smile, pretend that everything your daughters did and provided for their children was perfect parenting. Grandparents . . . Had he paid sufficient attention to the grandparents in the Dade case? To the Bruces and Matilda Carrish? It might perhaps be a good idea to call on these people in their own homes, make it all right with the Suffolk and the Gloucestershire police, and take a drive out there before the thaw. The roadways were clear and if no more snow fell . . .

If they didn't know more about their children's children than the parents themselves, they sometimes had insights denied to the mothers and fathers. Look how *he* knew Amy didn't like being thrown around by Chapman, he could tell from her stoical little face, her determination to be polite as she'd been taught, while Paul seemed to notice nothing. Sylvia was convincing herself her lover was good with children, but Wexford sometimes saw a look in Robin's eyes expressive of contempt. He would follow through this idea of his to see the Dade grand-parents in their own environment, make appoint-ments for soon, maybe as soon as possible.

But for now, the Dades themselves. He went alone. Theirs was the only house he was likely to enter at this time in which no decorations had been put up, yet he fancied the place would be shimmering with glitter and sylvan with green branches at a normal Christmas. Katrina opened the door to him, her face as the woman's in *The Scream* must have been just before Munch started painting it.

'No, Mrs Dade, no,' he said quickly. 'I'm not bringing you news, bad or otherwise. I only want to have a talk now the situation has changed.'

'Changed?'

'In that Ms Troy's body has been found.'

'Oh, yes. Yes. You'd better come in.' It was ungracious but less so than Roger Dade's behaviour who, when he saw Wexford, cast up his eyes in silence and retreated into the living room.

'I thought maybe you'd found my children,' Katrina said miserably, tears never far away. 'I thought maybe you'd found them dead.'

'Please sit down, Mrs Dade. I must tell you both that an extensive search is being carried out in the neighbourhood of Passingham Hall but so far nothing has been found.'

'What's the point of searching when the place is under snow?' said Dade.

'Apart from it's being a more than usually unpleasant task for the searchers, the snow isn't deep and the thaw has begun. Now I'd like you to tell me if either Giles or Sophie had ever been to Passingham St John? Did they ever mention the place?'

'Never. Why would they? We don't know anyone there.'

Katrina was less brusque. 'I'd never heard of Passingham St John till we were told they'd found – Joanna. And found her car. I've been to Toxborough but that was years ago and the children weren't with me.' At the emotive word she began to cry noisily.

'The car was found in the woods at Passingham Hall. It's the property of a man called Peter Buxton. Do you know him?'

'Never heard of him,' said Dade. 'You heard my wife say we don't know this Passingham place. What are you, deaf?'

The hardest thing, Wexford sometimes thought, was to keep your cool when spoken to like this by a member of the public, especially when you were quick-tempered yourself. But it had to be. He had to remember – and remember all the time – that this man's two children had disappeared, his only children, and were very likely dead.

Katrina, through her tears, gave her husband the sharpest look he had ever seen from her but said, instead of something helpful, 'Do you know when Joanna's funeral will be?'

'I'm afraid I don't.'

'I'd like to go. She was my very dearest friend, poor Joanna.'

After that, he thought another call on Peter Buxton might be helpful. He took Vine with him. This time they walked down the lane in the hope of seeing just how clear the entry to the woods was, the path the blue VW had taken, but the snow masked everything, all that could be observed in these conditions was that at the point where the path probably started and deep into the woods, the trees stood further apart, far enough apart to allow the passage of a car.

Buxton opened the door himself. Again it was too early in the morning for his wife. He looked like a sick man, destined for some coronary or arteriosclerosis crisis, his face the mottled grey and red of pink granite and as rough-surfaced. Blood-red veins made a lacework across his eyeballs. There was a faint tremor in his hands and his breath, which peppermint toothpaste hadn't much disguised, was a mixture of stale whisky fumes and some indefinable digestive enzyme, enough to make Wexford step back. He felt an unaccustomed urge to warn the man he was killing himself but of course he didn't. Newspapers and magazines were stuffed with articles about what happened when you ate rubbish and overdid the booze. He'd had Moses and the prophets. Let him hear them.

'Seems a good time to have a word, Mr Buxton,' said Vine breezily.

Buxton glowered. For him there had never been a worse time. He led them down passages to the kitchen, making Wexford think the drawing room, no doubt littered with yesterday's plates and glasses, might be unfit for morning entertaining. But this can't have been the case, for the kitchen was possibly worse, Christmas dinner cooking utensils, pots and pans and empty tins lying about. For some reason Buxton offered them a drink.

'Water, orange juice, Coke or something stronger?'

The reason was obviously so that he could have something stronger too. Wexford and Vine would have accepted tea if it had been available but it wasn't.

'Hair of the dog,' said Buxton with a ghostly

snigger, pouring Scotch. He gave the policemen fizzy water with a perceptible sneer. 'What was the word it was a good time to have, then?'

'Who knows this place apart from you and your wife?' Wexford asked. 'Who visits you here?'

'Our friends. The people who work for us.' Buxton uttered the first two words loftily, the second six with scarcely disguised contempt. 'You can't expect me to tell you the names of my friends.'

Vine was looking incredulous. 'Why not, sir? They've no reason to object if they've done nothing wrong.'

'Of course they've done nothing wrong. Chris Warren is a County Councillor and his wife Marion, well she's a . . .' Buxton seemed to have encountered some difficulty in defining exactly what Marion Warren was '. . . a very well-known lady in these parts.'

'And where might Mr and Mrs Warren live?' Vine wrote down the Trollfield Farm address Buxton reluctantly gave. 'And who else, sir?'

Their neighbours, the Gilberts, said Buxton. Perhaps he meant 'neighbour' in the biblical sense, thought Wexford, for there was no house within sight of Passingham Hall. 'They live in a very lovely mansion in the heart of the village.' Buxton sounded like a second-rate travel brochure. He didn't know the name or number of the house, he just knew it by sight, no one could miss it. More names were dragged out of him by Vine's persistence: village acquaintances, met on the Chardonnay party circuit, a couple of Londoners who had once been weekend guests. On the subject of those he apparently considered his social inferiors he was more expansive and, in the case of Rick Mitchell and his wife, vindictive. They were nosy, interfering people who probably snooped about all over his land in his absence. Suddenly he seemed to see that police enquiries, far from intruding on his privacy, gave him opportunities he was unlikely to find elsewhere.

'The same with that Pauline and her husband. She comes down here whenever she feels like it. Never mind keeping to a routine. I was here up in the wood – I don't think these people realise I enjoy walking on my own land – when who do I come upon but Pauline's husband strolling about with a very undesirable-looking fellow he introduces as a Mr Colman. A private detective. On my land. And that's just one instance. For all I know the whole neighbourhood's trespassing on my land when I'm not here.'

'Where is Mr Colman now?'

'How should I know? This was yesterday. Christmas Day, if you've ever heard of such a thing.'

Wexford nodded. It proved only that Search and Find Limited were keen as mustard. 'How long have you owned Passingham Hall, Mr Buxton?'

'Getting on for three years. I bought it from a man called Shand-Gibb, if that interests you.'

Buxton turned round – nervously, Wexford thought – as his wife came in. Today she was wearing a tracksuit, as white as the snow outside. Was she planning to go running, to find herself a local gym or was it just the day's preferred costume? He said good morning to her and she asked sharply what they wanted. He didn't think himself called upon to answer that. Buxton answered for him in a sulky voice while Sharonne pounced on the whisky, replaced the cap and carried the bottle away. She acted exactly as Wexford had once seen Sylvia respond to Ben's excessive consumption of mint humbugs from a jar and the expression on Buxton's face was, as far as he could remember, identical to Ben's. He looked both furious and mutinous.

'Is there anyone else you can think of, Mr Buxton?'

'No, there isn't. Are they still searching those fields? And when can we go back to London?'

'Yes to your first question,' said Wexford, 'and tomorrow morning to your second. But I'm not satisfied with your explanation about the discovery of the car, Mr Buxton, and I shall want to talk to you again.'

He and Vine didn't wait for protest. Outside the sun had come out and the thaw begun. Water dripped from the eaves of the house and the snow had begun to turn transparent. 'If an English heat-wave is two fine days and a thunderstorm,' he remarked, 'a cold snap must be twelve hours of snow and forty-eight of muddy meltdown.'

The lane, which an hour before had been under its crisp covering, was in parts like a running stream. Halfway up they met a party of searchers who had found nothing. Wexford had an uneasy sense of frustration. Logically, the Dade children should be somewhere within a reasonable distance, they had to be there, where else would they be? He tried to imagine a scenario in which all three of them were brought here by the perpetrator – by perhaps more than one perpetrator – all killed and Joanna left in the car which was then pushed over the quarry edge. What then became of the other bodies? There was no sense in taking them away while Joanna's body was left behind. Perhaps it wasn't bodies he had to think of but two living people. Had there then been two cars? One to be left behind as tomb for Joanna, the other to be driven away. The children taken away – where?

It was all too unreasonable to allow for the working out of a sequel. Who, for instance, were these two people, possibly a man and a woman, who had driven here in two cars? What was their motive?

How, above all, did they know of Passingham Hall grounds and the quarry in its heart. Suddenly he found himself thinking of the open space, the clearing in the wood, and he suggested to Vine that they go up there again before leaving.

This would be one of the areas from which the snow would take longest to clear, for nothing broke its smooth untouched whiteness and no foot had trodden it. From where they stood it looked like a lake of snow surrounded by a wall of leafless dark-grey trees of uniform size. There was no wind and nothing stirred their branches.

'Maybe this Shand-Gibb can help us,' said Vine.

Chapter 15

He had no memory for recent events. And in his case 'recent' meant the past two or three decades. Before that, his early and middle years, he could readily recollect. Wexford, of course, had come across this in old people before but seldom to this extent. Bernard Shand-Gibb could scarcely remember the name of his housekeeper, a woman not much younger than himself, whom he addressed as 'Polly – Pansy – Myra – Penny,' before getting it right and coming out with 'Betty!' on a shout of triumph.

It was a long time since Wexford had heard that accent. His was the speech of the old gentry, spoken by an upper class when he was a boy and liable to strike awe into those lower down the social scale, but now almost dead and gone. Actors had to learn how to do it, he had read somewhere, before playing on television in a drama of the nineteen twenties, learn to say 'awf' for 'off' and 'crawss' for 'cross'. Such an accent would have prevailed, he thought, when his own grandfather was young and the local rector, riding past him and his friends, cracked his whip and called out, 'Take your hats off to a gentleman!'

Shand-Gibb was a gentleman but a very gentle one, puzzled by his inability to remember his last years at Passingham Hall. 'I do wish I could recall something or someone, my dear chap,' he said in that incomparable voice, 'but it's all gawne.'

'Perhaps your housekeeper . . .?'

Mrs Shand-Gibb had been alive then and Betty had tended on them both. But she was a servant of the old school, not one to know or wish to know her employer's business. Wexford thought that if she had to refer to him it would be as 'the master'. She sat down in his company because Wexford had asked her to stay and asked her to sit down too, but she sat uneasily and on the edge of the chair.

'Can you recollect anything?' Shand-Gibb asked her in his mild, courteous way. He was not the sort of man to omit names or styles or titles when he addressed someone and he had made an effort to remember what she was called, had tried and failed, had struggled with it, mouthing names, but had failed.

'I'm sure I don't know, sir,' she said. 'I could try. There was the Scouts came to camp in the springtime and in the autumn too. They was good lads, never made any trouble, never left a mess behind them.'

'Did anyone else camp in the wood?' asked Vine. 'Friends? Relations?'

Shand-Gibb listened courteously, occasionally nodding or giving a puzzled smile. He was like someone who has tentatively claimed to understand a foreign language but when addressed in it by natives finds it beyond his comprehension. Betty said, 'There was never anything like that, sir. Not to *sleep*, there wasn't. The village had their summer fête there. Is that the kind of thing you mean? Regular they did that. In June it was and they put up a marquee in case of rain, sir, as it mostly did rain. They was clean too, never left a scrap of litter.' She considered. 'Then there was those folks that did their singing and dancing up there. On the Dancing Floor, sir.'

A smile of nostalgia spread across Shand-Gibb's face. A light seemed to come into his faded blue eyes, half lost as they were in a maze of wrinkles. 'The Dancing Floor,' he said. 'We used to have fine hot summers then, Mr Er – . I don't believe it ever rained in June. The whole village came to dance on Midsummer's Eve and made their own music too, none of your gramophones then.' The tape and CD revolutions had passed him by. A long-playing record was probably the last innovation he could recall. 'We danced on the Dancing Floor, the loveliest spot in Kent, high up but as flat as a pancake and as green as an emerald. We should go up there when the summer comes, Polly, er, Daisy, never mind. We should ask young Mitchell to wheel me up in my chair, what?'

Betty looked at him. It was a look of infinite sweet tenderness. She spoke very softly, 'You don't live at the Hall any more, sir. You moved away three years since. Another gentleman and lady live there now. You remember, don't you?'

'I do for a moment,' he said, 'when you tell me I do,' and he passed one shaky, veined hand across his brow as if the stroking movement might wipe away the mist that descended on his memory. 'I take your word for it.'

Wexford could imagine a maypole set up between the greening trees, a young girl, plump, fair, rustic, not beautiful by today's standards, not a Sharonne Buxton, brought to be crowned Queen of the May. 'These were people Mr Shand-Gibb gave permission to use the ground?' he asked.

'Not just anyone who asked,' Betty said quickly. 'If they was the sort that made a mess they never was allowed back. There was a couple wanted their wedding reception there. Mr Shand-Gibb said yes on account of him not being too well and Mrs Shand-Gibb –' she lowered her voice, though ineffectively '– in her last illness.' The old man winced, tried to smile.

'Ooh, the state they left the place in. Litter everywhere, tin cans and I don't know what. They had the cheek to want to come back for some party or other they was giving but Mr Shand-Gibb said no, he was very sorry, but not this time, and they took it badly. It was shocking how rude they was.'

Wexford took down these people's names but they were the only names he was destined to get. Betty could remember other applicants for the use of the dancing floor but not what they were called. Mr Shand-Gibb knew but she hadn't been told, it wasn't her place to be told, she incredibly said. She only knew the name of the bridal couple because Mrs Mitchell had talked about them, the whole village had talked about them.

'When you mentioned singing and dancing,' said Vine, 'were you referring to the people who got married?'

'That was another lot,' said Betty. 'These folks never made no mess. After they'd gone you wouldn't know they'd been there. Mind you, they made a lot of noise, singing you could call it but some would call it screaming and shouting. Didn't bother Mr Shand-Gibb, he let them come back the next year.' Her employer had fallen asleep. 'I don't reckon he could hear it from the house, poor old gentleman.'

Screaming and shouting, Wexford thought, as they drove back to Passingham Hall with the Kent police DC who was accompanying them. No doubt an elderly woman of old-fashioned ideas meant no more than that the gathering danced to the kind of music habitually heard in discos or reverberating from cars with their windows open. The Mitchells at the farm might know, would almost certainly be more helpful than a servant of the old school who knew her place and an aged man with a memory irretrievably gone.

Rick Mitchell and his wife Julie knew everything. That, at least, was the impression they liked to give. They knew everything and they were 'good people', the kind that swamp you with offers of food and drink, comfort and their time, when you come to call. That the three policeman would be calling they had been told in advance and Julie Mitchell had prepared a mid-morning spread, coffee and orange squash, scones, mincepies and a bakewell tart. Vine and the young DC tucked in. Wexford would have liked to but dared not. Rick Mitchell moved swiftly into a lecture on Passingham St John village life from the Middle Ages to the present day. Or that was what it seemed like to Wexford who found himself powerless to cut the man short, as one is when the speaker ignores one's interruptions and continues relentlessly on. He wondered if Mitchell had learned this technique from listening to interviews with Cabinet ministers on Radio Four.

But at last the man paused to draw breath and Wexford put in swiftly, 'How about this couple –' he referred to his notes '– a Mr and Mrs Croft who had their wedding reception in the wood? Where do they live?'

Mitchell was looking affronted. It was easy to tell what he was thinking. You come here and eat my food, the good home-baked cakes my wife has sweated over a hot stove for hours to make, and you can't even have the courtesy to let me finish my sentence . . . 'Down in the village,' he said sulkily. 'Cottage called something daft. What's it called, Julie?'

'I don't know if I'm pronouncing it right. It *used* to be called Ivy Cottage but now it's got some funny Indian name. Kerala or however you pronounce it.'

'She's Indian, the one that got married.' Rick Mitchell seemed to forget his grievance in the pleasure of imparting information. 'Got a funny Indian name. Narinder, if I've got my tongue round it right. The husband's as English as you or me.' He glanced uneasily at the Kent DC, an olive-skinned man with jet-black hair and dark-brown eyes. 'They've got a baby now, what they call mixed-race, it must be. I reckon it takes all sorts to make a world.'

'Mr Shand-Gibb's housekeeper has told us there were some people who used the wood, apparently several years in succession, and who made a lot of screaming and shouting. Does that mean anything to you?'

Whether it did or not Wexford was not to learn for some minutes. Both Mitchells broke into extravagant praise and regrets for the departure of the former owners of Passingham Hall. They were lovely people, of the old gentry, but not a scrap of 'side' to them.

'That was a sad day for Passingham when dear old Mr Shand-Gibb sold up,' said Julie Mitchell in the kind of lugubrious voice television newscasters use when they segue from an England soccer victory to the death of a pop singer. 'He was one in a million. A far cry from those new folks, those Buxtons, newvo rich yuppies they are.'

'You can say that again,' said her husband and for a moment Wexford was afraid she would. But she only shook her head more in sorrow than in anger and Mitchell went on, 'It's my belief he'd known that car had been there for weeks. Maybe put it there himself *and* what was inside it, I wouldn't put it past him. What was he doing there mid-week in the middle of December, that's what I'd like to know. Revisiting the scene of his crime, there is no other explanation. He knew it was there all right.'

Wexford was inclined to agree, not that he did so aloud. 'Let's get back to the visitors who made the music, shall we? The "screaming and shouting". Have you any idea who they were?'

The worst question you can ask a man like Rick Mitchell is one to which he doesn't know the answer. Far less bad is one which, if he answered truthfully, might incriminate him. Plainly he had no reply to make but that didn't stop him replying. 'Not exactly *who* they were, if it's names you're meaning. I know *what* they were, a bunch of vandals, if the way they parked their cars down the Hall lane is anything to go by. Terrible ruts they made in the grass verges and that sort of rut never comes out, it's there for good, a blot on the landscape . . .'

'And you could hear them shouting and yelling, Rick,' said Julie. 'You know you could. We were going to complain . . .'

'Not to Mr Shand-Gibb, mind. He'd gone by then. We had serious thoughts of putting in a complaint to Buxton. Didn't bother him, did it? He wasn't here when they were. Oh, no, he was up in London living it up, no doubt.'

'It didn't sound English, what they were shouting,' said Julie. 'I C, I C, it sounded like.'

'What, the letters I and C?' Vine asked.

'That's what it *sounded* like but it's not English, is it?'

This emphasis on Englishness must have aroused some vestige of conscience in Mitchell, for, as they were leaving, he remarked in a kindly tone to the Kent DC, 'You OK then, are you?'

Wexford went back to Kingsmarkham, leaving the other two to pursue enquiries in the village. He was going to a funeral, Joanna Troy's. She hadn't driven the car over the edge of the quarry, she had been dead before she was put into the car. 'Murdered?' he had asked Tremlett on the phone.

'No reason to think so, no reason at all.'

Except that her body had been removed from wherever death took place. Pains had been taken to conceal that body. And where were the Dade children in all this? The parents, at any rate, were at the funeral in St Peter's, Kingsmarkham, Roger Dade as well as his wife, and Katrina's parents too, if he was right in thinking the elderly man was her father. Now might be his chance to carry out his resolve of talking to the grandparents. Never mind that they wouldn't be in their own home. The Dades were feeling better, Wexford thought, they *look* better. They believe that because Joanna is dead and no other bodies were in the car, no other bodies have been found, Giles and Sophie are alive. Do I believe that, he asked himself. He couldn't find the slightest reason to think so and he knew those parents were relying on instinct and intuition rather than on reason.

It was a cold, wet day, icy inside a church the size of a cathedral. How many people know you don't have to have a funeral? How many know it's not necessary or prescribed by legislation to have voluntaries and glumly intoned prayers and hymns – invariably 'Abide with Me' or 'The Lord is my Shepherd' – if you don't believe and the dead person didn't believe? None of this lot had been inside a church for years, he thought. How much better it would have been for all of them to have had Joanna Troy's body cremated and afterwards held a quiet gathering of friends and family to remember her. At least there were only family flowers, a simple wreath of forced daffodils from Joanna's father and stepmother.

Ralph Jennings, the ex-husband, hadn't come but the neighbour, Yvonne Moody, was there, the woman who had told him she suspected Joanna's passion for Roger Dade. On her knees when everyone else was sitting or standing, weeping quietly. He noticed that Joanna's father didn't cry. His grief he showed otherwise, in an ageing that added a decade to his years. People hadn't yet discarded the habit of wearing black to funerals. All these mourners were in black but only Yvonne Moody and Doreen Bruce wore hats. They filed out of the church, George Troy clinging to his wife's arm, Katrina Dade holding her husband's unwilling hand, and got into the cars which would take them to the crematorium miles out in the country at Myfleet Tye. Katrina's parents weren't going. Wexford had been surprised to see them there at all but supposed they had come simply to support their daughter. The Bruces had their own car with them. As Mrs Bruce helped her husband into it and started the engine, Wexford got into his and followed them back to Lyndhurst Drive. He was on the doorstep before they had let themselves in.

Doreen Bruce failed to recognise him and assumed, for no reason, that he must be selling something. Even after he had explained, she wasn't forthcoming but announced that her husband had to rest, he had a bad heart, it was essential he lie down. She hadn't wanted him to come this morning. It wasn't as if they'd known Joanna Troy. Eric had had a coronary in October and since then had had to take things easy. Not that you'd know it the way he was always dashing about. To Wexford Eric Bruce looked far from 'dashing' anywhere. He was a thin little old man, pale and pinched, the last you would imagine to have a heart condition. He wasn't to be allowed to go upstairs but was led to the sofa in the living room and covered with a blanket. The black cat, lying on the shelf above a radiator, watched the fussy movements with feline scorn and stretched out one foreleg as far as it would go as if admiring its pointed claws.

Wexford was shown into the dining room, a not-much-used place made dark by the small diamond panes of its windows and the heavy ruby velvet curtains. Doreen Bruce sat opposite him, nervously drumming her fingers on the table. 'Sometimes,' he said, 'grandparents have a better knowledge of their grandchildren than those children's parents have. I know Giles and Sophie enjoyed staying with you – in Suffolk, is it?'

She probably called everyone 'dear'. It wasn't a sign of affection or intimacy. 'That's right, dear. Berningham. Where the American Air Force used to be but it's much prettier now all those ugly buildings have gone. You hear about these teenagers wanting nothing but clubs and amusements and worse but our two weren't like that. They love nature and the countryside, being out in the open air. Sophie used to cry when she had to go home. Not Giles, of course, dear, a boy wouldn't.'

'What did they do all day?'

She was puzzled. To her, obviously, the mystery was what they did at home in Kingsmarkham. 'Went for walks, dear. We take them to the beach. Eric and I don't think they're old enough yet to go alone. Well, Eric does, but you know what men are, said I babied them. Mind you, he liked their company all right, always wanted to be with Giles whatever he did. Of course that was before his coronary, dear.'

'When did they last stay with you, Mrs Bruce?'

'In August.' She came back with her answer very promptly. 'In their school holidays, dear. They wouldn't have been allowed to come for a weekend in term-time. Roger keeps their noses to the grindstone, you know.' An aggrieved note had crept into her voice. 'Homework, homework, homework night after night. I don't know why they don't rebel. Most teenagers would, from what I hear. Mind you, it's my belief they'd work hard without his lordship cracking the whip over them. They like their school work. At any rate, Giles does. He's a clever boy, is Giles, he'll go far.'

One point Doreen Bruce had made Wexford hit on. He asked curiously, 'Did you say Sophie cried when she had to go home?'

'That's right, dear. Cried like her heart would break.'

'A thirteen-year-old?' he said. 'Would you call her young for her age?'

'Oh, no, dear. Not really. It's not that.' Mrs Bruce's voice dropped and she looked cautiously in the direction of the closed door. Then she seemed to remember that her son-in-law wasn't in the house. 'It's more that she doesn't get on with her father. Giles is afraid of him but Sophie – well, she just hates being near him. Shame, isn't it?'

And this woman had described the Dades as 'not one of those dysfunctional families' . . .

Chapter 16

The Bruces' home was to remain unseen but Wexford's reaction on contemplating Matilda Carrish's was that theirs had to be a more congenial place for teenagers to stay in. But perhaps Giles and Sophie seldom had stayed there. Situated in an exquisite Cotswold village of grey-gold houses and cottages, hers was of the same stone as the rest of the dwellings in Trinity Lacy but apparently built in the eighties, stark, flat-fronted and with a low-pitched slate roof. Rather forbidding at first sight. It was possible Katrina Dade had vetoed the children's staying with their paternal grandmother. She seemed particularly to dislike her mother-in-law. What a lot of disliking went on in that family!

'Were they frequent visitors?' Burden asked when they were shown into a chilly, sparsely furnished living area.

'Depends what you mean by "frequent". They came occasionally. When I had the time. When they were allowed.'

Discreetly, Wexford eyed the room where they were. Its redeeming feature was the number of bookshelves filled with books which lined three of the four walls. He noted the sophisticated means of playing music, the computer stand with screen, obvious Internet access, printer and other unidentifiable accessories. Every piece of furniture, apart from the white or black chairs and sofa, was of pale wood, chrome and black melamine. On the bookless wall strange abstracts in aluminium frames hung side by side with photographs of inner-city squalor and industrial decay, which Wexford recognised as Matilda Carrish's own. She looked as chilly and as stark as her artwork, a long, lean woman with a flat back and etiolated legs in grey trousers and black tunic, round her neck and hanging to her waist a single strand of grey and white pebbles strung on silver.

She must be well into her seventies, he thought, and yet the last thing you think about when you look at her is that she's old. That in spite of the wrinkles, the white hair, the gnarled hands. 'You last saw them in October, I believe?'

She nodded.

'When you were together,' Burden put in, 'were you close? They were teenagers and this is hard to imagine, but did they confide in you?'

This time she smiled very slightly. 'They certainly couldn't be close to their parents, could they? My son's a bully and his wife's an hysteric.' She said it quite calmly as if she were talking about acquaintances whose behaviour she had occasionally observed. 'When she got the chance my granddaughter talked to me. Told me a little about her feelings. But it seldom happened. Her mother would have stamped on that.'

'Did they get on, Giles and Sophie? Were they good friends as well as brother and sister?'

'Oh, I think so. Sophie was rather under Giles's influence. She's inclined to do what he does. If he likes a piece of music, for instance, she'll like it.'

'What would you think of a theory that Joanna Troy was having an affair with your son? Or would have liked to have an affair with him?'

For the first time Wexford heard her laugh. 'One

never never knows with people, does one? But I wouldn't have thought him such a good actor. Of course, I never met Miss Troy. Maybe she would have liked a relationship with my son. There's no accounting for tastes.'

A chilling woman. This was her own child she was talking about. '"Her feelings", you said, Mrs Carrish. What about Sophie's feelings?'

'That would be telling, wouldn't it? But this is a serious matter, as you'll tell me if I don't say it first. Not to put too fine a point on it, she told me she hated her father and disliked her mother. You see, Katrina lets her do as she likes, then flies into a rage when she does it, and my son forbids every pleasure and keeps noses to the grindstone. What Sophie would really like would be to come and live with me.'

There it was again, much the same as what Doreen Bruce had told him, only couched in different terms. 'What did you say to that?'

'Mr Wexford, I will be frank with you. I don't love my grandchildren. How could I? I only see them two or three times a year. I feel – how shall I put it? – benevolent towards them, that's all. I wish them well. I love my son, I can't help that, but I don't much like him. He's boorish and conventional, entirely without social graces. I don't have many of those myself but I hope I'm more honest about things. I make no pretence at being a conformist. I do as I like. Poor Roger is unhappy because he never does anything he likes, hasn't for years.'

Frank, indeed, Wexford thought. When, if ever, had he heard a mother and grandmother talk like this? 'Katrina would never even consider letting one of her children live with me,' she said. 'Why would she, come to that? I wouldn't have let my children live with a grandparent. Besides, I'm selfish, I like living alone, I want to go on living alone till I die.

That's why I don't live with my husband, though we're on perfectly good terms.'

He was astonished. He had supposed she was a widow, that she had been twice widowed. Other people's mind-reading ability always amused him. It was gift he had himself. Matilda Carrish now demonstrated it. 'No, I divorced my first husband, Roger's father. He's dead now. My second husband teaches at a European university. He has his job and he prefers living abroad while I prefer living here, quite a simple and amicable arrangement. We spend some time together once or twice a year – oftener, incidentally, than I see Giles and Sophie.'

Burden had picked up on a word. 'You mentioned children, Mrs Carrish. You have another child besides Mr Dade?'

'A daughter,' she said indifferently. 'She's married, she lives in Northern Ireland. County Antrim.' Burden took this woman's name and address. He wondered if Matilda Carrish had a similar relationship with her daughter as that with her son, a gut feeling of love but without liking or respect or, probably, much desire ever to see her.

As they were leaving she indicated to them a colour print on the hall wall. A mezzotint, Wexford thought it would be called. It showed eighteenth-century buildings in some city that might have been anywhere in northern Europe. Matilda Carrish looked as if about to make some comment on it but she turned away, saying nothing.

On the phone Wexford said, 'Mr Buxton, I strongly advise you to do as I ask and come to Kingsmarkham Police Station tomorrow morning. I have already told you of the offence of obstructing the police in their enquiries. There is another, that of perverting the course of justice. You mustn't believe this is an empty threat. I shall see you here at twelve noon tomorrow.'

'I shouldn't mind coming down,' Buxton said in an aggrieved tone. 'There are a few things I have to see to. Can't you come to Passingham Hall?'

'No,' said Wexford. 'It's out of my way.' He paused. 'I shall expect you at twelve.'

If Buxton didn't come he would have a serious case against him. The idea of arresting the man rather appealed to him. The next phone call he made was to Charlotte MacAllister, née Dade. Her voice was uncannily like her mother's, crisp, cool and ironic.

'I don't know Roger's children very well. There's been no quarrel. I seldom go to England and they never come here. Katrina's afraid of bombs.' She paused to give a dry laugh. 'I say they never come here but Giles did come three or four years back when things were quiet. He came on his own and he seemed to enjoy being with my kids.'

Nothing there, Wexford thought. Then he remembered something. 'Do you know why they call their house Antrim, Mrs Macallister?'

'Do they? I've never noticed.'

'I don't think it's coincidence, do you? You live in County Antrim, your brother calls his house Antrim, yet you don't seem to be close.'

'Oh, that's easy. They lived here when they were first married. Giles was born here. Roger wasn't in real estate then. My husband and he had been at school together, best mates and all that, and my husband put him in the way of getting a job. That's why they came here, because of the job. He was a salesman for a computer supplier – computers were just becoming fashionable then – but apparently he wasn't very good at it. He hasn't inherited our mum's brains.' Implying that she had? Perhaps. 'Katrina was upset when he got the sack but she didn't want to leave. She loved the cottage they lived in, she wanted him to get work here. Then the pub in the village got an IRA bomb and she left fast enough after that.'

Buxton came. He looked ill. The whites of his eyes were pale yellow and his cheeks a network of broken veins. The suit he wore, a double-breasted pale-grey, seemed unsuitable for the time of year and his tie, too loosely knotted, was an inappropriate mélange of garden annuals, petunias, pansies and nasturtiums. Such cheerful, almost holiday, clothes contrasted ludicrously with the bags under his eyes and his thinning hair. In Wexford's pleasant office he seemed ill at ease.

'I've asked you to come here for two reasons, Mr Buxton,' Wexford began. 'The first involves a question you'll find easy enough to answer. The second may be more difficult for you – I mean difficult in the sense of awkward or embarrassing. But we'll leave that for now.' Buxton had turned his liverish eyes away and was looking at the pale chocolate-coloured telephone, studying it with fascination as if it were an example of radically innovative technology. 'You've already told us the names of various friends and acquaintances of yours who visit and know the lie of your land. Since then I've spoken to Mr Shand-Gibb, and he and his housekeeper mentioned various people and groups who borrowed what he calls the dancing floor for functions. There was, for instance, a couple who held their wedding reception there, and his housekeeper told me of a noisy group whose shouting and singing could be heard down at the house. Does this mean anything to you?'

Buxton's red face had gone redder. He gave the classic reply: 'It might do.'

'Yes, Mr Buxton, I know it might. It might mean

something to me, such as for instance, that a bunch of people out in the open on a summer night usually do make a lot of noise. Let me rephrase the question. Do you know who these people were and were they there with your permission?'

Buxton seemed to speak unwillingly as if the words were dragged out of him. 'They used to use that clearing in the wood when the Shand-Gibbs owned the place. When I moved in the man – the boss, the organiser, I don't know – he wrote and said could they carry on with it. Twice a year they wanted it, July and January – must be bloody freezing in January.'

'So you agreed?'

'I couldn't see any reason to refuse. Sharonne and me, we wouldn't be there on a week night, so we weren't bothered about noise.'

'So they've used it four or five times since you moved in?'

'I suppose so.'

'And since it's now January they're due to use it again shortly?'

'They won't now. Not after – what was in the quarry.'

Why was the man so cautious, so evasive? Suddenly Wexford knew. 'You charge a fee? They pay a rent?'

'A nominal rent,' Buxton said unhappily.

'And how much might "nominal" be, Mr Buxton?'

'I don't have to tell you that.'

'You do,' said Wexford laconically.

Perhaps Buxton's thoughts strayed to the charge of perverting the course of justice, for he no longer hesitated. 'A hundred pounds a time.'

A nice little earner, Wexford thought. Especially if it came in twice a year and a similar sum from other organisations using the wood. A welcome addition to one's income but not, surely, to the income of a man like Buxton. But, of course. He wasn't declaring it, it was tax-free. And he'd insist on cash. Dropped through the letter box in an envelope, no doubt. That was the reason for the shame and the caution . . .

'Who are these people? What do they use the clearing for?'

Shifting in his seat as if his buttocks itched, Buxton said, 'They're religious. That singing is hymns. They shout out, "I see, I see!" meaning they've seen angels or spirits or something.'

'I thought you'd never been here when all this was going on?'

'The first year they used it after we moved in I came down. I wanted to know what I was letting myself in for.'

'Who *are* they, Mr Buxton?'

'They call themselves the Church of the Good Gospel.'

Of which Giles Dade was a fervent member. This meant that, having visited the wood on several occasions, he would know it and know about the quarry. And others would know about it too and know him. Know him enough to abduct him and his sister, and kill the woman who was looking after them? Perhaps. There seemed no point in enquiring about other parties who had used the place for here was a direct lead to the missing boy, the first link between him and Passingham Hall. 'The man, the boss, the organiser', as Buxton put it, would undoubtedly be Jashub Wright, pastor of the Good Gospel Church . . .

Buxton confirmed this, astonished that Wexford could identify him. But instead of reassuring him this evidence of the Chief Inspector's apparent omniscience only seemed to frighten him further. He pulled a mobile out of his pocket and asked if it would be all right to phone his wife. Wexford shrugged, smiling slightly. At least the man hadn't asked to use *his* phone.

Sharonne, it seemed, hadn't been given prior notice of her husband's visit to Kingsmarkham and interview at the police station. Wexford could gather quite a lot from Buxton's evasive replies and although he didn't actually say, 'I'm at Passingham' – that would have been too blatant in this company – the words 'Passingham Hall' were used. What would Buxton do if she called him back on the Hall phone? Perhaps say he'd had to pop over to Guildford. Buxton was getting a dressing-down. From where he sat Wexford could just hear the shrill reproving words of a scold. He couldn't blame her. Chronic mendacity seemed to come so naturally to Buxton that he told lies when the truth would surely have been perfectly acceptable to hearer as well as speaker. For instance, why on earth tell the woman, as he now did, 'I must go, darling, I've got a business lunch in five minutes'? When he ceased to be besotted with the 'divine Sharonne' and began on an adulterous spree he would have had plenty of practice at alibi-making.

'Then I suppose I should say I mustn't keep you,' Wexford said smoothly. For all his lying and prevarication, Buxton hadn't yet learned how not to blush. 'Unfortunately, I haven't done with you quite yet. I told you I had a second line of enquiry to pursue and I expect you know what that is.' A nod, an uncomfortable shrug. 'When did you first see the blue VW Golf in the quarry? No, don't tell me December the twenty-first. I know you were aware of it before that.'

'It would have been a bit before,' Buxton said, the words again wrenched out of him.

'Rather more than a bit, Mr Buxton. The weekend of the fifteenth perhaps? The eighth? Even before that? The *first*?'

Of course Wexford was enjoying himself. How could it be otherwise? Normally a compassionate and considerate man, he felt no need to waste mercy on Buxton. He watched the man squirming and watched without compunction. Oh, what a tangled web we weave, as his grandmother used to say, when first we practise to deceive. The wretched Buxton said, 'I didn't come down on the fifteenth or the eighth.'

'So it was the first of December and at the same time the first weekend in December?'

'It must have been.'

'Well, Mr Buxton, you have wasted a lot of police time. You've wasted public money. But if you tell me no more lies and explain to me instead exactly what happened when you went up into the wood the first weekend in December, one week after Ms Troy and Giles and Sophie Dade went missing –' he paused, looking searchingly at Buxton '– I think it's likely the Director of Public Prosecutions will not decide to take this any further.'

He had taken pity on him but instead of relaxing Buxton looked as if he was going to cry.

Nothing of what Buxton told him could set a precise time on the arrival of the car in the quarry. But by Saturday, 2 December the body inside the car was decomposed enough to smell strongly. The weather was far from cold but it was, after all, midwinter. The air was moist and mild after that rain, and decay would have happened quite quickly.

'I haven't even got a theory,' said Wexford when he and Burden met in the Olive and Dove at the end of a long day. 'Can you come up with anything?'

'We know now that Giles could have directed whoever killed Joanna to the wood and the quarry but I don't think he and Sophie would have acquiesced in her murder, do you? It's more likely he told the perpetrator about Passingham Hall in all innocence. He didn't know what the perpetrator wanted. He and Sophie didn't even know Joanna was dead. They may have been killed before they could find out. Or they may have been taken away while Joanna was still alive. Even taken by Joanna in the car with whoever it was.'

'So where do the Good Gospellers come in?'

'They don't. Their only function in all this is that of introducing Giles to Passingham Hall.'

'I shall still want to talk to them again. More of them. Not just the Reverend Jashub. I'd like to find out exactly what happens when they have their open-air carry-on at Passingham Hall, when they turn into Blue Domers.'

'What's a Blue Domer?'

'Someone who doesn't go to church but says he prefers to worship outside, under God's "blue dome". Mike, I don't know how, still less why, but I think Joanna Troy was killed in the hall of the Dades' house and on that Saturday night.'

Wexford had been staring out of the window, staring at nothing, but now the void was filled with three people he knew, all crossing the bridge and hand in hand. In the glaring yellow lamplight he had recognised his former son-in-law and his two grandsons. Of course. It was Friday, the evening Neil had access to his sons and took them out. If they were crossing the bridge towards the centre of town they were most likely heading for McDonald's, the boys' favoured venue for supper.

'What are you looking at?'

'Neil and Ben and Robin. I've just spotted them.'

'D'you want to go outside and say hello?'

'No.' Wexford suddenly felt deeply sad. Not angry or frustrated or regretful but just sad. 'Let the poor chap have some time alone with his children. You know, Mike, that's the insoluble problem today. The media are always on about how men should learn to be good fathers but they seldom say a word about the father who doesn't get the chance. His wife has left him and she's got his children, she's *always* got his children. But are they therefore to stay together and be miserable together for years and years so that he can be a good father? And suppose she won't? I don't know the answer. Do you?'

'Marriage partners should stay together for the sake of the children,' said Burden sententiously.

'Easy to say when you're happily married.' Neil and his children had passed on out of sight. Wexford sighed. 'D'you want another?'

'Only if you will.'

'No. I'd better get home.'

Outside it was raining harder than ever. The Kingsbrook, once more in spate, tumbled and foamed along towards the dark tunnel mouth. Wexford wondered if the floods would come back and he thought with dismay of his garden. Burden gave him a lift home but refused an invitation to come in. Wexford made his way up to the front door, noticing water gushing from the outfall pipe that drained the gutters. There was nothing to be done about it. He let himself in, found Dora in the living room with her glass of wine, first of the two she would have that evening. She got up, kissed him, said, 'Reg, I've just had a very odd phone call from Sylvia.'

'Odd in what way?'

'She sounded a bit wild. She said Cal was pressurising her to marry him. That was her word, "pressurising", And she'd said she'd think about it but she wasn't ready for remarriage yet. You know the ridiculous way they talk these days. She wasn't ready for remarriage.'

'Thank God for that, anyway.'

'The boys were going out with Neil, it being Friday, and she said that once she was alone in the house with Cal again he'd start and she didn't like the way he bullied her.'

'Why can't she just leave him?' Wexford said irritably. 'After all, she's left one man, she knows how it's done. I suppose I should say, why doesn't she chuck him out, she's done that too.'

'I'd no idea you felt as bitter as that.'

'Well, I do. About both of them, him for being a pig and a boor, and her for being such a fool. D'you think the garden's going to flood again?'

Calling in at Passingham Hall to check on the state of the heating – he couldn't trust Pauline's judgement – Buxton found the man called Colman standing on the gravel sweep at the front of the house, staring up at his bedroom window.

'What the hell are you doing? Get off my property and don't come back.'

'Keep your hair on,' said Colman, using a quaint old-fashioned expression Buxton vaguely remembered on his grandfather's lips. 'No need to get aerated.' Swiftly he plucked a card from his pocket and held it out to Buxton. 'It's more in your interest than anyone else's that we find those kids.'

Buxton supposed it might be, though he didn't say so. 'Who are you acting for?'

'Mrs Matilda Carrish. Now why don't we go up into the wood and you show me exactly where you found that car – when was it, now?'

'Just before Christmas.' Buxton was getting nervous.

'Come off it. Rumour has it you knew that vehicle was there weeks before you said a word. I wonder why you kept so stumm?'

Buxton took him up into the wood and reconstructed for him an itinerary for the car to have taken once it had left the road at the top of the lane. After a while he began to find Colman congenial company, particularly as the enquiry agent was carrying on him a hip flask of whisky which he passed several times to Buxton. By the time they parted, Colman to drive to the Cotswolds, Buxton to London, they had agreed to keep in touch.

Sharonne was out and no note had been left for him. Buxton wondered uneasily if after that call he had made to her from Kingsmarkham Police Station she had phoned Passingham Hall and, receiving no reply, absented herself in order to punish him. It wouldn't be untypical. The phone sat on its little table, silent and accusatory, a small white instrument whose invention and subsequent universal use had probably caused more trouble in the world than the internal combustion engine. For some reason he lifted its receiver and dialled 1471 to obtain the number of the last caller. He didn't recognise it but he knew it belonged to none of those he and Sharonne called their friends nor to any tradesman or shop that he could recall.

When he went to fetch himself a drink he noticed that he was holding between his fingers and turning it this way and that, the card given him by the representative of Search and Find.

Chapter 17

At Antrim they were taking the entrance hall to pieces.

'Everything will be put back exactly as it was,' Vine said to Katrina Dade, more in hope than certainty. Katrina moaned and wrung her hands, finally retreating to the living room where she lay on a sofa with a blanket over her and her face buried in cushions.

The carpet had come up and a couple of floorboards. A brownish patch was scraped off the skirting board and a section of flooring with a red-brown stain on it lifted away from between the bottom of the clothes cupboard and the uncarpeted floor. Vine knew what he had to do next and he didn't fancy it, but a policeman's lot, he sometimes thought, was a series of unpleasant tasks he didn't fancy. DC Lynn Fancourt said kindly to him, 'I'll ask her if you like, Sarge. I don't mind. Really.'

Vine sometimes thought that if he weren't a happily married man with kids and responsibilities he wouldn't have been averse to a runaround with Lynn. She was just his type, old-fashioned sort of figure and lovely golden-brown hair. 'No, I'll do it. Now. Get it over with.'

He went into the living room and coughed. Katrina lifted a tear-blotched face from the cushions. Vine cleared his throat. 'Mrs Dade, I'm sorry to have to ask you this. Believe me, it's just a precaution. Don't read anything into it. But do you happen to know which blood group your children belong to?'

Katrina read everything into it. She set up a loud wailing. Vine looked at her in despair and called Lynn, who came in calmly, sat down beside Katrina and murmured softly to her. No brisk admonitions, no slapping of face. Katrina sobbed and gagged and stuck her fists in her eyes, laid her head on Lynn's shoulder, but eventually gulped out that she didn't know, she never dealt with that kind of thing.

'Would your husband be able to help us?'

'He's at the office. He doesn't care. Children are just something a man in his position thinks he ought to have. He's never *loved* them.' The emotive word set off fresh wails and floods.

Lynn patted her shoulder, said gently, 'But would he know about blood groups?'

'I suppose so. If there's anything to know.'

At this moment the front door was heard to open and close, and Roger Dade came into the room. Katrina once more buried her head in the cushions. As always on the lookout for someone to blame, Dade said aggressively to Vine, 'What have you been saying to her?'

Lynn answered, 'We need to know your children's blood groups, Mr Dade.'

'Why didn't you come to me first? You know she's a crazy hysteric. Look what you've done to her.' But he lifted his wife – tenderly for him – and put his arms round her. 'There, there, come on. You can't go on like this.' He looked up at Lynn. 'Their groups are on file upstairs. If I ask you what you want them for I suppose you'll say it's just routine.'

Neither officer answered. Dade sighed, disengaged himself from his wife's grip – she had locked both hands round his neck – and went upstairs. Vine looked at Lynn and cast up his eyes.

There was no reason to believe a triple murder hadn't been committed in that hall. Unless the absence of much blood might be a reason. The hall would be easy to clean, Wexford thought. No carpet, no rugs, the wood apparently coated with a hard stain-repellent lacquer that would resist blood as well as any other compound. He wondered if they even had enough on the samples to make comparison with Joanna Troy's group possible.

One of the Dade children, Sophie, had a blood group that matched hers, O Positive, the commonest. Giles Dade's group was A Positive. If the samples revealed only O Positive blood they still wouldn't know much, merely that Sophie might have been killed along with Joanna. On the other hand she might not. But if they showed A Positive as well there was a strong possibility it was Giles's. How about DNA comparisons? They already had hair from Sophie Dade's hairbrush. DNA would be discoverable on that if the hair had fallen out, not if it had been cut off . . .

He would be seeing Jashub Wright at midday. At his home, to ask him about the ritualistic meetings at the Dancing Floor. Lynn Fancourt, back from the Dades', went with him. This was his first visit to the semi-detached bungalow, its exterior coated with that most depressing of wall covers, grey pebble-dashing. No attention had been paid to the front garden until, apparently, someone had attacked grass, nettles and incipient saplings with a scythe. Presumably on one of the rare days when it wasn't raining. It was raining now, water staining the grey walls a deeper charcoal. Every time Wexford saw pebble-dashing he was reminded of long ago when he was seven and staying overnight for some reason with an aunt. The walls of her house had a similar surface. He had been put early to bed in a back bedroom while guests were entertained. The company sat under his window in deckchairs, his aunt and uncle, two old women – old to him then – and an old man with an entirely bald shiny head. Unbeknownst to them he watched them from his open window and, unable to resist the temptation, began picking bits of pebble-dashing off the wall and dropping them on to that bald pate. For a few moments he had the blissful satisfaction of seeing the old man brush what he thought was some insect off his head. Twice he did it, three times, and then he looked up. They all looked up. Auntie Freda came running up the stairs, grabbed her nephew and whacked him with a hairbrush, later the cause of much indignation to Wexford's mother. These days, he thought, as Lynn rang the doorbell and they waited, she'd have had her sister-in-law up before the European Court of Human Rights.

Thekla Wright answered the door. Wexford had never seen her before and was a little taken aback. She was blonde and very pretty but the way she was dressed – what did her clothes remind him of? It came to him when they were on the threshold of the living room. A photograph he'd once seen of the wives of a Mormon in Utah, polygamy long illegal but a blind eye turned to it. They had been dressed like Thekla Wright or she was dressed like them, her frock faded cotton print mid-calf length, her bare legs covered in fuzzy blonde hair, her feet in flat sandals of the Start-rite kind children had worn in his pebble-dashing days. Her long hair was looped up untidily with combs and grips.

He had expected to see Jashub Wright alone but

the pastor's wife opened the door to disclose inside a gathering that made him think of a function he had never attended but only heard about, a prayer meeting. He had to stop himself staring. Probably most of the chairs the Wrights possessed were arranged in a circle and on each one, eight out of the ten, sat a man. They weren't dressed in striped trousers and frock coats and they weren't wearing stovepipe hats but for a moment he had the illusion they were. All were in suits with shirts and ties. All had very short hair. They rose to their feet as one when he and Lynn came in and Lynn got some very strange looks. He thought Mrs Wright had left them because her baby was crying but perhaps not, perhaps she had gone because they excluded women from their counsels. But Jashub Wright stepped forward with outstretched hand. Wexford ignored it – he was practised in this – and introduced Lynn, expecting verbal disapproval. But there was none, only a rather oppressive silence.

Wexford sat down and Lynn did. Now all the chairs were occupied. Before he could begin one of the men spoke and he saw he had come to a conclusion too soon.

'I am an elder of the United Gospel Church. My name is Hobab Winter.' He glanced quickly at Lynn and away. In that glance a feminist would have detected fear of women. 'It's my duty to point out that females are not normally present at our meetings but we will make an exception in this case.'

Wexford said nothing but Lynn spoke up, as he was sure she would. 'Why not?' No one answered and she repeated what she had said. 'I'd really like to know why not.'

It was the pastor who replied, in a genial and friendly tone, as if Lynn couldn't fail to appreciate what he was saying. 'We must never forget that it was a woman who brought about man's fall.'

Lynn was evidently too stunned for an immediate riposte and when after a few seconds she opened her mouth, Wexford whispered for no one's ears but hers, 'DC Fancourt, not now. Leave it.' She said nothing but he was aware of the tremor of rage running through her. He spoke quickly. 'May I have your names, please? So that we know what we're doing.'

One by one the circle uttered them, preceded by their titles, Elder, Reader, Officer, Deputy. Very odd, he thought. 'Now would someone tell me about this ceremony that takes place in the wood at Passingham Hall twice a year in January and July? Presumably this is the cleansing ritual you once mentioned to me.'

'The ritual, as you call it, though we prefer another name, will not be taking place there this January. Not in view of the circumstances.'

'So if you don't call it that what do you call it?'

'It is our Confessional Congregation.'

They certainly weren't anxious to be forthcoming. Wexford looked at the circle of men. Some of them were vaguely familiar to him, he had seen them about in Kingsmarkham. Each face was calm, enclosed, mild. They were rather alike, not one could have been described as good-looking, all had roundish faces, all were clean-shaven with small eyes and small mouths, though the noses varied in shape and size and the hair colour varied where much hair could be seen. Every face was curiously unlined, though somehow he could tell the youngest was in his thirties and the oldest in his sixties. If he was still alive and if he stayed with them, would Giles Dade come to look like this one day?

'What happens at the Confessional Congregation?' he asked.

'Church members attend.' Jashub Wright was laconic. 'New members confess their sins and are absolved. Cleansed. Purified. As I said to you once before, their bodies and spirits are cleared of toxins. Afterwards biscuits and Coke and lemonade are served. Women are involved in the catering arrangements, of course.' Once again he smiled gently at Lynn who looked away. 'Miss Moody is in charge of that. The people are very happy, they rejoice, they sing, they claim the new member as their own. Each new member has a mentor – one of the elders, of course – assigned to him. Or her. To prevent him sliding back into sin.'

'Who did you say was in charge of the catering?'

'Miss Yvonne Moody. She is one of our most deeply committed members.'

They left the room for a brief interval.

'She came to us of her own accord, sir, and she did admit to knowing Giles Dade,' Lynn said. 'You can't say she's tried to deceive us.'

'No, I dare say not. But it's interesting in various ways, isn't it? She knew Joanna Troy well, she lived next door to her, and she knew Giles through her church. Not only that. She knew about the clearing Shand-Gibb calls the Dancing Floor and therefore the existence of the quarry and the way through the wood to reach it. I revoke "I dare say not". She *did* deceive us. She came to us of her own accord because she saw that as the best way to project her innocence. Let's go back in there.'

The circle of members was as they had left it, the faces still serene, mild, inscrutable. Wexford noticed what he hadn't before, a faintly unpleasant smell pervading the small room. It took him a moment to realise this was the odour of eight lounge suits, worn daily but dry-cleaned seldom. He sat down again.

'How are you – maybe I should say, how *did* you – get to the site of the Confessional Congregation? By car?'

'Certainly by car,' Wright said. 'Occasionally some people went by train and station taxi but these means are difficult as well as costly. Our members in general are not well-off, Mr Wexford.' The circle indicated its approval by vigorous nods. 'Besides that, there was always limited parking space at Passingham Hall and Mr Buxton didn't care for us leaving cars outside his house. Add to that the limited incomes of our members and you will understand that we usually attended three or four to a car. That is the prudent way.'

'So any members of the United Gospel Church', said Burden, 'would know how to get to Passingham St John, the location of the drive to Passingham Hall, the way into the wood and the whereabouts of the quarry?'

'Broadly speaking, yes.' It was the man called Hobab Winter who replied. Where did they get these names? Not from their godfathers and godmothers at their baptism, Wexford was sure. They must have adopted them later. 'Of course, as we've said, some would be passengers in other people's cars. Some can't drive. One or two come by train and take a taxi from Passingham Park station.'

If he had been going to say more, Jashub Wright cut him short. 'To what are these questions tending?'

Wexford spoke sharply, 'To finding, arresting and bringing to trial the murderer of Joanna Troy, Mr Wright. And to locating Giles and Sophie Dade.' He paused. 'Dead or alive,' he said.

Wright nodded silently but with an air of offence. His wife's voice from outside summoned him to the door and he held it open for her to pass through, carrying a tray. On it were ten tumblers of something pale-yellow and fizzy. Lynn took hers with an expression on her face that almost made Wexford laugh. The drink was lemonade but a surprisingly good home-made kind.

'I take it you are all present at Confessional Congregations? Yes. I'd like your full names and addresses and . . .' he dropped his bombshell '. . . I shall want to know where each of you were on Saturday, the twenty-fifth of November last, between ten a.m. and midnight.'

He expected a chorus of indignation but the faces remained impassive and only the pastor himself protested. 'Alibis? You're not serious.'

'Indeed I am, Mr Wright. Now perhaps you'll do as I ask and give your names to DC Fancourt.'

Wright made an attempt at a joke but his tone was sour. 'Round up the usual suspects,' he said.

Back in his office, Wexford regarded the list. The seven were called Hobab Winter, Pagiel Smith, Nun Plummer, Ev Taylor, Nemuel Morrison, Hanoch Crane and Zurishaddai Wilton. The first names were grotesque, the surnames uncompromisingly English. Not only were there no Asian names among them – he would have known that from the Good Gospellers' appearance – but none of Scots or Welsh origin, never mind any incomers from the continent of Europe. He wondered if all this meant they were subject to adult baptism when they joined the Gospel Church and received new names as people converted to Judaism did.

'Funny, isn't it?' he said to Burden. 'These odd Christian sects, they used to be called Dissenters, Nonconformists, I don't know what they are now, they all go on and on about the gospel but they're hooked on names out of the Old Testament, old Jewish names in fact, while Jews never are. You'd expect them to have names like John and Mark and Luke and whatever but they don't, they think those are Catholic names.'

'I know a Jewish chap who's called Moses, and you can't get more OT than that. And my sons are called John and Mark, but I'm not Catholic.'

'No, you're not anything and nor am I. Forget it. I know what I mean if you don't. Barry and Karen and Lynn are checking on alibis and we are going to see Yvonne Moody but this time we'll go to her.'

There was one question he had failed to ask the elders and officers of the United Gospel Church but it was to be some time before he realised what it was.

The little town house where Joanna Troy had lived looked forlorn. Perhaps that was only because they knew it was empty and its owner gone for ever. A bay tree in a tub which, if Joanna had returned home on Monday, 27 November, would no doubt have been taken indoors for the winter out of the rain, snow and frost, had succumbed to one of these dire weather conditions and become a shivering pillar of brown leaves that rattled in the wind. The rain had given way to a whitish mist, not dense enough to be called a fog but obscuring the horizon.

Inside one of the panes in a downstairs window of Yvonne Moody's house was pasted a notice which announced that a 'Winter Fayre' would be held at the Good Gospel Church, York Street, Kingsmarkham on Saturday, 20 January. 'All welcome. Tea, cakes, stalls, games and bumper raffle.' She made no secret of her affiliation, Wexford thought. But really he had no justification for supposing she did, only the sneaking feeling that an honest woman when referring to Giles Dade would have said, 'I've only come across the son, he belongs to my church,' instead of leaving out reference to the church altogether. When they were inside, seated in a cluttered living room that smelt strongly of springtime meadow air freshener, he asked her why not.

'It wasn't important,' she said and added, 'I didn't think it was your business, frankly.'

'But you thought it was our business to hear about a possible relationship between Roger Dade and Joanna?'

'It was useful information, wasn't it? Adultery contributes to murder. I know that. Not from experience, certainly not, but from what I've seen on TV. Half those serials and dramas are about that sort of thing. Of course I'm careful what I watch. Half those things I have to avoid, it wouldn't be suitable for a woman committed to Jesus as I am.'

She might be rather attractive, he thought, if she weren't bulging almost indecently out of her green jersey trouser suit. He looked, then out of politeness tried not to look, at the double bosom she seemed to have, her true breasts and the roll of fat underneath them and above her too tightly belted waist. Her dark frizzy hair was held back by an Alice band, the kind of headgear he believed no woman should wear after the age of twenty. She wore a lot of heavy make-up, so presumably the Gospellers hadn't latched on to biblical strictures against paint and adornment.

'Did you like your next-door neighbour, Ms Moody?'

'You can call me Miss. I'm not ashamed of my virginity.' Burden was blinking his eyes rapidly. '*Like* her? I didn't dislike her. I pitied her. We always pity sinners, don't we? I'd be sorry for anyone so lost to God and duty as to contemplate adultery with a married man. That poor boy Giles. I was sorry for *him*.'

'Why was that?' Burden asked her.

'Fifteen years old, on the threshhold of manhood, and subject to her influence. He was old enough to see what went on between her and his father if his sister wasn't. The corruption of the innocent makes you shiver.'

Did she always go on like this? Could her friends stand it? But perhaps she had none. 'When did you last attend one of the Good Gospel Church's Confessional Congregations, Ms Moody?'

She sighed, perhaps only because once again he had failed to pay tribute to her maidenhood. 'I couldn't go last July. I organised the food and drink but I didn't actually go. My mother was unwell. She lives in Aylesbury and she's very old, nearly ninety. Of course I realise this can't go on, she'll have to come and live here with me. These things are sent to try us, aren't they?'

Neither Wexford nor Burden had an opinion on this. 'So you haven't been for a year but you know the place pretty well? Passingham Hall grounds, I mean.'

Was she wary or was it his imagination? 'I don't know if I could find my way there if someone else wasn't taking me. Mr Morrison usually takes me, Mr Nemuel Morrison that is. And his wife, of course. I haven't a car of my own, I don't drive.'

'You don't or you can't?' Burden asked.

'I can but I don't. The traffic has become too heavy and too dangerous for me. I never go far except to my mother and I do that by train.' She began to tell them in detail the route she took from Kingsmarkham to Aylesbury, the train to Victoria, tube across London, train from Marylebone. 'I did once go to Passingham by train. All the cars were full, you see. It was an awful journey but worth it in such a good cause. It was Kingsmarkham to Toxborough, then the local train Toxborough to Passingham Park and then a taxi, but the taxi ride was only two miles. Mind you, I could afford a car. I've got a very good job in management.'

'We'd like to know where you were on the twenty-fifth of November of last year,' Wexford said. 'That was very likely the night on which Joanna Troy died. Can you account for your movements? The period we're interested in is from ten a.m. on Saturday until midnight.'

Questioning about alibis often elicited an angry response from people who were not necessarily suspects but simply had to be eliminated from enquiries. But seldom had either officer's simple query met with such a storm of indignation.

'You're accusing *me* of killing Joanna? You must be mad or very wicked. No one's ever said anything like that to me in all my life.'

'Ms Moody, you're accused of nothing. All we are doing is – well, crossing people off a list. Naturally, we have a list of the people who knew Joanna, that's all. *Knew* her. You're on that list just as her father and stepmother are and we would like to cross you off.'

She was mollified. Her face, which she had contorted into a grimace of fury and disgust, relaxed a little and her hands, closed into tight fists, loosened. 'You'd better cross me off here and now,' she said. 'I was in Aylesbury with my mother. I can tell you exactly when I went there and when I came back and I can do it without looking it up. I had a phone call from her neighbour on the twenty-third of November and went up there next day. Once again I had to get off work, take the rest of my annual leave. By the time I got to my mother's house she'd been taken into hospital. Anyone up there will tell you I was staying in her house that weekend and visiting the hospital twice a day – well, not the Saturday afternoon, she was having some procedures, had to be sedated, and there was no point in me going till next morning. The neighbours will all tell you I was in the house on my own all evening.'

'The neighbours', said Wexford as he and Burden enjoyed a quiet pint in the nearest pub, 'will tell us they didn't see her or hear her or hear any sounds from the house but they know she was there, where else would she be?'

'But we'll have to ask them. She could have got to Passingham Hall that evening and back probably but it would have taken a very long time. I'm sure she wasn't involved.'

'Maybe. Leave that for a moment and get back to Joanna herself. I think the contents of that overnight bag of hers point to the time they all three left, or perhaps I should say, were taken from, the Dades' house.'

'You mean it must have been late at night because Joanna was apparently wearing – well, a nightdress. That's what girls wear those oversize T-shirts for.'

'Do they, indeed?' said Wexford, grinning, 'And how would you know? But, no, that wasn't what I meant.'

'No, because she could just as easily have been killed on Sunday morning at that rate. She could still have been wearing that T-shirt.'

'Mike,' said Wexford, 'she was an early riser. Jennings told us so. Don't you remember? When he was talking about her energy? She always gets up at six thirty, he says, same at the weekends. Always gets showered and dressed, he said, or words to that effect. In that bag of hers she had two sets of underwear among the soiled clothes, one set for Friday, one set for Saturday, and one set *unworn*. Those were for Sunday. Therefore they were taken from the house on Saturday night and probably quite late at night.'

Burden nodded. 'You're right.'

'And now I'm going home,' said Wexford, 'to look up these loony names in the Old Testament and maybe the voters' list on the Internet too, find out what these Good Gospel people are really called.'

'What on earth for?' Burden asked as they began the walk back.

'For my own amusement. It's Friday night and I need a bit of hush.'

He wasn't himself capable of looking up the electoral register on the Internet but Dora was. In the past six months since this innovation came to their household she had learned computer skills.

'You don't want it downloaded, do you? It's miles long.'

'No, of course not. Just show it to me and tell me again how you scroll down or whatever it's called.'

There it was, on the screen before him. He had the addresses of the elders of the United Gospel Church and he viewed the register street by street. Just as he thought, not one of the elders bore the names their parents had given them. Hobab Winter had been – and in the register still was – Kenneth G. while Zurishaddai Wilton was George W. Only Jashub Wright of all the church hierarchy was still named as he had been at his baptism. Next Wexford turned to the Bible. This he could also have summoned on the Net but he had no idea how and didn't want to call Dora from her television serial.

He had told Burden he was doing this for his own amusement but there is nothing amusing about the Book of Numbers. All you could say for it was that it inspired awe and sent a shiver down the spine. It was something to do with the absolute obedience these people's God demanded from the Israelites. Had that too been handed down to these Good Gospellers along with their adopted names? He was looking these up, discovering that Hobab was the son of Raguel the Midianite and Nun the father of Joshua, when Dora came back into the room. She looked at the screen.

'Why are you interested in Ken Winter?'

'He's one of those Good Gospellers. An elder and he calls himself Hobab, not Ken. And he lives in this street, a long way down but this street.' The familiarity with which she had referred to the man suddenly struck him. 'Why, do you know him?'

'*You* know him, Reg.'

'I'm sure I don't.' said Wexford, who wasn't sure and now remembered how several faces at that meeting had seemed recognisable.

'He's our newsagent.' She was starting to sound exasperated. 'He keeps the paper shop in Queen Street. It's his daughter that delivers the evening paper, a girl about fifteen.'

'Ah, now I know.'

'I feel for that girl. Sometimes she's still in her school uniform when she starts that paper round. She goes to that private school in Sewingbury, the one where the children wear brown with gold braid. It's not right a girl of her age being out after dark and I really think . . .'

He was wondering whether all this was of any significance when the phone rang. Wexford picked up the receiver.

'Dad?'

The voice was unrecognisable. He thought whoever it was had a wrong number. 'What number do you want?'

'Dad, it's me.' Feeble, shaky, gasping. 'Dad, I'm on a mobile. It's so little, I hid it on me.'

'Sylvia, what's happened?'

'Cal – Cal beat me up and locked me in a cupboard. Please come, get someone to come . . .'

'Where are the children?'

'Out. Out with Neil. It's Friday. Please, please come . . .'

Chapter 18

To go himself would be wrong. The proper thing would be to send two officers, say Karen Malahyde, trained in dealing with domestic violence, and DC Hammond. But he couldn't have sat at home and waited. He phoned Donaldson for his car and he phoned Karen at home. She wasn't on duty but she didn't hesitate. By the time Donaldson got to his house she was there too.

'I must come,' Dora said.

'He may be violent,' Wexford didn't want to stop her but he had to. 'He *is* violent. I'll phone you when I find her. I won't leave you in the dark a moment. I promise.'

For the first ten minutes of the drive to the remote rural place where Sylvia – and once Neil too – had bought and converted the Old Rectory, Karen was silent. When she spoke it was to say she didn't understand, not *Sylvia,* Sylvia couldn't be a victim of this kind of thing.

'Not after all the time she's worked at The Hide. I mean, she's seen the results of it day after day. She *knows.*'

'When it's your personal life you see things from another perspective.' Wexford had been wondering the same thing. 'You say to yourself – and to others – "Yes, but this is different."'

The Old Rectory was a big house approached by a curving drive about a hundred yards long. The front garden, if such it could be called, for the house stood in its own grounds and was surrounded by garden, was overgrown with shrubs and overhung by tall trees. Maybe because of this Sylvia always kept the place a blaze of light when dusk came, for her own comfort, perhaps, or that of her sons. But tonight it was in darkness, total darkness, for not a glimmer showed or chink between drawn curtains. If the curtains were drawn. Even when Donaldson had driven up to the door it was impossible to tell. Rain dripped from the branches of trees and water lay in puddles on the paving stones.

The place looked as if no one lived there. When was Neil due back with the boys? Nine? Ten, even? They could lie in in the morning, they didn't have to go to school. Wexford made his way to the front door in the light from the car headlights and put his hand to the bell. It is a peculiarity of the parent–child relationship that while children invariably have a key to their parents' home the parents never have a key to theirs. Wexford's sixth law, he thought wryly, half forgetting what the others were. No one came to the door. He rang again. As he turned round a great gust of wind blew rain into his face.

What was he going to do if Callum Chapman refused to let him in? Break in, of course, but not yet. Karen got out of the car with a torch in her hand and shone the beam over the front of the house. All the windows were tight shut. Wexford went back to the door, pushed in the letter box and called through the aperture, 'Police! Let us in!' It was for Sylvia's benefit, not because he thought it would have any other effect. He could make his voice very loud and resonant, and projected it as energetically as he could when he called again. Maybe she could hear him, wherever she was.

He and Karen picked their way round the side of

the house. Doing this was impossible without getting very wet. Untrimmed shrubs, most of them evergreens, encroached on the path, their leaves laden with water. Rain dripped from the trees in large icy drops. Without the torch the darkness would have been impenetrable. As it was, its bulb cast a greenish-white beam, a shaft of foggy light to cut through the wet jungle and show equally wet long grass underneath. It lit up a red plastic football one of the boys must have kicked there in the summer and been unable to find.

'Does no one do any gardening round here?' Wexford grumbled, remembering as he'd said it that his own contribution to horticulture was sitting outside and admiring the flowers on a summer evening. Such a pursuit seemed unreal this evening, an illusory recall. 'The back door should be here somewhere, at the end of the extension.'

It was locked. Was it also bolted? The back of the house was as dark as the front. By the light of the torch he glanced at his watch. Just after eight thirty. What time would Neil bring the boys back and did he have a key? Very unlikely. Another one of Wexford's laws might be that the first thing an estranged wife does when turning her husband out of what had been their joint home is to take away his key.

Then he remembered. 'In the shed,' he said to Karen, 'in that outhouse place there, she used to keep a key to the back door. Neil made a kind of niche in a beam on the far side from the door. The theory was that no one could guess it was there.'

'The kind of person who might want to get in would guess all right,' Karen said. 'There's nowhere to hide a key and be sure it won't be found.'

'As I told her. She said she'd take it away but I wonder . . .'

At least the shed door wasn't locked. Inside it was

a gloomy place, mediaeval-looking with its beamed walls and a ceiling where the timbering came down so low that Wexford couldn't stand upright. There was no interior light and never had been. Once a cottage and home to a family, it had last been lit by candles. The motor mower, unused garden tools, plastic sacks and cardboard crates were no more than bulky shapes in the darkness. He took the torch from Karen and directed its light on to the fifth beam from the door, revealing ropes of cobwebs and an irregular round fissure in the black oak that looked as if it might have been a knothole. His hands must be larger than Neil's for only his little finger was small enough to reach inside. But reach it did and when he wriggled it about and then withdrew it something metallic dropped out on to the floor. He bent down to pick up the key, straightened with a cry of triumph and gave his head a mighty whack on the beam.

'Are you OK, sir?' Karen was all concern.

'I'm fine,' he said, wincing and rubbing his head, still seeing stars and floaters and coloured flashes. 'Good thing she didn't take my advice.'

So long as the door wasn't bolted . . . It wasn't. He turned the key in the lock and let them in. Laundry room first, then kitchen. Karen felt for switches and put the lights on. A meal had been eaten at the kitchen table, begun but not finished. Wine had been drunk, half a bottle of it, and most of it, he guessed, consumed by Chapman, for the glass where he normally sat was empty and the other, Sylvia's, full. Wexford walked out into the hall, switched on more lights and called out, 'Sylvia? Where are you?'

A door opened at the top of the stairs. It was rather near the top of the stairs, only about a yard from the top step. Chapman came out of it. 'What are you doing here? How did you get in?'

'I have a key,' said Wexford who, in case he didn't

know about its hiding place, wasn't going to tell him. 'I rang the bell twice and you didn't answer. Where's Sylvia?'

Chapman didn't answer. He looked at Karen. 'Who's that?'

'Detective Sergeant Malahyde,' she said. 'Tell us where we can find Sylvia, please.'

'Not your business. None of this is your business. We've simply had a row, normal enough, I should think, between partners.'

Suddenly Wexford knew where she would be. In the place she and Neil had called the dressing room, though it was really no more than a walk-in clothes cupboard. There was a lock on its door, he'd noticed that one day several years ago when Sylvia had the flu and he was visiting her. He set his foot on the bottom stair and when Chapman didn't move said, 'Come on, let me pass.'

'You're not coming up here,' Chapman said, and then, revealing he didn't know about the phone call, 'I don't know what's brought you here except maybe her usual whingeing but she doesn't want you and nor do I. It's between us, it's a private matter.'

'Like hell it is.'

Wexford went on up and tried to push past him. Chapman was shorter than he but a lot younger. He drew back his arm and struck Wexford a blow which failed to connect with his jaw but landed on his collar bone. Luckily, perhaps luckily for both of them – for Wexford was forced to think what the results of hitting him might be – the force Chapman had to bring to this made him stagger, lose his balance and tumble down the top stairs. He was up in a flash, his face red with rage. Wexford stood where he was, filling the square of carpet at the top, making a barrier which, to get past, Chapman would have had to make a fierce fight of it. And he was on the stairs again, his fists up, when Karen called his name. She called it softly.

'Mr Chapman!'

He turned. He ran down the stairs. Perhaps he'd decided, Wexford thought afterwards, that if he attacked a woman, *another* woman, her superior officer would be down those stairs in a flash to defend her. As he would have done, as he was starting to do. It all happened very fast. One second Chapman was reaching for Karen's shoulders, reaching perhaps for her neck, the next she had taken him in some kind of hold, thrown him into the air and cast him with a smash on to the hall floor.

'Well done,' said Wexford. He had forgotten all about those karate classes she had regularly attended last year and the year before. It worked. He had seen it done in the past but never so effectively. Within a moment he was putting on lights, making for the dressing room. Karen followed him.

'Sylvia!'

It was ominous that the silence was maintained. Why, come to that, hadn't she heard him the first time? Her bedroom door wasn't locked and nor was the one to the dressing room. He opened it. It was empty but for the rows of clothes on hangers.

'Sylvia, where are you?'

Not a voice but the sound of feet drumming on something. There were a lot of bedrooms in this house and all had cupboards in them. But Chapman had come out of the one at the top of the stairs . . . It was Karen who found her, in that bedroom, in the place they called the airing cupboard, though nothing had been aired in it for decades. The heat inside was tremendous, pouring from the boiler and an ill-insulated immersion heater turned full on. It must have been close on 40 degrees Celsius. She was sitting on the floor, sweat streaming off her, surrounded by the clothes she had presumably been wearing but stripped down now to a thin skirt and a T-shirt. Her ankles were tied together with what looked like a dressing gown belt but her hands were nearly free. No doubt she was managing to ease herself out of whatever bound them. He saw why she hadn't answered. Presumably after she'd made that call, but for some other reason, Chapman had taped up her mouth with sticking plaster.

He picked her up in his arms and carried her out, laying her on the unmade bed. While Karen worked gently on her mouth to ease the plaster off, he phoned Dora, told her all was well and no longer to worry. Then he turned back to look at his daughter. Karen removed the last stubborn edge of the plaster with a swift and probably painful rip. Sylvia put her hand on her upper lip and whimpered through her fingers. She had two black eyes, a dark-red contusion down her cheek and a cut between upper lip and nose that the plaster had covered, though covering it had obviously not been its purpose.

'He did this to you?'

She nodded. The tears welled up in her eyes. Rage filled Wexford with a burning tremulous heat. He felt as if he might explode with it as he heard Chapman returning, coming up the stairs. The power of rational thought had left him when the overwhelming anger poured in, possible consequences were forgotten, prudence cast to the winds. He swung round and fetched Chapman a heavy well-aimed punch to the jaw. It was remarkable that he could do it, he thought afterwards, for he hadn't hit anyone since boxing at school, but he had done it all right, he had done it as to the manner well-taught. Sylvia's lover lay sprawled on the floor, apparently unconscious, his mouth open. My God, thought Wexford, suppose he's dead?

Of course he wasn't. He began to struggle into a sitting position.

'Don't let him come near me,' Sylvia screamed.

'You should be so lucky,' muttered Chapman, rubbing his jaw.

'I want him out of this house. Now.'

Wexford thanked God for it. What would he have done if she had decided to forgive him? It might happen yet . . . Karen said, 'Can you come downstairs, Sylvia? Are you up to that? I'm going to make you a hot drink with plenty of sugar in it.'

She nodded, eased herself up with difficulty like an old woman. 'My face must be a sight,' she said. 'My body will be worse only you can't see.' She looked at Chapman with loathing. 'You can pack your bags and go. I don't know how you'll get to Kingsmarkham. Walk, I suppose. It's only about seven miles.'

'I'm not fit to walk,' he grumbled. 'Your bloody father has nearly killed me.'

'Not near enough,' said Wexford, and then, because it was the only way he could think of to be sure of getting rid of him, 'We'll take him. I don't want to but he'll never do it on foot.' That remark of Chapman's in the Moonflower suddenly came back to him, something about skiving off on the taxpayers' money. 'I'd rather see him dead in a ditch but it's only the good die young.'

They got Sylvia downstairs. He could see the bruises on her legs now. Why hadn't he understood when he saw that red bracelet-like contusion on her wrist at Christmas? Because he couldn't believe a woman who worked in a refuge for victims of domestic violence would herself put up with abuse from a partner.

Oddly enough, Chapman came too. A hangdog air had replaced his truculence. He trailed behind them, silent, looking as if he might start crying. Karen put the kettle on and made tea for Sylvia, herself and Wexford. Sylvia's was very sweet and milky, the way she never took it normally but which seemed to comfort her now. Colour came back into her battered face and she began to talk. Wexford had believed she would have preferred to defer explaining until Chapman was out of the way but she seemed to take pleasure, as he confessed he would have done, in telling it all in her attacker's presence.

'He wants to marry me. Or he did. I don't suppose he does now. He kept on and on at me and once or twice he hit me.' She looked at her father and cast up her eyes. 'I'm a fool, aren't I? I of all women ought to know better. I can only say it's different when it happens to you. You believe them when they promise not to do it again . . .'

Chapman interrupted her. 'I do promise, Sylvia. I won't do it again. I'll swear on the Bible, if you like. I'll make a solemn vow that I never never will. And I still want to marry you. You know all this only came about because you wouldn't marry me.'

She laughed, a dry little laugh that stopped because it hurt her. 'We had a really big row this evening. I said I wouldn't marry him and I didn't want him living here any more. I told him to go and he started on me. He knocked me down and punched my face. I got away from him and ran upstairs. I thought I could lock myself in my bedroom but that was a fatal mistake. It was better for him having me up there. Easier to get hold of the sticking plaster, for one thing.' Chapman got a look of such viciousness Wexford was nearly shocked. 'This house is so cold it's a good thing I was wearing so many clothes – well, it is in one way. I nearly died of the heat in that cupboard but it meant I had my mobile with me, in the pocket of my cardigan.'

Chapman hadn't known. He shook his head, perhaps at his own lack of foresight in not searching her before making her prisoner. Sylvia said, 'He came back later and taped up my mouth and tied up my feet and hands and put me in that cupboard, the *hot* cupboard. That was deliberate torture. I don't know what he meant to do next, go out maybe in *my* car, or wait till Neil brought the boys back. . . . Where are the boys?'

As she asked that question the doorbell rang. Wexford went to answer it. Ben and Robin rushed in, making for the kitchen. Seeing their mother in that state wouldn't be pleasant for them but they would have to know some time. He told Neil as briefly as he could what had happened.

'Where is he? Let me get at him.'

'No, Neil. Not you too. As it is, I shouldn't have hit him and God knows what he'll do about it. He's going anyway. The best thing will be for Sylvia and the boys to come and stay with us. I'll get Karen to drive them in Sylvia's car.'

'I'll take them,' Neil said.

Sylvia had apparently told her sons she had fallen down the stairs. She had come out of the bedroom where the airing cupboard was, it was dark, she had missed her footing and crashed down the entire flight. Whether they believed that this would also account for her black eyes Wexford couldn't tell. But they seemed satisfied with the explanation and excited, as children mostly are, at the prospect of going away for the night. Chapman, the fight knocked out of him, had gone upstairs to pack suitcases.

'Why did he turn all the lights off?' Karen asked.

'I don't know. He was always saying I was extravagant with electricity but it's my house and I paid the bills. I don't know what he thought would happen when Robin and Ben came back. Maybe he was going to tell them I wasn't feeling well and had gone to bed and keep me in there all night. He's capable of it. Oh, I'm such a *fool.*'

So Neil drove his family to Wexford's house while Wexford and Karen took Chapman with them. He had brought so many cases, boxes and plastic carriers, filling up the car boot, that Wexford was driven to wonder how many of Sylvia's possessions the man had filched. It was worth almost anything to be rid of him. No one spoke. Donaldson at the wheel was consumed with curiosity, his ears on stalks for the hints of enlightenment that never came. He was directed to drive to a district of Stowerton he wouldn't normally have associated with the chief inspector's daughter or anyone belonging to her. There, in a street that ran along the back of a disused factory, he was told to drop their passenger outside a run-down block of flats with a nameplate from which several letters had fallen and never been replaced and where only one of the four globular lamps above the entrance was working. Donaldson was preparing to carry those cases and boxes up the steps to this entrance but Wexford said no, leave them on the pavement.

Chapman got out and stood there, surrounded by his, and possibly Sylvia's, property.

'Goodnight,' said Wexford, his head out of the window.

The last they saw of him was a weary figure humping inelegant luggage across the pavement, along the path and up the steps. There was so much of it that he would have to make several journeys. Maybe that would be the last they saw of him and maybe not, Wexford thought, his experience of life telling him that couples when they parted seldom made a clean break of it but drifted together again and apart again, the whole sorry process punctuated with rows, reconciliations and recriminations. Not this time, please, not when it was his injured daughter . . .

How about charging Chapman with causing Actual Bodily Harm, say, or even resisting arrest? He thought not. This was *his* daughter. Was he going to pre-empt any accusations which might come from Chapman by first telling Freeborn what he'd done? Chapman could be revenged by accusing Wexford of assault, but he was unlikely to do this when it meant admitting he'd been laid low by a man much older than himself. Wexford couldn't honestly say he regretted what he'd done, for the blow he had struck hadn't been for Chapman alone but for all the ghastly men who had been in and out of his daughters' lives over the past years. The weedy bore Sylvia had been running around with between Neil and Chapman, the awful literary prizewinner and poet Sheila had gone about with, and back, back to her drama school days, the idiot called Sebastian something who had dumped his dog on them and which Wexford had had to take walkies. I won't think about any of it now, he thought, I'll force it out of my mind.

He said goodnight to Karen and thanked her for her help. When she had gone he asked himself what it was, what had happened that evening, which kept teasing at the back of his mind. Something to do with that staircase it was, and the way the bedroom door opened only a couple of feet in from the top riser. Anyone coming out of that room could easily fall down the stairs, as Chapman had fallen part-way when he had overbalanced after hitting Wexford. He concentrated. He revisited the scene in his mind's eye.

The configuration of staircase and bedroom door was the same at Sylvia's as at Antrim. A matter of awkward and clumsy design in both cases but safe enough if caution was used. Imagine, though, someone coming to that bedroom door . . . No, not 'someone'; Joanna Troy. Because he was in that room doing that weary everlasting homework, the homework his father insisted on over and above the call of school duty, and Joanna came to the door and knocked, maybe to tell him it was time to put the light out and go to sleep. Possibly Roger or Katrina Dade had asked her to see the children didn't stay up too late. Perhaps she had come before, even two or three times, and, exasperated, he had flung open the door and pushed her away.

It was impossible. No fifteen-year-old boy would do that unless he were a criminal psychopath in the making . . .

Chapter 19

There comes a time in every case if it is a complex one, when the investigating officer reaches an impasse, when there seems no way forward and no unexplored paths to go along. This is what had happened to Wexford in the Missing Dade Children affair. He had thought he had a strong lead in the matter of the Good Gospellers, but not one of the enquiries his officers had made revealed anything suspicious beyond the fact that they knew Passingham Hall woods and Giles Dade had been one of them. Each one of the elders had been alibi'd by his wife and, in some cases, by his children. Joanna Troy's past had interested him but it had mostly been concerned with things *she* had done and not with things done to her. Now that she was dead, probably murdered, her own offences were of little account. Who cared any longer that she had been accused of stealing a schoolboy's money? That her marriage had been a failure? Or that another boy had been attacked by her and years later died by falling over a cliff? She was dead, dumped in her car in the bottom of a waterlogged quarry. As for all the teenagers closely or remotely connected with her, Giles and Sophie, Scott and Kerry Holloway, Hobab Winter's daughter, children *would* figure in her life. She was a teacher.

The Dade children were probably dead too. Wexford knew very well how simple it may be to find a body when it has been buried in its own back garden or in next door's, how almost insuperable when the killer has disposed of it in some distant place, perhaps hundreds of miles away, which even he has never visited before. He knew he should be looking at the case from an entirely different angle to those which he had explored already. But which angle? Where to start?

Well, he could ask Lynn Fancourt about the Dade children's school friends, though most had been dismissed from the case. It was Sewingbury Academy's uniform that was brown and gold and which Dora said she had seen the Winter girl wearing when she did her father's paper round.

'What's her name?' he had asked her.

'One of those strange Bible names. Dorcas.'

'*Dorcas*?'

'I said it was strange. Come to think of it, it's not really any stranger than Deborah only one's fashionable and the other's not.'

Now he said to Lynn, 'Is she on the list?'

She scanned it. 'No. Was she Giles's or Sophie's friend?'

'I don't know. They're the same sort of age and they go to the same school. She lives in my road and she's the daughter of the Queen Street newsagent.'

'D'you want me to go round there and ask her if she knows Giles, sir?'

Why? What on earth was the point? He shook his head. 'If I decide to pursue it I'll go round there myself.'

Another disappointment. He consoled himself with his relief that at least his garden hadn't flooded again, while some low-lying properties in Kingsmarkham, especially those near the river banks, were once more inundated. Life at home now included Sylvia and her sons, for she was afraid to go home lest Callum Chapman come back. How could she tell whether he had a key or not? She had taken his key which he had mislaid and she had found in the bedroom they had shared. He might easily have had another cut during one of their quarrelsome periods when he was pressing her 'to make things permanent' and she was telling him that if he went on like that he would have to leave. To her father and mother she continued endlessly to explain how it was possible she had endured him for even a day after he first struck her, she who had been the most ardent and the most vociferous campaigner against violence in the home, she who had almost daily advised women to leave abusive partners whatever promises they made or undertakings they gave.

'It's different when it's happening to you,' she repeatedly said. 'It's a real person with good qualities, it's someone who strikes you as deeply sincere whatever else he may be.'

'Strikes you is right,' said her father, who had scant sympathy with all this now time had passed and her wounds and bruises healed. At least Chapman hadn't attempted to have him charged with assault. 'You could leave off the rest of that sentence. You're a grown woman, Sylvia, you're a mother, you were married for God knows how long. Whatever Chapman did to you you've only yourself to blame.'

Dora thought him very harsh. 'Oh, *Reg*.'

'Oh, Reg, nothing. She's a social worker, for God's sake. She ought to know a lowlife when she sees one.'

Relations between him and his elder daughter were fast returning to what they were before Sylvia left her husband and miraculously became a nicer person. And he was back in the morass of guilt he struggled to be free of by repeating to himself a kind of mantra: You must not show favouritism of one child over the other. But Chapman was gone and that was something to rejoice about.

One of the difficulties was that they still had very little idea when Joanna and the Dade children left Antrim. Let alone why. All of them had been there on Friday and overnight. Joanna had presumably still been there on Saturday morning and for part of the afternoon since her car was there. Giles was seen on Saturday afternoon, probably as late as half past two. On Sunday morning the car was gone. It was therefore reasonable to suppose that Giles and Joanna were alive and well by early evening on Saturday – but was it?

To Burden, over lunch in the Moonflower, he said, 'We know Giles went out at around half past two but we don't know when he came back. If he came back. We know Joanna was in the house because her car was seen on the driveway by Mrs Fowler and according to her father she never walked anywhere if she could help it. But we really have no idea where Sophie was. No contact was made with her, so far as we know, after she spoke on the phone to her mother in Paris on Friday evening at about seven thirty.'

Burden nodded abstractedly. He was ordering their meal with care. It had to be served fast, it had to be 'healthy food', to which he had lately become addicted, and it had to be as fat-free as possible for Wexford's somewhat raised cholesterol. Dragon's Eggs were still on the menu and another one, even worse, had been added: Flying Fleshpots.

'It sounds awful,' said Wexford, 'but I'm going to try it.'

'I shall ask Raffy about its fat content,' Burden warned, though he had little faith in an honest answer. And when this enquiry was put to him,

Raffy, efficient and smart as ever, replied that it was lowest in fat levels of any dish they served.

'It's got Lo-chol in it, sir, which has actually been clinically proven to lower cholesterol.'

'You made that up.'

'I'd never tell a lie, Mr Burden. Especially to police officers.'

Making a face, Wexford drank some of the sparkling water Burden insisted on. 'To return to our ongoing problem,' he went on, 'did Giles ever come back from wherever he went? We've no reason to suppose he ever came back and none really to think he didn't. Come to that, where did he go?'

'To the shops? To visit a friend?'

'Those Lynn questioned say they didn't see him the entire weekend. Scott Holloway tried to speak to him on the phone but failed. He may or may not have gone round there, he says not and it's not much use saying I don't believe him. And where was Sophie?'

'In the house all the time with Joanna, surely?'

'Maybe. But we don't know that. All we can be sure of is that Joanna, Sophie and Giles left the house or were taken from it some time on Saturday night.'

Burden said carefully, 'There's a strong possibility someone else came to the house on Saturday after the rain began. Just because no one saw him it doesn't mean he didn't come. It's even possible Giles brought this person back with him.'

'Scott? If Giles had called on the Holloways and taken Scott back to his house, Mrs Holloway would know. No, if Scott went there he went alone and, I think, much later.'

'So you're saying', said Burden, 'this is someone we haven't included in our enquiries.'

'That's right. Because he or she has left the country. We know, for instance, that Giles's and Sophie's passports are here and Joanna's is here, but we know nothing about anyone else's. And it's not much use to us if we don't know who this person is. Was Joanna killed at Antrim and killed by this person? Did it take place in the hall and was it caused by her falling or being thrown downstairs? As far as we know she never left Antrim until Saturday night and when she did leave Giles and Sophie were with her. Was this caller driving her car? It must have been someone they or one of them knew, that they invited in.'

'As we know, the neighbours saw no one,' said Burden, 'after Mrs Fowler saw Giles leave the house. But I'm inclined to think there was a visitor to the house that night and that he came by prior arrangement. Or it could have been a chance visit.'

Wexford's Flying Fleshpots and Burden's Butterflies and Flowers arrived, the former indistinguishable from lemon chicken, the latter prawns, bamboo shoots, carrots and pineapple fancifully arranged. A large bowl of prettily coloured rice accompanied these dishes. At the next table a very affectionate couple, who contrived to link his right hand and her left while manipulating chopsticks with the other, were both eating Dragon's Eggs.

Burden pursued his theory. 'He'd want to get her body away. We'll say he had some sort of grudge to settle. We've heard about Joanna beating up Ludovic Brown while they were still at school and there may have been other instances of the same thing. She did coach children for their GCSEs. Suppose she attacked one of them and the child's father wanted revenge.'

'Then he'd have gone to her home, wouldn't he?' Wexford objected. 'Not to the Dades.'

'He may have enquired of the neighbours, Yvonne Moody, say, as to where Joanna was. No, he couldn't have. She was away at her mother's. Perhaps he followed Joanna or his child told him she might be at the Dades.'

'I don't know.' Wexford was dubious. 'The logistics are a bit funny. Your X finds out where Joanna is, though how is a moot point, and he goes up to Antrim on Saturday evening. He knows he's got the right place because her car is outside. He rings the bell and someone lets him in.'

'Joanna might not have done if she recognised him as antagonistic to her,' Burden put in quickly, 'but Giles or Sophie would have.'

'Right. Presumably he makes a row. I mean, you're not saying he sits down and has a cup of tea with them and watches telly, are you? No, he makes a row and blusters but he can't do much in front of the kids. So he somehow gets Joanna out into the hall – this is the sticky bit, Mike – and he gets her there alone. Twirling his moustaches, our villain hisses something like, "I'm going to get you for this, my proud beauty" and whacks her round the head. She screams, falls over and hits her head on the side of the clothes cupboard. Giles and Sophie come running out. "What have you done?" They find that Joanna is dead. The body must be removed and hidden. So X persuades the kids to go off with him in Joanna's car? It must have been persuasion, not force. They weren't babies, they were fifteen and thirteen. The boy will be quite strong. Remember how tall he is. They could easily have resisted. But they don't, they agree to go. They make their beds, they put Joanna's clothes into her case, but they don't take a change of clothes for themselves. Why do they go? In case they might be blamed along with X? I don't much like this part, do you?'

'I don't like it but I can't think of anything better.' Burden drank some water. 'How did X get to the Dades' house? It must have been on foot, maybe part of the way by public transport. If he or she came in their car that car would still have been there on the

Monday. And they didn't leave in it, they left in Joanna's. Did he leave fingerprints? Maybe they were among the unidentifiable prints left about the house, many of them smudged by Mrs Bruce's fanatical dusting. Then there's the T-shirt with Sophie's face on it. Did X tell Sophie to bring the T-shirt so that he could drop it out of the window at the Kingsbrook Bridge as a red herring? That presupposes an intimate knowledge of the Dade family on his part.'

'It doesn't if he simply asked the children to bring something by which one of them could be immediately identified. But still . . . I don't know, Mike, there are so many holes in it and so many questions left unanswered.' Wexford looked at his watch. 'It's time I paid my visit to the Dades,' he said with a sigh.

'I'll come with you.'

It was more than two months since Joanna and the children had disappeared and in that time Wexford had made a point of calling on the Dades two or three times a week. Not to enlighten them, not to bring them news, but to show them they had his support. That their children weren't forgotten. Not that his calls were more warmly received now than at the beginning. Rather the reverse, for Katrina was more disturbed, terror-ridden and haunted than ever. Wexford thought that by the end of the first week she must have cried all the tears out of her but those weeping tanks behind her eyes still overflowed. Sometimes she was speechless, her face buried, throughout his visit, while her husband was either awesomely rude or else ignored him altogether. Strangely, though, he was out at work less often than when the children first went missing. He seemed to make a point of being at home when Wexford arrived, perhaps only to see how far he could go before the Chief Inspector rebelled and stopped coming. Wexford was determined this wouldn't happen. Until the children were found or the case was closed he would continue to pay his visits, however these parents chose to treat him.

The rain had stopped. It was cold and misty but already it was noticeable that the dusk came a little later and in spite of the wet, something in the air hinted at the dreadful sterility of winter left behind. The front door of Antrim was opened by Mrs Bruce. Never more than a week seemed to go by but she was back staying with her daughter, with or without her husband. The horror of his visits was lessened when she was there, simply because she behaved like a civilised human being, greeted them, offered them tea and even thanked them for coming. And she was old enough to say 'Good afternoon', instead of the habitual 'Hiya' or 'Hi, there', with which most householders met them.

Unfortunately, Dade was at home. He took no notice of Wexford beyond favouring him with a hard stare before returning to his paperwork, apparently a sheaf of estate agent's specifications. Katrina was in an armchair, sitting the way children sometimes do, her head and body facing into its back, her legs curled up under her. For a moment Wexford thought he was to be ostracised by both of them, left in silence but for Doreen Bruce's polite chatter. Burden, who came more rarely, stood looking incredulous. But then Katrina slowly turned round, her legs still up on the chair seat, and clasped her arms round her knees. In these two months she had got even thinner, her face gaunt, her elbows sharply pointed.

'Well?' she said.

'I'm afraid I've no news for you, Mrs Dade.'

In a crazy sing-song voice she intoned, 'If their bodies, their bodies, could be found, could be found, I'd have something, something, something, I'd have corpses to bury.'

'Oh, shut up,' said Dade.

'I'd have a stone to write their names on, their names on, their names on . . .' It was reminiscent of Ophelia and her mad dirge. 'I'd have a grave to put flowers on, flowers on . . .'

Dade got up and stood over her. 'Stop that. You're putting it on. You're acting. You think you're very clever.'

She began to sway from side to side, her eyes shut, tears trickling from between the half-closed lids. Doreen Bruce caught Wexford's glance and cast up her eyes. Wexford thought Dade was going to hit his wife and then he knew he wasn't, it was Sylvia's experience gone to his head. Dade's violence was all in his tongue. As Jennings had said Joanna Troy's was in hers. Mrs Bruce said, 'Would you like a cup of tea?'

She went away to make it. Dade began to walk about the room, stopping to look out of the window, giving a meaningless shrug. Katrina folded herself up, her head down on her knees, the tears gushing now and, because of her hunched and twisted position, running down her bare legs. Wexford could think of absolutely nothing to say. It seemed to him that he had extracted from these parents every detail of their children's lives that they were prepared to tell him. The rest he must deduce, they wouldn't help him.

The silence was the heaviest and the longest enduring he had known in that house. Katrina lay back with her eyes closed as if asleep, Dade had removed the cap from a ballpoint and was making notes on his property specification, Burden sat contemplating his own knees in immaculate grey broadcloth. Wexford tried to reconstruct what Roger Dade's own childhood might have been, using hints the man had dropped as to having been too much indulged when young. No doubt Matilda Carrish had allowed him and his sister the almost total freedom that was coming into fashion for children, free expression, liberty to do anything they liked without correction. And he had hated it. Perhaps he had disliked the unpopularity which resulted from the rudeness and ill manners it encouraged. If so, he hadn't done much to eradicate that aspect of things in his own character, only apparently determined that his own children should receive the reverse of this treatment, an old-fashioned severity and discipline. The result had been that one of them disliked him, the other feared him, which seemed to be constituent parts of the attitude he had to his own mother . . .

Mrs Bruce was taking a long time . . . His thoughts wandered to Callum Chapman. The man had overbalanced and fallen down the stairs. Not on account of his clumsiness or loss of control but simply due to that space at the top of the staircase being too narrow for safety. That's what happened here, he thought. Joanna fell down the stairs. Or someone pushed her. X pushed her. She would no more have died than Chapman had if she hadn't struck her head on the side of that clothes cabinet. There was a little blood and a dislodged tooth crown . . .

Katrina's mother came back, bearing a tray with a teapot on it and a large home-made simnel cake, marzipanned and browned under a grill. It was years since he'd seen a simnel cake and it was irresistible. A look from Burden and a minuscule shake of the head he chose to ignore and allowed Mrs Bruce to lay a big slice on his plate. It was so delicious and its sweetness so comforting that Dade's glance of disgust passed over him and left him unscathed. Mrs Bruce made conversation about the weather, the nights drawing out, her husband's heart and the tedious journey here from Suffolk, while Burden replied to her in polite monosyllables. Wexford ate his slice of cake with huge enjoyment and saw to his surprise that Dade was doing the same thing. He thought about Joanna and the staircase. Did X push her down it or did she stumble and fall in the dark? Perhaps neither. Perhaps X chased her along the passage at the end of which was Sophie's room, chased her and she fell down the stairs because she couldn't avoid them. And when was it? On the Saturday afternoon? No, later. In the evening? It must have been dark and maybe there were no lights on upstairs. But if she had been upstairs in the late evening or night and X with her, that must mean X was a lover . . .

Dade interrupted this reverie. He had finished his cake, shaken the crumbs off his lap on to the floor and turned to Wexford. 'Time you left. You're not doing any good here. Goodbye.'

Both officers got up, Wexford seriously wondering, in spite of his resolve, how much more of this he could stand. 'I will see you in a day or two, Mrs Dade,' he said.

It was Ken Winter's wife who admitted him to the house. Her first name was Priscilla, as he knew from the voters' list. Never having seen her before, he had expected an older and even dowdier version of Thekla Wright. Priscilla Winter was dowdy enough but the shabbiness of her clothes, the old slippers she wore and her rough red hands were not what was first noticeable about her. Wexford was struck, almost shocked, by her bent shoulders, the result possibly of repeatedly hunching them in a vain gesture of protecting face and chest, her withered look, the way her eyes peered fearfully at him.

Her husband wasn't yet home. Recognising him, she said this before he had uttered a word.

'It's your daughter I'd like to see, Mrs Winter.'

'My daughter?' To be the mother of a fifteen-year-old, she was very likely no more than in her late forties. Her wispy grey hair, uncut for years by the look of it, hung about her shoulders. No doubt the Good Gospellers banned hairdressers. 'You want Dorcas?'

The girl was good-looking, though there was something of her father in her oval face and regular features. Her darkish hair was very long, tied back with a brown ribbon, but to Wexford's surprise, the brown and gold school uniform had been changed for the universal teenagers' wear of jeans and sweatshirt. Dorcas looked surprised that a grown-up had been asking for her.

'No paper round this evening?' Wexford said.

'I was late back from school. Dad's got one of the boys on it or he's doing it himself.'

Priscilla Winter said, as if an attack had been intended on her husband, 'It's not a big round.' She recited its route like a child saying its tables. 'Chesham and this road and Caversham and Martindale and Kingston to the corner of Lyndhurst.'

She shuffled across the floor to open a door for them. Dorcas could have done that but she left it to her mother and, pushing past her, led Wexford into a sitting room. If not the most important person in the household, she plainly ran her father a close second – even though she was a girl. That spoke of a weakness in Winter's religious principles in the face of paternal love. There was television in this room, for the girl's benefit, Wexford thought, but no books, no flowers, no houseplants, no cushions or ornaments. Heavy curtains of a nondescript colour shut out night and rain. The only picture was a pale landscape, innocent of trees, animals, human figures or clouds in its sky. The room reminded him of the lounge a third-rate hotel provides for its guests when they complain of nowhere to sit but their bedrooms.

Mrs Winter said timidly, as one making a daring suggestion, 'Would you like a cup of tea?'

He had wondered if tea was included among banned stimulants, but apparently not. 'I shan't be stopping more than a minute or two,' he said, remembering the glories of the simnel cake, 'but thank you.'

'You will have heard about the missing young people,' he said to Dorcas. 'Giles and Sophie Dade. I've been wondering how well you knew them and what you can tell me about them. They're fairly near neighbours.'

'I don't know them. Well, I know what they look like but not to speak to.'

'You go to the same school and you and Giles are the same age.'

'I know,' the girl said. 'But we're in different forms at school. He's in the A form.'

'Where *you* should be,' said her mother. 'I'm sure you're clever enough.'

Dorcas cast her a glance of contempt. 'I really don't know them.'

Wexford had to accept it. 'And I don't suppose you've ever had private coaching from Miss Joanna Troy?'

'She doesn't need that,' said Priscilla Winter. 'I told you, she's clever. The only private teaching she has is her violin lesson. That reminds me, Dorcas, have you done your practice for your lesson tomorrow night?'

It seemed strange to him that Dorcas didn't know the Dades but he couldn't see why she should lie. He thanked her and said goodnight to Mrs Winter. The damp, dark night received him but he hadn't far to go. On the way home he met no one and no one passed him. He let himself into his own house, warm and well-lit and with a comforting smell of dinner in the air, and almost tripped over the evening paper which lay on the mat, damp and sodden at the edges as it always was these days.

Chapter 20

Sylvia remarked apropos of nothing that she thought of going home next day. Neil had promised to fetch her and the boys and take them home to the Old Rectory. The light in Dora's eyes was unmistakeable. Wexford could tell, as if he had read her mind like a book, that she was thinking there might be a reconciliation there, Sylvia and Neil reunite, remarry, live together as they once had, but this time it would be second time lucky and happiness ever after. Had she forgotten that Neil had at last found himself a new girlfriend? After Sylvia had gone to bed he said gently, 'It won't happen, you know, and if it did it would be a bad thing.'

'Would it, Reg?'

'When they got married it was sex and when that went there was nothing. It can't be revived, it's too late. But one day she will find someone to be happy with, you'll see.'

Brave words, but he was less sure himself. In the morning he said goodbye to his daughter and kissed her, and all was well again. More or less. He was sitting in his office, thinking more about her than the Dade case when the phone rang.

'Hello. Wexford.'

'I have Detective Superintendent Watts, of Gloucestershire Police for you, sir.'

'Right. Put him on.' Gloucestershire? No connection with the county came immediately to mind.

Maybe another mistaken sighting of the Dade children. They still came in.

A voice with a pleasant burr said, 'Brian Watts here. I've got a piece of news for you. We've a young girl who says she's Sophie Dade at the station here . . .'

'You have?' A surge of excitement, then reason returned. 'We've had dozens of kids saying they're the Dades and dozens of people who've seen them.'

'No, this one is her all right. I'm as sure as can be. She got hold of the emergency services on a nine-nine-nine call at six this morning. Asked for an ambulance for her grandma. She reckoned the old lady had had a stroke and she was right. Pretty good for a thirteen-year-old, wouldn't you say? Anyway, she's here.'

'Any sign of the boy?'

'You're greedy, you are. No, it's just the girl and she won't say where she's been or how long she'd been with this Mrs Carrish. She's not said a word about her brother. Have you got someone who could come up here and fetch her home?'

'Sure. Yes, thanks. Thanks a lot.'

'You sound gobsmacked.'

'Yes, well, I am. That's exactly what I am. Has Roger Dade been told about his mother?'

'She's in hospital in Oxford. The hospital will have informed next of kin.'

'So he'll know *a* young girl was with her when she had her attack?'

'Maybe. Not necessarily.'

To say something to Roger and Katrina Dade? Better not, he thought. Not yet. The hospital wouldn't be interested in telling him who called them beyond saying it was a young girl.

It might not be Sophie. In spite of what his caller

had said, there was more than a strong possibility it wasn't. The difficulty was that the rules said he couldn't question her without one of her parents or a responsible adult present. Waiting for Karen Malahyde and Lynn Fancourt to come back with the girl, he asked himself if he would recognise her. He got out her photograph and looked – really for the first time – at her face. The previous time he had seen it he had noted in passing that she was pretty and had elements of her mother in her expression, but not then having seen Matilda Carrish, hadn't observed the resemblance. By the time she was thirty this girl would also have hawk-like features, a Roman nose, thin lips. Her eyes were curiously large, their colour dark but otherwise unidentifiable, the fierce light of intelligence gleaming in their depths.

What was she doing in Matilda Carrish's house? Even more to the point, how long had she been there? She must be very cool and collected for one who was after all still a child. He imagined her awakened in the night, in the deep dark of a February morning, by the sound of a crash, made by her grandmother falling to the floor. Most people of her age, surely, would have run crying to a neighbour. She had phoned the emergency services. Once she knew they were coming and her grandmother would be looked after, had she contemplated running away again but decided it would be useless, that she hadn't a hope? Where would she go? Perhaps, too, though he hadn't suspected it, she loved her grandmother too much to leave her.

He ate lunch in the canteen, watched the rain falling. Karen phoned to say they were on their way back with the girl. He looked at the clock on the wall, looked at his watch, decided it would be wrong to put it off any longer and dialled the Dades' number. Mrs Bruce answered.

'Mr Dade or your daughter?'

'Katrina's asleep, dear, and Roger's gone to Oxford to visit his mother in hospital. She's had a stroke. He heard this morning.'

Wexford was at a loss, but he made a decision. 'There was a child with her when she was taken ill. It seems likely it's Sophie.'

The astonished silence and then the gasp told him no one in the Dade household had been alerted.

'Will you ask Mrs Dade to phone me when she wakes up?'

Doubts began as he put the phone down. Suppose it wasn't Sophie? He would have told Katrina Dade her daughter was coming home when it wasn't her daughter and he could just imagine Roger Dade's reaction to that when he found out, the enormous fuss he would make to the Chief Constable. Wexford went down in the lift. He wanted to be there when the two women officers came back with the girl. As the crow flew, or any other bird come to that, it wasn't all that far to Oxford, but in the current state of traffic it took a long time. And it was always worse when it was raining, which meant that these days it always was worse. Three o'clock, ten past. The swing doors opened and Burden came in, back from wherever he had been.

'D'you think it's her?'

'Don't know. I've told the mother it is. Who else would it be with Matilda Carrish at that hour of the morning?'

'She may have someone living in to look after her.'

'Sure,' Wexford said drily, forgetting that he too had doubted the girl's identity. 'Nothing more likely than that this someone is a thirteen-year-old paranoid schizophrenic who tells people she's her employer's granddaughter.'

The car came on to the forecourt, sending up a

cloud of spray. Lynn was driving. He saw the girl get out, then Karen, Lynn last. It was still raining and they hurried in. He knew at once, there was no doubt. She wore the brown anorak missing from her home and shrugged herself out of it once she was inside the swing doors.

'Well, Sophie,' he said. 'We'll need to talk to you but not now. First you have to go home to your parents.'

She looked straight at him. Few people had eyes like hers, almond-shaped, slightly tilted, exceptionally large, as near dark-green as human eyes ever get. She was less pretty than in her photograph but more intelligent-looking, more formidable. The camera loved her; reality did not. 'I don't want to go home,' she said.

'I'm afraid you must,' Wexford said. 'You are thirteen years old and at thirteen you don't have a choice.'

'Karen says my father is at the hospital with Matilda.'

'That's right.'

'I'll go, then. At least *he* won't be there.'

She allowed herself to be helped back into her jacket and led back to the car by Lynn. 'A bit of a little madam, sir,' said Karen.

'You could say that. Will you tell Mrs Dade I shall want to talk to Sophie later? We'll say six o'clock. And one of them must be with her. If Mrs Dade isn't up to it Mr or Mrs Bruce will do.'

Now he was anxious to do everything by the book. First, he phoned Antrim again and this time spoke to a hysterical incoherent Katrina, managing at last to understand that she had phoned her husband on his mobile, or rather, her mother had, and told him. Wexford decided it would nevertheless be wise for him to do the same. Not having the mobile number and scarcely trusting Katrina to give it to him, he phoned the hospital where Matilda Carrish was and eventually was able to leave a message for Dade with someone who barely spoke English.

The temptation now was to indulge in speculation. How long had she been with Mrs Carrish? All the time or only part of it? Why had Matilda deceived them? And where, now, was Giles? Whatever he guessed would very likely be wrong. Imaginary solutions usually were. He must wait.

The rain had ceased and it had grown very cold, perhaps colder than it had been all winter. A sharp wind dried the pavements. In February it wasn't quite dark by five forty-five but the greyish-red sun was down and dusk had begun. The sky was dark-blue and jewel-bright, as yet starless. Karen drove him up to Lyndhurst Drive and, to his surprise, it was Dade who opened the door. He was considerably chastened and so forgot to be rude.

'There was no point staying up there. She's unconscious. It's my belief she won't survive this.'

A lay person's opinion is never of much value in these matters but Wexford said he was sorry to hear that and they went inside. 'I can't get a word out of my daughter,' Dade said, 'but that's par for the course. I never can.'

Wexford thought that boded better for him and Karen. They went into the living room where he had spent so much time in the past weeks. Katrina was there, looking madder than he had ever seen her. 'Like one of the witches from *Macbeth*,' whispered Karen, who wasn't usually given to a literary turn of phrase, and Wexford, normally only exasperated by Sophie's mother, felt a serious concern for this woman whose hair looked as if she had been tearing it out and whose mouth hung open as if she had seen and was seeing some dreadful vision. He said nothing to her because he didn't know what to say.

'You want someone with her when you question her, right?'

'I'm obliged to, Mr Dade. You or –' no, obviously not '– or one of your parents-in-law.'

'She won't talk at all if I'm there,' Dade said bitterly. He went back to the open door and called out in the sharp harsh voice all too familiar to Wexford, for it had been directed often enough at him, 'Doreen! Come here, will you?'

Doreen Bruce came in and went up to her daughter, giving her her arm. 'Now, dear, the best place for you is your bed. It's all been too much.'

Once more they waited. There was no sign of Sophie. Was Doreen Bruce putting Katrina to bed? Dade sat down in an armchair, or rather, lay down, his arms spread out over its arms, his legs apart, his head thrown back in the characteristic attitude of anguish. Wexford wondered what he had expected to see in this house. Relief and joy and sweetness and light? Something like that. He could no more tell how people would react in an extreme situation than he could predict the answers to the questions he would ask Sophie. If she ever came. At that thought, her grandmother brought her into the room. She looked at her recumbent father and immediately turned away her head, twisting her neck as far round as she could, as ostentatiously as she could.

'Where shall I sit?'

That was too much for Roger Dade and he bounced upright. 'Oh, for God's sake,' he yelled at her. 'You're not at the bloody dentist's.' He left the room and banged the door.

'You sit here, Sophie,' said Mrs Bruce, 'and I'll sit in this chair.'

Wexford noticed that the girl had changed her

clothes since she got home. Under the anorak she had been wearing a pair of trousers that were a little, but not much, too large for her and a sweater that was wrong in some indefinable way for a girl of her age. He realised now that those must have been Matilda's clothes. She had taken nothing with her when she left except those, as people rather oddly put it, she stood up in. Now she was dressed in her own jeans and a T-shirt, unsuitable for anyone on such a cold evening, especially in a house where the central heating was inefficient. She didn't seem affected by it. Those disconcerting eyes gazed at him.

'You will have realised, Sophie, that I want to talk to you about what happened here the weekend of twenty-sixth of November?'

'Of course I have.'

'You're prepared for that?'

She nodded. 'I'm not hiding anything. I'll tell you all of it.'

'Good. You remember that weekend?'

'Of course I do.'

'Joanna Troy came here to look after you and your brother. She came on the Friday, is that right? Would I be correct in saying she arrived at about five?' A nod. 'What did you do that evening?'

'I had homework,' she said. 'I went to my bedroom and did my homework. My father's conditioned me to homework. I'm like one of that Russian guy's dogs. Come six and I'm doing my homework.' She sniffed. 'My mother phoned from Paris. I didn't speak to her, Giles did. He was downstairs with Joanna, watching TV, I guess. Joanna made us supper. Baked beans, it was. Baked beans and toast and bacon.' She made a face. 'It was skanky.'

Karen translated. 'That means "nasty", sir.'

Sophie looked incredulous, presumably because he hadn't understood what the whole world must understand. 'The bacon was skanky, it was soft. After that we watched some shit on TV. Joanna told us to go to bed when it got to ten. I didn't argue and Giles didn't.'

Karen said, 'Did you like Joanna, Sophie?'

As if three times her age, she said, 'Is that relevant?'

'We would like to know.'

'All right. I'm not my father, you know. I mean, rude and nasty to everyone. I'm mostly quite polite. No, I didn't much like Joanna and Giles didn't. He did for a bit and then he went off her. Not that that made any difference, we still had to have her here.'

'And next day?' Wexford asked.

'We got up. We had breakfast. It wasn't raining then. Joanna wanted to go to the Asda – you know, out on the bypass – and we went with her. Wicked way to spend a Saturday, wasn't it? She bought a lot of food and she bought wine, though there was plenty in the house. We all had lunch at the Three Towns Café in the High Street and she said she'd got a friend coming over for supper, that was why she'd bought the food.'

Wexford sat up straighter. 'A friend? What kind of friend?'

'A man.'

She was either a very good liar or all this was true. And it meant he had been right. She continued to look at him with that steady gaze and now she took hold of a lock of her long brown hair and twisted it into a spiral in her fingers. 'We went home and Giles went out. I don't know where so don't ask.'

'When did he come back?'

'I don't know. I was upstairs doing more homework, the stuff my tutor set me. When I came down Giles was there and Joanna was getting supper. Me and him, we just went cotch, he watched TV and I surfed the Net. Maybe it was six by then. Is this what you want?'

Karen nodded. 'Exactly what we want. "Going cotch" means relaxing, sir.'

'Considering what she'd given us, supper was going to be wicked,' said Sophie. 'Three courses. Avocados and grapefruit in something she called a coulis, some dumb-ass fish – I hate fish – and some sort of fruit tart with cream.'

'Did the friend come?'

A slow nod from Sophie. 'At around half-six. Peter, she called him.'

It was a common name. He must hear more before he jumped to conclusions. 'At around half-six' she had said.

'And his other name?'

'No one said. It was just Peter.'

'Had the evening paper come by then?' Wexford asked. He would ask Dorcas Winter but he wanted her version.

'I can't remember. I know it came. I suppose that girl brought it, the one that goes to our school. It was wet and we dried it on the radiator. God knows why, it's always full of shit.'

Doreen Bruce flinched but didn't interrupt.

'When we'd had the food Joanna wanted to know if Giles was going to church. "In this rain," she said. He must have told her in the morning he'd be going. He said he wouldn't because the service was on Sunday and that gamey Peter teased him a bit about church. Giles didn't like it, but he gets a lot of that. You know, "Going to be a vicar when you grow up, are you?" – that kind of crap.'

Once more Mrs Bruce drew in her breath. Probably Sophie had been more guarded in her speech when she stayed with her. Wexford said, 'What did he look like, this Peter?'

'A dumb-ass. Ordinary. Not in very good shape. Old.'

What did that mean from someone of thirteen? 'How old?' It was almost useless asking.

'I don't know. Not as old as my father.'

He left it. She hadn't given him much to go on but she hadn't eliminated the suspicion she'd raised either. 'Did Scott Holloway come?' he asked.

'Him? Yeah, I guess so. The bell rang but we never answered it.'

'Why not?'

'We just didn't.'

Perhaps that was standard practice in this house. 'Go on.'

'We had supper and watched *Jacob's Ladder* on TV. That guy Jacob got shot in a siege. Then Joanna and Peter said they were going to bed.'

She looked at Wexford, her head on one side. What he saw in her expression, in her eyes, shocked him more than if she had screamed obscenities at him. A wealth of knowledge was there, of adult experience, of a weary worldly wisdom. He wondered if he was imagining it or if he had guessed the reason, and when he looked at Karen he saw that she was thinking the same thing. There was no need to tell Sophie to continue. She needed no encouragement.

'They'd been feeling each other up, deep kissing and all that, you *know*. They didn't care about us being there. He was going to shag her, it was obvious. She didn't say anything about us going to bed, she'd forgotten us. That was when the doorbell rang.' She looked up and at him. 'I was too interested watching what they did to answer it. But when they were just kissing we did go to bed. It was about half past ten. I went to sleep. I don't know when it happened, maybe around midnight. The noise woke me, a scream and a crash, and footsteps running down the stairs. I didn't get up straight away. If you want to know the truth, I was scared, it was *scary.* I got up after a bit and went down the passage, and Giles was just standing there, outside his room. You know, it's right at the top of the stairs. He just stood there, looking down. Peter was down there, bending over Joanna, feeling her neck and her pulse and all that. He looked up and said, "She's dead."'

There was absolute silence for a moment and then that silence was shattered by the phone ringing. It rang only twice before someone in the hall picked it up. Wexford said, 'No one called the emergency services? You did that when your grandmother was taken ill but not when a woman fell downstairs. Why was that?'

'I wasn't the only one there, was I?' She had become aggressive. 'It wasn't for me to do anything. I'm only a child, like my father's always telling me. I haven't got any rights.' The same thought as he had had before came into Wexford's mind. Apparently unmoved, he shuddered inwardly. 'Peter tried to lift Joanna up but she was too heavy for him. He asked Giles to help him and they put her on the sofa. There was some blood, not much. Peter got a cloth and wiped it up and he asked me where there was a scrubbing brush. Always ask a woman, don't they?'

She was suddenly a forty-year-old feminist and her voice had grown strident. Doreen Bruce had gone quite white, her hands trembling on the arms of the chair. Karen asked her if she was all right. She nodded, the living symbol of an aghast older generation.

'I wasn't going to do it,' said Sophie. 'It was him pushed her down the stairs.'

'You didn't see that?'

'It was obvious. He said, was there any brandy? Giles got it for him and he drank it. Then he said he'd like another one but he'd better not, seeing as he was going to drive . . .'

The door opened and Roger Dade came in. Sophie stopped talking abruptly, fixed him with an insolent stare. He said, 'That was the hospital. My mother's dead. She died half an hour ago.'

Doreen was the first to speak. 'Oh, Roger, how sad. I *am* sorry.'

He took absolutely no notice of her, simply repeated, 'She died half an hour ago.' Then he turned with noisy violence on his daughter, shouting at her, 'That's your fault, you little bitch! She'd be alive now if you hadn't given her all that trouble. You've been a liar since you were born and you made her tell lies and turn against her nearest and dearest . . .'

Wexford got up. 'That's enough,' he said. 'You've had a shock, Mr Dade. You're not yourself.' He feared the man was only too much himself, but it was useless continuing now. Was the girl at risk? He thought not. Anyway, she had her grandmother, her *surviving* grandmother, for what that was worth. 'We'll go now. We'll see you tomorrow.'

Dade had calmed down into a disgruntled misery and laid himself in a chair in the attitude he had adopted earlier. Wexford thanked Sophie, told her she had been very helpful. After a fashion very unusual for him, he felt he had had about as much as he could take for one day. Mrs Bruce came up to him after the girl had gone, said apologetically, 'I don't know where they learn those words. They don't pick them up at home.'

Wexford wasn't so sure of that. He patted her on the arm. 'They all do it. It's a phase. Best ignore it, I think. Ten o'clock tomorrow morning?'

She nodded rather miserably.

Outside, the evening was colder, the sky clearer, a moon that looked as if it had been soaked in soapy water sailed above the trees. Against his face the air felt fresh and damp. He got into the car beside Karen.

'You were thinking what I was thinking, weren't you?'

'What would that be, sir?'

'That though Dade dislikes his daughter and she hates him, there has been more between them than there should have been.'

'You mean, *he's* done things *he* shouldn't have.' It was a reproof but he let it pass. 'Something has to account for her not wanting to go home while he's there. It makes me want to vomit.'

'Me too,' said Wexford.

The car turned into the street where he lived and she dropped him at his gate. He hadn't said anything about Peter. It was too soon.

Chapter 21

He hadn't asked the girl where her brother was. Because he knew she wouldn't tell him? Even supposing she knew herself. It was already clear to him that this Peter had driven them away in Joanna's car with Joanna's body in the boot.

'Why take the children with him?' Burden asked when they met in the morning.

'He couldn't trust them not to tell anyone what they'd seen,' Wexford said. 'But I think they went willingly. Sophie can't wait to get away from home. Her mother's crazy and I've a suspicion her father's been abusing her.'

'You're not serious.'

'It's not something I'd joke about, is it? I want a bit more to go on before I go to the Social Services. It could all be in my head.'

'How much of what she says do you believe? Is she a liar?'

Wexford thought about it. 'I don't know. In details perhaps, not in the essentials. For instance, the three of them didn't have lunch at the Three Towns Café. The staff there know the kids and no one saw them on the Saturday. The way Sophie talked about Peter at first sounded invented but when she said he and Joanna were feeling each other up . . .'

'She used those words?'

'Oh, yes, and then she said he was going to "shag" her. The obnoxious Dade says she's a liar but that's when I knew she was telling the truth. That, too, is when I wondered if he'd been assaulting her. It's just what abusive fathers do say, that the child is a liar. And abuse is well-known to give children a precocious – well, sophistication. They have a knowledge inappropriate for their time of life, like those two in *The Turn of the Screw*.'

Burden's initiation into literature by his wife hadn't extended to Henry James. 'So you're going to see her again this morning?'

He nodded. 'Matilda Carrish died, you know. It's in the paper. Along with Sophie's reappearance, only there's no connection so far as they know. Better that way. Sad really, isn't it? If Sophie were dead it'd be the lead story, but she's alive and well, so it merits a paragraph. Matilda's obituaries will follow tomorrow, I suppose. Newspapers have them all prepared in advance of celebrities dropping off their perches. I wonder why she – well, harboured Sophie instead of doing the responsible thing.'

'Maybe Sophie told her what you suspect about her dad.'

'That would be quite something to hear about your own son. But I dare say she'd had enough shock-horror about ruthless Roger to take it in her stride.'

'I don't know if you've noticed,' said Burden, 'but those missing children posters are all over the place this morning. More than ever. No one's told Search and Find Limited that Sophie's turned up.'

'They'll know by now. Of course, there's no one *to* tell them now Matilda Carrish is dead.'

'Unless she's given them some payment in advance,' Burden said, 'they'll call their dogs off. They'd be daft to expect to recover what they're owed from Roger. Some hopes.'

When Wexford and Karen got to Antrim only Mr and Mrs Bruce and Sophie appeared to be at home.

No explanation for the absence of Roger and Katrina Dade was offered and Wexford didn't ask. He didn't want to know. The first question he put to Sophie was unexpected. She had obviously hoped to be allowed to proceed with the departure of the three of them from the house, and for a moment she looked disconcerted.

'Where is Giles now?'

She shook her head slowly. 'I don't know. I *really* don't know. I'm trying to be helpful but I can't be because I just don't know.'

'Because your grandmother didn't tell you?'

'I asked. Matilda said it was better for me not to know so that if anyone asked me like you're asking now I wouldn't have to lie, I just wouldn't know.'

It made sense. Matilda Carrish had sent Giles somewhere to be safe. . . . But safe from what? And why had she done it? Why had she done any of it? Why receive the children in the first place? Now was the time to test Sophie's truth-telling. 'Where were we? Ah, yes, you heard a noise and a scream and came running out of your room . . .'

'We'd got past that.'

'Maybe. I'd like to hear it again, though.'

She caught on where many three times her age hadn't seen through his ruse. She knew quite well what he was doing. 'Giles came out of his bedroom. It's right at the top of the stairs. Peter was down in the hall feeling Joanna's neck and her pulse. He looked up at us and said, "She's dead." After a bit he tried to lift her up but he couldn't and he had to get Giles to help him. They put her on the sofa. Peter got a cloth and wiped up the blood, there wasn't much, but he said he needed a scrubbing brush and water. I told him where it was and he fetched the brush. But before he started on it he said he needed brandy and

Giles gave him some but he wouldn't have another because he was going to drive.'

'All right, Sophie, that's fine.' He wasn't imagining it, she looked triumphant.

'He scrubbed the carpet,' she said, 'and wiped the side of the cupboard and then he said we must pack up her stuff to take with us.'

'Take with you where?' Karen asked.

'He didn't say. He just said we had to get Joanna's body out of there. OK, I know what you're thinking – why didn't I just say no? I don't know why. I don't know why Giles didn't. I suppose we thought we'd helped him clear up and I'd packed Joanna's case and Giles had helped lift her, he helped carry her out to the car as well. We were sort of involved, you see. Look, I thought if we stayed I'd have to tell my father, I could imagine the questioning, all his shit, you don't know how he goes ballsing on. We'd get blamed, I knew that.

'It was pouring with rain, they got soaked out there. I put on my old anorak because Peter said the yellow one would attract attention, though there wasn't any attention, it was one in the morning and raining like the end of the world was coming . . .'

Karen interrupted. 'What were they wearing, Joanna and Peter? When she went down the stairs, however it was?'

'She had just a T-shirt on, a long one that sort of came to her knees. He was in pants, you know, underpants. Nothing else. But after he'd cleaned up in the hall he put on the clothes he'd been wearing, jeans and a shirt and a sweatshirt. We all went upstairs and Giles and me, we got dressed and we made our beds, we made them look the way they do when the cleaner does them.' She laughed. 'You can if you try. Then we shut all the bedroom doors. No, before that Peter said to take something with us to make it look as if we'd drowned. He said there'd be flooding and the river would – what do they call it? Burst its banks.'

'He said *that*?' Almost for the first time she had said something Wexford simply couldn't believe. The man was a prophet? That was before any of the floods began.

'Why not?' She sounded aggressively like her father. 'It was on the news at ten. There were flood warnings out all over the south.'

'All right. What did you take with you?'

'A T-shirt with my face on it and my name. It was cool but it got too tight. We had one done for me and one for Giles when we were in Florida.'

'So you left the house – at what time?'

'It was about two by then. He had to put the windscreen wipers on at double speed or he wouldn't have been able to see, it was raining so hard . . .'

'Wait a minute,' said Karen. 'This was Joanna's car, right? What about his car? He arrived in the evening by car, didn't he?'

Sophie hadn't thought of that or she genuinely didn't know? Hard to tell. 'He never said. Maybe he didn't come in a car, he could have walked, or else he left his car out in the street.'

'Unless he came back for it on the Sunday – a risky thing to do – it would still be there if he had.'

'Well, I don't know. You can't expect me to know everything.' Wexford thought she was going to repeat that she was only a child but she didn't. 'The river *was* rising. You could still get over the Kingsbrook Bridge but it looked as if you soon wouldn't. Peter said to drop the T-shirt over the wall – what d'you call it? The parapet – and I did. Did anyone ever find it?'

'Oh, yes, it was found.'

'I want it back. It was groovy. Did they think we'd drowned?'

'Some did.'

'I bet my mother did. She's poop, you know. Two tracks short of a CD, Giles says. Or he did when he was skill. Before he got all Christian and good. D'you want to know what happened next?'

'Yes, please.'

'I hadn't a clue where we were going. I thought it didn't matter. I just thought Peter would look after us. He seemed sort of quite kind and friendly. I did notice when we went across the county boundary. There was a sign by the road said "Welcome to Kent".

'I was quite interested by then in where we were going. Peter knew. He wasn't just driving somewhere, anywhere. We left the main road and came to a village and there was another sign saying it was a place called Passingham St John.' Sophie pronounced it as it was spelt. 'Peter said that was wrong,' she said, 'it should be Passam Sinjen. You could tell he knew it well.

'He drove down a track – well, more a sort of lane. About halfway down was a track leading into a wood. It was quite wet and manky, and I thought the car might get stuck but it didn't. There was a big open space and on the other side of that was this quarry. All in among the trees. Peter stopped there. He said we were going to sit there for an hour because it was still only about three and once we'd got rid of the car we wouldn't have any shelter. It was still raining but not as much as it had been at home. I think I fell asleep for a bit. I don't know if Giles did. When I woke up it was still raining but not as much.

'Peter got Giles to help him carry Joanna into the driving seat. I sat in the back while this was going on, but he made me get out to help push. We all pushed as hard as we could till the car went over the edge. It didn't turn over, it just slid and bounced a bit and came to a stop when it got caught in bushes. You could still see it all right but only if you really looked.'

'All right,' he said. 'We'll break for ten minutes.'

'You could tell he knew it well,' she had said. He had driven there in the dark, in the rain, apparently without difficulty. He was called Peter . . . Yet Buxton had seemed such a fool. If all this were true – and how could it not be? – he must be a consummate actor.

They went back into the room and Mrs Bruce came in with Sophie. She brought three cups of tea on a tray and a glass of Coke. Her granddaughter looked at it and said, 'Real people drink it out of the can.'

'Just for once then, you'll have to be an unreal person, dear.'

Karen began the questioning. 'You and Giles and Peter were in the wood at – what? Four o'clock in the morning? – with no car and no future plan. Is that right?'

The girl nodded. She made a face over her Coke.

'There's a house at the bottom of the lane. Did you go to the house?'

'I didn't see any house. I didn't know there was one. We went to the station.'

Like some commuter on a routine journey to the office . . . 'What station?'

'I don't know. Passingham something. Passingham Park. There's not a park there. It means people can park their cars but there weren't any there. It was too early.'

'How did you get to Passingham Park?' Wexford asked.

'We walked. I suppose we had to. It was a long

walk along a lot of lanes but Peter knew the way. They were just opening the station when we got there. We were very wet, soaked through. Then that dumb-ass Peter said he was leaving us, we were to stay away for a week and then we could go back home and say what we liked, he'd be out of the country by then. He wrote down an address and gave it to Giles and said we could stay there. The first train would be along a bit after five. We went into the station and he bought tickets for us. Out of the machine. We had to go over the bridge but he didn't come with us. He gave Giles some money and said goodbye and good luck or something like that. We waited on the platform and the train came along at around five fifteen.'

'That would be the Kingsmarkham–Toxborough –Victoria main line?' Karen said.

'I suppose. It did go to Victoria because that's where we got out. We were still thinking then that we'd go to the address Peter had given us but Giles said, no, we'll go to Matilda. It was a bit past six, too early to phone her, but we had to get across London to Paddington Station and we got into a muddle about that. We haven't been in the London tube much and when we changed from the first line we got into a train going the wrong way, so it was nearly seven when we got to Paddington. Giles had some money of his own and the money Peter had given him. The cafeteria was open and we bought rolls and cheese and bananas and ate them, and we had two cans of Sprite and then Giles went to find a phone box. He's got a wix phone but he'd left it at home.'

'A mobile,' said Karen.

'Matilda said to come straight away, she'd come to Kingham station and meet us. Kingham's the nearest station to where she lives. We bought two tickets to Kingham and got a train at seven thirty . . .'

'Wait a minute,' said Karen. 'Your grandmother just said to come straight away? Giles had presumably told her you'd left home and gave her some reason for that and she didn't want to know any more, she didn't question any of this, she just said to come? I don't believe you, Sophie.'

'I can't help that. That was what happened. She didn't like my parents, you know. She couldn't stand Mum.'

'Even so . . . Let it go for now. You went by train to Kingham, your grandmother met you there and you stayed at her house with her. No one thought of phoning your parents to say you were safe? Peter only told you to stay away for a week. Why didn't you go home after a week?'

She shrugged. 'I don't know. I hate it here and I liked it with Matilda. Matilda was deep . . .'

'Deep?' Wexford looked helplessly at Karen and Karen said, 'I think it just means "cool", sir.'

Sophie made a disgusted face. 'Giles had gone, anyway. He went away next day. I didn't want to be at home alone with *them*.'

'Giles went away?' Wexford said. 'Where did he go? Why did he?'

'Matilda said he ought to go. They didn't talk about it in front of me, so I don't know what she said or why. I told you. If I didn't know I couldn't tell, could I?'

'The police came – where were you then?'

She smiled, then laughed. 'The first time I just went up into one of the bedrooms. Matilda said they wouldn't search for us, not in the home of an old woman and a celebrity, she said. Then, when *you* came, I hid in the cupboard in the room where you were talking. I thought how manky it would be if I sneezed.'

'And all this', Wexford said, 'was set up by Matilda

Carrish? She knew how anxious your parents were, she must have known every police force in the country was looking for you, she even came to us to complain we weren't doing enough.'

'She thought it was funny. She left me alone in the house that day she went to London with strict instructions not to go out. I never did go out. I didn't mind, it was raining all the time. I'd done enough walking that night to last me my life.'

'How about these private investigators? These Search and Find people? She took them on, she must have made a down payment. Do you know anything about that?'

'She said it would make people think she couldn't be to blame. It was cool, wasn't it? Really skill. She knew they'd not search her place and they'd never find Giles, she said.'

Wexford shook his head. Usually able to see the funny side of almost everything (as his wife put it) he found nothing in the least amusing here, in spite of the girl's twitching lips and barely suppressed enjoyment of the situation. For all that, his next words hadn't been intended to bring her down to earth quite so violently.

'Well, she's dead now. She's beyond explaining to us.'

Sophie knew she was dead as well as anyone did, but this reminder crushed her. She lifted a suddenly woeful face. 'She was jammy, I loved her and she loved me. That's more than anyone else does. Excepting Giles, she was the only one I loved.' And she broke down in a storm of tears.

At the beginning of this case, Wexford said to himself, I said they weren't the babes in the wood. Now I'm not so sure.

*

In the afternoon they began again, but this time Burden was with Wexford and her father with Sophie. Wexford didn't like it and Sophie obviously loathed him being there but there was nothing he could do. Understandably, Doreen Bruce had had enough. But he was sure Roger Dade's presence would make the girl clam up. He hoped he wouldn't have to reprove him too often for interfering. Of Katrina there had been no sign all day.

As it happened, Dade hardly spoke and certainly he made no attempt to stop his daughter speaking, but sat with closed eyes in morose silence, seemingly indifferent to police questioning and Sophie's answers. Though he began by once more probing into Matilda Carrish's extraordinary willingness to take in and hide her grandchildren, Wexford's aim at this session was to discover as much as he could of Giles's possible whereabouts. He was disinclined to believe the girl when she insisted she didn't know. But he started with Matilda.

'I find it hard to believe your grandmother took you in without question. She simply agreed to take you in and lie to the police? Did she give you any explanation, tell you, for instance, why she was doing this?'

'She didn't say anything about it,' Sophie said. 'Giles told her what had happened to us and I told her. We told her in the car going back from the station. She just said she was glad we'd come to her.'

Dade opened his eyes and looked at his daughter. It was an unpleasant look but Sophie didn't flinch. Wexford persisted, 'You'd done nothing wrong.' Concealing a crime? Hiding a body? 'I'll correct that. You'd done nothing yourselves to Joanna. Why didn't she phone your parents? You'd told her about Peter. Why not phone the police and tell them what you'd told her?'

Sophie was beginning to look uncomfortable. 'She never even thought of that, I'm sure. She just wanted to look after us and see we didn't get into trouble.'

He left it. 'Your brother can't have left the country,' he said. 'His passport is here. When did he leave your grandmother's house?'

She had already told him but again he was testing her. 'It was early on the Sunday morning we got to Matilda's. I slept a lot that day and so did Giles. We were tired, we'd been up all night. But in the evening Matilda said he ought to go first thing in the morning, she'd been making arrangements on the phone. He ought to go before our parents told the police we were missing. By the time I woke up it was all fixed. She drove him to the station. She said it was best for me not to know where he was going and then I couldn't tell anyone who asked.' She looked triumphantly at him. 'Like you,' she said.

The sheet of water that covered most of the road reminded him of the winter floods. Not again, *please.* The rain had stopped but it was obviously no more than a lull. He was putting out the recycling box on to the pavement, and thus breaking one of the local authority's rules. You weren't supposed to put the newspapers, cans and bottles out till the following morning but the rain might be torrential in the morning . . .

It was a funny thing, he thought, how you were always distracted from this task by reading whatever was on top of the pile. You wouldn't normally read it when you'd sat down with the newspaper it was in, you wouldn't dream of reading a piece about waterproof mascara or Burmese cats or the latest fifteen-year-old pop sensation, but somehow you couldn't resist it in these particular circumstances. The article that caught his eye was on a cookery page.

It happened to be lying open on the top, although the date on it was a week ago. Its illustrations in full colour, it showed a starter of avocado and grapefruit in lime coulis, a monkfish confection and a *tarte tatin* with cream . . .

But wait a minute, wasn't that the menu Sophie had described as Joanna preparing for this dinner on the fateful Saturday night *three months ago*? He looked at it again, standing there in the road, under the street lamp. Coincidence? He didn't think so. More likely, it was proof of the extent to which the girl had lied. She had read that page while at her grandmother's and remembered its details when they were needed . . .

Chapter 22

Since he and Sharonne were detained there over Christmas, Peter Buxton had not been back to Passingham Hall. Events had given him a dislike of the place. He had even thought of selling it. But could he sell it while the discovery of a body in a car in the grounds was fresh in people's minds? He had tentatively suggested the possibility of selling to Sharonne but she had been adamant. She had been aghast, then furious.

'But we must have a country place, Pete.'

'Why must we? Sell it and we could buy a bigger house up here. Think about it. We haven't been there for two months. I don't suppose we'll go again before Easter, if then. The council tax still has to be paid, and Pauline. The house eats up fuel.'

'What am I going to say to people? That we don't have a country place? Oh, no. I should coco.' Incongruously, since she so obviously wanted to hold on to Passingham Hall, she added, 'Besides, nobody would buy it. Not since you advertised the fact there was a dead body in the grounds.'

The Warrens had invited them to their Silver Wedding party. The anniversary itself was on Valentine's Day but that happened to fall on a Wednesday that year so the party was fixed for Saturday the seventeenth. It was to be a big affair, half the county there. Sharonne was determined to go.

'Of course we're going, Pete. Why ever not?'

'You go,' Peter said daringly.

'What, and leave you here on your own?' As if he were a child or senile, as if he were likely to set the place on fire or invite other women in. 'Absolutely not. God knows what you'd get up to.'

What was that supposed to mean? What he'd get up to! Was she as pure as driven snow? That phone number was still hovering beneath the surface of his mind, he had long known it by heart. Every time he came home and found himself alone with the phone, he dialled 1471 but its records had never divulged that number again.

He would have to go to Passingham some time. It was obvious he must either go there or sell it, and Sharonne wouldn't let him sell it. Peter was beginning to think the unthinkable and wonder what exactly he got out of his marriage. He could see what he put into it – money, companionship, money, obedience, money, a continual yielding to pressure – but what did Sharonne put in? Herself, he supposed, herself. He felt most frightened and most like shying away from the whole subject when he began asking what that self amounted to. A caring – but deceitful? – bossy, clothes horse . . . Last week he had asked her about starting a family and she had reacted as if he had suggested she navigate the globe single-handed in an open boat or make her own clothes or something equally fantastic. They had never discussed it before. Naïvely, he had supposed all women wanted babies just as he had supposed they could all cook.

Of course, they went to Passingham. As they were leaving on the Friday evening the phone started ringing. After three rings it stopped and switched over to the answering service. It never crossed Peter's mind that this might be Kingsmarkham Police calling to fix a time to interview him. After all, he could check the message on Sunday night.

As they turned down the lane towards the Hall she began on the body in the car.

'They never would have found it if you hadn't phoned and told them.'

'Well, I did phone. It's too late now.'

'When all's said and done, I think we're very lucky the Warrens asked us. They must be very tolerant people to overlook a thing like that. Most people would give us the cold shoulder.'

'Don't be ridiculous,' said Peter in a rough tone. 'We didn't put that car there. We didn't put that woman in it. It was just our luck.'

'Well, *I* know that, but others don't. Others would say there was no smoke without fire and we must have had something to do with it.'

'You mean *you* would.'

It was in a state of mutual resentment that they entered the house, Peter lugging all his wife's three suitcases, one under his arm, two dragged behind him, a task she said was obviously his to perform. He reached for the light switch but the bulb was defunct and for a few moments they blundered about in the pitch dark. As Sharonne located the panel of switches in the drawing room but before the light came on, the phone began to ring. Peter felt for it, knocked the receiver off and was crawling about the floor feeling for it when light poured out from behind the half-open drawing room door. Kicking over the largest of Sharonne's suitcases in his haste, he gasped out, 'Hello?'

'I seem to have phoned at a bad time,' said a voice he recognised as belonging to Chief Inspector Wexford. 'Kingsmarkham Crime Management.'

'What do you want?' Sharonne was standing in the doorway, watching him intently. 'It is a bad time, very bad.'

'I'm sorry about that. I'm not at liberty to be tactful

about these things. You'll be staying at Passingham for the weekend?'

'Why?'

'Because I'd like to talk to you tomorrow morning as a matter of urgency, Mr Buxton.'

Peter looked at Sharonne's stony face, thought with a disloyalty that amazed him, how anger reduced her to ugliness, and wondered how he could keep from her whatever it was this policeman wanted. He said a cautious, 'All right.'

'You have a car with you? I'd like you to come here. In the morning.'

The Warrens' lunch party . . . 'What time in the morning? Early preferably.'

'I was thinking of eleven.'

'Could you make it ten?' Sharonne was listening intently. 'Ten would suit me better.'

'It wouldn't suit me,' said Wexford. 'I'll see you at eleven.'

What could he say? In Sharonne's presence, he dared not ask what the police wanted this time. He thought only of the blamelessness of his life these past six weeks. Surely they hadn't found anything else on his land . . .? He dared not ask. Wexford said he would see him at eleven in the morning and rang off. Peter carried the suitcases upstairs and dumped them on the bedroom floor. The house felt damp and chill as the central heating began to cool. He went downstairs and after a good deal of grubbing about in the kitchen, dislodging stacks of heterogeneous rubbish, receipted bills, empty cardboard boxes, plastic bags, out-of-focus photographs, used matchbooks, triple A batteries, keys that locked no known doors, at last found a 100 watt light bulb in the back of a cupboard. Once he had managed with some difficulty to slot it into the socket, he went into the by now cold drawing room and poured himself a large Scotch.

'Did you take my cases upstairs?' said Sharonne. Getting a surly nod in response, she remarked that she was disappointed to see him lapsing back into his old drinking habits. 'You've been so good about it lately.'

Not all worms turn but some do. 'I haven't been good. I haven't cut down on my drinking, I've just done it when you weren't there. I'm a grown man, *Mummy*, I'm not a child. No one tells me what to do.' He picked up his whisky. 'I'm going to bed now. Goodnight.'

They had shared their bed but distantly, each one lying on an extreme edge. Peter woke up very early and got up. He couldn't lie there wondering if something else had turned up on his land, those children's bodies, for instance, or clothing or some weapon. He should have asked. But he couldn't, not with Sharonne looking at him so accusingly. So far she hadn't said a word about that telephone conversation.

It was still dark but dawn was coming. A fine precipitation, halfway between drizzle and mist, hung in the greyish air. In Barbour, rubber boots, country gentleman's tweed cap and gauntlets, he explored the wood, expecting at any moment to see blue and white crime tape showing brightly among the tree trunks. But there was nothing. The Dancing Floor lay passive within its encircling trees, a brighter green than he had ever seen it, quagmire green, bog green, in the increasing light waterdrops glittering on every blade of grass. No one could walk on it at present, still less dance. His search yielding nothing that might be construed as incriminating, he felt a little better and he returned to the house with a renewed appetite for breakfast.

He was making toast and, in some trepidation,

boiling an egg, when Sharonne appeared unprecedentedly early. She had cleaned up her face before going to bed but not removed her eye make-up so that this morning she looked as if she had received a double whammy during the night. In her not very clean white dressing gown and with her hair sticking up in tufts, but not in a fashionable way, she was an unappetising sight.

'You never told me', she said, 'who that was on the phone last night.'

'The office,' he lied.

'You're never going into the office at eleven this morning?'

'Why not?'

'Well, for a start, what for? You never work on Saturdays. You once said it was a rule, no one in your firm worked on Saturdays or Sundays. Not ever.'

Peter didn't answer. He took the pan off the ring and rather clumsily cut the top off his egg. It had boiled hard, the way he disliked it. Sharonne sat down at the table and poured herself some coffee.

'You're not going to the office, are you? I can read you like a book, Pete. That wasn't the office on the phone, it was someone else.'

'If you say so.' He might say much the same to her concerning phone calls, but he didn't. He was afraid.

'Well, we're due at the Warrens by twelve thirty at the latest and I hope I don't need to remind you Trollfield Farm is fifteen miles away. So you'd better not be wherever you're going for more than half an hour.' She studied his face, reading him like a book. 'I know who it was,' she said. 'It was the police.'

He shrugged.

'You're going to Toxborough police station. Well, Trollfield Farm is between here and Toxborough, so that's all right. What do they want? I thought all that business was over. What have you been doing, Pete?'

'Me? I haven't done a thing. I never have done. All I did was find a car with a body in it.'

She stood up, hands on hips. 'No, that wasn't all you did. All you did was go and look at it, mess about with something that was no business of yours. All you did was go and tell the police and bring them here so that this place has got a bad name and we'll never be able to sell it.'

'But you don't want to sell it!'

'That's got nothing to do with it. It'd be all the same if I did, you never take any notice of what I want. And now they suspect you of something else. Putting that car there, I expect, and maybe you did – how would I know? I'd be the last to know.'

Peter picked a piece of toast out of the toaster and hurled it across the room. He tipped the remains of his egg into the sink. 'It's not Toxborough, it's Kingsmarkham. And there's no way I can get back here before half past one.' Like a child, he added, 'So there!'

She stared at him, gathering her rage for an outburst.

'And you can't have the car,' he said. 'I want it.'

'If you go to Kingsmarkham,' she shouted, 'and I can't go to the Warrens, I'll never speak to you again.'

He found the nerve that had been in abeyance for three years. 'Good,' he said.

The single sentence of that altercation that stayed in his mind was the one she had uttered about the police suspecting him of putting the car in the quarry. Maybe they did, he thought as he began the drive to Kingsmarkham, maybe that was what it was all about. But they *couldn't*. On what grounds? He didn't know the dead woman, he didn't know those missing kids. He should have asked that policeman. But Wexford's tone had been so cold and repressive that he had sensed he'd get no more out of him on the phone.

At two minutes to eleven he drove on to the parking area outside Kingsmarkham Police Station. Before he had opened the driver's door, a young policeman was saying very respectfully to him, 'Sorry, sir, you can't park here.'

'Where can I park then?' Peter asked irritably.

'It'll have to be in the street, sir. On the "pay and display", sir, if you please, not the residents' parking.'

'I know that. I'm not a resident of this place, thank God.'

It took him more than ten minutes to find somewhere to park in a side street and walk back to the police station, so that when he was shown into Wexford's office the Chief Inspector was pointedly looking at his watch. But the interview, which he by now expected to be a gruelling interrogation, lasted no time at all. Wexford only wanted to know what he had been doing on the afternoon and evening of 25 November of the previous year. Of course he couldn't produce an alibi, though he could have done for almost every other Saturday night of the year, Sharonne enjoying such a very social lifestyle. In fact, that was why he remembered that Saturday without reference to his diary. Simply because, almost uniquely, they had been home alone together.

Wexford seemed not at all perturbed. He didn't even seem interested. He thanked Buxton for coming, made a few remarks on the weather and then said he'd escort him downstairs to the front entrance himself. They took the lift and crossed the black and white checkerboard floor towards the swing doors. He vaguely thought he recognised the girl of thirteen or fourteen who was sitting on an upright chair next to an elderly woman. Her picture had been in the news lately. For being murdered? For winning something? Having not yet seen a morning paper, he couldn't remember. She was gazing at him in a rude, brash sort of way but he soon forgot her.

He had been so short a time in the police station that he had a good chance of getting back to Passingham by noon. It was still only twenty-five past eleven when he got back into his car. Unfortunately for him (and for the victims of the accident) a container lorry had hit a car full of holidaymakers as the driver overtook a line of vehicles this side of the Toxborough turn-off. The traffic queue extended back from the crash site for two miles by the time Buxton reached the tail end of it. Eventually, when an ambulance had taken away the injured, when the broken and twisted metal that had been a people carrier was cleared from the road and the lorry towed away, the line of cars slowly proceeded towards Toxborough and London. The time was twelve twenty and it was ten to one when Buxton reached the Hall.

He knew Sharonne must be still there, however enraged and threatening, because he had the car and she no means of getting to Trollfield unless she'd called a taxi. If she'd done that she'd have had to explain to the driver she hadn't got a car. That wasn't Sharonne's way. But she wasn't there. He went round the house calling her name, a large whisky in his hand. Someone must have called for her, someone must have taken her to the Warrens. Well, she'd be back.

Later, on the news, he saw that Sophie Dade had been found or come home of her own accord. It wasn't clear which of these possibilities was the true one. So that was the girl he'd seen at the police station. There was a little whisky left in the bottle. He might as well drink it. It was wasteful leaving dregs.

Reminding himself that what Sharonne had been to was a lunch party, he saw that it was after six. Soon afterwards he fell asleep and dreamed about the phone number disclosed to him when he dialled 1471. Once, just once. The chap had never phoned again. Because Sharonne had cautioned him not to? It was pitch dark and very cold when he woke up. Finding that it was four in the morning was a bit of a shock. Once again, though this time in a shaky state, he toured the house calling her name. She wasn't there, she hadn't come back. Maybe the phone number man, the lover, if he was a lover, had driven her back to London. After a hair of the dog and some work with an electric toothbrush to get the foul taste out of his mouth, he dialled his London number, got his own voice asking him to leave a message.

He slept again. He phoned his London home again, eventually phoned the number that had been haunting him. An answering service responded, only repeating the number he had dialled but giving no name and asking very tersely for the caller to leave a message. The only satisfaction he got, if satisfaction it was, was from the voice being male. By the middle of the morning it was plain to him that she had left him and instead of sadness, he felt a terrible rage. He took Colman's card out of his pocket and dialled not the main phone number but that of the man's mobile. Colman answered smartly.

'It's Peter Buxton. I want your people to act for me.'

'Sure. A pleasure. What might we be searching and finding?'

'Evidence for divorce,' said Buxton, and he explained.

'You're behind the times, Mr Buxton. Under the Matrimonial Causes Act, 1973, you can get a no-fault divorce in two years and the waiting time's since been reduced to one year.'

'I don't want a no-fault divorce. There's plenty of fault – on her side. And I want it fast.'

'Let me just give a rundown of our charges,' said Colman.

Thus the Buxton marriage was the first relationship to come to grief through the case of the Missing Dade Children.

Chapter 23

Matilda Carrish's funeral took place in the same church and the same crematorium as Joanna Troy's had a month or so before. There the resemblance almost ended. True, Roger Dade was at both and the same unfortunate clergyman officiated at both, intoning the same contemporary version of the funeral service to a similarly apathetic and vaguely agnostic group of mourners, but Katrina Dade was not there to see her mother-in-law laid to rest, nor were her parents. Attendance was poor. Perhaps, Wexford thought, more friends of Matilda, neighbours, fellow artists from the world in which she had moved for so long and with such distinction, might have come along if she had been buried in her local cemetery and the words of committal recited in her village church. It had obviously been Roger Dade's decision to do otherwise.

Dade sat in a front pew, looking sullen, beside a woman who looked not in the least like him nor like Matilda but who, Wexford nevertheless thought, must be his sister. She was a heavy woman with a full face and tightly curled hair. What was her name? Charlotte something. He had once spoken to her on the phone. Would talking to her face-to-face be of any use? Then he remembered the man Matilda Carrish had married, an old man who lived abroad and was now her widower. But there was no one in the front pews it could conceivably have been. Sophie had come into the church and seated herself as far from her father as it was possible to be. She had decked herself out in deepest unrelieved black – not difficult for any teenager these days. Matilda Carrish had sent her brother away and taken the secret of his hiding place with her to the grave. But why? Why? To keep him away from this Peter? If so, what was Peter's interest in the boy? Probably not a sexual interest at all but fear of Giles telling what he had seen at Antrim on that Saturday night. In that case, why had Matilda not sent Sophie away too? She had seen as much as he and possibly more.

He ought to be able to reason out *where* she had sent Giles. Was it possible he had gone to her daughter's house? If so, the daughter had left him behind to come here, but no doubt in the care of her husband and children. It was a place he could have gone to without a passport. As a kind of minor celebrity, Matilda most likely had friends everywhere, abroad as well as here. But he couldn't have gone abroad because he had no passport . . . Would a friend living in, say, northern Scotland harbour a boy who was involved in a murder inquiry and whom the police wanted to question? Matilda had and birds of a feather flock together . . .

The coffin was carried in. The sparse congregation rose as a dismal voluntary was played, and Wexford's earlier impression was confirmed. Very few people had come. There was no choir and no one with a strong voice among the mourners. They broke into a ragged version of – what else? – 'Abide with Me'. Just where could Giles Dade possibly be abiding at this moment?

All the members of Wexford's team that could be spared had spent the previous day questioning George and Effie Troy and Yvonne Moody about

Peter. The results weren't helpful. Only George Troy seemed to recall Joanna mentioning a Peter but he had similar recollections of her talking about an Anthony, a Paul, a Tom and a Barry. Effie interrupted to say that these weren't boyfriends but children she had taught and this had thrown George into confusion. Yvonne Moody's replies were useless. She was obviously predisposed to a need for Joanna to have no friends apart from herself and possibly other women. Reluctantly, she had at last admitted she had seen men – she called them boys – going to Joanna's house for private coaching. One of them might have been a Peter.

The coffin was removed and placed in the car that would transport it to the crematorium. Only the officiating clergyman seemed to be accompanying Matilda Carrish on her last journey. Wexford watched her driven away. Dade had come down the steps from the church with Charlotte something. He gave Wexford a sullen glare, muttered to his sister. Wexford expected a putting of heads together, a whispered colloquy, before both of them ignoring him. But Dade's sister turned in his direction, smiled and came over, hand extended.

'Charlotte Macallister. How do you do?'

'I was sorry to hear about your mother,' Wexford said insincerely.

'Yes. What on earth was she doing, hiding those children? I think she must have gone quite mad. Senile dementia or something.'

She was the least likely victim of senile anything, he thought. 'Giles is still missing, of course,' he said. 'But he's alive . . .' A bellow from Dade momentarily took his breath away.

'Sophie! *Sophie!*'

The girl was running out of the churchyard, running as fast as only a thirteen-year-old can. Her father yelled because he was powerless to stop her. He clenched his fist and stamped.

'Very bad for the blood pressure,' Charlotte Macallister said calmly. 'He won't make old bones if he goes on like that.'

'It occurred to me in there', said Wexford, 'that your mother might have sent Giles to you.'

'It did, did it? Well, I'm sorry to disappoint you but I'm not so much a chip off the old block as that. And if I fell in with her plots my husband wouldn't. He's a high-ranking officer in the Royal Ulster Constabulary and a pal of Sir Ronald Flanagan. Bye-bye. If you need me I'll be staying with Roger and Katrina for a couple of days.'

Wexford and Burden lunched together, not at the Moonflower, but in the police canteen. Burden sniffed his fish and made a face.

'Something wrong with it?'

'No. Not really. Cod ought to smell of something, it ought to smell nice. This smells of nothing, it might be cardboard – no, polystyrene. That's what it looks like.'

'Talking of fish,' said Wexford who was eating ravioli, 'this whole Peter story is fishy, don't you think? No one's heard of him. Katrina hasn't, Yvonne Moody hasn't, and they were apparently her closest friends. Her father and stepfather haven't. And I'll tell you something else. It may be coincidence but I had another look at that cooking piece I told you about and it was written by someone with Peter for a first name.'

Burden raised his eyebrows, nodded. 'None of the Dade neighbours saw anyone come to the house that Saturday evening except Dorcas Winter. They didn't even see her, only knew she'd been because the paper was there.'

'Why would Sophie invent him? Besides, *could* she invent him? A man called Peter she might, and the name she got from a magazine, but the things he did and said? His pushing Joanna downstairs, clearing up the blood, driving the car and knowing about Passingham? Knowing how it was pronounced?'

'He could be called something else,' Burden said. 'On the other hand, none of these people even knew of a man in Joanna's life. Why should she conceal him from her family and friends? She wasn't married.'

'Very likely he is, though. All we know is who he's not, and he's not Peter Buxton. Sophie was adamant about that. In fact, when I asked her after he'd gone she was so indignant that I might even think so for a moment that she was almost in tears. I'd say she passionately didn't want Buxton to be this Peter – and that in itself is odd.'

'It's not odd,' Burden said slowly, pushing fishbones to the side of his plate and the khaki-coloured peas to join them. 'It's not odd if she invented Peter and panicked when she saw we took it seriously, when she realised that here was a real person who could be accused of a crime he didn't commit.'

'Then, if she invented Peter, who *was* in the house and accidentally or purposely, killed Joanna Troy?'

'Someone she doesn't want us to know about. Someone she's protecting.'

'Then we'll have to talk to her again,' Wexford said.

'By the way, the Buxtons are splitting up. I met Colman in the High Street, taking down posters. He told me. Not very discreet of him, was it?'

There had been a funeral and, in other circumstances, he would have let a day pass, but no one except Sophie had shown much grief for Matilda Carrish.

Even hers, Wexford felt, was the grief of a child whose whole future, eagerly anticipated, is before her and who knows, anyway, that in the nature of things the old must die. What kind of a mother had Matilda been that Roger Dade seemed to regard her as one who caused almost less nuisance by dying than by remaining alive? Perhaps the kind he had imagined, well-intentioned, an ardent believer in free expression, but neglectful too, pursuing her own (lucrative) interests while leaving her children to pursue theirs. Or was it that Dade was simply a congenitally unpleasant man? And why, why, why had the woman taken those children in and defied the police forces of an entire country to find them?

He notified the family that he and Burden would return in the late afternoon to speak to Sophie once more. Fortunately it was Mrs Bruce he saw. Dade's reaction would have been less amiable. This time, surprisingly, it was her mother who chaperoned her at the interview, but she might as well have not been there, for she sat silent for almost the whole time, lying back in an armchair with her eyes closed. Also present was Karen Malahyde. 'I need you as interpreter,' Wexford said to her and then the girl came in. Once more she was all in black and a dancing devil with horns and trident had appeared on her forearm. It looked like a tattoo but was probably a transfer.

'Sophie,' he began, 'I'm going to be very frank with you in the hope that you'll be frank with me. Four hours ago when I was having my lunch with Mr Burden here we discussed the man you call Peter . . .'

She interrupted him. 'He *is* called Peter.'

'Fine. He's called Peter,' said Burden. 'I expressed my doubts about Peter's existence. None of your neighbours here had seen anyone come to this house that evening. Scott Holloway denies coming here. Only Dorcas Winter came, delivering the evening paper, and she didn't come in. But Mr Wexford thought Peter must exist because he doubted if you could have invented him. You might have invented a man called Peter but not the things he said and did. Above all, not the way he pronounced Passingham. What do you have to say about all that?'

Her eyelids flickered. She looked down. 'Nothing. It's all true.'

'Describe Peter,' Burden said.

'I did. I said he was ordinary, a dumb-ass.'

'What did he look like, Sophie?'

'Tall. Not in good shape, quite ugly. His face was starting to go red. Dark hair but going bald.' She screwed up her eyes, apparently in an effort to think. 'One of his front teeth crossed a bit over the one next to it. Droopy mouth. Maybe forty-five.'

She had described her father. But even by the wildest stretch of imagination and the wildest manipulation of alibis, Peter couldn't be Roger Dade. At the relevant time he had been in Paris with his wife, as attested to by a hotel keeper, a travel agent, an airline and the Paris police. A psychologist would say she didn't know many men (as against boys) and had described her father as the one she knew best and most strongly disliked and feared – in other words, a man she thought capable of violent crime.

'Sophie,' Wexford said, 'what became of the piece of paper Peter gave you with an address on it?'

He hadn't asked her that before. It had seemed unimportant. He was astonished to see her flush deeply. 'Giles threw it away,' she said.

He was more certain she was lying than he had been at any of her other replies. 'Did you look at it before you decided to go to your grandmother? Was it something about that address which made you decide going to your grandmother would be better?'

'Giles looked at it. I didn't.'

He nodded. He glanced at Katrina. She appeared to be fast asleep. 'Giles hadn't got his mobile with him. He made the call to your grandmother from a call box. How did he know the number?'

'She was *our* grandmother. Of course we knew her phone number.'

'I don't think there's any "of course" about it, Sophie. You only saw your grandmother once or twice a year. You had seldom been to her house before. No doubt you had her number in an address book at home. Your parents probably had it on a frequently used number directory in their phone at home but what you're saying is that you knew the number by heart, you had it in your memory or Giles's.'

The girl shrugged. 'Why not?'

'I think you decided to make for your grandmother's *before you left this house.* I think you knew where you were going from the start.'

She made no answer.

'Who spoke to her, you or Giles?'

'It was me.'

'All right,' Wexford said, 'that will do for today. I'd like to speak to Mr and Mrs Bruce, please. Where are they?'

That awoke or at least stirred Katrina. She sat up. 'My parents are sitting up in their room. They went up there because they've had a row with Roger. They're going home tomorrow, anyway.' Her voice rose until it became somehow frighteningly high-pitched. 'And I'm going with them. I'm going with them for ever.'

Sophie said, 'Take my father with you.'

'Don't be more stupid than you can help. I'm going with them because I'm leaving him. D'you understand now?'

'You're poop.' The girl spoke roughly but she

sounded afraid. 'What about me? I can't be left alone with him.'

Katrina looked at her and tears of self-pity welled. 'Why should I care about you? You didn't care about me when you took yourself off, you and your brother, when I thought you were both lying dead somewhere. It's time I started thinking of *me.*' She addressed Wexford. 'Having your child murdered or disappeared or thinking they have mostly leads to the mother and father splitting up. It's quite common. Haven't you noticed?'

He didn't answer this. He was thinking of Sophie, thinking fast and wondering.

'We'll be leaving in the morning. Early. If you want my parents they're in Giles's room. Just go up and knock on the door. I had to put that bitch Charlotte in the one they'd been using. Apparently she can only sleep in a room where the bedhead is to the north. I'll put it all behind me tomorrow, thank God.'

Wexford motioned to Burden to come outside into the hall with him. The house was very silent and seemed otherwise empty. Probably Roger had taken his sister out somewhere. Wexford said, 'No time like the present. We'll take Sophie into that other room, the dining room or whatever, and you ask her. Ask her outright. I can't leave it another day.'

'You can't do that, Reg. She's thirteen.'

'Oh God, so I can't. Then it'll have to be in the mother's presence.'

But when they went back Katrina had fallen asleep or was giving a very good imitation of someone who had. She lay curled up like a cat, her knees under her chin, her head buried in her arms. Sophie sat staring at her fixedly like someone watching a wild animal, wondering what it would do next.

Wexford said, 'Why do you dislike your father so, Sophie?'

She turned towards him, it seemed reluctantly. 'I just do.'

'Sophie, you seem very well-informed about sex. I'm going to ask you outright. Has he ever touched you or tried to touch you in a sexual way?'

Her reaction was the last either police officer expected. She started to laugh. It wasn't dry or cynical laughter but true merriment, peal on peal of it. 'You're all poop, the lot of you. That's what Matilda thought, that's why she let us come. Her own dad did it to her when she was a kid. So she let us come and said she'd hide us. But I put her right, though I don't think she believed me. He's skanky but he's not that bad.'

Burden glanced at Katrina. She hadn't moved. 'So fear of your father's, er, attentions isn't what makes you dislike him?'

'I get pissed off at him because he's just never never nice to me. He shouts at me and he's skanky. And he's always nagging me to go to my room and work. I can't have my friends here because it's a waste of time, *he* says. I'm supposed to work, work, work. I only like get books and CDs and gear as presents for working. It's the same for Giles. Is that enough for you?'

'Yes, Sophie,' said Wexford. 'Yes, thank you. Tell me something else, then. When did you set your grandmother straight about your relationship with your father? As soon as you got to her house? The same day, the Sunday?'

'I don't remember exactly when but it was before Giles went away. We were all three there, Matilda and Giles and me, and Matilda asked me why we'd left and I told her and she said was it really more about something my father did to me. I'd heard about that stuff, it's always on the TV, but it never happened to me and I told her so.'

'In that case, if she was satisfied that your father was no more than strict and a bit bullying with you, why didn't she then call your parents or the police to say where you were or that you were safe?'

With a shake of her head and a brandishing of arms, Katrina woke up. Or came out of her self-induced trance. She put her feet to the ground. 'I can answer that.' As seemed to happen almost every time she opened her mouth, the tears started. But instead of constricting her speech or causing her to gag, they simply rolled down her thin cheeks. 'I can tell you why she didn't. She took my children in to get revenge on me. Because I told her when she was here in October that I wouldn't let them see her again. Not ever. Well, when they were grown-up I couldn't stop them but while they lived here with us I'd keep them apart if it took the last breath in my body.'

'Do you mind telling us why you wouldn't let their grandmother see them again?'

'*She* knows.' Katrina pointed a shaking forefinger at her daughter. 'Ask her.'

Wexford raised an enquiring eyebrow at Sophie. The girl said nastily, 'You tell them if you want. I'm not going to do your dirty work for you.'

Katrina pulled her sleeve down over her hand and used it like a handkerchief to wipe her streaming eyes. 'She was going to stay a week. My husband –' she put extreme scorn into the word '– said we ought to have her for a week. I didn't want that. She looked down on me, always did, because I'm not supposed to be clever like her. Well, the third day she was here I went up to Sophie's room to tell her her tutor had phoned to say he couldn't give her a lesson next day and when I opened the door she wasn't there and she wasn't in Giles's room, and I found all three of them in Matilda's room. They were all in there and Matilda was sitting on the bed smoking *pot*.'

'Mrs Carrish was smoking cannabis?'

'That's what I said. I started screaming – well, anyone would. I told Roger and he was *incandescent*. But I didn't wait to see what he'd do, I told her she'd have to go, there and then. It was evening but I wasn't going to have her in my house a minute longer . . .'

'You'd better tell what Matilda said, not just you,' Sophie said scornfully. 'She said she was doing what she always did to relax. If we didn't ever relax, she said, we'd get sick and be too ill to pass exams. It was harmless if we wanted to give it a go, she said, but she wouldn't give us any, she was sure we had plenty of chances to get it. Oh, and said my father was full of shit and he'd make us full of shit too.'

'Stop using that filthy language,' Katrina said at the top of her voice, and to Wexford in a more subdued tone, 'I even packed her bags for her, threw all her fancy clothes, all her black designer stuff, I threw it into her cases and put them outside on the doorstep. My husband fetched her downstairs – for once he asserted himself with *her*. I'd never seen that before. It was nine at night. I don't know where she stayed, some hotel, I suppose.' Suddenly she screamed at him, 'Don't look at me like that! She was an old woman, I know that. But she didn't act like one, she acted like a fiend, getting my children on to drugs . . .'

Sophie cocked a thumb at her mother. 'What she means is she thinks Matilda hid us to get back at her and I reckon she's right.'

'It was her revenge,' said Katrina, sobbing now. 'It was her way of getting revenge.'

Not for the first time, Wexford wondered what the people who talked so glibly about 'family values' would say to a scene such as the one he had just witnessed and the revelations he had heard. But come to that, wouldn't he, if in Katrina's place, have done just what Katrina had done, if more calmly? What had possessed Matilda Carrish to do something more readily associated with pushers a quarter of her age? No doubt it was because she had used cannabis herself, perhaps regularly for years, and she genuinely believed it a harmless relaxant.

He and Burden went upstairs. Wexford thought he had known who 'Peter' was and, broadly speaking, what had happened that night from the point when Sophie had described her father. But he had truly seen the light when she insisted they had memorised Matilda's phone number, when he knew the whole operation had been planned before they left Antrim.

He knocked at the door of Giles's bedroom and Doreen Bruce's voice asked who it was. Wexford told her and she came to open it. Her husband was sitting in a small armchair he recognised as having been brought there from the living room, the book he had been reading lying face-downwards on the bed. Giles's religious artefacts and posters had disappeared.

Wexford came straight to the point. 'Mr Bruce, can Giles drive a car?'

Afraid of the law, as many people of her generation are, his wife immediately plunged into excuses. 'We told him he must never try to drive before he'd got a licence and insurance and all that. We explained it was fine for him to practise on the old airfield but he couldn't take his test till he was seventeen. And he understood, didn't he, Eric? He knew it was all right for Eric to teach him on the old runway when he came to stay with us and he had to save driving for when he was with us, that was his treat here, something to look forward to.'

Yes, of course, the airstrip at Berningham, once a United States base . . .

'You took him out in your car, did you, Mr Bruce?'

'It was something for him to do. And I enjoyed it. We all enjoy teaching, don't we? Be a different matter if we had to do it for our livings, I dare say.'

'We'd have taught Sophie too, dear,' said Mrs Bruce, 'but she wasn't keen to learn. I think the truth was she wasn't keen to learn from a couple of oldies. Well, you can understand it, can't you?'

'Mind you, he was a good student,' said Mr Bruce. 'They are at that age. Giles can drive as well as I can – better probably.'

'Talk about reversing into a marked space,' said his wife. 'I've never seen it done so well. You could drive a cab in London, I said to him, though of course he'll do something a lot superior to that, won't he?' She looked up into Wexford's face. 'He will, won't he, dear?'

He understood. 'I'm sure he will.'

'We're leaving tomorrow and – and Katrina's coming too. I hope it's only temporary. Frankly, I've never cared for Roger but still I hope it's not a permanent break. I hope it won't come to divorce for the children's sake.'

That would make the second partnership to come to grief as a result of this case, Wexford remarked as he and Burden went down the stairs. Sophie and her mother were still where he had left them. Katrina had lapsed back into sleep, the place and condition she escaped to. Sophie's eyes were fixed inscrutably on her.

'You said Matilda drove Giles to the station,' Wexford said. 'That would be Kingham station?'

'She drove him to Oxford.'

'And was he going to Heathrow from Oxford? Was he going to catch a domestic flight?'

For a moment she was perfectly silent. Then she screamed at the top of her voice, waking her mother, 'I don't know!'

It was wet and by now very dark, a starless, moonless night, though not yet six in the evening. Wexford and Burden stood under a lamp-post, in its brassy yellow light.

'Scott Holloway's father is called Peter,' said Wexford.

'How do you know?'

'I don't remember how. I just know.'

'He can't be *the* Peter. Sophie would have recognised him. For God's sake, he lives practically next door.'

'Nevertheless, let's go and find out a bit more about those Holloways.'

Chapter 24

Peter Holloway no more fitted the generally accepted image of a lover than his son would in a few years' time. He was tall enough but stout with it and moon-faced. Sitting very comfortably by a fire of real logs, a cup of some warm milky drink beside him, the newspaper on his knee, he looked as if this was his natural role and habitat. For no other occupation could he be so well adapted. Scott and his sisters were also in the room, all seated at a table playing Monopoly, and when Mrs Holloway sat down in an armchair next to a small table on which lay pale-blue knitting, Wexford felt he had strayed into a 1940s advertisement for some cosy aspect of family life.

Burden rushed straight into the middle of things. 'Did you know Joanna Troy personally, Mr Holloway?'

The man sat up a little, startled and defensive. 'I never met her. My wife sees to that sort of thing.'

'What sort of thing? The children's education?'

'All that sort of thing, yes.'

Wexford had his eyes on the boy. The Monopoly game had been suspended, apparently at Scott's wish, for one of his sisters still held the cup with the dice in it in her hand while the other's face had taken on a look of exasperation. Now the boy turned round and looked at his father.

Wexford said sharply, 'What time did you go to the Dades' house, Scott?'

It was a good thing the police weren't armed. He could cheerfully have shot Mrs Holloway. 'He told you, he didn't go there.' She had picked up her knitting and her fingers worked frenetically. 'How many times does he have to tell you?'

'Scott?' said Wexford.

He had been made in his father's image. He wasn't quite as fat – yet. His face was as round and his eyes as small. Piggy eyes, they used to be called, Wexford remembered.

'I know you did go there, Scott.'

The boy got up. He stood in front of Wexford. It was possible that at that school he went to they taught children to stand when they were addressed by a teacher. 'I didn't go in.'

'What did you do?'

'I went round there. In the evening. It was – I don't know what time, maybe nine or a bit earlier.' He said to his mother, 'You and Dad were watching TV. I went up the road to their house. There were lights on, I knew they were in. *Her* car was there.'

'Whose car, Scott?' said Burden.

'Miss Troy's, Joanna's.'

'And you changed your mind about going in when you saw her car? Why was that? She'd been your teacher too, hadn't she?'

He gave no answer, but he blushed. The dark-red spread all over his face until it was the colour of raw beef. Like a child half his age, he muttered, 'Because I hated her. I'm glad she's dead,' and before the tears gathering in his eyes could fall, he rushed from the room.

'She's got a new one.'

Dora's words greeted him as he walked in the door.

'Who's got a new what?'

'Sorry, that wasn't very clear, was it? Sylvia's got a new man. She brought him in here for a drink. They were on their way to a – well, a political meeting. There was to be a lecture. "The Way Forward to a New Left" or something like that.'

Wexford groaned. He sat down heavily in the middle of the sofa. 'I suppose he's tall and handsome and thick and deeply boring, is he? Or weedy and buck-toothed and brilliant and rude?'

'Not any of those. He looks a bit like Neil. He's quiet. Sizing up the situation, I imagine. Oh, and he teaches politics at the University of the South.'

'What's his name?'

'John Jackson.'

'Well, it's different. He's not a Marxist, is he? Not these days? Not in the twenty-first century?'

'I don't know? How am I supposed to know?'

'I wonder what Neil will say,' said Wexford rather sadly. He hoped the man would be good company, not a bore, kind to the children. But he strove always – though not always with success – not to worry about things he couldn't change. He believed his daughters loved him but nothing he could say or do carried much weight with them any more. Their contention was the usual one in any family disagreement, that a parent can't understand, and who was to say they weren't right?

Dora went back to her book. He switched his thoughts back to the Dades. Their family disagreement had been far from usual. Examining it while alone, he wondered if it was the world's first instance of a grandmother introducing her teenage grandchildren to drugs. He was prepared to give Matilda – dead Matilda – the benefit of the doubt and concede that it was probably done because she really believed cannabis would be therapeutic to these over-stressed children. She had been using it for so long herself, she might even have a medical reason, arthritis for instance, and rather than harming her it had taken away pain. Now he remembered the faint scent of it, no more than a hint, a breath, he had noticed when she passed him in his office.

In any case, those children would have been offered harder and more dangerous drugs every day at their school gates. Of course, that didn't in any way exculpate Matilda, and it was no wonder the parents were enraged. Katrina had turned her out of the house and her own son had supported his wife. No doubt it was dark. Very probably it was raining. No taxis were ever to be found in the Lyndhurst Drive–Kingston Gardens area. She would have had to walk, carrying those cases, as far as the station taxi rank or, instead, to the nearest hotel. Most old women would have been seriously distressed but Matilda wasn't most old women. She would have been angry, furious, or, as Katrina might put it, *incandescent.* Well, she had had her revenge.

Had Scott Holloway had his? Almost certainly not. As far as Wexford could see at present, all he had said established that Joanna and the Dade children were still in the house at nine and the only Peter in the case, apart from Buxton, had been watching television with his wife.

Before he got the chance to talk to Burden next day, something else happened. He had a visitor. How she ever got past the front desk he didn't know but guessed it was because they were short-staffed. Experienced people were all away with flu and temps were taking their place in the network that separated him from the public. She walked in and the girl who showed her up presented her as Ms Virginia Pascall. Wexford had never heard of her. He noticed – he couldn't help it – that she was young, still in her twenties, and quite startlingly beautiful. Apart from all that, the exquisite features, the long red-gold hair, the spectacular legs and stunning figure, he saw something else, stark madness in her blank blue stare and twisting, writhing hands.

'What can I do for you, Ms Pascall?'

Send for the attendants in white coats with the tranquillising syringes? She sat down on the edge of the chair, immediately jumped up again, put her hands on his desk, leant towards him. He could smell something on her breath, the scent of nail varnish perhaps or some sweet but non-alcoholic drink. Her voice was sweet, like the smell, but jerky and brittle.

'You have to know, he wants you to know, he killed her.'

'Who did he kill, Ms Pascall, and who is "he"?'

'Ralph. Ralph Jennings, the man I'm engaged to. The man I *was* engaged to.'

'Ah.'

'He's had secret meetings with her. It was a conspiracy. They were plotting to kill me.' She began to shudder. 'But they quarrelled over how to do it and he killed her.'

'Joanna Troy?'

Once he'd uttered the name, Wexford wished he hadn't. Virginia Pascall made a noise midway between an animal's roar and a human scream, then it was all screaming. For a moment he had no idea what to do. No one came. He'd have something to say about that once he'd got rid of her. But she stopped as abruptly as she'd begun and fell into the chair. It was as if the paroxysm had released something and for a while she was at peace. She leant across the desk and he looked into eyes which, in colour only, were normal human eyes.

'That night he killed her, I can prove he wasn't with me. I can prove anything. He ran her down in his car, you know. Her blood was on the wheels. I wiped it off and smelt it. That's how I know it was hers, it smelt of her, foul, stinking, disgusting.'

You were supposed to humour people like this. Or you were once. Perhaps in these psychiatric times that was no longer true. On the other hand, it couldn't do any harm. 'Where is he now? Is he at your home?'

'He's gone. He's left. He knew I'd kill him if he stayed. He ran her down outside our house. She was on her way to see me. Me!' The unsteady, sweet voice leapt an octave. 'He killed her to stop her coming to me. He drove backwards and forwards over the body till the car was all over blood. Blood, blood, blood!' She sang it, her voice reaching scream level. 'Blood, blood, blood!'

It was at this point that Wexford pressed the alarm bell on the floor under his desk.

'What happened then?' Burden asked over their coffee.

'Lynn came running and a couple of uniforms I've never seen before. One of them was a woman. This woman didn't fight them, though she spat at Lynn. I said to send for Crocker but they were already on the phone to Dr Akande.'

'Was she always like that or has the Joanna business driven her over the top?'

'I don't know. The main thing is for poor old Jennings that he's left her at last. That makes the third couple to split up through the Dade affair.'

'I'll be very surprised if George and Effie Troy make a fourth or Jashub and Thekla Wright, for that matter.'

Wexford managed a smile. 'Odd, though, isn't it? I think that's the only wise thing I've ever heard Katrina Dade say, that it's common for couples to split up when their child is missing or killed.'

'You'd expect a loss like that to bring them closer together,' Burden said.

'I don't know. Would you? Isn't it likely that they depend on the other one in ways they never have had to before? And that other, who has always seemed strong or comforting or optimistic, suddenly shows they're none of those things. They're just as weak and helpless as the other one and that seems to show they've been living for years under an illusion.'

'Maybe, but that wasn't what you wanted to talk about, was it?'

'No, I want to talk about Giles. Now it's pretty obvious Sophie invented Peter. She probably thought him up on the journey here from Gloucestershire. I'm sure Matilda was never told about him. So who did Matilda think had killed Joanna?'

'Whoever it was drove the car. Someone drove it.'

'Giles can drive.'

Burden said nothing, raised his eyebrows.

'You're looking astonished but you shouldn't be. You know what kids are, you've got three. I guarantee even that small one of yours is talking about the day he'll be allowed to drive a car. They're all mad to drive pretty well from the time they can walk. Giles might be a religious fanatic but he was no exception. His grandfather Bruce taught him on an old airfield.'

'I should have guessed,' Burden said ruefully.

Wexford shrugged. 'There were just the two of them escaping from Antrim, Giles and Sophie. Sophie and Giles. That's all. With a dead body in the car. Maybe in the boot. And they knew all the time they were eventually making for Trinity Lacy and Matilda. They knew she was "cool". Remember the pot-smoking.'

Burden gave a dry laugh. 'I must say that boy's

religious faith doesn't seem to have had much effect on his moral character. As for the girl . . .'

'You see them like that, do you? I see them as victims, truly as babes in the wood.'

'None of this is getting us any further with what Matilda did with Giles.' This was one of the times when Burden almost lost patience with Wexford. 'Where he is now, I mean. Where did she get him away to? Some friend we don't know about? What friend would consent to shelter a boy who'd just killed a woman . . .'

'Hold hard a minute. Is that what you're saying, that Matilda *knew* Giles killed Joanna Troy?'

'Or that Sophie did. But it wasn't Sophie she sent away. And if this friend wasn't told Giles was a killer, what were they told?'

'God knows,' said Wexford. 'This was Monday and Giles's picture was all over the papers by the following Wednesday. He would have been quickly recognised.'

Burden shrugged. 'Nevertheless, their friendship for or relationship to Matilda was such that they agreed to shelter him. It must be so and he has to be here. He couldn't get out of the country. Well, he could get to Shetland or the Channel Islands or Ireland but his aunt in Ulster hasn't got him, so who else is there in Ireland?'

Wexford turned to him, staring but at the same as if he were not seeing him. 'What did you say? About Ireland. Say it again.'

'I just said "Ireland". No, "Ulster".'

'Stay a minute. Don't go away. Something has just occurred to me. Suppose a British citizen born in Northern Ireland has a sort of dual citizenship . . . I'm going to phone the Irish embassy.'

*

He phoned Dade and sprang a surprise, one he'd sprung on Burden half an hour before. 'Giles,' he said, 'has he an Irish passport?'

Dade had groaned when he heard Wexford's voice. 'I suppose it's slipped your mind that this is Saturday?' Now he answered grudgingly, 'Well, yes, he has. Seeing he was born in Northern Ireland, he was eligible, and when he passed the Common Entrance to get into his school – did spectacularly well, in fact – well, I applied for an Irish passport for him. It was what he wanted. God knows why. Look, you're not saying he was planning this four years ago, are you?'

'Very unlikely, Mr Dade. I expect he thought it might come in useful. I wish you'd told me about this passport before. Why didn't you?'

'Because (a) I forgot about it and (b) I didn't suppose a son of mine could act the way he has done and do the things he's done. You'll be telling me next he killed that bitch Joanna Troy.'

Wexford didn't answer. 'Mr Dade, I'd like your permission to search your mother's house. With the cooperation of the Gloucestershire police.'

To his surprise Sophie came on an extension. He heard a soft click and then her breathing. 'Search all you like, as far as I'm concerned,' Dade said. 'The place won't be mine till we've got probate. You want me to ask my mother's solicitors?'

He had never been so willing to meet them halfway. Perhaps misery had sweetened his nature, though in Wexford's experience it seldom did improve anyone's.

'If you'd be so kind.'

'May I know what you're searching for?' A sarcastic edge to the question deprived it of its apparent politeness.

'I will be frank with you,' Wexford said. 'I want to

find the whereabouts of your son. And that's as good a way as any of making a start.'

'She knows.' He too had heard the breathing. 'She knows where he is.'

'I do not!' Sophie shouted it at the top of her voice.

'I'd fetch it out of her only I know you people would be down on me like a ton of bricks if I laid a finger on her.'

On the way there, and accompanied by two officers of the Gloucestershire Constabulary, Wexford sat silent in the car, his thoughts turned to his last visit there. All the time he had talked to Matilda Sophie had been in the house, concealed and laughing. Could anyone be blamed for taking it for granted no grandmother would give sanctuary to a child in opposition to that child's parents, to her own son? That was what he had done. By now he ought to know better than to take anything for granted. Yet only a few days ago he was assuming that no social worker who spent her time witnessing domestic violence and its results would willingly continue to live with a man who beat her.

His heavy sigh fetched a glance and bracing words from Burden. 'Cheer up, it may not be true. We're nearly there.'

Already Matilda's house had an unlived-in look and a stuffy, airless atmosphere. It was very cold. Regardless of the possibility of frozen pipes and subsequent water damage, the heating had been turned off. Wexford suggested that Burden and one of the Gloucestershire officers should begin the downstairs search while he and the other officer started on the upper floor.

The difficulty was that he had no idea what they were looking for. Perhaps he had simply supposed that this would suggest itself when they began. One thing would lead to another. He found himself rather distracted by Matilda's photographs, which proliferated up here even more than on the ground floor. At least, he assumed they were Matilda's, though they were unlike any of those he particularly associated with her and which her reputation rested on. These, on the staircase wall and following its angle, seemed to be views of a city with a large Gothic cathedral surmounted by twin spires, the same city pictured on the wall by the door that he had noticed last time. Between them was a print in sepia of what might have been the same city except that the cathedral had onion domes.

He was wasting time. He went into the principal bedroom, the one that had been Matilda's. He turned his attention first to the wardrobe and the pockets of coats and jackets, and when this yielded nothing, to the drawers of a desk and those of a tall chest. Matilda Carrish had kept no letters. What unpaid bills there had been, what bank statements, cheque-books, insurance policies and all the rest of the paraphernalia of modern paperwork, had been removed, no doubt by the firm of solicitors and executors of the will Roger Dade had spoken of. Wexford thought he had never before investigated such a barren desk. In the pigeonholes were four ballpoints and a fountain pen as well as that outdated substance, ink in a dark-blue bottle.

Inside the two clothes cupboards and the two chests of drawers all was neat and orderly, hanging garments, folded garments, black silk socks, no frivolities in the shape of old lady's lavender sachets or dried rose leaves. Creams and lotions in a top drawer but no make-up. Matilda Carrish had no doubt decided that at her age she must leave lipstick and eye shadow behind for ever. He never quite knew what made him open a particular jar labelled 'moisturiser'. Perhaps it was only because it looked, from the scratched lid and partly worn-off label, as if it had been long in use. He unscrewed the top and found himself looking at a brownish, rather fibrous, powder. The smell was unmistakeable. There is no more unique and distinctive scent. Cannabis sativa.

Well, there was bound to be some. All his find did was help confirm what the Dades had already told him. He found one thing in the bottom drawer that told him, along with the cannabis, that Matilda had been human after all: a thick pigtail of black silky hair, apparently cut off while still in its plait. Whose was it? Sophie's? Charlotte's? But Sophie's hair was brown and Charlotte's fairish. Wexford decided, and this made him smile to himself, that it must have been Matilda's own. Cut off, perhaps, sixty or seventy years ago and kept all that time. But hair never decayed, never disintegrated, lasted while teeth crumbled and nails fell to dust . . .

He turned his attention to her books, and found himself immediately diverted by their contents. It always amazed him that an officer could conduct this kind of search and, once he or she had flipped a book open and shaken it, give it no further attention and show no curiosity as to what it was about or who had written it. But it often happened and he had often wondered at it. These books held no revealing or incriminating documents. As well as the contemporary ones he came upon Cobbett's *Rural Rides* and Gilbert White's *The Natural History of Selborne*. There was some Thesiger, Kinglake's *Eothen* and T. E. Lawrence's *Seven Pillars of Wisdom*. Incongruously, a child's book was beside it, a book with a picture of a cartoon cat on its jacket and the title in some incomprehensible language.

He passed on to the spare bedrooms. In one the Gloucestershire officer was carefully removing small objects from a drawer, a comb, a couple of postcards, a music cassette, a tube of some cream a cosmetic company gave away as a 'free' gift, and laying them on top of a chest. Like those in the main bedroom, the books on the shelves here held no revealing or incriminating documents or photographs; they were travel books, mostly. He began taking them out in quest of some paper or card that might have been laid between the pages but also found himself, as he always did find himself in this situation, looking closely at them and reading extracts.

The cameras were no doubt downstairs along with rolls of film. If she had still worked, Matilda had by this time probably acquired a digital camera as well as the trusted conventional sort – or whatever the term was. What had he expected from this chest? The kind of treasure trove he hadn't found in the desk, presumably. But there was nothing. Underclothes, three pairs of tights, unworn and still in their transparent wrapping. The trouser-suited Matilda would have worn socks. And here they were, many pairs, nearly all of them fine black silk. Downstairs Burden had found the cameras. They had a cupboard to themselves along with tripods. But that was really all which had come to light apart from an address book in which a lot of the pages were quite blank. He looked curiously at the many phone numbers whose codes proclaimed them to be in foreign countries. Matilda had more friends abroad than here but there might be an easier way than by calling every one of those numbers . . .

This time, tired as he was, he had to go to the house. A phone call wouldn't do. Signs of the absence of women – Sophie hardly counted – were already apparent. Takeaway had been eaten by the two sole occupants and its remains, foil containers, greaseproof paper, plastic carriers, as well as a pungent spicy smell, lingered in the dusty living room. Roger Dade's breath smelt of garlic and tikka marsala.

Retreating a little, Wexford said to Sophie, 'In your grandmother's house is a children's book in a Scandinavian language and there are some photographs, apparently taken by her, of a city that looks as if it might be somewhere in northern Europe. Can you tell me anything about that?'

'I didn't know,' Sophie said, and he believed her. 'I've never seen the book and I never noticed the pictures.'

'The language', Dade said, 'is probably Swedish. My stepfather, as I suppose I'm bound to call him, lives in Sweden. I hardly know the man. I've only met him once. They were married over there and my mother used to go over a couple of times a year but that all stopped when she got past seventy-five. They may have divorced for all I know.'

Wexford tried to imagine a situation in which one didn't know one's mother's husband and didn't know whether she was divorced or not, tried and failed. But he believed Dade. It was typical. Probably it would be equally useless asking the man where in Sweden but he could lose nothing by trying.

'I told you. I thought I made myself clear. I only met the man once. All I know is he's called Philip Trent – Carrish was my mother's maiden name – and at one time he was a university lecturer or whatever the term is.'

'He wasn't at your mother's funeral.'

'If you're implying no one told him you're wrong – as usual. My sister tried to phone him and then she sent an e-mail. Whether or not it got there I wouldn't know. Probably he just couldn't be bothered to come. Maybe he's dead himself.'

*

All he could get from Charlotte MacAllister was a messsage on her answering machine. He thought of trying to find her husband, the 'high-ranking officer' in the Royal Ulster Constabulary, and then he decided the Internet might be easier. Some clever operator at work could find Philip Trent. He knew he was himself incapable of it. He could manage to name the universities of Sweden from an encyclopaedia and that was all. Stockholm, Uppsala, Lund . . . A young woman with a degree in computer studies, saying this was easy and implying, just, that with her talents she was capable of better things, got down to sorting out websites.

He began to walk home. He would have his dinner, hear the latest on Sylvia's new man – and please let it be cheerful encouraging news this time – and then come back for the search results. A fine, almost smoky, rain was falling, the kind of rain that is nearly mist, damp rather than wet, a mild hindrance to breathing. He saw Dorcas Winter, parcelled up in rainproof layers, delivering evening papers ahead, just turning out of Kingston Gardens into his own street. The large red plastic bag of papers she pushed along on what looked like a supermarket trolley. The rain was nearly as bad as fog, obscuring figures, turning them into ghostly shapes on a worn-out TV screen.

Wexford was quite close to the delivery girl before he saw it wasn't a girl at all but the newsagent himself. 'Good evening,' he said. At first the man failed to recognise him, then he did. 'Oh, good evening. Not a very good one, is it?'

'What's happened to Dorcas?'

'Gone to her violin lesson. I couldn't find anyone else to do the round.'

'If you've got a minute,' said Wexford, 'I'd like to

ask you something. You remember the Confessional Congregation last July? You were there?'

'Certainly I was there.' It was interesting how, as soon as the subject was changed from the mundane to matters of the Good Gospel Church, from being an ordinary pleasant tradesman Kenneth 'Hobab' Winter became pompous and self-important. 'I am always present at significant church functions. I am an elder, remember.'

'Yes, well, can you tell me how Giles Dade went to Passingham St John that night and how he returned to Kingsmarkham?'

'By what means of transport, do you mean? As a matter of fact, I can, as I was closely involved. There was no car available to take the boy. Many of our members, you must understand, came straight to the Congregation from their places of work. Mrs Zurishaddai Wilton escorted him on the train from Kingsmarkham to Passingham Park and thence by taxi to Passingham Hall. The return journey was made in my car, driven by me and accompanied by my wife and Mr and Mrs Nun Plummer.'

'Was he upset? Distressed?'

'Who? Giles Dade? Not at all. He was happy and relieved. "Bubbly", I think one could say.'

'Really? He had just confessed what sins he had to confess. It must have been embarrassing, not to say – well, disturbing, with the congregation all chanting.'

'Not at all,' said Winter again, urbanely this time. 'People feel cleansed and liberated. It's a kind of God-given psychoanalysis. Giles felt free for the first time in his life as people do when they confront God after cleansing.'

'Thank you,' said Wexford. 'That's very helpful. I may as well take my paper. Save you delivering it.'

Smiling, Winter passed over the *Kingsmarkham Evening Courier* with a hand in a wet woollen glove.

'Well, goodnight, then.' He was a normal man again.

Wexford walked to his house, imagining the feelings of Giles Dade on that car journey. He must have made some kind of confession, perhaps of the kind of clumsy and unsatisfying sexual adventures a boy of fifteen would have had, confessed too to teenage shoplifting indulged in for bravado and the occasional pre-Matilda spliff. Then, fresh from the howling mob 'shouting and singing', he had to travel home sandwiched no doubt between the Plummers and facing the uncompromising backs of Mr and Mrs Winter. Yet he had been 'bubbly'? It was a word in popular use which Wexford loathed and here it seemed singularly inapt. Perhaps the other passengers in the car had congratulated him, inducing in him a kind of mad euphoria. That was the only explanation that seemed reasonable.

He was back in his office by eight and had been there only five minutes when the computer studies woman walked in with a couple of sheets of A4 on which he could see text in unmistakable Internet type.

Philip Trent wasn't dead, but very much alive and living in Uppsala. His name hadn't been in the address book. Perhaps no one would enter a husband's name and phone number into a personal directory, however apart or estranged they might be. She would have known it by heart.

Chapter 25

Ice and snow were to be expected, a kind of Ultima Thule on the northern edge of the world. He supposed he was lucky to be sent. Police officers normally looked on it as a perk to be sent abroad – only he was ungrateful enough to wish that, in March, it could have been Italy or Greece. Maybe where Burden would be going next day on his fortnight's leave, the south of Spain.

But it was Sweden. He had managed, at last, to speak to Philip Trent. And after one short phone conversation he knew, in Vine's words, that he had 'a right one here'. The old man spoke much the same kind of English as Mr Shand-Gibb, former owner of Passingham Hall, but Trent's had a faintly alien intonation to it, not an accent – he was plainly a native English speaker – but the slight lilt that comes from habitually speaking a Scandinavian language. He admitted, without shame or apparent guilt of any kind, that Giles Dade was staying with him in his house in Fjärdingen, a district of Uppsala. A quarter or 'farthing' in mediaeval times, he explained kindly, though he hadn't been asked, and Wexford thought of *The Lord of the Rings* and hobbit country where counties were similarly named.

'Oh, yes, Mr Wexford, he's been here since early December. We spent a pleasant Christmas together. A nice boy. Pity about the fanaticism but I don't think we shall hear much more of it.'

Indeed? 'He must he fetched home, Professor Trent.'

An efficient young woman who spoke perfect English had revealed Trent's rank to him and that he formerly held the Chair of Austro-Asiatic Languages (whatever they might be) at the University of Uppsala and that now, although well past the retirement age of sixty-five, he retained his own office for research purposes at the university as one of its distinguished former faculty members.

'I am not up to travelling, as you will appreciate. Besides, I am too busy, I have my research to do here. Investigation of Khmer, Pear and Stieng, for instance, is still in its infancy, a situation not helpful to linguisticians and brought about by the warfare which raged for such an extended period over Cambodia.' He spoke as if the only consequence of that war was its effect on the languages spoken by the people. 'Perhaps you could send someone?'

'I thought of coming over myself,' said Wexford tentatively.

'Did you? We're enjoying rather pleasant weather at present. Cool and fresh. I suggest you put up at the Hotel Linné. It enjoys very attractive views across the Linnaean gardens.'

When he had rung off Wexford looked up Austro-Asiatic Languages in the encyclopaedia and found there were dozens if not hundreds of them, mostly spoken in south-east Asia and eastern India. He wasn't much wiser, though he managed to connect 'Khmer' with the Khmer Rouge. The section on Uppsala was more rewarding. Not only the botanist Linnaeus came from there, but also Celsius, the temperature man, Ingmar Bergman and Dag Hammarskjöld, second secretary-general of the United Nations, while Strindberg had attended Trent's university. He wondered what Trent had meant by 'rather pleasant weather'. At least, it wouldn't be raining . . .

At Heathrow he went into a bookshop and searched the shelves for something to read on the flight. A guide to Sweden he already had. Besides, he wasn't looking for a travel book but anything, fiction or non-fiction, which might spontaneously take his fancy. Much to his surprise, among the 'classics', he found a little slender book he had never before heard of: *A Short Residence In Sweden, Norway and Denmark* by Mary Wollstonecraft. Confessing to himself that he had never come across any work by Mary Shelley's mother apart from *A Vindication of the Rights of Woman*, he bought it.

The flight went at five. It was a mild day, very damp and misty, though no rain had fallen since the previous evening, but Wexford had rooted out his winter coat, a very old tweed affair, unworn for several years and superseded by raincoats. He laid it across his lap, settled down in his seat and opened his book. Unfortunately, Mary Wollstonecraft had spent more time in Norway and Denmark than in Sweden and while in that country had visited no more than Gothenburg and the extreme west. Wexford's hope that she might have given him a picture of Uppsala in the last years of the eighteenth century faded fast. It would, anyway, be very different today, as would the diet of smoked meat and salt fish denounced by the author, and the pallid, heavy appearance of the people. Certainly the poverty would be past and gone but the 'degree of politeness in their address' might, he hoped, remain.

He had decided to proceed straight to the Hotel Linné and meet Giles and Professor Trent first thing next morning. By now the Uppsala police knew all about Giles and the possibility of further spiriting him away was gone. Wexford had written 'Hotel Linné, Uppsala' on a piece of paper but the taxi driver at Arlanda Airport spoke enough English to understand his directions.

It was dark. The drive took them along a wide, straight road through what seemed to be forests of fir and birch. The houses he saw, or made out through the fairly well-lit darkness, looked modern, uniform in materials – red-painted weatherboarding, leaded roofs – if varied in design. Then the lights of the city in the distance showed him with dramatic impact a huge cathedral standing on an eminence, a black silhouette, its twin spires pointing at the jewel-blue starlit sky. In Matilda's mezzotint it had onion domes. Only in the very old pictures were there Gothic spires. He didn't understand, unless the images weren't of Uppsala at all but of some other north-European city.

A formidable castle on another hill, serene buildings he thought might be baroque, a fast-flowing black river. He got out of the taxi and the driver patiently sorted out his kronor for him. Oddly enough, he felt he could trust the man not to swindle him, something that wouldn't be true everywhere. Outdoors only briefly, he was chilled to the bone by the bitter cold. But inside the Hotel Linné it was cheeringly warm. Everyone spoke English, everyone was polite, pleasant, efficient. He found himself in an austere room, pale, rather bare but with everything he could possibly need. Boiling hot water gushed out of the taps. He had eaten on the plane and wasn't hungry now. In some trepidation he followed the hotel's telephone directions and dialled Philip Trent's number. Instead of a flood of Swedish, Trent's voice said, 'Hello?'

Wexford told him he had arrived, would see him in the morning at nine thirty, according to their prior arrangement. Trent, who conformed uncomfortably to clichéd images of the absent-minded professor, so much so that his manner seemed assumed, had apparently forgotten who he was. Wexford wouldn't have been surprised to have been greeted in Wa, Tin or Ho, some of the Austro-Asiatic languages he had discovered existed. But Trent, saying vaguely that he must 'come back to earth', agreed that nine thirty 'would do'. Coffee was generally available at that time. He managed to imply that he was living in a restaurant.

'My house is on the corner of Östraågatan and Gamla Torget. That is "East Street" and "Old Square" to you. More or less.' That was more or less the meaning or was the house more or less there? 'It's on the river. You can ask the hotel for a plan.'

Philip Trent sounded profoundly uninterested in his visit. Wexford had a long hot shower and went to bed. But the street outside was noisier than he had expected. Just as the place was clean and cold, austere and not very populous, so he had anticipated utter silence. Instead, the voices of young people and their music reached him, the sound of something being kicked into the gutter, a motor bike noisily started up, and he remembered that this was a university city, Sweden's oldest, its Oxford, and one of the oldest in Europe, but nevertheless full of modern youth. He sat up in bed reading Mary Wollstonecraft on the ease of Swedish divorce and the superiority of the little towns to similar places in Wales and western France. Eventually quiet came and he slept.

The morning was bright and cold. But where was the snow? 'We haven't had much for many years,' said a multilingual girl serving breakfast, or rather, directing guests to the buffet tables. 'Like all the world, we are affected with global warming.' She added severely, looking into Wexford's eyes, 'Are you knowing Sweden has the best environmental record in the earth?'

Humbly, he said he was glad to hear it. She returned to his table with a plan of the city she had procured for him from reception. 'There. Fjärdingen. Not very large, all things are very easy for you to find.'

It was early still. He went out into the 'Farthing' and found himself in a place the like of which he had never seen before. It wasn't that it lacked the modern appurtenances of the west. Far from it. He suddenly realised how odd it was, how refreshing in more senses than one, to see the latest models of cars, an Internet café, a CD shop, fashionably dressed women, a smart policeman directing traffic, yet at the same time smell pure crystalline air, unpolluted and clean. The sky was a pale sharp blue, scrawled over with wind-torn shreds of cloud. Some of the buildings were modern but most eighteenth-century, yellow and white and sepia, Swedish baroque. They would already have been here if Mary Wollstonecraft had passed this way. Not many cars were about, not many people. Walking towards the Linnaean gardens, he recalled that the entire population of this large country was only eight million, less than three million in Wollstonecraft's time.

He really only wanted to step into the gardens or look into them over the wall because the night before he had started out he had quickly read up on Linnaeus and his earth-wandering journeys to find new species. It wasn't the best time of the year unless you were a plant enthusiast and expert, everything was still asleep, waiting for a later spring than England enjoyed. He thought of his own poor garden, swamped by unnatural rains. If it was true that this nation had the world's best environmental record, would their thoughtful prudence save them from coming catastrophes?

It was nine o'clock. He heard the chimes begin and, as if it were immediately above him, the deep-throated tolling of a clock striking the hour. Quickening his pace, he began to walk in the direction of that sound and, as buildings opened and parted to afford him a panorama, saw the great cathedral standing before him on an eminence. A line of prose came back to him, he had read it years ago, he couldn't remember when or where, but it was from the writings of Hans Andersen who, visiting this city, spoke of the cathedral 'lifting its stone arms to heaven'. It was exactly like that, he thought, as the final stroke of nine died away. The Domkyrka was crimson and grey, clerical grey, dark and austere, huge, formidable and as unlike any cathedral he knew as could be imagined. Only its straight lines and pointed arches recalled English Gothic. It made cathedrals at home look cosy. Below and beside it hung the buildings of the university, Odins lund and high above, the vast bastion of the castle with its two cylinder towers capped in round lids of lead. He was looking at the picture Matilda Carrish had hung on her staircase, even the sky was the same, pale, ruffled, a north-edge-of-the-world backdrop, but the cathedral's spires in her mezzotint had been onion domes . . .

Too early yet to make his way to the man who had been her husband. He came to a modern, rather ugly street of the kind of shops he most hated in English cities, the kind of architecture everyone dislikes but which goes on being used; then, turning his back on it, to the river. Called the Fyris, it scurried along to divide the town. Ice-cold and glittering dark-blue its little waves looked as they rushed and tumbled towards the bridge and the next bridge and the next.

Standing on this one, he was glad of his old tweed coat and he noticed everyone was more warmly wrapped than they would have been in Kingsmarkham. Scarves and hats and boots protected them from the knife-blade wind and the icy bite of the air. He watched his own breath make a beam of mist.

It would be pleasant walking along this river bank in summer, past the little shops and cafés, watching the boats. When would summer come? May or June, he supposed. On the western side he walked to the next bridge and, looking across the river, realised he had reached his destination. According to the map, that was Gamla Torget on the other side and the river bank street that ran into it, Östraågatan. So the ochre-coloured house, three floors high, its plain windows in its plain façade each with its pair of useful shutters, must be Trent's. The shutters were open now, the panes of glass gleaming in the thin sunlight. Like them, the front door was painted white. No Swedish architect, he thought, had wasted time or money on spurious house adornment, and the result was peaceful, calming, serene, if a little stark. As the cathedral clock chimed the half-hour, he crossed the bridge and rang Professor Trent's doorbell.

Trent himself would answer it, he had supposed, or whatever might be this cool and progressive nation's idea of a servant, the maker of nine-thirty coffee perhaps, a young girl rather like the severe waitress at the Linné. Very unexpected was to come face-to-face with a boy of sixteen, dark, extremely tall, but with the almost fragile thinness of adolescence.

'Philip said I should let you in,' Giles Dade said. 'I mean he said *I* should and not anyone else.'

Chapter 26

The warmth he had come to expect but not the eighteenth-century interior and early-Victorian furniture, white and blue and gleaming gilt. Everything awesomely and most unacademically clean. The boy hadn't spoken again. He was a good-looking boy with regular features, dark-blue eyes and luxuriant dark hair, which Wexford fancied had been left to grow for three months, perhaps the first time such laxness had been permitted. He showed Wexford into a living room that spanned the ground floor of the house. Almost the first things he noticed were the books in a bookcase like the one Matilda had and with more pictures of a tailless cat on their jackets. *Pelle Svanslös,* he read on a spine, not attempting to pronounce it. More pale delicate furniture, a ceiling-high stove in one corner encased in white and gold porcelain tiles, and a view of the river from the front windows and of a small bare garden at the back.

The old man who joined them within a moment or two was tall and nearly as skinny as Giles. Perhaps once, half a century ago and more, he had looked like Giles, and he still had the copious hair, now quite white. His expression was not so much irritable as preoccupied, distrait. It was apparent he looked on this development as an intrusion on a largely unvarying scholarly life.

'Well, yes, good morning,' he said in his Shand-Gibb voice. 'Please don't trouble yourself about this. I shall not be going to the university this morning. Don't feel you have to, er, speed things up.' He brought out this phrase as if uttering an outrageous piece of recent slang. Wexford understood he was dealing with a man so self-absorbed that he genuinely believed others must be exclusively concerned with anxieties about his comfort. 'Take your time. Sit down. Oh, you are sitting down, yes.'

He turned to Giles, addressed him in what was presumably Swedish, to which Giles responded in the same tongue. Wexford had to stop himself gaping. Trent said, when the boy had gone, 'A very simple language to learn, Swedish. All the Scandinavian languages are. Nothing to it. Inflected, of course, but in an entirely logical way – unlike some I could name.' Wexford was afraid he might but do so and with examples, but he continued on the subject of Swedish. 'I picked it up myself – oh, a hundred years ago – in a month or so. Giles is taking a little longer. I thought he should occupy himself usefully while here. Naturally, I have seen to the continuance of his education – and not only in that particular respect.'

He spoke as if Giles's missed schooling was the only aspect of his flight likely to give anyone much concern. Wexford was for a moment struck dumb. But when Giles returned with coffee pot and cups and saucers on a tray, he addressed the boy.

'Giles, I intend to return to the United Kingdom this afternoon on the two thirty p.m. flight to Heathrow and I have a ticket for you as well. I expect you to return with me.'

He also expected resistance from one or both of them. But Giles said only, 'Oh, I'll come.' He poured coffee, handed Wexford a cup and the milk jug. 'I know I have to go back. I always knew I'd have to some time.'

The old man was looking out of the window, not as if pretending tact or insouciance but surely because he really was thinking of something quite other, Palaungic syntax perhaps. The boy looked up, looked straight at Wexford, his face taking on that curious collapsing look, a crumbling or melting, that precedes tears. 'I'll come with you,' he said. An effort was made, his face set and there were no tears. 'How is my sister?'

'She's fine.' She wasn't but what else could he say? Certainly not at this stage that she had been abandoned by their mother. The scalding coffee alerting him and waking him in a bracing way, he turned his attention to the owner of this house. 'May I know what possessed you, Professor Trent, when you gave shelter to Giles? What were you thinking of, a responsible man, a respected scholar of your age? Didn't you consider your civic duty if nothing else?'

'"Possessed" me,' said Trent, smiling. 'I like that. I used to think, when I was young, how amazing it would be to be actually possessed. By some kind of spirit, I mean. Would it bring with it the gift of tongues, for instance? Imagine being suddenly endowed with the ability to speak Hittite?' Giles's shocked expression halted him. 'Oh, come on, Giles, you've given up all that fundamentalist nonsense, you know you have. You've told me so often enough. You know very well it's not possible to be possessed by a demon, gift of tongues or not.'

'I used to think', said Giles, 'that Joanna was possessed by one. They said a demon was what made people behave like that.' He didn't specify who 'they' were but it was apparent he meant the Good Gospellers. 'They said *I* had a demon that made me do what I did.'

'You know better now, an enlightened young person like you.'

Wexford thought it time to put a stop to this. 'Professor Trent, you haven't answered my questions.'

'Have I not? What were they? Oh, yes, something about my civic duty not to harbour fugitive criminals. Well, I've never supposed I had a civic duty and Giles isn't a criminal. You've just said that yourself.' He broke into a flood of Swedish and Giles nodded. 'I'm not particularly responsible either, I've never had the least interest in law or politics or, come to that, religion. I've always considered I had quite enough to do elucidating the knotty problems of the languages spoken by seventy million people.'

More incomprehensible asides to Giles prompted Wexford to say testily, 'Please don't speak in Swedish. If you persist I must ask to talk to Giles alone. I may do that, he is over sixteen now. I take it that your late wife telephoned you and asked you to receive Giles?'

'That is correct,' said Trent slightly more affably. 'Poor Matilda. She knew I would do anything for her except live in the United Kingdom of Great Britain and Northern Ireland.' He shuddered artificially. 'She knew I was exactly the man to give sanctuary to someone fleeing its justice. Besides, my housekeeper had moved up to Umea and it seemed to me Giles might be an adequate substitute for a while. I am, oddly enough, quite a domesticated man, but I need some assistance. I must tell you, I've grown quite attached to this boy. He performed a few tasks about the house, running errands, making the beds and the coffee – now is that an example of zeugma, Giles?'

Giles grinned. 'No. It would be if you'd said, "making haste and the coffee". Yours is syllepsis.'

'Not quite but we won't go into it now,' said Trent. 'I would have been a good deal less happy, Inspector, if Matilda had sent me a fool. The housework accomplished would hardly have been a compensation for lack of mental ability. Am I coming close to solving your problems?'

Wexford didn't answer. He saw that pursuing this was useless. And what did he intend to do if he got some sort of admission out of Trent? Have him extradited? The whole notion was ludicrous. Perhaps all he was after was that rather contemptible goal, revenge. Not quite abandoning the idea of it, he said, 'You are aware, Mr Trent, that your wife is dead?'

At that Giles turned away his face but Trent said only, 'Oh, yes, I knew. Matilda's daughter told me. I might have gone to the funeral – not that I approve of funerals – and even if it had meant passing the time of day with Giles's appalling parents, but I could hardly leave Giles here alone. Apart from all that, I had just reached a crucial point in my research into the early proliferation of Pear, what I believe is called a breakthrough.'

'I won't ask you what Ms Carrish's motive was. In asking you to receive Giles, I mean. I know what it was.'

Giles looked at him enquiringly but he didn't elucidate. 'You travelled on your Irish passport,' he said. 'Before you left your home with Sophie you phoned Matilda, knowing she would help you, and she suggested you bring your Irish passport with you but leave the British one behind – to fool the police. Am I right?'

Giles nodded. 'What happened to Matilda?'

'She had a stroke,' Wexford said. 'Sophie was with her. She'd been with her all the time. She phoned the emergency services and then, of course, she had to give herself up. There was nothing else for it.'

'We should have done that in the first place, shouldn't we? Phoned the emergency services, I mean.' He didn't need an answer. He knew what

Wexford would say, what everyone would say. 'I thought no one would believe me. They'd think what Matilda thought and they wouldn't be so – so understanding.'

'You can tell me about it on the flight,' Wexford said. 'And now you'd better get your things together. We'll take ourselves to the airport, have some lunch first.'

Trent had been silent through most of this. Now he turned round and fixed his eyes, cold and blue as the Fyris, first on Wexford, then on the boy, and there they lingered. 'If I'd known it was going to take such a short time I wouldn't have rearranged my schedule.' You could hear the quotation marks clanging into place on either side of the final word. 'I suppose I can get up to the university now before any more time is wasted.'

'I'll come back,' the boy said eagerly. 'You know what we said. In two years' time I'll come back here to the university.' In the silence which followed he looked at Wexford. 'I will, won't I?'

'Let's hope so,' Wexford said. He turned to Trent. 'Tell me something. The cathedral here has two Gothic spires. When it was built in the fourteenth century it must have had Gothic spires. But in the prints I saw in Ms Carrish's house from the eighteenth and nineteenth centuries it's the same cathedral but it's got onion domes. Why?'

Trent looked deeply bored and at the same time harassed. 'Oh, there was an enormous fire here and the towers fell down or something like that and they put those onion things there and then at the end of the nineteenth *they* were out of fashion so they tore them down and put Gothic spires up again. Ridiculous.'

'Could I . . .' Giles said to him, 'could I have a copy of *Pelle*? Kind of as a souvenir?'

'Oh, take it, take it,' said Trent testily. 'And now if you'll excuse me . . .'

At the duty-free Wexford bought perfume for Dora, bearing in mind Burden's pre-Christmas advice on this subject. Giles drank a can of Coke and Wexford, without much enthusiasm, a small and very expensive bottle of sparkling water. The boy was subdued and quiet, evidently fearful of this return home and reluctant to leave the country that had received him. He still stared nostalgically out of the airport windows towards where the flat plain of Upplands lay.

The flight was delayed but only by twenty minutes. Wexford gave Giles the window seat. As they took off the woman in the seat across the aisle crossed herself, a little shamefacedly it seemed to Wexford. The boy, who had also witnessed this, speaking for the first time since they fastened their seatbelts, said, 'I've given up all that.'

'All what?' Wexford thought he knew but he needed to ask.

'You'd call it fundamentalism.' Giles made a face. 'The Good Gospel, all that. What happened cured me. I thought – I thought they were – well, what they said, *good*. I wanted to be good. I mean, in the widest possible sense – d'you know what I mean?'

'I think so.'

'You see, the way people behave – I mean people my age – makes me feel sick. My sister's getting that way. The sex and the words they use and the way they – they sort of mock anything religious or moral or whatever. The foul stuff on TV, I mean comedy shows and that. And I thought – I thought I wanted to keep myself away from all that, keep myself *clean*.

'The church I went to wasn't any good. That was St Peter's. They didn't seem to know what they believed or what they wanted. The Good Gospel people seemed so sure. There was just one way for them, you did all those things they said and you'd be all right. That's what I liked. Do you see?'

'Maybe. Why did you want the book?'

'*Pelle Svanslös*? *Svanslös* means "the tailless one". They're children's books about a cat and his friends, and they all live in Fjärdingen, near where I was. I had to have something to remind me.'

'Yes. You liked it there, didn't you? Now why don't you tell me what happened that weekend when Joanna came to stay? I've heard your sister's version and most of it wasn't true.'

'She tells lies all the time. But it's not her fault.'

'Now I want to hear the truth, Giles.'

The aircraft had begun its journey along the runway, proceeding slowly at first, then faster as the captain called to cabin crews to take their seats for take-off. Smoothly they soared into the air, from blue sky into blue sky for there was no cloud barrier to break through.

'I'll tell you the truth,' the boy said. 'I've wanted to do that for a long time but I've been – I've been afraid.' His face had whitened and as he turned his head to look at Wexford his expression was desperate. 'You have to believe me. I didn't – kill Joanna. I didn't do anything to her, not anything at all.'

'I know *that*,' Wexford said. 'I knew that before I found out where you were.'

Chapter 27

'There seem to be a lot of people getting off scot-free,' grumbled the Assistant Chief Constable.

'I wouldn't say that, sir,' Wexford said robustly. 'We've a murder charge, one for concealing a death, another for wasting police time. Even if the boy gets no more than probation and a period of community service, his conviction will be on his record for ever. I very much doubt, for instance, if the Swedish authorities will let him enter the country to attend the University of Uppsala when the time comes, which is what he wants to do.'

'And you call that punishment?'

'For him it will be. His sister's punishment is to have to go on living with their father.'

He had submitted his report to James Freeborn and explained it in detail. Now he was due to meet Burden and enlighten him. It was, of course, a wet evening in April, the fields surrounding Kingsmarkham permanently waterlogged but not under water. From where Wexford walked down the High Street towards the Olive and Dove those meadows simply looked a brilliant fresh green in the yellow clouded sunset. At the Queen Street turning he made a detour. Curiosity impelled him and, sure enough, the newsagent's, normally open until 8 p.m., was closed 'until further notice'. Perhaps it was a sign, perhaps this was the moment to stop taking that absurd anachronism, a provincial evening paper. Who needed it? Who wanted it? Still, if it disappeared many would lose their jobs and there were other newsagents in the neighbourhood to distribute it . . .

His digression had made him a little late. Burden was already in their 'snug', the small room tucked away in a back region but still with access to the saloon bar, the only corner of the drinking areas of the hotel, as Wexford sometimes said, to be free of music, fruit machines, food and children. Nor were there posters asking who wanted to be a millionaire, the local and live version of the television programme, no advertisements for tugs-of-war or clairvoyant dog contests, attractions it had long been assumed at the Rat and Carrot, and was now assumed all over the town, to be demanded indiscriminately by everyone. The snug, where Burden stood with his back to an enormous coal fire in a small grate, was a very small room with brown woodwork and brown-papered walls on which hung very dark pictures of a vaguely hunting-print kind. At least, from what you could make out in the gloom, they were of animals on foot and men on horseback chasing things through bracken, bramble and briar. If no one had smoked much in this room for several years, time was when many had. As the bar rooms of the Olive and Dove were never decorated and probably never had been since the beginning of the twentieth century, the smoke of several million cigarettes had mounted to the once cream-coloured ceiling and stained it the dark mahogany of the furniture.

Two tables and six chairs were the snug's only furniture. On the table nearer the fire stood two tankards of beer, two packets of crisps and some cashew nuts in a dish. It was enormously, but not unpleasantly, hot. Burden, deeply tanned from his holiday, was dressed in one version of his weekend garb, a tweed suit with caramel shirt and tie that fortuitously matched the ceiling.

'Raining again,' Wexford said.

'I hope you've got more to say than that.'

Wexford sat down. 'Too much, I dare say you'll think. It's nice here, isn't it? Quiet. Peaceful. I wonder if this will be the end of the United Gospel Church. Probably, for a while.' He took a swig of his lager, thought of opening one of the crisp packets but changed his mind with a sigh. 'All the time we thought this case was about the Dade children but it wasn't. Not really. They were just pawns. It was about the conflict between the Good Gospellers and Joanna Troy – or, rather, people like Joanna Troy in the broadest sense.'

'What does that mean?'

'I'll explain. There was an aspect of the Good Gospellers we knew about but to which we neglected to give the importance it deserved: their keenness on "purity". I should have paid more attention to it because it was one of the first things about the church's aims that Jashub Wright mentioned to me. He talked about something he called "inner cleanliness" and all I could think of was Andrews Liver Salts, which, in case you're too young to know, was a constipation remedy when I was a child. "Inner cleanliness" was their slogan. I suppose that's why I didn't pay any attention to the fact that it was also the Good Gospellers' slogan. Only they didn't mean what today is called clearing the body of toxins, they meant sexual purity, *chastity*. Unchastity was the prime sin new converts were expected to be open about when they were brought to the Confessional Congregation.'

'I don't imagine', said Burden, sitting, 'that Giles Dade had much of that to confess. He was only fifteen.'

'Then there you'd be wrong. He had some revelations for that bunch of latter-day saints or however they think of themselves. But we'll leave him for the moment and get back to the Good Gospellers themselves. Like many such fundamentalists, they weren't much concerned with other sins, things that maybe you and I would call sins, if we were inclined that way. I mean violence, assault, bodily harm, cruelty, stealing, lying and simple unkindness, none of that bothered them. And I get the distinct impression from Giles that they would have been impatient with anyone who wasted their time confessing to hitting his wife or neglecting his children. It was sex they were concerned with, pre- and extramarital sex, fornication and adultery, most of it in their view caused by women and their tempting ways, rather in the way the early fathers of the Roman Catholic Church thought about it or some modern American cults. Sex, according to Giles, must in their view be confined exclusively within marriage and not too much of it there. Ideally, it should be restricted to the procreation of children.'

Burden nodded. 'Sure, but where does Giles come in?'

'Let's move on to Joanna Troy now. Joanna was apparently an entirely normal young woman, clever, gifted, nice-looking, a good teacher and potentially a successful person with a full life ahead of her. But she had already done a good deal to make that full life look unlikely.'

'What do you mean?'

Wexford looked up at the window, at the rain lashing against it and the dusk deepening outside. The curtains, of figured brown velvet, looked as if they had never been drawn since someone first hung them on their mahogany pole thirty or forty years before. He got up and tugged at them, releasing clouds of tobacco-smelling dust. As they met across the window the decay of years showed in the transparent ragged areas where they were coming apart. Both of them laughed.

'I only wanted to shut out the weather,' Wexford said and, after a pause, 'You asked me what I meant. When Joanna was a teenager she was attracted by her contemporaries, like most people of her age. At fifteen she lost her mother. What that meant to her we shall never know and I'm not a psychologist, but I'd guess she was very traumatised by that loss, especially as her sole parent then was that dreary old windbag George Troy with about as much understanding as a flea. Maybe an effect of it was to make her revert to childhood and to the companionship of children, though she was no longer a child. Maybe if she had had brothers none of this would have happened.

'The first thing to happen, or the first we know about, was the incident at school with Ludovic Brown. He was younger than she, probably prepubertal, and when Joanna made advances to him he was frightened and repelled her. She did all she knew how to do then – she fought him. He wouldn't, shall we say, love her? – so she beat him up. Revenge and anger and the misery of rejection all went into it. The consequences of that we know. His death, was an accident, quite separate from this case.

'Joanna must have had other relationships with boys, some of them satisfactory, but as she grew older and the ages of the boys remained the same, that is in their early or mid-teens, her tastes began to look unnatural. But she was trapped in adolescence by the trauma of her mother's death which happened when she was sixteen.'

Burden interrupted him. 'Are you saying Joanna Troy was a paedophile?'

'I suppose I am. We think of paedophiles as men and their victims as either girls or boys. Older women having a taste for young boys doesn't seem to come into the same category, largely, I think, because most men, when told about it, tend to make "Aarrgh" noises and say they should have been so lucky.'

Burden pulled a face that had a grin in it. 'I wasn't going to say that but they do have a point. You know me, you think I'm a bit of a prude, but even I can't imagine a boy of fifteen with all that testosterone slurping about inside him saying no to a good-looking woman ten or twelve years older than himself.'

'You'd better imagine it, Mike, because it happened. Only say seventeen years older. But first came Joanna's marriage. Ralph Jennings was in his early twenties when she met him but he looked years younger. Those very fair people do. Unfortunately, they also age correspondingly faster. I think Joanna believed Jennings might be her salvation. He was a passive yes-man but quite bright, a potential high earner, they had plenty in common. Perhaps if she was with him she'd stop fancying boys ten years her junior. This proclivity of hers, after all, wasn't just a nuisance, it was as much against the law as if she'd been a middle-aged man and the boys girls in their teens.

'But, sadly for her, Jennings started to go bald. His face reddened. Domestic life ruined his boyish figure. Sex was not only no longer the fun it had been, it was becoming distasteful. The marriage broke up. But Joanna remained in Kingsmarkham and in her prestigious job teaching at Haldon Finch. Instead of controlling her impulses towards boys of fourteen or fifteen, she let rip, as people so often do when some long-term relationship comes to an end.' Wexford paused, thinking of Sylvia, wondering how many more there would be before things worked out for her. 'She was in exactly the right place for a female paedophile, wasn't she?' he went on. 'A mixed school where she taught students of the age she most fancied. And in a much better position than her male counterparts, for young girls who may often have been raped or at least seduced are far more likely to complain than boys enjoying sex for the first time.

'Damon Wimborne didn't complain. He would happily have continued his relationship with Joanna for months if not years. You talk of testosterone but we forget the idealistic aspect, we forget how prone young boys are to worship and put the adored one on a pedestal. Damon was in love with Joanna, "whatever that may mean", as Jennings and a more eminent person put it. But it's a sad fact that for some people, having a sexual partner in love with them is the most off-putting thing. It put Joanna off and her feelings for Damon cooled to a point of – nothing. But in a way, she was still a teenager and always would be. Teenagers are rude to their contemporaries – and others – and they say bluntly what they think. She told him she was no longer interested in no uncertain terms, probably brutal terms. We misquote that most popular of aphorisms and say, "Hell hath no fury like a woman scorned." But the lines are: "Heaven hath no rage like love to hatred turned, nor hell a fury like a woman scorned." Love can turn to hatred in men as well as women and that's what Damon's did. He was scorned and he needed to lash back. Physically, he was a mature man but he was only fifteen, his mind was fifteen. He said he'd seen her steal a twenty-pound note from his backpack . . .'

'Yes. It fits.' Burden tapped Wexford's tankard. 'Another?'

'In a minute. The head teacher couldn't understand why Joanna didn't fight it and clear her name. But Joanna dared not do that. Everything would come out if she did. She knew her career as a teacher was over, there was no help for it. Resign now and make a new career for herself, be self-employed so that within reason she could do as she liked. She owned her house without encumbrances, she had the use of her father's car, she had her qualifications and the opportunity was there . . .'

He was interrupted by the arrival of the barman. 'Another round, gentlemen? I thought I'd pop in because we've a coach party and we may be a bit busy over the next half-hour.'

Wexford asked for two more halves, glancing complacently at the untouched crisps and nuts. 'Some months before she had made the acquaintance of Katrina Dade. I can't imagine Katrina was much company for a woman like her but she was a sycophant and people of Joanna's sort, clever, prickly, paranoid, immature, they like sycophants, they like to be buttered up all the time, flattered, told how brilliant they are.'

'This may be particularly true', put in Burden, 'when the flattered looks free and independent, self-supporting and successfully feminist, and the flatterer is disturbed, dependent, always seeking role models and someone to adore.'

'I see evidence of that psychology course Freeborn made you take.'

'Maybe, and why not?'

The barman came back with their order and two packets of a different variety of crisps. 'On the house, gentlemen,' he said kindly. 'I see you've drawn the curtains. Shut out the floods, eh?'

'Floods?'

'The river's rising just like it did in the winter. Those old curtains haven't been drawn since they went up in nineteen seventy-two and it shows, doesn't it?'

Wexford shut his eyes. 'I just hope my garden's all right.' He waited till the barman had gone back to his coach party. 'Still, as far as I know we've still got the sandbags. To return to Joanna, she didn't know of Giles's existence at that time, just that Katrina had two children. Katrina gave up being school secretary and now neither of them was at Haldon Finch but they went on seeing each other and eventually Joanna went to Katrina's house.'

'I take it that all this time Joanna was managing to indulge her sexual tastes with young boys? These were the "men" Yvonne Moody had seen going to the house and they had ostensibly come there for private tuition?'

'That's right. Then, at Antrim, Joanna met Giles Dade. He was fourteen at the time but that wasn't too young for her. A stumbling block was his commitment to religion, first to the Anglicans, then to the United Gospel Church. But Joanna had offered her services to the Dades as a child-sitter, the best possible way she thought she could get to know Giles. Oddly, like a lot of teachers, she wasn't very good with children. Sophie disliked her from the first, Giles, in the grip of religious mania, simply wasn't much interested, and Joanna did nothing to win their trust or their affection. I gather she just gazed at Giles and started touching him, his arm or his shoulder or running a finger down his back, and he didn't understand what on earth it meant.

'That was one of her problems. Another was that though the Dades occasionally went out in the evenings they never went away overnight. Joanna simply wasn't getting anywhere and her suggestion to Roger Dade that his son might like to come to her for private tuition also failed. Dade might be a bully and a tyrant but he recognised a good brain when he came across one. In this case, two. He knew both his children were academically clever – in a way he never had been – and perhaps he was even stricter because of this, he was determined their talents wouldn't be wasted, they must be encouraged to get on. But not with Joanna Troy. Her services simply weren't called for. Giles had taken a French GCSE when he was only fourteen and got an A star. German wasn't on his curriculum. What could Joanna teach him?

'French conversation. Or so she thought. She began coming round – at her own invitation – to instigate French conversation with him, to watch videos in French and encourage him to read French classics. It wasn't a very successful move because Giles had changed courses since then and was working hard at Russian along with history and politics. French he had done with for the time being. That Giles is very quick at languages was shown, I think, by his picking up Swedish in a matter of weeks, and at that time it was Russian – a very difficult language – he was concentrating on. His spare time, such as it was, he devoted to the United Gospel Church. In a few months' time he was due to be received into that church after he had attended the Congregation in Passingham woods and made his confession.'

Burden said ruefully, 'He had very little to confess then, I suppose.'

'Nothing more than a bit of backsliding about going to church and possibly lack of respect to his parents, something else the Good Gospellers were very hot on. But in the spring the Dades went away for the night. It was the annual dinner and dance of Roger's firm's parent company and, for a change, it wasn't held in Brighton but in London. They would have to stay overnight. I don't know if Joanna overheard them discussing this and offered her services or if Katrina asked her. The only thing that matters is that Roger and Katrina went to this function and Joanna stayed the night with Giles and Sophie.

'It was a Saturday and one of those Saturday evenings rather than Sunday mornings when the Good Gospellers held their weekly service. Giles told me that Joanna, who arrived at about five, tried to stop him going. She insisted on speaking French to him in order to stop Sophie understanding, a stratagem you can imagine maddened the volatile Sophie who also has a very good brain, only her talents lie in the areas of maths and science, not languages.

'Giles, who is considerably more sophisticated now, had very little idea of why Joanna insisted on sitting close up to him and talking to him – in French – in what he describes as "a wheedling way". He's quite open and frank, and he says the way she behaved reminded him of actresses flirting on television, "making up to men", as he puts it. In real life he had known nothing like it but it made him uneasy. Still, he went to church but he had to come home again.

'It was only half past nine but apparently both Joanna and Sophie had gone to bed. He went up to his bedroom, relieved not to have to talk to Joanna any more. Much as he dislikes his parents, he found them infinitely preferable to Joanna Troy. He undressed, went to bed and sat up memorising grammar from a Russian textbook in preparation for a lesson on the Monday morning. Joanna came in without knocking. She was wearing a dressing gown which she undid without a word and dropped to the floor. He says he sat there, staring blankly at her. But something happened which he describes as "horrible".

He doesn't know, I quote, "how it could have happened". He was aroused, and violently so. Things were utterly beyond his control. He hated Joanna then but he wanted her more than he had ever wanted anything in his life. I think we both know what he meant and further explanation isn't necessary. He was only fifteen and this was his first experience.

'He held out his arms to her, he couldn't help himself. He wasn't himself, he says, and for a while he really believed he'd been possessed by a demon – to use Good Gospellers' language. Joanna got into bed with him and the rest is obvious – in the circumstances inescapable.'

Chapter 28

Wexford drew back a corner of curtain and they watched the coach party leave, stumbling towards their single-decker through deepening puddles, through stair-rod-straight rain, coats protecting hairdos, umbrellas up, one man with a newspaper over his head. It was a copy of the *Evening Courier*.

'I'm going to phone Dora.'

The message service was switched on. He cursed modern innovations, thinking how extremely mystified his own parents would have been by a man's ability to phone home, be spoken to by his own self and then address that self with an abusive expletive which would be recorded for himself to hear whenever he chose. Burden listened with an impassive face while he spoke these thoughts aloud, then said, 'Go on with all that sexy stuff about Giles and Joanna.'

'Ah, yes. I think Giles felt at first as most boys of his age would: astonishment, a certain amount of fear, gratification that things had – well, worked, and even pride. He was still enjoying the situation when Joanna came back early next morning and a couple of weeks later when Joanna came for the evening while the Dade parents went out. Sophie was in the house but in her room. However, in the following week she challenged Giles about it and he told her. There was no risk, she'd have been no more likely to tell Roger or Katrina than he would.

'But her knowledge of the affair, if we can call it that, eventually gave her that daunting sexual sophistication which made me believe for a while that she must have been abused and that her father was abusing her. No one was. She was just privy to Giles's activities then and his changed attitude later.'

'His changed attitude?'

'Oh, yes. You see, at first he made no connection between what was going on between him and Joanna and his religious affiliation. Or so he tells me. They were in separate compartments of his life. Then, one Sunday morning, he was in church when brother Jashub preached a sermon on sexual purity. That was in early June. You might say if you were a Good Gospeller and given to biblical metaphor, that the scales fell from his eyes. Moreover, he had been told that he must make his public confession at the Confessional Congregation in July. Suddenly he saw that what had seemed a wonderful enhancement of his life, great fun at its lowest and sublime at its highest, was just a squalid sin. He would have to end it and make Joanna understand.

'He was only fifteen. He began by cancelling an apppointment he had to go to Joanna's house. He never had been there, this was to be a first, and he told her it was too risky for him. His mother would find out. As luck would have it, the Dade parents weren't going anywhere in the evenings so Joanna's services wouldn't be called for. The Congregation date came and he was taken to Passingham Hall woods. There was a shortage of cars and various participants were starting from their places of work, not from home, so he was escorted to Passingham by train and thence by taxi, from which he acquired his knowledge of how to get to Passingham Park station. For the return journey there were plenty of cars and drivers willing to take him back. He came back in a car with four Good Gospellers. It must have been a right squeeze.'

Burden interposed, 'Do you feel like eating something? I don't mean these so-called nibbles. Shall I see if this place can rustle up a sandwich?'

While he consulted a menu the barman had brought, Wexford went out into the porch. The rain had eased a little. He picked someone's umbrella out of the stand, thinking how awkward it would be if the owner panicked and accused him of stealing it. But he would only be a minute. He stepped out on to the forecourt, avoiding puddles.

What had he expected? That the Kingsbrook Bridge would be under water? Certainly the river had risen and become once more a rushing torrent. This was the point at which Sophie had thrown her T-shirt over the parapet. Conditions must have been very much the same as now, the water rising but the bridge still passable, rain descending so steadily it seemed it must never cease. Giles had driven on, gaining confidence with every mile, Joanna's body in the boot of the car. Did he think, when he was on his way to dispose of it in Passingham woods, of the journey he had made home from there on that previous occasion? Had they, that sententious bunch in Nun Plummer's car, cited for him the example of the virginal Joseph resisting with iron chastity Potiphar's wife? I bet they did, Wexford thought. They weren't Catholics, so the temptation of St Anthony wouldn't have come into it . . .

He ran back into the hotel, opened and shut the umbrella to shake off the raindrops and replaced it in the stand.

Burden was back in the snug with more lager – time to watch it now – and toasted sandwiches ordered. 'So he confessed all that in public, did he?' he said.

'In front of a howling mob, you might say,' Wexford said. 'Singing and dancing, as Shand-Gibb's housekeeper put it. His only comfort must have been that no names were mentioned. They had allowed that. He was absolved, of course, on the usual grounds that his behaviour mustn't be repeated. And he was assigned a mentor to guide and watch over him. One of the elders to see he didn't sin again.

'He didn't intend to. That congregation had shaken him, as it might have shaken someone three times his age. Once again he told his sister about it but he said nothing to Joanna, he just did his best to avoid her and he was successful. At what cost to himself we don't know but I can guess at. In September his grandmother Matilda Carrish came to stay. An uncomfortable visit, I imagine, owing to the dislike of Katrina for her mother-in-law and Matilda's contempt for Katrina. I think she only went there because she was worried about Sophie. Why she thought she had any grounds for worry I don't know and now we never shall know. Perhaps it was only that as a child she herself had been sexually abused by her own father and she suspected Roger of having the same proclivities. She was wrong but we suspected the same and we were wrong too.

'Was the subject discussed between her and Sophie? Sophie is such an accomplished liar that it may be impossible to find out. I think of myself –' Wexford looked rueful, raising his eyebrows '– as a good lie detector but that child runs rings round some of the worst villains in that department I've ever interrogated. Pity you can't do GCSEs in mendacity, she'd be in the A star category. Maybe she inherited her talent from her paternal grandma who's no slouch at lying herself.

'Anyway, what Matilda did succeed in doing was establish a strong bond between herself and her son's children. It wouldn't be an exaggeration to say that in those three days they came to love her. Here was a grown-up person who took them seriously, who wasn't always yelling at them or weeping over them, and who perhaps said before she left that if they ever needed her she'd be there. They only had to phone. One phone call would fetch her. Needless to say maybe, Giles said nothing to her about the Joanna business. Why would he? He was trying to put it behind him.'

Wexford ate a sandwich and then another. As he savoured the hot melted butter, the rare but not too rare roast beef, the capers and raw red onion, he felt he could see his waistline expanding. Few writers on the subject seemed to point out that delicious food makes you fat and the kind no one wants to eat doesn't. There must be a reason for this but he didn't know what it was.

'Get to the crucial weekend, Reg,' said Burden.

'The crucial weekend, yes. When his mother told him Joanna would be coming while she and his father were away, Giles was seriously worried. Since the Congregation he had become far more conscious of the need for chastity than he ever had been before. Well, he had scarcely been at at all conscious of it before. Now he agreed that continence must be a good thing, something worth adhering to until he got married. He had heard several more sermons on the subject and the Good Gospel elders, starting with lectures in the car home from Passingham, had taken it upon themselves to keep him up to the mark. Incredible as it sounds, they even instituted a couple of one-to-one tutorials. One of these was conducted by Pagiel Smith and the other by Hobab Winter. Brother Jashub was also around quite a bit, dispensing admonitions and threats. They all made extramarital sex into a far worse sin than cruelty, untruthfulness, fraud and even murder.

'Up till that time Giles had never specifically named his sexual partner to any of them,' Wexford went on. 'But now he was growing more and more worried by the day. She was coming to stay in a fortnight's time, in a week, in a few days. After church on Sunday, the nineteenth of November, he spoke to the Rev. Mr Wright, and told him everything. Joanna would be coming to stay in his home in the absence of his parents on the following Friday. Jashub called a council of elders, all of them bent on keeping Giles pure.'

'That poor kid,' said Burden.

He passed Wexford the sandwiches. Taking one, Wexford thought how, as long as he could remember back in their relationship, when there had been four sandwiches, Burden had had one and he had had three and when there had been eight he had had six and Burden had had two. This happened now and it was no doubt the reason why he was always thinking of battling with his weight if not actually battling with it, while Burden remained thin as a teenager. He sighed.

'As we know, the Dade parents went away on Friday the twenty-fourth in the morning and Joanna came in the late afternoon. One part of Giles hoped she would have forgotten everything that had passed between them, but we won't be surprised to learn that the other part of him longed for her to remember. She remembered all right, came to his room on the Friday evening and the rest was inevitable. Not without a struggle on Giles's part, though. He told her what he now believed, that this was very wrong, and she laughed at him. In a couple of weeks he'd be sixteen and what they were doing would no longer be illegal. She had misunderstood.

'Sophie knew all about it. She had watched Joanna's advances to Giles throughout the evening and translated them neatly for my benefit into passages between Joanna and "Peter" His name, of course, was an invention, unconsciously adopted from the author of that recipe article. It didn't take much imagination as it must be one of the commonest names there are. She didn't know that two real Peters were connected with the case, and if she had I dare say she'd only have thought it funny.'

'What happened next day?'

'All that shopping and cooking described to me by Sophie was rubbish. She got the dinner menu out of a newspaper supplement that wasn't published until two weeks ago. Not quite clever enough, but still she's only thirteen, there's plenty of time for improvement and by the time she's twenty she'll be the most expert spinner of fictions we're ever likely to see. Far from accompanying Joanna and Sophie on this food-buying spree and having lunch out with them, Giles went round to Jashub Wright's, told him what had happened and that he was fearful of its happening again. What should he do? Resist, he was told, be strong. There's something ridiculous these days about the image of a young highly sexed man keeping himself chaste for what is a wholly imaginary concept of the man we call Jesus – who never said a word about sex outside marriage – but not to these people. Giles was to resist *in His name* and he would get help.

'By the time he got back to Antrim, the rain had begun. He looked forward with dread to the evening ahead of him. Remember there was no "Peter", there was no dinner guest and no elaborate meal. There were just the three of them, each in his or her way tense about what was to come: Sophie curious and excited, Joanna preparing to break down a resistance which only added spice to the whole affair, Giles struggling to keep her at a distance, desperately wishing, he says, that he had the practical aid of a lock on his bedroom door.'

'But wait a minute,' said Burden, 'you've told me Giles wasn't involved in Joanna's death, but there were only the three of them in the house?'

'At that time there were only the three of them in the house. But the situation changed. By six it was raining very hard indeed, as you'll remember. The newspaper, the *Evening Courier* was late on account of the rain but at just before six thirty it came. The person who delivered it didn't ring the doorbell but Giles heard the paper fall on to the mat and went out to fetch it.'

'Where does Scott Holloway come into all this?'

'Scott hated Joanna. I'll tell you why I think this was. Sophie wasn't the only one Giles told about his relationship with Joanna. When it first began and the guilt hadn't started he told Scott too, let's say he boasted to him about his – well, his conquest, his experience. When Scott found himself booked to have private coaching from Joanna he hoped for the same thing to happen but Joanna rejected him. The poor boy isn't exactly attractive, is he? No wonder he hated her, gave up his lessons and when he saw her car outside Antrim that Saturday evening, went straight back home to avoid seeing her.

'The occupants of Antrim went to bed early, Giles in two minds. He knew now that he was safe, though in many ways safety was the last thing he wanted. Joanna's advances to him while they sat on the sofa watching television, advances she barely bothered to conceal from Sophie, had quite naturally excited him almost beyond bearing. Yet he knew he was safe. Knowing his dilemma, Sophie refused to go to bed and leave them until Giles had gone. She went upstairs at the same time as Joanna and watched her go to her bedroom.

'Half an hour later Joanna was lying dead at the bottom of the stairs. She had been pushed down or thrown down, and by someone who saw himself as opposing the Great Dragon, the Antichrist. His mission accomplished, he left Giles to clear up the mess and, presumably, face the music. This, Giles thinks, wise after the event, was intended as his punishment, for with these people confession and absolution are not enough. There must be atonement. Besides, Giles had sinned again since he confessed at Congregation. He had repeated his sin, the same sin. Only after he had left the house did Sophie come out of her room and saw what had happened.

'The first thing they did was phone their grandmother. They were in a blind panic and she had said she would always be there for them. She was. She was a rock and a sanctuary. The children calmed down. She saw their difficulty, she understood Giles's terror of his father, of the law, of the discovery of his behaviour with Joanna – but she thought he had killed Joanna. She didn't believe in the intervention of a third person and nor did Sophie. They were liars, you see, and liars think the rest of the world lies like they do. Of course, a sensible woman would have advised them to phone us at once, waste no more time, but Matilda Carrish wasn't very sensible. Clever, even brilliant, talented, but neither sensible nor wise. Bring your Irish passport, she told Giles. Leave Joanna where she is and leave her car and come here as soon as you can get here.

'They obeyed her to a certain extent. They would go, but why not go in Joanna's car and take her body with them? Sophie didn't believe Giles's story, so the police wouldn't. If Joanna's body was here and they weren't, wouldn't the police assume them guilty?

But if there was no body . . . Giles was only fifteen and he had been enormously afraid but I think some spirit of adventure came into it now. He could drive and he wanted to drive. Freedom was what was in Sophie's mind. Get away from here, get away from those parents. Make it look, they both thought, as if Joanna is still alive and has abducted us . . .'

Wexford's phone was ringing. Dora's voice said, 'Have you been trying to get me? I'm at Sylvia's with her and Johnny.' *Johnny*? Things had been moving fast. 'Where are you, anyway?'

'In a pub.'

'I see. If you've been worrying about the rain, there's no water lying anywhere near our garden but we've still got the sandbags and if there's any sort of threat Johnny says he'll come and put them up against the wall. See you later.'

'Do you know what *Plus ça change plus c'est la même chose* means?'

'No,' said Burden.

'It's pretty well the only bit of French I do know,' Wexford said. He went on unfairly, 'It's just that Sylvia's new chap sounds just the same as the last one.'

Burden said in a nasty tone, his upper lip curled, 'You are a master of suspense, aren't you? You love it. You even get better at it. I reckon you've been working on it.'

'I don't know what you mean,' said Wexford.

'Who killed Joanna Troy, is what I mean.'

'I'm coming to that. Let's go back a few hours to the evening paper delivery.'

'The *what*?'

'Wait. It's important. We all have the same Queen Street newsagent round my neighbourhood and Lyndhurst Drive is my neighbourhood. As you know, Antrim is only a few streets away from me. The round begins, not in Queen Street itself, nor does it touch Godstone Road. Therefore it also fails to take in most of Lyndhurst Drive, but starts in Chesham Road, follows my road, Caversham Avenue, Martindale Gardens, the north side of Kingston Drive, back along the south side and ends on the corner of Lyndhurst Drive and Kingston Drive. The last house in Lyndhurst is covered by the round and is always the last house at which a paper is delivered. That house, as you know, is Antrim. The person who delivers the *Kingsmarkham Evening Courier* is usually but not invariably a girl much the same age as Giles Dade and Scott Holloway, Dorcas Winter. On Saturday the twenty-fifth of November she didn't deliver those papers. She *seldom did on a Saturday*, because she had a violin lesson. Her father took over.

'He delivered the papers on foot and got very wet in the process. When he came to the last house, which was of course Antrim, he didn't have to ring the doorbell because Giles heard the paper fall on to the mat and went to the door. But even if Joanna had heard it and gone to the door it wouldn't have worried him. He had his excuse ready. Seeing that he knew Giles, they were both members of the same church and, more than that, he was Giles's mentor, assigned to him and teacher and guide. Could he come in and dry himself before returning home?'

'Members of the Good Gospellers, you mean?'

'The newsagent', said Wexford, 'is Kenneth, alias Hobab, Winter.'

Chapter 29

'He has already appeared in court, as you know,' Wexford said, 'on a murder charge and been committed. Charging Giles with concealing a death can't be avoided, though I hope to drop a wasting police time charge. The good things that have come out of it are that he's turned his back on the Good Gospellers and they seem to be in the process of disbanding, he's learned another language which he's going to take along with other GCSEs in a couple of months' time and he seems to be on slightly better terms with his father. Sophie won't be charged with anything. Frankly, I think any court would take her word against police and expert witness evidence. We'd be wasting our time.'

'Get back to Hobab Winter,' said Burden.

'You'll remember that during the afternoon Giles had appeared before Jashub Wright and an emergency session of the elders. Hobab, of course, was present. Something we're working on now is whether they all knew what Hobab planned to do, whether they all planned it, or if he did it off his own bat. Giles doesn't know. They dismissed him with those cryptic words that he would "get help". He thought it likely help would come from his mentor and, as you can imagine, he half wanted it and half wanted anything but. When the paper came he saw he had guessed right.

'Hobab came into the living room and was

introduced to Joanna and Sophie. He was even *given a cup of tea*. I know. You may well laugh. Something like that was a possibility we'd thought of and dismissed as ludicrous. His raincoat was hung up in the hall over a radiator, his shoes dried in the kitchen and the woollen gloves he was wearing also put on a radiator to dry. His other clothes weren't wet apart from his trouser bottoms and these he left to dry on him.

'Hobab intended to kill Joanna, of that I'm sure. If he had left her injured but alive she would hold him, and therefore the Good Gospellers, responsible. Marks were found on her, you'll remember, indicative of her having been beaten about the face and head. Also he took another step to conceal the fact that he'd been in the house. Unknown to Joanna and Sophie, he remained there. When his gloves were dry – this is important – and his shoes wearable, Giles took him upstairs to his own bedroom. As far as Sophie and Joanna knew, this hadn't happened. According to Giles, they thought he had taken his raincoat from the hall and left the house. In Giles's bedroom, with Giles's Bible to read, he sat in a chair and waited. He intended, Giles says, to wait all night if necessary, to prevent further sin being committed.

'Joanna, presumably made confident by Giles's succumbing to her the night before, repeated the process downstairs. Giles says he didn't encourage her and of course he must have been mindful all the time of the presence of Hobab Winter upstairs. However, after he had gone into his bedroom for the night Joanna came to the door and once again she didn't knock. Perhaps if she had she might have saved her life, if she had been a little more tentative and a little less presumptuous.

'As it was, Hobab leapt from his chair and manhandled her from the room. Beat her with his fists and banged her head against the wall. No doubt he used all sorts of imprecations to her, calling her the Scarlet Woman and the Great Dragon, whatever. She screamed – it must have come as a great shock to her – and from the very top of the staircase, Hobab threw her down, more than satisfied to see her strike her head against a corner of that cupboard.'

'Ah,' said Burden. 'I see. And he just left the house? He left two children to deal with it.'

'I think he barely noticed Sophie's presence downstairs. After all, she was a girl, maybe growing up into another Joanna. His own daughter he probably thinks of as the only female worth saving. Besides, Sophie didn't come out of her room until he had left. She's a sound sleeper. Yes, he left Giles to it and walked the short distance to his home through the driving rain, very likely congratulating himself on a successful mission.'

'Did he really think he could get away with it? He didn't know Giles and Sophie would leave and take the body with them.'

'And would anyone have believed Giles if he said the man delivering the evening paper had pushed Joanna down the stairs? A man who left no traces behind him? Someone Joanna had never even met? Someone Sophie knew had gone home hours before? Remember that Sophie too thought Giles guilty. Any of the elders of the Good Gospel Church would have alibi'd Hobab. His wife had done so, as all their wives had alibi'd them. Look how the elders behaved after the disappearance of the three was known. They – Jashub Wright certainly – acted not only innocent, but indifferent. Unchastity is the most heinous of all sins to them. Violent death didn't matter much, especially if in a good cause, and lying in court would have been a mere peccadillo, easily excused.'

'So this respectable newsagent, this pillar of his

church, having led a blameless life, suddenly ups and kills a young woman with savage violence. A bit way out, isn't it?'

'It would be if what you've said were true.'

'What do you mean?'

Wexford said thoughtfully, 'You know I don't talk about these things at home. No more than you do. Dora picked up something about this case, she was bound to, managing the Internet for me, but Sylvia knew nothing till she saw the very brief bit about Hobab appearing in the magistrates' court. Saw it in the *Evening Courier*, by the way, which pretty well justifies its existence for me. She came round – with that Johnny, of course – and told me about something that happened one night when she was on the helpline at that women's refuge of hers.

'It was a couple of years ago. The woman who phoned in wouldn't give her name. Not at first. She said her husband had beaten her up and she was afraid to be in the house when he came back from his prayer meeting. Sylvia thought that bizarre enough for a start but she told the woman to take a taxi and come to The Hide. As you've guessed it was Priscilla Winter, Mrs Hobab Winter. Her nose was broken, she had two black eyes, and bruises all over her.'

'And an elder of the Good Gospel Church had done that?'

'Oh, yes, and not for the first time. Though the first for a long while. He regularly knocked her about, once *knocked her downstairs*, when their daughter was little, but this was the first time for a couple of years. The reason for it was that he'd come home and found her having a cup of tea with a male neighbour. The pity was that she only stayed at The Hide two nights and then she went back home. She couldn't leave Dorcas, she said.'

'She'll be free of Hobab now,' said Burden. He took

his raincoat from the dusty old wooden coat rack and helped Wexford into his. They went out into the High Street. The rain had lessened to a thin drizzle. 'But I still don't see how you can be sure it was murder. A savage attack, yes, a tragic accident, even manslaughter. But murder?'

'Oh, didn't I say?' Wexford put up the umbrella he was carrying. 'After he'd dried his gloves, Winter kept them on all the time. Not for warmth. It was a mild night and the heating was on. He meant to kill her and he kept his gloves on to avoid leaving fingerprints in Giles's room and on Giles's Bible. If it doesn't sound too psychodiagnostic, I'd say he was killing his wife at the same time and maybe a lot of other women too.'

'And I', said Burden, forgetting all about his psychology course, 'would say he was a total villain.'

'Do you know,' said Wexford, 'I've taken someone else's umbrella, one of the coach party and they've gone now. I think that's the first time in my life I've ever stolen anything.'

Read on for Chapter One of Ruth Rendell's thrilling new novel to be published by Hutchinson in October 2003

THE ROTTWEILER

Chapter 1

The jaguar stood in a corner of the shop between a statue of some minor Greek deity and a jardinière. Inez thought it said a lot about the world we lived in that to most people when you said 'jaguar' they took it to mean a car and not an animal. This one, black and about the size of a very large dog, had once been a jungle creature someone's grandfather, a big game hunter, had shot and had stuffed. The someone had brought it into the shop the day before and offered it to Inez at first for ten pounds, then for nothing. It was an embarrassment having it in the house, he said, worse than being seen in a fur coat.

Inez only took it to get rid of him. The jaguar's yellow glass eyes had seemed to look reproachfully at her. Sentimental nonsense, she said to herself. Who would buy it? She had thought it might seem more attractive at eight forty-five in the morning but it was just the same, its fur harsh to the touch, its limbs stiff and its expression baleful. She turned her back on it and in the little kitchen behind the shop put the kettle on for the tea she always made herself and always shared these days with Jeremy Quick from the top floor.

Punctual as ever, he tapped on the inside door, and came in as she carried the tray back into the shop. 'How are you today, Inez?'

He, and he alone, pronounced her name in the Spanish way, Eeneth, and he had told her the Spanish in Spain, but not in South America, pronounced it like that because one of their kings had had a lisp and they copied him out of deference. That sounded like an apocryphal story to her but she was too polite to say so. She handed him his teacup with a sweetener tablet in the spoon. He always walked about, carrying it.

'What on earth is that?'

She had known he would ask. 'A jaguar.'

'Will anyone buy it?'

'I expect it will join the ranks of the grey armchair and the Chelsea china clock that I'll be left with until I die.'

He patted the animal's head. 'Zeinab not in yet?'

'Please. She says she has no concept of time. In that case, I said, if you've no concept of time, why aren't you ever early?'

He laughed. Inez thought, and not for the first time, that he was rather attractive. Too young for her, of course, or was he? Not perhaps in these days when opinions about that sort of thing were changing. He seemed no more than seven or eight years her junior. 'I'd better be off. Sometimes I think I'm too aware of time.' Carefully, he replaced his cup and saucer on the tray. 'Apparently, there's been another murder.'

'Oh, no.'

'It was on the news at eight. And not far from here. I must go.'

Instead of expecting her to unlock the shop door and let him out, he went back the way he had come and out into Star Street by way of the tenants' entrance. Inez didn't know where he worked, somewhere on the northern outskirts of London, she thought, and what he did had something to do with computers. So many people did these days. He had a mother of whom he was fond and a girlfriend, his feelings for whom he never mentioned. Just once

Inez had been invited up to his top-floor flat and admired the minimalist décor and his roof garden.

At nine she opened the shop door and carried the bookstand out on to the pavement. The books that went in were ancient paperbacks by forgotten authors but occasionally one would sell for 50p. Someone had parked a very dirty white van at the kerb. Inez read a notice stuck in the van's window: *Do not wash. Vehicle undergoing scientific dirt analysis.* That made her laugh.

It was going to be a fine day. The sky was a soft pale blue and the sun coming up behind the terraces of little houses and the tall corner shops with three floors above. It would have been nicer if the air had been fresh instead of reeking of diesel and emissions and green curry and the consequences of men relieving themselves against the hoardings in the small hours, but that was modern life. She said good morning to Mr Khoury who was (rather optimistically) lowering the canopy at the front of the jeweller's next door.

'Good morning, madam.' His tone was gloomy and dour as ever.

'I've got an earring that's lost its what-d'you-call-it, its post,' she said. 'Can you get it repaired if I bring it in later?'

'I shall see.' He always said that, as if he was doing you a favour. On the other hand, he always did repair things.

Zeinab, breathless, came running down Star Street. 'Hi, Mr Khoury,. Hi, Inez. Sorry I'm late. You know I've no concept of time.'

Inez sighed. 'So you always tell me.'

Zeinab kept her job because, if Inez were honest with herself and she nearly always was, her assistant was a better saleswoman than she was. She could have sold an elephant gun to a conservationist, as

Jeremy once said. Some of it was due to her looks, of course. Zeinab's beauty was the reason so many men came in. Inez didn't' flatter herself, she'd plenty of confidence but she knew she'd seen better days, and though she'd been as good-looking as Zeinab once upon a time, it was inevitable that at fifty-five she couldn't compete. She was far from the woman she had been when Martin first saw her twenty years before. No chap was going to cross the street to buy a ceramic egg or a Victorian candlestick from her.

Zeinab looked like the female lead in one of those Bollywood movies. Her black hair came not just to her waist but to the tops of her slender thighs. In nothing but her hair to cover her she could have ridden a horse down Star Street with perfect propriety. Her face was as if someone had taken the best feature from the faces of half a dozen currently famous film stars and put them all together. When she smiled, if you were a man, your heart melted and your legs threatened to buckle. Her hands were like pale flowers on some tropical tree and her skin the texture of a lily petal touched by the setting sun. She always wore very short skirts and very high-heeled shores, pure white t-shirts in summer and pure white fluffy sweaters in winter and a single diamond (or sparkling stone) in one perfect nostril.

Her voice was less attractive, her accent not the endearing musical tones of upper-class Karachi but nearer Eliza Doolittle's Lisson Grove cockney, which was odd considering her parents lived in Hampstead and, according to her, she was practically a princess. Today she was wearing a black leather skirt, opaque black tights and a sweater that looked like the pelt of an angora rabbit, white as snow and downy as a swan's breast.

She walked daintily about the shop, carrying her teacup in one hand and in the other a rainbow-coloured feather duster, flicking dust off silver cruets, ancient musical instruments, cigarette cases, thirties fruit brooches, Clarice Cliffe plates and the four-masted schooner in a bottle. Customers didn't realise what a task it was keeping a place like this clean. Dust soon gave it a shabby look as if the shop was seldom patronised.

She paused in front of the jaguar. 'Where did that come from?'

'A customer gave it to me. After you'd gone yesterday.'

'*Gave* it to you?'

'I imagine he knew the poor thing wasn't worth anything.'

'There's been another girl murdered,' said Zeinab. 'Down Boston.' Anyone not in the know might have thought she was talking about Boston, Massachusetts, or even Boston, Lincs, but what she meant was Boston Street, NW1, which ran alongside Marylebone Station.

'How many does that make?

'Three. I'll get us an evening paper the minute they come in.'

Inez, at the shop window, watched a car which was pulling into the kerb behind the white van. The bright turquoise Jaguar belonged to Morton Phibling who dropped in most mornings for the purpose of seeing Zeinab. No vacant meter was required as his driver sat in the car waiting for him and if a traffic warden appeared, was off circling round the block. Mr Khoury shook his head, holding on to his luxuriant beard with his right hand, and went back indoors.

Morton Phibling got out of the Jaguar, read the notice in the back of the dirty van without a smile and swept into the shop, leaving the door ajar, his open camel hair coat billowing. He had never been known to utter any sort of greeting. 'I see there's another young lady been slaughtered.'

'If you like to put it that way.'

'I came in to feast my eyes on the moon of my delight.'

'You always do,' said Inez.

Morton was something over sixty, short and squat with a head which must always have looked too big for his body, unless he had shrunk a lot. He wore glasses which were not quite shades but deeply tinted with a purple glaze. No beauty and not, as far as Inez could tell, particularly nice or amusing, he was very rich, had three homes and five more cars, all of them resprayed some bright colour, banana-yellow, orange, scarlet and Caribbean-lime. He was in love with Zeinab; there was no other word for it.

Engaged in sticking a price label to the underside of a Wedgwood jug, Zeinab looked up and gave him one of her smiles.

'How are you today, my darling?'

'I'm OK, and don't call me darling.'

'That's how I think of you. I think of you day and night, you know, Zeinab, at twilight and break of dawn.'

'Don't mind me,' said Inez.

'I'm not ashamed of my love. I trumpet it from the housetops. By night in my bed I sought her whom my soul loveth. Rise up, my love, my fair one and come away.' He always went on like this, though neither woman took any notice. 'How splendid in the morning is the lily!'

'D'you want a cup of tea?' said Inez. She felt the need for a second cup; she wouldn't have made it specially.

'I don't mind if I do. I'm taking you to dinner at Le Caprice tonight, darling. I hope you haven't forgotten.'

'Of course I haven't forgotten, and don't call me darling.'

'I'll call for you at home, shall I? Seven thirty do you?'

'No, it won't do me. How many times do I have to tell you that if you call for me at home my dad'll go bonkers? You know what he did to my sister. D'you want him sticking a knife in me?'

'But my attentions are honourable, my sweetheart. I am no longer married, I want to marry you, I respect you deeply.'

'It don't make no – I mean, it doesn't make no difference,' said Zeinab.

'I'm not supposed to be alone with a bloke. Not ever. If my dad knew I was going to be alone with you in a restaurant he'd flip his lid.'

'I should have liked to see your lovely home,' said Morton Phibling wistfully. 'It would be such a pleasure to see you in your proper setting.' He lowered his voice, though Inez was out of earshot. 'Instead of in this dump, like a gorgeous butterfly in a dungheap.'

'Can't be helped. I'll meet you at Le whatsit.'

In the little back kitchen, pouring boiling water on three teabags, Inez shivered at the thought of Zeinab's terrible father. A year before Zeinab came to work at Star Antiques, he had nearly murdered her sister Nasreen for dishonouring his house by staying overnight in her boyfriend's flat. 'And they didn't even do anything,' said Zeinab. Nasreen hadn't died, though he'd stabbed her five times in the chest. She'd been months recovering in hospital. Inez more or less believed it was true, though no doubt exaggerated, that her assistant risked death if she got herself any suitor except one approved of, and chaperoned by, her parents. She took the tea back into the shop. Morton Phibling, said Zeinab, had gone off down the road to buy them a *Standard*.

'So we can read about the murder. Look what he's given me this time.'

Zeinab showed her a large lapel pin of two roses and a rosebud on a stem, nestling in a bed of blue satin.

'Are those real diamonds?'

'He always gives me real diamonds. Must be worth thousands. I promised to wear it tonight.'

'That won't be a hardship,' said Inez. 'But you mind how you go. Having that on show puts you in danger of being mugged. And you want to remember there's a killer at large who's well-known for stealing something off every girl he kills. Here he is, back.'

But instead of Morton Phibling it was a middle-aged woman in search of a piece of Crown Derby for a birthday present. She had picked up a paperback on her way in, a Peter Cheyney with a picture of a strangled girl on its jacket. Appropriate, thought Inez, charging her 50p for it, and wrapping up a red, blue and gold porcelain plate. Morton came back and courteously held the door open for her. Zeinab was still gloating over her diamond roses, looking like an angel contemplating some beatific vision, thought Morton.

'I'm so glad you like it, darling.'

'It still don't – doesn't – give you the right to call me darling. Let's have a look at the paper, then.'

She and Inez shared it. 'It says it happened quite early last night, about nine,' read Zeinab. 'Somebody heard her scream but he didn't do nothing, not for five minutes, when he saw this figure running away down past the station, a shadowy figure, it says, man or woman, he don't know, only it was wearing trousers. Then he found her – they haven't identified her yet – lying dead on the pavement, murdered. They don't say how it was done only that her face was all blue. It would have been another of them garrottes. Nothing about a bite.'

'That bite business is all nonsense,' said Inez. 'The first girl had a bite mark on her neck but they traced the DNA to her boyfriend. The things people do in the name of love! Of course they called him the Rottweiler and the name has stuck.'

'Did he take anything of hers this time? Let me see.' Zeinab scanned the story to its foot. 'Wouldn't know, I suppose, seeing they don't know who she was. What was it he took the other times?'

'A silver cigarette lighter with her initials in garnets from the first one,' said Morton, showing his considerable knowledge of jewellery, 'and a gold fob watch from the second.'

'Nicole Nimms and Rebecca Milsom, they was called. I wonder what it'll be off this one. Won't never be a mobile, I reckon. All the bastards on the street nick mobiles, wouldn't be like his trademark, would it?'

'Now you be careful coming down to Le Caprice tonight, darling,' said Morton, who seemed not to have noticed the jaguar. 'I've a good mind to send a limo for you.'

'If you do I won't come,' said Zeinab, 'and you've called me darling *again*.'

'Are you going to marry him?' said Inez when he had gone. 'He's a bit old for you but he's got a lot of money and he's not so bad.'

'A bit old! I'd have to run away from home, you know, and that'd be a wrench. I wouldn't like to leave my poor mum.'

The bell on the street door rang and a man came in, looking for a plant stand. Preferably wrought iron. Zeinab gave him one of her smiles. 'We've got a lovely jardiniere I'd like to show you. It came over from France only yesterday.'

In fact, it had come from a junk shop having a clearance sale in Church Street. The customer gazed at Zeinab who, squatting down beside the jaguar to pull this three-legged object out from under a pile of Indian bedspreads, turned her face up to him and lifted from it the two wings of black hair like someone unveiling a beautiful picture.

'Very nice,' he mumbled. 'How much is it?' He didn't demur, though Zeinab had added twenty pounds on to the agreed price. Men seldom tried bargaining when she was selling them something. 'Don't bother to wrap it up.'

The street door was held open for him as he struggled out with his purchase. A shy man, almost bowled over, he took courage once on the pavement and said, 'Goodbye. It was very nice to meet you.'

Inez couldn't help laughing. She had to admit business had taken a turn for the better since Zeinab had worked for her. She watched him go off in the direction of Paddington Station. He wasn't going to take it on a train, was he? It was nearly as tall as he. She noticed that the sky had clouded over. Why was it you never seemed to get a fine day any more, only days that started off fine? The dirty white van had gone and another, cleaner, one was being parked in its place. Will Cobbett got out of it and then the driver got out. Inez and Zeinab watched from the window. They saw everything that went on in Star Street and one of them usually provided a running commentary.

'That one that's got out, that's the one called Keith what Will works for,' said Zeinab. 'He'll be going down the Edgware Road to the building materials place. He always comes over here on account of it's cheaper. What's Will doing home at this hour? He's coming in.'

'I expect he's forgotten his tools. He often does.'

Will Cobbett was the only tenant who hardly ever came through the shop. He went in by the tenants' door at the side. The two women heard his footsteps going up the stairs.

'What's with him?' said Zeinab. 'You know what Freddy says about him? He says he's a couple of dips short of a limbo.'

Inez was shocked. 'That's nasty. I'm surprised at Freddy. Will's what used to be called ESN, educationally sub-normal, but now it's "learning difficulties". He's good-looking enough, I must say, learning difficulties or not.'

'Looks aren't everything,' said Zeinab, for whom they were. 'I like a man to be intelligent. Sophisticated and intelligent. You won't mind if I go out for an hour, will you? I'm supposed to be having lunch with Rowley Woodhouse.'

Inez looked at her watch. It was just gone half past twelve. 'You'll be back around half past two then,' she said.

'Who's being nasty now? I can't help it if I've no concept of time. I wonder if you can go to a class in time management? I've been thinking of an elocution course. My dad says I ought to learn to speak right, though him and mum have got accents straight out of downtown Islamabad. I'd better go or Rowley'll create.'

Inez recalled how Martin had taught elocution for a while. That was before *Forsyth* and the big-time, of course. He'd been teaching and taking bit parts when she first met him. His voice had been beautiful, too patrician for a detective inspector on the television now but not in the eighties. She listened to Will's footsteps drumming down the stairs. He ran out to the van, his toolbag in his hand, just as the traffic warden arrived. Then Keith appeared from the other direction. Inez watched the ensuing argument.

Bystanders always do watch confrontations between traffic wardens and hapless drivers, wistfully hoping for a punch-up. Inez wouldn't go as far as that. But she thought Keith ought to pay up, he ought to know a double yellow line when he saw one.

She waited while two blonde women with thickly painted faces wandered round the shop, picking up glass fruit and figures which might or might not have been Netsuke. They were 'just looking', they said. Once they had gone, checking that the doorbell was in working order, she went into the kitchen at the back and switched on the television for the one o'clock news. The newscaster had put on that expression presenters such as he are (presumably) trained to assume when the first item is grim or depressing, as in the case of the girl murdered in Boston Place the night before.

She had been identified as Caroline Dansk of Park Road, NW1. She must have come down Park Road, thought Inez, crossed over Rossmore and gone down into Boston Place on her way to somewhere, perhaps to the station. Poor little thing, only twenty-one.

The picture switched to the trainline out of Marylebone and the street running alongside it, with its high brick wall. Quite upmarket, the houses smartened up and trees planted in the pavement. Police were about and police vans and crime tape everywhere, the usual small crowd gathered behind, seeking what it could devour. No photograph of Caroline Dansk yet and no TV appearance of her distraught parents. That would come in due time. As no doubt would a description of the object her killer had taken from her after he had stifled her life out with that garrotte thing.

If it was the same man. They could only tell, now the biting had proved a nonsense and therefore the sobriquet inappropriate, by the stealing of one small object. These young people had so much, thought Inez, all of them with computers and digital cameras and mobile phones, unlike in her day. A sinister expression that, as if everyone had her day and when it was over started on the long decline into night, twilight first, then dusk and finally the darkness. Her day had come quite late in life, only really begun when she met Martin, and it was after he died that the daylight began to dim. Come on, Inez, she said to herself, that won't do. Get yourself some lunch, as you've no Rowley Woodhouse or Morton Phibling to get it for you, and switch on to something more cheerful. She made herself a ham sandwich and got out the Branston pickle but she didn't want any more tea, a Diet Coke would be all right and the caffeine would wake her up for the afternoon.

I wonder what he's taken off this girl? I wonder who he is and where he lives, if he has a wife, children, friends. Why does he do it and when and where will he do it again? There was something degrading in speculating about such things but almost inescapable. She couldn't help being curious, though Martin could have helped it, risen above such relish for ugly details. Perhaps it was because he was obliged to involve himself in fictitious crime each time he acted in a *Forsyth* production, that he wanted nothing to do with the reality.

The doorbell rang. Inez wiped her lips and went back into the shop.

Live Flesh

1

The gun was a replica. Spenser told Fleetwood he was ninety-nine per cent sure of that. Fleetwood knew what that meant, that he was really about forty-nine per cent sure, but he didn't attach much weight to what Spenser said anyway. For his own part he didn't believe the gun was real. Rapists don't have real guns. A replica does just as well as a means of frightening.

The window that the girl had broken was a square empty hole. Once since Fleetwood arrived had the man with the gun appeared at it. He had come in answer to Fleetwood's summons but had said nothing, only standing there for perhaps thirty seconds, holding the gun in both hands. He was young, about Fleetwood's own age, with long dark hair, really long, down on his shoulders, as was the prevailing fashion. He wore dark glasses. For half a minute he stood there and then he turned abruptly round and disappeared into the shadows of the room. The girl Fleetwood hadn't seen, and for all he knew she might be dead.

He sat on a garden wall on the opposite side of the street, looking up at the house. His own car and the police van were parked at the kerb. Two of the uniformed men had succeeded in clearing away the crowd which had gathered and keeping it back with an improvised barrier. Even though it had now begun to rain, dispersing the crowd altogether would have been an impossible task. Front doors stood open all the way down the street with women on the doorsteps, waiting for something to happen. It was one of them who, hearing the window break and the girl scream, had dialled 9–9–9.

A district that was neither Kensal Rise nor West Kilburn nor Brondesbury, a blurred area, on the borders of nowhere in particular. Fleetwood had never really been there before, had only driven through. The street was called Solent Gardens, long and straight and flat, with terraces of two-storey houses facing one another, some Victorian, some much later, from the nineteen twenties and thirties. The house with the broken window, number 62 Solent Gardens, was one of these newer houses, the end of a terrace of eight, red brick and pebble dashing, red pantiles on the roof, black and white paintwork, a pale blue front door. All the houses had gardens at the back and gardens at the front with lonicera or privet hedges and bits of lawn, and most of them had low brick or stone walls in front of the hedges. Fleetwood, sitting on a wall in the rain, began to wonder what he should do next.

None of the rapist's victims had mentioned a gun, so it would seem as if the replica had been recently acquired. Two of them – there had been five, or at any rate five who had come forward – had been able to describe him: tall, slim, twenty-seven or twenty-eight, olive skin, dark longish hair, dark eyes and very black eyebrows. A foreigner? Oriental? Greek? Perhaps, but perhaps just an Englishman with dark-skinned forbears. One of the girls had been badly hurt, for she had fought him, but he had used no weapon on her, only his hands.

Fleetwood got up and walked up to the front door of number 63 opposite to have another talk with Mrs Stead, who had called the police. Mrs Stead had fetched out a kitchen stool to sit on and put on her winter coat. She had already told him that the girl's name was Rosemary Stanley and that she lived with her parents but they were away. It had been at five minutes to eight in the morning, one and a half hours ago, when Rosemary Stanley had broken the window and screamed.

Fleetwood asked if Mrs Stead had seen her.

'He dragged her away before I got the chance.'

'We can't know that,' Fleetwood said. 'I suppose she goes out to work? I mean, when things are normal?'

'Yes, but she never leaves the house before nine. Ten past as often as not. I can tell you what happened, I've worked it all out. He rang the doorbell and she went down in her nightie to answer it and he said he'd come to read the electric meter – they're due for this quarter, he'd know that – and she took him upstairs and he had a go at her, but in the nick of time she bashed the window out and uttered her desperate cry for help. That's the way it's got to be.'

Fleetwood didn't think so. For one thing the electricity meter wouldn't be upstairs. All the houses in this part of the street were the same and Mrs Stead's meter was just inside the front door. Alone in the house on a dark winter morning, Rosemary Stanley would hardly have opened the door to a caller. She would have leaned out of the window to check on him first. Women in this district had been so frightened by tales of the rapist that not one of them would set foot outside after dark, sleep alone in a house if she could help it, or open a front door without a chain on it. A local ironmonger told Fleetwood that there had been a boom in the sale of door chains these past few weeks. Fleetwood thought it more likely the man with the gun had forced an entry into the house and made his way to Rosemary Stanley's bedroom.

'Could you do with a coffee, Inspector?' said Mrs Stead.

'Sergeant,' Fleetwood corrected her. 'No, thanks. Later maybe. Still, we must hope there won't be a later.'

He crossed the road. Behind the barrier the crowd waited patiently, standing in the drizzle, coat collars turned up, hands in pockets. At the end of the street, where it turned off the main road, one of the PCs was having an argument with a driver who seemed to want to bring his lorry down here. Spenser had predicted that the man with the gun would come out and give himself up when he saw Fleetwood and the others; rapists were notorious cowards, that was a well-known fact, and what did he have to gain by holding out? It hadn't been like that, though. Fleetwood thought it might be that the rapist still believed he had a chance of escape. If he was *the* rapist. They couldn't be sure he was, and Fleetwood was a stickler for accuracy, for fairness. A few minutes after the 9–9–9 call a girl called

Heather Cole had come into the police station with a man called John Parr, and Heather Cole had said an attack had been made on her in Queens Park half an hour before. She was exercising her dog when a man had seized her from behind, but she had screamed and Mr Parr had come and the man had run off. Had escaped this way, Fleetwood thought, and entered 62 Solent Gardens for refuge from pursuers rather than with the intention of raping Rosemary Stanley because he had been baulked of Heather Cole. Or that was Fleetwood's guess.

Fleetwood came the nearest he had yet been to the Stanley house, opening the small ornate wrought-iron gate, crossing the square of wet bright-green grass, making his way round the side. There was no sound from the interior. The exposed side wall was sheer, without drainpipes or projections, with three small windows only. At the back though, the kitchen had apparently been extended and the roof of this extension, which was no more than eight feet from the ground, could be reached by scaling the wall against which grew a sturdy thornless climber – a wisteria probably, thought Fleetwood, who in his leisure hours was fond of gardening.

Above this low roof a sash window stood open. Fleetwood was proved right. He noted access to the garden from a lane at the back by a path of concrete slabs leading past a concrete garage. If all else failed, he thought, he or someone could always get into the house by climbing up the way the man with the gun had.

As he came round the front again, the voice shouted at him. It was a voice full of fear but it was itself none the less frightening for that. It was unexpected and it made Fleetwood jump. He realized he was nervous, he was afraid, though he hadn't thought of this before. He made himself walk, not run, on to the front path. The man with the gun stood at the broken window, the window from which he had now knocked out all the glass into the flowerbed below, holding the gun in his right hand and the curtain back with his left.

'Are you in charge here?' he said to Fleetwood.

As if he were running some sort of show. Well, perhaps he was, and a successful one to judge from the avidity of the audience, braving rain and cold. At the sound of the voice a noise came from them, a crowd-sigh, a collective murmur, not unlike wind in the treetops.

Fleetwood nodded. 'That's right.'

'So it'd be you I'd have to make terms with?'

'No terms are going to be made.'

The man with the gun now appeared to consider this. He said, 'What's your rank?'

'I'm Detective Sergeant Fleetwood.'

Disappointment was apparent in the thin face, even though the eyes were hidden. The man seemed to think he merited a chief inspector at least. Perhaps I'd better tell Spenser his presence is required, thought Fleetwood. The gun was pointing at him now. Fleetwood wasn't going to put his hands up, of course he wasn't. This was Kensal Rise, not Los Angeles, though what real difference that made he didn't know. He looked into the black hole of the gun's mouth.

'I want a promise I can come out of here and have half an hour to get away in. I'll take the girl with me and when the half-hour's up I'll send her back here in a taxi. OK?'

'You must be joking,' said Fleetwood.

'It'll be no joke to her if you don't give me that promise. You can see the gun, can't you?'

Fleetwood made no reply.

'You can have an hour to decide. Then I'll use the gun on her.'

'That will be murder. The inevitable sentence for murder is life imprisonment.'

The voice, which was deep and low, yet colourless – a voice which gave Fleetwood the impression it wasn't used much or was always used economically – turned cold. It spoke of terrible things with indifference.

'I shan't kill her. I'll shoot her from the back, in the lower spine.'

Fleetwood made no comment on this. What was there to say? It was a threat which could provoke only a moralistic condemnation or shocked reproach. He had turned away, for he noticed out of the corner of his eye a familiar car arriving, but a gasp from the crowd, a kind of concerted indrawing of breath, made him look up at the window once more. The girl, Rosemary Stanley, had been pushed into the empty square from which the glass had gone and was being held there, her stance suggesting a slave pinioned in a market place. Her arms were grasped in other arms behind her back and her head hung forward. A hand took hold of her long hair and with it pulled her head back, the jerking movement causing her to cry out.

Fleetwood expected the crowd to address her or her to speak, but neither of these things happened. She was silent and staring, statue-still with fear. The gun, he thought, was probably pressed into her back, into her lower spine. No doubt she too had heard the man's statement of intent. So intense was the crowd's indignation that Fleetwood fancied he could feel vibrations of it. He knew he ought to say words of reassurance to the girl but he could think of nothing not absolutely false and hypocritical. She was a thin little girl with long fair hair wearing a garment that might have been a dress or a dressing gown. An arm came round her waist, pulled her back, and simultaneously, for the first time, a curtain was drawn across the window. This was in fact a pair of thick-looking lined curtains that drew tightly together.

Spenser was still sitting in the passenger seat of the Rover reading a sheet of paper. He was the kind of man who, when not otherwise occupied, is always to be found perusing some document. It occurred to Fleetwood how subtly he was grooming himself for future commanderhood: his abundant thick hair just silvering, his shave cleaner that ever, the skin curiously tanned for deep midwinter, his shirt ice-cream transmuted into poplin, his raincoat surely a Burberry. Fleetwood got into the back of the car and Spenser turned on him eyes the blue of gas flames.

In Fleetwood's view, his reading had, as always,

informed him of everything that was irrelevant while contributing nothing to the cooling of crisis.

'She's eighteen, left school last summer, works in a typing pool. Parents went to the West Country first thing this morning, left in a taxi around half-seven, a neighbour says. Mrs Stanley's father in Hereford had a coronary. They'll be informed as soon as we can reach them. We don't want them seeing it on TV.'

Fleetwood immediately thought of the girl he was to marry next week. Would Diana find out he was here and worry? But no TV camera crew had appeared, no reporters of any kind yet, as far as he knew. He told Spenser what the man with the gun had said about a promise and getting away and shooting Rosemary Stanley.

'We can be ninety-nine per cent sure it's a replica,' said Spenser. 'How did he get in there? Do we know?'

'By means of a tree growing against the rear wall.' Fleetwood knew Spenser wouldn't know what he was talking about if he said wisteria.

Spenser muttered something and Fleetwood had to ask him to repeat it.

'I said we'll have to go in there, Sergeant.'

Spenser was thirty-seven, nearly ten years his senior. Also he was growing rotund, as perhaps was appropriate for a commander-to-be. Older than Fleetwood, less fit, two grades up in rank, Spenser meant by his 'we' that Fleetwood should go in there, maybe taking one of the young DCs with him.

'By means possibly of the tree you spoke of,' Spenser said.

The window was open, waiting for him. Inside was a man with a real gun or a mock gun – who knew? – and a frightened girl. He, Fleetwood, had no weapon at all except his hands and his feet and his wits, and when he talked to Spenser about being issued with a firearm the Superintendent looked at him as if he'd asked for a nuclear warhead.

The time was a quarter to ten and the man with the gun had made his ultimatum at about nine twenty.

'Are you going to talk to him at all, sir?'

Spenser gave a thin smile. 'Getting cold feet, Sergeant?'

Fleetwood took that in silence. Spenser got out of the car and crossed the road. Hesitating for a moment, Fleetwood followed him. The rain had stopped, and the sky, which had been uniformly grey and smooth, was now broken into grey and white and patches of blue. It seemed colder. The crowd now reached as far as the main road, Chamberlayne Road, that runs over Kensal Rise to meet Ladbroke Grove at the bottom. Fleetwood could see that the traffic in Chamberlayne Road had been halted.

Up at the broken window in the Stanley house the drawn curtains moved about in the light wind. Spenser stepped on to the muddy grass from the comparative cleanness of the concrete path without a pause, without a glance at his well-polished black Italian shoes. He stood in the centre of the grass, legs apart, arms folded, and he called up to the window in the authentic voice of one who had ascended the ladder of rank in the police force, a chill clear tone without regional accent, without pretension to culture, almost uninflected, the note of a sensitively programmed robot: 'This is Detective Superintendent Ronald Spenser. Come to the window. I want to talk to you.'

It seemed as if the curtains fluttered with greater violence but this might only have been the wind blowing coincidentally.

'Can you hear me? Come to the window, please.'

The curtains continued to move but did not part. Fleetwood, on the pavement now with DC Bridges, saw the camera crew elbowing through the crowd – unmistakable newshounds, even if you couldn't see their van parked on the street corner. One of them began setting up a tripod. And then something happened to make all of them jump. Rosemary Stanley screamed.

The scream was a dreadful sound, tearing the air. The crowd acknowledged it with a noise like an echo of that scream coming from a long way off, half gasp, half murmur of distress. Spenser, who had started like the rest of them, stood his ground, digging in his heels, positively sinking into the mud, his shoulders hunched, as if to show his firmness of purpose, his determination not to be moved. But he didn't speak again. Fleetwood thought what everyone thought, what perhaps Spenser himself thought: that his speech had caused the action that had caused the scream.

If the man with the gun had done as he was bidden and come to the window, it would have provided a distraction, under cover of which Fleetwood and Bridges might have climbed up the house and gone in at the open window. No doubt the man too knew that. Fleetwood felt strangely comforted, though. There had been no detonation. Rosemary Stanley hadn't screamed because she had been shot. Spenser, having demonstrated his fearlessness and his phlegm, turned from the house and slowly walked across the soggy grass, the path, opened the gate, came out on to the pavement, gave the crowd a blank dispassionate stare. He said to Fleetwood, 'You'll have to think about going in.'

Fleetwood was conscious of his photograph being taken, a shot of the side of his head and a bit of profile. It was Spenser's face they really wanted a picture of. Suddenly the curtains were flung apart and the man with the gun stood there. It was funny the way it reminded Fleetwood of the pantomime he and Diana had taken her niece to at Christmas: a pair of curtains thrown apart and a man appearing dramatically between them. The villain of the piece. The Demon King. The crowd sighed. A woman in the crowd uttered a high-pitched giggle of hysteria, which was abruptly cut off as if she had laid her hand across her mouth.

'You've got twenty minutes,' said the man with the gun.

'Where did you get the gun, John?' said Spenser.

John? thought Fleetwood. Why John? Because Lesley Allan or Sheila Manners or one of the other girls had said so, or just for Spenser to have the satisfaction of hearing him say, 'My name's not John'?

'These replicas are very good, aren't they?' Spenser said

conversationally. 'It takes experience to tell the difference. I wouldn't say expert knowledge, but experience, yes.'

Fleetwood was part of the crowd now, caught up in it, as was Bridges. They were pushing their way through it towards the main road. How long could Spenser keep him talking? Not long, if all he could do was mock him, take the piss about that gun. From behind him he heard, 'You've got just seventeen minutes.'

'All right, Ted, let's talk.'

That was better, though Fleetwood wished Spenser would stop calling the man with the gun by phony Christian names. He was out of earshot now, out beyond the crowd and in the main road, where the traffic was jammed solid. He and Bridges went down the alley, closed to vehicles by an iron bollard, that became the lane at the back of the houses. The Stanley house was easy to find, distinguished by the ugly concrete garage. By this time the man with the gun might easily have closed that sash window, but he hadn't. Of course, if the window had been closed, it would have made it virtually impossible to get into the house, at any rate to get in silently, so Fleetwood ought to have been pleased, he thought, that John or Ted or whatever his name was hadn't thought to close it. But instead it struck him with a sense of vague cold dismay. Surely if the window hadn't been closed, this was not inadvertent. It had been left open for a purpose.

Now they were once more near enough to hear Spenser's voice and the voice of the man with the gun. Spenser was saying something about letting Rosemary Stanley out of the house before they could begin bargaining. Let her come down the stairs and out of the front door and then they could start making terms and conditions. Fleetwood couldn't hear the man's reply. He put his right foot up on to the wisteria where it bent at almost a right angle, his left foot a yard higher into the fork and then hauled himself on to the extension roof . . . Now all he had to do was swing his leg over the sill. He wished he could still hear the voices but he could hear nothing but the groaning of brakes on the main road, the mindless sporadic hooting of impatient drivers. Bridges started to climb up. It was odd the things you noticed at times of tension and of test. The last thing that mattered now was the colour the windowsill was painted. Yet Fleetwood took note of the colour, Cretan Blue, the same shade as that on the front door of the house he and Diana were buying in Chigwell.

Fleetwood found himself in the bathroom. It had green-tiled walls and on the floor creamy-white tiles. Footprints, made in liquid mud and now dry, crossed it, growing fainter as they reached the door. The man with the gun had come in this way. Bridges was outside the window now, bracing his weight on the sill. Fleetwood had to open the door, though he couldn't think of anything he had ever wanted to do less. He was not brave, he thought, he had too much imagination, and sometimes (though this was no time to think of it) it seemed to him that a more contemplative, scholarly life would have suited him better than police work.

From here the traffic sounds were very faint in the distance. Somewhere in the house a floorboard creaked. Fleetwood could also hear or feel a regular throbbing but this, he knew, was his own heart. He swallowed and opened the door. The landing outside was not at all what he had expected. It had a thick pale cream carpet and at the head of the stairs there was a polished wooden handrail and on the stair wall were little pictures in gilt and silver frames, drawings and engravings of birds and animals, and one of Dürer's *Praying Hands*. This was a house where people were happy and where loving care had been expended on its furnishings and its maintenance. A surge of anger came to Fleetwood because what was happening in the house now was an assault on this quiet contentment, a desecration.

He stood on the landing, holding the handrail. The three bedroom doors were all closed. He looked at the drawing of a hare and the drawing of a bat with a face that was vaguely human, vaguely pig-like, and wondered what there was about rape that made any man want to do it. For his part he couldn't really enjoy sex unless the woman wanted it just as much as he. Those poor girls, he thought. The girl and the man with the gun were behind the door to the left of where Fleetwood now stood – on the right, as far as the observers outside were concerned. The man with the gun knew what he was doing. He wasn't going to be fool enough to leave the front of the house unmanned while investigating what went on at the back.

Fleetwood reasoned: if he shoots me, I can only die, or not die and get well again. His imagination had its limits. Later on he was to remember what he had thought in his innocence. He stood outside the closed door, put his hand to it and said in a bold clear voice, 'This is Detective Sergeant Fleetwood. We are in the house. Please open this door.'

There had not been total silence before. Fleetwood realized this because there was total silence now. He waited and spoke again.

'Your best course is to open this door. Be sensible and give yourself up. Open the door now and come out or let me in.'

It had hardly occurred to him the door might not be locked. He tried the handle and it gave. Fleetwood felt a bit of a fool – which, in a curious way, helped. He opened the door, not flinging it; it flung itself, being the kind of door that always swings open to hit with a crash the piece of furniture immediately to the right of its arc.

The room burst into view before him like a stage set: a single bed with blue covers and blue bedspread thrown back, a bedside cabinet with on it a lamp, a mug, a book, a vase containing a single peacock feather, walls papered in more green and blue peacock feathers, wind blowing through the broken window, lifting high the emerald-green silk curtains. The man with the gun stood with his back to a corner wardrobe, pointing the gun at Fleetwood, the girl in front of him, his free arm round her waist.

He had reached a pitch of dangerous panic. Fleetwood could tell that by the change in his face. It was scarcely the same face as that which had twice appeared at the window, having been overtaken by animal terror and by a regression to instinct. All that mattered to this man now was self-preservation; he had a passion for it, but in this passion there was no wisdom, no prudence, only a need to escape by killing all who hindered him. Yet he had killed no one, thought Fleetwood, and he held a replica gun . . .

'If you put that gun down now,' he said, 'and let Miss Stanley go, let me take Miss Stanley downstairs . . . if you do that, you know the charges brought against you will be minimal compared to what they might be if you injure or threaten anyone else.' And the rapes? he wondered. There was no proof yet that this was the same man. 'You need not drop the gun. Just lower the hand you're holding the gun in. Lift your other arm and let Miss Stanley go.'

The man didn't move. He was holding the girl so tightly that the veins on his hand stood out blue. The expression on his face was intensifying as his frown deepened; the skin around his eyes creased further and the eyes themselves began to burn.

Fleetwood heard sounds at the front of the house. A scuffling and a thud. The sounds were drowned in rain noise as a sudden hard shower lashed the unbroken upper part of the window. The curtains blew in and ballooned. The man with the gun hadn't moved. Fleetwood didn't really expect him to speak and it was a shock when he did. The voice was strangled with panic, not much more than a murmur.

'This gun I have is not a replica. It's for real. You'd better believe me.'

'Where did you get it?' said Fleetwood, in whom nerves affected his stomach rather than his throat. His voice was steady but he was beginning to feel sick.

'Someone I know took it off a dead German in 1945.'

'You saw that on TV,' said Fleetwood. Behind him Bridges was standing in the short passage behind which were the banisters and the stairwell. He could feel Bridges's breath, warm in the cold air. 'Who was "someone"?'

'Why should I tell you?' A very red tongue came out and moistened lips which were the same olive shade as the man's skin. 'It was my uncle.'

A shiver went through Fleetwood because an uncle

would be the right sort of age, an uncle would be in his fifties now, twenty-five or thirty years older than this man. 'Let Miss Stanley go,' he said. 'Why not? What have you got to gain by holding on to her? I'm not armed. She's not protecting you.'

The girl didn't move. She was afraid to move. She sagged over the supporting arm that held her so tightly, a small thin girl in a blue cotton nightdress, her bare arms goose-pimpled. Fleetwood knew he must make no promises he wouldn't be permitted to keep.

'Let her go and I can guarantee it will count very much in your favour. I'm not making any promises, mind, but it will count in your favour.'

There was a thudding sound which Fleetwood was pretty sure was someone putting a ladder with padded ends up against the wall of the house. The man with the gun didn't seem to have heard. Fleetwood swallowed and took two steps into the room. Bridges was behind him and now the man with the gun saw Bridges. He lifted the hand which held the gun an inch or two and pointed it up towards Fleetwood's face. At the same time he drew his other arm from round Rosemary Stanley's waist, as if pulling his nails hard across the skin. And indeed the girl did give a shuddering whimper, shrinking her body. He pulled his arm back very sharply and kneed her in the back so that she staggered and fell forwards on to all-fours.

'I don't want her,' he said. 'She's no use to me.'

Fleetwood said quite pleasantly, 'That's very sensible of you.'

'You've got to make me a promise though.'

'Come over here, Miss Stanley, please,' Fleetwood said. 'You'll be quite safe.' Would she? God knew. The girl crawled, pulled herself up, came towards him and held his sleeve with both hands. He repeated it though. 'You're quite safe now.'

The man with the gun also repeated himself. His teeth had begun to chatter and he gobbled his words.

'You've got to make me a promise.'

'What, then?'

Fleetwood looked past him and, as the wind raised the curtains almost to ceiling level, saw the head and shoulders of Detective Constable Irving appear at the window. The DC's body blocked half the light but the man with the gun didn't seem to notice. He said, 'Promise I can go out of here by the bathroom and give me five minutes. That's all – five minutes.'

Irving was about to step over the sash. Fleetwood thought, it's all over, we've beaten him, he'll be quiet as a lamb now. He took the girl in his arms, hugged her for no reason but that she was young and terrified, and thrust her at Bridges, turning his back on the man with the gun, hearing behind him the chattering voice say, 'It's real, I warned you, I told you.'

'Take her downstairs.'

Above the banisters, on the wall down which the staircase ran, hung the reproduction of those praying hands, a steel engraving. Across the front of it came Bridges to hold the girl and take her down. It was one of those eternal moments, infinite yet swift as a flash. Fleetwood saw the hands that prayed for him, for them all, as Bridges, whose body had obscured it, moved down the stairs. Behind him a heavy foot dropped on to the floor, a sash slammed, a chattering voice gave a cry, and something struck Fleetwood in the back. It all happened very slowly and very quickly. The explosion seemed to come from far away, a car backfiring on the main road perhaps. There was no more pain, and no less, than from a punch into the base of the spine.

He saw as he fell forward the loosely clasped beseeching hands, the engraved hands, sweep upwards above his view. Slumping against the banisters, he clutched on to them, slipping down as might a child holding on to the bars of a cot. He was fully conscious and, strangely, there was no more pain from that punch in the back, only an enormous tiredness.

A voice that had once been soft and low he could hear screaming shrilly: 'He asked for it, I told him, I warned him, he wouldn't believe me. Why wouldn't he believe me? He made me do it.'

He made me do – what? Nothing much anyway, Fleetwood thought, and holding on to the bars, he tried to pull himself up. But his body had grown heavy and would not move, heavy as lead, numb, weighed down or pinned or glued to the floor. The red wetness spreading across the carpet surprised him and he said to all the people, 'Whose blood is that?'

2

All his life, for almost as far back as he could remember, Victor had had a phobia. A teacher at college to whom he had been unwise enough to mention it had called it chelonophobia, which he claimed to have made up from the Greek. He made stupid cracks about it whenever the opportunity arose, such as when the Principal's cat wandered into the lecture room one day or when someone was discussing *Alice in Wonderland*. Victor had his phobia quite badly, to the extent of not wanting to hear the creature named or even to name it himself in his thoughts, or to see a picture of it in a book or some toy or ornament made in its image, of which many thousands were in existence.

During the past ten years and a bit he had neither seen it nor heard it spoken of, but sometimes it (or one of its allotropes) had come to him in dreams. That had always happened and presumably always would, but he fancied he was a bit better about the phobia than he had used to be, for he no longer screamed aloud in his sleep. Georgie would have told him if he had. Even when he only moaned a little Georgie made enough fuss about it. One of those dreams had come last night, his final night in there, but he had learned by now how to wake himself up, which he did, whimpering and reaching out with his hands for reality.

The girl came for him in her car. He sat beside her in the front but he didn't look out much, he didn't really want to see the world yet. It was when they stopped at a red light and he turned his head aside that he saw the pet shop, and that reminded him he would be a prey to his phobia once more. Not that there was anything of that sort in the window, no reptiles of any kind, but a white puppy and two kittens playing in a pile of straw. He shivered just the same.

'You all right, Victor?' the girl said.

'Fine,' he said.

It was Acton they were going to – not his favourite place, but they hadn't given him much choice. Somewhere not totally unfamiliar, they had suggested – Acton, say, or Finchley or Golders Green. Well, Golders Green might be on the expensive side. He had said Acton would be all right, he had grown up there, his parents had died there, he had an aunt living there still. He found looking out of the car and seeing the familiar place, the same yet changed, still there, still going on while he had been a decade away, almost unbearably painful. That was something he hadn't expected. He closed his eyes and kept them closed until he felt the car turn and head northwards. Hanger Lane? No, Twyford Avenue. This was motherland and fatherland all right. They weren't going to stick him in the same street, were they? They weren't. Mrs Griffiths's house in Tolleshunt Avenue was three or four streets further west. Victor thought he would have liked to stay sitting in the car for ever but he got out and stood on the pavement, feeling dizzy.

The girl led the way. Victor followed her up the path. She had one of those handbags that are divided into many compartments with zip-up sections and extraneous purses, and from one of these she took a ring with two keys on it, one of gold metal, one of silver. It was the gold one she inserted into the lock, opening the door. She turned and gave him a reassuring smile. All he could see at first was the staircase. Most of the hall was behind it. The girl, whose name was Judy Bratner and who had asked Victor to call her Judy from the start, led the way up the stairs. The room was on the first floor, its door opened by the silver metal key. Victor was surprised to see how small the room was, for Judy had told him what the rent would be, though he would not be paying it, and he stood on the threshold for a moment, letting his eyes travel from the tiny sink and draining board in one corner to the curtainless window with its cotton blind and thence to the beanpole figure of Judy and her earnest well-meaning dedicated face.

The blind was down and Judy's first self-appointed task was to raise it. Some diffident apologetic sunshine came in. Judy stood by the window, smiling more confidently now, as if she had personally caused the sun to shine and had created – by painting it on canvas perhaps – the view. Victor went to the window and stood beside her, looking out. His right shoulder was a good six inches from her left shoulder but nevertheless she flinched a little and moved fractionally to the right. No doubt she couldn't help it, it was a reflex action, for she would know about his past.

Looking down, he could see the street where he had been born and brought up. Which house it was he couldn't be precisely sure from here, but it was one of those in the terrace with the grey slate roofs and the long narrow gardens separated from each other by chestnut paling fences. In one of those houses, for the first time, he had seen it . . .

Judy spoke regretfully and as if she had had to brace herself to do it. 'We haven't been able to come up with any sort of job for you, Victor. And I'm afraid there's no prospect of anything just at this moment in time.'

How they talked! He knew about unemployment, how it had come up like a cloud during the latter part of his lost years and now hung fog-like over the whole country.

'You might go to the Job Centre yourself once you've settled in here. Of course you'd have to be open about your . . .' She sought a word, preferably a euphemistic piece of jargon.

'Antecedents,' he said flatly.

She seemed not to have heard, though her face coloured. 'In the interim,' she said, 'it will take you a while to find your feet here. Things will seem a bit strange at first – externals, I mean. But we've talked about that.'

Not as much, in fact, as Victor had expected. Other prisoners, coming to the end of their terms, had been gradually acclimatised to the outside world, taken out for a day, let out for a weekend. Nothing like that had been done for him and he wondered if there had been new rulings on release techniques for long-term prisoners. Newspapers found their way into the prison and there was no ban on reading them daily, but they were not *serious* newspapers, the kind known as 'quality', and they gave you headlines and pictures rather than information. For instance, after that talk with the governor which had taken place early on, there had hardly been any news about the policeman.

Then, six months before his release was due, his 'rehabilitation programme' began. He was told about this in advance but all that happened was that Judy Bratner or her colleague, a man called Tom Welch, came to talk to him for half an hour once a fortnight. They were voluntary associates of the Probation and After-care Service or some such thing, though emphatically not to be called prison visitors. Exactly what they were and whom they were Victor had never found out, because Judy and Tom, though kind and bent on helping him, treated him as if he were a very stupid illiterate twelve-year-old. He didn't care because he didn't want to know. If they would do as they promised and find him somewhere to live and tell him how to get the Department of Health and Social Security to keep him, that was all he wanted. Now what he wanted was for Judy to go.

'Oh, I almost forgot,' she said. 'I have to show you where the bathroom is.'

It was at the end of the passage, down six steps and round a corner, a small cold room painted the green of tinned peas.

'All you can possibly want, you see.'

She began explaining to him how the room heater could be made to function by the insertion of twenty-pence pieces and the water heater fifty-pence pieces. Victor couldn't recall ever having seen a twenty-pence piece. It was one of those new coins. There was a pound coin now too, he seemed to remember. They walked back along the passage. A strip of beaded wood, which Victor thought was called a chair rail, ran along the wall at waist height, and on the plaster above this rail, in letters no more than half an inch high, someone had written in pencil: *The shit will hit the fan.*

'Now I'm going to leave this number with you, Victor, so that you can give us a call if there's anything bothering you. Well, there are two numbers, just to be on the safe side. We don't want you to feel you're out on your own. We want you to feel there are some supportive people who do genuinely care. Right?'

Victor nodded.

'Of course, needless to say, I or Tom will pop back in a day or two to see how you're making out. Did I tell you the pay phone's on the ground floor, just back of the stairs? You'll need five- and ten-pence pieces for that. Now you're OK for money, aren't you, till your DHSS comes through? I'm afraid Mrs Griffiths, who owns this house, she does *know*. I just thought I'd tell you, but there's no way she couldn't be told.' Judy's face screwed up with the agonizing effort of it. Her working life consisted in recounting horrible unpalatable truths – there is no job, there is no security, comfort, ease, peace, future – and it was beginning to show on her troubled pinched face. 'I mean, we always have to tell them because they'd find out, you know. Actually, Mrs Griffiths has been on our books quite a while.'

What did that mean? That half or all the other tenants were also ex-prisoners? Ex-criminals?

'But she doesn't live on the premises,' Judy said with the air of one telling first the bad news, then the good. She seemed to be searching for a remark with which to take her leave and grabbed at a whole clutch. 'It's really a nice area, not at all rough. This is a quiet street, not a through road. You might think about joining things, making friends. What about an evening class?'

Over the banisters, he watched her go downstairs. The front door closed behind her. He wondered if he were alone in the house. There was no internal sound at all. He listened and heard Judy's car start up, then a heavier vehicle with a diesel engine park further down the street, the shriek of a woman, followed by a ringing laugh. Victor went back into his room and closed the door. Judy or someone had placed on the draining board and the shelf beside it a wrapped loaf, a carton of margarine, long-life milk, canned mince and canned beans, tea bags, instant coffee and granulated sugar. The staples of English working-class diet as seen through the eyes of a social worker.

Victor examined the sink, the taps, the small cylindrical water heater, familiarizing himself with the place. Between sink and window was a cupboard, of triangular shape, formed by constructing a frame with a door in it across this corner of the room. Inside it hung his few clothes, some of which, he saw, were those he had possessed in that far-off time before his imprisonment. Everything he had owned then had gone into his parents' keeping, and both his parents were now dead, his father having died first and his mother a mere six months later. Victor had been told he might be temporarily released to attend his parents' funerals, but he had not wished to do so. It would have been embarrassing.

The bed was a single size, made up with pink nylon sheets, two multicoloured blankets manufactured in the Third (or maybe Fourth or Fifth) World and a cover that had seen better days as a french-window curtain. The tape through which the hooks had been inserted was still attached to it. The only chair in the room was of Korean cane and there was a cane and glass coffee table on the stout frame, on which someone – the graffitist prophet of disaster? – had stubbed out a hundred cigarettes, giving almost but not quite the effect of pokerwork. Upon the slippery linoleum, red-patterned with cream rectangles so that the impression given was of ravioli in tomato sauce, lay two small rugs of green nylon fur.

Victor looked out of the window. The sun had gone in and the roofs of West Acton lay red and grey and terracotta under a pale grey sky across which a large gleaming unidentifiable aircraft was making its way to Heathrow. There was no wind and it was very clear. A main road could be seen along which traffic flowed in a metallic stream. This road was just behind the gardens of the street where his parents' house had been – or, rather, where stood the house his parents had rented for the duration of their married life. He was glad they were dead – not from any conventional or sentimental standpoint, such as shame at having to confront them or fear of giving them pain, but simply because here was one additional trouble and stumbling block out of the way. Yet he had loved his mother deeply, or had told himself he had so often that he believed it.

When he had gone to prison he had supposed he would begin regular sessions with a psychiatrist, for in pronouncing sentence the judge had repeated the jury's recommendation that he should receive psychiatric treatment. But he had never seen a psychiatrist – on account he supposed of shortage of funds or shortage of psychiatrists – and the only time it had been suggested that treatment might be meted out to him for a possible mental instability had been when he was asked, only two years ago, if he would care to volunteer for group therapy as part of an experiment carried out by a visiting sociologist. Victor had refused and no more had been said. But while he had been awaiting the summons to a psychiatrist in those early days he had sometimes turned over in his mind what he would say to this man or woman when the time came. Most of all he had thought about his phobia and the grotesque way it had begun and about the panics and the violent anger. He had asked himself too why the child of happily married middle-class parents, whose childhood had been for the most part uneventful and contented, should have needed to make motiveless unreasoning attacks on women.

A psychiatrist might have come up with some answers. On his own, Victor had not been able to supply any. And he became angry when he thought about his anger, panicky and confused when he tried to examine his panics. Sometimes he thought of them as symptoms of some disease he had caught, for they could not have been inherited nor yet brought into being by ill-usage or neglect when he was young. In prison what he had felt most of the time, more than any other emotion, was self-pity.

One day the Governor had sent for him. Victor thought it might be to tell him that his father, who had been unwell, was worse or even dying. But in fact his father was not to die for another five years. A prison officer took him to the Governor's office and sat down in a chair specially provided for such custodians, more or less between Victor and the Governor, who was in any case protected by his large oak desk. The warder sat in the way warders and policemen waiting for something or keeping a watch on people always do sit: upright, legs apart, hands folded in lap, and wearing an expression of blank idiocy.

'Well, Jenner,' the Governor said, 'we thought you might care to have some news of the progress made by Detective-Sergeant Fleetwood. Am I right?'

'Yes, sir,' said Victor. What else could he say? He would have liked to say he didn't care and it was nothing to him. He would have liked to pick up the inkwell from the desk and hurl it at the Governor's head, seeing the ink drip down the Governor's chin like black blood on to his immaculate collar. But he wanted to get the maximum remission. In those days he longed to get out.

'Sergeant Fleetwood has been in Stoke Mandeville Hospital for a year now. That is the orthopaedic hospital, you understand, which means specializing in injuries to the spine and limbs.'

It didn't mean that. It meant correcting deformities. But the Governor was an ignorant bastard who spoke to everybody alike, as if they were all the same illiterate boneheads.

'I'm glad to tell you he has made great strides . . .' The Governor seemed to realize what he had said and, pausing, he cleared his throat. 'Of course he cannot walk without a mechanical aid, but there are hopes he may one day be able to do so. He is in good spirits and will soon be leaving hospital to make a life for himself in his own surroundings.'

'Thank you, sir,' said Victor.

Before the trial, while he was on remand in custody, he had read articles in the newspapers about Sergeant Fleetwood. He had never felt pity for him, only contempt and a kind of exasperation. If Fleetwood had been sensible, had listened to him and believed him, if he had believed him when he said the gun was a real gun, Fleetwood would be a fit vigorous man today, a man leading a normal life and doing his job. But he hadn't listened and Victor had lost his head. It was something he did in times of great stress or pressure; he always had. He lost his head, panicked and did things in that panic. Which was why it had been wrong to charge him with and convict him for attempted murder. He had not *intended* to kill or even maim or hurt Fleetwood. Panic came over him like a kind of electric suit, fitting him as a second skin, prickling him all over, crawling on him, tingling and sending into his hand an impulse that pulled that trigger and fired that gun. That was the only way he could describe what one of his panics was like: an electric suit full of tingling wires.

There had been a sentimental article about Fleetwood in one of the popular tabloid papers. It said that his first name was David and he was twenty-eight (the same age as Victor) and engaged to be married to a girl called Diana Walker. There was a picture of her and him taken at their engagement party. The article made much of the fact that Fleetwood had been due to get married the following week. He hadn't got married but his girlfriend told the paper that they were only waiting for Fleetwood's superficial injuries to heal. She was going to marry him just as soon as she could. Never mind if he couldn't move, couldn't walk and might never walk again, she was only too happy to have him alive. They would win through, the two of them together. It was being together that was important. There was nothing in the article about Victor Jenner. Of course there couldn't be – nothing about what a monster he was and how it was a pity people like him couldn't be flogged within an inch of their lives – because that would be *sub judice*. But there was a great deal about what a wonderful policeman Fleetwood had been. The way they wrote about him, his brilliant brain, sweet nature, invincible courage, unselfishness, powers of judgement and deductive faculties, made you wonder why he wasn't at least a chief superintendent or maybe Attorney General.

Victor saw him as the instrument whereby he had been sent to prison for fourteen years.

After that interview with the Governor, Victor had never been told another word about Fleetwood. He didn't see newspapers every day. Sometimes he didn't see a newspaper for weeks on end. But one day, some two years later, he did read a paragraph about a charity concert at the Albert Hall organized in aid of the dependants of injured policemen, and this concert had been compèred by David Fleetwood. There was no picture but the paragraph mentioned that Fleetwood had introduced the performers from his wheelchair.

Most of what went on in the prison the Governor knew nothing about. Word had got round as to details of Victor's conduct before he shot the policeman; the other men in the prison knew he was the Kensal Rise rapist and they all had a kind of virtuous antipathy towards rapists just as they did towards child molesters. It was all right to beat old ladies over the head in tobacconists' shops and break into the till, it was OK to rob banks; but rape was something else again, beyond the pale.

Victor knew what it was like to be raped now. Four of them raped him one night and Cal, who later became his instructor in the office furniture shop, told him afterwards that maybe that would teach him not to do it again. In pain and bleeding but not on this occasion in a panic, Victor fixed him with a cold stare and managed, though there were tears on his face, a small tight smile. He was staring and smiling at such ineffable ignorance of human nature and life and the way men are.

Did something like that teach you not to do it again? Victor didn't know. His eyes, while he had been dwelling on the past, had been fixed mesmerically on what he thought was the roof of the house he had lived in as a child, a red patch among other reds and greys, the white of streets and the green of gardens. He shook himself and blinked his eyes to break the hypnosis.

It was April. The clocks had gone on three weeks before and the days were long and light. Immediately below this window was a garden of sorts with a shed in it, four dustbins and a rusted filing cabinet. In prison he had worked in the office furniture shop, making filing cabinets like that one and stands for photocopiers and swivel chairs. Of course that couldn't be one of his grown old, for items made by prisoners were not allowed to be sold to the general public. Mrs Griffiths's garden wasn't the kind you sat in or gardened in but the kind you ran out into with a bag of rubbish or to fetch a bucket of coal. A good many similar junk-filled backyards were visible as well as tended gardens, but otherwise it was all backs of houses. Victor wondered if Judy and Tom had purposely arranged it this way to avoid Victor's seeing people walking along when he looked out of his window . . .

What they wouldn't want him to see were women.

Was he crazy to think like this, to attribute such caution to others? As soon as he went out he would see women. They were half the human race. Judy and Tom might not know, he told himself, and Judy might have flinched and drawn away from him for quite some other reason.

It wasn't, after all, for rape that he had gone to prison but for attempted murder.

3

That first night he lay in bed listing in his mind all the things he had to do. He hadn't been able to bring himself to go out, for as soon as he opened the door and stepped on to the landing and heard voices from below and a girl's laugh, the electric suit had begun to fit itself around his body and his limbs, fastening itself at the neck and constricting his throat, prickling his wrists and ankles and squeezing his chest. Into the room he had retreated, gasping for breath. He had covered his head and the upper part of his body with bedclothes and lain on the bed for some half an hour. Then he got up and made himself tea and baked beans on bread, taking strong deep breaths all the time to steady himself. It took a deliberate effort of will and great concentration to make himself think of practical things but at last, after it got dark and he was lying in bed with the blind down and the top light and bedlamp on, he succeeded. The DHSS first, then register with a doctor, go to the bank and find out about his money. Then a telephone call to his aunt in Gunnersbury. Then the Job Centre.

Great changes must have taken place, out there in the outside. Some intimation of this had come to him during the ride home with Judy. He fancied London looked dirtier and the people shabbier, and it all somehow looked *bigger*, though he could have imagined that. And he knew nobody, he had no friends, he was utterly alone. He remembered boasting in the old days that he didn't know what loneliness was, he liked his own company, but now he was less sure. Doubts came to him as to what he meant by his own company, as to exactly what that was.

He had shared a cell for so long in a building full of

people that he found himself afraid of the comparative solitude of this room. But he finally did sleep and his sleep was crowded with dreams. He had always been a great dreamer and had dreamed a lot in prison, especially the dream about the road through life and the houses and, of course, inevitably the phobia dream, but never about the house in Kensal Rise, at 62 Solent Gardens. Now, after more than ten years, he did. He was in that bedroom again, an animal in a den with the hunters coming first by the back way, then by the front. As a hostage the girl was hopeless because he could only kill her and then what could he do? At this point in the dream Victor realized he was dreaming, for things had not actually happened quite like this. He thought he would wake himself out of the dream before it got to the bad part.

Fleetwood opened the door and came in – only it wasn't Fleetwood, it was himself, or his mirror image. Victor heard himself shouting at Fleetwood to send a real policeman, not someone disguised, and Fleetwood, as if he understood, metamorphosed before his eyes, growing taller and thinner and paler. Behind him, on the wall, hung a picture, a line drawing or engraving, whose subject Victor could not make out, but which he feared.

'I'm dreaming,' Victor said, and he closed his eyes and opened them again, willing himself to wake, but the dream refused to go. 'This is a real gun,' he said to Fleetwood. 'I got it from my uncle who was a high-ranking officer in the German army. You'd better believe me.'

'Of course I believe you,' Fleetwood said, and then Victor knew there wasn't going to be a bad part to the dream. 'You can have ten minutes to get away in. I'm not looking, see? I'm looking at this picture.'

Fleetwood turned his back and looked at the picture, leaning on the banisters. It wasn't what Victor thought it might be but a pair of praying hands. With his arm round the girl, Victor went past him into the bathroom; only, when they got there, it wasn't a bathroom but his Aunt Muriel's house in Gunnersbury, and his mother and father were there and his aunt and uncle, having tea. When his mother saw the girl she got up and said, 'Hallo, Pauline, you *are* a stranger.'

Victor woke up. The room was full of sunshine. He reflected on his dream. How many people had to dream of things that happened ten years before and of people who were dead or disappeared because they knew no one new? Of course knowing no one worked both ways. He didn't know them – and they didn't know him. That, however, was something which would rapidly change. It would soon change if he registered with a doctor, made himself known to his fellow tenants and did what Judy had suggested in the way of joining evening classes.

He would have to tell everyone he encountered who he was and where he had been for the past ten years. He would either have to do that or tell elaborate lies. Change his name, for a start, say he had been ill or living abroad. If he was going to do that, he must do it from the start. He mustn't even stay in this house longer than was strictly necessary. First, though, it was absolutely essential to go out. Rather as a man who has been in a motor accident knows he must as soon as possible get into a car and drive it again or he never will, Victor knew he must go outdoors. It had been bad getting into Judy's car and being driven here. Everything had seemed very big and changed and unreal. And that was nothing to how it would feel if he were on foot with no strong capsule of glass and metal to protect him. But go he must, and this morning.

He waited, lying in bed, until the sounds in the house ceased. The night before he had calculated that there were four other occupied rooms in the house, so when he heard the front door slam four times he got up. There might be more people, of course, wives who didn't work or old people, but that was a chance he had to take. As it happened, he met no one on his way to or from the bathroom. He dressed in clothes that had been his before his arrest, a pair of grey worsted trousers and a green velvet cord jacket. The trousers were tight on him and he had to draw in the belt under his belly, for he had put on weight in prison, on account no doubt of the stodgy food.

Getting out wasn't easy. He went back twice, once because he thought he hadn't closed the window, and the second time – by then he was at the foot of the stairs – because he thought he might be cold and need a sweater. The big sunny windy terrible outdoors received him like icy water receives a naked diver. He gasped for air and the air rushed in to fill his lungs. For a while he had to stand still and hold on to the gatepost. This, presumably, was the agoraphobia from which his Auntie Muriel said she suffered. At any rate, his mother used to tell him she hadn't been out of doors for five years. If she felt like this, he could understand it.

Presently he began to walk slowly along the street in the direction of Acton High Road. This led him past the house where he used to live. He walked along fearfully with a powerful sense that he was being followed. Every few seconds he found himself looking round sharply but there was never anyone there. He thought what a lot of cars there were, cars parked everywhere, double, treble the number there had been ten years ago. A woman came out of her front door and slammed it. The sound made him jump and he almost cried out. Outside the gate of his parents' house he stopped and looked at it.

His mother hadn't been a fussy or even very careful housekeeper and in her day, from the outside certainly, the place had had a drab look. There had been curtains of different, and not very attractive, patterns at all the windows. Now every window was festooned with snowy white net, gauzy flounces ruched and looped up like a girl's petticoat. Victor had a strange feeling of breathlessness and an indefinable discomfort when this particular comparison came to him. Girls didn't wear petticoats, did they? Not unless fashions had changed drastically. He relaxed a bit when he remembered that his mother herself had possessed just such a petticoat, white and frilly and stiffened, in the mid-fifties, when such garments enjoyed a vogue.

The stucco surface of the house had been painted white as icing on a Christmas cake and the woodwork a bright emerald green. On either side of the front door were green and white tubs with cypress trees in them. Victor realized that the house looked so well tended because its occupants owned it. You took more interest in the appearance of a house when it was yours. His grandmother, his mother's mother, had been the original tenant, and when his parents got married they went to live with her. That was just after the Second World War. His grandmother died a few months before he was born and his parents continued with the tenancy, the rent being so low and the housing shortage so acute. His mother had been a happy woman who had had the good fortune to fall in love, marry the man she was in love with and remain in love with him for the thirty-five years until he died. Victor had never been in love and couldn't imagine what it would be like. His mother had been only fifty-seven when she died. His father, who was ten years older, had died first. He had had a stroke five years after Victor went to prison and after that could only get about in a wheelchair. Propelling himself along the pavement one summer morning – on this very stretch of pavement, Victor supposed, between here and the corner – he had keeled over and died, running the wheelchair into a brick wall and overturning it. The cause of death was a massive heart attack. What his mother had died of Victor didn't know, though the death certificate which he had been shown gave the cause as coronary disease, which was surprising because she had been a strong woman. She had survived his father by only six months. But perhaps it wasn't so surprising, for her husband had been her whole life, the heart and core of her existence. Victor had sometimes tried to imagine how life had been for his mother on her own, but he had simply been unable to see her without his father.

From babyhood Victor had been used to the society of demonstrative people. His mother was young and pretty and his father was always touching her, putting his arm round her and kissing her. They never sat in chairs but always on the settee, holding hands. When he looked back (as he did when rehearsing what to say to the psychiatrist), he was never able to see his parents singly or recall times when he had been alone with his mother, though these must have been numerous, as for instance after school before his father returned from work. They never quarrelled, as far as he could remember. They were kind, affectionate parents too, and if Victor's mother always seemed to favour her husband over her son, as in the case of serving him first at table or giving him preference when it came to titbits – this was the hungry aftermath of war – Victor would have told the psychiatrist that this was only what he would have expected, his father being older and bigger and more powerful than he.

His parents had few friends and almost the only visitors to the house were relatives. They were all in all to each other, locked in an exclusive relationship of companionability, devotion and sex. Victor's mother answered all his questions about sex carefully and fearlessly so that by the time he was five he knew how babies were made and knew too that parents went on doing that thing that makes babies, the man pushing his willy into the lady's bottom, even when they don't want babies but because it was right and, his father said, what men and women were for. His father drew diagrams for him – well, he didn't exactly draw them, he traced them out of a book, which rather disillusioned Victor – and answered questions his mother couldn't or wouldn't answer, such as what wet dreams were and how it felt to want to do that thing that made (or did not make) babies.

For all that, he never really connected it with his own parents. Once, when he was about six, getting up to go to the bathroom, he had passed their bedroom door and heard his mother groaning: 'Don't, don't – Oh, no, no, no!' and then she gave a low howl like an animal. But she had looked so happy before she went to bed! With that howl still in his ears, he remembered her soft rippling giggle, her sidelong smile at his father, her hand caressing the nape of his neck. Victor wasn't at all afraid of his parents but he was afraid to go into the room. Just the same he screwed up his courage and tried the door handle. The door was locked.

Next morning the first thing he heard when he woke was

his mother singing. She was singing a pop song of the time called 'Mr Sandman, bring me a dream'. There was a line in it that went 'Tell me that my lonesome nights are over'. She came into Victor's bedroom still laughing at something his father had said and she gave Victor a morning kiss and said it was a beautiful day and swept the curtains back to let the sun in. So he knew it was all right and that she wasn't hurt but happy. He even wondered if he had dreamed what he had heard, if in fact Mr Sandman had brought him this dream like in the song. He still wondered that. Certainly he had never listened outside that door again, which was why he had been utterly flabbergasted when, years later when Victor was in his twenties, he heard his father telling someone what a nuisance he had been when a little boy – 'a pest', his father called him – always wandering about the house at night, and he had once been found fast asleep on the threshold of their bedroom.

The night before his seventh birthday he had seen them doing that thing. Later on, he had read in a magazine – the *Reader's Digest* probably – that this is called in psychiatrist's terms 'the primal scene', and in another article that seven is regarded as the onset of the age of reason; in other words, you know what you're doing after that, you're responsible. It was the night before his birthday, and he knew they had bought him a present and hidden it somewhere and he was unashamedly looking for it. It was the same on Christmas Eve. He went about hunting for his presents, and they knew it, he thought; they knew it and half enjoyed his curiosity, playing up to it and hiding the presents in unlikely places.

He wanted a cat or a dog but didn't think there was much chance of his getting either. As third best he hoped for a rabbit. They had more or less promised a 'pet'. He got out of bed at about half past nine, having been unable to sleep, and came downstairs looking for his present. There was no television in those days, or at least there was, but they didn't have it. His parents had the radio on in the evenings. Soft music was coming from the living room. He opened the door very quietly, to check if they were sufficiently occupied not to be aware he was out of bed. They were sufficiently occupied. His father, with a shirt on but no trousers, was humping up and down on top of his mother, who lay on her back with her skirt up and her blouse undone on the brown velvet settee.

It was not so much the movements they made as the noises, a kind of sucking slurping, his father puffing and gasping, his mother giving long sighs and short squeaks. It was not so much the noises as the movements, the way his mother thrashed from side to side, the way his father bounced and drove. It was both. He need not have worried about disturbing them. A shotgun (he thought years later) let off in that room wouldn't have disturbed them.

He turned round and went away. Into the kitchen. He wanted a sweet or a biscuit, though this was forbidden after teeth-cleaning, he wanted something sweet for comfort. They possessed a small fridge but no sweet things were kept in it. The larder was a walk-in cupboard with a stone floor, a wire-mesh window in the door and an airbrick to the outside. Victor wasn't tall enough to reach the door handle but the door wasn't quite closed and he took hold of the edge of it and pulled it open.

A huge shell. A head reared up from under the rim of it, snake-like but blank and dull-eyed, questing, moving from this side to that, two armoured feet sluggishly waving, the whole of it an inch or two from his face. He screamed. He covered his face and his ears and his eyes and rolled on the floor, screaming. His father and mother had finished, for they heard him and came running, fastening their clothes and calling out to him. His mother picked him up and held him, asking why, why? Afterwards he understood, he accepted explanations. It was his birthday present, kept for the night in a box on the larder floor, but he hadn't seen the box or the straw or the wire netting. Only the tortoise. They gave it away, of course, to the Macphersons down the road.

That was the Macphersons', five houses down. Perhaps they were still alive, though the thing he had named once in his thoughts but wouldn't again couldn't be. Mrs

Macpherson might at this moment be watching him from her window. What had his mother told the neighbours? She would have had no chance of concealment. For days the papers had been full of him and then again at the time of his trial. He wondered if in fact she had cared so very much. It had been he, after all, and not his father who had been taken from her and shut up in prison.

Victor moved away from the gate, for he had been leaning on it. Round the back there, behind the side gate, was a little paved sunny yard where his mother had grown tomatoes in pots, and one of the windows – or in this case a grid – that gave on to the yard opened out of the larder where the – thing had been in its wire-netted box. It occurred to Victor for the first time that only a very slatternly housekeeper would have thought of keeping an animal, a creature like that, in a larder overnight, and for some reason he shivered. His life would have been different if he hadn't opened that larder door, but perhaps not so very different.

Victor gave the house a last look. He hadn't really lived there since he had left school and gone to the polytechnic. It was a pity his parents hadn't bought it so that he rather than the landlord might have had the – what sort of sum did a house like that fetch now? Twelve thousand pounds? Fifteen? He was astounded by what he saw in the estate agent's window when at last, his confidence very gradually increasing, he reached the High Street.

Forty thousand for a house like that! What then was his bus fare going to cost him? Suppose he wanted to take a taxi? Victor was reminded of a joke which had been going the rounds before he went to prison and inflation had begun to take off. Alan that he worked for had told him.

'There was this man who thought he'd take advantage of inflation. He had himself put to sleep and frozen for twenty years. When he woke up the first thing he saw was a letter from his stockbroker, a year old, saying his investments were worth a million pounds. He went down the road to the callbox to phone his stockbroker and as he was feeling in his pockets for some small change he read the instructions on the pay phone and they said: dial the number you require and when you hear the ringing tone insert nine million pounds . . .'

It wasn't apathy or fear that kept him from doing more than make sure of his Social Security payments. He found himself increasingly reluctant to root himself here in Acton. After a week of freedom he had succeeded in avoiding contact with all the other occupants of the house, and he had seen neither his landlady nor her agent. His rent was paid direct. Presumably the DHSS believed – and with justification – that, if they gave the rent money to the tenant, the tenant would keep it for his own use. There would be time enough to register with a doctor when he was ill.

Reading newspapers and magazines daily gave him instruction in current ways and current parlance. There was an expression 'to psych up' which he couldn't remember having heard before. Victor psyched himself up to go to the bank and find how much was in his deposit account – or he was in the process of psyching up, telling himself that once he was in the bank talking to the manager or whoever he wouldn't feel afraid, when something happened to drive him out. He had been almost a week in the room in this house when contact with another human being was forced upon him. There came a tap at his door at ten one morning and when he opened the door, sick and cold with trepidation, he found a woman outside announcing that she was Noreen and that she had come to clean his room.

'I don't want the room cleaned,' he said. 'It doesn't need cleaning. I can't afford to pay for that.'

He hadn't used his voice much in the past week and hadn't resorted to talking to himself, so his speech sounded stilted and strange in his ears. Noreen was not apparently sensitive to these nuances. She walked in, pushing a vacuum cleaner.

'That's all taken care of,' she said. 'It comes in your rent.' She looked round her. 'Doesn't need it! You could have fooled me.'

She set to work with furious vigour, yanking the bed away from the wall, piling the cane chair and table and rugs into the middle of the room, the vacuum cleaner already switched on though immobile, as if it needed to warm up. She was a small rather pretty woman of about thirty-five with long greasy curly dark hair. Her body was rather plump and bulgy but her legs were thin with fine slender ankles. She wore a black cotton skirt, mauve tee shirt and Scholl sandals. Victor felt an unexpected shocking violent surge of desire for her.

He edged away and stood between the cupboard and the sink. The electric panic suit began to enclose him. In the past week he had been glad that he felt nothing. Why did this urge grip him now? She was not much to look at, this Noreen, and she smelled of sweat. She wasn't very young. Was it because he was in his own place and feeling reasonably safe while outside he was still afraid and astonished most of the time? He wanted to whimper and bleat like an animal. He wanted to scream.

Noreen shouted above the sound of the vacuum cleaner, 'If you've got anything to go out for, I should go out now. Then you won't be under my feet. I usually get done in half an hour.'

He put on his jacket and edged past her, walking with his hands on the walls. The years in prison hadn't killed it then. Had he ever supposed they would? Outside the door, on the landing, he fell on his knees and crouched forward with his head on the floor. He rocked back and forth. The vacuum cleaner whined and groaned and hiccupped behind the door. Victor banged his forehead on the floor. He lurched to his feet and staggered down the stairs. With his room taken over, there was nowhere for him to hide. He thought of a line he'd read somewhere once, long ago. No doubt he'd come across it in that mixed English–Sociology–Economics course he'd started at the polytechnic. For this is hell, nor am I out of it. He hadn't the least idea who had said that, but this was hell and he was in it up to his neck.

The money his parents had left him was in a deposit

account at the local branch of Lloyds Bank. There had originally been something in the region of a thousand pounds but out of that had had to come the cost of his mother's funeral and payment for the removal of the furniture. Victor forced himself to walk to the bank, teeth gritted, hands stuffed in his pockets. Part of the way he walked almost blind, his eyes half closed, his head bent so that he was looking down at the pavement.

In the bank everything was so easy that he wondered what had stopped him coming days before. He gave his name, which the bank teller didn't recognize, which obviously meant nothing to him, and though he couldn't give the account number, this hardly seemed to matter. They found out everything like that on computers now. Victor, who barely knew what a computer was, felt ignorant and awed.

His account contained only just over three hundred pounds. A slip of paper, folded in half, was passed to him via the little trough under the grille. They were a lot more security-conscious in banks than they had been ten years ago. Cal had been inside for doing a bank, he remembered, and Georgie for holding up a postmaster in some Hertfordshire post office at gunpoint while his mate helped himself to a couple of hundred old-age pensions. Three hundred pounds – and that included the accumulated interest over five or six years.

Victor didn't want to use the phone that was attached to the wall in the area behind the stairs. He might be overheard. It was always impossible to tell whether or not the house was empty. There was a pair of phone boxes outside the Job Centre, both unoccupied. Victor looked at what was on offer in the Job Centre window. The number of jobs going was at variance with what he had been told by Judy but no doubt when you came to apply they would turn out either to be filled or not what they seemed. There was even one that might suit him: 'Skilled or semi-skilled metalworker/cabinet maker wanted for office furniture workshop.' In the days he'd worked for Alan it had been as a driver in Alan's car-hire company. He could drive all right, drive anything, and he could make filing cabinets – but what was he going to tell them when they asked about his previous experience?

He pulled open the door of the first phone box. There were no directories and when he tried to use the phone he found that it was dead. In the next box not only was the phone dead but the receiver had been cut off and laid on its side in the metal box where the directories should have been. Victor couldn't understand it. His face must have expressed his bewilderment for, as he came out of the box, a woman walking past said to him, 'Them two've been vandalized, love. They've been like it for weeks.'

Victor thought it was outrageous that people could go about doing damage like that and getting away with it, going unpunished. He had been going to phone his aunt but now he asked himself what was the point? Whenever he chose to go there, she would be in. She never went out. Noreen might have finished cleaning the ravioli linoleum by now, but very likely she would still be in the house. He wasn't going back while she was still there.

He began walking down Gunnersbury Avenue, for he couldn't get up the courage to take a bus. Traffic on its way to Heathrow pounded past him at rush-hour volume, though it was only eleven in the morning. It made him wonder what it would feel like and how he would feel if he tried driving a car again after ten years. This used to be what his mother had called a 'select area', but Victor had always thought it bizarre, rows and rows of large neo-Tudor houses, every square foot of their surfaces adorned with half-timbering, their roofs steeply pitched and their windows leaded and glazed with stained glass. It might not have been so bad if there had been space enough, if each house had been allotted half an acre of land, but instead they were crammed together. Mostly, the front gardens were rockeries with steps winding up through them to the front door. His aunt's was a corner house with the front door a studded oak medieval imitation and a kind of granite cliff hung with rock plants supporting the porch.

Muriel Faraday had married late. She was older than his mother but Victor was sixteen before she got married. He could remember going to the wedding because it was just after his 'O' Level results had come in and at the reception his father went about telling people his son had eight 'O' Level passes, which had embarrassed Victor. The marriage had been in some registry office, he couldn't remember where, and Muriel had worn high heels and a big hat which had made her look huge beside the stooping elderly man who was her husband. Sydney Faraday was the owner of three prosperous greengrocery shops, a widower with grown-up children. Victor's mother told him that Muriel had stipulated that if she agreed to marry him there was to be no question of her ever serving in one of the shops, not even to help out in an emergency.

Victor and his parents derived no benefit from Muriel's new prosperity, though his mother had had high hopes of fruit out of season and a discount on new potatoes. 'Not so much as a punnet of strawberries,' she used to say. It would have been difficult for such presents to be handed over since his mother invited people to the house or accepted invitations very rarely and his aunt, soon after her wedding, developed a phobia about going out. On only two or three occasions had Victor gone to his aunt and uncle's house, for Christmas dinner twice and one other time, but he remembered perfectly where it was.

Before going up the steps to the front door, Victor walked down the steep ramp to the garage at the bottom. This garage was half timbered and had little diamond-paned windows like a country cottage on a calendar. Victor looked through one of the windows at the furniture inside, all of it covered up with his mother's curtains. On top of the curtains bric-à-brac from his mother's shelves and cupboards lay in heaps – cups and plates and vases and ashtrays and paperweights and candlesticks. Where one of the curtains had slipped, he could see the bedhead from his parents' bed, old gold quilted satin across the padded buttoned surface, from which hung a long thick cobweb.

A concrete staircase, winding and rustically uneven, led

to the front door. All around it loomed artificial outcroppings of stone, hung with trailing plants and partly obscured by dark fan-shaped growths of horizontal conifers. For as long as Victor could remember – from the time, that is, when Muriel married Sydney and moved in here – garden statuary had relieved the gloomy starkness of these escarpments, creatures cast in concrete: a frog, a rabbit, an owl with painted yellow eyes, and a tortoise. Fortunately for Victor, the tortoise was the least obtrusive, for the stone on which it stood was the one nearest to the box hedge and half covered by fronds of juniper. Giving it only a cursory glance, you might have taken it for a stone itself. Victor, of course, had never approached it nearer than these steps, had never looked at it except out of the corner of his eye. Now he noted only that it was still there, neither more nor less obscured than it had been last time he was here, more than a decade ago. Either the juniper had not grown or else it was purposely kept trimmed back to this level.

The front door looked as if it hadn't been opened for months or as if it were in fact the entrance to some fortress and his summons, by means of the bell that must be rung by pulling a twisted iron rod, would call forth a doorkeeper in chain mail holding a club. Victor hesitated before pulling it. He didn't want that furniture, he had nowhere to put it, and even if he had possessed an empty house waiting to be furnished, almost anything would have been preferable to these pieces in which memories and pains and shames were somehow petrified. But perhaps he hadn't really come for that at all, perhaps he had come to see Muriel, who was his only living relative, the only link left in that flesh and blood chain that anchored him to the past.

She might be dead. They wouldn't have bothered to tell him that in prison. She might be bedridden or in a home. The house didn't look lived in. But it hadn't looked lived in when he had come on Christmas Day with his parents; there hadn't been a paper chain or a card on display. He reached for the iron rod and pulled the bell.

All the windows down the street that he could see, all

diamond-paned casements with curly metal handles in wooden mullions, gleamed with a kind of black glitter, but those in his aunt's house seemed to have a grey mist on them, a dusty bloom that had been rained on and then filmed with more dust. He rang the bell again. This time he heard something. Absurdly – because this was his old aunt he was calling on, he reminded himself, a nothing, nobody that mattered – he felt the tingle of panic, electric tremors in his shoulders and down his back. He drew in his belly and put back his shoulders and breathed deeply.

The door came ajar slowly, drawn open with extreme caution, a crack, six inches, a foot. An old face peered out at him, twitching, mouse-like. She had aged so that he would hardly have known her, would not have known her in the almost impossible eventuality of their encountering each other elsewhere. He stared, his throat constricting. She had been a mountainous woman with a big floury-painted puffy face that used to remind him when he was a teenager of some elaborate cake in a patisserie window, powdery white with cherries on it and marzipan, surrounded by a golden frill. The cake had fallen into ruin, dust and cobwebs where the icing had been, a furriness as of mould on the spongy cheeks. The stout body, once tightly corseted, was wasted and bent. Muriel wore a pink net or snood on the wispy grey hair that in former times had been peroxided, a dirty blue wool dressing gown and dirty blue feather mules.

Victor didn't know what to say. He swallowed. He waited for her to say something and then he understood she didn't know him.

'It's Victor,' he said.

She stepped back, putting a hand up to her mouth. He walked into the house and shut the door behind him. She spoke in a hoarse whisper. 'Have you escaped?'

He would have liked to kill her, he could imagine doing that. And then he understood that she was afraid.

'What do you mean, escaped?' he said roughly.

'There's four more years for you to go.'

'Haven't you ever heard of remission for good behaviour?'

Horrified, she stared at him. She looked him up and down, her hands holding her face claw-like. A thin nervous giggle came from her.

'Good behaviour!' she said. 'I like that – good behaviour.'

From distant times he remembered where the living room was. He pushed the door open and went in. She followed him, shuffling.

'I thought you must have got out over the wall.'

He took no notice. The living room was full of newspapers and magazines. Against the wall opposite the fireplace four tower blocks of magazines reached from the floor to the ceiling. The impression was that the building had ceased only because the ceiling was reached. In the embrasure of the bay window, newspapers were piled, broadsheets on the left and tabloids on the right, to a height of about four feet. More magazines filled the area between the refectory table top and the floor beneath, the three bookcases, the alcoves on either side of the fireplace, even the sofa and one of the armchairs. A small space in the centre of the carpet only was free of them, this and the armchair draped with a blanket in which his aunt presumably sat in front of the television.

And she never went out! How did one old woman who never went out assemble this hoard of paper? If you never threw anything away, he thought, if you took one daily paper and two weeklies, say, and two or three monthlies and you never threw anything away . . . Had she always been like this? He couldn't remember. He turned round to her.

'You've got my furniture.'

It occurred to him, immediately he had spoken, that she would probably start in about how generous she'd been, what it would have cost him to have the furniture stored, and so on. But she only said, 'It's in the garage.'

'Could you take me, please?'

She shook her head. 'It's outside,' she told him, as if some people had garages in the centre of their houses. 'You can go through the kitchen and in the back way. There's keys. I'll get you the keys.'

She shuffled along through the house and he followed her. Her husband had been well off and it was a big house, furnished with big expensive over-upholstered furniture from the thirties. The dining room had a lot of magazines in it too, arranged in similar pillar-like stacks. If no one had cleaned the place for several years, there had been nothing much to make it dirty. Pale soft dust was everywhere and a dusty smell. The kitchen looked as if no one had cooked food in it for a long time. His aunt opened a drawer and took out a bunch of keys. She had guarded his property well, for three separate keys were needed to open the garage door. She wasn't a bad old girl really, he thought. Maybe it was natural she'd been frightened when she first knew who he was. He had suspected her of malice and censoriousness but she was only a bit ga-ga. In the ruined face he could see something of his mother, which was odd because his mother had been lovely, but it was deep in the eyes, a something in the shape of the nostrils, the modelling of the temples. This made Victor feel strange, weak, worse in a way than he had when he knew his mother was dead.

He unlocked the garage door, using the three keys. Even then it stuck and he had to put his shoulder to it. No one had been in there for a long time. Victor stood on the threshold, gazing at his past, his childhood, cradled in these beds and mattresses, in these tables and chests and chairs, all of it shrouded in the multicoloured fabric that had covered the windows and kept the outside at bay.

Closing the door behind him, he pushed his way into the depths of it. He moved like someone who finds himself in a thicket or maze composed of trees he must not damage. The furniture smelled of his mother's house, a smell he had not been aware of while he lived with her, but which he at once recognized as personal and unique: his father's tabacco, beeswax, witch hazel, Coty *L'aimant* talcum powder. Victor found himself inhaling it as if taking in gulps of fresh air and he had to stop himself doing this.

He closed his eyes, opened them, took hold of the hem of a curtain and tugged at it. Revealed beneath was the settee, upholstered in brown velvet, on which his parents had used to sit holding hands and on which, on the night of the tortoise, he had come upon them making love. Folded on its cushions was a brown check travelling rug. Pressed up against its back was a wheelchair.

This must be the wheelchair his father had been confined to. After his father had suffered that first stroke Victor had never seen him again but his mother had continued to visit the prison, not noticeably cowed or dispirited by the atmosphere or even distressed by her son's being in there. She had been tranquil and talkative as ever, and he didn't think it had been put on for his benefit. Why should she have worried? She had his father, who was all she had ever wanted. He remembered her talking about this wheelchair and how clever he was at managing it, 'whizzing along the pavements'. That was the phrase she had used.

Victor wondered why it had been kept. It should have been handed over to the social services surely, that was obvious. Why hadn't someone written to him about it? The solicitor, for instance, who had been executor of his mother's will, had arranged with his aunt for this storage of the furniture, and neatly abstracted his own fee from Victor's legacy. What persons in their right mind had thought *he* would have a use for a wheelchair?

He covered it up again. All this stuff would have to be sold, that was the only thing to do with it. Walking along Acton High Street, he had passed a junk shop with a notice outside that said: *Flats and houses cleared and good prices paid*.

The door locked once more with the three keys, Victor went back through the house. It was a very quiet house that might have been in the depths of the country rather than in a London suburb on the main route to Heathrow. He called out, 'Auntie Muriel?'

There was no answer. He came to the dining-room door and saw her inside, leaning over the table which was covered with pieces of paper. Victor went into the dining room. He saw that the pieces of paper were cuttings from newspapers and magazines, all neatly clipped out, not torn, as if prepared for a scrapbook. Perhaps they *had* been prepared for a scrapbook, perhaps that was his aunt's design. When he saw what they had in common, he felt a great wave of heat, like a breaker in a warm sea, wash over him, flood up to his face and over his head. He felt sick, not because he cared or was remorseful, but because he thought she must have taken all these magazines, all those papers and periodicals, just for this, to this end. He held on to the edge of the table and gritted his teeth. That was nonsense, of course, no one would do that, and yet . . .

He swung round and took hold of her by the shoulders. She made a little gibbering noise and cringed. He had meant to shake the life out of her, but he let her go, though roughly enough to send her staggering so that she almost fell.

The cuttings on the table were all accounts, stories, photographs of David Fleetwood and the life he had led since Victor shot him ten years before.

4

Having only two topics of conversation, the Second World War and the greengrocery trade, Sydney Faraday had talked exhaustively about battles and beetroot, the former slightly dominating. He had been a sergeant with a tank regiment, part of Montgomery's Second Army that swept across northern Germany in the spring of 1945. One of his favourite stories was how he and a corporal and a private had gone into a farmhouse kitchen near the Weser, found the occupants gone, nothing to eat but a sucking pig roasting, in fact ready to eat at that moment, in the oven. Another was the one about the gun. Outside Bremen Sydney had found a dead German officer lying in a ditch. He was still holding a gun in his hand which led Sydney to believe (on no other evidence) that he had shot himself out of despair at the way the war was going. On the altruistic grounds of not wanting the man branded a suicide, Sydney took the gun and kept it. It was a Luger.

'A German military small-bore automatic pistol,' Sydney would explain to the company, rather in the manner of an encyclopedia.

The first time Victor heard this story had been after Christmas dinner. He was only seventeen and still going about with his parents. He heard it again ten years later when his mother said she never saw him these days and then nagged him into going with them to Muriel's on Christmas Day. Things were just the same: the same undercooked defrosted turkey, this time with canned potatoes, for there had been technological progress during the intervening decade, and greens that were perhaps sub-standard for the shop. While they ate the shop-bought, home-boiled pudding and drank the only pleasing constituent of the meal, Sydney's port, Sydney told the story of the German officer and the gun once more. Victor's mother murmured, though to no avail, that she had heard it before. Muriel, who had no doubt heard it many many times, interjected mechanically with 'My goodness!' and 'I say!', uttered expressionlessly as if she was learning these exclamations as part of a minor role in a play. She had grown fat, and the more fat she became the more withdrawn. It was as if whatever spirit she had ever had was being steadily suppressed, muffled and smothered under layers of flesh.

At the time Victor couldn't precisely remember from ten years before the exact words Sydney had used in telling the story of the dead German officer, but he didn't think they varied much from the present version. Perhaps the narrative had filled out a bit.

'So I thought, poor old devil, he must have been at the end of his tether. No future, I thought, nothing to look forward to. I reckoned on him being found and his wife and kids back home getting told he wasn't a hero, he wasn't killed on active service. Oh, no, he done himself in. You know how you get arguing with yourself on what's right and what's wrong. I thought to myself, Sydney, the only good German's a dead German, you know that.'

'My goodness!' said Muriel, deadpan.

'But somehow, I suppose the truth is we've all got the quality of mercy in us somewhere, somehow I couldn't leave him there to be branded a rotten coward. I picked up his dead stiff hand, cold as ice it was, I remember like it was yesterday, and took that Luger and stuck it in my pocket and never said a word to no one. That was a little secret between me and the dead, my own private mark of respect.'

'Can I have some more port?' said Victor.

Sydney pushed the bottle at him. 'And you won't believe this but I've still got that Luger. Oh, yes. I can show it to you any time you care to see it. For some reason I've treasured it. It's not a matter of getting it out and having a gloat over it, not a bit. I just like to remember it sometimes and think to myself, you will pass this way but once,

Sydney Faraday, and any good you can do, do it *now*. Well, that was my little bit of good when we was sweeping across to victory in old Monty's wake.'

Nobody asked to see the gun. Victor was thinking of asking when Sydney announced that he would go upstairs and fetch it. The Luger was wrapped in a white silk scarf, the kind of thing men used to wear with evening clothes. Victor's mother asked if it was loaded and when Sydney sneered that of course it wasn't, what did she take him for, handled it gingerly while remarking that it hardly seemed right on Christmas Day.

Sydney wrapped the gun up again and returned upstairs with it. The moment he was out of the room Victor excused himself to go to the bathroom. He went quietly up the stairs. At the top on the left was Sydney and Muriel's bedroom, a big room with a pink flowered carpet and a pier glass in the middle of the floor. Victor glanced quickly in there, then turned down the passage towards the bathroom at the end. Sydney's stooping form could be discerned inside the second bedroom (there were four) lifting up the eiderdown on a brass bedstead. He didn't seem to have heard Victor pass by.

At that time Victor had scarcely thought of needing a gun. Rather, he had reflected that a gun was a precious thing to possess because it was rare and it was forbidden. But in the following May he made an attack on a girl on Hampstead Heath and the girl had had some sort of training in martial arts, which wasn't very usual back in the seventies. She managed to throw Victor and escape. He remembered Sydney's gun.

Sometimes Victor thought how wrong it had been of Sydney to put temptation in his way like that. If Sydney hadn't boasted about the gun and shown it off, he, Victor, would never dreamed of such a thing being in Muriel's house, and in default of that gun, of course, he would never have acquired one. And if he had never acquired a gun . . .

Even then he didn't think much about it until Sydney fell ill and went into hospital. He was suffering from lung cancer, and a year or so later he was to die of it. Muriel had scarcely set foot outside the house for years but she had to go and visit Sydney. Victor learned all this from his mother, who told him how Muriel would only go to the hospital if she went with her, arriving in a taxi at Muriel's door to collect her. For a long time Victor's mother had had a key to her sister's house.

The next time the two sisters were due to go hospital visiting, Victor went to Gunnersbury. He watched the taxi come and his mother climb the mountain path between the alpine plants and horizontal conifers. His mother let herself into the house and came out five minutes later with the obese figure of Muriel clinging to her arm. Muriel had on a big black hat with a wide brim and a black silk raincoat, as if she were anticipating Sydney's death and was already in mourning. A few minutes after the taxi was out of sight, Victor let himself in with the key he had had copied from his mother's. It was a bit stiff and new and for a second or two he thought it wasn't going to move the lock. It did.

He wondered where that key was now, what had happened to it. There was no particular use he could think of for it, but just the same he liked having things of that sort, they made him feel safe and rather powerful. It must have got lost six months later when all his possessions were transferred to his parents' house. What, for that matter, had happened to the gun? Presumably, the police had held on to it, though it wasn't theirs any more than it had been Sydney's. It rightly belonged to the German government, Victor supposed.

He went straight up the stairs, which were of dark polished wood with a runner down the middle of the treads of red turkey carpet. How dark this house always was, even in the height of summer! The gloomy upper floor smelled of camphor and as if the windows were never opened. Victor entered the room with the brass bedstead and lifted up the eiderdown. A stone hot-water bottle and a metal bedpan lay on the bare mattress, but no gun.

Victor looked inside the hot-water bottle and inside the bedpan, he looked through the folded clothes in the chest of drawers, setting mothballs rolling out of sleeves and sock toes. The carpet was blue with a faded pattern round the border of yellow grapes and green vine leaves. He lifted up the carpet, he searched the wardrobe, he opened a wall cupboard full of shoes and boots, its upper shelf containing a small library of western novels in paperback: *The Man Who Rode to Phoenix*, *The Secret of Dead Eye Ranch*. It was his temper, his anger, which helped him that time. In a rage he kicked at the shoes in their wooden trees, overturning them. Underneath, a floor-board was loose. Victor could lift the board up with his fingers. Inside was a cardboard shoebox and inside the box was the Luger wrapped up in Sydney's fringed white silk scarf. What Sydney hadn't mentioned was that he had also taken off the German officer four rounds of ammunition. Probably that sort of rifling of a corpse would have been harder to explain on grounds acceptable to Sydney's vaunted morality.

Sydney didn't die until Victor had been nearly a year in prison. He had been out of hospital and home again when Victor made use of the gun – totally unaware, Victor often thought, how much he shared responsibility for the maiming of Fleetwood. He and Fleetwood and the girl Rosemary Stanley each had a share in that responsibility: Sydney for taking the gun in the first place, Fleetwood for refusing to believe in its evident reality, the girl for her stupid screaming and breaking of that window. People never thought of how much they might embroil others in their careless behaviour.

He hoped, though, that Sydney had been made to feel something of his guilt when, after the shooting, the police had gone to him and asked about the gun, how he had come by it and why he had given it to his wife's nephew. Even on his sickbed they hadn't spared him but had pestered him until he told them everything. That must have been one time, Victor thought, when he hadn't enjoyed boring guests with that particular after-dinner story, when he couldn't have put across all that *spiel* about how moral and caring he was.

*

In an interview he had given to a Sunday newspaper Fleetwood had talked quite frankly about his life and his feelings, less so to a women's magazine. Or the women's magazine had cut out the bits it thought might make its readers uncomfortable. He spoke about not being able to walk, about foregoing all those athletic activities which had been important to him, running, playing rugger and squash, going on walking holidays. He mentioned – not for the newspaper, only the magazine – how he had become fond of reading. One of the ventures he had begun on was studying for a degree with the Open University. He read novels and biographies and poetry, had joined the London Library as well as two book clubs. Gardening interested him and he enjoyed planning a garden, though he had to have someone else to do the work for him. He was considering as a hobby learning to make musical instruments, an organ perhaps or a harp.

In the middle of the newspaper article, just when the reader might have started thinking that being paralysed and confined to an orthopaedic chair for the rest of one's life wasn't so terrible after all, Fleetwood said, 'I suppose the worst thing is what most people don't think of, that I'm impotent, without sex. I can't make love any more and it's pretty unlikely I ever will. People forget that that gets paralysed too, they think it's solely a matter of not walking. It's the hardest thing to bear because I like women, I used to love women, their beauty, you know. That's all lost to me in a real sense, I have to face it. And I can't marry, I couldn't do a woman that sort of injury.'

In another cutting, which pre-dated the Sunday paper story by some years, was something about how Fleetwood's fiancée hadn't married him after all. There was a picture of her with him when he was fit and well and another picture of her sitting beside his wheelchair. She was slim and fair-haired, very pretty. The magazine the cutting came from wasn't particularly harsh to her or lacking in understanding. It quoted her without much comment, asking its readers at the end of the piece how they would feel in her situation: *Write in and let us know your views.*

'I loved David – well, I still do,' she had told them. 'I started off with high hopes. Good resolutions, I suppose you'd call them. The fact is, I just wasn't a big enough person to take it. I want a real marriage, I want children. I wish I could be a better person, more of what he expected, but I think it's better to know it now, to face up to it now, than to have tried marriage and failed.'

The sickly sentimentality of it made Victor cringe but he went on reading. The cuttings were laid out on the table like a pack of cards for some elaborate patience game. They spanned Fleetwood's life from the day in the house in Solent Gardens to the present, or almost to the present, the latest being dated the previous Christmas. There was the story about the charity concert Victor had read of while in prison. A photograph of Fleetwood accompanied it. He sat in a wheelchair on the stage with, on one side of him, a famous comedian whose name had been a household word for years before Victor went to prison, and on the other, a beautiful long-legged girl in a spangled leotard who leaned over him with her arms loosely about his neck. More photographs were inserted into an account in a magazine of some of the physio-therapeutic treatment Fleetwood had undergone. One of those showed the former policeman sitting in a garden with a yellow labrador dog; another, in a later story, had him at his father's funeral, holding a wreath of pink and white roses in his lap; a third was in the text of an interview with Fleetwood in which he said he was moving out of London, it was even possible he might emigrate to Australia or New Zealand. In all there were fifty-one cuttings on the table – not quite a pack of cards – and the last of them was about Fleetwood distributing presents to children in an orthopaedic hospital. He had travelled to the hospital from where he now lived, in a place in Essex called Theydon Bois.

Victor, who would scarcely have known his own aunt, whose own face in the mirror sometimes seemed unfamiliar to him, would have recognized Fleetwood without any introduction or caption. Once in his life he had seen him, for Fleetwood had been too ill to attend the trial, but he would have known him anywhere. That face was printed on his memory more indelibly than his mother's. It was a firm square solid face with regular features and a rather large long mouth. The eyes were dark (and now mournfully sad), the eyebrows black and very nearly straight, the hair dark, thick and wavy. It was a face not unlike his own. There was no question of a twin-like resemblance, but they might have been taken for brothers. They belonged to the same physical type, as if to the same tribe of tallish, well-built, even-featured people. Victor raised his head and looked at himself in the large oval steel-framed mirror which hung on the opposite wall and saw threads of grey in his hair, an indefinable ageing of the skin, something old and tired and experienced in the eyes which was similar to that in Fleetwood's own. They were each thirty-eight, which was young yet, but Fleetwood had ruined both their lives by refusing to believe an evident truth.

His aunt had come creeping back into the room. She went behind the table, keeping the table between them, as a means of defence perhaps. On the hand which held together the two sides of her dressing gown was a magnificent diamond ring. The clustered diamonds formed a dome half an inch in diameter and a quarter of an inch thick. It was a ring that should have adorned the lily-white hand of youth. Victor thought how rich Sydney must have been, better off than any of them had thought. He said to her, 'What made you save all this lot?'

Her expression was truculent and spiteful. 'Somebody had to.'

It was a senseless remark. 'Why did they? What's the use of raking up the past? I've got to put all that behind me.'

She was silent, looking at him, her tongue moving across the almost closed lips, a habit of hers that he could remember from early childhood. Then she said, 'There's some might say you ought to feel shame for what you did.'

It was useless arguing with people like her. They had stereotyped minds that ran along grooves of stock response and the commonplace. 'Anyway, I don't want this stuff,' he said. 'I'm not interested.'

'I never said you could have it,' she said. 'It's mine. That took me years to do.'

She spoke as of a work of art, a book she had written or tapestry embroidered. Like a child who is afraid of having its hand slapped, she began gathering up the cuttings, casting cautious glances up into his face. A reek of camphor came from her and he stepped back, disgusted.

'I'll see about getting someone to move the furniture. I'll phone you.'

'You'll be lucky if you get an answer.'

'What's that supposed to mean?'

She had put the cuttings carefully away into two quarto-size brown envelopes. Probably she had some secret hidey-hole for them, and Victor shuddered a little when he remembered hiding places in that house.

'There's some funny types phone,' she said. 'You wouldn't believe the things I've had said to me. Me, at my age. So now, mostly, I don't answer.'

'OK, I'll come round and tell you.'

The envelopes were merely tucked in among the magazines, halfway down the *Lady* stack. 'It can't be too long for me,' Muriel said, her tone ordinary, mildly disgruntled, not matching the malevolence of the words. 'I'd sooner have your chairs and tables than you, and that's the truth. What you've done's enough to turn a person's stomach.'

Outdoors was becoming familiar to him, less alarming. He had been on a bus and, to the amusement of the other passengers, expressed his amazement at the magnitude of the fare. Returning, he had tried the tube and the tunnels hadn't bothered him or the crowds. For days he had concentrated on getting used to London, to losing the terrible self-consciousness that had made him feel everyone was looking at him and everyone knew. Walking along Acton High Street, he followed a girl part of the way – that is, she was walking along and he was behind her, going in the same direction. She wore spiky heels and a short skirt which made him feel uncomfortable. He wouldn't express it to himself more strongly than that. It made him feel uncomfortable, that was all. Suppose it had been night time, though, and one of the paths crossing Ealing Common rather than this densely populated place, what then? He refused to answer the question.

The shop where they bought furniture and cleared flats was at the bottom of Grove Road. On the pavement outside was a rack of old books no one would buy either for their content or their decoration value, and just inside the window a tray of Victorian jewellery, rings and pendants and buttons. The stuff for sale inside reminded him of Muriel's own furniture, big, ugly, uncomfortable and shabby. A stuffed peacock with its tail feathers spread in a threadbare fan perched on the back of a chaise longue upholstered in horsehair and black leather.

A boy of about eighteen in jeans and a denim jerkin came out and asked Victor if he could help him or did he just want to browse round? Victor said he had some furniture he wanted to sell. It was really a valuation he wanted.

'You'll have to see Mr Jupp,' the boy said.

'All right.'

'Yeah, but he's not here, is he? He's up the other shop. I mean, you could go up there if you felt like it or I could pass on the message.'

'I could go if it isn't far.'

'Salusbury Road – well, sort of Kilburn. You want to go to Queens Park on the Bakerloo.'

Victor didn't realize until he got there and saw the name Harvist Road. Everything seemed to be spelled wrong around here, or spelled in an unlikely perverse way, that made him feel uneasy or as if mocked. But it wasn't that which caused him to pause outside the station, lean against the wall and momentarily close his eyes. Solent Gardens was a turning off Harvist Road. A step or two or three westwards and you were in Kensal Rise.

He had told Muriel he wanted to forget, to put the past behind him, but he was walking along Harvist Road in the opposite direction to where Jupp's shop was and remembering how, ten years before, with Sydney's gun in his pocket, he had been in the park that lay to the right here very early in the morning.

In those days he had got into the habit of roaming London at all hours. Possessing the gun gave him confidence. With the Luger in his pocket he felt invincible, a victor indeed. Had Sydney, home again by then, ever missed it? Had Muriel been told? If they had, no hint of this had filtered through to Victor living up in Finchley in his 'studio' flat, driving cars for Alan to airports and stations. In the mornings he would sometimes get up at five and go out while it was still dark. His hours were strange and irregular anyway, meeting planes as he often did at six in the morning, taking home to Surrey or Kent party-goers who at midnight or later had drunk too much to drive themselves. That morning in the late autumn he had been on his way to Heathrow, due there at nine thirty to meet, in the best of the limousines, an Arab businessman and take him to the London Hilton. What had happened to the limousine? Victor had sometimes wondered since. Leaving home at five, he had parked it round the back here, in Milman Road. And then he had walked about, feeling an excitement rise in him that he couldn't have called pleasant but which he needed to have, the trembling, breathless, choking feeling Cal had told him he felt when he looked at a pornographic photo. Cal hadn't used those words but that was what he meant, and Victor had recognized this as the feeling he had when he contemplated forcing some woman, any woman. At seven thirty he had entered the park that lay to the north of Harvist Road.

The girl was exercising a dog, a very small dog. She had just taken it off the lead and watched it run into the bushes when Victor seized hold of her. He caught her from behind, hooking one arm round her neck and clamping his hand across her mouth. That was to stop her crying out. She hadn't needed to make a sound because she was seen. A man had been in among the trees, having 'stepped in there for natural purposes', they said at the trial, which meant standing up against a bush for a pee. That was just Victor's ill-luck.

He didn't forget the gun but he didn't use it. He ran. He hadn't been certain whether both of them chased him or just the man, but it came out at the trial that it was both, and two or three others they picked up along the way. Like a pack of hounds after a miserable fox. Round those back streets he had run, doubling back and hiding, still thinking then about shaking them off and finding the car and getting off to Heathrow, still hoping. He had found himself in that lane between back gardens, a place of broken concrete pavings and garage entrances and padlocked gates. One gate wasn't padlocked though and he had gone in, up the path, bent double so they shouldn't see him over the fence, ducking down at last into a corner made by house wall and fence. It was then that he had heard the throb of a taxi's diesel engine and a front door slam. The occupants of the house were leaving it, were going out. If they were going out at this time of the morning, he had reasoned, it would be for the day.

He climbed up on to the extension roof and in through a bathroom window that had been left open a crack at the top. It was a sash window with nothing to hold it and it had slid down easily. By then his pursuers were lost or at least were soundless and invisible. He crouched for some minutes on that bathroom floor. Then, because he was sure the house was empty, he went out on to the landing. He crossed the landing and looked through the crack of a barely open door, and because he could see nothing or not enough he pushed the door a little and the girl in bed inside, the girl called Rosemary Stanley, sat up and screamed at the sight of him, jumped up screaming and ran to the window, smashed it with a hairbrush and screamed 'Help me! Help me!' to the outside world.

The strange thing was that the house meant nothing to him as he looked at it now. No doubt it was the same house, 62 Solent Gardens, the end of a terrace, but he would not have recognized it on sight alone. He walked along the opposite side of the street, looking at it. The uneven plaster surface had been painted chalk white and the front door was a different colour – wasn't it? Victor couldn't remember whether he had ever seen the front door. The broken window had been mended. Of course it had, years ago. Yet somehow when he had thought about that house while in prison he had always seen it with the window broken and the wind blowing in and lifting the curtains. That had been one of the most frightening things, that billowing curtain, for each time it lifted he had expected to see a policeman on a ladder outside. And then, at last, he had seen one. He would never know why he had aimed the gun at Fleetwood and not at the policeman on the ladder outside the window.

A woman came out, walked to the gate and leaned over it, looking to the right and then to the left. She was about forty, dark and plump, and there was no way she could be either Rosemary Stanley or Rosemary Stanley's mother. The Stanleys must have moved away. She went back into the house, leaving the door a little ajar. Victor turned round and walked back past the house towards Harvist Road and Salusbury Road and Jupp's shop.

In that room with the girl it had all seemed unreal. This can't be happening, was what he had thought over and over again. The police had insisted he meant to rape the girl but this had never crossed his mind. Indignation was what he had felt, indignation and amazement that all this could have happened, the police outside and police trying to get in, a state of siege in fact, sirens sounding, a crowd gathered and watching – and all because he had put his arm round a girl's neck and run away and tried to find refuge in an empty house . . .

Jupp's shop looked exactly like the one in Acton. There was a trough full of secondhand books out on the pavement and a tray of Victorian jewellery just inside the window. A bell jangled when he opened the door. Inside it was different, with less furniture and a case of pin-stuck butterflies, clouded yellows and commas and red admirals, instead of the stuffed peacock. On a red marble table stood an ancient cash register priced at thirty-four pounds. Victor couldn't imagine why anyone would want to buy it. A dusty green velvet curtain at the back of the shop was pulled aside and an old man came out. He was tall and strong-looking with big calloused hands. His face was the purplish red of morocco leather, against which his mass of creamy white hair, worn rather long, and the yellowish-white shaggy moustache made an almost violent contrast. He had little, bright, red-veined blue eyes.

'Are you Mr Jupp?' said Victor.

The old man nodded. He was one of those people who always stick out their lower lips when they nod. For his age he was extraordinarily dressed in a pair of denim jeans, a red shirt and a black pinstriped waistcoat, which he wore unbuttoned. Victor explained what he wanted, that he had a houseful of furniture to be valued and a buyer found for the items.

'I could come and have a shuftee,' said Jupp. 'Where is it? Not out in the sticks, I hope.'

Victor said it was stored in the garage of a house in Gunnersbury.

The lower lip went out over the upper as Jupp nodded. 'So long as you don't get things out of proportion,' he said. 'I mean, no delusions of grandeur about mum's priceless antiques and all that jazz.'

'How did you know it was my mother's?' said Victor.

'Well, ask yourself, cocky, who else's would it be? Poor old mum's gone at last and left you her bits, which is the last thing you want to be lumbered with, them not being your Louis Kangs or your Hepplewhite, whatever you might wish others to believe.'

'It's good furniture,' Victor protested, beginning to feel aggrieved.

'I daresay. So long as we don't have to hear about *valuations* and *finding a buyer*. What I do is clear flats and houses, right? I have a shuftee and tell you a price, and if you like it I clear the lot, and if you don't you go elsewhere and find a bigger sucker than what I am. *If* you can. Right? You happy with that?'

'OK, but I'll have to warn her you're coming. My aunt, I mean. It's my aunt's place where it is. I'll have to go round and tell her you're coming.'

'Don't break no speed records,' said Jupp. 'It'll be a good fortnight. I'm up to my eyebrows for the next fortnight. How about we say two weeks tomorrow, cocky? You give me the good lady's address and I'll be there three on the dot.'

Victor gave him Muriel's address. Jupp wrote it down and Victor's own name as well. Victor waited for the name to be recognized but it seemed to mean nothing to Jupp, who closed up his order book, took a packet of Polo mints out of his pocket and offered one to Victor.

Not liking to refuse, Victor took a mint. Jupp hesitated reflectively, contemplating the mint on the top of the pack, rather as a man who is trying to give up smoking stares with longing and disgust and doubt and hunger at the next cigarette. After a second or two he gave a small sigh, folded the torn paper over the exposed mint and restored the pack to his pocket.

'Mustn't indulge myself,' he said. 'I used to be addicted to these things something shocking, hooked you'd say. Twenty packets a day was nothing to me and thirty was more like it. Luckily, I haven't got my own teeth or they'd have gone for a Burton. Nowadays I've got it down to five. A steady five and I'm happy, or let's say I can take it, I can live with it. I don't suppose you can understand that, cocky?'

Although he had never been subject to an addiction, Victor could understand it only too well. It made him feel uncomfortable and in a way he wished he hadn't come to Jupp, but he didn't want to have to go searching for another secondhand furniture dealer, so he said he'd see Jupp at Muriel's on Thursday fortnight at three in the afternoon.

This time he avoided the tube and got on to a bus instead. Going over the hump of bridge by Kensal Rise station, he caught sight from the window of a newsagent's board on which was scrawled: *Acton Girl in Rape Horror*. He turned his head sharply away but at the next stop he got off the bus, went into the first newsagent's he came to and bought a paper, the *Standard*.

5

The story was a short one, at the foot of the page. A girl from Acton Vale had been raped in Gunnersbury Park on the previous evening, her jaw broken by blows, her face cut. A gardener found her after she had lain all night where her attacker had flung her, in a shrubbery of laurels. Reading it gave Victor a strange feeling, a faint dizziness, a nausea. In the past he had sometimes read accounts of rapes he himself had committed during his marauding of London from Finchley to Chiswick and from Harlesden to Leytonstone, one of Alan's cars parked somewhere as, *en route* to fetch a client, he looked for what the more sensational papers called his 'prey'. In those days the police and judges and juries and the general public had been far less sympathetic towards rape victims and far less condemnatory of rapists than they now were. The consensus of opinion had been that the victims asked for all they got and that the rapists were tempted beyond control. High-ranking police officers were not above suggesting that victims should 'lie back and enjoy it'. It seemed to Victor, reading the *Standard*, that things had changed a lot. This had registered with him even while he was still in prison, that what with Women's Lib and women campaigning against the way rape victims were treated and the attitude of the court changing, rape was regarded with a severity unthinkable ten years ago.

Here, on an inside, page, were some figures. He read them as he walked along. Out of 1334 cases of rape 644 men had been proceeded against. A variety of sentences had been imposed on those found guilty. Twelve of the men had been given life imprisonment, eleven of them seven to ten years' imprisonment, and fifty-six had been given two to three years. It was interesting, he thought, that in only three cases had a restriction order been made under the Mental Health Act. Yet, speaking for himself, personally, he knew that the acts of rape he had performed had been beyond his control, had had nothing to do with will, had been as involuntary and as distinct from any decision or purpose of his own as his firing the gun at Fleetwood. Did that mean he was mad when he did these things or at least not responsible for his actions?

Having now walked all the way down Ladbroke Grove, reading his paper and just staring at the blurring print, thinking, wondering how in the future he would control that which admitted no control, Victor got on a bus that would take him home. A faint feeling of regret for the prison he had left took hold of him, a certain nostalgia for that brutish sloth and lack of any responsibility. He had been looked after in there and safe, and if it had often been uncomfortable, always boring, a waste of life, there had been no worries and, later on, no fear. He read the story of the Gunnersbury Park rape once more as he walked up Twyford Avenue, raising his eyes just before he reached the house. Tom Welch was sitting outside the gate in his car. He got out when he saw Victor coming, putting on an over-warm, jovial expression.

'I guessed you wouldn't be long. I thought I'd wait for you.'

It was a week since Judy had brought him here but Victor hadn't bothered to get in touch with the after-care people. They ought to be relieved, he thought, they must have enough on their plates.

'How are things? How have you been getting on?'

Victor said he was OK, he had been getting on all right. Going up the stairs, Tom talked in a very hearty way about the weather and about the neighbourhood, that this was really the best part of Acton and these houses particularly attractive. When he saw the writing about the shit hitting the fan he laughed rather too loudly and said he hoped that wasn't Victor's handiwork. Victor said nothing. When they were inside he made Tom a mug of Nescafé, thinking that later on he would have a drink. At last, after all these years, he would have a drink. Go out and buy himself a bottle of wine, maybe.

'Any prospect of a job?' Tom asked.

Victor shook his head. He had forgotten about trying to get a job, it had seemed unimportant. There were so many other things to think about and handle and live with.

At one time he had felt very differently. After one year at the polytechnic, they had refused to have him back because he had made such a mess of his first-year exams. He had done so deliberately. The course wasn't hard and he was sure he could have taken a good degree but it felt like school and he was sick of school. He wanted to work and make real money.

Jobs were not a problem in the late sixties. He could take his pick. He tried the Civil Service and he tried a bank, but both bored him. His father began to get heavy, making vague threats, so Victor left home and took a flat, paying rent in advance with an insurance policy which had matured when he was twenty-one. He had a new job selling cars. The showrooms were in North Finchley, his flat not far away in what the estate agent called 'Highgate Borders', and he was engaged to a girl he had met at the polytechnic and who was still a student there. If Pauline's temperament had been different in one respect, he sometimes thought, his whole life might have been changed, none of this might have happened. He would be happily married – for didn't all the psychologists say that the children of the happily married had themselves the best chance of happiness in marriage? – he would be a father, a householder, prosperous probably, respectable, content. But Pauline . . . what a piece of ill-luck that this woman of all women was the one he had taken up with! He didn't want to think about her now.

He could see that Tom, who was still talking about employment and unemployment, had his eyes fixed on the newspaper Victor had bought, which lay folded with the page uppermost on which the headline was 'Rape and its Aftermath'.

'You're sure you're all right,' Tom now said. 'There's nothing you're in need of?'

What on earth did he mean by that? What would he say if Victor answered that yes, there was plenty he was in need of? His youth back again, a place of his own far from here, a decent job he'd enjoy doing – and another thing too, something that just at present he wouldn't even name to himself. His eyes strayed to the open newspaper, the word on the page, and he felt the blood go out of his face and a shiver touch the nape of his neck.

Tom said, 'Look, Liz said to tell you to come and have Sunday lunch with us some time. I mean, why not this coming Sunday, Victor? Will you do that?'

Victor sensed the effort behind the invitation. He had the impression Tom had had to conquer an enormous distaste for the task, would have given a lot to forget it, but duty impelled him, social conscience forced him. Of course Victor didn't want to go, he wouldn't go, but he couldn't think of a reason for saying no. He said yes, he'd come, while making a private decision not to turn up when the time came.

After Tom had gone, Victor sat in the window, looking down over the roofs of houses, over the roof of the house where his mother and father had lived, and thought about things. It was seeing the house in Solent Gardens that had brought this about, even though he had resolved not to think about the past. He couldn't help it. It was funny how people expected you to mean the things you said, he thought. Judges and juries and policemen and psychiatrists and social workers and just about everyone took it for granted you meant what you said, though they didn't mean what they said, and of everything that was ever said, Victor estimated, only about a half or less was meant. They had called him a psychopath on the grounds of something he had said while he was in that bedroom with Rosemary Stanley. They took it as evidence of his cold-bloodedness and his intent to shoot Fleetwood.

'I won't kill her,' he had said to Fleetwood out of the window. 'I'll shoot her in the back, in the lower spine.'

Fleetwood hadn't been at the trial to repeat that, but Rosemary Stanley had and half a dozen witnesses. It never occurred to any of them that he hadn't meant it. In fact, he could remember exactly why he had said it. The evening before, at home in Finchley, he had been reading the evening paper, this same *Standard*, only they called it the *Evening Standard* in those days, and there was a piece in it about some old war hero, an ex-airman with a VC, who was paralysed through a spinal injury. And there was a bit by a doctor in the article writing about what happened to you when you got shot down there, in the 'lower spine'. The words had come back to him as he talked out of the window and he uttered them as if by inspiration, as the nastiest thing he could think of just at that moment. It was his bad luck that when he shot at Fleetwood – never having fired a gun before, hardly knowing where and how to aim – the bullet had struck him just where Victor had threatened to shoot Rosemary Stanley. Why he had fired at all he didn't know.

He had been so frightened, so intolerably frightened, in the worst panic of his life. Somehow, he had always thought, if he had been able to make them understand that, they would have let him off. But they never understood. They barely stopped to listen. And yet they must all have known fear, have been frightened out of their lives, just as every day they made remarks and comments, excuses and threats which they did not mean even at the very time of uttering them, which stemmed from fear or boredom or simply from not knowing what else to say.

Victor picked up the *Standard* and read the rape story again. The girl's name wasn't given but she was twenty-four, a hairdresser from Old Oak Road. She was 'recovering in hospital', her condition 'satisfactory'. Victor wondered who it was that had attacked her in that park so near to Muriel's house and where he was now and what he was thinking. He turned the page and his eyes met those of David Fleetwood, sitting in his wheelchair with his dog beside him.

The story was a chatty piece. Fleetwood was writing his

memoirs, in fact had written them, and this autobiography was to be published in the autumn. There was talk of a sale of television rights. The photograph showed Fleetwood sitting in the garden at the front of his house in Theydon Bois, where he had been living for the past three years. Victor thought of the houses which stood in his life like landmarks. It was as if his life were a road and, as this road curved, another house of disturbing or even terrible significance came into view. His parents' house first of all, the one whose roof he could see, then Muriel's grotesque Tudor pile, the house in Solent Gardens with its broken window and the wind blowing in to lift the curtain, now this one, Fleetwood's house in Theydon Bois.

Of the four the latter was the most attractive, part brick, part dark weatherboard, with a gable and latticed windows, a porch over an oak-studded door, a large integral garage, climbing plants, roses perhaps, half covering the wall and now coming into leaf. The front garden was neat and well tended, a garden pretty enough to be on a seed packet or advertising something – a hosepipe, say, or a lawn mower. Tulips filled the bed under the front windows and some sort of blossoming tree was in flower. On a birdbath a pigeon had obligingly perched, or perhaps the bird was made of stone. Fleetwood sat in his wheelchair, his knees covered by a rug, one hand on his labrador's head, the other holding some sheets of manuscript. He had been interviewed by the *Standard*'s reporter, talking about the book mostly, though not mentioning the actual incident that had caused his paralysis. Yes, he did feel pleased about the book; he would be getting a substantial advance from his publishers; but no, he wasn't planning to do any more writing in the future. Marriage? He didn't think so, though of course it was possible. Well, yes, he did have a girlfriend. Clare, she was called, and she had typed the manuscript for him.

It was all right for some, Victor thought, folding up the paper and putting it under the bamboo table out of sight. Money, success, a woman, a nice house – Fleetwood had everything; and what did he have? A furnished room, a sum of money in the bank that was very small by today's standards, an aunt whose property he just might inherit if she forgot to make a will. If she remembered to make one, he certainly wouldn't inherit anything. Muriel, anyway, though she looked a hundred, couldn't in fact be more than in her mid-sixties and might very likely live twenty years.

His youth he had lost. It was pointless looking at it in any other way. Those years he had spent in prison were the best years of a man's life. That was the period of life when the best things happened to you, when you got on and when you settled down. Alan, for instance, who was the same age, would be married now with a house of his own and flourishing business. Victor had slaved for him, sweated his guts out getting up at all hours and often not going to bed at all, worked for him for five years after he got fed up with selling Fords, and Alan hadn't even come to see him in prison, hadn't so much as written. Pauline, he thought, would be married now to some poor devil who had perhaps adjusted to what Victor had never been able to accustom himself to: her icy impenetrable coldness. Well, no, not impenetrable, for he had penetrated on numerous occasions a limp flaccid body which lay passive as blancmange while Pauline studied something on the wall with intense concentration, her mind elsewhere. Once he had observed her counting on her fingers, doing sums. After a while this affected him so that he wilted inside her. Pauline hadn't seemed to notice. That had been around the time when she had begun being more wakeful and active during their sexual moments, wakeful and active to the extent of chatting about what her mother had said to her on the phone that morning and her history tutor's comments on her latest essay. Victor had got up and put his clothes on and gone out into the dark and raped a girl who was taking a short cut home through Highgate Wood. The girl had been terrified and had shouted and fought. It wasn't like doing it to a dead sheep with a chit-chat tape playing. It was wonderful. She had cried out, 'Don't, don't, don't – Oh, no, no, no!' She howled like an animal. 'Oh, no, no, no!'

It took Victor some time – by then he had committed three more rapes – to remember where and in what circumstances he had heard that before. When he did remember, he refused to think about it. It seemed disgusting, blasphemous almost, to think of that. By then Pauline and he had parted. But if she had been warm and loving, greedy for sex as he had read that women in the 1970s inevitably were, if she had been all this and his wife, would he ever have attacked the two women on Hampstead Heath, the girls on Wandsworth Common, Wanstead Flats in Epping Forest? That Christmas, if that different Pauline, that transformed Pauline, had been with him instead of gone five years before, would he have been so interested in Sydney's Luger and a few months later stolen it?

That night he slept badly and dreamed a lot. When Tom had been gone an hour or so he had gone out and bought a bottle of wine and drunk it all. It was the first alcohol he had tasted for nearly eleven years. It made him drunk, which was what he wanted, though he didn't want the after-effects. His dream was an enlarging of that fantasy of his about his life as a road and the houses which appeared as he rounded the bends in it. Only this time, after Muriel's house and before 62 Solent Gardens, there came into view along the road the block of flats in Finchley High Road where he had lived with Pauline and the house in Ballards Lane where he had been renting the top floor at the time of his arrest. He walked on, though the surface which had been smooth was now rough like a cart track, with stones and rocks in his path like the stones in the mountainous front garden at Muriel's. The house in Solent Gardens stood alone, having been lopped off from its fellows in the terrace, and the upper window was still broken, the wind blowing in and lifting the curtain. Why, in his imagination and his dreams, did he always see it from this side, the outside, when from that aspect he had glimpsed it only once, when they had brought him out between two policemen, his hands manacled?

The next house along the road that he came to was Fleetwood's with its gable and its black weatherboard and climbing roses, but it wasn't the last. The last was the prison where he had spent half his adult life, a red-brick sprawl with a forest of chimneys sprouting out of its red roofs.

Why did prisons always have so many chimneys, he asked himself stupidly as he woke up. It wasn't as if they were warm places or distinguished for their cooking or the standard of their laundry. His heart was pounding, his head throbbed and his mouth was bone dry. Because he couldn't go back to sleep again, he got up, drank pints of water straight from the tap, his mouth over the tap, and sat by the window, looking hopelessly out over Acton. It was dawn, pearl-grey and misty, the swell of traffic noise mounting already, birds starting to sing. All the gardens he could see were filled with small trees coming into leaf and flower, green and white and pink, so that a muslin-pale haze of colour lay like a thin printed cloth over earth and brick and stone. Hating the human race, Victor thought with an anger that made him clench his fists how all these householders were so mean and grudging that they wouldn't even plant a tree unless it was a fruit tree they could get something out of.

Why had his life been passed in these dreary suburbs? He had never lived anywhere interesting or different, though there were plenty of interesting places he had passed through on his way to the airports at Heathrow and Gatwick and Luton and Stansted. Like most Londoners born north of the river, he found it hard to contemplate living south of it. The west side of London he had enough of and he told himself he hated the north. Go east then, a long way, to Epping perhaps or Harlow, or as far as Bishops Stortford.

Three hours later he was once more making his way down Gunnersbury Avenue towards Muriel's house in Popesbury Drive. This was the way he had regularly driven to Heathrow. He missed the use of a car. Would he ever have one again? He supposed he could go out to Epping –

if he was serious about that – by bus or coach or all the way to the end of the Central Line.

A lot more trees had come into leaf in the week since he was last here. Over the craggy outcroppings up to Muriel's front door the hanging plants had burst into masses of purple flowers, pink and mauve and purple and puce, so bright they hurt the eyes. Victor could hear Muriel scuffling about inside, fumbling at the door. She knew who it was – she had seen him from the window or she had guessed. The blue dressing gown and the mules she wore were the same, and so was the smell of camphor, but the pink snood with which she had covered her hair had been changed for a brown one. She peered suspiciously out at him, grudgingly easing the door open, widening inch by inch the gap between door and door frame until it was just wide enough for Victor to pass through.

'What d'you want this time?'

He might have been some importunate beggar always bothering her for money or meals rather than a nephew whom she had seen only twice in ten years. Needless to say, Muriel hadn't been to see him in prison either. If she wouldn't set foot outside for her husband's funeral, she'd hardly have gone prison visiting. Yet he had never done her any harm. You couldn't call taking that gun harming her, and if the police had come here questioning her about it and searching the place, no one had blamed her, no one had put her away for ten years. He followed her into the living room, explaining about Jupp and how he would be coming to look at the furniture two weeks from today.

The room was stuffy with a fine fug built up. A large electric fire with two elements was switched on. Muriel had made herself a cosy haven or enclave in front of this fire, an island in the sea of magazines. There was the armchair in which she had been sitting with two cushions in the back of it and a pillow in a dirty white pillowcase, a plaid rug over one arm, a footstool that looked like a hassock pinched out of a church, a table on each side of it, one with a library book on it, a pair of glasses and a bottle of aspirins, the other containing a pile of magazines, a ballpoint pen and a pair of scissors. Instead of returning to her chair, Muriel stood there hesitantly, looking at him with a truculent stare. From a distant part of the house a whistle started up and rose to a scream.

Of course Victor knew quite well what this must be, or he knew within a split second. At the start of it though, he gave a slight jump and for some reason this brought a grin to Muriel's face.

'I was going to make myself a coffee,' she said.

Victor followed her down the passage to the kitchen. Muriel shuffled along, the belt of her dressing gown trailing behind her. For some reason she never fastened the belt but preferred to hold the sides of the dressing gown together with her left hand. The kettle was jumping about on the gas and squealing. Muriel was very slow. She put a spoonful of instant coffee into each cup, calculating that they contained precisely the same amount by studying the individual grains and tipping an extra grain off the top of the second one with a knife. Victor's nerves couldn't stand the bouncing and squealing and he pushed past her to lift the kettle off the gas. She looked at him in resentful surprise. She opened the fridge and removed a small carton of double cream. This went on to a round tray with one of the cups of coffee, a sugar basin and two biscuits on a plate. The biscuits were of the kind made for children called Iced Bears, shaped like teddy bears with coloured sugar on them. On to a second, smaller tray Muriel put the other cup of coffee and pushed it across the table to Victor.

He could hardly believe his eyes. The tray with the cream and biscuits she meant exclusively for herself, she was hugging it to her with her hands round its rim. He didn't even merit a teaspoon. But what was the use of arguing with her? He reached across the table for the sugar, climbing over her hands, so to speak, in order to do so, like someone scaling a fence that surrounds a forbidden park. Taking his cup, he went out into the garage to have another look at the furniture. It was wonderful how material, mere pieces of coloured fabric, could awaken so much in the memory. Covering a bedstead and some sort of chest were the curtains which had hung at his own bedroom windows when he was a boy. They must have been of very good quality to have lasted so long, a pattern of bluish-green and red blocks on a black and white background, postwar and early fifties' fashion. He could clearly remember lying in bed and looking at that pattern, the sunlight shining through and making them transparent, or else they would be opaque when there was darkness outside. He would lie there waiting for his mother to come upstairs and tuck him in and kiss him goodnight. Sometimes, before he could read, he hoped for a story as well. She always promised to come but she seldom did; she was with his father, distracted by his father's greater glamour, stronger desirability. The neglect wasn't bad enough to make him cry, though, and he would fall asleep with the last thing printed on his retina those curtains patterned in bluish-green and red blocks on a black and white background.

Perhaps he shouldn't let Jupp have all this furniture. If he was going to find himself somewhere to live in Epping, he might need it. Suddenly Victor knew he wouldn't be able to live with the furniture which had surrounded him when he was a boy. It was painful even to look at it. The curtain patterns, for some reason, were the worst, but the beds were bad too and that brown velvet settee. The only thing, he decided, he felt all right about was his father's wheelchair, and that was perhaps because he hadn't been there when his father had got it and he had never seen his father using it. Victor drank his coffee and covered up the bed and chest again and asked himself why he was suddenly taking it for granted that he was going to live in Epping. Surely he hadn't decided on that? He had never really been to Epping, just passed through on his way to Stansted, and once of course stopped off in the Forest near a pub called, he thought, the Robin Hood. And there, a good quarter of a mile from the road, in a glade of bracken and birch trees, he had come upon a woman walking alone, not young or pretty or in any way attractive to him, but a woman alone . . .

Victor went back into the kitchen. His aunt had gone. He found her back in her armchair in front of the electric fire in the close camphor-smelling fug, cutting a piece out of a sheet of newsprint with her scissors.

'I've got something to show you,' she said.

'No, thanks. I know what it is.' Out of the corner of his eye he had seen the photographed corner of Fleetwood's house, a section of gable, an inch of chimney stack.

She took no notice but went on cutting, holding the paper and the scissors right up close to her nose. 'He's writing a book,' she said. 'It's going to be all about his past life.'

'I know,' said Victor. 'I've seen the paper. You're not telling me anything I don't know.'

'You'll be in it.'

He felt anger beginning to mount again, hot liquid rising in the vessel of his body.

'There's bound to be a long bit in it about you, with pictures.' She laid the scissors down, folded the cut piece of paper in two. Her face was raised up towards his, the sagging flesh of her neck hanging in a double pleat from her chin. 'It's only what you deserve,' she said.

Victor had read somewhere that walking or any vigorous exercise frees the body of tensions and calms anger. He didn't find this to be true in his own case. Making his way back to Gunnersbury Avenue, he was filled with murderous rage, to the brim now. The lack of understanding maddened him, not just in his aunt, in everyone, all those people who couldn't see why things happened, how things could happen to you almost without your being aware of them, and then – you were punished for ever, and even then they said it wasn't enough.

He would be in Fleetwood's book. Victor wasn't much of a reader, he had always preferred films and television, but if he ever read anything it was biography and memoirs. If Fleetwood were to write a book about his life, indeed had done so, Victor would be in it, with a chapter to himself probably, with photographs of himself. While his trial was going on, newspapers had used a studio portrait of himself taken at his mother's request at the time of his twenty-first birthday. His mother wouldn't have given it to a reporter, so Muriel must have done. Another photograph was the one of him being brought out of 62 Solent Gardens between two policemen. Probably both these would be in Fleetwood's book – unless he could stop it by some legal means, though he didn't know how to go about this and was afraid anyway that it might cost a lot of money.

Could Fleetwood say what he liked about him in the book and he have no redress? No doubt, Fleetwood would call him a psychopath and those words he had shouted out of the window would be quoted again: 'I'll shoot her in the back, in the lower spine!'

When she had stood in the witness box and repeated those words, Rosemary Stanley had cried. She had stumbled over the words and begun to weep – a very effective method, Victor had thought, of getting all the sympathy of the court, as if she didn't have enough already. That would doubtless be in Fleetwood's book, even though he wasn't at the trial. And Fleetwood's book was going to be on sale everywhere, in paperback as well, turned into a film for television. The idea made Victor feel sick. As soon as he was back in his room, he took the *Standard* from the rack under the bamboo coffee table in order to read the article again, to learn from it what he could. But he had left the paper folded so that the Gunnersbury Park rape story was uppermost and a line caught his eye, a kind of subheading in quotation marks: 'Rape is not a sexual act but an act of aggression'. Some psychiatrist had said it. He was wondering what it meant, how screwing a girl could be anything but sexual, when the front doorbell rang. Victor had heard that bell ring before, usually in the evening when one of the other tenants had gone to answer it. Whoever it was it couldn't be for him and he wasn't going to answer it now. The bell rang again. Victor heard footsteps and then voices. Someone had opened the front door and this surprised him, very slightly alarmed him, for he had been nearly certain there was no one in the house.

Footsteps started up the stairs. He *knew* they would go past his door and on up, they had to, there was no one who could possibly want him. There were at least two people coming upstairs. The knocking on his door was like thunder, the kind of thunder that makes you jump because it is preceded by no warning flash of lightning. Victor's calm, his sanity, his euphoria, vanished and he felt panic like a mass of tingling wires. He opened the door, aware of how vulnerable, how helpless, he must look.

Outside stood a woman in a hat and two men in the kind of leisure wear the police thought disguised them. Victor knew the woman must be Mrs Griffiths, his landlady. He knew it from the expression on her face, forbearing, patient, virtuous yet mildly disapproving, the kind of look worn by someone who is socially conscientious enough to take ex-convicts into her house, along with all the inevitable consequences.

'CID,' said the older man, the one in the heather-mixture tweed jacket. 'Can we have a word, Vic?'

6

No one ever called him that. Vic – he hated it, it sounded like the stuff his mother rubbed on his chest when he was a child. And what right had they to call him by his Christian name anyway? He heard the younger one, the one in the distressed leather jacket, say, 'Thanks very much, Mrs Griffiths. Sorry to bother you.' They didn't call *her* Betty or Lily or whatever her name was. But he had been in prison, of course, and therefore forfeited his human dignity, his right to respect for ever and ever.

They came in and Distressed Leather shut the door.

Heather Mixture said, 'Nice little place you've got here.'

Victor said nothing. The palms of his hands tingled, he felt a creeping in his shoulders as if an insect was crawling across his back. He sat down. They didn't.

'Don't suppose you need to go out much. Haven't got a job, have you?'

Replying to this with a shake of his head, Victor wondered if he would be able to find a voice. His throat had closed. He would have liked to ask what they wanted rather than endure all this facetious preamble but he didn't dare experiment with speech. They were both staring at him but at least Distressed Leather had sat down.

'Still, you've been out today, need a breath of fresh air sometimes, no doubt. We're having a nice spring, aren't we? It's often the way after a bad summer. But you wouldn't know about that really, would you, having been – what shall we say – out of circulation at the time? Most people in your situation, Vic, find going out a bit of an ordeal at first. But it hasn't taken you that way, am I right?'

Victor lifted his crawling shoulders.

'No, it hasn't taken you that way,' repeated Heather

Mixture. 'You've been out, you've faced the world. How many times have you been out, would you reckon? Every day, every other day, twice a day? How about last Monday, for instance? Did you go out then?'

His voice came, less than a voice but better than a croak. 'Why d'you want to know?'

Even as he spoke, he knew. Nonetheless, it was a horrible shock to him. On Monday night a girl had been raped in Gunnersbury Park, he had read about it in the *Standard*; he had bought the *Standard* and read about it on his way back from Jupp's. He hadn't been to prison for rape, he had been in prison for shooting David Fleetwood, but once he had been convicted, before sentence was passed, he had asked through his counsel, on his counsel's advice, for two cases of rape to be taken into consideration. This had been done expediently in case the police tried to charge him with these offences once he had served his sentence. Victor's counsel was not to know that those two instances were not the only rapes Victor had committed.

He hadn't wanted to mention them at all, he hadn't wanted to bring it – his nature – out into the open. But he had, he had yielded to persuasion. And now the police knew. He must be on a file somewhere, a file on one of these computers which had taken over the world while he was inside. Victor didn't want to think, now, of the implications of that.

'Let's play it this way,' said Heather Mixture. 'You answer my question first. How about that?'

'I went to see my aunt.'

Heather Mixture's facial muscles didn't move but a grin twitched at Distressed Leather's mouth.

'And where might this lady live?'

'Gunnersbury.'

They went stiff and still. For a moment.

'As to your question, Vic, I think we can forget that, don't you? You know very well what we're on about. You know what you are and we know. It would save a lot of time and trouble if we all got in the car and went down to the police station.'

They wanted to carry out some tests. Heather Mixture had all sorts of amusing euphemisms for being in prison, bringing them out one after another, for the sake of seeing Victor's discomfiture perhaps and Distressed Leather's twitching sycophantic mouth. At first Victor refused, saying he wanted his lawyer. The name of the solicitor who had briefed counsel for him nearly eleven years ago he still remembered, but not the man's office address or phone number. Nor did he have a five- or ten-pence piece for the phone. Heather Mixture said he could have his solicitor, no problem, easiest thing out, he could phone him from the police station. At that Victor gave in because he thought they could probably eventually *make* him go to the police station, though how he didn't know.

The girl's name was Susan Davies. She was in hospital and would be there for a long time. She had described her attacker as being between twenty-five and thirty-five, dark-haired, of medium height. They told him all that. When Victor pointed out that he was thirty-eight, Heather Mixture said most people liked being taken for younger than they were and, anyway, you didn't age so fast when you were sheltered from the world in durance vile.

They told Victor they would like to do a blood test. Victor said he wanted his lawyer. Nothing easier, said a detective inspector Victor hadn't seen before, but when he asked for a phone directory the detective inspector said he couldn't quite lay hands on one just at that moment and why didn't Victor go over to the lab with Sergeant Latimer (Distressed Leather) and have his blood tested while he looked for a phone book? Of course Victor went. He was considerably unnerved. Latimer explained something to him he hadn't known before – perhaps it wasn't generally known or hadn't even been discovered before he went to prison. This was that some men are what are called 'secretors', that is, their blood group can be detected from their semen and other body fluids. There was no knowing whether or not Victor was a secretor without carrying out tests.

Victor now saw that it was very much in his own interests

to have the tests done. He stopped worrying about finding a solicitor. All he wanted was to get out of there and get home – exonerated. He hadn't raped Susan Davies but he could already see that *circumstantially* he wasn't going to be able to prove he hadn't been in Gunnersbury Park at the relevant time. There were no witnesses he could produce that he had been at home. And his Aunt Muriel – if it was imaginable that anyone could get any sense out of her – could only say that he had been with her for a couple of hours in the afternoon. The blood test would prove it. Three quarters of all people were secretors, Latimer said.

They kept him hanging about there until they got the results of the tests. Nothing more was said about a telephone directory and Victor didn't mention it. It was early evening and they had brought him a hamburger and a cup of tea before they told him the results. Well, they didn't exactly tell him, they wouldn't, they merely said he could go home, they wouldn't want to be seeing him again. Like Judy and Tom, only more so, they treated him as if he were sub-human, sub-intelligent. Victor said he supposed he must be a secretor then. That's right, the detective inspector said. What blood group was he, Victor asked, not expecting an answer, expecting to be told this was a police station, if he didn't mind, not a Harley Street consulting room. But the inspector told him, laconically, dismissively. It appeared that he was B positive. Did that mean anything to him? Victor left.

On the way home he went into a wineshop and bought a quarter bottle of whisky and twenty cigarettes. Soon after he went to prison he had stopped smoking, though it was possible to smoke in there at certain prescribed times. But he had stopped. Now he felt he needed something strong and comforting to drink. At least he hadn't succumbed to panic, he hadn't fallen into raving madness and tried to grab, hit or shake them. He congratulated himself on that. The cigarettes and the scotch would take care of this shaking which had taken over his hands and sometimes his knees too from the moment he left the police station.

He let himself into the house. Mrs Griffiths, in hat, coat

and gloves, was in the hall talking to a young woman Victor had never seen before. The young woman looked away. Mrs Griffiths gave him a tight smile which Victor knew meant it was one thing having ex-convicts in one's house but only if they had turned over a new leaf. It was seven years since he had smoked a cigarette. The first puff made his gorge rise and he vomited into the sink. He sat down on the bed shivering.

Things suddenly presented themselves to him with an awful clarity. While it had obviously been in his interest to have those tests done at that particular point in time, taking the long view it was a disaster. They had found out his blood group, they had found he was a secretor, and on top of that was the misfortune that he belonged to a rare blood group. Victor remembered incongruously an occasion years and years ago watching a television show in which the comedian Tony Hancock appeared in a sketch about blood groups. The point was that he turned out to have the rarest known group, AB negative. B positive, which was Victor's group, wasn't as rare as that but still only six per cent of the population belonged to it.

Every time there was an attack on a girl in West London – in the whole of London and the Home Counties, come to that – and there was evidence that the perpetrator was a B secretor, they would come to him. But that was one thing, that could be borne, since there would be few cases. What if he himself were the perpetrator? Victor knew the time would come when he would want to assault a girl again. There was a part of him which said it wouldn't, that he would struggle for his own sake to avoid this, but at the same time he knew that the struggle couldn't be wholly effective.

He poured some of the whisky into one of Mrs Griffith's thick moulded glasses, the kind that are given away with a sale of more than thirty litres of petrol. There was no question of vomiting that up. It warmed him and swam into his head. If the time came when he attacked a girl, *when* the time came, they would do whatever you did do to a computer, type it like a typewriter probably, and up would come a printout: Victor Jenner, 38, 46 Tolleshunt Avenue, Acton, W5, secretor, blood group B Pos . . . And it would, must happen every time, only there wouldn't be 'every' time – there would be the once and the last, for after that he would be in gaol for the rest of his life. He could imagine the judge calling him a 'dangerous animal' who would have to be locked up 'for the safety of the community', a 'wild beast' who, unless permanently restrained, would indiscriminately ravish women and murder men. The thing was that he wasn't really like that at all, Victor thought; he was frightened and panicky and alone. He would have liked help but he didn't know where to get it – certainly not from Tom or Judy, who would offer evening classes and community service.

How different must be the life of David Fleetwood whose fault all this was! Fleetwood was safe, secure, housed, pensioned. His sexual problems had been taken care of in the soundest, most final way. Victor, sitting on his bed drinking whisky in the darkening room, thought he wouldn't mind *that* solution to his own dilemma. Then the desire, the temptation, the uncontrollable urge, would be gone for ever. And most of all Fleetwood had respect. Everyone respected him, positively worshipped and honoured him. If he had had to go to a police station for tests, they would probably have called him sir. It was ironical really. Fleetwood had brought all this about by his obtuseness, yet it was he who had all the glory and Victor who got all the stick, on and on for years. Perhaps Fleetwood had done it on purpose, Victor thought. Human behaviour was incomprehensible, everyone knew that. Perhaps Fleetwood had got himself shot on purpose, knowing he would get looked after for life and that people adored a crippled hero.

Victor walked along Twyford Avenue towards the High Street. He had passed two dreadful nights and a bad day. Both nights he had wakened up with his heart racing and his body all a-prickle. The first time he had lain there weeping, then turning his face into the pillow to muffle the screams he couldn't otherwise control. In the morning he had met a fellow tenant on the landing, a man, who had asked him if he had heard anything in the night, someone crying, for instance, and a noise like bedsprings repetitively jerked. Victor muttered that he had heard nothing. Most of the day he had slept, finding it easy to sleep, escaping thankfully into sleep as a respite from life. But that night the panic came upon him with redoubled force, enclosing him in its straitjacket way, convulsing his limbs with a kind of spasticity, so that he could not lie still but had to jump out of bed and seize and manhandle the nearest object. This happened to be the cane chair, which he found himself grasping and pounding, up-down, up-down, first against the wall and then on the floor. His teeth were clenched and he could hear himself make a kind of growling sound.

One of the legs split off the chair and hung by a strand of raffia. Spent and gasping, Victor flung himself on the bed. Almost immediately someone knocked on his door. Victor took no notice. His heart was beating so hard that it hurt him with its pumping as if it would pump its way out through his chest wall. Whoever had knocked at the door shouted that they wanted to know what the hell was going on. Victor staggered to the door, put his mouth close to it and whispered that it was nothing, it was over. 'For Christ's sake,' said the voice.

Victor had no more sleep. He got up very early and went out on to the landing with a bar of soap and a pot scourer and erased the writing on the wall. There was no point in it any more. It had happened. The shit had hit the fan.

He went to the library to see what he could read up about blood grouping. There was quite a lot of literature about it. Victor knew he was an intelligent person – someone had measured his IQ for him when he was at college and it had come out at 130 – and usually able to grasp scientific data, but blood grouping was too much for him. It was too complicated and abstruse for him to follow. What he did gather was that the ABO system had been discovered as far back as 1900 but that since then a dozen or so other systems had been found, including the Rhesus one, and all these could be tested for, thus fining down even further the possibilities of whose blood was whose. There was the MNS system, the Lutheran, the Kell, the Yt and the Domrock. Why, it looked as if the time would come when everybody's blood group would turn out to be different from everybody else's.

But later he began to think about it more rationally. He had never been charged with rape and rape had never been proved against him. Besides that, he intended never to attack a woman again. If he could survive ten years in prison without attacking a woman, surely he could survive the rest of his life. 'Rape is not a sexual act but an act of aggression,' the newspaper had told him. Was it anger then that made him attack women, and if he could otherwise handle his anger would that make him stop wanting to attack them?

Tom lived in North Ealing, up near Park Royal station. Victor didn't think that the house was likely to be a landmark along his road, it being small, semi-detached and one of those between-the-wars council houses that proliferate in north-west London, though Tom probably owned it. An overturned tricycle lay on the patch of grass in front and beside it a teddy bear face-downwards, looking as if someone had shot it in the back. Victor winced and wondered why he had had to think of that comparison. He hadn't meant to come at all but to spend the day working out some plan for the future, walking first, continuing with the business of accustoming himself to the outdoors, then in his room, calculating how much money he had and how much he could muster. But he had got no further than Ealing Common when the rain began and he went into the tube station to take shelter. It wasn't going to stop, it was coming down in summer tempests. Park Royal was only two stops up the line and at least he would get his lunch cooked for him.

The tricycle was covered with water drops and the teddy bear looked wet, though the rain had now stopped. Tom's children must have abandoned them to run indoors. Victor didn't much like children. A thin woman in trousers and a flowered apron opened the door to him, smiling much too enthusiastically and assuring him in a very hearty way how delighted she was to see him, how she and the children had been looking forward to meeting him. A curious memory came back to Victor as he entered the living-dining room. It was of a newspaper article he had read years ago, long before he went to prison, in which the theory was put forward that no one can be in prison for more than five years and remain quite sane. A psychiatrist had written it, someone who called himself a behaviourist. Victor hadn't remembered that all the time he had been in prison, but he did now, and with a kind of jolt or shock – but he didn't know why he remembered it, there being nothing about Liz Welch or the small shabby cluttered room to bring it to mind.

'Tom's just popped out to get a bottle,' she said. 'Wine, I mean. Would you like a can of beer for now?'

They lived in the kind of hand-to-mouth way, Victor thought, which obliged them to run out to a wineshop whenever anyone came. There was very likely a single can of beer in the house. He had never drunk beer, didn't like it. The Welches were poor. Tom didn't get paid for working for the after-care people, he was a schoolteacher by profession, but Victor didn't feel particularly sorry for him. It seemed to him insane to marry and lumber oneself with all this.

The children came in, subdued, staring. The little girl wore steel-framed glasses. The boy, who was younger, had a bandaged knee through which the blood was beginning to ooze. When he saw the blood he burst into loud cries, was taken on to his mother's lap and comforted. Mrs Welch talked to Victor about the weather, other topics not being safe.

'All this rain day after day,' she said, unwinding the bandage. 'There hasn't been a day in the past week without rain. As bad as last year, isn't it?'

She realized what she had said and blushed. Victor enjoyed her discomfiture. He wondered if it was Tom who had told the police where he was to be found. But Tom didn't know about his history as a rapist, did he? Tom came in while Liz was re-bandaging the child's knee. It had come on to rain again and water was streaming off his bright blue nylon cape. He shook hands heartily with Victor, produced the bottle of Bulgarian red wine he had gone out to buy and said they would be all right now.

Victor suddenly decided against telling Tom he intended to move away from London. The less anyone knew about his movements the better. If they had been alone, he might have mentioned his fears about appearing in Fleetwood's book and asked where he could go for advice about taking legal steps. But he wasn't going to talk about it in front of this woman – he hoped she would wash her hands before she served the food – or this squalling boy or the girl who since she had come into the room had done nothing but stand in front of him and stare.

Lunch came at last. It was roast pork, apple sauce, tinned peas and old potatoes that were boiled, not roasted, followed by a Sainsbury's raspberry and redcurrant tart with custard made from powder. It reminded Victor of better Sunday dinners in prison. Tom talked about television programmes and Victor said he was thinking of renting a television set. This seemed to thrill the Welches because it gave them an opportunity to recommend various rental companies and compare what they knew of rival costs. Tom went outside to make coffee while Liz cleared the table.

Left alone with the children, Victor hid himself behind the *Sunday Express*. As far as he could see, there was nothing in it about rape or Fleetwood. The extraordinary thing was that on an inside page he came upon a photograph of a man on a horse riding in Epping Forest. It seemed to mean something, it seemed as if fate was pointing him that way. And of course it wasn't all that extraordinary. It was well known, for instance that things went in threes, that you had only to come upon a new name or place for it to recur twice more that day. He was startled by a fist banging on the paper from behind and he drew it away, not intending to lower it. But the little girl caught hold of the top of the paper and pulled it down, bringing her face close to his over the top of it.

'What's a lag?' the child said.

Victor muttered, 'I don't know.'

'My daddy told my mum we'd have to have one of his old lags over on Sunday.'

Sometimes Victor thought he had educated himself from magazines. Most of the information stored in his brain seemed to have come from them. Perhaps reading magazines ran in his family or perhaps it was a passion that showed itself only in himself and Muriel, for he couldn't remember his father or mother ever reading anything much. But he could remember Muriel bringing him comics when he was very young, and perhaps the habit had started then.

An article in a magazine had led him to believe he might cure himself of his phobia. This was years ago, before prison, before the house in Solent Gardens, before he took Sydney's gun. The article said that the method it outlined was derived from modern psychotherapy treatment – only you proceeded on your own without the psychotherapist. You began by looking at pictures of the thing you feared. A week or two before this, a nature magazine had been among the ones Victor had bought and the centrefold was devoted to a feature on terrestrial turtles of North America, principally to the courtship ritual of the gopher tortoise. Catching a glimpse of this, barely more than that, Victor had slammed the magazine shut and put another magazine on top of it so that he shouldn't even see the cover. The cover was innocuous enough, being of a butterfly poised on the lip of an orchid, but because Victor knew what was inside, this innocent and in fact very beautiful photograph was enough to start a shiver up his spine. He did not throw the magazine away though, because there was another article in it he very much wanted to read – if he had the courage to touch even the outer pages again. Up till he had read the piece about the modern psychotherapy, he hadn't had that courage. Well, he would try.

In his teens, while he was still at school, they had gone on an educational visit to the Victoria and Albert Museum. In the museum was a Staffordshire teapot of the Whieldon type, circa 1765 – he could remember all that, he would never forget – made in the shape of a tortoise in tortoiseshell-patterned pottery. There it was, in front of him, eyeing him, a totally unexpected sight. Victor had fainted.

No one knew why. He wasn't going to tell them. Imagine letting one's schoolfellows find out about a thing like that. Boys of that age would have no mercy. The teachers who were with them thought he was ill, and in fact the incident had occurred not long after he had come back to school after having had flu with bronchitis. Since that time his phobia had been worse, had grown very slowly but progressively worse, until it reached a point where he not only couldn't look at a picture of the thing, he couldn't touch the book in which the picture was or even approach too closely the shelf or table where the book was. He suffered all this secretly, privately, in silence. Pauline had a tortoiseshell-backed hairbrush which he could touch, he could just touch it, but he disliked it and he didn't care to hear it called by name.

Of course one could pass through life encountering the land-dwelling turtles of the family *testudinae* only rarely. It wasn't like having a phobia for cats or spiders. But fainting in the V and A had really frightened Victor, just as these horrid glimpses in magazines frightened him, or the effect they had on him did. What would happen were he to see a real one?

With the aim of curing his phobia or attempting to cure it, he opened that magazine at the centrefold and made himself look. At first it was a dreadful experience, making him feel shivery, queasy and weak, then starting up a barely controllable shuddering. But he followed instructions. He told himself that this was a harmless reptile, that these were mere photographs of this harmless reptile, rendered in glossy colour on to paper. They could not hurt him and he was free to close the magazine whenever he chose. And so on.

Up to a point it worked. He could look at those pictures. He could get quite blasé about them, though he would experience a great tiredness, a feeling of total exhaustion after one of these sessions. He went to the library, looked 'tortoise' up in the *Encyclopedia Britannica* and obliged himself to fix his eyes on the most awful picture he had ever seen in his whole life: a colour photograph of *testudo elephantopus*, the giant Galapagos tortoise, a huge reptile four feet long and weighing three hundred pounds. Fortunately, the picture of it was very small.

The next step would be to visit a pet shop. His nerve failed him. The article of instructions also failed because what was essential was the presence of the psychotherapist, if only in the role of a supportive human being. Victor couldn't do it on his own. He actually phoned a pet shop and asked them if they had any tortoises – he spoke the word aloud on the phone! – and they said they had and he started to go there, but he was worn out by the effort of it and his spirit was broken. What was the point anyway when you scarcely ever saw the things, or even their pictures, unless you went out of your way to find them?

But he fancied he had never been quite so bad since then. Some progress had been made, some success achieved. He could walk past pet shops now, he didn't have to make detours to avoid them, and he could look at the covers of nature magazines and touch them, despite what might, what just possibly might, be inside. Since his emergence from prison, this slight emancipation he felt he had from his phobia wasn't put to the test until four or five mornings after his panicky crashing about in his room.

Someone knocked on his door at about nine thirty in the morning. It was Mrs Griffiths, whom Victor got a good look at for the first time. She was dressed rather as a woman might have been for a Buckingham Palace garden party taking place some thirty years before: a navy blue suit, frilly blouse, straw hat with a white nylon flower in it, white gloves and very high-heeled white openwork shoes.

Pinned to the left lapel of the suit jacket was a gold brooch in the shape of a tortoise, its shell formed of stones which might or might not have been sapphires.

'There've been complaints about you, Mr Jenner,' she said.

She didn't pull her punches or hesitate or preface her words with an 'I'm afraid' or 'you won't mind my saying'. She charged straight in, speaking in a coarse near-cockney voice very much at variance with her genteel appearance. Victor had given the brooch one glance, swallowed, and now was looking away. But he didn't feel like fainting, he didn't even feel sick. He even thought he would be able to look at it again provided he fixed his eyes on the blue stones and avoided the tiny gold protruding head.

'Banging about in the night,' she said. 'Stamping. Knocking on the wall and I don't know what.' He could see her eyeing the furniture for chips or missing legs. 'What were you up to?'

'I have bad dreams,' he said, his eyes going back to the brooch.

'Just have them lying down in bed next time,' she said and, aware of his hypnotic gaze and perhaps also of the pallor of his face, 'I hope you're all right, Mr Jenner. I hope we're not going to have any trouble. For instance,' she said, 'are the police likely to come back?'

'No,' said Victor. 'Oh, no.'

It would be a good idea to move as soon as possible, Victor thought after she had gone. When he closed his eyes, he could see that brooch, a glowing dark image on a white background, but gradually it faded and disappeared.

7

There was a tube map on the station platform just as there had always been on stations. Victor didn't bother to look at it because the indicator informed him that the next train due would be going to Epping. It wasn't quite at the extreme other end of the Central Line but almost. A small subsidiary line went on to North Weald and Ongar during the rush hours. He stood on the platform with a return ticket for Epping in his pocket, waiting for the train that would go no further than Epping. Later on, in the weeks to come, he was to wonder what would have happened if he had looked at that tube map. Would his life have been utterly changed, have run along a different track, so to speak, an alternate line? Certainly he might have changed his mind about going to Epping that day. But in the long run, probably not. Probably, by then, he was committed to certain steps, to certain inevitable courses, even though these were not known to his conscious mind.

The journey was long and slow, for the line soon entered the tunnel, and would not emerge again till the eastern edge of London. Victor had bought *Ellery Queen's Mystery Magazine* and *Private Eye* to read. The train began filling up at Notting Hill Gate. An elderly woman, very overweight, cast longing glances at his seat and sighed each time she was jostled or someone pushed past her. Victor wasn't giving up his seat to her. Why should he? No woman had ever done a thing for him; they had been positively antagonistic to him: his neglectful mother, that malicious old bag Muriel, Pauline, Rosemary Stanley, who had screamed and broken a window when he threw himself on her mercy, that hard-faced Griffiths woman. He owed women nothing and he felt rather resentful when a man of her own age got up to give this one a seat.

The train finally emerged from the tunnel after Leyton. Victor had never been this far along the line before. This was deepest suburbia, the view being of the backs of houses with long gardens full of grass and flowers and pear trees in bloom running down to the track. Four more stations of this sort of thing and then, after Buckhurst Hill, a burst of countryside, part of the Green Belt encircling London. Loughton, Debden, and what seemed to be an enormous estate of council houses with industrial areas. The train came out into more or less unspoiled country again, slowed and drew to a stop. The station was Theydon Bois.

Victor stared at the name. He hadn't looked at the tube map and it had never occurred to him that Theydon Bois would be in this particular forest corner, adjacent to Epping. Essex, the *Standard* had said, and of course this was Essex, metropolitan Essex but still Essex. It was one of the biggest counties of England, extending from Woodford in the south as far north as Harwich. The effect on Victor of seeing that name, the letters of the two words seeming to stand out and vibrate, was one of sickening shock. He stood up and stared at it, leaning across the seat, resting his hands on the window ledge. The doors closed and the train began to move. Victor turned away and looked unseeing into the face of a fellow passenger, a middle-aged man.

The man grinned at him. 'Theydon Bois,' he said, 'or Theydon Bwah, as the natives don't call it,' and he sniggered at his joke.

Victor said nothing. He sat down again in a daze. This, then, was where Fleetwood lived. Out there, somewhere beyond the station buildings and the trees, was the house with the weatherboard and the gable, the roses round the door and the birdbath in the garden. If he had looked at the tube map, Victor thought, he would have seen where Theydon Bois was and he wouldn't have come. If he closed his eyes he could see that name, Theydon Bois, in dazzling white letters that vibrated a little, that danced. He wished very much that he hadn't come, for he felt nauseous now, a real physical sickness. And what was the point of his coming to Epping anyway? What did he think he would get out of it? He couldn't afford to buy a place and there would be no flats to let here, there never were in places like this. As if he would think of living only a mile away from Fleetwood!

The train stopped at Epping and Victor got out. This was the end of the line anyway. He had hesitated, thinking he might just as well stay in the train and go back again, but it was his feeling of nausea that stopped him. Fresh air would help that. He imagined being sick in the train with people looking.

Epping hadn't changed much as far as he could see. The High Street seemed a bit quieter, if anything, less congested, and there were street signs which seemed to indicate that new roads to divert the traffic, motorways, had been built during those lost ten years of his. The wide market place looked much the same, as did the water tower shaped like a castle with a single turret sticking out of one corner that you could see from miles away, the grey stone church, the big triangular green and the tall shady trees. Victor walked from one end of the town to the other, from the Forest side of the tower up to nearly as far as St Margaret's Hospital. He didn't see much, the process of seeing, of registering what he saw, seemed to have gone into abeyance. All he could think about was Fleetwood and the fact that Fleetwood was no more than a mile or two away from him, over that hillside, to the south-east. Or perhaps even nearer, for when Theydon Bois people went shopping surely they would come here?

Walking back, down the hill, he was aware that he was looking for Fleetwood. There were a lot of cars parked and Victor looked at all of them, seeking the sticker of a pin man in a wheelchair disabled people have on their car windows. If Fleetwood were shopping in the town he would himself be in a wheelchair. Victor caught sight of a wheelchair outside a supermarket and he approached it with a return of that sick feeling. But already, from a distance of fifty yards, he could see that the occupant, whose back was to him, had fair hair. As he passed the seated figure, glancing back, swallowing the saliva which had gathered in his mouth, he saw a boy with drawn-up knees and twisted spastic hands.

It was still early, not yet midday. The rain Liz Welch had bemoaned came back in a sudden squally shower with a rumble of thunder over the Forest. Victor went into a place that was half café half wine-bar and had a cup of coffee and because it was raining and nearly lunchtime anyway, a hamburger and salad and a strawberry yogurt. The sickness was gone. So was the rain, for the time being, and the sun had come out with tropical heat and brilliance, shining on the puddles and wet pavements and making them too mirror-bright to look at.

Victor studied the boards outside newsagents' shops. Several furnished rooms to let were advertised, two or three in Epping itself, one in North Weald and one in Theydon Bois. He noted down phone numbers. The North Weald one said 'inquire within' but when he went into the shop the girl behind the counter said she knew for a fact that room had gone weeks before, months before, they just hadn't bothered to take the advertisement out, she didn't know why.

'Could I walk to Theydon Bois from here?' he asked her.

She looked at him, a grin on her face. 'Maybe *you* could. I know I couldn't.' She thought he was interested in the room advertised on the next card. 'I expect that one's gone too. Most of the stuff's out of date.' She spoke with the indifference to an employer's interest of someone whose job is boring and uncongenial.

He had no intention of walking to Theydon Bois and he had no idea why he had asked the question. As for living there . . .! He left the shop and started to walk in the direction of the station. If he wanted to live outside London, what was wrong with somewhere along the river, Kew or Richmond, for instance, or in the far north on the borders of Hertfordshire? There was a train waiting but it was a long time before it departed. An elderly woman with a carrier bag got into the train. He and she were the only people in the carriage. Victor soon realized that there was something wrong with her, that she was probably more than a little mad, or at any rate suffering from delusions. She wore a long red flowered skirt and a sweatshirt with a number on it like an American baseball player's, highly unsuitable garments for someone of her age, but her shoes and stockings were of the most conventional and she had an old lady's knitted hat tied under the chin with knitted strings.

At first she merely sat, smiling and nodding, shifting her bags about, placing one to the right and the other to the left of her, then both on the right, then both between her knees. The train doors shut, trembled and came open again. She got up, leaving the bags where they were, tripped to one end of the carriage and slid down the window between it and the next, ran all the way down to the opposite end and did the same to the window there. At the open doors she leaned out, looking up and down the sunlit deserted platform. Victor realized that she was playing at being a guard and a cold shiver went down the length of his spine. She was at least seventy. He couldn't remember ever having seen a guard in a tube train even in the old days, though they did have them, they did exist, and she was playing guards. He knew this but it still made him jump when, leaning out, she shouted, 'Mind the doors!'

Either it was coincidence or she knew something he didn't know, but even as she spoke the doors began to close. She sprang inside, rubbing her hands together with evident satisfaction. She said to Victor, 'All aboard for Liverpool Street, Oxford Circus, White City and Ealing Broadway!'

Victor said nothing. He was embarrassed but he felt something worse than embarrassment. He remembered the thought that had come back to him the day before, at the Welches, how the behaviourist had said that prison drove everyone mad who was in there more than five years. He, Victor, had been there twice as long as that. Already he sensed in himself strange currents of behaviour, divergences from the norm and impulses he could barely understand. Would he one day become like this old woman? She was sitting opposite him again, shifting the bags, mouthing whispers, smiling. The train had gathered speed and was heading towards Theydon Bois. She skipped up the aisle between the seats, seized hold of the handle on the door at the far end of the carriage and struggled to open it. The awful thought occurred to him that she might be intending to throw herself out. He didn't know what to do. Her bags remained on the floor opposite him and he saw one of them move. He saw a slight movement inside one of the bags and the top of it seem to swell and sink. There might be some animal inside there – a rabbit? The thing he didn't care to name? – or it could simply have been the plastic of the bag itself responding to temperature changes. But Victor didn't think it was that. He got up and stood by the doors. She came and stood close beside him, looking up into his face.

The train seemed to take hours pulling into Theydon Bois. It came almost to a stop, gathered speed again and finally stopped in the station. The doors opened and Victor got out, tremendously relieved. He meant to run up the platform and get into the next carriage and he hardly knew why he stood there instead, savouring relief. She called out behind him, 'Mind the doors!'

He watched the train depart, taking the madwoman with it. Afterwards he thought he would have got out of the train anyway, his fate or stars or destiny or something decreed that he get out of the train, but for the moment he felt angered by what had happened. He would probably have to wait half an hour for the next train.

It was a waste of money as well as time, he thought as he left the station and gave up the return half of his ticket. Now, when he had finished whatever it was he was going to do in Theydon Bois, he would have to buy a single ticket to West Acton. And what was he going to do? Look for Fleetwood's house, a quiet little voice answered him.

The place was much bigger than he had expected. A huge green space traversed by an avenue of trees filled the centre of it. Around this green were houses, a church, a village hall, and roads from it that looked as if they might lead to more estates of houses. Victor walked along past a parade of shops, feeling vulnerable and wary. He had already noticed a car parked with a disabled sticker on the windscreen. But thousands of people had those. Alan had told him once that they were easy to get hold of. Your doctor would let you have one for nothing much worse than corns or a twinge of gout. There was no reason to suppose that this car, parked outside the shops, belonged to Fleetwood. And there was nowhere to be seen a man in a wheelchair or a man on crutches. Victor caught sight of his own face reflected in a shop window, dark, rather drawn, the eyes feverishly bright but the eye sockets becoming dark as an Indian's, the short black hair threaded with grey over the temples and with grey showing in the combed-back bit above the forehead. A thought that was rather more fanciful than those he usually had came to Victor: that age was like frost which passes leaving a whitening behind it and a withering and a shrivelling, a blight that destroys all the bright signs of hope. Would Fleetwood even know him if he saw him now?

The former policeman, if photographs didn't lie, had barely changed at all. But then what had he had to change him? In and out of hospitals, waited on, cared for, cosseted, he had led a sheltered preserving life, had done nothing and undergone nothing to make him look old. Victor had a momentary vision of that bedroom at 62 Solent Gardens once more, of himself standing with his back to the cupboard, holding Rosemary Stanley in front of him, his arm round her waist, and of the door being thrown open and Fleetwood standing there – Fleetwood, who could have had no prevision that a few minutes only were to pass, two or three at most, and after that for the rest of his life he would never stand or walk again. For two or three minutes only they had looked at each other and spoken to each other before he let the girl go to Fleetwood and she threw herself into his arms. Perhaps it had been five minutes in all before the wind blew the curtain out and under the lifted curtain he saw the man on the ladder outside and Fleetwood had turned his back and Victor had shot him. For five minutes at most they had studied each other's faces, looked into each other's eyes, and Fleetwood had refused to believe, pinning enough faith on his refusal as to turn his back and, as it were, challenge Victor. The challenge had been taken up and the gun had gone off, but before that they had got to know each other's faces better than each knew his mother's face, as well as each knew his own looking back at him from the glass.

Or was it all in his imagination? Was it nonsense and did he only feel he would recognize Fleetwood with such ease because he had been reminded of that face by pictures of it in a heap of newsprint? There had been no pictures of him for Fleetwood to see since those early ones, himself leaving 62 Solent Gardens between two policemen and another that Victor tried to forget: a faceless photograph that would be no use to Fleetwood for identification purposes, of the man accused of disabling him hustled into a police van waiting outside the court, a dark coat flung over his head.

Victor looked over his shoulder. He saw a woman with a bandaged leg come out of a shop and get into the car with the disabled sticker. Looking for Fleetwood's house, be began to walk the winding roads, the network of roads where the gardens were pretty with pink and white blossom, trees spread with veils of green, houses of which so many were in the style of Fleetwood's, built at the same time and of similar materials, but which were nevertheless not the same, of which none was the *one*.

The road he was on was a loop that brought him back to face the green. Beyond it and its trees were what seemed in the distance to be more pretty, blossoming, garden-bordered roads, more houses of brick and plaster and weatherboard with creepers climbing them and tulips in their flowerbeds. Victor crossed the road and walked across the green, feeling misgivings now, not doubting he would recognize the house when he saw it, but deploring the method he had chosen of finding it. Why hadn't he done the obvious thing, gone into a post office or a phone box and looked up Fleetwood in the phone directory? Anyone would be able to tell him where Fleetwood's particular road was, he wouldn't need a plan of the place.

By now Victor had reached the avenue of trees, a metalled road which bisected the green diagonally. It would lead him back to the centre of this village suburb and to the parade of shops. A double row of oaks formed the avenue and Victor had scarcely come within the shade of their branches when he saw something which made his heart give a lurch, then begin a bumpy painful beating. From the far end of the avenue, approaching him quite slowly under the trees and on the crown of the metalled surface, were a man and a girl, and the man was in a wheelchair.

They were a long way from Victor and he could not see their faces or discern much about them except that the girl wore a red blouse and the man a blue pullover, but he knew it was Fleetwood. The girl wasn't pushing the wheelchair, Fleetwood was manipulating that himself, but she was walking close by it and talking animatedly. It was a place where voices carried and Victor heard her laugh, a clear, happy, carefree sound. This would be Clare, he thought, this would be the girlfriend called Clare. In a moment, even if they proceeded at this slow pace, he would be able to see their faces and they his; he would be looking on Fleetwood's square-shaped, fresh, regular-featured, dark-browed face, for the first time in the flesh for ten years, for only the second time ever. Victor made no conscious decision to avoid the confrontation. His motor nerves did it for him, turning him swiftly aside off the avenue on to the grass again, carrying him over the grass on to the main road where the garage was and the row of houses and the pub, so that by the time he reached the opposite pavement he was running, running for the station like someone who has no more than one minute in which to catch his train.

8

In the old days Victor used to buy at least two daily newspapers and an evening, the *Radio Times* and the *TV Times*, the *Reader's Digest*, *Which?* and *What Car?* and sometimes even *Playboy* and *Forum*, though the former bored him and the latter made him feel sick. Cal's preoccupation with pornography, soft and hard, was beyond his understanding. Driving for Alan, Victor had a lot of waiting about to do, and it was while sitting in cars waiting that he did most of his reading. He even tried really high-powered periodicals sometimes, the *Spectator* or the *Economist*, but after a while he realized that he was only doing this to impress the client, who would be stunned to see the hire-car driver engrossed in literary criticism or polemics. Most days the coffee table in the Finchley flat had a heap of papers and magazines on it, though Victor had never hoarded them the way Muriel did.

A psychiatrist writing in the *Reader's Digest* had said how people's life-style patterns have a way of reasserting themselves even if circumstances have changed and a period of enforced disruption has intervened. That just about described what had happened to him, if you like long words, Victor thought, and the patterns were reasserting themselves, at least the habit of buying newspapers and magazines was. As to other habits and patterns, they could lie low as long as they pleased. He had got back into the way of buying two dailies and an evening paper and reading them from front to back, reading everything that was in them, and that was how he came upon the paragraph about the arrest of a man for raping that girl in Gunnersbury Park. A small paragraph on an inside page, that was all. The man's name was omitted but it said that he was twenty-three, lived in Southall, and that he had appeared that morning at Acton Magistrates' Court and been committed for trial. Victor wondered if he too were a secretor with a not too common blood group. At least it meant the police would leave him alone now – until the next time, of course.

None of the papers had anything in them about Fleetwood. There was no reason why they should have had, for Fleetwood wasn't a celebrity whose every movement was news. Probably there wouldn't be any more until this book of Fleetwood's was published. Victor told himself that it was on account of the book and the probability that he would figure in it that he thought about Fleetwood so much. At first he had bitterly regretted running away at the point when it seemed that he and the former detective sergeant must inevitably meet, though he knew it was panic which had made him run and therefore something over which he had little control. And after a while he told himself it was for the best, for what could they have to say to each other but give vent to anger and recrimination? Yet what of the book? Was he going to appear in the book and in such a light that everyone he met who had read it would shun and hate him?

Tom called round one morning to tell him he had heard of a job going if Victor was interested. A local wineshop owner wanted a driver for his delivery van and Tom had seen the vacancy advertised in the shop window. It was the place he had been out to that Sunday morning to buy the Bulgarian claret.

'You'd have to explain about your background,' Tom said awkwardly.

'Considering there'll be about a hundred people after the job and I'll be the only one who's done ten years inside, I'll be a really likely candidate, won't I?'

'I don't want to seem to take an authoritarian attitude, Victor, you know that, but you do have to think a bit more positively.'

Victor decided that while he was here he might as well ask him. He showed Tom the *Standard* article about Fleetwood's book.

'I'm not qualified to tell you if it would be libel,' Tom said, looking worried. 'I just don't know. I shouldn't think he could just say anything he likes about you but I honestly don't know.'

'I suppose I could ask a solicitor.'

'Yes, but that'll cost you, Victor. I'll tell you what. You could make inquiries at the Citizen's Advice Bureau; they'll have a lawyer come there and give advice for free.'

Instead of the Citizen's Advice Bureau, Victor went to the public library, where they had telephone directories covering the whole country. There he looked up Fleetwood and found him entered as Fleetwood, D.G., 'Sans Souci', Theydon Manor Drive, Theydon Bois. Victor knew that the name of the house was French but he didn't know what it meant. He went over to the dictionaries section and looked up *souci*. *Sans* he already knew. The translation was 'without care' or 'carefree', which was an odd name for a house, he thought. Had Fleetwood given it that name himself and was he without care? Perhaps he was. He had nothing to worry about, no awful past to forget, uncertain future to dread. He didn't need a job, he would have a nice fat pension, and growing older wouldn't make much difference to him.

Victor didn't want to drive a wineshop van, the idea was grotesque. Besides, it wouldn't be driving, or not much. It would be humping great heavy cases up staircases in blocks of flats. But he went by tube up to Park Royal and found the shop, a poky little place with its windows pasted over with cheap offers and amazing bargains. There was no job advertisement, and when Victor went inside to inquire he was told that the vacancy had been filled.

Walking back to the tube, he realized he would have turned it down even if it had been offered to him. Taking that job would have meant staying here, either going on living in Mrs Griffiths's house or finding somewhere else in the neighbourhood. He still wanted to move out, to move a long way away. In his mind's eye he saw Epping once more, the forest and Theydon Bois with its green and the avenue of trees. It was pervaded in his memory by a kind of tranquillity, a soft sunlit peace. But Fleetwood lived there, thus making it impossible for him to live there too, and Victor felt building up inside him a second resentment of Fleetwood, as if the man were again ousting him from the proper course of his existence. His conduct had consigned Victor to prison for the best years of his youth. Now he was expelling him, as from paradise, from the only place in the world where he felt he wanted to live.

Ever since he had come back from Theydon Bois, ever since that long long journey from one outer end of London to the other, he had had a sense of unfinished business. He should not have run away, he should have stood his ground. A strange idea kept confronting him whenever he was walking along Twyford Avenue, as he now was, or sitting in his room or lying on the bed, letting the magazine fall, concentrating no more – an idea that, once he had seen Fleetwood and spoken to him, the spell would be broken. For instance, he would no longer feel unable to find a place to live in Epping or even Theydon Bois itself, for there would no longer remain a fear of running into Fleetwood by chance or of having, each time he went out, to be on the watch to avoid meeting him. Why, it was possible once they had resolved things, that they might meet quite casually in the street or under those trees in the avenue and simply pass each other with a hallo and maybe a remark about the weather. Possible but not too likely, Victor had to admit. There was the book to take into account, after all, and the fact, never to be done away, of the great injury Fleetwood had inflicted on him. No doubt, some would say, most did say, that this had only been tit for tat, and Fleetwood too had been injured. So well and good, Victor thought, but you measured injury surely by its long-term effects and Fleetwood was contented now, a famous, honoured person, soon to be a bestselling author, a man who lived in a house called 'Carefree', while he . . . There was no use going into it all again. Nothing made any difference to the fact of the unfinished business, the business he was never going to feel easy about until he had finished it.

In Mrs Griffiths's house, on the ground floor, in a dark

corner behind the stairs, was a pay phone. A cupboard had once been there and, later on, its walls and door had been taken away, to make more space, Victor supposed. When you stood by the phone and looked up, you could see the underside of the stairs treads, raw wood still, unpainted, though the house was getting on for a hundred years old. Tenants, over the years, had written telephone numbers in pencil and ballpoint on the raw pitch pine of those stairs.

Victor had copied Fleetwood's phone number down on the same piece of paper on which Tom had written the address of the wineshop. Now he wrote it on the wood of the stairs and, on an impulse, 'David Fleetwood' beside it, having a confused idea in his mind of recording it there for future users of the phone to look at and wonder about while they waited for the pips to cease and their calls be answered. He wrote Fleetwood's name and then he dialled Fleetwood's number. He was pretty sure he was alone in the house. At this hour he usually was and by lunchtime Noreen had always gone. The bell began to ring.

It rang seven times and then the receiver must have been lifted, for the sharp repetitive sound of the pips started. Victor, holding the phone with its lead at full stretch, was squatting on the floor, for he did not trust himself to stand – that is, for his legs to support him. He had a ten-pence piece in his hand and he stretched up and pushed it into the slot. A man's voice said, 'Hallo? David Fleetwood.'

Victor had sunk on to his knees. The voice was unchanged. He would have recognized it whatever words it had spoken, without the utterance of that name. The last time he had heard it, in that bedroom, it had said in fainter tones, 'Whose blood is that?'

Now Fleetwood spoke again, on a note of slight impatience. 'Hallo?'

Victor had never used Fleetwood's name. In that room he had naturally not addressed him by name. He spoke it now, but hoarsely, in a whisper.

'David.'

He didn't wait to hear what Fleetwood had to say next. The receiver slipped out of his hand and swung on the length of its lead. Victor got to his feet and replaced it in its rest. He heard himself give a kind of groan and he stood with his forehead pressed against the stair tread that had Fleetwood's name and phone number written on it. Why hadn't he spoken to Fleetwood? What was the matter with him? He should have explained to Fleetwood who he was and, if Fleetwood had hung up on him, so what? It wouldn't have hurt him, it wouldn't have done him any actual harm. Fleetwood probably wouldn't have hung up on him but would have been distantly polite and might actually have agreed when Victor asked if he could come and see him and talk about the book.

The voice rang and echoed in his ears. He went upstairs and lay face-downwards on his bed. Fleetwood's voice continued to speak inside his head, saying the things he had said during the hour that passed between his arrival in Solent Gardens and his collapse on the landing floor, shot in the back. Victor could remember every word that had been said as clearly as if he carried a tape cassette inside his brain which he had only to push into a slot and switch on.

'That's very sensible of you. Come over here, Miss Stanley, please. You'll be quite safe.'

Victor had said that Fleetwood had to make him a promise.

'What, then?' The same note of impatience as on the phone just now.

The request then for escape by means of the bathroom window and for five minutes to get away in – a five minutes' start, like when kids played hide and seek. But Fleetwood had promised nothing, for just at that moment the other policeman appeared at the top of the ladder, the wind blowing the curtain in and up to reveal him.

'Take her downstairs,' Fleetwood had said.

The gun went off in Victor's hand, filling the room, the little house, with the loudest noise he had ever heard in his life, shaking his body with a shock from toe to head, driving shock through him so that he almost fell. But it was Fleetwood who had fallen, sprawling forward on to the banisters, clasping them with his hands and slipping down, down, silent while Victor shouted, a silence and a shouting that seemed to endure for an infinite age, until Fleetwood's calm voice intruded upon it and said, 'Whose blood is that?'

Victor remembered it all, his mind playing the tape. When, then, had Fleetwood told him he didn't believe the gun was real? He must have told him, and over and over again, for it was this which had challenged Victor to shoot him, to prove he wasn't lying, but somehow Victor could not fit these statements of disbelief into the recording. They had to be there, though, for they had certainly been uttered. Perhaps he was too confused now, knocked sideways by the experience of hearing that voice again, to remember properly.

Getting off the bed, he looked at his face in the mirror, pushing his face up close to the glass. He looked pale and drawn, his eyes unnaturally bright and the sockets dark as bruises. A muscle worked at the corner of his mouth. Chorea, it was called, 'live flesh'. He had read an article about it once in the *Reader's Digest*. The mirror had become hateful to him and he took it down, laying it face-downwards on the shelf by the sink. Mrs Griffiths (or Noreen) provided him with a clean towel each week on Mondays, a thin almost threadbare towel, larger than a hand towel but very small for a bath size and always of a sickly shade of pink. Probably the intention was to match the pale pink nylon sheets. Victor took his towel and the piece of soap from the sink and went along the passage to the bathroom. Because he had only two ten-pence pieces left with which to feed the water heater, he got rather a small bath, not the kind you could relax in and be comforted by. He put on clean jeans and the one good shirt he had and the jacket that had been among the clothes he had had in Finchley, a velvet cord jacket in dark green for which he had paid the then enormous sum of twenty-five pounds. It looked a bit shabby and indefinably out-of-date but it was the best he could do.

By now he wasn't panicky or upset or frightened. He

was excited. He was so excited that he had to stop himself running the quarter-mile or so to West Acton station. Although he had walked, although he had made himself walk nonchalantly, and had positively strolled into the station, his voice was breathless and hoarse when he asked for a return ticket to Theydon Bois.

A man serving petrol at a filling station opposite the green told him where Theydon Manor Drive was, pointing to the far side of the green and away up to the left. It was three thirty in the afternoon and Victor had had no lunch, not even a cup of coffee. But he wasn't hungry. The idea of food was slightly nauseating. He began to walk up the avenue of trees.

The weather was much the same as it had been that last time he was here, just a week ago, heavy showers followed by bursts of bright, quite hot, sunshine. Water still lay in puddles at the side of the road. The blossom had blown down during that week and petals lay everywhere in pink and white drifts. Apple blossom was coming out now and white fool's parsley. Victor walked up the avenue of oaks where he had seen Fleetwood and the girl coming towards him. Suppose Fleetwood always went out in the afternoons? Suppose he were out now? If he were out Victor thought he would just wait for him to come back, though the idea of waiting, of any sort of inactivity, was intolerable. He had to stop himself running.

Following the directions the garage man had given him, Victor crossed the top of the green on the right-hand side of a tree-fringed pond. Theydon Manor Drive started here, a road that might have been a country lane and where the houses looked as if they had been built within the confines of a beautiful and varied wood. Tall chestnut trees were in full bloom, each bearing hundreds of creamy-white candle-like blossoms. Wall-flowers, the colours of a Persian carpet, bordered lawns of a rich soft green, and late narcissi and tulips filled tubs and window boxes as if flowerbeds alone were inadequate to support all the flowers people here had to have. The houses were all different, of varying sizes, all standing alone and surrounded by garden. Victor saw Sans Souci ahead of him when he had reached number 20. The road bent a little to the right and Fleetwood's house was facing him diagonally.

It was one of the smaller houses, less grand and imposing than it had looked in the photograph. The front lawn with the birdbath was no more than fifteen feet by twelve. The bird on the rim of the fluted stone font was no longer there, so it had been a real one after all. Fleetwood was no longer there either and nor were the tulips, their heads all neatly snipped off. He must employ a gardener, Victor thought, for all was trim and well kept, the grass cut and the edges clipped, the climbing rose wired to its trellis. Breathless now, though he had not run, Victor stood for a while looking at the house. On the white-painted gate the name Sans Souci was lettered in black but above the front door, an oak door with studs, was the number 28. Victor could see no signs of life, though he hardly knew what signs he expected.

He had come all this way in a white heat of excitement and need, but now he had arrived at his goal, a reluctance took hold of him. Even now there was nothing to prevent him turning round and returning the way he had come. Some idea of the self-reproach and bitterness and disgust this would cause stopped him. He moistened his lips, swallowed, put his hand to the gate. His fingers touched the black letters of the name that were slightly raised above the level of the white board. Although this was a shady place because of the trees and shrubs, numerous and tall, the path that led up to the front door was bathed in sunshine. There was a feeling in the air that a period of settled weather, of summer, was about to begin. The sun fell on Victor's face, deliciously warm. He wondered whether to ring the bell or use the knocker which was of brass, its clapper the figure of a Roman soldier. It was the bell he decided on, drawing his breath in sharply as he put his finger on the push and pressed.

No one came. He rang the bell again and still no one came. Of course, if Fleetwood were alone in the house, it would take him a little time to answer the bell, since he must necessarily propel himself to the door in his wheelchair. Victor waited, feeling nothing, preparing nothing to say. The air was pervaded with a sweet floral scent that he had smelled before, long ago, but could not place. For the third time he rang the bell. Fleetwood must be out.

Victor looked through two front windows into a comfortably furnished room where there were bookshelves full of books, pictures on the walls, flowers in vases. On a coffee table the *Guardian* lay folded with, beside it, a packet of cigarettes, an agate table lighter and what looked like an address book. He moved on round the house but there were no more windows except one that obviously had on the other side of it a bathroom or lavatory. The floral smell was far stronger here as Victor rounded the side wall and came to the back of the house, to the back garden; he saw that it came from a climbing plant covered with a dense mass of pinkish-golden blossom, a honeysuckle perhaps. It hid from his view the whole of the back of the house. He took a few steps further along the path, then turned to look back. On the stone terrace that ran the entire length of the house, at this end of which the honeysuckle hung in a drapery of colour and scent, a girl was standing and staring at him. She was standing behind a circular teak garden table from the centre of which protruded the shaft of a sunshade, its blue and white striped canvas not yet unfurled.

It was the girl who had been with Fleetwood in the avenue the previous week. Somehow, although on that occasion he had seen her only from a distance, he was sure of this.

'Hallo,' she said. 'Did you try to ring the bell? It's not working, there's a loose connection or something.'

He took a step or two towards her, across grass, up to the edge of the terrace. Smiling a little, assuming probably that he was some meter reader or salesman, she bent across the table to put the sunshade up.

'What was it you came about?'

He made no answer, for the canvas sprang into a broad

umbrella and the girl stepped aside, thus revealing open french windows behind and on the threshold of them, where a ramp had been built, a wheelchair in which David Fleetwood sat, his hands resting on the wheels. It was clear that he did not at first recognize Victor, for his face wore a look of polite inquiry. Victor was choked and silenced by a curious indefinable emotion, yet in the midst of this, or on another level of mind, he was aware of a pleased feeling that Fleetwood in life looked much older than in his pictures. His tongue passed across his lips. He had not foreseen Fleetwood's failure to recognize him and he was at a loss for what to do. Fleetwood, manipulating the wheels with practised hands, rolled the chair down the ramp and stopped about a yard from the table. Victor said, 'I'm Victor Jenner,' and, 'You'll know the name.'

The girl didn't. She had drawn one of the striped canvas chairs up to the table and sat down in it. Fleetwood's face, squarish, brown-skinned with the black brows and the clear blue eyes, had undergone a slow change. The expression was not so much grim as wondering, incredulous.

'What did you say?'

'I said I'm Victor Jenner.'

'Good God,' said Fleetwood. 'Well, good God.'

The girl looked at him inquiringly. He said, 'Clare, you were going to get us a cup of tea. Do you mind? You wouldn't mind if I asked you to leave us alone for five minutes, would you?'

She stared at him. 'Leave you alone? Why?'

'Please, Clare. Do this for me.' His voice had become urgent, almost as if he were – afraid.

'All right.'

She got up. She was a beautiful girl. With wonder that he should notice such a thing at such a moment, this fact registered in Victor's brain along with all the other wonders. He found himself half stunned, confused, by her looks, by the cloud of blonde hair, the honeysuckle skin, the small perfect features. Those eyes, that were a clear bluish-green, turned doubtfully from Fleetwood to him, then back to Fleetwood. 'You'll be all right?'

'Of course I will.'

She went into the house. At first she moved with hesitation, then more quickly, disappearing through what was probably the doorway to a kitchen. Fleetwood spoke in a calm steady voice. Once a policeman, always a policeman, Victor thought. But Fleetwood sounded as if he were forcing himself to remain calm, exercising that control Victor always envied in others.

'Why have you come here?'

'I don't know,' Victor said and he didn't know, he really didn't know now why he had come. 'I wanted to see you. I've been – out three weeks. Well, a month nearly.'

'I know that,' Fleetwood said. 'I was told.'

He had an air of recalling that he had been told much more than that, that he had somehow been *warned* about Victor's being once more at large, or having been told had warned himself to be on his guard. His strong lean brown hands were gripping the wheels of the orthopaedic chair.

'I didn't expect we should meet – like this.'

Rather desperately Victor repeated, 'I wanted to see you.'

'Was it by any chance you who phoned at lunchtime?'

Victor nodded. He wet his lips, pushed the back of his hand across his mouth. The edge of the table dug into his thighs and he pressed his hands heavily on it.

'Sit down, won't you?' Fleetwood said more gently, and as Victor lowered himself into one of the chairs, 'That's right.' He seemed relieved or as if recovering composure. 'Would you like a cigarette? No? I shouldn't either, I smoke too much, but I feel in need of one now. That's rather an understatement. I'm glad it was you who phoned.'

Victor found himself holding on to the seat of his chair, grasping the corners of the canvas-covered cushion. 'Why – why are you glad?'

'I used to get some pretty unpleasant phone calls. Not so much obscene as, well, violent, insulting. Anonymous letters too. But the phone calls were a bit – well, upsetting. And they've started again lately.'

The girl called Clare was coming back, carrying a tray. 'They're disgusting,' she said. 'They call David "cop" and "fuzz", and the main theme seems to be that it was a pity that thug didn't finish the job and shoot him dead.'

Victor made a small inarticulate sound. It was evident that Clare supposed him to be some friend of Fleetwood from the past before she had known him. And Fleetwood himself was taken aback by what she had said. He drew on his cigarette, exhaled, said, 'This is Clare Conway. If, as I suppose, you found out where I was from the story in the *Standard*, you'll know who she is.' He paused as Victor gave an infinitesimal nod. 'Where are you living yourself?'

The voice had a sort of authority about it, commanding though kind. Perhaps it was this quality which made Victor reply like someone making an application for a job or a document, 'Forty-six, Tolleshunt Avenue, Acton, West Seven.' He added, 'I've got a room.'

Clare was looking puzzled and wary. She passed a teacup to Victor and indicated the sugar basin. Her hands were small and brown, rather plump-fleshed with tapering fingers. She wasn't a thin girl but no one would have called her plump either, well made perhaps, full figured. When she leaned forward to take back the sugar basin and pass it to Fleetwood, Victor saw the tops of her round smooth breasts above the neckline of her white and pink dress. Her eyebrows, like moth wings, were drawn together in perplexity.

Fleetwood lit another cigarette from the stub of the first.

'I will have one,' Victor said. 'Please.'

'Sure,' said Fleetwood, and he pushed the packet across the table.

The first inhalation made Victor's head swim. One of those sick feelings to which he was prone rose up into his mouth. He closed his eyes, bending across the table.

'Come on,' Fleetwood's voice said. 'Bear up. Are you all right?'

Victor muttered, 'I'll be OK in a minute. It's years – years since I smoked.'

Forcing his eyes open, he stared at Fleetwood, and Fleetwood said in a tone that was no longer steady, 'You know, when you first came here and said who you were, I thought, he's going to do what that phone caller said, he's going to shoot me again. He's going to finish the job.'

Victor said stupidly, 'I haven't got a gun.'

'No, of course you haven't.'

'I didn't do it on purpose!' A voice burst out of Victor almost without his volition. I didn't mean to. I'd never have done it if you hadn't kept saying the gun wasn't real.'

Clare had sprung to her feet. The blood poured into her face and it was crimson. Victor smelled a heavy wave of honeysuckle scent, as if brought about by the movement of the air, by the energy of them all, for even Fleetwood had moved all of himself he could move, flexing and tensing his upper body, leaning forward with hands upraised.

'Do you mean this is the man who shot you?'

Fleetwood shrugged. 'That's what I mean, yes.' He flung himself against the back of the chair, turning his head to one side away from her.

'I don't believe it!'

'Oh, Clare, you know you do believe it. You only mean it's such an amazing thing to have happened, that he – that Victor – should have come here. Do you think I'm not amazed?'

An extraordinary sensation of warmth touched Victor's skin like the sunlight had on the path, but this warmth penetrated and seemed to fill his body. It was prompted by Fleetwood's use of his Christian name. But even as he felt it he was aware of the girl's eyes on him, of the look on her face, an expression of the kind of hatred and disgust a woman's face might show when confronted by a poisonous reptile. She had even drawn her hands up from the surface of the table and crossed her arms over her breasts, a hand on each shoulder.

On a note of infinite scorn she said, 'What have you come for? To apologize?'

Victor gazed down at the brown polished bars of teak, at the blue china cup and saucer, the cigarette smouldering, its long accumulation of ash dropping on to the stone paving of the terrace.

'Did you come to apologize for ruining his life? For

taking half his body away from him? For smashing his career? Is that why you're here?'

'Clare,' said Fleetwood.

'Yes, it's Clare and if that means, stop, Clare, control yourself, watch what you're saying, I won't, I can't. If you can't express how you feel, I'll express your feelings for you. I'll tell this thing, this animal – no, because animals don't do that, not to each other, not to their own species – this *subhuman* what he did to you, the pain and the suffering and the misery and the loss, what you've been through, the hopes raised and dashed to the ground, the pain and struggle, the awfulness of realizing what paralysis means, the . . .'

'I would much rather you did not.'

It was steely, the voice, the same which had said, 'I'm not making any promises, mind, but it will count in your favour.' And it repeated her name.

'Clare. Please, Clare.'

Victor had pulled himself to his feet. He stood unsteadily, holding the edge of the table, looking down into the cup at the tea leaves in the dregs, a pattern like islands. His head ached from that all-pervading perfume.

'He went to prison for ten years, Clare. In most people's opinion, that would be payment enough.'

'He sent you to prison for life!'

'That really isn't true,' Fleetwood said. 'That's an exaggeration and you know it.'

'It's what you said yourself last week. Those were your own words.' She moved a little way round the table towards Victor. He had an idea she might be about to strike him and he wondered what to do.

'You've come and you've seen,' she said. 'I hope you're satisfied with what you've seen. He isn't going to walk again, whatever the papers may say, and he knows it and all the doctors know it. Crudeness is what people like you understand, so I'll be crude. He isn't going to fuck again either. Not ever. Though he does still want to. And now you can get out. Get out and don't ever come back. Go!' she shouted at him. 'Go, go, go!'

He looked at neither of them again. Behind him she was crying. He had a confused impression that she had collapsed or thrown herself across the table and was crying. From Fleetwood there was no sound. Victor walked back around the side of the house in the sunshine that was hotter and brighter though the afternoon had worn on. A pale-coloured creamy-grey dove with a darker band round its neck sat on the rim of the birdbath, drinking the water. Victor closed the gate that was named 'Carefree' behind him, feeling nothing, feeling drained and empty and weak. But as he made his way to the station, walking on the springy green turf, a tremendous anger, familiar and welcome, invaded his body and filled those empty spaces with a seething heat.

9

Anger fed him and buoyed him up and sustained him. It was a source of enormous energy which he wanted to keep, not rid himself of. There was no real temptation to punch and pummel the bed and the furniture. He sat in his room feeding on his anger, directing it against that girl – that fat, showy, noisy blonde, he called her in his furious mind, that loud-mouthed bitch with her tits sticking out of her dress who used the sort of filthy language he had always hated to hear on a woman's lips. Fleetwood had said nothing, not a word of reproach – supposing he felt he had a reason for resentment – but that girl who probably hadn't been around Fleetwood for more than a year of two, who took it upon herself to sit in judgement on *him*, who raved and screeched . . . Now Victor's anger dictated to him all the things he might have said if he had thought of them, how in front of Fleetwood he might have put her down, squashed her with some well-chosen words that entirely exonerated him and revealed the truth – that no one was responsible, that it was fate, the force of circumstances and destiny which had inflicted such terrible injury upon the man she loved.

That night he dreamed of rape. From boiling energy he was potent and inexhaustible, ravishing women like a soldier sacking a town, faceless women that he seized upon in the dark. And when he had done with them he raised them by the shoulders and battered their heads against the stone ground. He walked among the women, dead or unconscious, despoiled, lying in their torn clothes, their blood, holding a torch in his hand, looking for Clare's face but not finding it, never finding it, looking instead at the worn flaccid cheeks and loose mouth of Muriel and jumping away with a cry of horror.

Whether it was the dream or the night itself or sleep which took away his anger he didn't know, but by the morning it was gone and it didn't return. A certain partial satisfaction replaced it, that he had after all, in spite of everything, seen David Fleetwood and talked to him. David, he said, to himself, savouring the name and repeating it, David. How would it have been if David had been alone and the girl not there, out perhaps or just not existing? Though he could form no very clear idea of what might have taken place in the absence of the girl, he had a profound feeling it would have been good, pleasing to both parties. Each might have acknowledged his personal share in their fates, his imprisonment and David's disablement, admitting that neither was more to blame than the other, but that the good thing which had come out of it was their ability to confront one another and discuss the subject. Of course that hadn't happened because that foul-mouthed blonde bitch had intervened, yet Victor felt it *would* have happened – it was, so to speak, there waiting to happen. The necessary goodwill was present on both sides.

Victor bought a lot of magazines, picking likely-looking ones off the shelves at W. H. Smith's and more from the station bookstall. He also bought a packet of cigarettes, he didn't quite know why, for he didn't really want to smoke and he certainly couldn't afford to. The way he lived, eating out, buying wine and now cigarettes, he wasn't going to be able to live on the DHSS money and soon he would be making inroads on the small capital left to him by his parents. He would have to get a job.

Reading his magazines, he realized he was looking for an article or feature about David Fleetwood. Now he *wanted* to read about David, there was, of course, nothing to read. That was Sod's Law. But David wasn't a singer or an actor or TV personality, only someone who'd been – well, brave, was how you'd put it, Victor thought. There was no doubt he had been brave, though foolhardy was another word, but yes he had shown courage that time at 62 Solent Gardens. Victor had to admit it. They had both shown a good deal of bravery and – what was the word his father used to use? – grit.

Did David know about the rapes? The police had always, as far as Victor knew, assumed, or half assumed, that he was the man responsible for several cases of rape carried out in the Kilburn–Kensal-Rise–Brondesbury districts of London. And he was responsible, there was no doubt about it, for this was a district his route to Heathrow led him through. But nothing had ever been proved against him and he had never been charged with rape. Yet because Heather Cole had told the police, and repeated it at his trial, that he was the man who had taken hold of her in the park, he was immediately stamped as a rapist, *the* rapist. Then, for safety's sake, he had asked for two incidents of rape to be taken into consideration. That perhaps had been a mistake and had added to the assumption that he intended to rape Rosemary Stanley, whereas he had entered the house only to hide and his encounter with Rosemary Stanley had been as much of a shock to him at it was to her. To assault her had never crossed his mind, any more than while in prison or after his release he had thought of rape. A man was not responsible for his dreams, they were something else.

Since he had never been convicted of rape and nothing in that way proved against him, the police had no right whatever to make these assumptions. At his trial, all the time, there had been this undercurrent of belief that rape was behind it all, attempts at rape the underlying cause of what prosecuting counsel had called 'the final tragedy'. The real cause, finding refuge from his pursuers and reacting to David Fleetwood's taunts, was never mentioned. But all this could give him no clue as to whether David knew about the rapes and if he had passed on what he knew to the girl, Clare. He might not know; he had still been in hospital at the time of the trial, and if he were fair-minded, as Victor had begun to believe he was, even if he had heard hints that Victor and the Kensal Rise rapist were one and the same, he might presume a man innocent until he was proved guilty. Not, Victor told himself, that he cared what the girl thought, but David's opinion was another matter. It was so long since he had raped anyone, and he never would again, that it seemed terrible he should be stigmatized for this thing in his past. Shooting David was one thing, that had been an accident, brought about by circumstances, by loss of control and will over his own reactions, by David's own folly, but the rapes were in another category, regrettable, something Victor could imagine he might one day feel remorse over, especially about the girl he had hurt in Epping Forest. He wouldn't like David to know about that, he wouldn't care for it at all.

In vain he looked through his magazines for some note or paragraph about David. He had started going to bed early, there was so little to do, and he lay there reading a short story about an old man, a French peasant farmer, who, instead of keeping his money in the bank, plastered it into the walls of his house, the notes folded up and wrapped in strips of the plastic bag the farm fertiliser came in, thrust between the laths, then daubed and painted over. No night passed without dreams, and in this night's dream he was in a train, on the Northern Line, going towards Finchley. No one was in the carriage but himself and then, at Archway, his mother got in with David Fleetwood. David could walk, but not well; he had a stick and he hung on to Victor's mother's arm. They took no notice of Victor, they behaved as if he wasn't there, as if no one was there, whispering to each other, putting their faces close and then kissing. They kissed each other passionately as if they were alone. Victor jumped up and shouted and protested that it was disgusting what they were doing, it was indecent, that this was a public place, and woke up shouting, sitting up in bed and shaking his fist.

This was the day he was due to meet Jupp in Muriel's house but he very nearly forgot about it. At lunchtime he bought the *Standard* and saw a driving job advertised in it, a mini-cab driver wanted, and the attractive thing was that it said 'car provided'. The firm was in Alperton. Victor went straight up there on the tube to look for the mini-cab company in Ealing Road.

Few people, he thought, would have got hold of the *Standard* before he had, and any who had would probably have obeyed the advertisement and telephoned. It might be that he would be the first applicant to present himself. In his one pair of good trousers, a clean shirt and the velvet jacket, he knew he looked presentable. Before buying the paper he had by a lucky chance had his hair cut. For a while he had considered growing it long again, the way it had been on the day of his arrest, but that was old-fashioned and he, too, was growing rather old for it now. In a few weeks' time he would be thirty-nine.

The mini-cab company he found in half a shop, a very small poky place, not much more than a cupboard, where a middle-aged woman with streaked blonde and brown hair sat answering two phones. He wasn't used to women being bosses, for there had been far less of this when he went to prison, and he knew he had got off on the wrong foot when she corrected his assumption that she was a sort of secretary–receptionist and that the boss was somewhere else. He never found out her name. She wanted a reference from his last job, she wanted to know why he hadn't had a job for ten years. *Ten years*?

'My God, with women it's babies,' she said. 'It can't have been that with you, where were you, in gaol or something?'

She was joking but he said no more. So angry he could have leaped on her and seized her by the throat, he made a mammoth effort at control, turned round and left the place, slamming the door with all his strength behind him. The shop shook. The shop next door shook, and an assistant came to the window to see what the noise was. Victor looked back and saw old furniture, a brass bedstead, vases, a plant stand in the window behind her. With a jolt it reminded him of his appointment with Jupp – at Muriel's house in Popesbury Drive at three. It was ten to now.

At least he could sell that furniture and get some money by this means. He got back into the tube at Alperton and it took him down to Acton Town, the nearest station to

Muriel's. If anything, the purple flowers which overhung the rock slopes of Muriel's garden were even more purple today and their stems had grown longer, so that the stone ornament Victor avoided looking at was entirely concealed. He stared defiantly in its direction, feeling nothing. Since he was last here a laburnum of a particularly violent acid yellow had come into bloom. Two women chatting on the pavement were examining the laburnum and saying how lovely it was, what a wonderful sight, but Victor didn't think it was lovely or that flowers were inevitably beautiful just because they were flowers. Somewhere inside his brain he seemed to smell that honeysuckle once more, though none of the flowers here was scented and the only smell was a faint one of diesel fumes.

A van with J. Jupp printed on the side of it was parked on the ramp that led down to the garage, backed up to the garage doors. Victor went round the back way, through the side gate, into the area between the garage and the back door of the house. The rear garden was a wilderness, blossoming apple trees rising out of grass that reached halfway up their trunks. Victor tapped on the back door, tried the handle. To his surprise it wasn't locked. His aunt and Jupp were sitting at the kitchen table, drinking tea.

What had Jupp said or done to put Muriel so unusually at ease, to get into the house and make his way to the kitchen? Victor seemed to have interrupted a conversation, at least an anecdote of Jupp's, to which Muriel listened avidly. They both seemed rather sorry to see him. Muriel had her pink hairnet on and the left-hand earpiece on her glasses, which had apparently been broken, was done up with pink sticking plaster. At last Jupp got up and, saying this wouldn't buy the baby a new frock, followed Victor out to the garage. Today he had on the trousers of the suit of which the black pinstriped waistcoat was a part and with them a black tee-shirt and long ginger suede jacket with fringes. His long hair and walrus moustache looked thicker and more luxuriant, on account perhaps of recent shampooing. He took a Polo mint from his pocket and put it in his mouth.

'Remarkable woman, your aunt,' said Jupp. 'Had a fascinating life. It's not often you'll find a person frankly admit they married for money. I call that honest. Been a good looker too – there's what you might call remnants of it still.'

Victor said nothing. They might not have been thinking of the same woman.

'Pity about her never going out, though. If you don't mind me saying so, you ought to make an effort there, get her moving, put a spot of salt on her tail, eh?' Victor did rather mind him saying so. He began to unlock the door. 'What was she doing then, storing all your stuff for you? You been away?'

The only reason Muriel wouldn't have told him the truth was because she hadn't yet had the chance, Victor thought. When he was a little boy, very small, he had hated his parents talking about a time before he was born. That there had been a time when he didn't exist he hadn't been able to bear, and he had cried and stamped when his mother spoke of it. It was the first memory he had of outbursts of anger. Because that time of non-existence was intolerable to him, he had started saying he had been in New Zealand. When his mother spoke of 'before you were born', he corrected her and said he was in New Zealand. He said it now to Jupp.

'I was away a long time. I was in New Zealand.'

'Really?' said Jupp. 'Nice. Very nice. Let's have a looksee then. Let's have a shuftee at some of the movables.'

He pushed his way about among the furniture, pulling off the curtains, the gold folkweave and the green rep, and Victor's bedroom curtains with the red and green squares on the black and white background, pulling them off and tossing them aside, peering under table tops and tapping surfaces with a rather long fingernail. Victor wondered if he was checking for woodworm. The wheelchair he pushed back and forth like someone trying to get a child off to sleep. Victor noticed that the wheelchair was the same make as David's, though his looked like a later model. Jupp stuck out his underlip.

'I tell you what, I'll give you four hundred pound for the lot.'

Victor was disappointed. New furniture, he had seen from looking in shop windows, was very expensive. Secondhand furniture too had rocketed in price. Why, when he had wanted a few bits for his flat, the dealers couldn't give old sideboards and dining tables away. Things had changed. The three-piece suite alone was surely worth four hundred pounds.

'Five hundred,' he said.

'Now wait a minute. I've got to pay a fella good wages to come over here with me and clear this lot. I've got to pay for juice and maintenance of the van. I've got to lose half a day in the shop.' He took another mint, looked at it and put it back in his pocket.

'I reckon that wheelchair's worth a hundred,' said Victor. 'Look at it, as good as new.'

'There's not exactly a boom in the wheelchair market to be honest with you, cocky. Suspending an invalid carriage on a chain from your lounge ceiling hasn't caught on in Acton, it's not what you'd call chic, right? Four hundred and twenty.'

They compromised at four hundred and forty pounds and Jupp said he would come back and pick the stuff up next Wednesday. He looked at the thigh-high grass in Muriel's garden and said what a wicked waste when there were lionesses and cubs looking for homes. Victor went back into the house. Muriel was washing up cups and saucers. She washed a cup, rinsed it, dried it on a teacloth, put it inside a cupboard, then began on the process with a saucer. Saying he needed to go to the bathroom, Victor went along the passage and up the staircase with its runner of red turkey carpet. It would not have been true to say nothing had changed when he had made this same journey just a little less than eleven years ago in search of Sydney's Luger. The house was much dirtier. Had it been Sydney who did the housework? Or was it simply that Muriel had done none since he died? The once polished edges of the stair treads lay under a layer of grey fluff and the carpet itself was coated with a mat that consisted mostly of hairs, Muriel's hairs presumably, shed and left to lie over the years. The sun was shining outside, even as it had been on that evening when he had let himself in with the key he had had cut, when Muriel and his mother had gone to see Sydney in hospital, and as on that evening the interior of the house was dark. It was gloomy and still and dark and everything was now coated in dust. Perhaps the windows had never been opened all those years. The camphor smell was still there and allied to it, mingling with it, the sharp sour choking odour that is the smell of dust itself.

Once it had been a handsome house, for it had been built at a time when materials were relatively cheap, when fine hard woods were plentiful and when, somehow, there had been more time and more skill and craftsmen to create panelling and carved wood and unusual mouldings for cornices. And yet the builders or maybe the architect had gone too far so that the thickly leaded windows excluded more light than they let in and the curtains completed the job, curtains that some big store – Whiteley's, he guessed, or Bentall's – had made to order and hung themselves, swatches of thick velvet or heavy slub silk, lined and interlined, pleated and flounced and looped back with tasselled cords. They had never been cleaned or even brushed, and dust and powdered cobweb lay in their folds. Victor gave a twitch to one of the curtains in the room where he had found the gun in the hiding place under the cupboard floor. A cloud of dust flew out into his face, making him cough. The dust lay so thick on the carpet that you could no longer see the pattern of yellow grapes and green vine leaves; only a vague impression was received of a bluish-grey pattern.

The western novels were still on the shelf, undisturbed for more than a decade. He left the room and went into his aunt's bedroom. A big mirror, framed and swinging, mounted on two uprights, stood in the middle of the pinkish flowered carpet. Pink and white crêpe-paper roses filled the fireplace, a decade of soot having fallen on to and spotted their petals. The bed, unexpectedly, was made and in the middle of it lay a pink fluffy dog, the zip fastener in its belly open and revealing the white nightdress which must be the one Muriel put on when she took off the nightdress she wore by day.

The story of the French peasant in his mind, Victor thrust his hand under the pillows, between under-blanket and mattress. He pulled open the drawers in the bedside cabinets, opened the doors of the wardrobe, which he found full of Sydney's suits. A search of the pockets afforded him nothing. A section of the side compartment of this wardrobe was crammed with old handbags, navy and black and wine-coloured and white, cracked and split, their metal fastenings tarnished, their clasps broken. Victor pulled a black one out, it was imitation crocodile skin, and felt inside. The crackle of notes made him catch his breath. But he had been up here too long, he would be back next week when Jupp took the furniture. Without counting the money, he helped himself to a handful of whatever colour those notes were, closed the bag again, shut the wardrobe door and ran downstairs.

Muriel was sitting by her electric fire, busy with her scissors, with copies of *Country Life* and *Cosmopolitan*. She seemed to be compiling a scrapbook of events in the life of the Duchess of Grosvenor.

'You were a long time,' she said to Victor.

She had a way of looking at him which was similar to the way a mouse looks emerging from its hole: wary, suspicious, sharp, perceptive and entirely self-absorbed. He could almost see her nose twitching, whiskers vibrating, eyes making quick nervous movements. The ring that was a dome of diamonds was on her finger; perhaps she never took it off.

His hand in his jacket pocket, he could feel the crisp notes there, one, two, three, four – at least four, maybe five, it was hard to tell. They might be tenners.

'I want to tell you something,' she said.

He moved across the room, he stood by the window. It was just as stuffy there, the dense smell of mothballs and old unwashed clothes, of ageing newsprint and dust burned on the heater element, was just as strong, but you could see daylight, you could even feel the warmth of the sun struggling through the dirty diamond panes. The long yellow plumes of the laburnum hung against the glass.

Muriel said, 'I never fancied making a will. I'm superstitious, I suppose, don't want to tempt providence.' She looked up from her cutting, up at the ceiling, as if God had taken up his residence in her bedroom and had his ear to the floor. 'But there comes a time when you have to do what's right and not what you want, and I knew the right thing was to make sure you never got hold of anything that was mine.'

'Thanks very much,' said Victor.

'So I made my will the day after you was here last time. Jenny next door that goes to the shops for me, she got a will form and took it to my solicitor and he's done what I wanted and I've got it signed and witnessed. You can see a copy if you want. I've left the lot to the British Legion. That would have pleased Sydney. I said to myself, poor old Sydney devoted his life to pleasing you, Muriel, and now you can do this to please him.'

Victor stood staring at her. He could feel that pulse beginning to beat at the corner of his mouth, the twitch of live flesh. His hand in his pocket felt the money and he rubbed his fingers over the notes.

'The Legion do a lot of good,' said Muriel. 'They won't waste it. Sydney would turn in his grave if you got your hands on it.'

'He was cremated,' said Victor.

It was the only time he had scored with a parting shot, uttered it at the right time instead of thinking of it afterwards. He slammed the front door behind him like he had slammed the door at the mini-cab place. Walking home by the back streets, up towards the Uxbridge Road, he took the notes out of his pocket. There were five of them, two twenties, one ten, two fives. The possibility that there might be twenties among the notes hadn't occurred to him and his spirits rose. Losing Muriel's house and her money was hardly a misfortune since he had never counted on getting them. The malevolence of her glare and her words grated on him, though. The attitude she had taken towards him, a combination of fear and dislike, made him glad he had taken the money and wish he had helped himself to more.

Victor had never stolen anything before, unless you counted chocolate bars nicked off the counters at Woolworth's when he was still at junior school. Everyone did that and it was more a game than delinquency. As an adult he had rather prided himself on his honesty. He and Alan and Peter, the other driver, had had a system whereby they shared their tips, which were sometimes substantial, and Victor had almost always rendered his up in full for the share-out. Once or twice the temptation had been too much for him – as, for instance, when that American, on a first visit, had confused pounds with dollars and given him twenty-five – but generally he had been honest. He told himself that, if Muriel's something she had to tell him had been different, had been, say, the very opposite of what she had told him, that she had made a will in his favour, he would have taken that money back upstairs and restored it to her handbag. Now his only concern was that she might miss it. What if she did? She was hardly likely to call the police in over her own nephew, however much she might hate him.

On the strength of what he had from his parents, was going to get from Jupp and what he had taken from Muriel, Victor went into one of the High Street shops half an hour before it was due to close and bought a television set.

Since he had come to Mrs Griffiths's house Victor had received virtually no mail. All he ever got were communications from the DHSS. Letters and cards were spread out on the table in the hall by whoever came out first and picked the mail up off the doormat. On Friday morning he had been promised delivery of his television set and when ten o'clock had passed with no sign of it – between nine and ten was the time named – he came downstairs to check that the doorbell was working. Electric doorbells can go wrong, as he had recently learned. He only looked at the mail on the table because there might have been a card from the TV people explaining why they hadn't come or saying when they would come. Between two postcards of foreign seaside places lay an envelope addressed in a strong upright hand to Victor Jenner, no 'Mr' or 'Esq.' or anything. The postmark was Epping.

Victor forgot about the television. He took his letter upstairs. His throat drying, the tension that preceded nausea getting a hold on him, he sat down on the bed and split the envelope open. The letter was typewritten on both sides of a single sheet and signed 'Clare Conway'. Victor read:

Dear Victor Jenner,

You will be surprised to hear from me after the way I spoke to you on Monday. May I say that you took that very well? A lot of people would have shouted abuse back at me and I think you would have been justified if you had done that. This letter is in part an apology. I had no business or right to speak to you like that, I wasn't involved, the injurer or the injured, I was just being as I often am a bit too partisan.

I am trying hard to say what I have to say but it isn't easy. I'll try again. David and I think it was very brave of you to come here, a very brave thing indeed to do because you couldn't know what sort of reception you would have, and in fact you had about as bad a one from me as possible. You didn't say why you came, though of course it was obvious you did so because you felt you wanted to make some sort of restitution to David. I imagine you as having been haunted by events and feeling the need to take some positive action as soon as you could.

I'll admit here and now that I wouldn't be writing to you if it was your conscience only that was in question. You have to deal with that in your own way. It's David I'm concerned about as I have been almost since I first met him nearly three years ago. David is a wonderful person, easily the most just and honest and generous-minded, the most *complete*, person I have ever known, which seems an odd thing to say, since physically of course he is anything but complete. You can't be aware – no one can except those who are very close to him – how, in spite of being able to forgive and accept, he is still as haunted by what happened in that house in Kensal Rise eleven years ago as I suspect you are. He dreams of it, every possible association reminds him of it, the memory of it comes back to him every day, but the worst thing is that he can't resign himself to it as having been inevitable. He *regrets*. I mean that he is always thinking of what might have happened, what might have been avoided rather, if he had acted differently or maybe said different things.

The point is, though, that since seeing you and talking a little to you last Monday, in spite of everything, in spite of *me*, he seems easier in his mind. At least I think he seems easier. And when I said I was going to write to you he welcomed the idea and said he would like to see you. You see, I am convinced that if you two could talk a bit more and tell each other what you felt, really talk this thing out, a lot might be resolved. David might at last be able to resign himself to what his life is going to be for the rest of it and you – well, it might solve things for you too and bring peace of mind.

I hope this doesn't sound too high-flown – or worse, like some sort of psychotherapist. If you have read this far you will have guessed what I'm going to ask. Will you come and see us? I know it's a long way for you, so please come for the whole day, a Saturday or Sunday, and please make it soon. I'd like to think it was a good destiny that made David keep your address in his head. He has a good memory – too good, I sometimes think.

In the hope that we shall see you,

Yours,

Clare Conway

Victor couldn't remember the last time he had been really happy. It must have been before he went to prison, for certainly there had been no happiness since, not even when he knew he was going to be released and was released; resignation, yes, and a degree of contentment, the relative calm that came between bouts of anger and panic, but happiness never. The last time was probably when he knew he had got the Ballards Lane flat or when, six months before he took Sydney's Luger, Alan had promised him a future partnership in the business. It was an unfamiliar feeling but he recognized it: happiness. Like anger, only differently, without the burning pain and the beating heart, it filled the vessel of body and mind with the effervescence of a sparkling wine. It reached his lips and made him laugh aloud, he had no idea why.

There was no phone number on the letter and he had thrown away Tom's piece of paper. When the television man had been, he would have to go back to the library. He went down to the hall, stood looking at the phone, wishing he could remember David's number and then, turning his head, he saw it. He had written it on the raw wood of the underneath of the stair treads and David's name beside it: David Fleetwood.

His hand was shaking and he had to grasp his wrist in the other to steady it. Because of that tremor in his fingers, he couldn't be sure he had dialled the number correctly but he must have done, for when the pips sounded and he put his ten pence in, Clare's voice answered.

He said, his voice uneven with excitement, 'It's Victor.' They weren't likely to know another Victor, so there was no need to say his surname.

'It's good of you to get in touch so quickly.' She had a beautiful voice, low and measured, a little formal, things he hadn't noticed when she was abusing him. 'I feel,' she said, 'a bit embarrassed talking to you. I was so awful.'

'Oh, forget that.'

'Well, I'll try. I do hope this call means you'll come. When will you come? When would it suit you? We'd like it to be soon. I've a job, and David sometimes has to go to hospital for checks, but apart from that we're always here, we don't go out much. It's complicated for David to go out – we have to make so many arrangements in advance.'

'I could come any time.'

The doorbell rang and he knew it must be the television man but it seemed no more than a distant nuisance, something he wouldn't allow to be an intrusion.

'Could you come tomorrow?' she said.

10

Sixty pounds didn't go very far these days when you were buying clothes. Having parted with almost all of what his parents had left him on the purchase of the television set, Victor had decided to spend the money he had 'had' from Muriel on a pair of trousers, a shirt, a pair of shoes. He preferred to put it like that, what he had 'had' from Muriel, rather than what he had 'taken'. It was Ealing where he went shopping, the district being rather more upmarket. Half the money went on the trousers and half on the shoes, a shirt as well being beyond his means. He was more than ever convinced that he needed a job, and a long way away from here, where so much reminded him of Muriel and Sydney, of his parents and his youth.

Victor had never really had any friends. This was probably because his parents hadn't had any. Of visitors to the house he could only remember Muriel and later, once or twice, Muriel and Sydney, a neighbour who occasionally came to tea and a married couple called Macpherson whose society his mother lost because she did not, as his father put it, 'keep friendship in repair'. She had never cared for intruders into the unit formed by her husband and herself. They were all in all to each other, as Victor once heard her tell Mrs Macpherson, and besides this, she found entertaining, even in the most modest way, too much for her, it made her hysterical. When Victor was at school she didn't encourage him to bring other boys home and because of this he seldom got asked back to their houses.

It was for his ninth birthday that the idea of a party was mooted. He would never forget the circumstances but he could no longer remember whose idea it had been, his mother's or his father's. The birthday was in June but plans for the party were made weeks ahead. Victor's mother thought invitations ought to be sent out but she didn't know how to word them, so although a great deal of energy was expended on worrying nothing was actually done. If it was a fine day the party could be held in the garden, but who could tell, in England, if 22 June would be a fine day or not? Victor's mother didn't want all those little boys – there were no prospective little girl guests – in her house. She wasn't a houseproud woman but she could not contemplate the idea of all those little boys running about. Victor had not been allowed to say anything about the party at school. He had been forbidden to issue invitations by word of mouth, but of course he had hinted that a party would be held. Then there was the food. It was really a question of which kind of food would be least messy and least trouble to prepare. Victor had been to a party where the children threw the food at each other and he had been unwise enough to mention this at home. His mother talked about the party every day and she talked about it as if it were a watershed on this side of which lay unimaginable stresses and anxieties and problems and on the far side, if it could ever be attained, a glorious peace and freedom. Sometimes she cried about it. One evening – it was the first week of June and no invitations had been sent – she burst out crying and asked why had they ever considered having a party, what had got into them, were they mad? Victor's father calmed her down and cuddled her and said they didn't have to have a party if she didn't want to. This made an amazing difference to Victor's mother, who dried her eyes and smiled and said they really didn't, did they? She immediately became happy and put the radio on and made Victor's father dance with her. She danced and sang 'Mr Sandman' and they never had the party.

When Victor was older he sometimes found himself on the perimeter of one of those groups which are formed of a nucleus of two friends with two or three lesser friends and a few hangers-on. Victor was one of those hangers-on. He never had much to say but he wasn't a good listener either. Silent or laconic, he lived in a world of his own, as one of his teachers said in a school report. If a girl at his school didn't have a boy to go out with by the time she was fourteen, she felt less than a girl, inadequate and unattractive, but no such stigma attached to a boy with or without a girlfriend. At the time he went to the polytechnic Victor had scarcely spoken to a girl and he had certainly never been alone with one.

Pauline chose him, not he her. His mother, who didn't like her, said she wanted someone to get married to and wasn't too particular about who it was, as long as he was young and nice-looking and with a potential for making a good living. Victor had been very nice-looking in those days, everyone said so. He was somewhat vain of his appearance and was glad when the fashion came in to grow one's hair long.

Pauline had friends but he never got on with them. Women's voices irritated him, the pitch of them, their flexibility and rise and fall. Nor did he feel much need for a male friend. Alan was the nearest he ever had to a friend, but they seldom saw each other out of working hours and working hours were spent in separate cars. They had nothing in common but age and sex. Alan had a wife and child in Golders Green, a girlfriend in Camberwell, and was obsessed with vintage cars and rugby football. Victor could take an interest in the cars but that was about all. It wasn't much of a friend, he thought, who deserted you when you were down on your luck, never even wrote you a postcard. He had never had a friend but now perhaps that was about to change. The novelty of it excited him. As he put on his new trousers, his new shoes, he began to feel new himself, a person in the process of being re-made, his past shadowy this morning as if it had all taken place in a previous life – in New Zealand, in fact.

And yet, of course, without that past he would never have got to know David. A pretty costly way of making a friend, he thought, as he got into the train, and a picture of prison came before his eyes, notably the night when Cal and the other three had raped him. Why did he have to think of that now? Settling in his seat, opening the first of the magazines he had bought, he wiped it away.

It was a beautiful day, the best day they had had since he came out. The sun was as hot as late summer, though it was still only May. Clare had said 'about one' but he intended to be punctual, he intended to get there on the dot of one. Too late it occurred to him that in some circles it was considered polite to take flowers with you on these occasions or maybe a bottle of wine. Flowers would be like coals to Newcastle. Perhaps he could give them *New Society*, *Country Life* and *Time* Magazine, which still looked quite new and as if unread.

There were people all over the green, throwing balls about and playing games and exercising dogs. Victor loitered, for it was only a quarter to. He remembered the room at Theydon Bois he had seen advertised on the newsagent's board and he wondered if it were still vacant. The place was so green and peaceful, the air so fresh compared to London, and yet London was only about fifteen miles away. He started walking slowly towards Theydon Manor Drive, feeling the sun on his face, thinking how impressed they would be by his appearance, his trim haircut, his new clothes. The scent of the honeysuckle he could smell all the way down the street and it quickened his excitement, his alert feeling of expectation.

He had supposed Clare would open the door to him. This time he didn't make the mistake of pressing the bell but rapped with the Roman soldier door knocker. No one came and he waited. He waited, knocked again, and held his breath, afraid. The door was opened by David, which accounted for the delay. David had reached from his wheelchair and opened the door and sat there with a smile on his face.

'Hallo, Victor. Is that right or would you rather be called Vic?'

'I'd rather Victor,' said Victor.

He put the magazines down on the hall table. It was the first time he had set foot inside the house, which was cool and rather dark, but not dark in the way Muriel's was, for there was a feeling here that these rooms were a kind of refuge from the sunshine, but that if you wanted it you had only to throw open doors and windows and curtains for light to pour in. The hall floor was carpeted in a glowing ruby red. On the stairs was a lift, which ran on a rail above the banister and which was large enough to accommodate David's wheelchair.

'It's good of you to come.'

Victor couldn't think of a reply to that. Just when he could have done without it, when he needed to make a good impression, the chorea had come back, making his left eyelid twitch. He followed David into the room with the french windows. David was wearing the same baggy slacks he had had on last Monday but on top he wore a tee shirt and he said to Victor to take off his jacket if he wanted to. And help himself to a drink, the drinks were on the sideboard. Victor poured himself a measure of whisky, rather a large measure. He needed it – both to help him talk to David and for the confrontation with Clare which would surely happen at any minute. David, watching him, was lighting a cigarette.

'What about you?' Victor said.

He shook his head. Victor felt he was being subjected to a fascinated examination. David seemed to be watching his every movement with a compulsive interest as if he were wondering how it was that this man could perform routine tasks like other men, pour liquid from a bottle into a glass, walk across a room, seat himself. Perhaps he was imagining it, though. Perhaps David was silent, smiling now, only because he too was at a loss for words.

Inspiration came to Victor.

'Where's the dog?' he said.

'Mandy?' said David. 'Oh, she died. She got old and died.'

'I saw her in the newspaper photograph,' Victor said.

'She wasn't a puppy when I had her. She was two. They don't usually live past eleven, those labs. I miss her. I keep thinking I see her, you know, in a doorway or lying up against my chair.'

Victor didn't say any more because Clare came in.

He wondered how he could ever have called her fat, even when he was hating her, when nothing was too bad to think about her. She was one of those women who are both slim and plump. Her figure was perfect. It was just that she wasn't one of those stick-insect girls who pose (he had noticed) in designer clothes in magazines. She wore a dark blue skirt and a white shirt and her face was without make-up. You could see it was without make-up in this midday light; those colours, the rosy-gold and the soft pink and the feather-brown brows were natural.

She had written to him and spoken to him on the phone, she expected him to come and knew he had come, but when she saw him her face reddened. She blushed and smiled slightly, putting one hand up to her cheek as if she could wipe the blush away. He held out his hand to her, though he hadn't done this to David. She shook hands with him and he thought how this was the first time he had touched a woman for years and years . . . Only it wasn't, for he had touched Muriel, held her and shaken her, when first she showed him the cuttings about David.

'Victor, we thought we'd eat our lunch outside, if you'd like that. We get so little summer, it seems a pity not to take advantage of it, but if you hate eating outside please do say.'

He couldn't remember that he had ever tried it but he wasn't going to admit to that. Clare had gin and tonic and David white wine mixed with Perrier water, and Victor showed some interest in the Perrier water, which had hardly been around when he went to prison – or at any rate wasn't the universal drink and mixer it had since become.

'Not before you-know-what,' said David and the ice was broken. You could almost hear the tinkling of it as it broke.

'Well, a lot of things have changed,' Victor said.

'I know. I was – out of the world too for quite a while. In and out, anyway. And when I came out I'd always find something new people were talking about or eating or drinking.'

'Or saying or singing,' said Clare. 'Five minutes away and you lose your grip. But you were ten years away, Victor, and you haven't.'

The compliment pleased him. 'I read a lot,' he said.

They had lunch. It was cold soup, white and green and lemony, and an onion and bacon flan with a salad. Clare had done the cooking and she was a good cook, which somehow he hadn't expected. The whisky had had an effect on Victor, which the wine they drank reinforced. His tongue was loosened and he talked about the room in Mrs Griffiths's house and Acton and Ealing, which, after all, were his native heath, but he added how he would like to move away, move outside London. He'd got a job in marketing coming up, he said, for he couldn't bear them to think him indefinitely unemployed and without prospects. A proper flat was what he would really like with a kitchen of his own so that he too could cook. In fact, he had scarcely cooked anything ever beyond scrambled egg and cheese on toast but as he said it he believed it, and he told Clare what a good cook she was, as from one culinary expert to another.

'You'd think he'd marry me, wouldn't you, Victor? I've proposed to him often enough but he always turns me down.'

Victor didn't quite know how to take this. He looked sideways at David.

'I've been living with him for two years now. It's time he made an honest woman of me.'

David said gravely, 'I've never made a dishonest woman of you.'

A chill seemed to fall across them. It was as if the sun went in. Victor thought he understood what was implied but he wasn't quite sure.

Clare said rather brightly, 'After we've had coffee we thought you might like to go out for a walk. I mean, we'll all go. The forest is beautiful in May, it's the most beautiful time.'

For a moment he was alone with David once more while she cleared the table. The ice seemed to be forming again and Victor sought desperately for words that would dissolve it. He fancied that, though silent and calm, David kept his eyes on him unblinkingly. The scent of the honeysuckle, still overpowering, was past its best, sickly now, cloying, a rotten sweetness.

'Up there on the horizon,' David said suddenly, 'at night you can see the lights of the new motorway. I say "new" but it's been there three years now. Yellow lights go all the way along it and they're on all night, like a kind of phosphorescent yellow ribbon winding over the fields. It's a pity really, it spoils the rural character of the place. You'll see later on. Sometimes I think of leaving here, of going a long way away – well, of emigrating.'

'I thought of emigrating, but who'd have me? I'd have to be open. Anywhere I'd want to go to, they wouldn't have me, with my record.'

David said nothing. He had clasped his hands together and was holding the left hand tightly in the right, making white knuckle bones. Victor began to talk about getting a job when you had a record, about having to tell the truth to a prospective employer, and then he remembered how he had said he had a job lined up. But before he could correct the impression he must be giving David, Clare came back and asked him if he would mind helping her with the dishes. Victor was rather surprised, for he had never done anything about the house while Pauline was living with him and he had never seen his father lift a finger to help his mother. But he followed Clare because he didn't know how to refuse. It was a well-appointed kitchen, full of the usual equipment and gadgets and a lot more unusual ones besides, the kind of bars and ramps and handles specially designed and installed for the convenience of a disabled person. Clare, of course, hadn't always been here to look after David. She handed Victor a tea towel but there weren't many dishes to do as David had a machine which Clare had already loaded.

'I wanted to be alone with you for a moment,' she said.

Bending over the sink, she kept her face turned away from him.

'I have to tell you that when I wrote to you and talked to you on the phone – I did that to please David. I wanted to kill you. It seemed unreal, your coming here, I mean *you*, the man who actually shot David and maimed him for life. And yet at the same time it seemed too real, the right thing, the only possible right outcome – and I couldn't handle it. Do you understand what I mean?'

Victor wasn't sure that he did, though he thought she must be praising him for coming here, congratulating him, and he was conscious of a warm feeling of pleasure.

'I thought,' she went on, 'that when you came here I wouldn't be able to keep it up, I mean being nice to you, treating you politely. I've been crazy with worry ever since we spoke on the phone yesterday, wishing I hadn't asked you to come, anything but that. But now you're here, as soon as I saw you in fact – I knew it would be all right. I suppose I'd seen you either as a sort of monster or else as a – well, an instrument of evil, I suppose. And then I saw you again and of course I realized you were just a man, a human being, who must have done what he did because he was unhappy or afraid.'

'The gun went off by accident,' Victor said. *Had* it? He could no longer remember. 'It just went off in my hand, only no one believes that.'

'Oh, I can believe it,' she said, and she turned to look at him. 'I sometimes think life is all like that, a matter of random happenings and chance and accident.'

'You're right there,' he said with feeling.

'Take me meeting David, for instance. I'm a radiographer at the hospital in Epping, so you'll say that's not chance, that's one of the obvious ways people meet. He must have come to me for X-rays. But he didn't, he's never been to St Margaret's. All his treatment's been at Stoke Mandeville – he's going back there in a couple of weeks time. We met in the dry cleaners in Theydon. The wheels of his wheelchair got locked on the step and I freed them for him – it's wearing out, that wheelchair, he needs a new one. But the point is, it was just chance we met. I passed the shop, not meaning to go in, but the sun had come out and it was warm, and I thought, why don't I take off this jacket here and now and get it cleaned? And I did and David came in and we've been together more or less ever since. That was two years ago last September.'

'Do you live here, then?' Victor asked her.

'Oh, yes.' She laughed. 'I'm pretty committed. I've thrown in my lot with David, there didn't seem an alternative. I told you he's a wonderful person.' She looked at him defiantly. 'I'm lucky.'

Every inhabitant of Theydon Bois was out for a walk this afternoon, it seemed. Most of them knew David and spoke and smiled and even those who didn't know him gave him looks of sympathy and admiration. Victor wondered what it must be like to receive people's regard in this way. He walked along on one side of the wheelchair with Clare on the other, past the pond, across the green and up the road that led into Epping Forest. Clare said she thought it one of the most beautiful parts of the forest because it was hilly and with open clearings between the groves of trees. There were silver birches everywhere with pale spotted trunks and a covering of new green leaves like a sprigged veil. The whole place looked as if newly made because of the freshness of the young foliage, the brilliant thick green grass and the flowers that grew among it, yellow and white and star-like. Yet the birches, the preponderance of them, awakened in Victor an uneasy memory which increased the further they walked. For a moment, for more than a moment, the panicky idea invaded him that David and Clare knew, that every detail of his past in all its circumstances was known to them and they were bringing him to the scene of the rape he had committed here to test or mock him. For it was here, on this very spot, that it had happened.

The girl had been ahead of him in her car on the Epping New Road, heading north. He was on his way to pick up a couple and their daughter at Stansted airport but he was very early. Where the girl was going he didn't know, but he followed her car round the Wake Arms roundabout, out by the second exit and down this road. He had had no idea that it led to a place called Theydon Bois. But here, at this point where Clare was suggesting they leave the road and follow one of the clay rides among the trees, she had parked her car and left it, to walk her little dog. The dog was too small to help her. Victor recalled how its yapping had maddened him. It was this as much as anything which had made him beat the girl so badly, the only time he had ever done this, punching her face, clasping her head in his hands and pounding it against the ground, finally stuffing her own tights into her mouth. The dog had yapped and then howled, staying by its owner's unconscious form, while Victor drove away, hearing those thin reedy howls in the distance behind him. In the papers it said that the dog had saved the girl's life, for a passer-by heard it and came to find her. By that time Victor was stowing the Stansted passengers' baggage into the boot of the car.

He could actually recognize one of the trees here, a gnarled oak with a hole in its trunk shaped like an open screaming mouth. He must have fixed his eyes on that hole in the tree trunk while he was raping the girl and the little dog howled. Sarah Dawson, her name had been. Victor realized by now that Clare and David had no idea of the associations of this place for him. It was simply a place they liked to come to. The rape of Sarah Dawson had taken place at least twelve years ago and they had probably never heard of the case. Why, Clare wouldn't have been more than about fifteen herself then, he thought.

How could he have done such a thing? What had impelled him to harm that girl, to cause her such pain and terror, to beat her until her jaw had been broken and she had to have operations and orthodontic treatment? Victor had never before asked himself such questions, they were a novelty to him, and he felt stunned by the inquiries he was making of himself. But they were too much for him and he shirked deeper probing. He knew only that these events were long in his past, far away, never in any circumstances to be repeated.

'You're a very quiet man, aren't you, Victor?' Clare said as they sat down for a while on a smooth grey beech log.

He thought about it. 'I've never had much to say.'

'I must seem an awful chatterer to you.'

'It's all right when there's something worth talking about.'

'David and I talk all day long,' she said.

She smiled at David and he reached for her hand and took it in his. They *had* been talking all the time, Victor realized, on about the people they knew, and the forest and plants and trees, and where they would go for their holiday, and Clare's job and the people she worked with. It mystified him a little, for such conversation was unfamiliar to him. David began asking him if he liked it here and he said he did, that he thought of living here and looking for work. Victor felt disappointed because neither David nor Clare said they thought this a good idea or that they would help him to find something and keep their eyes open.

But when they were back at the house and Clare had left them alone together – to prepare a meal, Victor thought, but afterwards he wondered – David asked him if he would mind if they talked a little about that morning at 62 Solent Gardens . . . Victor said he didn't mind. David, who hadn't had a cigarette all the time they were out, lit one now and Victor had one too, just to be sociable.

'I've never been able to confront what happened that day fairly and squarely,' David said. 'I mean, I've resented it and raged about it. I've lamented my fate, if that doesn't sound too melodramatic. Well, even if it *does* sound melodramatic. It was a melodramatic thing that happened there that morning. But what I'm saying is, I've never had a long cool look at it and tried to re-live it. I've never talked it through – even to myself.'

Victor nodded. He could understand that David might feel like this.

'I've simply assumed I did it wrong. I've assumed I handled it badly – well, I handled *you* badly. Do you remember every detail of it like I do?'

'I remember it all right,' Victor said.

'I was in the front garden and I said to you that if

you murdered Rosemary Stanley you'd get life. Do you remember that?'

Again Victor nodded. He found he was pushing out his lower lip the way Jupp did.

'And you said you wouldn't murder her, you'd just . . .' David's voice broke off and he wet his lips. He leaned forward in his chair and seemed to be trying to speak.

Victor thought he ought to help him out. 'Shoot her in the lower spine,' he said.

'Yes. Yes, you do remember. At the time I – we – all of us – thought it was a terrible thing to say. It was so cold-blooded. I suppose it was what someone told me counsel said at your trial: 'a statement of cruel intent'. And then, of course, later, you actually did do that to me. I'm finding this extraordinarily hard to say, Victor. I thought I would and it isn't any easier than I expected. The thing is, I felt you meant all along to – well, *do that to someone* – and the someone happened to be me.'

'I didn't mean to,' Victor said. 'It was just something to say. I'd read something the night before in a magazine about – what's it called? – paraplegia and being injured down there. I do read a lot. It stuck in my mind.'

'And that was why? Is that really true?' David's voice was full of wonder.

'Of course it is,' Victor said.

'You only made that threat because of something you'd been reading? So if, for example, you'd read about shooting someone in the shoulder and disabling their right arm, you might have threatened that instead?'

'Right,' said Victor.

Clare came back then and they had supper. It was cold stuff on a tray, pâté and cheese and different kinds of bread, a fruit cake and apples and grapes and a bottle of sweetish flowery German wine. They drank that bottle and David opened another. The evening remained warm and they sat around the table on the terrace, the air pervaded with the heavy scent of honeysuckle, a violet dusk closing over the garden. To protect them from the mosquitoes, Clare had set up a 'zapper' and against this glowing blue ring the insects cast their frail bodies to be electrocuted with a snap and a hiss. Victor was rather amused by this effective method of control and said, 'There goes another!' with great satisfaction each time the device hissed, so that David's attitude astonished him. David couldn't stand it. He said that, if it was a choice between sitting out here and listening to this slaughter and going inside with the windows shut, he'd rather go inside. For an ex-policeman that was almost unbelievable, Victor thought.

They did go inside and Clare played records, country music and then some English folk songs, and the dark came down and at last Victor said he ought to be getting back. It was late – though not too late for the last train – and the idea was forming in his mind that if he hung it out long enough they might ask him to stay the night. He wanted to see what the place looked like first thing in the morning, hear the dawn chorus of birds, the garden when the sun came up. He imagined having breakfast here, Clare in her dressing gown perhaps, he imagined the smell of the coffee and the toast. But when he said he must be going neither of them suggested anything about staying the night, though Clare did say they would let him know if they heard of any flats or rooms going and she gave him a copy of the local paper to look at the accommodation page.

When he left, they came part of the way with him to the station. The wheelchair set up a squeaking and again Clare said it was wearing out.

'He charges about so much, Victor, he wears them out like other people wear out shoe leather.'

Victor thought this a bit tactless but it made David laugh. When they were down on the green, David pointed to the horizon and the crest of yellow lights that spanned the length of it, the bright necklace of the motorway that strung out the whole length of the skyline. It brought London nearer, it made Victor feel Acton wasn't all that far from Theydon Bois. He shook hands with David and then he shook hands with Clare, though this seemed strange with a woman, but it would have been stranger still to have kissed her.

He turned back twice and the first time they too turned and waved to him. The second time he could still make out their shadowy figures in the distance but although he looked for a long time, watching them recede into the dark, they didn't turn their heads again.

Victor was sitting in the almost empty train, reading the paper Clare had given him, looking out occasionally as Leytonstone was passed and Leyton and the train entered the tube tunnel, when it came to him that he had forgotten all about David's book. He had forgotten about the book and had never mentioned it or whether he might figure in it.

11

His mother used to say that you only needed to write thank-you letters to people if you stayed with them overnight. It wasn't necessary just for a meal or a party. How she could make these rules Victor hardly knew, for he had never known her eat a meal (apart from those Christmas dinners at Muriel's) away from her own home, still less stay the night in someone else's house. All day Monday he thought about writing to Clare or David or both of them but he didn't know how he should address the envelope. 'Mr David Fleetwood and Miss Clare Conway' looked clumsy and perhaps tactless and anyway perhaps the 'Miss' should come before the 'Mr'. Nor could he think of anything to write except 'thank you for having me', which was what kids said when they had been to tea. In Victor's life were huge gaps, empty spaces, where other people had social experience. He was only now aware of it. He could phone them but then they might think he was trying to get another invite for himself. He was, but he didn't want them to realize it.

The accommodation page in the local paper had afforded him nothing – or nothing that was attractive to him. Only one advertisement looked hopeful but, when he phoned the woman who had a two-room flat to let, she asked for a thousand pounds' deposit. Victor, having put the phone down, thought that of course once Jupp had paid him for the furniture he would be in a better position, but it was essential then that he made no more inroads on his capital. If he didn't hear from Clare or David by the end of the week, and so that they didn't think he was on the cadge, he would invite them to have a meal with him. There must be good restaurants in the neighbourhood, there always were in places like that, and Clare drove a car – well, a Land Rover. He hadn't seen the Land Rover, it was shut up in the garage, but she had told him that they had one and that it was specially equipped to take David's wheelchair. If he hadn't heard from them by Friday, that was what he would do. There were ways of paying for the meal without breaking into his inheritance.

Jupp was already there when he got to Muriel's on Wednesday morning. He and Muriel were having coffee in the dining room and a man whom Jupp said was his son-in-law was starting to load furniture on to the van. For once Muriel was properly dressed with a skirt on and a flowered blouse, stockings and lace-up shoes instead of nightdress and dressing gown. She had combed her hair and smeared some red on her mouth. The only thing unchanged was the camphor smell. She had taken a fancy to Jupp, he could tell that, and they were having digestive biscuits with their coffee and a chocolate Swiss roll.

Victor said he would go out and give the son-in-law a hand. Instead he went quietly upstairs and into Muriel's bedroom. This room was over the living room, not the dining room where Muriel and Jupp were, so they were less likely to hear him. At their age they were probably a bit hard of hearing anyway.

Muriel had been too busy dressing up for Jupp to make the bed. Two nightdresses, grubby nylon entrails, sagged out of the unzipped belly of the pink toy dog. One of the windows was open, a fanlight. Much more of this and she would be behaving like a normal person. Victor opened the door of the wardrobe and a draught from the window blew the skirt of Muriel's black silk raincoat up into his face. That was the coat she had worn on the evening Victor's mother took her in a taxi to the hospital, and in their absence Victor had gone in and taken Sydney's gun. Perhaps he could get hold of another key of Muriel's and have another one cut from it.

The handbags were there in the shelf section in just the same positions as he had left them last time, the black imitation crocodile one at the front. Now, with Jupp keeping Muriel occupied downstairs, he had more time – time to look as well as feel. He unclasped the bag and saw the notes inside, neatly arranged, a wad in each of the bag's stiff corded silk compartments. The familiar feeling of sickness rose into his throat. He tried to breathe deeply and steadily. Why shouldn't he take David and Clare out somewhere really nice, buy them a really good meal? The reading he had done in the past weeks had taught him that a really good meal for three people, even out in the outermost outer suburbs, might cost getting on for a hundred pounds. Why shouldn't he spend a hundred pounds on them?

He pulled out one of the wads, emptying the compartment. Some of the notes were fifties, rich-looking, golden-green. He couldn't remember that he had ever seen a fifty-pound note before – they were new, or new to him. This must be Muriel's accumulated pension, he thought, that Jenny next door fetched for her as her accredited agent. There must be some sort of form she had to fill in to appoint an agent to fetch her pension. He should be so lucky! Then what did she use to pay for her shopping and all those magazines? Cheques to the paper shop, no doubt, and maybe cheques to a grocer. Why not? He didn't wonder why she hoarded all this money in cash. He knew why. It made her feel safe having plenty of money about the house, money in every cupboard for all he knew, in every drawer, stuffed inside shoes and the pockets of coats as likely as not. He understood because, in her position, in any position where cash was plentiful, he would do the same.

Sydney had left her a lot. The pension was superfluous, icing on a rich cake, but the kind of icing you take off and leave on the side of your plate. She wouldn't know how much cash she had and she certainly wouldn't know how much was missing. He took all the notes out of the next compartment and then distributed all that remained between all the compartments, counting as he did so. The next bag he opened was empty but a red leather one with a lot of gilt decoration on it contained a bundle of tenners fastened together with a rubber band. Victor took twenty notes out of the bundle. That made five hundred pounds. He could hardly believe it.

No doubt, later on, he would be back for more and he would want to know whether she had touched the bags in the meantime. His own belief was that she had packed as much into these particular receptacles as she intended to and had moved on to another 'bank', a shelf or drawer or box perhaps not even in this room. He pulled a hair out of the crown of his head and laid it lightly across the clasp of the black crocodile bag. There was no way now that anyone could move those bags without dislodging the hair.

Downstairs he heard Jupp's voice. He and Muriel were coming out of the dining room and Jupp, of course, would go straight to the garage where Victor was supposed to be. It probably didn't matter too much but he had better go down. Inadvertently he caught a glimpse of himself in the pier glass. The furtive look on his face, mean, sharp and calculating, took him aback. He drew back his shoulders, squaring them. He raised his head. If Muriel hadn't said that about leaving her property and money to the British Legion, he wouldn't have helped himself to her money. Or at any rate he would have put back what he had taken if the reverse had been true and she had announced she was leaving it to him. Never would he have thought of coming back for more. It served her right. In a properly constituted legal system there would be a law compelling people to leave their property to their own flesh and blood.

Jupp didn't comment on his absence or ask him where he had been. He was about to put Victor's father's wheelchair into the van, was pushing it up the ramp. Almost everything was gone and the curtains lay in a crumpled heap on the floor. Victor had a wonderful idea. David's wheelchair was wearing out, Clare had said so twice. Why shouldn't he give David this one? It was a good wheelchair, anyone could see that, and his father had only used it for about six months. It was an Everett and Jennings orthopaedic chair, leather and chrome, and Victor thought what a marvellous present it would make for David. Of course

David had that house and nice furniture and obviously didn't want for anything, but he would only have some sort of disability pension to live on (not a great hoard of inherited capital like Muriel) and no doubt couldn't just go out and buy a new wheelchair when the fancy took him.

'Want a mint, cocky?' said Jupp, holding out the packet.

'You can give me one,' said the son-in-law. 'I reckon I do you a favour every time I take one of them things, like when a person takes a smoker's fags. It's a kindness to them, keeping them off their poison.'

'I'm not as bad as that, Kevin,' Jupp said humbly. 'I'm a thousand times better than what I was. You wouldn't call me addicted, would you? Dependent maybe, but addicted, no.'

'He's a mintaholic,' said the son-in-law, laughing. 'Joseph Jupp MA, Mintaholics Anonymous.'

'I don't want the wheelchair to go,' said Victor. 'I've changed my mind and I'm keeping it.'

'Now he tells me,' said Jupp. He pulled the wheelchair out from where he had stowed it between a bookcase and a pile of cushions. 'I shall have to knock a bit off the purchase price. No doubt you've taken that into account. Four hundred.'

'Four hundred and twenty,' said Victor.

Jupp gave the chair a shove and it careered down the ramp. 'Four hundred and ten and that's my final word. Do you think your auntie'd come out for a drink with me? Or maybe the cinema?'

'She never goes out.'

Another mint went into Jupp's mouth. He had finished the packet and he screwed up the paper wrapping and threw it into the back of the van. 'She never got dressed either, did she? But look at her this morning. Quite the glamour girl. I think I shall go and try my luck. Faint heart never won fair lady.'

'Christ,' said the son-in-law.

'Don't be like that, Kevin.' Jupp's hand went to his pocket but the supply was exhausted. He said to Victor,

'I'm a widower, by the way, in case you was thinking it wasn't all above board.'

'It's nothing to me,' said Victor. He held out his hand, palm uppermost. 'I'm a bit pressed for time.'

Jupp wrote him a cheque. He was left-handed and he wrote slowly in a sprawly round hand. The cheque smelled of mint. What with his mints and her camphor, they would make a fine pair, Victor thought disgustedly. He let Jupp go back into the house and, leaving Kevin seated on a spur of rock among the purple trailing flowers, he went round the house to see if a key might be concealed somewhere under a loose paving stone or flowerpot. But there was nothing.

On the garage floor lay the brown checked travelling rug that had always been draped over one end of the settee. To conceal a cigarette burn made by his father, Victor had discovered when he was about eight. On an impulse, he picked it up, folded it and put it on the seat of the wheelchair.

'That'll have to come off the purchase price,' said Kevin, winking. 'No doubt you've taken that into account.'

Because Kevin meant to be funny, Victor managed a smile. He said goodbye and went off, pushing the wheelchair. Instead of going the direct way home, he crossed Gunnersbury Avenue and walked along Elm Avenue towards Ealing Common. There was no one about, it was very quiet, a dull weekday morning with rain threatening. Sure he was unobserved, Victor sat down in the wheelchair and covered his knees with the rug. Manipulating it looked easy when David did it. He thought he would have a go and see how easy it was. The wheels had chromed metal hoops attached to them of slightly smaller circumference. These you pushed forward and they drove the larger wheels round.

There was something quite pleasant and gratifying about making the chair move along. Victor took one of the paths across the common. He felt rather like the way he had when he had first mastered the technique of riding a bicycle. It brought a new dimension to daily life. A woman was coming towards him with a retriever on a lead. Victor's first thought was that he must get out of the chair because this woman would think it odd or be shocked by what he was doing, but immediately he realized that of course she wouldn't be. She would simply take him for a handicapped person who was obliged to use a wheelchair. And this, in the event, was what happened. It was interesting to observe her behaviour. Although Victor was on one side of the path and she on the other and a good six feet separated them, she drew in the dog's lead, shortening it to less than a yard's length, gave Victor a quick searching glance, then looked away with an assumed indifference as if to say: Of course I know you are a cripple, but to me, sophisticated creature that I am, you are no different from anyone else and I shan't commit the social solecism of staring at you, so don't imagine I am wondering what is concealed under that rug or what brought you to what you are now.

Victor was sure he could read all this in her reactions, and it intrigued him. There was no doubt that in a wheelchair one was the centre of attention. He met and passed several more people and the feeling he often had when on foot, that he might as well not be there, that he was invisible, that no one took a bit of notice of him, was replaced by a sensation that in this new guise he affected everybody. No one who saw him was immune from his effect. It might be pity they felt or embarrassment, resentment, guilt or curiosity, but they felt something, those who stared, those who ostentatiously did not stare and those who stole at him sideways glances. When he came to the lights at the big crossing where the Uxbridge Road crossed the North Circular a big man came up to him and said, 'Don't you worry, mate, I'll see you over,' and when the lights changed and the traffic stopped, shepherding Victor, walking along by the side of the chair, 'Let them wait, that won't do them any harm.'

Victor thanked him. He was enjoying himself. Something else he realized was that he had always hated walking, though he had never confessed this before, even in his innermost thoughts. One thing about prison, exercise might have been compulsory but there had been nowhere to walk to. For the most of his adult life, prior to prison, he had had a car to drive. The wheelchair was hardly a car and it would be out of the question in bad weather, but in some ways it had advantages over a car, it had attractions, Victor acknowledged, as two gossiping women jumped aside to let him pass, that cars didn't have. He caught himself up on that when he realized the enormity of his thoughts – a man with the full use of his legs wanting to be confined to a wheelchair!

It wasn't easy getting the chair up the stairs at Mrs Griffiths's, but there was nowhere to leave it downstairs. Victor thought how good it would be if the phone under the stairs were to ring at this moment and for it to be Clare. He would tell her about the wheelchair being a gift for David and she would be delighted and probably come over as soon as she could in her car and take him and the wheelchair back to Theydon Bois, and this time perhaps he would be asked to stay the night. The phone didn't ring, of course it didn't. Clare would be at work, doing her radiography at St Margaret's Hospital.

The wheelchair was more comfortable to sit in than anything provided by Mrs Griffiths. Victor sat in it by the window, looking at the roof of his parents' house and reading *Punch*. The roof was all that could be seen of the house for the leaves were thick on the trees now and the spotty green and pink and white veil had become a blanket of foliage. In the garden below, weeds had grown up as high as the woodpiles and oil drums: nettles and thistles and a pink flower as tall as a man. Victor counted his cash. With his last social security payment he had just on a thousand pounds in hand. The magazines he had bought contained plenty of advertisements for restaurants recommended in the *Good Food Guide* or by the AA or Egon Ronay. Victor sat in the wheelchair reading them and wondering where it would be best to go. If he hadn't heard from David and Clare by Saturday, he decided, he would ring them on Saturday morning and ask them to have dinner with him that evening. He had never taken anyone out to dinner before, apart from eating in cafés with Pauline and once or twice going to the steak house in Highgate with Alan.

Victor thought he wouldn't go out at all on Friday. It would be awful if he were to go out and David were to phone and there was no one here to take the message. At various times throughout the day, which was very long and passed slowly, he told himself that he had no reason to believe David would phone, he hadn't said he would phone. Probably he and Clare were waiting for him, Victor, to phone them and thank them for last Saturday. At three in the afternoon, when he was bored and sick with waiting, Victor went down and dialled David's number. There was no reply. He sat in the wheelchair reading last Sunday's *Observer* colour magazine for half an hour and then he went back to the phone and tried again. Still no reply. He would leave it for two hours, he thought, and at five thirty he would try again.

On the stairs, coming down at twenty past five, he heard the ringing begin. He ran down and lifted the receiver. It was Clare.

Her voice had a strange effect on him. He didn't want her to stop talking, her voice was so lovely, warm and rich and with an accent few women in his circle, such as it was, had possessed. She spoke rather slowly and precisely, yet with a kind of breathlessness that was very charming. He was listening to the tone of her voice and its quality, not the sense of what she said, so he had to ask her to say it all over again.

'It's a flat, Victor. Not here but at a place called Epping Upland. The house belongs to someone my mother knows. Her husband has died and she wants to let part of her house. She's going to advertise but she won't for a week or two, so now's your chance. I haven't said anything to my mother. I thought I'd wait until I'd asked you.'

Victor said he would like to see the flat and Clare said he could fix that up with Mrs Hunter himself. She would give him Mrs Hunter's phone number and address. Victor realized she wasn't going to invite him to Theydon Bois or even say anything about seeing him again. The beginnings of nausea cramped his chest.

'There's just one thing I'd suggest, Victor. I'm not advising you to be dishonest – I'm sure you wouldn't take that sort of advice anyway – but I wouldn't say anything about the past to Mrs Hunter if I were you. It's not as if – well, what you did you're likely to repeat. It's not as if you did something likely to affect a person letting you a flat, I mean stole something or – well, committed a fraud or anything. Please forgive me for mentioning it.'

Victor swallowed. He said, 'That's all right.'

'David and I have talked it over and we agreed we wouldn't say anything about who you were even to my mother.'

'Thanks,' Victor said, and, 'I thought of changing my name,' though he had not in fact thought of this until that moment.

'That might be a very good idea. Well, fine. Now let me give you Mrs Hunter's phone number. Have you got a pen?'

He wrote it down mechanically. Epping Upland was probably miles away from Theydon Bois, almost the other side of Essex, very likely. They wanted him a long way away. Had he done something he shouldn't last Saturday? Had he blown it in some way?

'Right, I'll have to ring off now,' she said. 'We're going out.'

'Clare,' he said, his mouth dry, 'I'd like to – I mean, would you and David have dinner with me tomorrow? Somewhere nice, somewhere out near you. I'd really like to take you out but I don't know any places.' He felt spent with the effort of making this long speech.

'Well . . .' she said. That single word sounded doubtful. Did it also sound pleased? 'We couldn't tomorrow.'

Disappointment was an actual pain. He crouched down on the floor, doubling up his body in an effort to ease it.

'Victor? Are you still there?'

'I'm still here,' he said hoarsely.

'Would a night in the week be possible?'

'Oh, yes. Any night. Monday?'

'Let's say Wednesday, may we? And shall I book somewhere? Would you like that? I'll have to arrange with them about getting David's chair in. We always have to make sure restaurants can do that.'

The best place, Victor said. The best place she knew, she mustn't worry about expense. He would call for them, would that be all right? He would rent a car. Why not?

'Of course not, we'll go in ours. Come early, come about six.'

He asked her to remember him to David, please to give David his best regards. She sounded surprised when she said she would, surprised and a bit puzzled. Amazed he could afford all this hospitality, he thought, as he returned to his room. Epping Upland wouldn't be all that far from Theydon, very likely no more than three or four miles. He thought he could remember noticing a signpost to it on those trips he used to make to and from Stansted. When he was living in Mrs Hunter's flat he would be able to ask Clare and David over for a meal. By then, of course, he would have a new name. He wondered what he should call himself. His mother and Muriel had had the maiden name of Bianchi. Their grandfather had been Italian, from southern Italy, which accounted for Victor's own darkness of hair and eyes. He didn't fancy calling himself by an Italian name. Faraday then, after Sydney? Pauline's surname (doubtless changed long ago) had been Ferrars but he didn't want to be reminded of her. It would be easy enough to pick a name out of the phone book.

Victor phoned Mrs Hunter, giving the name of Daniel Swift and saying he was a friend of Clare Conway. She said he could come and see the flat on Wednesday if he wanted to. Not knowing how far Epping Upland might be from Theydon Bois and wanting to be absolutely sure of getting to David's by six, Victor said he would come in the morning. He would come at eleven thirty. He forgot to ask what rent Mrs Hunter would want or when the flat would be available.

On Tuesday he went out shopping, this time to the West End. He couldn't wear the green velvet jacket yet again. To go out to dinner surely you needed a suit. If only he had a car of his own! The possibility of ever owning a car seemed remote. He went into the men's department at Selfridge's and bought a dark grey suit. It cost him two hundred pounds. To go with the suit he bought a grey and cream striped silk shirt and would have got a grey tie, only the assistant told him flatteringly that this was rather dull for a man of his age and recommended instead a rich leaf green with a single diagonal cream stripe.

Dressed in his new clothes, he set off early on Wednesday morning – too early, for he was at Epping by eleven. A station taxi took him to Epping Upland and Mrs Hunter's house. It was rather a long way and Victor hadn't seen any sign of public transport, though there must be some, and he disliked the idea of walking all this distance. He asked the taxi driver to wait and was glad he had done so, for it turned out that, although she had said nothing of this on the phone, Mrs Hunter wanted a married couple for the flat and help in the house in lieu of some of the rent. Victor returned to Epping, the whole empty day stretching before him.

At any rate, dressed like this and with money in his pocket, he could buy himself a good lunch in one of the hotels. It was a very good lunch he had and he found himself very respectfully treated, no doubt because of the suit. Victor realized, as he was eating his crème caramel and drinking the last of his wine, that it was nearly two weeks since he had been in a panic or felt angry. Those great angers that took told of him and took control of him, changing him physically so that his skin burned and he felt literally as if his blood was boiling, they seemed remote. So did the panics that enclosed his limbs in an electric suit that tingled and shocked where it touched. He was changing. As he thought this, he was aware once more of a feeling that must be happiness and with it came a gentle luxurious calm.

Beginning at the tower end of the town, Victor went into

every estate agent to ask what they had in the way of unfurnished flats to let. There was none, but some had furnished flats and houses on their books, their owners protected by leases which stipulated strictly limited tenancies. The DHSS would, of course, pay his rent but would they pay *any* rent? A hundred pounds a week, for instance? It seemed unlikely. Victor decided he must ask Tom or Judy about that. He bought a local paper, though it was nearly a week old. He had a look at a newsagent's board, not the one he had been to before, and wrote down two phone numbers, both with the Epping exchange.

By the time he had tried these two numbers – one advertising a flat, the other a room – and had got no reply from either, it was nearly three thirty. If he walked slowly to the station and got a train and then walked slowly to Theydon Manor Drive, surely he wouldn't be too early at David's? Well, he would be early but only about an hour and David wouldn't mind.

Just as a journey can be very long when one is late so it can be accomplished with amazing speed when one has time to kill. The train was waiting and as soon as Victor got into it the doors closed. Last time he had travelled from Epping to Theydon Bois that old woman had been in the compartment with him, the one who ran up and down playing guards and had some live thing with her in a carrier bag. This afternoon he was alone. About an hour ago the sun had come through and it was quite hot, the carriage full of almost static motes of dust suspended in the rays of light. It was still only ten to four when he got to Theydon.

He walked very slowly across the green, not wanting to sit down on a seat, still less on the grass, for fear of marking his suit. At ten past four he could bear it no longer. He could feel his calm threatened by a strange stretched feeling that was part boredom, part exasperation with the dilatoriness of time, part an undefined fear. Unwilling to let it mount any further and destroy his new self, he began to walk rapidly towards Sans Souci.

The garage doors were open and the garage was empty. Victor knocked at the front door, a smart double rap with the Roman soldier. No one came, so he walked round the side as he had done that first time. The honeysuckle smell had grown stale and petals lay everywhere. On the terrace, in his chair, David sat fast asleep, his head hanging forward at an awkward angle. For a moment or two Victor stood watching him. Hanging like that, David's face looking puffy, the cheeks pendulous. He looked old and sick and sad.

Victor moved quietly towards the table and sat down in one of the blue and white canvas chairs. Almost immediately, though Victor was sure he had made no sound, David woke up. He woke up, blinked, and seeing Victor there, made an involuntary movement of recoil. It was a flinch, made with shoulders and head, and at the same time he rolled the chair a foot or two back towards the french windows.

'David,' Victor, said, 'I know I'm early. I thought you wouldn't mind.'

David took a moment to recover. He passed his fingers across his forehead. He blinked again. 'That's all right. I was fast asleep.'

Victor wanted to ask him if it was he that he was afraid of, that he had flinched from, or if anyone would have had that effect. He would have liked to ask but of course he didn't. David's cigarettes and lighter were on the table and an empty cup that had had coffee in it. Victor didn't look at David but at the wall behind him, where a rambler rose climbed, its stems laden with clusters of creamy buds.

David said, 'You look very smart, what my father used to call "Sunday-go-to-meetings".'

'My father called it that too,' said Victor, though he had no memory of his father actually ever saying this. He began telling David about the flat and David said it was pity Mrs Hunter hadn't thought to mention that bit about a married couple to Clare's mother.

'I've got something I want to give you,' Victor said. 'A present. I want you to have it. I couldn't bring it with me though, it's too big and awkward.'

'I'm intrigued. What is it?'

'A new wheelchair. Well, it's not absolutely new, it was my father's. But it's hardly been used.'

David looked at him, a steady blank stare. In a way that gave the impression of stiff lips, of lips frozen perhaps, he said, 'I've got a new wheelchair, this one. Didn't you notice? I got it at the end of last week.'

And then Victor did notice it, the shiny chrome, the smooth new grey upholstery. He passed his tongue across his lips. The glassy stiff expression on David's face had crumpled and he was smiling. He was smiling in the way people do when they don't want to seem to be smiling, yet at the same time want the person they are talking to to see there is cause for amusement.

'*You* wanted to give *me* a wheelchair?'

'Why are you smiling?' Victor said.

'You lack a sense of humour, Victor.'

'I expect I do. There hasn't been much in my life to be humorous about.'

'Never mind, then. It was the irony that struck me, but never mind.'

It took Victor a moment or two to see what David meant but he got there, he did see. He got to his feet and stood, holding the edge of the table.

'David, I didn't shoot at you on purpose. It was an accident. Or rather, I lost control through you taunting me. I wouldn't have shot you if you hadn't kept on saying the gun wasn't real.'

David breathed deeply, looking at him eye to eye.

'I said that?'

'Over and over. You kept on saying the gun was a replica, that it wasn't real. I had to *demonstrate* – can't you understand?'

'I never once said the gun wasn't real,' David said.

Victor couldn't believe it. He would never have thought David capable of lying. An abyss seemed to open before him and he held on to the table to stop himself from falling in.

'Of course you said it. I can hear you now. "We know the gun isn't real," you said. Four or five times at least.'

'It was Superintendent Spenser who said that, Victor. From the front garden.'

'And you said it too. When we were in that room, you and me and the girl. You've forgotten, I can understand that, but I haven't. That's why I shot you. It wouldn't – it wouldn't do you any harm to admit it now.'

'It would do me a lot of harm to admit to something that never happened.'

'Unfortunately, there's no way of proving it.'

'Yes, there is, Victor. I have a transcript of your trial. Detective Bridges gave evidence and so did Rosemary Stanley. Both of them remembered very clearly what was said. Counsel asked them both if I ever asked if the gun was real or suggested it might not be. Would you like to see the transcript?'

Silent now, Victor nodded.

'If you'd like to go into the living room, the room at the front of the house, you'll find a roll-top desk on the right-hand side of the door. It has three drawers and the transcript is in the top one.'

The house smelled of lemon polish and faintly of David's cigarettes. It was cool and very clean. The living-room door was held open to the extent of about a foot by a stone doorstop that from a distance caused Victor a tremor of alarm but it turned out to be a crouching cat. Victor went into the living room. On one side of the fireplace, its grate laid with a pile of birch logs, was the desk, and on the other, on a low table, stood a photograph of Clare in a silver frame. She wasn't smiling but seemed to be looking at whoever looked at the photograph with a rapt mysterious gaze. Victor opened the top drawer of the desk and took out a blue cardboard folder to which was attached a label with the typewritten words: *Transcript of trial of Victor Michael Jenner*.

Presumably, David meant him to read the relevant part of the trial proceedings outside in his presence. Victor went back to the garden where David, having rolled the chair closer to the table, was lighting a cigarette. He sat down opposite David and began to read. It was quite silent in the garden but for the irregular throbbing hum made by a bumble bee drawing the last pollen from the honeysuckle. Victor read Rosemary Stanley's evidence and James Bridges's evidence. He could remember nothing of any of this. It was a blank to him, the trial no more than a blur, a confused memory of injustice and persecution. David sat smoking, his eyes fixed on the far end of the garden, which was enclosed by trees and a hedge of blossoming red may. The familiar sick feeling was taking hold of Victor, combined with a tingling he knew to be the start of panic. That afternoon, finishing his lunch, he had spoken (or thought) too soon. He forced himself to re-read the evidence. He re-read the cross-examination. An exhalation of smoke from David, a rather harsh sighing sound, made him look up. He became aware, perhaps for the first time, of the angle of the other man's legs, their utter useless *deadness*. They were like the limbs of dead men seen in battlefield pictures.

Victor jumped up. He stood trembling.

'Victor,' David said.

Almost without knowing what he was doing, Victor had crashed his fist hard down on the teak slats of the table. Again David rolled the chair back.

'Victor, here's Clare now,' he said. 'I can hear the car.'

Saying nothing, Victor turned away and went into the house. It seemed extraordinarily dark in there. He walked blindly across the room and came up against a wall and stood with his forehead pressed against it and the palms of his hands. It was something that had hardly ever come to him before, to understand that he was wrong, that he was at fault. The floor and ceiling of his world had gone and he hung in space, he hung on the wall with his forehead and his hands.

Victor let out a low animal moan of pain, turning blindly. He felt his body come up against another body, his face touch skin, soft warm hair veil him, arms enclose his shoulders. Clare had come in and without a word taken him in her arms. She held him lightly at first, then with increasing tender pressure, her hands moving on his back, up to his neck and head, to bring his head into the curve of her shoulder. His lips felt the warmth of her skin. He heard her murmuring gentle comforting things.

Holding her now, letting her hold him, indeed pressing his body into hers with a voluptuous abandonment as he had yielded it in the past to warm water or a soft bed, he felt the last thing he would have expected, a swift springing of sexual desire. He was erect and she must feel it. There was no embarrassment, he had gone too far into despair and horror and now a kind of joy, too far into intense emotions, for anything so petty. He was aware only that his feelings, here and now, were new, never before experienced in quite this way or for this reason. He held her hard against the length of his body and, raising his head, moving his face against hers, across the soft skin with a sensuous trembling delicacy, would have brought his lips to her lips and kissed her had she not, with a whispered something he couldn't catch, disengaged herself and moved away.

12

In the next two weeks Victor saw David and Clare several times but Clare never put her arms round him again or kissed him or even touched his hand. They all knew each other well now, they were beyond shaking hands, they were friends, or so Victor expressed it to himself. He had lost his shyness about arranging meetings. It was better for him to phone them anyway. He could hardly hear the phone bell when he was up in his room and most of the time there was no one else to answer it.

That evening at the restaurant in the old part of Harlow where they had had dinner, Victor hadn't said much. He had listened to the other two talking. Silence had always seemed to come naturally to him, and when he spoke he used clipped sentences, merely stating facts. He liked the sound of David and Clare's voices, the rhythm of them, the rise and fall, and he marvelled that they could talk so much when they really had nothing to say. How was it possible to go on and on like that about a piece of roast duck and where you had had it done like that before, or about something called 'cuisine naturelle' and something else called 'tofu', or the appearance and ages and professions – all guesswork this – of the couple at the next table? After a time he scarcely heard their words. He thought about David and what he had done to him and how David had forgiven him. Why, all these years, had he convinced himself he had been goaded into shooting David by David himself? Perhaps because he had never quite wanted to admit to himself that he could lose control without provocation. Whatever David said to him or proved by that transcript, he, Victor, was still left asking himself why he had done it and what that provocation could have been.

Their talk, though, had brought him closer to David. And much closer to Clare. Victor couldn't help wondering quite what he would have done, how he would have coped. if Clare had not come in at that moment and comforted him. He had no words, or few, to say to her when they were together but at home he talked to her. He carried on a silent inner conversation with her all the time, something he had never done with anyone before. She never replied but that was somehow unimportant. Her replies were implicit in what he said to her and the questions he asked. He sat in the wheelchair, looking out over the green rustling treetops, talking to her about his parents' house and his parents and the exceptional devotion they had for each other. He asked her if she thought he ought to go out more, take more exercise. It would be better for him to read books, wouldn't it, rather than all these magazines? And then, getting up and going out, he would ask her in the newsagent's which magazine to buy today.

Another remarkable thing was how he kept thinking he saw her. She never came to Acton – in fact she had told him she had never once been there – but time after time he fancied he saw her ahead of him in the street or in a shop or getting into a tube train. It was always someone else, of course it was, some other pretty girl with fine-spun flaxen hair and golden-pink skin. But for a moment . . . Once he was so sure he called her name.

'Clare!'

The girl who came down the library steps didn't even turn her head. She knew he was calling someone else.

It was funny how David had receded into the background. Of course he *liked* David tremendously, he was his friend, but he didn't think about him much any more. One way and another, Victor had got hold of a good many ideas about the mind and the emotions, among other things by reading *Psychology Today*, and he wondered if he had, so to speak, *exorcized* David by the talks they had had, by the revelation that had been made, by 'talking it through'.

It was possible. He realized now how much he had thought about David, how exhaustively he had been obsessed by him, between leaving prison and going for the first time to Sans Souci. Now, when he wasn't thinking about Clare and talking to her, his mind dwelled on his parents and particularly on the love they had had for each other. Once, he now understood, he had resented that love, had been jealous of it perhaps, but he no longer felt like that. He was thankful his parents had been happy together and when he remembered the settee embraces it was with indulgence rather than distaste.

He sat in the wheelchair most of the time he was at home. It was comfortable, and if he was going to have to keep it in his room it might as well be put to use. Once or twice he tried an experiment. He sat in the wheelchair and pretended he couldn't move his legs, that he was dead below the waist. This was very difficult to do. He found it easier if he covered his legs with the travelling rug. Then he attempted to lift himself out using only the power of his arms, talking all the time to Clare but unable to decide whether she approved or not. Once he fell over on the floor and sprawled there, lying immobile until he told himself that of course he could get up, *he* wasn't paralysed.

The first time he went to Theydon after the three of them had had dinner together it was to take them a present – well, a present for David really since it wasn't Clare's house and Clare wasn't married to David or even a girlfriend in the usual sense of the word. Since it wasn't possible to give David the wheelchair – and he saw now that this had been a tactless idea – he must give him something else. That was what you did. If you suggested a present to someone and it wasn't acceptable, you found an alternative. What the alternative must be was obvious – a dog. David's dog had died and he missed it, so he must have a new dog.

Victor bought *Our Dogs* magazine. There were a great many advertisements in it for yellow labrador puppies. He was amazed at how expensive dogs were, a hundred pounds was the norm and, for certain less usual breeds, two hundred, wasn't uncommon. Victor rang up the nearest dog breeder to advertise and, when he was told puppies were available now, went up to Stanmore. Fortunately, the tube went there, the Jubilee Line that had been enlarged and changed its name since he had gone to prison. He found that you couldn't just buy a dog the way you bought a TV set. The breeder wanted all sorts of promises and guarantees that the ten-week-old bitch would be going to a good home. Victor told the truth. Objections melted away when the dog breeder heard that his puppy's new owner would be the heroic policeman David Fleetwood whose case he remembered well from eleven years back. Victor paid for the dog and arranged to pick it up on Wednesday. It wouldn't be of much benefit to Clare, he thought, in fact might be rather a liability, so he went to the perfumery department at Bentall's and selected a whole range of St Laurent Opium, eau de toilette and talcum and bath stuff and soap, but when he told the salesgirl that Clare was young and blonde she persuaded him to change to Rive Gauche. The dog cost him a hundred and twenty pounds and the perfumes not far short of a hundred. Victor still had his driving licence and it was still valid. He went to the car-hire place in Acton High Street and rented a Ford Escort XR3.

By a piece of luck David had wheeled himself round to the front of the house and with secateurs was clipping the dead heads off those spring flowers which were within his reach. Again Victor was early. He had allowed himself two hours to get here from Stanmore and thanks to the motorway had done it in less than an hour. The puppy, in a wicker basket shaped like a kennel that Victor had bought specially, cried all the way.

David propelled the wheelchair up to the gate.

'Victor, you've got yourself a car! You didn't tell us.'

It's on hire, Victor was on the point of saying. But the admiring light in David's eyes – admiring of him surely, as well as the Escort – he didn't want to see go away and be replaced by that more usual patient polite look.

'It's not new,' he said, remembering the B on the licence plate.

'Well, maybe not but it's very nice. I like that shade of red.'

Some explanation was necessary, Victor felt. Suppose David were to think he had stolen the car or the money to pay for it!

'My parents left me a bit,' he said.

'What's in the basket?' David said.

The puppy must have fallen asleep. It had been silent for the past ten minutes. He lifted out the kennel basket and at that moment Clare arrived. The Land Rover looked shabby beside the Escort, and Victor felt sorry for her and David but proud at the same time.

'It's not our birthdays, Victor,' she said when he gave her the package wrapped in coloured paper.

Savouring his surprise, Victor opened the top of the basket, lifted out the plump, cream-coloured, velvet-skinned puppy and put her into David's lap. Afterwards he knew he must have imagined their looks of dismay. He *was* a pessimist and a bit paranoid sometimes, he knew that; he did tend to think people distrusted him and disliked the things he did. Anyway, within seconds David was cuddling the little dog which snuggled up to him, and stroking its head and saying, how lovely, what a beautiful animal, and, Victor, you shouldn't have.

In the back garden the dog gambolled about, examining everything, digging a hole in a flowerbed. Clare said, though she was smiling, 'I don't know how we'll ever train her with me out at work all day. Mandy was trained when David got her. But oh, she is sweet, Victor! What will you call her, David? How about Victoria?'

'Her proper name is Sallowood Semiramis.'

'I daresay,' said David, laughing. 'Dogs should have simple, ordinary names. Sally will do very well.'

Victor decided to keep the hire car for a few days because he would be coming back to see them during the following week. In the meantime he drove about the outskirts of London a good deal, looked at two flats in metropolitan Essex, one in Buckhurst Hill and one at Chigwell Row, and rejected both. He imagined Clare sitting beside him in the passenger seat and he talked to her as he drove, though without moving his lips or making a sound. He asked her if she thought he ought to buy a couple of pairs of really good shoes, a raincoat and a spare jacket, and he sensed that she thought he should. Not much now remained of the nine hundred and ten pounds.

Returning to Mrs Griffiths's house, Victor passed Tom, who was on foot as usual, a long way from West Acton station but evidently bound for there. It struck Victor for the first time how shabby Tom always looked. He was wearing trainers not real shoes, a thin pale blue nylon zipper jacket and badly worn Lois jeans. Tom turned round as Victor pulled up alongside and called his name. His pale puffy spectacled face peered out between black fuzzy beard and black fuzzy hair.

'Hop in. I'll give you a lift.'

'You *have* come up in the world,' said Tom.

Victor said he had a job, out in Essex. He was commuting at present but soon he would move. As soon as he had said this, he realized he could no longer ask Tom about whether the DHSS would pay the rent of a hundred pound a week flat for him.

'You're looking well, Victor. Work obviously agrees with you. What's the job exactly?'

Victor told him a lot of lies. The gist of them was that he had been taken on by an estate agent's in Epping, where business at this time of year was brisk.

'Do you want me to jot down your business address in case you move before I see you again?'

Victor pretended not to hear. 'Here you are. West Acton,' he said.

While he had the car he had another errand to perform. He drove down Gunnersbury Avenue in the stream of airport traffic but, instead of taking the car right up to 48 Popesbury Drive, he parked it round the corner and approached Muriel's house on foot. The idea came to him that he would find Jupp there, a permanent resident perhaps, at least Muriel's steady friend, a 'boyfriend', if that wasn't too grotesque a word. Muriel might even marry

Jupp and then it would be he and not the British Legion who came into her money.

An unexpected sight met his eyes as he came in view of the house. Jupp's van was nowhere to be seen. The front door was ajar. Where Kevin had perched himself, on a broad flat grey stone that protruded from the rock plants, squatted a man in jeans and a vest with a pair of shears in his hands. He had been cutting back the grey attenuated seed heads which were all that now remained of those millions of purple flowers that had hung over the stone ridges like a drapery of thick fuzzy cloth. Victor hung about, not wanting to be seen. The man gathered up armfuls of cut seed heads, laid them on a barrow which he had lugged up on to the cliff top, and humped the barrow away over the stones in the direction of the garage. He went round the side of the house, leaving the side gate swinging behind him. Victor cast a quick glance in the direction of the lowest stones but the shearing hadn't progressed so far and they were still covered. He ran up the steps and in at the front door.

There was no one in the hall and the doors to the ground floor rooms were shut. The chances were that Muriel was behind one of them. Victor went upstairs and into a bedroom he could not remember ever having entered before. Like the one where, under the floorboards, he had found the gun, this room contained a bed, a chest of drawers and a chair. The differences were that a wooden-framed swinging mirror stood on the chest of drawers, the curtains were a dull yellow-gold and the carpet gold with a dark brown border. Dust covered everything, gathered in fluffy nests in the folds where the curtains were looped back, lying so thickly on the top of the chest that it took a moment or two to see that the wood was partly covered by an embroidered runner. Victor pulled open the top drawer. It was empty, lined with brown paper, on which the activities of woodworm had left small pyramids of sawdust. The second drawer was the same but contained a man's underwear and socks. The bottom drawer was full of money.

Not full, that was an exaggeration. At first it looked like the other, empty, lined with brown paper. But it was too shallow. Victor lifted up the sheet of paper that lay at the bottom and the money was underneath, not in bags or in any way wrapped, but in neat stacks of pound notes and fives, hundreds of them, arranged in blocks as carefully as Muriel's magazines.

He skimmed the top. He took a quarter of an inch or so from the top of each of the twenty stacks and filled his pockets, glad he was wearing the padded cotton jacket, fashionably bulky, that he had just bought. You could have stuffed pounds of paper into those pockets without it showing. Out on the landing once more, he remembered the hair he had placed over the clasp of the mock-crocodile handbag. It would be as well to check. The house was silent, he could hear nothing. Muriel had made her bed today but for some reason the pink dog, zipped up for once, plump and glassy-eyed, had been placed on the pink satin dressing table stool, from which vantage point it seemed to watch Victor's movements. He opened the wardrobe door, knelt down and looked at the bag. The hair was till there.

What would Clare think if she could see him now? The thought came to him uninvited, unwanted, as he crossed the landing. When advising him not to talk about his past to Mrs Hunter, she said, 'It's not as if you stole something . . .' The circumstances were different, though, he thought. It wasn't stealing in the usual sense of the word, for if he had not been sent to prison unjustly, for something which had been an accident and not deliberate, Muriel would certainly have willed him her money and probably given him some of it in advance as people did (he had read in the *Reader's Digest*, in an article about Capital Transfer Tax) to avoid death duties. If, if . . . If Sydney hadn't happened to look into that ditch outside Bremen in 1945, if his attention had been distracted, for instance, by a low-flying aircraft or a vehicle on the road, he would never have seen the dead German officer with the Luger in his hand, so the gun would never have been under the floorboards here and Victor would never have taken it in preparation for it to go off in his hand and paralyse David for ever . . .

He had reached the foot of the stairs and was in the hall when the living-room door opened and Muriel came out with a young woman who looked just like Clare. Or so Victor thought for about ten seconds. Of course she wasn't really like Clare at all, being ten years older and twenty pounds heavier and with a face that was Clare's pushed about and melted and remodelled. But just for a moment, the colouring, the hair, the green-grey eyes . . .

Suddenly Victor knew how Muriel would introduce him. She would say that this was her nephew who had been in prison. But he had misjudged her, she didn't introduce him at all.

'This is Jenny from next door.'

The voice was about as different from Clare's as could be, shrill but lifeless, with a false warmth.

'And you must be the nephew I've heard so much about.'

Heard? What could Muriel have said about him?

'I expect you'll be wanting to do a bit for her now you're back. We do the best we can, I pop in and out, but it's a drop in the ocean really and we've got our own lives to lead. I mean, you need a *team* in that garden, not just one man, but now you're back you'll want to pull your weight.'

'Back?' he said, waiting for it.

'Muriel told me you'd been in New Zealand.'

Victor couldn't look at her. Was it, could it be, coincidence? Or did Muriel remember thirty-five years back, visiting her sister, and hearing her sister's little boy insist that there was never a time when he wasn't alive, only a time when he was in New Zealand? Certain it was that Muriel was ashamed of his, Victor's, past and didn't want to associate herself with that past. She didn't want her acquaintances, Jupp, this woman, to know.

Jenny had taken from her a shopping list so long that the items on it covered both sides of the sheet of paper. With it Muriel handed her a blank cheque which was made out to J. Sainsbury PLC and signed Muriel Faraday. I should be so lucky, thought Victor. Had she seen Jupp again? Had she been out with him? She was dressed – or undressed – as before, in nightdress and dressing gown, brown snood and pink mules. Victor thought she wasn't going to say a word to him, but he was wrong.

Her nose twitched, mouse-like. 'What did you come for?'

'I thought I might get you a bit of shopping in,' he said.

Jenny chipped in at once, luckily cutting off whatever retort Muriel was preparing. 'Oh, that's all right, no bother, I promise you. I'm not saying that once you get to know the ropes, I mean, once you've settled back and got into a routine, I mean, then you're at liberty to do your bit. But just at the moment – I mean, Brian'll run me to Sainsbury's in the morning and, to be perfectly honest, I do such a big shop there myself that her little bits and bobs don't actually make an iota of difference.' She and Victor had moved towards the front door together while she was talking. Muriel followed them only so far. Not only did she not go out, but she seemed to fear contact with fresh air or even the sight of outdoors from inside. She hovered in the background clutching with both hands the two sides of her dressing gown. Jenny said, 'Bye bye now. You can expect me like six-ish tomorrow, so mind you have the sherry ready and the dry roasted peanuts.' She winked at Victor, pulling the door closed behind her. 'What a life! Might as well be in the tomb already. I never miss a thing, I don't mind telling you, there's nothing goes on down here I don't see from my windows, and I can tell you that, until you came home and that old boy that eats the mints started coming, she never saw a soul but us from one year's end to the other.'

'Have you seen me come, then?'

'This is your fourth time in as many weeks,' said Jenny with alarming accuracy. 'If you want to get past me, you'll have to come Saturday lunchtime. That's when Brian takes me to do my big shop, isn't it, Brian?'

Looking around him at the garden, Brian said, 'I've not even skimmed the surface, not the surface.'

'If I'm going to start doing a bit for her, I'll have to have a key,' said Victor. He felt awkward but he pressed on. 'Could I have a loan of your key to get one cut?'

'We haven't got a key, Vic, not one of our own, that is. Don't you know where the key lives? Well, you wouldn't. I should leave that now, Brian, you'll only overdo it and I shall be up with your back half the night.' She pointed towards the hedge. 'Under the tortoise, Vic. The key's under the tortoise.'

22 June would be Victor's birthday, his thirty-ninth. He couldn't remember ever having celebrated his birthday beyond receiving presents from his parents in those early years. The time his mother and father had talked about a party for him and his mother had grown distraught at the prospect, they had in fact taken him to Kew. There isn't much in botanical gardens for a boy of eight but his mother was fond of Kew. She quoted something about wandering hand in hand with love in summer's wonderland, and she and his father did wander hand in hand, smelling the flowers and saying how beautiful it all was. Victor said to himself, as he drove past Woodford Green where the chestnuts had blossomed and shed their petals, that this year he would celebrate his birthday. He would do something with Clare and David before David had to go back into hospital.

The car he had kept for a further day – well, the weekend, for he would return it to the hire company on Sunday evening. He wore his new cotton padded jacket, two shades of grey, dove and slate, with slate binding, Calvin Klein jeans and, not to seem too exclusive, a dark red Marks and Spencer sweat shirt over the grey and cream striped shirt. On the back seat of the car were two bottles of German wine, Walsheimer Bischofskreuz, and two hundred cigarettes. A breeze was blowing and the sun was shining. It wasn't a bad day, warm enough to have the window open on the driver's side. Victor had never been one to play the radio in cars. He liked silence. From the drawer in the chest in Muriel's second spare bedroom he had helped himself to four hundred and sixty pounds. Unable to bear the prospect of waiting, he had counted the notes the moment he was back in the car. How much cash did that mean Muriel actually had in the house? Thousands? As much as, say, ten thousand? It was a well-known fact, one was always reading about it in the papers, that old people stashed away huge sums in their homes. It wasn't unusual, it was more normal than otherwise.

The hair had not been moved from the clasp on the handbag, so therefore Muriel had no idea as yet that any of her savings were missing. But suppose she did get that idea, suppose she found out, would she do anything about it? By this, Victor confessed to himself, he meant tell the police. Her behaviour led him to think she wouldn't. She had said nothing about his past or his prison sentence in the presence of either Jupp or Jenny next door, and this must mean she wanted to keep it dark, for she was malicious and uncharitable and there was no way she would have been discreet out of consideration for his feelings. If she discovered that he had been helping himself to the contents of her bags and drawers – to a fraction of what they contained, in fact – the chances were that she would berate him, would demand it back, but would do nothing more. The respectability of her family, as it appeared to other people, was important to Muriel.

If only he could acquire a car, Victor thought, he could start his own car-hire company, doing for himself that which in the old days he had done for Alan. He could buy a new car for six thousand pounds or two secondhand ones and take on another driver . . . With these ideas running pleasantly through his head (a flat in Loughton, for instance, a phone-answering service, journeys to the three London airports a speciality), he took the second exit out of the Wake roundabout and drove down the hill, through the forest, to Theydon.

It was a Saturday, so Clare would be at home. Victor's thoughts turned away from David and towards her as he drove into Theydon Manor Drive and he was aware of a mounting apprehensive tension, with a sick edge to it. Last night he had dreamed once more of the road that was his path through life with the significant houses on either side of it. There had been no temptation to enter any of the houses until he reached Sans Souci, which came into view round a sharp bend in the road. The part of the road that bent also passed through a dark wood of fir trees planted very close together in regular rows. Beyond the wood Sans Souci lay bathed in sunshine. Victor went into the front garden and helped himself to the key which was kept under the birdbath. He let himself into the house and called their names. 'Clare!' first and then 'David!' For a while there was no sound and then he heard someone laughing, two people laughing. The living-room door opened and Clare came out with David beside her, only David wasn't in his wheelchair, he was walking. He was well again, not paralysed, and he was walking.

Clare said, 'Look, a miracle!'

A terrible feeling of sickness and despair had come over Victor, for he knew, he couldn't tell why, that now David could walk again he had lost them both. But almost immediately he had woken up and the relief was tremendous, the knowledge of reality after that strange and frightening dream.

He didn't want to remember it now. He parked the car and walked round the side of the house. David had said he would be sure to find them in the garden if it was a nice day. The honeysuckle smell had been replaced by a scent of roses. Clare was mowing the lawn with an electric Flymo on a long lead and David was watching her from his wheelchair under the blue and white umbrella. She switched off the power and came towards him.

'Hi, Victor!'

Smiling, David raised one hand in a kind of salute. They were easy with him now, they accepted him, he was almost like a family member. Clare was wearing a cream-coloured cotton dress with an open shirt neck and big puffed sleeves. The dress was held in at the waist by a wide belt of saddle-stitched leather in a shade of deep tan. She had on flat sandals with thongs. Her hair, newly washed perhaps, instead of hanging to her shoulders, stood out in a shimmering gauzy cloud. In his dream she had been much less beautiful than this and when he thought how he had found a resemblance between her and Jenny next door he felt that somehow he had betrayed her.

The little dog Sally was on David's lap but she jumped off when she saw Victor, uttering surprisingly mature barks which made them all laugh.

'You shouldn't bring us all these things, Victor,' Clare said when she saw the wine and cigarettes.

'I like to. I can afford it.'

'You're wasting your substance on *our* riotous living,' David said. 'One day you're going to need that inheritance of yours.'

That inspired Victor to tell David about his plans for a car-hire company. David seemed to approve of this, but he thought it wisest for Victor to start in a small way, with just one car.

'We'll employ you when David has to go to Stoke Mandeville,' Clare said.

'Especially if you arrange to have the kind of vehicle the size of a large van with a ramp for taking a wheelchair up and an anchorage for the chair when it gets there and a specially designed seat belt.' David was smiling all the while he said this and Victor didn't think he was mocking him. How could he be? David really did need all those things and Clare's Land Rover did have them. He, Victor, was being over-sensitive and had doubtless imagined the sideways look Clare gave David and the very slight warning frown.

Lunch was salmon with a mayonnaise Clare had made green by putting finely chopped herbs in it, cucumber salad and French bread. Victor had never had that sort of salmon before, only the tinned kind and once or twice the smoked. Then they had strawberries and cream. David lit a cigarette.

'Would you mind fetching me something, Victor?' he said. 'You'll find it on the table where Clare's photograph is. In a brown envelope.'

'It's his book,' said Clare.

'There goes my surprise!'

'But, darling, Victor must know about your book. It was the article about your book that told him where you lived.'

'So it was,' said David.

His steady gaze rested on Victor and that small ironical smile was again on his lips. David's face had that heavy jowly look today that Clare said it had when he had slept badly the night before. Victor got up and went into the house, into the living room, pushing back the reclining cat doorstop. Clare's eyes met his from the silver photograph frame. He would like to have that picture, he thought, and he wondered if there was any way he could contrive to take it. But it was in such a prominent place and David evidently valued it . . .

The feeling he had was comparable to his sensations when they had taken him for that walk in the forest – that, contrary to all outward evidence, they were in fact mocking him, conspiring together to be revenged on him, leading him to this place only to confront him with the most despicable aspects of his past. Again he felt it as he picked up the large brown envelope. In some form or other inside here was David's book. Was David going to ask him to read it (even read it aloud?) in order to discover terrible revelations made about himself? Was he, Victor, pictured inside and described as a 'psychopath', 'a cold-blooded criminal', 'a sex maniac'? Suppose it were so, what was he to do?

He stood, holding the envelope, realizing that he dreaded looking inside. There was a sudden temptation to leave the house by the front door, taking the envelope with him, and drive away. He went back through the house and out into the garden once more. The little dog had fallen asleep on the lawn. Clare was bending over David's chair, her arm round his shoulder, her cheek against his. For one who had boasted that he didn't know the meaning of loneliness, Victor felt very alone, an outsider, lost. He thrust the envelope at David.

'Have you ever seen galley proofs before?' David said. 'I must confess I never had. Fascinating!' He was smiling and Victor knew that he was tormenting him. 'I'm supposed to read these and mark them for the printer – find typographical errors, you know, and maybe mistakes of my own.'

They were just the pages of a book, page one and two, for instance, on one side of the sheet and three and four on the other. In the text a word had been circled in red and a hieroglyphic made in the margin.

'How do you know what to do?' Victor said.

'*Pear's Encyclopedia* has all the proofreader's marks.'

There were no pictures, of course, and no cover or jacket, just this thick mass of printed pages. On the first page was the title: *Two Kinds of Life* by David Fleetwood. Their eyes on him, feeling sick, Victor leafed through the pages, but haphazardly, and blindly, seeing nothing but a dancing mass of black and white swirls.

Clare spoke gently. 'Victor, there's nothing to worry about.'

'Worry?' he said.

'I mean, there's nothing about you in there. The book's just what it says – two kinds of life. The life David had as a police officer and all that involved and the life – well, afterwards. It's really to show people life isn't over because one becomes a paraplegic, it's about all the things David has managed to do: get his Open University degree, for one thing, travel, go to concerts, learn to play a musical instrument. Did you know he not only plays the violin, he learned to make violins? That's what the book's all about, it's cheerful and forward-looking, it's full of hope.'

'Poor old Victor,' said David. 'What *were* you afraid of?'

Once Victor had hated and feared him. A wave of that old hatred broke over him now, of bitter resentment, for he knew that David had followed his thoughts every step of the way to this end. David had known how he felt and had kept him tantalized, believing perhaps that Victor had been screwing himself up to ask about the book ever since their first meeting a month before. Little could he have known that Victor had been too happy in his new friendship even to give the book a second thought till now . . .

'Look,' Clare said. 'Here's the only bit that mentions Solent Gardens.'

Victor read it. The thoughts he had had about David evaporated. Perhaps it had all been in his imagination. He knew he was sometimes paranoid, prison made one paranoid, said those supposedly in the know.

> The siege of Solent Gardens – never much of a siege and of very short duration – has been described too often elsewhere for me to say much about it. In a few words then, I was shot and the shot crippled me for life. These days, now that times have changed, some would say for the worse, the police engaged in that exercise would almost certainly have been issued with firearms and the likelihood is I would not have been shot . . .
>
> But 'jobbing backwards' is a useless and destructive practice. The past is past. I was shot in the lower spine, my spinal cord was severed, and my body below the waist permanently paralysed. My last memory for a long time was of lying in a pool of blood, my own blood, and asking, 'Whose blood is that?'
>
> The next months of my life, my second kind of life, were passed in Stoke Mandeville Hospital, which is what the following chapter is about.

'There's to be a foreword by a senior police officer,' said David, 'in which he is going to outline the siege. But without mentioning you by name, we decided on that.' He grinned at Victor. 'My publishers didn't like it, and that's the truth. They were scared of libel, I think. So no pictures, Victor, and no hard words, right?'

That might be true, about the publishers, Victor thought, but it was true too, he was sure of it, that David intended him no malice. David understood that it had been an accident. Why then did his eyes, lingering on Victor more constantly surely than usual, hold always that glint of irony, that tolerant amusement? Why did he seem to be watching Victor as if he were waiting – yes, that was it – waiting for him to do something terrible again, to have perhaps another disastrous accident of which he, David, would be the victim?

He replaced the proof sheets in the envelope and turned his eyes on Clare, his look full of gratitude. She it was who had read his thoughts and interpreted his anxiety, she who had given him comfort before he asked for it. Her ringless hand lay on the table, the hand on which David refused to place an engagement ring, a wedding ring. Victor longed to cover it with his own and hold it, but he did not dare.

13

The birthday was still two weeks off. Victor had cunningly ascertained that David and Clare were doing nothing in particular that Sunday night but would be together at home as usual. He said nothing about his surprise, only taking care to tell them it would be his birthday on that date, for he was confident they would all meet during the next fortnight.

Driving home – very late, in the small hours of Sunday morning – he made up his mind that he would leave it to them to phone him. Of course they could get hold of him if they wanted to, he was nearly always at home in the evenings, and if he left his door ajar he could hear the phone. Perhaps it had been a bit over the top going to see them twice in one week; he must be careful not to overdo things at this early stage. Why, they all had years and years before them. It would probably take a whole year or more to become really close friends. Victor wondered as he drove along the empty road between the beech woods, past the dark slopes and the paler clearings of the forest, if the day would come when they might all live together, sharing a house somewhere. The idea was an attractive one, he running his car-hire business and, if it were as prosperous as he thought it might be, Clare working for him, entering into partnership with him, while David, whose book was bound to be a success, entered on a third kind of life, the life of a writer. He wished, though, that he had that photograph of Clare. He could have asked her to give him a photograph. Why hadn't he? Fear of looking silly, he thought. Next time he saw them he would give them a photograph of himself and ask for pictures of them. That way they wouldn't know it was specially Clare he wanted a photo of.

Dressed in his new suit, Victor went a few days later to a photographer who had his studio at Ealing Green. The photographer seemed rather surprised by his request and assumed at first that Victor wanted his picture taken for a passport. Apparently it was rare for grown men on their own, without wife or child, to want portraits of themselves. And Victor sensed a real disappointment because he didn't smoke a pipe and wouldn't hold a dog or a golf club. However, the photographs were taken and Victor was promised a selection of shots from which to make his choice within the next few days.

He bought the *Tatler*, the *Radio Times*, the *TV Times*, *What Car?* and *House and Garden* and sat in the wheelchair reading them. In the evening he watched his new television set with the sound turned down and the door open so that he should hear the phone. On the Friday Clare did phone – to ask him if he realized he had left his sweater behind. She had parcelled it up and sent it to him by recorded delivery that morning. This was the red Marks and Spencer sweatshirt she was talking about and Victor hadn't missed it for the weather had been very warm, but he wished it had been his jacket he had left behind, or something with a more exclusive label on it.

Clare didn't invite him over but she did say, just as she was ringing off, that she would be seeing him. Victor liked that, the casual acceptance of himself as a friend, nothing formal about it, no need to say how enjoyable last Saturday had been, how lovely his wine, how they looked forward to meeting again. That was past, they were beyond that. And he told himself he was glad *not* to be asked. If he went there this weekend the birthday celebration might be made that much more difficult. There should be pauses in friendship, he thought, there should be breathing spaces. But after she had rung off he stood there in the darkening hall, still holding the receiver in his hand, and then speaking aloud into the mouthpiece what he had not said to her when she was at the other end of the line: 'Goodnight, Clare. Goodnight, darling Clare.'

That was not a word he had ever used to anyone before in his whole life. He picked up the pencil off the top of the phone box and wrote on the wood beside David's name and phone number: Clare.

In the food hall at Harrod's Victor looked at delicatessen, cheeses and cold meats and fish and salads. He looked at cakes and fruit, pricing items, unable to make any sort of selection in the face of this plenty, this excess, this amazing choice. But he would come back here next Saturday and buy everything he wanted for his birthday dinner. He would hire the car again. It was a pity he couldn't hire a refrigerator.

The prints arrived from the photographer, who stressed that they were unfinished, they were rough yet, just a guide. Victor thought that even in their present state they were quite good enough for him. He had not known that he appeared so young. His good looks were less marred by those prison years than he had thought. It was a serious, handsome, rather reserved face that looked back at him, the mouth sensitive, the eyes with their sombre experiences alone betraying that the man in the portrait was past his twenties. In one he was in profile, in the other two he was facing forward with his eyes slightly turned. Should he have the picture for David and Clare framed or simply give it them in the cream-laid deckle-edged paper folder the photographer would provide? He put the question to Clare in his thoughts but as usual she did not answer him.

Muriel had a refrigerator. Indeed, she had a very large refrigerator with large freezer compartment, necessary for someone who lived as she did. But Victor was loth to ask her if he could keep the food he was going to buy at Harrod's in her fridge overnight. She was quite likely to say no. Besides, he had a curious feeling that now he had begun using her house as a kind of bank there could be no relationship between them any more. They had ceased to be aunt and nephew. She had seen to that really by her aggressive attitude towards him.

In a way Muriel's house was like a bank with a machine on the outside (they didn't have them before he went to prison) where you stuck in a card and dialled a secret number and your money came out. Only here you merely needed the key and a certain amount of nerve. At the moment he didn't need any more money, he had enough to tide him over the next week or so. Victor walked along Acton High Street, pausing to look at refrigerators in a showroom window. Once he had his flat he would certainly need a fridge but at present he had scarcely room for one, the wheelchair took up so much space.

Returning, he passed Jupp's shop. In the middle of the window, behind the tray of Victorian jewellery, stood his father's writing desk. The price ticket, hanging from a string, was turned so as to be invisible from the street, a technique common to antique and secondhand dealers. But in this case it hadn't been turned quite enough, for by dint of bending his head down almost to touch his knees and twisting his head round, Victor could read, writen in biro, the sum: £359.99. And Jupp had given him only £410 for the whole lot! He must have known even then that the desk was an antique. And if the desk was worth so much, what about the rest? Probably his furniture had been worth nearer four thousand than four hundred pounds.

He understood though, as he looked at it and at his mother's pair of matching brass candlesticks which stood on top of it, that it was too late to do anything about this now. But he went into the shop just the same. The doorbell jangled. Prominently placed, some few feet inside, was the brown velvet settee on the arm of which someone had put the stuffed peacock, its clawed feet concealing the cigarette burn his father had made. It was not Jupp or the boy but Kevin who came in from the back.

'He's making a packet out of me, isn't he?' Victor said. 'He's asking nearly as much for that desk as he gave me for the lot.'

'Absolutely. It's daylight robbery,' said Kevin cheerfully. 'Well, he's not in it for his health, is he? And talking of health, you'll never credit it but he's given up them mints. Given them up total, cold turkey.'

Victor wasn't interested. The entire contents of his parents' house were spread around Jupp's shop, but for a few items which Victor supposed he had already sold or else transported to the place in Salusbury Road. He walked about reading price tickets: £150 for the dining table and six chairs, £25 for his parents' double bed (scene of so many love transports and cries for more, masked as distress), £10 for the buttoned satin bedhead, £75 for a bookcase and £125 for a glass-fronted china cabinet.

'D'you fancy a coffee?' said Kevin, coming in from the back once more. 'You may as well.' Victor followed him, ducking under the looped-up curtain. A saucepan was starting to boil over on an electric hob, white froth bubbling up and leaping over the sides before Kevin could reach it. 'It's no use crying over spilt milk,' he said.

The room was furnished like a kitchen but with armchairs and an ironwork table with a marble top of the kind you sometimes see in pubs.

'Do you live here?' Victor said.

'Are you kidding?' Kevin handed him a mug of boiled milk and water with half a spoonful of powdered coffee in it. 'Sugar? He's been giving your auntie a bit of a whirl, if you can credit it. I don't know what's come over the old Joe of late. He's been taking her out.'

'She never goes out.'

'Well, it's a manner of speaking, innit? "Taking out" – what does it mean? Anything from buying a chick a half of Foster's to screwing her out of her brains. He's got to have something to take his mind off his withdrawal symptoms.'

'He lives here then, does he?' Victor was determined to stick to the point.

'Nobody lives here,' Kevin said patiently. 'The wife and me, we live up in Muswell Hill, and old Joe's got a maisonette over the shop down Salusbury. Satisfied? So why do we have them chairs and a fridge out the back here? On account of if you're in this business you may have long periods of the working day, to say the least, when not a sod comes in. Right?'

'Can I put something in your fridge to keep overnight? Over Saturday night, that is.'

'What's wrong with your own?'

Victor explained that he hadn't got a fridge. Kevin took some convincing. Apparently, it had simply never occurred to him that there might be people – ordinary people living around him, not aboriginals or Amish – who didn't possess refrigerators.

'Would you credit it?' he said, looking at Victor with new eyes, and he began talking about the refrigerator he shared with Jupp's daughter, the largest and most efficient on the British market, of vast cubic footage and equipped with freezer, ice-maker and compartment for chilling drinks and dispensing them from a tap. At last Victor managed to elicit from him that the shop would be open until six on Saturday and he, Kevin, would be 'unofficially' opening it until midday on Sunday. 'Strictly against the law but highly favourable to the tourist trade,' he said.

Victor was prepared to point out that Jupp owed him something, the way he had practically stolen his furniture, but Kevin needed no more persuading. They never kept anything beyond milk and maybe half a dozen cans of beer in the fridge here. Victor was welcome.

'About twelve on Saturday then,' Victor said.

Suppose Jupp were to *marry* his aunt? Stranger things had happened. And after all it must be this which Jupp had in mind, for he could hardly be interested in her for sex or company. It must be her money. Victor let himself into Mrs Griffiths's house, into the warm musty silence, the quiet of the long day when he would be alone there. The parcel on the hall table was for him, addressed in Clare's hand. The sweatshirt, of course, and with it a current copy of the local weekly paper. Victor hoped for a letter as well, but the enclosure was a postcard with a drawing on it of a statue and a square and some buildings he thought Clare might have done herself but which said on the back: *Versailles*, Raoul Dufy. She had written: 'I thought you might need this in case we don't meet for a while. Love, Clare.'

He took it upstairs with him. He put the sweatshirt on, though it was rather too warm to wear it, and sat in the wheelchair, studying the note again. What did 'for a while' mean? A few days? A week? A month? Of course it didn't really matter what it meant as he would be going over there on Sunday to surprise them anyway. She had put 'love' when she might easily have written 'yours'. Last time she had written 'yours'. She could have put 'yours sincerely' or 'yours affectionately' or even 'yours ever' but she had put 'love'. You didn't write 'love' unless you had quite a strong feeling for a person, did you? He couldn't imagine writing 'love' to anyone – except her . . .

The sweatshirt had been handled by her, folded by her. He could smell her on it, a definite though faint scent of the Rive Gauche that he had bought her himself.

Advertised in the paper was a likely-sounding flat. It had probably gone by now, Victor thought, but he phoned the number just the same, standing in the hall with his eyes on Clare's pencilled name on the underside of the stairs. The flat was still available, fifty pounds a week and in Theydon Bois itself. Victor imagined seeing Clare and David every day. They would call in on him on the way back from their walks and sit outside with him under a striped sunshade, drinking white wine. It was a ground-floor flat, large bedsit with 'patio', kitchen and bathroom. A garage was also available for rent, if desired. Victor arranged to see the flat on Sunday afternoon. Without thinking very much about what he was doing, just doing it because it seemed right and what he wanted to do, he bumped the wheelchair down the stairs and out of the front door. Once he was in Twyford Avenue he got into the wheelchair and sat down and covered his legs with the brown checked travelling rug. It was a warm day but not warm enough to make the rug look silly.

Victor made his way on to Ealing Common. In the distant past such places had been attractive to him because of their potential. There he could find women alone. There, no one was in earshot of their cries. Dogs he had always found singularly ineffectual in coming to the aid of their owners, though it was also true to say that he had never attacked women accompanied by large dogs. He parked the chair under some trees. A child playing with a ball was called sharply away by its mother – in case it should be a nuisance to the handicapped man, he thought. The rapist he had once been seemed like a different person, and this was not simply because he was currently in the role of a disabled man. Rape itself had become as alien to him as to any normal ordinary citizen. Why had he done it? What had he got out of it? He asked Clare, who was listening sympathetically, but as usual she didn't reply. It was because he was always angry, he thought, and now he wasn't angry any more, nor could he imagine a cause of anger.

He turned round and went home. A young girl who looked a lot like Clare came to help him over the crossing at the Uxbridge Road, walking beside his wheelchair and holding the back of it. His arms were tired by the time he reached the corner of Tolleshunt Avenue, but when he got out of the chair to push it back to Mrs Griffiths's house his legs felt stiff from disuse.

Next day he had the hire car again and by a piece of luck managing to get the same one. He parked it in Harrod's car park, securing the last vacant space. In the food hall he bought asparagus and raspberries, smoked trout and quails, which he hoped Clare would know how to cook, tiny English new potatoes, the first of the season, herb butter, clotted cream, *mange tout* peas, brie and Double Gloucester and a goat's cheese that looked like a swiss roll with icing on it. He bought champagne, Moët et Chandon, and two bottles of Orvieto.

It cost nearly a hundred pounds. Victor hadn't known you could spend a hundred pounds on such a small amount of food. He drove to Jupp's shop. Jupp himself was there, trying in vain to sell an ugly *art nouveau* lamp to a woman who had obviously come in only to look round. Kevin, of course, hadn't bothered to tell him about the arrangement he and Victor had made.

'Bit of a peculiar request, isn't it?' he said lugubriously to Victor. 'A bit bizarre?'

'Your son-in-law said it would be all right.'

'I daresay. He thinks he owns the place, reckons he's monarch of all he surveys. You do as you like, cocky, make yourself at home.'

Jupp was wearing his jeans and the striped waistcoat but an incongruously formal white shirt and tie with a regimental crest. With the tip of his finger he removed something from the underside of a mirror frame and slipped it into his mouth. Victor went back to the car and fetched the box of food, noticing as he came back that his father's desk had gone. Munching his chewing gum, Jupp stood holding the fridge door open. He eyed every item Victor put inside and at the sight of the champagne his shaggy white eyebrows went up.

'Didn't I tell you not to spend it all at once, cocky?'

'You're making enough profit out of it, I should say,' said Victor.

Jupp slammed the fridge door. 'All's fair in love and war.' He didn't explain how love or war entered into a straight commercial transaction. Victor said he would be back for the food next morning, and left.

In fact he went back quite early, before ten, because he had wakened up in the small hours with the awful thought that suppose they didn't open the shop this particular Sunday, suppose Kevin simply forgot? Kevin, however, was there. He helped Victor re-pack the food, having peeled off and flung away a gob of gum he found adhering to the fridge door handle.

'Disgusting, innit? He's got an addictive personality. He'll be smoking next.'

This reminded Victor to buy some cigarettes for David. He also got a packet of Hamlet cigars. Back at Mrs Griffiths's house, he dressed carefully, casual today in a new dark blue tee shirt he had bought, dark blue cord jeans and the two-tone grey padded jacket. It was when he was lacing up his new shoes, perfectly plain fine grey leather, the most expensive pair he had ever owned, that he remembered it was his birthday. All this was in honour of his birthday yet he had forgotten the occasion in the complexity of preparations. He looked at himself in the mirror. Thirty-nine today, his fortieth year entered upon. No one had sent him a card – but who was there that knew his address except David and Clare? He was aware though of an uneasy feeling, a slight feeling of let-down, but he refused to let himself think about the reason for it: that David and Clare, who had been told it was his birthday, had not sent him a card.

At noon he set off, the box of food in the boot of the car, and in a stout brown envelope on the seat beside him the portrait photograph of himself which had arrived by yesterday's post. Victor had four hundred pounds in the pocket of his jacket, all that was left of the money he had drawn out of his 'bank' at Muriel's.

He had lunch in an hotel at Epping and drove down Piercing Hill to Theydon Bois. It struck him that he was living in the kind of style he had always aimed at and never quite achieved before: driving a smart new car, well dressed, lunching in good restaurants, about to choose a new and attractive home for himself, then to entertain his friends to a luxurious meal. The past was there still but it wasn't even like a bad dream, being too distant and impersonal for that; it was like someone else's past or something he had read about in a magazine.

The flat was part of one of the older houses adjacent to the forest. It was very small, a single room with french windows that had been converted into three. The 'patio' was a little bit of concrete outside these windows with trellis round it, overhung by a clematis at present covered by myriad creamy-white flowers. The woman who owned the house and whose name was Palmer told him it was a clematis and that the blue flower in the narrow border was bugle and that the iron table and chairs were new and of the best quality. Victor didn't think much of the chipboard furniture, the broken wash basin and the haircord carpet, but he imagined living here and eating out on his patio and having David and Clare drop in several times a week. On the phone, remembering what Clare had advised, he had given his name as Michael Faraday and now he repeated it, quite liking the sound of it. Mrs Palmer wanted a deposit of a month's rent and a reference. Victor handed over two hundred pounds and promised a reference, thinking that perhaps Clare would help him there, it being she after all who had suggested the assumed name and discarding of the past.

It wasn't yet four. Victor thought David and Clare might still be out for their walk, if indeed they had gone today. Bright and sunny when he left Acton, it had clouded over and grown colder, and as he drove slowly alongside the green a few drops of rain dashed against his windscreen. He hung about till half past, sitting in the parked car reading *Time Out*.

Rain was falling steadily by the time he drew up outside Sans Souci. They wouldn't be out in the garden today. He rapped on the front door with the Roman soldier knocker, the box of food and bottles at his feet. A curtain in one of the front windows moved and Clare peered out. He couldn't conceal from himself that, at the sight of who it was, her face was overspread with a look of blank dismay. The smile which replaced this was unnatural and forced. He felt suddenly very cold.

Clare opened the door. She was wearing white cotton trousers and a blue shirt that made her look very young and holding the puppy in her arms. Clare always looked young, she *was* young, but now she looked about eighteen. She said, 'Victor, what a surprise!'

'I meant it to be a surprise,' he said, speaking in an awkward mutter.

She looked at the box. 'What have you brought this time?'

He didn't reply. He picked up the box and took it into the house and stood there, aware of something different, aware of a sense of something missing or lost.

'I'm afraid David isn't here,' she said. 'They asked him

to go into hospital a week earlier than arranged. They specially wanted it and it was all the same to him. He's coming home tomorrow.'

Then Victor knew what was missing, the smell of David's cigarettes.

'Don't look so disappointed!'

'I'm sorry. It was just . . .'

'You'll have to put up with me instead. Come and meet Pauline.'

He had a horrible feeling of a possible trick again. She had arranged it, she had fixed it, and Pauline Ferrars was waiting behind that door for him, fetched from her hiding place, discovered, brought here to confront and taunt him. But of course it was quite some other Pauline, some friend or neighbour, a girl of about Clare's own age, dark-haired, pretty, wearing a gold wedding ring.

They had been drinking tea and the teapot was there and two mugs and biscuits on a plate. While Clare went away to fetch another mug he tried to talk to Pauline. He said it had been a nice day but it wasn't any more. She agreed. Clare came back and began talking about David, the treatment he was having, some kind of electric shocks to the spine that was still really in its experimental stages. She was going to fetch him home herself, would be taking the day off to do so, because he liked that better than going in the kind of ambulance that had been provided before.

Victor felt more than disappointed. He was bowled over and stunned. In this woman's presence he found it impossible to speak and he had already convinced himself that she had come for the day, for the evening. The absurdity of his plan, his 'surprise', unfolded before him and he saw how stupid it had been, indeed how childish, not to phone and check that they would both be at home and free. But when Pauline got up and said she must go – it was nice to have met him, she said. How could it have been? – he felt marginally better. He felt something might be retrieved and, though he was embarrassed, he was also rather pleased when Clare came back from seeing Pauline out to say that she couldn't help noticing the champagne in the box and what were they celebrating?

'My birthday,' he said, and because he couldn't resist it, 'I did tell you.'

'Oh, Victor, of course you did! I do remember. It was just that all this with David and him going to hospital early and getting things ready – it went out of my head.'

'It doesn't matter.'

'You know it does. You know it matters a lot. I think I know what's in the box. Things for a celebration dinner, is that it? Wine and food and lovely things?'

He nodded.

'Come on. Let's unpack them and see.'

Victor suggested they drink the champagne while they did this.

'Wouldn't you like us to save it till David's home? You could come back one day in the week and we could have it then.'

'*Today's* my birthday,' Victor said.

She was kneeling on the floor and she looked up at him with a sudden smile that was joyous and somehow conspiratorial, perhaps in appreciation of the childlike directness of his reply. She wrinkled her nose. He hadn't felt much like smiling but he managed it. The things that came out of the box made her gasp.

'We couldn't possibly eat all this anyway, just the two of us!'

Victor opened the champagne. She had two glasses standing ready. It hadn't been his lot in life to open champagne very often and when he had done so in the past there had been something like an explosion followed by a mess but now the operation was smoothly done and every foaming drop caught in Clare's glass.

'Can you cook all this stuff ?' he said.

'I can try. They do look pathetic, the quails, rather like four and twenty blackbirds baked in a pie.'

'Cooking will make a lot of difference,' said Victor.

'It had better.' Clare lifted her glass. 'Happy birthday, Victor!'

He drank. He remembered her face of dismay appearing at the window when first he knocked at the door. A layer of paranoia seemed to peel itself off his mind; he saw something more rational beneath and all kinds of understanding became less remote.

'If you wanted to be on your own this evening,' he said, 'if you'd rather I went, I wouldn't mind. I really wouldn't.'

She put out her hand and laid it on his arm. 'I'd like you to stay.'

It was clear that she meant it. He was very conscious of her touch, of the weight of that small brown hand, though it lay lightly, almost hoveringly, on his sleeve. He had a curious impulse to bend his head and press his lips to it. She took her hand away, sat back smiling at him.

'Of course I want you to stay. We owe you a lot, Victor.'

He stared, sensing sarcasm.

'I know that sounds strange, considering – well, if it hadn't been for you, David wouldn't have been in this state in the first place. That's true, of course. But we're different people at different stages of our life, don't you think?'

Didn't he! Passionately, he nodded, holding his fists clenched.

'The man who shot David isn't the man who's here with me now, he isn't the man that David can talk to and – well, somehow straighten things out, get things into perspective. And even that first man, David doesn't see him as a monster, as evil, any more. He's beginning to understand. Victor, there was a time when I thought David would go – mad. He was heading for a complete breakdown. He couldn't talk about the shooting, he certainly couldn't have written about it, and that's really why it's not in his book – not because of compassion for you, if that's what you thought. And then you turned up. First he thought you'd come to kill him and then, believe it or not, he thought he'd like to kill you.'

Silently Victor listened, watching her face.

'Then he started to *like* you. There is something – I must find the right word – *lovable* about you. Did you know that? I think it's because you seem very vulnerable.'

It might have been the champagne, though Victor didn't think so, but something seemed to move and tremble and unfold inside his body. Her words repeated themselves on his inward ear.

'Yes, lovable,' she said. 'I know David feels it. Forgive me if I say I don't think he quite trusts you yet, not entirely, but think how he has been hurt. He will, he will come to it. He'll adjust himself to life finally through you.'

Victor felt as if she had given him a magnificent birthday present. There was nothing material she could have given him to please him half so much. He would have liked to say so but he was unable to express these thoughts, they stuck on his tongue and he was struck silent. He packed the food back into the box and carried it out to the kitchen. The windows were awash with rain, the green and flowery garden a distorted blur through glass than ran with water. She came in carrying the champagne, took his hand and gave it a squeeze.

'Clare,' he said, holding her hand, 'Clare.'

In the end they decided not to eat the quails but to keep them in the fridge for when David got back. Clare cooked the asparagus and they ate the trout and then the raspberries with cream. They ate at the kitchen table and Victor loved the informality of it, the red and white check cloth Clare laid on the pine table, the red candle in a pewter candlestick that it was dark enough by eight to light, so wintry and twilit did the rain make Theydon Manor Drive that evening.

He told her about the flat he had put a deposit on. Clare said what he had fantasized she might say, though had not truly imagined she would.

'We'll be able to drop in when we're out on our walks.'

Victor said, 'He's back in hospital now – is there, does that mean there's a chance they'll cure him? Can he get better?'

She lifted her shoulders. 'Who knows, one day? It's not a subject I know much about. David knows everything about it, you'll have to ask him.' She smiled at his incredulous look. 'Yes, I mean it. It would do him good to talk.

But a cure . . .? Not at present, not at this stage of – well, knowledge. They experiment on him a bit – with his full consent, of course. By his desire even. That's why he's there now. But no miracles are going to happen, Victor. I'm not going to go there tomorrow morning and be met by a reception committee of joyous doctors with David walking in the midst of them. At best his reactions may be giving them some ideas to work on.'

He wondered if her mention of the following morning was a hint to him to go. But these suspicions he knew to be symptoms of a paranoia he was beginning to shed. She had asked him to stay, she wanted him here. He helped her with the dishes. He opened one of the bottles of Italian wine.

It was curious that, until then, he had really felt no desire for her. Several times he had remembered how she had caught him in her arms that afternoon when David had shown him the proofs of the book, and how he had responded to that embrace. But desire of that kind for women was something he had hardly ever felt, not since Pauline anyway, and to compare Pauline with Clare was a travesty. He recalled his response to Clare as an isolated phenomenon, interesting and even pleasing but something he might never feel again. When she had touched him, laid her hand on his arm and held his hand, he felt something that was distinct from desire, something he might define as mysteriously involved with what she called his vulnerability, his quality of being lovable. Yet things had now changed and he was aware as they moved about the kitchen of an alteration of consciousness, a shifting of his relations with her. He wanted her to embrace him again.

She blew out the candle and they went into the living room. The television set was there and he expected they would watch television. He had come to think of this as what you did in the evenings, what everyone did as a matter of course, a way of life. Clare put on a record instead. It was the sort of music he had always told himself he didn't like, sounding old and alien, *historical* music played on instruments no one used any more. She handed him the sleeve to read and he saw it was a harpsichord suite by Purcell. The cold sweetness of it poured into the room and his contentment went and he was filled with unhappiness, with grief almost and a sense of waste, with loneliness.

He said, 'Can I have that picture of you?'

'Can you have it? You? You mean have that photograph in the frame?'

He nodded. Then he remembered. 'I've got something for you. Something else, I mean. I nearly forgot.'

The envelope containing his photograph he had left on the passenger seat of the car and he got it out but he didn't re-lock the door. He would be going soon. The rain had stopped and the air was bluish, cold, very clear. A white moon had risen, screened by a nimbus, and on the horizon the yellow ribbon of the motorway could be seen, the lights sending a bright shimmer up into the dark sky. She got up as he came in and took the photograph from his hands. The music had changed, was warmer, a dance it sounded like, though still from a long way in the past.

'Did you have this taken specially?'

Put like that, it made him sound a bit of a fool. He nodded.

'Thank you,' she said. 'You can't have that picture of me, that's David's, but I'll give you another.'

He watched her search through the desk. A conviction formed itself and strengthened and became absolute that he couldn't drive home that night. It would somehow be beyond his powers. The loneliness that would sit beside him would overpower him and take over; like some hitch-hiker bent on violence, it would attack and subdue him and leave him for dead. He could tell her some lie, he thought, like not being able to start the car, anything, any subterfuge in order to stay.

Without turning her head, reading his mind surely, she said, 'It's late, Victor. Why don't you stay the night? I'll have to leave very early in the morning but you won't mind that.' She laughed, spun round in her chair. 'To tell you the truth, I don't much like being here alone. Pauline's been staying with me but her husband's back from a trip and she's had to go.'

He tried to sound casual, offhand, as if it were he doing her the favour. 'I could do, no problem.'

The picture she gave him was different from the one in the frame, taken longer ago, a young, almost childlike Clare. He sat staring at it, staring as he would hardly dare to gaze at the living woman. She'd give him the spare room where Pauline had slept, she said, David's room being so full of gadgets and aids for the handicapped. Her voice, he noticed, had taken on a strange, strained note. She had drunk rather a lot of wine, more than he remembered she had permitted herself at other meals he had shared with her. Her cheeks were flushed and her eyes seemed very large. He thought, she will kiss me again when she says goodnight to me.

A need to postpone that parting took hold of him. He was looking at her in silence, gazing now as he had gazed at her picture. She had been talking, conventionally enough, about tomorrow's trip, the long drive across country, and he entered into this, asking her questions about the route, offering to drive her himself – an offer which was rejected – and all the time keeping his eyes on her face with a yearning that increased to a nearly physical reaching towards her. At the same time he was aware of a reciprocal reaching in her towards him. He thought he must have imagined this but he wasn't mistaken, he couldn't be, and he remembered she had said he was lovable. Inwardly he trembled, though his body and his hands remained steady. His feelings were quite different from what they had been that time she embraced him, more diffuse, more tender, less rapacious.

This was the word he used to himself and it made him shudder. He said suddenly, harshly, 'What do you know about me? My past? What has David told you?'

She said steadily, 'That you were in a house with a girl, a sort of hostage, and David had to go in and rescue her and you shot him. Do we have to talk about it?'

'Is that all?'

'I think so.' She got up and he too rose. She stood looking at him, just standing there, her hands by her sides. 'It's late. We don't have to talk about that tonight.'

The hungry anxious look she had that he couldn't define. He had never seen it in a woman before. He had never before taken a woman in his arms and cupped her head in his hand and brought her face to his and kissed her lips. It was his thirty-ninth birthday but he had never quite done that before. The feelings it aroused in him were unexpected and new, tremendous, overpowering yet not somehow clamouring for immediate swift satisfaction.

She responded to his kiss quite differently from that last time, for he felt she was as desirous as he. Her kiss explored his mouth and her body pressed its curves into his hard muscles and vulnerable nerves. And then she twisted away, stood for a moment gazing at him in a kind of panic, the back of one hand against her lips. Puzzlement made him silent, left him at a loss. In these matters he had no experience. She left the room and when he followed she had disappeared. The hall was empty. He looked into the kitchen but there was no one there, only the little dog Sally curled up in her basket. He switched off the lights and went up the stairs where the railway for David's lift spanned the banisters.

Upstairs he didn't know the rooms, didn't know where to go and went into David's by mistake. Violins in various stages of construction, one finished, lay on a pine bed. A wide arch led into a shower room big enough to take the wheelchair under the water jets. He turned back. His heart was beating painfully and he half wished he had gone home, even through the cold moonlight, even with loneliness for a companion. The house was silent. Through a landing window he could see the golden thread of the motorway draped across plains and hills.

He drew a deep breath and opened a door and saw her waiting for him, sitting naked on the side of her bed, lifting her eyes to meet his, extending her hands to him without a smile.

14

In the night they both awoke at the same time. Victor woke and found that they had slept embraced and now her eyelids moved and her eyes opened. He couldn't remember putting the light out but he must have, for he saw her face now by white moonlight. Her breasts were very full and soft and he held them in his hands, which was another thing he had never done before last night. Lovemaking for him before had been an attack and a swift pumping, an explosive discharge, a gasp and a rolling off; and this not only with the women he had assaulted – that was still something else, something even further removed and less sexual – but with Pauline, who had somehow embarrassed him, had made him treat her body as a hole with a bit of flesh round it. Clare had not had to teach him to make love – he would not have liked that from a woman, any woman – but making love had come naturally with her, came naturally now, as he explored her body with his hands, the delicate tips of his fingers, his tongue and a murmuring stroking whispering of his lips. And he could not have anticipated the rewards, the sensation of her melting and flowing under his touch, of unfolding around him and receiving him with a kind of sweet loving gratitude.

She was not an active woman, the kind he had read of in magazines. A thrashing of limbs, a manipulation of his flesh, a riding and exultant cries he could not have borne, could not have coped with, nor any demanding initiative. Easily, with a dreaming reserve, thinking not of present gratification but of a lifetime of rarefied pleasure, he postponed his climax until he felt the pressure of her hands tighten on his back, until her lips joined to his whispered, 'Now!' The night before it had not been quite like that, not as perfect for her as for him, not an absolutely shared moving of the world. Years of dismay and bewilderment tiptoed away. His body filled with light and he knew that precisely the same thing had happened to her, the blood in their veins different, recharged.

'I love you,' he said, unfamiliar words that he had read but never thought to utter.

She was gone when next he awoke. The curtains were pulled back and it was a white-grey morning, dull of sky, a white rose, paler than the clouds, blossoming on a rambler, framed in one of the window panes. Clare came in, dressed, bringing him tea, sitting on the bed, dressed like someone's efficient secretary in a grey flannel suit and a red blouse with a bow. She kissed him and pulled away smiling when he tried to take her in his arms.

'Let me drive you. Let me get up and drive you.'

'No, Victor. I have to fetch David on my own. You must see that.'

Of course he saw. He could see plainly in her face what she was thinking, nothing changed her affection for David, her loyalty to him, any more than it could change Victor's. She had made a promise and she must keep it. After all, in a way she *was* David's secretary, his nurse or a loving sister.

'I'll get up and make myself scarce,' he said. 'I'll get off home.'

She nodded. 'We'll meet soon. I'll phone you.'

'I'd like to see David, you know.'

She seemed surprised. 'Yes, of course.'

He heard the Land Rover move out of the garage directly below his bed. He heard it move away, the change of gear, the pause as the bigger road was reached. When he could hear it no longer he got up and dressed and tidied up, washing their cups and her breakfast plate and the teapot. Eating didn't appeal to him, he didn't want breakfast. In the living room he found the photograph of herself she had given him. Clare, he said to the picture, Clare. He gazed at it, sitting in an armchair and holding the photograph in front of him and gazing. Why hadn't he understood all these weeks that he was in love with her? Because it had never happened to him before. His parents' need for each other's exclusive company he now understood and he wondered why he had been so blind and so deluded.

He slipped the photograph inside the envelope in which his own had been contained. He left his own lying on the table. Originally, he had been going to write across the corner of it, the way famous people do, write a message to both of them and sign it. He couldn't do that now, so he just left it.

It was still not eight o'clock. He went out to the car and heard a heavy distant hum like aircraft. It was the motorway, laden with morning traffic. The needs of the day and its pressures began to close on him, ordinary life coming back. He was due to return the car this morning but there was no way now that he could get it back by nine. He would have to pay for an extra day. Mrs Griffiths too must be given notice that he was leaving and perhaps Tom or Judy told. He thought about these things and then Clare, the image of her, the memory of her voice, drove them away. He drove back to Acton with his head full of Clare, his body intermittently excited by awareness of certain aspects of her, but not daring to think too intensely of what she looked like naked or the things they had done together. Even to remember her eyes opening in the moonlight made him tremble and a long shiver run the length of his spine.

And what next? They had said nothing about telling David, though Clare had agreed when Victor said he would like to see David, understanding what he implied by this. David himself would probably understand what had happened. He might even be pleased. After all, he might be very fond of Clare, he might share his house with her and depend on her for so much, but he couldn't be her lover, he could never give her what he, Victor, had given her last night. If he were really fond of her he would want her to have a love life and probably be glad it was with someone like Victor who would really love and cherish her and care about her.

Victor took the car back and because it was only ten past nine they didn't charge him for the extra day. He walked home to Tolleshunt Avenue, feeling strong and fit and young, in spite of having been thirty-nine yesterday and drinking nearly two bottles of wine. Upstairs in his room he sat in the wheelchair, imagining what it must be like to be David, alive only above the waist, capable of thinking and speaking and eating and drinking and moving the wheelchair but not of much else. Of course if he couldn't do it because the nerves or whatever it was down there were dead, it stood to reason that he couldn't want to do it. Victor knew he wanted to do it because he got erect whenever he even thought of Clare like that. Sitting in the wheelchair he was erect now, a bulge holding out the brown check travelling rug that he had pulled over his knees. How ridiculous and grotesque! He jumped out of the wheelchair and lay face-downwards on the bed but the bed brought her image to him again and suddenly there came a fierce painful longing for her to be here, painful because there was no hope of that today. Or was there perhaps? When would she get back? When would she phone him? He imagined her driving through June-green England, up the motorways, on the little winding roads through villages, thinking of him surely as he was thinking of her, a gold-skinned girl with paler gold hair in a secretarial suit and red blouse with a bow . . .

Presently he made himself get up and sit at the table with the bamboo frame adorned with cigarette burns and write to Mrs Griffiths. A week's notice only he would give her. She wouldn't be the loser, for the DHSS were paying her. He calculated that Clare would just about be there by now but when the phone rang downstairs he thought he had miscalculated and she was already home. As soon as she had got home she was phoning him! He ran downstairs and took off the receiver and a woman's voice asked if that was Curry's. A wrong number. It would be better to go out somewhere than sit here waiting for the phone, but he knew he wouldn't go out.

Committing himself utterly to her, he thought about

what they would do, where they would live. In the new flat for a while, presumably. He would have to get work, start the car-hire business he had already had ideas about. Would she, he asked himself, would she – one day – *marry* him?

Although it brought a kind of havoc to mind and body, causing him a physical torment of a kind he had never known before, he was unable to keep himself from thinking of how she had responded to him, with such sweet abandonment, almost with *relief*, as if this was what she had been aching for for a long time. She had given herself to him, old-fashioned expression he had once heard his mother use, though disparagingly – 'She gave herself to him and of course she regretted it.' Clare, he was sure, would never regret it, but it was true that she had given herself, making a joyful loving gift of it, the better to receive. He loved her and she loved him. There was a rightness about it all which had begun the day he saw the name Theydon Bois on the station and after that had begun the search for David. A lucky day for Clare, who had been rescued from a life that was no life for someone as young and lovely and capable of giving love as she was.

In the evening she phoned him. It was quite late, about ten, and he had given up hope of hearing from her that day. In a way he hadn't expected to hear and he wasn't unhappy or anxious. But the phone ringing and then her voice, that was a bonus.

'Victor? It's Clare. David's asleep. He's had an exhausting day.'

'When can I see you?'

'David's been asking about you. He wondered how you'd feel about coming over on Saturday.'

'I mean, when can I see *you*?'

She was silent, thinking. He began to understand that there might be difficulties. At first there were going to be difficulties. Of course it wouldn't be all plain sailing.

'I don't suppose you said anything to him, did you?'

'Said anything?'

'Well, told him.'

'No, Victor, I didn't tell him.' He could see her face as clearly as if this were a phone with a television screen. It swam in the darkness of the hall like a spirit face, a beautiful floater on his retina. On the underside of the stairs her name was written: Clare. 'Do you want to see me before Saturday?'

'Of course I do. Don't you want to see me?'

'Yes.'

His heart, which had been a prey to doubts suddenly, to terrible groundless fears, leaped with joy. He couldn't sing, had scarcely ever tried, but he would have liked to sing now. Tenors in operas, crowing with love and happiness, grief and tragedy, he could understand them now. 'When, Clare?'

'Not tomorrow. I can't. Wednesday, after work, five thirty in Epping. Could you manage that, Victor?'

He could have managed Wednesday at five thirty in Marrakech, he thought.

'Not a pub. It'll be too early anyway. On Bell Common, we could meet there, Victor. I'll park the Land Rover in Hemnall Street, just in from the High Street at the common end.'

'I love you,' he said.

It was an awful dream he had – 'unnecessary', he told himself. Why was it necessary for him to be visited with a nightmare like that? Of course, whatever the psychologists might say, you could account for dreams by what had happened to you on the previous day. And on this day, in the *Standard* he had bought himself, along with *Reader's Digest* and *Punch* and *TV Times*, was a paragraph that, though tucked away, leaped to Victor's eye. Things about rape always did, even though it no longer concerned him. This said that the man they called the 'Red Fox' – because he had red hair? A red face? – who had raped a seventy-year-old woman in Watford had now made a similar assault on a teenage girl in St Albans. How did they know it was the same man? Because of the descriptions which the women had given?

Victor didn't think about it. Or he thought he didn't think about it. Who knew what went on in the unconscious mind? If you knew, it wouldn't be unconscious, and that was the catch. Before going to sleep he read an article in *Reader's Digest* about the unconscious mind. And then, very soon after sleeping, it seemed, he fell into this dream. No road this time and no houses. He was in the wheelchair, out for the evening, crossing a common on which were areas of woodland. At one point he came to a bridge across a stream. It was a narrow bridge, of wooden planks, precarious and rickety, with a handrail made of rope on each side. A man on the far side, a kind of bridge keeper, came across to help Victor, walking backwards himself and pulling the wheelchair, telling Victor to close his eyes and not look down over the edge. Victor thanked him and continued along the path, which now entered one of the small dark woods. A woman was walking among the trees. She wore a long duster coat or mackintosh of black silk and over her head an embroidered black veil like a mantilla.

When she saw Victor approaching she turned to look at him, standing in an attitude of pity, of yearning sympathy, with both hands clasped in front of her. Victor jumped out of the wheelchair, ran towards her and, seizing her in his arms, threw her to the ground and tore at her clothes. She wore a mass of petticoats, layers and layers of stiff lace petticoats, and he tried to rip them away, burrowing in the starched crackling stuff with his hands, pushing with his face, his nose, like a snuffling pig. There was nothing there, nothing beneath, no flesh, only a clothes prop of wooden sticks. He tore off all the clothes, a wardrobe full, and the veil which was not one veil but two, three, a dozen, a wad of silky dusty black gauze, and underneath, under the last filmy layer, lay the photograph of Clare, her eyes looking up into his.

Nightmares recede quickly. Who had ever been troubled by a bad dream for more than an hour or two after waking? Nor could the dream spoil his feeling for the photograph. He took it with him down to Acton High Street and found a shop that did framing three or four doors up from Jupp's. They said they could do it on the spot and Victor chose an oval frame of walnut-coloured wood – perhaps true walnut. In Jupp's window, among the Victorian bric-a-brac and jewellery pieces was a gold locket shaped like a heart with a delicate chasing on it of flowers and leaves. He would have bought it, he would have gone in there and bought it for Clare, even though that meant putting more money into Jupp's pocket, but as he pushed the door open an inch or two and the bell began to jangle he noticed that the brown velvet sofa now had a label with 'sold' in red attached to it. Jupp came into the shop from behind the curtain, masticating gum, but Victor had turned away. He would buy a present for Clare elsewhere. Gold lockets, or gold anything come to that, were thick on the ground in London junk shops.

It was a pity that he couldn't have the car, but when he went to the car-rental place all they had available was a small Nissan van, the red Escort being out on hire. Besides, he was getting short of money again and after he had bought Clare a present it would be time to return to the 'bank'. A distaste for these transactions of his now began strongly to affect Victor. He didn't want to deceive her any longer about his possession of a car or lie to her about the source of his income. The idea that she might find out about his raids on Muriel's house appalled him, for he sensed that the justifications he made to himself would weigh nothing with her. 'It isn't as if you went to prison for stealing,' she had said. A vague unformed vision was slowly taking shape in his mind that Clare would lift him out of his past, just as knowing her had already absolved him from anger and panic and violence.

By mistake he got into a train that was going no further than Debden, and there he had to get out and wait for the Epping train. It was a warm white-skied day, sultry, the air full of flies. There had been a big blue-bottle buzzing against the windows of the carriage, trying to get out, seeking the sun. Victor had read in a magazine an article about how insects, searching for freedom or a way home, look to the sun to guide them. He had been glad to get out of the train, away from that frantic buzzing.

For some reason he fancied that Clare would want to see him dressed as he had been on his birthday, which he thought of and expected always to think of as the day they had found each other. He wore his dark blue cords and the same dark blue tee-shirt but it was too hot for the padded jacket so he carried that slung over his shoulder. Sometimes he caught sight of himself reflected in windows and he thought how much younger he looked since he had come out of prison, how much weight he had lost, and how his good looks, which he had once been proud of, had returned. There was no doubt that he looked years younger than poor David with his jowls and his excess couple of stone. In the train he had been thinking about David and thinking too that there was an alternative way for him to react. He might be bitter and resentful, he might say that Victor had ruined his life and now compounded the injury by stealing his girl. Uneasily, Victor remembered how Clare had said that David liked him but hadn't quite learned to trust him – yet.

A train had come in. It wasn't the shuttle service but another train from London, this time going all the way to Epping. Victor got into an empty carriage, the second from the rear. The doors were starting to close when the mad old woman came through them, holding in front of her a covered basket.

She put the basket on the floor between the long seats but, instead of sitting down herself, went up and down the carriage opening the windows. Victor looked at the basket, which was covered over with a piece of torn green towelling and which was distinctly moving up and down, a welling and subsiding movement, as if some culture worked underneath. It was the same uneven motion that had caused the shuddering of the carrier bag on that previous occasion. Victor could not keep from staring at it, though he did not want to. No culture, no activated yeast or fungus, could writhe with such vigour. It was as if she kept a pair of snakes in that basket.

The train drew into Theydon Bois and Victor got up to go into the next carriage. But the old woman blocked his egress – though surely not purposely – standing between the open doors with her arms in ragged red cotton sleeves spread wide to span them, calling out in accents which were a mimicry of an Indian's sing-song, 'Mind the doors! Please to mind the doors!'

He sat down again, too late to reach the other door. What did it matter? She couldn't harm him and in two or three minutes they would arrive at Epping station. He tried to read the *Essex Countryside* magazine. She was kneeling up on one of the seats at the far end writing something in a tiny cramped hand on an advertisement for mouthwash. Victor's eyes wandered back to the covered basket. There was no longer any movement under the green towel and it might have been eggs she kept in there or a couple of cabbages.

Why cover it with a towel then? Perhaps there was no accounting for the actions of the insane. He read a few lines about Morris dancers in Thaxted, then looked, because he could not control his eyes, back at the basket. If it was what it might be under that towel, if it showed itself or part of itself, what would he do, what would become of him? To be shut in this confined space from which escape was impossible with the object of his phobia, at this old creature's mercy too, when once she *knew* – that was the stuff of which his worst nightmares were made. For know she would, once she saw his reaction. Control would be impossible. Breaking into a total body sweat, he stood up. His eyes were on the basket but from the corner of the right one he could see her, kneeling there, looking at him.

The towel moved, slipped back. He gave an involuntary cry. It was a guinea pig's furry snout that appeared, waffling, a guinea pig whose coat was ironically in the colours and combination they call tortoiseshell . . . He breathed. The train drew in to Epping and the old woman picked up the basket, flinging the towel over the guinea pig with the swift quelling gesture of someone blanketing a parrot's cage. Victor tore off the return half of his ticket.

Somehow he didn't think he would be needing it but, on the other hand, if David was sore with him . . .

This business of always being early was something he would have to get out of. Whenever he wanted to be somewhere very much, he was about an hour early and that hour, passing it, was like getting through a day. He walked up from the station, taking it slowly, remembering the last time he had been here, before he knew Clare, when he scarcely knew she existed. If he turned right at the top of the hill he could go along to St Margaret's Hospital and wait outside the gates for her. But the main gates might not be the only exit, he thought, there might be other ways. He wandered through the town instead and in a little antique shop, much smarter and prettier (and more expensive) than Jupp's, bought Clare a Victorian ring of gold clasped hands on a silver band. The shopkeeper put it in a blue velvet box lined with white satin.

To kill time he walked Bell Common from one end to the other. The forest looked deep and dense, all the pale green of beech and birch darkened by summer, the grass under his feet starry with white and yellow flowers. In the still heavy air languid insects moved.

The Land Rover he saw in the distance, parked along a curve in the road, under chestnut trees. It had arrived while, for a moment, his head had been turned away. He wanted to run to her, though he would look a fool if he ran, but he ran just the same. The passenger door swung open. He climbed up inside and took her in his arms almost before he saw her. She was in his arms and he was kissing her, smelling her skin and tasting her mouth and pushing his fingers through her hair, before he could even have said whether she had make-up on her face or her dress was pink or white. She struggled a little, laughing, gasping, and then he was more gentle, taking her face in both his hands and looking at her, eye to eye.

Afterwards he could not remember how she had begun what she had said, the first words she used. Not precisely. And this was a merciful dispensation, for it was bad enough remembering what came later. He could remember only from the onset of his anger.

'You love me,' he said just as the anger began. 'You're in love with me. You said you were.'

She shook her head. 'Victor, I never said that.'

He could have sworn she had. Or was it only he who had kept saying it? Who had kept saying, I love you. 'I don't understand any of this.'

She said, 'Could we get out of here, please, and sit on the grass or something? Sitting so close to you, looking straight at you, it makes it hard.'

'I'm repulsive to you, am I? You could have fooled me.'

'I didn't mean that. You know I didn't.'

'I don't know anything any more,' he said, but he got out of the car into a wilderness of dead white sky and stuffy fly-laden air and dry grass. They walked in silence. She dropped suddenly to the ground, hid her face in her hands, then turned to him.

'Will you believe me when I say I honestly didn't know you felt like this? I know you said you loved me but people do say they love people. It's emotion makes them say it, being happy, it doesn't mean much.'

'It means the world to me.'

'I thought you felt the way I do. I like you, Victor, you're attractive too, very physically attractive. And I'm . . .' She looked down at the ground, the grasses and the flowers, her fingers pulling a daisy to pieces, stripping petals from the yellow calyx. 'The kind of lovemaking David and I do – it's all right, it's fine. Sometimes though, it's just not enough. I've got to learn to make it enough and I will. I've never,' she said very quietly, 'broken down, weakened, whatever you like to call it, before.'

He was horrified. 'You and David – make love? How can you? I don't know what you mean.'

She said a little wearily, 'Think about it, Victor. Use your imagination. His hands aren't paralysed. Or his mouth. Or his senses, come to that.'

'It's revolting.'

She shrugged. 'Never mind anyway. It isn't your

concern, is it? I was attracted by you. Still am, come to that. You were attracted by me. We were looking for comfort too and it was raining and – well, we had too much wine. We were alone together and frustrated and we fancied each other. I'm trying to be honest and not shirk things so I will say that I knew – well, I knew on Monday morning, we wouldn't just pass it over, forget it, I knew there'd be repercussions. That's why I got up so early. I was a bit aghast at what I'd done, Victor. For it was what *I'd* done. I know very well you wouldn't have touched me if I hadn't – instigated things.'

'Too right I wouldn't,' he said.

Ignoring that, she said, 'You're not really in love with me, Victor. You don't know me. You know scarcely anything about me. We've met just six times, and five out of those six times David's been there too.'

'What has that to do with it? I knew I loved you,' he said, believing it himself, 'from the first moment I saw you.'

'When I was so horrible to you?' She was smiling now, tried a laugh. 'When I abused you and used foul language? I'm sure you didn't, Victor. I don't – well, I don't make a practice of sleeping around casually, I've already said that, I think, but this time . . . Victor, can't we just say that we do like each other very much, we are attracted, and that Sunday night was good and lovely and we'll always remember it? Can't we do that? Look, it's six now. Let's go into the Half Moon and have a drink. I *need* a drink and I'm sure you do.'

Anger, at this stage, made him cold and condescending. 'You've already said you drink too much.'

'I don't think I quite said that.'

'In any case, it doesn't matter. None of this matters because I don't believe any of it. You couldn't pretend about something like this. You weren't *pretending* on Sunday night. It's now you're pretending so as not to hurt David, you're sacrificing yourself for David. Well, I won't have it. D'you hear me, Clare, I won't have it! Aren't I as important as he is? Hasn't my life been spoiled as much as his?' An idea came to him. 'I suppose you haven't dared tell him, is that it?'

She turned her head away. 'I didn't think it would be necessary to tell him.'

'Look at me, Clare. Turn round. I want to see your face.' He saw that she had become rather pale. 'Of course you're afraid to tell him. I'll tell him, I don't mind. You wouldn't spoil both our lives for the sake of ten minutes' unpleasantness, would you? Sticks and stones can break my bones,' he said, 'but hard words can't hurt me.'

'You don't understand at all.'

'I understand that you're nervous and you don't want a fuss. Look, why don't you take me back with you now and we'll both talk to David, we'll talk to him together.'

'That's impossible.'

'All right. You go. You go home now and just act as if nothing had happened and I'll follow in an hour. Don't say anything to him, I don't want you upsetting yourself. This is between David and me anyway.'

'Victor,' she said, 'can't you see we're worlds apart, you and I? The way we talk and think, the way we look at life?'

'What does that matter?' he said. 'That's not important. We didn't think like that on Sunday night and we won't again.'

'I would rather you didn't come tonight,' she said carefully.

'When then?'

'Oh, Victor, what's the use? Can't you *see*?'

'You go back to David now,' he said, 'and I'll follow in an hour.'

He smiled encouragingly at her. Her eyes were on him and she had a trapped look. Well, that was understandable, seeing what lay ahead of her. He slammed the door and she started the Land Rover. It occurred to him she must think he had his car with him, could get to Theydon without trouble. That was what he wanted her to think, wasn't it?

Momentarily the feeling came to him as he watched the Land Rover turn out into the main road that he would never see her again. That was ridiculous, she wasn't going to run away. It was a quarter past six. There was no need to take that stipulated hour too literally. Anyway, it was he who had stipulated it. He felt excited and energetic, tingling with excitement, but not afraid. David couldn't do anything to him beyond saying a few hard things. It would take him an hour to walk to Theydon and he decided to walk, the alternative being the train.

The motorway disappeared into the ground here, came out on the other side of the hill and wandered away, bearing its load across the meadows. But all you could see of it was the wall on top of the tunnel that might have been enclosing someone's garden. Victor walked down a winding country lane without a pavement, green-hedged and overhung with trees, past a golf club, the garden gates of big houses, through a bit of forest, coming out into Theydon by the church. The sun had come out and it was going to be a fine evening. Theydon Manor Drive was full of roses, hedges of white and red, circular beds of roses in many colours, roses climbing over porches and pergolas. Everything is coming up roses, he thought, another expression which he couldn't remember from before he went to prison.

Faint heart never won fair lady. Who had said that? Jupp, he remembered, going courting Muriel. It rather annoyed him to think of Jupp – and of Muriel, come to that – in this connection; the comparison with his own case was grotesque. At the gate he paused, though. There was a precipice on the other side of that front door. Clare had put the Land Rover away and shut the garage doors and for some reason that troubled him. He would have expected her to leave it out in the street. But of course she thought *he* had a car . . .

He went up to the front door but he didn't knock. He lifted the knocker and, instead of letting it fall, restored it quietly to its original position. Not looking in at the windows, he walked round the side of the house, came into the back garden, which seemed full of roses. On Sunday it had been raining too much to notice them. He turned his face slowly towards the house. The french windows were open. Inside the room, just inside the open windows, David was sitting in his wheelchair with Clare very close beside him in another chair. There was an impression that they had retreated in there from outside, for on the garden table was a jug of water with melting ice in it, a glass and David's cigarettes. Victor couldn't remember seeing David and Clare sit like that before, close together, holding hands. The way they were sitting was curious, as if they were waiting together for something awful to happen, for death or destruction, for the ultimate disaster. He remembered a picture he had seen years before, in a school history book. It was of the Goths or Huns or someone coming to Rome and the members of the senate waiting for them, sitting with impassive dignity for a horde of barbarians to come and bring desecration with them. Clare and David reminded him of that.

He said, 'David,' and, 'I expect Clare told you I was coming.'

David nodded. He didn't speak but his eyes moved from Victor's face down his body. Victor had his hands in his pockets, having placed them there because they had started to shake. David was looking at Victor's right hand in his jacket pocket and Victor knew at once, sensed beyond question, that he thought he had a gun there.

Clare had got up. Her face was pale and her eyes seemed very large. She was wearing the cream cotton dress with the big sleeves. Had she been wearing that in Epping when he kissed her? He couldn't remember. He took his hands out of his pockets. They were steady now. Taking a step or two forwards, he came up to the table, as to a barricade set up for battle, and lowered himself into one of the chairs.

'Clare has just said she'll marry me,' David said.

Victor shook his head. 'No.'

'I refused to ask her. You know that. She asked me again just now and I've said yes.'

'There are a few things I have to tell you,' said Victor, 'which may make you change your mind about that.'

'I've already told him the few things, Victor,' said Clare.

'Did she tell you I fucked her? Not once, on and on, all night.'

'Of course she told me. Don't be so melodramatic. That may happen again in the years to come – Oh, not with you, there's not much chance of that. With others. She says so herself. I know my limitations, Victor, and she knows them. Neither of us pretends life is what it isn't – unlike you.'

'I want to marry David,' Clare said. 'It's what I've wanted ever since I first got to know him.'

Victor trembled. He had a sensation all over his body of vibrating needles in the flesh.

'What did you tell her,' he said, 'to make her change her mind?'

'She hasn't changed her mind.'

Victor wouldn't have said it if he hadn't been so angry.

'Did you tell her I'd raped women?'

'No.'

Clare made that flinching movement that was like Judy's shrinking away when he had stood beside her at the window.

'I don't believe you,' Victor said.

'Is it true?' said Clare.

'Ask him. He's poisoned your mind against me. I should never have let you go back to him. I knew what he was, I always knew, and I thought – I thought we could be *friends*.'

He got up and moved, watching with pleasure as David tried to remain still and upright, to hold his ground. But David couldn't keep himself from shrinking, from drawing his hands back and gripping the wheels. Clare made a movement of protest, half shielding David with her arms. Victor saw red. He crashed his fists down on the table and the glass flew off and shattered on the stone. Victor picked up the water jug and hurled that on the ground too. Water flew on to David with splinters of glass and he covered his face with his arm.

'I wish I'd killed you,' Victor said. 'They couldn't have

done worse to me than what they did if I'd killed you. I wish I had.'

Somewhere in the house the puppy had begun to bark like a real watchdog.

15

When he left David's house Victor walked for a while aimlessly, having no idea of destination, unable to think of anywhere he wished to be. Prison might be the best place for him, the only place, and if he killed David he would go back to prison. He hadn't a gun but it was possible to get a gun. It was possible to get anything if you knew how, if you had money. He found himself heading for the forest, passing the house where he had paid a deposit on a flat. He would never live in Theydon now, never set foot in the place again except to see David once more. His head full of images of David shot, David bleeding, David sprawled on the floor, he went up to the door and rang the bell.

Mrs Palmer behaved in rather a frightened way. Afterwards Victor thought this must have been because he had acted wildly and talked wildly, he must have appeared scarcely sane to her. Clare had receded from his consciousness and David's image filled it. The woman didn't argue, she said he could have his deposit back and gave him a cheque. Victor thought he would spend the money on a gun.

He began to walk up the hill that led through the forest, by means of a steep winding hill, towards the junction of main roads. It was a little after half past eight. Anger had started to boil up in him, taking the form of a fierce energy. He could have walked for miles, he could have walked all the way to Acton, and still not have used up that rage-stimulated energy. It was not Clare he was angry with, it wasn't her fault; she had simply bowed to a greater strength, as women must do. If she hadn't been there, he thought, he would have taken David by the throat and strangled the life out of him. But what power David had!

What power a man could have from a wheelchair, a man who was only half alive!

Occasionally a car passed him, going up to Loughton or down to Theydon. Once he saw a man walking in the depths of the forest with a big grey gambolling dog, an Irish wolfhound. There were stretches of open green in the forest here, of fine cropped turf, and wide areas where only the unfurling fronds of bracken grew, branched, tall, green as the trees, and there were copses of birches with thin white trunks and trembling leaves. The sun set in a smoky red glow and the sky grew briefly pale, greenish-gold as if stripped, as if peeled of cloud. Victor was angry and full of energy and now he was afraid, because he asked himself what could become of this anger, how could he live with it? What happened to you if anger conquered you?

Then he saw the girl in the forest.

First he saw the car, which was empty. It was parked at the entrance to one of the rides which lead through the forest, in mud ruts, now dried, made previously by a much heavier vehicle. She was sitting, with her back to the parked car and the road, on a log of wood among the bracken. Victor, who would not have thought of things in this way even a week before, decided that she was waiting to meet a man. Clare had waited to meet him in the same sort of way, an illicit way. This girl too had a possessive jealous commanding man at home, so she had to meet her lover secretly, in a lonely, unwatched place.

Only it wasn't unwatched. She was dark and thin, not at all like Clare. It was nine fifteen and she was early perhaps, their arrangement being for nine thirty, but he didn't reason or work things out, he was beyond that. She was quite unaware of his presence, unhearing of his footfalls on the grass behind her, for he could see now what absorbed her. In the dusk she was making up her face. With her handbag open and a small mirror propped on it, she was pencilling her eyelids. Hardly daring to breathe, he stood a yard behind her and watched the red-tipped fingers take hold of the implement that would mascara her lashes. This was an operation to be postponed until she got here, an act that would arouse suspicion if carried out at home.

He came a step closer to her, hooked his left arm round her neck and pressed his other hand across her mouth. A scream tried to burst out of her into the palm of his hand. The contents of the handbag went flying. She struggled like a creature in a net, wriggled like a landed eel. He was immensely strong, his own strength amazed him. It was easy to hold her, to manipulate her, to throw her to the ground in a nest of bracken and stuff into her mouth the scarf that had fallen from that handbag. He was erect like a brass rod, hot as fire and painful with anger. His free hand fumbled with his fly but she was limp now, her head and neck twisted to one side, her hands not fighting him but pressed under her body. He dragged down her tights, his fingers going through the filmy stuff as fragile as a cobweb.

Dimly he was aware of something cracking. He heard a sharp crack and thought it might be a breaking bone, she was all bones, iron hard and unyielding. He pushed against cold dry resistant flesh and felt, suddenly, a sharp excruciating pain in his chest. It was a stinging blow he felt and he lurched off her body, seeing blood, *smelling* blood. He cried out in pain and disgust. There came more pain, as of needle pricks, and he heard the roar of a car's engine, wheels crunching on dry clay, the rev of a motor whose driver gives the accelerator a final flip before he brakes. Victor leaped to his feet. Blood was running down his chest. The girl, her mouth full of scarf, red silk trailing from her mouth like more blood, held a triangle of broken mirror in her hand. Underneath her body, on a stone perhaps, she had contrived to snap that handbag mirror and use one of the slivers as a weapon.

He plunged for the cover of the trees, doing up his clothes as he ran. Behind him he heard a man's voice call, 'Where are you? What's happened?'

A cry, a sobbing, silence as she was caught, held, comforted. Victor didn't dare to stop, though he could feel blood flowing out of the largest of the wounds, pumping out even, a pulse throbbing and a darker stain spreading out over the dark blue tee-shirt. He ran deeper in among the trees, having no idea where he was heading. It would be dark soon, it was nearly dark now. Running in the forest wasn't easy if you left the paths, for underfoot it was all brambles and stinging nettles and the endless bracken. And all the time he was listening for pursuers. They would follow him, he thought, just as, on the day he took refuge in Solent Gardens, Heather Cole and the man in the park had followed him. The brambles caught at his trousers and he stumbled and righted himself, but next time he fell, plunging forward into a damp hollow full of thorny tendrils.

Victor knelt there, listening. His hands stung from contact with nettles. He was sure he was still bleeding. There was no sound behind, no sound anywhere but the faint buzz, insect-like it was so far away, of a distant aircraft. Big splayed chestnut leaves, vegetable hands, damp and cold, touched his face. He got up, still listening. No one was following him and then he knew why. The couple were illicit lovers, each of whom, probably, had given false excuses as to where they were going to a husband and a wife or to other, more legitimate or accredited, lovers. Chasing him, telling the police about him, would be to blow their cover, to bring down the wrath of those others on them, perhaps to end their affair. He shivered with the relief of it. But fear took over almost immediately. How badly had she hurt him? Suppose he bled to death?

It was too dark in here to see anything. He could feel the blood on his chest, though, its warm wetness. The sky above him was still visible as a pale glowing greyness, but the tops of the trees were black bunches, festoons of black leaves. There must be a path somewhere, places like this were always traversed by hundreds of paths. It wasn't really country, more like a big park really, not much wilder than Hampstead Heath.

The segment of forest he was in, he calculated, must be bounded by the Theydon road he had come from, the road from Loughton to the Wake Arms, Clays Lane and Debden

Green. Once, a lifetime ago, he had had to drive someone from Debden Green to Cambridge and he had some idea of the neighbourhood. He couldn't go back the way he had come; in spite of his reasoning, that would be too risky. It was too dark to see what time it was, perhaps no more than ten. David had brought him to this. Why hadn't he killed David that time in Solent Gardens?

After a very long time had passed Victor did reach some sort of path or ride. By then he had revised his view of Epping Forest being a kind of outer London park. It was huge and dark and confusing, a maze. He followed the path he had found, or perhaps it was another path, an offshoot of the first one. He had no idea where it went. It seemed to him that he was covered with blood, not only on his body but on his hands, for while groping his way along, he had tried to hold the sides of the worst wound together and staunch the flow. At least he had succeeded in staunching it. The blood had clotted and he could feel the crust of it mixed with forest dirt. He put out his hands to touch the obstruction ahead of him, thinking it might be yet another huge smooth trunk of a beech tree, and came up against a man-made close-boarded fence.

Feeling along it, he came upon a gate. It wasn't locked. Victor went through it and found himself in someone's back garden, a vast garden of lawns and trees, shrubs and glistening in the middle of it a pond, a smooth sheet of water in which the stars were reflected. At the far end of the lawn, up by the house, light from a bedroom window fell on to this lawn in the form of two yellow rectangles. With a sense of horror, he thought: I could climb up there and go in and find Rosemary Stanley in bed, and she will scream and break the window and David will come . . .

To reach a road, a way of escape, he would have to pass the side of the house. Victor was afraid to do this, he had had enough, he was aware all of a sudden that he was tired to exhaustion point, he was worn out. Adjoining the fence, by the gate where he had entered, was a wooden shed. The door had a padlock on it but the padlock hung loose and the door came open when he turned the handle. Inside it was dry and stuffy and smelling of creosote. It was also pitch dark but Victor could just make out, lying on the floor, what he thought was a pile of netting, the kind of thing gardeners use for protecting fruit bushes from birds. He shut the door behind him and flung himself face-downwards on the pile of nets.

By four it was light. He had no idea how long he had slept, perhaps as much as five hours. Very bright pale light from a newly risen sun was coming in through a small window high up under the eaves of the shed. Victor looked at his hands. He tried to look at his chest but the largest wound was too high up to see and, besides, his tee-shirt was a mess of matted blood sticking to skin and hairs. A way must be found of cleaning this up before he got into a bus or train.

Leaving the shed and then the garden itself by the gate in the fence, he came out on to a forest path which led to a road. He saw how near he had been last night to one of the main roads. Not that it would have been of much use to him at midnight. On the other side of this road was a pond, one of the forest ponds which once were gravel pits, its surface clear and brown with long flat leaves floating on it. A truck went past, then, in the opposite direction, a car. But there was very little traffic yet. Victor crossed the road and, kneeling down, bathed his face and hands in the water of the pond. It wasn't cold, nor was it very clean, but brown, rather oily, stagnant. It more or less served his purpose and he dried himself as best he could on the lining of his jacket.

The road downhill seemed to lead towards houses and away from the forest. After about half a mile he realized that he was in Loughton, approaching the High Road. The traffic was just beginning and there were one or two people about. He stopped a man and asked him the way to Loughton station and the man told him, not eyeing Victor in any particularly curious way, so he guessed he must be presentable and not a figure of horror.

*

A scar would always remain. The wound should have been cleaned and stitched, for it was more than an inch long with sides which still gaped and showed dirt inside. Perhaps, even now, it wouldn't be too late to stitch it, but Victor knew he wasn't going near any doctor. The girl might go to the police, there was always that possibility. If she and her boyfriend could think up some story for her being there, she might go to the police. In any case, Victor thought, he could be wrong. She could have been meeting him there because she lived at home with her parents and he lived at home with his and there had been nowhere but the forest to make love.

She had made a nasty mess of his chest. Apart from the major wound there was a mass of smaller cuts. It had been painful getting his shirt off. In the end he had given up and lain in the bath to soak it off and the bath water had gone brown as with rust. His jacket would have to be cleaned. He emptied out his pockets and found the cheque and the blue velvet box containing the ring he had bought for Clare.

His anger was still there, for he had done nothing to assuage it, but it was simmering indignantly rather than exploding. Also he was now able to reason out how he should have behaved, where he had gone wrong. Of course he should have gone back to Sans Souci with Clare in her car. His mistake had been his own pride, he could see that. Had he sacrificed his happiness and hers out of a refusal to admit that the red Escort was a hire car which had had to go back? If they had gone in there and confronted David together, how different things might have been! David only understood violent action, force, for once a policeman, you were always a policeman. Victor knew he should have gone with Clare and he should have done the talking, told David some home truths, forcibly removed Clare. What could David have done – from a wheelchair?

The little ring with the joined silver hands on a gold band – he wouldn't throw it away, he would keep it, Clare would wear it yet. Victor put sticking plaster on his chest and then he dressed, the striped shirt, denim jeans, green velvet jacket. He sat in the wheelchair and counted his money. Under sixty pounds remained, though he had this week's social security payment to come. Still, there was the cheque, his deposit on the flat returned to him, two hundred pounds. He unfolded it. She had made it out to M. Faraday.

When he came back from taking his clothes to the cleaners, Victor phoned David. It amused him to remember how shy he had been of phoning David that first time, how unable to speak beyond uttering his name when David had answered. Things were very different now. He dialled David's number and waited impatiently, tapping with his fingers on the underside of the stairs.

'Hallo?'

'David, this is Victor. I just wanted to say that thanks to you I had a pretty horrendous night, missed the last train and all that. I'm lucky to be alive, what with one thing and another. I don't think I handled things very well last night but that won't matter in the long run. You'll have to make up your mind, you know, that Clare and I are going to be together, she wants me and I want her and that's the way it is. Right?'

David didn't say anything but he hadn't rung off.

'I shall be talking to her later today and making arrangements, but I think we ought to be civilized about this. I think you owe it to me to give me a hearing. Anyway, I'd like to talk the whole thing through with you. You know it helps us both to talk things through.' It cost Victor something to say this and he didn't really mean it anyway. It was a sop to David. 'I'd like us to go on being friends. I know Clare will want to go on being your friend.'

'Victor, let's get this straight,' said David. 'It was a mistake our meeting in the first place. A lot of harm's been done, maybe irrevocable harm. The best thing we can do now is try to get back to where we were before, pick up the pieces. We shan't be seeing each other again.'

This superior attitude made Victor furious, in spite of his determination to remain calm.

'You've lost her, David,' he shouted into the phone. 'Make up your mind to it, you've lost this war. You're defeated.'

He crashed down the phone before David could replace his receiver. Upstairs again, sitting in the wheelchair, he counted the money once more, contemplated the ring. Maybe he could sell it to Jupp. Their love, his and Clare's, had no need of rings, of material bonds. He read the magazines he had found in a wastepaper bin, the *Sunday Times* colour magazine and something called *Executive World*, and the *Standard*, which he had had to pay for. The man they were calling the 'Red Fox' had raped a woman in Hemel Hempstead but there was nothing about a girl being attacked in Epping Forest. He watched Wimbledon on television until six and then he dialled David's number, resolving to put the phone down if David answered.

It was Clare who said hallo.

'Clare, darling, you know who this is. Have you been all right? I didn't like leaving you with him but what was I to do? I should never have left you to face him alone. We won't make any more mistakes, we'll do the right thing from now on.' Victor thought he had never talked so much or so articulately in his life before. He was proud of himself. 'I'm longing to see you. When can we meet? I'm going to be perfectly honest with you and confess something. That car isn't mine. I only hired it. I just let you think it was mine because – well, I suppose I wanted you to think well of me.' The words streamed out, it was easy. 'Am I forgiven? Well, I know you won't care about that, not really. And you know I'll come any distance to meet you if I have to walk every step of the way. We'll have to face it, it's going to be tough for the next few weeks, making him see reason among other things. But we'll be together and we'll come through all right.'

'Victor,' she said in a small distressed voice, 'this is my fault. I know that, I'm sorry.'

'Sorry?' he said airily. 'What have you got to be sorry about? Absolute nonsense.'

'David didn't want me to speak to you, he said it was

better not, but that would have been such a cowardly thing . . . I still have a lot of explaining to do. I shall always feel guilty if I can't say them.'

'You can say anything you like to me, darling, everything. When shall we meet? Tomorrow? In that Half Moon pub of yours?'

'Not tomorrow,' she said. 'Monday. Six o'clock. I'll tell David what I'm going to do. I know he'll think it's the right thing.'

'I love you,' Victor said.

He replaced the receiver, well pleased with the result of his call. Someone unlocked the front door and Mrs Griffiths came into the hall. She was wearing white gloves and a different navy blue straw hat, this time with a small spotted veil.

'Oh, Mr Jenner,' she said, 'you've saved me a climb,' as if his room was up Ben Nevis or on the tenth floor of a liftless tower.

He stared blankly at her, his head full of images of Clare.

'Some policemen were here again yesterday, asking for you. At about five in the afternoon.'

His heart missed a beat and then steadied. Five o'clock was four or five hours before he had encountered that girl in Epping Forest.

'It isn't pleasant, Mr Jenner.' Mrs Griffiths looked about her, craned her neck to peer up the staircase, said in lowered tones, 'Mr Welch and those after-care people, they did give me to understand there wouldn't be any trouble. However, I do understand from your note that you're leaving and what I wanted to know was – well, precisely when?'

Victor had forgotten that he had committed himself to leaving. Writing that letter she called a 'note' seemed so long ago, so much had happened since. He had nowhere to go.

'At the end of next week,' he said, and corrected himself. 'No, this coming Monday.' He wouldn't let Clare go back to Sans Souci this time. He and she would go to a motel, the Post House at Epping, for instance.

'Do you know you're bleeding through your shirt?' said Mrs Griffiths.

The wound had come open again. Exulting at the sound of Clare's voice, at her calling him by his name, he had flung his arm out wide, expanded his chest. He bathed the wound at the sink in his room, put a fresh piece of plaster on to it, drawing together the sides of the cut. Sitting in the wheelchair, he watched Wimbledon on television, an exciting women's singles.

It was one of the tortoise dreams he had that night. He was back in the shed at the bottom of that garden in Loughton, lying on the nets, aware, though it was dark, of a pile of stones in one corner. One of the stones came alive and began to walk, to approach his bed. Victor saw the scaly feet moving rhythmically like very very slow clockwork, the shell swaying, the head that was a snake's yet stupid, myopic, wobbling from side to side as if attached to a rusty pivot. He shouted and tried to get out but the door of course was locked and the window inaccessible, so he backed against the wall and the thing came nearer, dull-eyed, slow, relentless, and Victor screamed and woke up screaming, the sound coming not in a thin cry as was so often the case with nightmare screams but as yells of agony and fear.

Footsteps sounded on the stairs and someone banged on the door. It was the same voice that had protested once before, the time Victor had pounded on the floor and walls.

'What's going on in there?'

'Nothing,' said Victor. 'I had a dream.'

'Christ.'

He got up, had a bath and changed the dressing on the cuts. At nine, when he knew Clare would have left for work, he phoned David.

'Hallo?'

David sounded wary. He probably had a good idea who it was and he was scared.

'Yes, it's me again, David,' Victor said. 'I don't know if Clare told you I'm meeting her on Monday and that'll be it. She won't be coming back to you after that, she'll be coming away with me. I think it's best to be perfectly honest about this and keep you informed about everything we plan to do.'

'Victor, Clare isn't planning to do anything with you.' David spoke in a patient slow way as if to a child, which annoyed Victor. 'Clare is going to stay here with me and marry me. I think I've already told you this.'

'And I've already told you Clare is meeting me on Monday and coming away with me. Are you deaf or something?'

'Clare and I will both meet you, Victor, and we'll try and talk sensibly about all this.'

'If you come with her on Monday,' said Victor, 'I'll kill you,' and he rang off.

He went out and collected his social security money, his clothes from the cleaners, and, passing Jupp's shop, took the ring out of his pocket and looked at it. There was nothing in the jewellery tray priced at more than fifty pounds, which meant that the most Jupp was likely to give him for the ring was twenty-five. The brown velvet sofa had gone and Kevin was lugging out from the back a rather battered green and gilt chaise longue to put in its place. Victor stood there for a moment, watching him stand the peacock on top of the big gilt scroll that ran along its back.

Victor got into the train at Ealing Common and went up to Park Royal. Not to Tom's this time but to the shop next to the wineshop which he remembered from his previous visit and which was called Hanger Green Small Arms. In the window were all sorts of weapons, it was an armoury of a kind, but Victor knew that very little but the shotguns and rifles were real. He went in and asked about a replica Luger. The man hadn't got one but he offered Victor a Beretta instead, the kind James Bond used to have, he said, before he changed to a Walther PPK 9 mm. It was a large heavy automatic pistol, precisely and in every detail the twin of a real one, but it fired nothing, it wasn't even equipped to fire blanks. The price was eighty pounds, which would leave Victor with just four pounds to live on till the next social security came through. But he didn't hesitate. He had had an idea about cashing that cheque.

On the way home he bought a magazine called *This England* that came out quarterly. He couldn't afford it, he could barely afford food, but there was an article inside about Epping Forest. What had become of all the leftover food from Sunday, he wondered. The quails, for instance. Probably David had eaten them. He wasn't going to demean himself by inquiring but he would phone David again just the same. He might as well use up all the coins he had left on phoning David.

'Hallo?'

'It's Victor,' said Victor. 'As if you didn't know.'

'I don't want to talk to you, Victor. We've nothing to say to each other. Please don't keep phoning like this.'

'*I*'ve got plenty to say to *you*. I'm coming over to see you tomorrow when Clare's at home and this time you won't get the chance to attack me with broken glass. I think you understand me.'

'*What*?'

'You heard,' Victor said. 'If I went to a doctor and showed him the wounds on my chest, you could be charged with causing grievous bodily harm. I'll phone Clare later. Just leave her to answer, will you? Have the decency to do that. It'll be about eight.'

He rang off. Five ten-pee coins remained in his pocket and a pound note and a pound coin. There was half a loaf of bread in his cupboard, a can of tomatoes and about a quarter of a pound of Edam cheese. Tomorrow he would go and see Muriel. He went out and spent the pound note and the pound coin on twenty cigarettes, a pint of milk, a bar of chocolate and the *Standard*. There was nothing in it about rape, either in Hertfordshire or Epping Forest. He sat in the wheelchair smoking and watching television. When the tennis went off and the news came on, he removed, with considerable pain, the dressing from the biggest wound on his chest and covered it with a fresh strip of sticking plaster. Of course he didn't really think David had made those cuts, he wasn't mad, he knew very well they had been made by the thin dark girl in the forest, but he wanted David to think he thought it. David might begin to believe it himself.

Waiting till eight to phone Clare was impossible. He ate some bread and cheese and smoked a cigarette, went downstairs and dialled David's number. It was twenty-five past seven.

David answered, though Victor had warned him not to.

'You've no right to stop her speaking to me when it's what she and I want.'

'It isn't what she wants, Victor. And I may as well tell you this is the last time you'll be speaking to me because I'm going to have the phone number changed.'

Victor started to laugh, he couldn't help it, because David was going to all that trouble when he, Victor, couldn't phone anyway because he hadn't any coins left.

'Victor,' said David, 'listen to me a minute. I don't bear you any ill will, you must believe that. But I think you need treatment, you're sick. For your own sake you need treatment. You need to see a doctor.'

'I'm not mad,' said Victor. 'Don't worry yourself about me. If prison couldn't drive me round the bend, you won't. And I do bear you ill will, a hell of a lot of ill will. Don't think you've seen the last of me. You can tell Clare I won't let her down, I'll never give her up, right?'

But David never answered for the pips started and Victor hadn't another ten-pee piece to put in. He put the receiver back and with the pencil that was kept on top of the phone box blacked out David's name and phone number that he had written on the underside of the stairs. Of course it was Clare's phone number too but that didn't matter because by now he knew it by heart . . .

Tomorrow, he thought, when he had some money, he would go to Theydon Bois and take the Beretta with him. David had been very foolish, last time, refusing to believe in the reality of a real gun, but once bitten, twice shy. This time he would believe. Just as he had once before failed to believe that that real gun was real, so this time he would not fail to believe a fake gun was real. While Victor held

David motionless with the gun, Clare could make her escape from the house. They would go in the Land Rover. He was glad now that he had confessed to her about the red Escort only being hired and about the rapes too, come to that. She knew all about him, he had no secrets from her, which was the way it should be . . .

16

He was going to have to lift that thing up, move it to one side and take the key from underneath it. Fearfully he glanced in its direction and then quickly away. Once more he climbed over the rocks and looked in through the diamond panes. Muriel was still asleep in her chair and no amount of ringing at the doorbell, the shrill clanging made by tugging at the iron bellpull, would awaken her. He even wondered if there might be something wrong, if she had perhaps had some kind of seizure.

There might be a chance of getting in the back way. Victor went round the side of the garage and tried the back door. It was locked, of course. The back garden had become a hayfield which the wind ruffled and made paths through. Once he had done what he came for, he was going to take the tube to Theydon and remove Clare from that house at gunpoint. The Beretta was in the pocket of his grey padded jacket, heavy, weighing it down a bit on the right-hand side. David had confessed that first time that he was afraid of him, afraid he had come to 'finish the job'. Victor didn't anticipate much resistance from David. The pressing thing was to get into this house. It was already two o'clock and he had been hanging about, ringing that bell, trying door and windows for nearly an hour.

Muriel slept on, an empty plate and cup on one of her side tables, magazines, scissors, a paste pot on another. It was a warm day, even the wind was warm, but she had one element of the electric heater on, a single bar glowing red. Victor couldn't smell it out there but he could imagine the stench of burning dust.

He climbed over the stones and stood on the one also shared by the rabbit and the frog. Frogs he didn't mind, or snakes, come to that, or crocodiles even. He could cheerfully have touched the skin of a toad. He moistened his lips, swallowed, forced his eyes on to the stone tortoise. It's stone, he said to himself, it's just a lump of stone. They made the thing in wax or clay and then they made a mould round it and then they cast it. They pour some sort of mortar or fine concrete into the moulds. Hundreds, thousands, they make like that, they're mass-produced. Telling himself all this didn't make much difference. I'll have to work on it again, Victor thought, try and finish what I started all those years ago. Clare will help me, Clare's used to healing. Meanwhile, he had to get into the house, therefore he had to take the key from under the – thing. Tortoise, he said, tortoise.

The flesh on his upper lip began to jump. He tried to hold it still with his hand. Then he imagined that his finger was a scaly leg pressed against his mouth and a shudder went through him, actually jerking his body. If I touch it I will faint, he thought. Suppose he were to go next door and ask Jenny or her husband to move it for him? That was full of difficulties. They would want to know why. Then when he'd got the door open one of them might come in with him and he didn't want that. He knelt down and closed his eyes. Why did he immediately think of those last moments in the house in Solent Gardens and of David thrusting the girl down the stairs and turning his back? Because of the picture of the praying hands on the stairwell wall? Perhaps. He was kneeling now, with his eyes closed, in a ridiculous attitude of prayer.

He told himself to think of anything rather than of what he was doing, about to touch a stone facsimile of the object of his phobia. Think of David, think of those last moments, of the gun going off. Those were bad things but infinitely preferable to this thing. He leaned forward, holding out his hands, clasped the thing, feeling the stone coruscations on its shell. It was surprisingly heavy, which helped. The real thing would not have been as heavy. Holding his breath, he set it down, felt for the key and found it. To replace the thing on the spot from which he had removed it was beyond his powers. He stood up, clutching the key, and retched. His stomach was empty, luckily, he hadn't wanted lunch and was without money, anyway, to pay for it. Twice he heaved and retched, shivering with nausea, but recovered enough to feel the whole street must be watching him. It seemed as if the operation had taken hours but when he looked at his watch he saw that his sufferings had endured for a little over one minute.

He unlocked the front door and went in. She awoke immediately, or perhaps was awake before he even put the key in the lock. She called out, 'Is that you, Joe?'

Victor thought how he might have saved himself a lot of anguish. He walked into the living room. The heat was stifling, the smell of burning dust as he had imagined it. Muriel had her brown hairnet on but she was dressed, in a flowered silk dress which should have had a belt but didn't and stockings rolled down to her ankles and fur-lined bedroom slippers. She contorted herself into that peering attitude, hunched forward, head on one side, looking up with nose twitching.

'What are you after?'

A gust of anger swept through Victor, or, rather, swept upon him and remained. It seemed to grow, to mount, like yeast working, bubbling up. What had she done to herself, he thought, to make her look so like his mother? It was a resemblance he had scarcely noticed before. If his mother had lived, without his father, would she too look like this now? The notion was almost unbearable. There was something about her face. The jawline was fuller and firmer. She didn't have false teeth, as far as he knew, but she didn't have many of her own left either. It must be a plate she wore, that she should wear all the time, but had put in because of Jupp, to present a more attractive appearance for Jupp. He remembered why he had come.

'I needn't go into details,' he said, 'but I gave this woman to understand my name was Faraday and she's given me a cheque made out to M. Faraday. All I'm asking is for you to sign on the back of it for me.'

'The police came here again,' she said.

'What do you mean?' he said. 'When did they come?'

'When was the day it rained? When Joe was here.'

'How should I know? Monday? Tuesday?'

Before his night in the forest, he thought, breathing again.

'They'd been to you,' she said, 'but you weren't there. For rape, they said. It made me go cold all over, it turned me up. The Red Fox they're looking for and maybe that's you, they said.'

The Hertfordshire rapist. That was why they had been to Mrs Griffiths's then.

'Your poor mother,' said Muriel.

'Never mind my mother. My mother's dead.'

His mother's face looked at him, aged, distorted, whiskered, twitching like a mouse, blear-eyed, but still her face. Victor, convulsed now with anger, had the curious sensation that Muriel was a subtle tormentor placed here by some higher power to torture him in most refined and subtle ways, in ways specifically designed to suit him, as if details of what most flicked his raw places had been fed into a computer and the resultant print-out had been presented to Muriel as a guideline. Only Muriel wasn't Muriel but an avenging angel or devil elaborately disguised. Why hadn't they fed in the worst thing? Or had they? Would she, in a moment, open a cupboard and show him . . .?

As if to follow the course of his fantasy, she got to her feet. She lifted up the cup and saucer in her left hand, put two fingers of her right hand into her mouth and drew out a dental plate with seven or eight teeth on it from the lower jaw. Victor, watching in horror, heard himself make a sound of protest. She dropped the teeth into her teacup.

'That's better,' she said, and her face wasn't his mother's any more, but the eyes were, suddenly pale blue and sparkling. Victor closed his own. 'What was it you wanted?' she said.

Again he tried to explain about the cheque, but he gagged on the words, anger closing his throat.

'Speak up,' she said, the cup in her hand, the molars all grinning out of it. 'What did you tell them my name for?'

He couldn't answer.

'Two hundred pounds. There's some swindle going on, I daresay. It's bound to be crooked if it's you.' She came very close, head turned, peering up. 'What stopped you forging my name?'

What had? He had never thought of it. He took her by the shoulders to thrust her away and she cringed under his touch.

'Don't you . . .!' she cried. 'You'd better not . . . Oh, no . . .'

Immediately and with horror he understood what she meant. It was rape she feared. Broken old creature that she was, his ruined mother that she was, she feared rape at his hands and, while dreading it, her eyes nevertheless sparkled. She trembled, tense and fascinated. She peered into his face, reached up to take his hands away, shuffled backwards, one step, two steps, the cup with the teeth falling on the floor, rolling across the carpet.

He was aware for the first time since entering the house of the gun weighing down his pocket. He put his hand into his pocket and took out the gun and struck at her with it. It struck the side of her head and she reeled, screaming out. Victor struck again and again, raining blows with an automatic hand, energy flowing out of a great bowlful of anger in the centre of his body, running down his right arm in a charge of very high voltage. The blows struck at his mother and at all women, at Pauline and Clare and Judy and Mrs Griffiths. From the first blow he was blind, dealing out anger mindlessly and unseeing, doing what all the rapes had been about.

Muriel's screams became moans, then grunts. It was when they ceased, when the silence came, that he opened his eyes. He continued, however, to beat the gun against its target, though that target was no longer solid but a pulpy mass. He was aware, too, that in order to continue this frenzied pounding he had fallen on to his knees. A warm sticky wetness covered him and his hands were glutinous with it. He rolled on to the floor, rolled away from her, both hands clutching the wet slippery gun.

The first thing he did was cover up the body. It was a dreadful sight. He couldn't bear it. He picked up the hearthrug that lay in front of the electric fire, a thin worn vaguely Turkish-patterned thing, and threw it over the bloody mass that had been Muriel. When she was hidden from his sight he felt less as if the end of the world had come. He was able to breathe again. But as he stood there, holding on to the back of the chair Muriel had always sat in, he did ask himself how it was possible for men to do murder and afterwards not die or go mad but carry on with their lives, making their escape, covering their tracks, denying, forgetting. He asked himself and he had no sooner asked than he was doing these things, turning off the electric heater, closing the door, climbing the stairs.

In the pier glass in Muriel's bedroom he caught sight of his reflection and gave an involuntary cry. He had known there was blood on his hands and he meant immediately to wash, but this he had not expected. The sight of himself frightened him. He was splashed with blood and soaked in blood as if he had plunged his arms and face into a bowl of it like some wallowing butcher. The cotton padded jacket was dark with blood, his shirt red with it, and a great dark stain spread across the front of his jeans as if from a wound in his own body. It was so horrible that there and then he began stripping off his clothes, feeling the kind of panic that made him in his haste rip cloth and tear off buttons. The blood had seeped through to his skin, thin, pale and dabbled like meat juice. He staggered down the passage to the bathroom, retching and sobbing.

Washing would be ineffectual; only a total cleansing by immersion would do. He filled the bath, kneeling on the floor with his head pressed against the cold enamel while the water flowed in. Whatever device heated the water in this house Muriel had kept turned low and it was a tepid bath that he had, shivering as he soaped himself. Rubbing his body dry on a thin grubby towel, he thought of clothes, he must find clothes to put on.

The bloodstained heap in the bedroom sickened him again. It was as if a second body lay there. He began pulling open drawers, finding only women's underclothes, pink corsets, their elastic sides stretched out of shape, brown lisle stockings and tan-coloured silk stockings, locknit knickers, bloomers rather, in pink and white, petticoats with wide straps and deep round necks. His own nakedness was horribly alien to him, awkward, embarrassing, a source of shyness. Naked, he moved and walked clumsily, and he realized that he had hardly ever in his life been naked for more than a moment or two, except during those hours with Clare. The thought of her made him shut his eyes and clench his hands on the hard edge of the chest of drawers.

Muriel's dressing table contained no male underwear but in the top drawer was a jewel case. Victor left the drawer open and the lid of the jewel case open. He went into the bedroom where he had found the greater part of the money. The chest in this room had Sydney's underwear, what remained of it, in its third drawer. Victor put on old man's white cotton underpants, yellow with age, reeking of camphor, an Aertex vest, a pair of matted navy blue socks darned with brown. The bottom drawer was still half full of money, mostly pound notes. He took them. In the next bedroom he emptied another drawer of five-pound notes. Back in Muriel's bedroom he opened the wardrobe and emptied out all the handbags. They contained hundreds of pounds.

Victor dressed himself in a suit of Sydney's in light brown tweed and a cream cotton shirt he found hanging on a hanger with the price tag still on it. How ancient must it be, yet never worn? Sydney had paid two pounds nine shillings and eleven pence three farthings for it. Dressed, Victor felt better, he felt clean and sane and as if to continue with life, some sort of life, would be possible. In Muriel's jewel case the ring with the dome of diamonds lay on top of a pile of gold chains and glass bead necklaces. He put it in his pocket and replaced the case in the drawer. The money he stuffed into his pockets until they bulged with it. The nightdress case dog, pink nylon viscera looping out of its belly, watched him with dead glass eyes.

Why shouldn't he clear the house entirely of money? He might as well have it all now. From the cupboard where the gun had been he took a small brown leather case of the sort that his father had used to call an attaché case and stuffed the money into it. He searched all the bedrooms, the fourth one as well, the one he hadn't been into before, and he found notes everywhere, in a plastic carrier bag under a pillow, two tenners under the base of a lamp, a bundle of fivers in the firegrate basket, tucked under a soot-powdered silver paper fan. There was almost too much money to go into the case and it was with difficulty that he fastened the clasps.

The house had grown dark, darker than its normal daytime twilight. Victor had forgotten about time but he thought it must be evening. He looked at his watch and saw that it was not quite three. All this earthquake had taken place in less than an hour.

It was pouring with rain, a dense glittering rain, straight as glass rods. Victor went downstairs, noticing when he reached the bottom how, on his way up, he had left bloody footprints on the hall carpet, footprints which faded and grew indistinct as they mounted the stairs. The rain would wash his shoes clean, cleanse the pale leather of those dark splashes.

The hallstand was hung with coats piled one on top of the other. It had been like that for as long as he had known it. Mixed up with and supported by the coats were a couple of umbrellas. By unhooking the topmost coat, Victor caused the whole accumulation to subside, sinking in a heap to the floor. From among it he pulled a man's raincoat, Sydney's presumably, left here when it was taken off for the last time a decade ago. It was a trenchcoat, black and shiny, of some plastic or rubberized material, and Victor chose it because it looked totally waterproof. He put it on and did the belt up. It was a bit long for him but otherwise it fitted.

He remembered the key, though not where he had left it. Among his clothes? In there with the body? To replace it under the tortoise would in any case be an impossible task. He also remembered the gun. With closed eyes he opened the living-room door and when he opened them he knew that, contrary to the laws of nature and experience, he had hoped to see Muriel sitting in her chair, scissors in hand, the electric element on. As it was, the rug hid the worst of it, and no blood splashes had reached the walls. He crept across the carpet past the dental plate and the teacup, picked up the gun by its barrel between fastidiously extended forefinger and thumb. It was gummy with clotting blood. This was, in a way, the worst part of all, closing the door again, carrying the gun to the kitchen and washing it under the cold tap, seeing the clots swirl in the water and stick at the plug hole, thinking inescapably that it was of this stuff that he too was formed.

'Whose blood is that?' – my own.

He hadn't wanted to remember those words. He pushed them away, dried the gun on Muriel's grubby teacloth, stuck it into the raincoat's right-hand pocket. The rain made a glass wall beyond the porch. Victor stepped outside, put up the umbrella and closed the door behind him. Jenny next door's car was parked outside her house, which it hadn't been when he came. Victor remembered something, that it was Saturday and Jenny and her husband went shopping on Saturdays. No doubt they had been at the shops when he arrived and had returned while he was – upstairs. They would have things with them they had bought for Muriel, as soon as the rain stopped would come to look for the key . . .

Probably they had already seen him. Jenny had told him she missed nothing of what went on in the street. Standing by the gate, at the foot of the stone hillside, Victor understood that it was too late to cover his tracks. As soon as anyone entered that house it would be known who Muriel's killer was. He felt calm, caught in an irrevocable destiny. All he could do was postpone the discovery of the body.

He mounted a similar flight of steps, through similar

escarpments, spars and outcroppings, pulled a similar bellpull, though setting this one in motion resulted in a chime such as a clock makes at the half-hour. Jenny came to the door. He saw the look of Clare again, a debased, spoiled Clare, and he had a sensation of something falling out of his body, leaving him hollow.

'Hallo, Vic, I didn't recognize you for a minute. You do look smart. All got up like a dog's dinner.'

Sunday-go-to-meetings . . .

'She said to fetch the stuff you got her.'

The days of finding an ability to express himself were over. He was inarticulate again, half dumb.

'There was only teabags and a Swiss roll, Vic. You want to come in a minute? OK, if you're pressed for time.' She was away a few seconds, came back with two paperbags. 'Here you are then, but I can easily pop them in later myself.' He saw that she was looking at his shoes, grey shoes into which the blood had soaked in great black patches.

'She's not too good. She doesn't want to be disturbed.'

'Right. I can take a hint. On your bike, Vic. I'll be seeing you.'

Because she might be watching he took the two paperbags round the back of the house. And left them on the kitchen window sill to the depredations of the rain. Tomorrow or the next day, he thought, Jenny next door would find Muriel's body. He walked home, carrying the suitcase full of money, and it wasn't until he was nearly there that he asked himself what he was going back to Mrs Griffiths's house *for*?

From the corner of Tolleshunt Avenue he saw the police car. Victor was calm still and he knew very well nobody could yet know about the murder of Muriel. The police had called on him for some other reason, the usual reason. They were still pursuing inquiries about the Red Fox, or else the woman in Epping Forest had complained. He hesitated and as he waited two men, one of them the detective constable he had dubbed Distressed Leather, came out of Mrs Griffiths's house and got into the car. Even then he thought it wasn't going to move off, but at last it did, sending up a spray of water out of the overflowing gutter.

They would be back, of course, and very soon. He dreaded meeting Mrs Griffiths or the man who complained about his violent nights. But there was no one. Victor climbed the stairs and let himself into his room. There he changed his shoes, uncaring of the grey ones which he left behind for the police eventually to find. He opened Sydney's attaché case and put into it the one thing he cared about taking with him: Clare's photograph.

No, there was one other thing – the wheelchair.

Victor folded the brown blanket and laid it on the seat. He banged the door behind him, having taken a last look at the cigarette-burn pattern round the bamboo table, the ravioli linoleum and the green rugs, the television set on which most of his parents' money had gone. He bumped the wheelchair down the stairs. Outside the front door he got into it and covered his knees with the rug. The rain had thinned to a drizzle. Victor propelled himself along the street towards Twyford Avenue, down the wet puddled pavement, under the dark green heavy-foliaged trees that dripped water denser than raindrops. The suitcase with the money in it and Clare's photograph were on his lap under the rug.

Just as he reached the corner the police car came back, slowed, and passed him. He was not Victor Jenner but a handicapped man in a wheelchair. About a mile from Mrs Griffiths's house, when he had manoeuvred the wheelchair to the limit of his strength, he got out of it and noticed something he had not seen before, that had not occurred to him before. It would fold up. He folded it up and, when a taxi came, took the folded wheelchair into the back with him.

17

Victor lay on the bed in his hotel room. This was in Leytonstone, about halfway between Acton and Theydon Bois. The taxi driver had refused to take him any further and Victor had been too tired to think about hire cars or tube trains. While he had been in prison tourism in London had vastly increased and hotels like this one had been opened all over the inner and outer suburbs, conversions of big old houses they mostly were, charging much lower rates than those in central London. Not that the cost need have bothered Victor. He was carrying with him thousands of pounds in his suitcase – how much he didn't know, he was too tired to count. Enough, anyway, more than enough, to find a place for him and Clare to live in, to set up a business or to go abroad if she would prefer that.

There was a phone in this ground-floor back room but it was useless phoning her. David would be sure to answer. Much better to leave it till tomorrow, when he would go there with the money and the gun. It was still early in the evening but he had stripped off Sydney's suit and lay in Sydney's curious old underwear, wondering if he ought to dress again and go out to eat, but each time he thought of food he remembered rinsing the clots of blood off the Beretta and nausea came up into his throat.

His three possessions furnished the room: the gun, the wheelchair, the attaché case full of money. The hotel management had provided a built-in cupboard, a built-in counter with mirror, bed and television set. Victor lay watching television. The news came on, and two or three hours later came on again. But there was nothing about Muriel, nor would there be until Jenny next door went in

– perhaps not till next Saturday, he thought. He rolled over and fell asleep.

David's phone number had gone out of his head and the only record of it he had he had blacked out on the underside of Mrs Griffiths's staircase. Directory Enquiries gave it to him and Victor phoned the number at about ten in the morning, resolving to replace the receiver if David answered. But no one answered. He wrote the number down on the inside of the attaché case. They were out for a walk probably. It was a fine day, the clouds and rain of Saturday dispersed, the sky clear and the sun shining. Victor looked out of his window on to old London suburban gardens, shorn weedless grass, pear trees, a yellow brick wall. He couldn't bring Clare here.

One of the wounds on his chest had gone a purplish colour and the area around it was swollen. A bit of glass was probably inside there but it hurt too much to squeeze. If he got blood poisoning, David would be responsible, he thought, and in his mind's eye he saw David leaning forward out of that wheelchair, lunging at him with a sliver of glass. But he needn't worry about it, for that was something Clare would deal with as soon as they were together. He asked Directory Enquiries for the number of the Post House Hotel at Epping, phoned them and booked a double room for that night.

Trains were less frequent on Sundays and he waited twenty minutes on the platform at Leytonstone, holding the folded wheelchair, carrying the attaché case, the raincoat slung over his left shoulder, for it was too warm to wear it. On the village green at Theydon children were playing ball games, people were walking dogs. He looked for David and Clare, thinking they might be walking Sally but then he remembered that Sally mustn't go out yet, not until she was past her hardpad and distemper immunization.

Victor wheeled the chair along. It was too heavy to carry. He laid the attaché case, the brown travelling rug and the raincoat across the seat. Although it was a hot day, all the windows in Sans Souci were closed. He looked through the windows, looked through the side window of the garage and saw that the Land Rover was gone. At the back of the house the french windows were closed and the blue and white sunshade furled. He noticed something else. It upset him disproportionately, yet there was no reason to be upset by something which he could remember his mother once telling him was normal for this time of the year, for the end of June. There were no flowers out. The spring flowers were over and the roses cut, the summer ones and late roses not yet in bloom and the garden was all green, just green.

Victor banged on the french windows to make the dog bark but there was no sound from inside. So they had taken her with them wherever they had gone. He decided to go back to Leytonstone and wait there, come back again this evening. The wheelchair was a nuisance but he couldn't very well just leave it in the street. At a newsagent he bought two Sunday papers and read them in the train. In a pub in Leytonstone he had sandwiches for lunch, a glass of wine and then another, aiming to sleep the afternoon away. The idea of getting mildly drunk appealed to him and he had two double whiskies in a pub further along the High Road, a place where urban blight and perhaps a threat of road widening had closed shops and offices and where abandoned houses had their windows boarded up. There was something desolate about the place on this hot sultry day, few people in the streets but lots of traffic and a reek of engine vapours. A long way in the distance, perhaps over Epping Forest, thunder rumbled.

The mixture of drinks went to his head, bringing him a carefree feeling. He passed a woman in a wheelchair being pushed along by an elderly husband, so he got into his own wheelchair, covered his knees and propelled himself along. People got out of his way, cast him the familiar looks of sympathy, embarrassment, guilt and fear, took a self-conscious pride in assisting him across roads. Because he was confused and muzzy-headed from the drink it never occurred to him to wonder (until he was inside there) what the people at the Fillebrook Hotel would think about the man who walked out of their front door that morning and returned in the afternoon a cripple. But a different staff was on duty. The girl in reception reacted of course, but not with astonishment or anger, rather by rushing to open further an already open pair of glass doors and running ahead of him to unlock his room door as if he had lost the use of his hands as well as his legs.

He lay down on the bed and slept off the drinks he had had, waking with a headache, the kind that seems to prick the inside of the scalp. Before he went to sleep he must have switched the television on, for it was on now, a congregation of devout, earnest-looking people singing hymns. He switched channels on to London Weekend, got what appeared to be a detective series and turned the sound right down. Dialling the Theydon Bois number, he thought that the best thing might be to ask the hotel the name of a local minicab company, then get them to drive him out there and pick Clare up. The phone was answered and David said hallo. Of course he wouldn't think it was Victor because for the first time he wasn't calling from a pay phone.

'I'd like to speak to Clare Conway, please.' Victor put on a higher pitched, 'posher' voice than his own and David, though suspicious, seemed deceived. 'This is Michael.'

'Michael who?'

'Faraday,' said Victor.

There was silence. He thought it was working all right and then he heard a whispering and Clare's voice say, 'My God!'

Victor felt the corner of his mouth begin twitching with live flesh. Clare came to the phone and her voice was strange with a tremor in it.

'Victor, where are you? Please tell us where you are.'

Us? He said nothing. His eyes had wandered to the silent television on whose screen had appeared Muriel's house, a Tudor keep standing like a fortress on its rocks, but not a fortress, not inviolable, its front door standing open. He moved the receiver slowly away from his mouth, his arm gradually falling, Clare's voice speaking out of it his name over and over.

'Victor, Victor . . .'

The picture on the screen had been replaced by another, by his own photograph, the one he had given to Clare.

Her betrayal stunned him. For quite a long time he was unable to move. He was just capable of putting the receiver back into its rest but not of turning up the sound on the television. What more could it tell him, anyway, beyond the facts that Muriel's body had been found and the police were looking for him? Clare must have given the police his picture. No doubt David had compelled her to do this but just the same . . . He would have died before he gave up hers, Victor thought. That was where she and David had been all day, with the Acton police, for Muriel's body must have been found either last night or this morning.

Could they trace his call? Victor didn't know, though he had a vague idea calls from private phones couldn't be traced. Was a hotel number private? He put on the raincoat, got into the wheelchair, covered his knees with the rug and laid the attaché case on the rug. In the right-hand pocket of the raincoat the Beretta felt heavy and bulky. It wouldn't work but it was a comfort to him.

Something told him that this would be his last chance to make a phone call for a long time. He dialled the Theydon Bois number, knowing they would answer, knowing they were longing to talk to him. It was David again.

'You know who this is.'

'Victor, please listen to me . . .'

'*You* listen to me. I've got a gun and it's real. You'd better believe me. It's a Beretta and it's for real. You make them believe that if you don't want someone else getting what you got.'

He crashed down the phone. The photograph he had given Clare – the memory of that giving made him wince with pain – was an excellent likeness. He had a sudden mental picture of the reception girl watching the London Weekend six-thirty news in some back office, seeing that face and then coming out into the hall and seeing it again. The wheelchair protected him, of course; in some subtle way the wheelchair even changed his face. He emerged from the room. The hall was empty. With no idea of where to go, Victor bumped the wheelchair down the single step and out on to the pavement and, turning in the opposite direction from the trains, the railway underpass and the High Road, wheeled himself into a hinterland of Victorian streets that led nowhere he knew.

After a time he came to the forest. He had vaguely known that Epping Forest reached all the way down here and he understood that he was facing the southernmost tip of it, urban forest with little grass and no flowers, and only brown trodden earth underfoot. He began propelling the wheelchair along the Whipps Cross Road in a westerly direction. A police car passed him quite slowly. Victor now remembered that he had checked into the Fillebrook Hotel in his own name and understood that it would only be a matter of time, perhaps of minutes, before the management realized who their last night's guest had been. He must get out of the district, think where ultimately to go and what to do. The money would take care of him. With money you could do anything, go anywhere.

Taxi drivers who had been out all day wouldn't have seen television. Victor was afraid to get up out of the wheelchair in the open like this. It would be a suspect act, drawing attention to himself. He turned into a side street, got out of the chair and folded it up, dragged it behind him out into the Whipps Cross Road and hailed a taxi. The driver looked at him indifferently, without interest. He seemed disappointed that Victor wanted to go to Finchley and not central London.

If he showed signs that he knew or suspected, Victor thought, if he spoke in a suspicious way on that radio phone of his, he would press the barrel of the gun into his back and command him to drive to some deserted country place. But nothing like that happened. It had become a gloomy grey evening, stuffy and close. A fork of lightning flickered in the heavy clouds on the horizon that Victor thought was Muswell Hill. That sharp point sticking up was the spire of St James, Muswell Hill. He would go there. No one would expect him to go there.

The storm broke late that evening. In the hotel Victor had found in Archduke Avenue, Muswell Hill, television sets were not provided in the rooms, nor were phones. But they had ground-floor rooms vacant in a single-storey annexe at the rear. Victor checked in as David Swift. The management were solicitous, helpful, opening doors for him, running ahead to check that the room door was wide enough to admit the wheelchair.

Everywhere up here, even ground-floor rooms, had panoramic views over London. He sat in the wheelchair and watched the storm fight its way across a sky of cloud plains and cloud mountains. He hadn't eaten since lunchtime but he didn't want to eat. A feeling of malaise had begun to take hold of him in the taxi and was still with him, not the nausea he so often felt in times of stress, but a light-headedness, something like fever. Perhaps it was only that he had drunk too much at lunchtime. He was aware too of a rapid pulse. Before he went to bed he felt in the pocket of the raincoat to make sure the gun was there but he must have felt in the left-hand side, for there was nothing in the pocket but a half-used packet of mints. The gun was in the other side all right.

Victor slept and dreamed of David. David was well and walking again, back in the police force and put in charge of the hunt for Muriel's killer. He didn't suspect Victor, in fact he wanted to discuss it in all its aspects with Victor, talk it through. The case must be concluded by tomorrow because David was getting married tomorrow. His bride came into the room in her wedding dress but when she lifted her veil and showed her face it was not Clare but Rosemary Stanley. Victor woke up with a feeling of stiffness in his neck and jaw. It must have been the way he had been lying on this hard mattress and latex pillow. There was something ridiculous, he thought, in a man dreaming of weddings. Only women dreamed of weddings. He slept again, but very fitfully, and got up at seven.

The stiffness in his face and neck was still there. It was probably something to do with this chorea he had been having, though there were no jumping muscles this morning. His pulse still raced. He dressed in the same underwear and shirt, having no other, but making up his mind to go out and buy some as soon as the shops opened. It had rained all night and the day was heavy and humid, cold-looking.

He had no desire to eat and fancied anyway that it might be a painful process, the way his jaw felt. On the table in the hallway lay the morning papers. Victor, slowly propelling himself in the wheelchair, took a *Daily Telegraph* back to his room.

The murder had made the front page. There was a photograph of Muriel as Victor remembered her from when he was a teenager, at the time of her marriage, a moon-faced smiling Muriel wearing thick make-up and pearl studs in her ears. Jupp had found the body. There was an account of some of the things he had said, such as that he had been going to marry Muriel, that he was 'devoted' to her. On Saturday night he had gone to her house – to see her, yes, but principally to fetch something he had left behind last time. He had a key to the house and had let himself in at about eight in the evening. The first thing he saw was a footprint in blood on the hall floor, only he hadn't of course known then that it was blood.

Victor wondered what it was that Jupp had left behind and why the *Telegraph* didn't say what it was. Surely it would have been more usual to say 'left my umbrella behind' or 'left my scarf'. Perhaps it *had* been an umbrella and that was the one Victor had taken and abandoned in Mrs Griffiths's house.

His knees covered, the attaché case with him because he was afraid to leave it behind, Victor manoeuvred the wheelchair along Muswell Hill in search of underwear, socks and a shirt or two. Shop assistants were attentive, polite, one rather embarrassed. He bought the clothes he wanted but the buying of them brought him none of the pleasure he had felt when he had spent money on his grey jacket, his suit and those grey shoes. His head throbbed and he felt as if he were at a remove from reality, out of touch somehow, his grasp of life lost. Even the realization that Clare was gone from him for ever, that he would never see her again, brought him a resigned sadness rather than pain. Perhaps this was insanity, that might be what it was, the prison years they said drove you mad catching up with him at last.

At the pedestrian crossing in Fortis Road opposite the cinema he waited with four or five other people for the traffic to stop. Then a terrible thing happened. Coming towards him from the other side as soon as the cars had pulled up were a man and woman arm-in-arm, and the man was Kevin, Jupp's son-in-law.

He glanced at Victor, then stared hard. Victor had no choice, there in the middle of the road, but to move towards him. They came up to each other, eye to eye, but there was no recognition in Kevin's face. He had thought Victor was Victor – and then thought better of it. The wheelchair had disguised him, had kept him from discovery, would save his life. Kevin didn't even look back. He said something to the woman Victor supposed was Jupp's daughter, and the two of them went into a shop. Victor remembered now that Kevin had told him he lived in Muswell Hill.

Being in the wheelchair made him invisible or, rather, changed him into someone else. He understood that for safety's sake he must confine himself to it, become a handicapped person, as David was.

18

Back in his room, Victor counted the money. There was something over five thousand pounds. He had been right in guessing that Muriel kept thousands of pounds in the house; probably there had originally been as much as seven thousand. He couldn't be certain of the exact sum he had brought away with him, for he seemed to have lost his powers of concentration. Whatever ailed him it couldn't still be half a bottle of wine and two whiskies from lunchtime yesterday. If you could get flu in July, it might be flu he had, for he felt hot and then shivery by turns. He put the money back into the attaché case but set Clare's photograph up on the table by his bed.

It would soon be twenty-four hours since he had eaten, yet he had no desire for food. He shivered but he felt hopeful, cheerful even. The money would last a good while, so long as he got out of these hotels and found a room. It would have to be a ground-floor room, of course, and the work he got would have to be work suitable for a disabled man, but there were schemes catering for such people, he had read. Getting a job as a handicapped person might be *easier*, life in this wheelchair as David Swift might be altogether easier and happier.

Victor didn't dare have a bath. It would be too complicated and dangerous trying to get the wheelchair along the passage, down steps, into the bathroom. Instead he washed standing up at the basin. The wound on his chest had an ugly inflamed look about it and the edges of it gaped open, ragged snarling lips. He knew he should have had it stitched but it was too late now.

There was no mirror over the basin, the only mirror was

on the inside of the clothes-cupboard door, so he dressed in his new underwear and shirt before starting to shave.

When he opened the cupboard and looked in the mirror he got a shock. It wasn't just on account of the wheelchair that Kevin had failed to recognize him. His face had changed. There was something skull-like, rigid, about it, while the eyeballs seemed to start from his head. His dark skin could never have become really pale but it was livid rather, olivine, deathly sick. It was no wonder after what he had been through, he told himself, no wonder at all.

The evening paper would be on the street by now. It was midday. Although it was warm, Victor was shivering with cold and he put the raincoat on. He told himself that he must not only look disabled but think himself into the *persona* of a disabled man, resigning himself to the confinement of the wheelchair, allowing no possibility of separation from it. It must become as much a part of his mobile self as his shoes were.

Fear of meeting Kevin again made him turn the wheelchair in the other direction, towards Highgate Wood. He came to some shops, one of which was a restaurant where he thought he might have lunch. In the newsagent's next door he bought the *Standard*, *What Car?* and *Here's Health*, this last because he thought his condition might be due to not eating properly and it might tell him what he ought to eat. He manoeuvred the wheelchair a little way into the wood and sat reading the *Standard*. It said that the police were very anxious to interview Victor Michael Jenner, Muriel Faraday's nephew, who had left his home in Tolleshunt Avenue, Acton, and spent the night following the murder at an hotel in Leytonstone, E11. Victor remembered that he had registered there as Michael Faraday, seeing this now as reckless behaviour. However, he was safe enough here, protected by the wheelchair. A lengthy description of him followed, so lengthy as to be continued on an inside page, but Victor didn't bother to turn the page. The print danced and formed black and white wavy patterns, chevrons and parabolas. His hands felt too feeble to make the effort of holding it and it slid from his lap.

Victor watched it fall on to the ground and the magazines after it and he let them lie, lacking the strength to retrieve them. This area of woodland, though dusty and buzzing with flies, yet reminded him of the forest at Theydon where he had attacked the girl long ago, where David and Clare had taken him, where he had tried to rape the woman who sat making up her face and who, breaking the mirror under her in the leaf mould, in the fibrous, spore-ridden, mealy earth, had stabbed . . . Or had David done that in the garden? Or Clare, with a sliver from the broken water jug? Or he himself? Victor couldn't remember. His eyes closed. He saw before them feverish images, curtains blowing ceiling-high at a broken window, his mother's face and Muriel's, blending, separating, a train roaring out of a black tunnel, and he fancied he could smell honeysuckle. A stuffed peacock perched on a sofa screamed and his mother's voice crooned to Mr Sandman to bring her a dream . . .

He awoke and forced himself to move, though he was weak and disorientated. Eating would be impossible. The little restaurant was called Terrarium and he could see a big green glass tank inside which probably contained trout from which customers chose one to be caught and cooked for them. It seemed to Victor a distant outlandish prospect, a custom from another world. Wearily and slowly he made his way back to the hotel. It was no more than two or three hundred yards but it seemed a mile and sometimes he had the illusion he was travelling backwards, as in one of those frustrating dreams, the kind in which everything is geared to stop you going where you want to go and attaining what you want to reach.

The television was on in a kind of lounge place, watched by a single old woman. For a moment he thought it was the old woman in the train, the one who played guards and travelled with a guinea pig, for she was dressed the same and wearing the same woolly hat. But when he looked again his vision seemed to clear and he saw that he had been quite mistaken, that she was even smart with pretty white hair and a blue dress on. He was steering the wheelchair towards the open door when a woman's voice called, 'Mr Swift!'

How strange that there should be a real Swift staying here, he thought.

'Excuse me, Mr Swift.'

The receptionist spoke it almost into his ear this time. She must think him deaf or mad.

'We found this on the floor of your room.'

It was a diamond ring. He was going to deny ownership but, as he stared at the dome of diamonds, he seemed to see Muriel's hand form around it, her dirty-nailed wrinkled finger slipped through it. Hadn't he once thought it should adorn some fair young hand?

'Thanks,' he said through jaws that had grown stiff. He was beginning to find it difficult to open his mouth.

When he was counting the money he must have pulled the ring out of the attaché case with the notes. He sat for a while, gazing unseeing at the television, his head throbbing with pain. Now he was aware of a kind of spasm in his chest, though a long way from the wound itself. Perhaps he should lie down, try to sleep. A young man had taken over from the girl receptionist while Victor was in the lounge and Victor fancied that he gave him a long and searching look.

'Everything all right, Mr Swift?'

It was the kind of question a hotel manager would ask a disabled guest and Victor decided he had been imagining things. He nodded and went on to his room. The wound looked the same, angry, festering, swollen. It must be blood poisoning he had, so what he had said to David had not been far wrong. That would account for the racing pulse and the fever. His forehead felt burning hot and there was sweat on his face. He wondered what his temperature was, very high no doubt, a hundred and two or three, as it had been long ago when he had had scarlet fever and his mother had laid her hand on his forehead like this. He lay on the bed and tried to concentrate on future plans, ignoring his fluttering heartbeat. If he moved out of London and used half the money to buy a car, once the fuss had died down he could leave the wheelchair and set up in the minicab business. Was it possible, even now, that Clare might join him? If only he could see her, if only he could *explain* . . . Her photograph seemed to grow very large, her face to float out of it with that mysterious smile, that gaze fixed on a point far beyond him.

He wasn't well, of course, hence these delusions, imaginings, near-hallucinations. Perhaps it was due to malnutrition. He read an article in *Here's Health* about harmful food additives and another one about mineral deficiency in contemporary diets. Not much the wiser, puzzled by his own physical sensations, never before experienced, he fell asleep.

The sky had been growing dark with storm clouds before he lay down on the bed and when he woke up it was raining. Victor looked at Muriel's diamond ring, which he had put on the bedside table beside Clare's photograph. That would have been a better ring to give Clare than the little one with the clasped hands but he couldn't see his way to giving it to her, he couldn't even think at the moment of an approach to her. What dim light there was in the room the cone of diamonds caught and flashed, twenty diamonds and a large single one in the centre, Victor counted. There had been nothing in the *Standard* about a missing ring (or, indeed, about anything missing from Muriel's house) so it might be quite safe to sell it. What a piece of luck if it should turn out to be worth a lot, thousands and thousands, say.

Victor felt stiff all over, not just his face. He must expect that, he thought, as the result of sitting in the wheelchair all the time and exerting muscles in his arms hitherto not much used. In time he would get used to it, he would adjust. It probably wasn't improving things to starve himself either. He must eat. He must force himself to eat even if he didn't much want to.

The temperature had dropped and it was cold for a July evening. Victor put on the raincoat, wondering for the first time what had possessed Sydney to purchase and wear such an unlikely garment. It was plastic, presumably, not leather, a grainy-ridged surface to the black shiny fabric, and no doubt absolutely waterproof. Sydney had surely been no more than five feet nine and it must have come down nearly to his ankles. Victor came out of his room, finding the propulsion of the wheelchair rather heavy-going. People went in for races in these things, he had seen them on television – how could they do it? His arms felt weary.

The girl receptionist was back on duty. In the lounge the old lady and a couple of German tourists, a man and a woman, were watching the weather forecast that followed the six o'clock news. Frontal systems moving across the Atlantic, a deep depression to the west of Ireland, more rain to come. Between the reception desk and the front door was a circle of wicker chairs with a glass table in the middle of them covered with papers. A man Victor hadn't seen before sat in one of the chairs, reading the ABC London Street Atlas, or at any rate looking at it. He glanced up indifferently as the wheelchair passed.

Under the dripping trees Victor proceeded up the Muswell Hill Road towards the little restaurant called Terrarium. It had been a chambermaid, he supposed, who had found Muriel's ring on the floor of his room. How much more of his property had been examined, investigated? Had she, for instance, found the gun? It had been in the raincoat pocket, hanging up at that time inside the clothes cupboard. Victor put his hand into the right-hand pocket and felt the gun there. He manipulated the wheels, rhythmically pushing on the hoops of chrome, decided he had better transfer money from the attaché case to his pockets before he entered the restaurant, not risk drawing attention to himself by revealing all those wads of notes while seated at a table.

The doorway was only just wide enough to admit the wheelchair. A waitress pushed furniture aside so that he could reach a table. Victor felt in the left-hand pocket of the raincoat where he had put two ten-pound notes and his hand encountered the half-used packet of mints. Immediately he knew whose this raincoat was. It hadn't belonged to Sydney but to Jupp. This was the item Jupp had left in Muriel's house and had gone back to fetch on Saturday evening, had forgotten on a previous occasion because it had been raining when he arrived and not when he left. The newspaper had not specified its nature because the raincoat was so distinctive-looking, because they guessed that Muriel's killer would wear it and could be identified by it.

Victor broke into a sweat and his body was seized by cramps as in some immobilising dream. Luckily he was alone in the restaurant but for two girls who sat studying the menu. His instinct was to take off the raincoat but this could only be done with great difficulty while sitting down. Victor asked the waitress where the men's room was. Through that door, down the passage, there were just two shallow steps. The smell of food made him feel sick, he knew he would be unable to eat anything. He must remove the raincoat, hide it, go. As he began to move the chair again he felt something terrible happening to his face, the jaws clamping shut, his eyebrows dragged up as a frown corrugated his forehead.

In the men's room he struggled out of the chair, took off the raincoat and tried to roll it up. He transferred the gun and the notes to his jacket pocket and left the raincoat in a heap on the floor. The mirror above the washbasin showed him his frowning face and his teeth bared in a ferocious grimace. I am going mad, he thought. Why do I look like this? As he willed his face to relax, the rigid muscles of his neck to slacken, his body went without warning into a violent convulsion. His back arched as if it would split in two, his arms and legs shot in all directions. Victor gasped with pain and tried to cling to the edge of the washbasin. It was awful the tricks fear and shock could play on you.

Trembling and tense, shuddering, he had seated himself once more in the wheelchair when the door opened and the man who had been sitting in the hallway of the hotel reading the London Atlas came in. He nodded to Victor and said good evening. Victor tried to nod but he couldn't speak. Back in the passage, moving towards the door that led into the dining area, he wondered if he should try to see a doctor. If he saw a doctor privately there would be no need of medical cards and National Insurance numbers. With the footrest of the wheelchair he pushed the door open, entering the restaurant for the first time from this angle. Ahead of him, on a table that divided the diners from the cash desk, stood the green glass tank, lit from behind by bright tubular lights, furnished with feathery fronds and weed streamers, swarming with green reptilian shell-backed creatures.

He closed his eyes. He drew a long noisy breath.

'They're terrapins,' he heard the waitress say.

A kindly tone, a gratuitous piece of information offered to the disabled, who from the look on his face was also very likely mentally wanting. Show the poor man our menagerie, out terrarium . . .

He curled his fists on the chrome hoops. She was moving the chair nearer to the tank to show him. Victor had no control left. He staggered to his feet out of the wheelchair, hearing gasps, hearing one of the girls in the corner give a cry. The waitress was staring at him open-mouthed, her eyes round, her hands still on the handles of the chair. He grabbed the attaché case in his left hand. The door from the passage opened and the man who had been in the hotel foyer came in, stopped, took in everything, understood as only a policeman sent there to understand could do. He said, 'Victor Jenner?'

Victor pulled out the gun and pointed it at the waitress. She gave a whimpering cry. She was a small dark girl, Indian perhaps, or partly Indian, olive-skinned with black eyes in dark eye sockets. The policeman side-stepped between the tables, wary-eyed, tense.

Victor said, 'It's a real gun. You'd better believe me.'

That was what he tried to say. Something else came out, some broken mumble, some gagged jerky grunting that was all his locked jaw would allow to escape. But it didn't matter what he said. The gun spoke for him, the gun was enough. Behind him, behind that swarming dreadful green tank, he was aware of more people coming, standing, their breath audible. The two young girls had got under their table, under the overhanging cloth.

'Put that gun down, Jenner. That isn't going to do you any good.'

Because he knew he couldn't, because it was all right to make this threat this time, Victor said, 'I'll shoot her in the back.' The words came out as a series of grinding jerks. He turned the girl round, spun her with a stiff left hand, stuck the barrel on the Beretta into her thin back, her young knobby spine. 'Out of that door,' he said, and because she couldn't understand, pushed her with the gun towards the passage door. There was no way, ever, he could pass that tank, not if his life depended upon it.

Not one of the others moved. They believed in the gun. The waitress was crying with fear, tears flowing down her cheeks. She stumbled to the door, sobbed because she had tried without success to push it open.

'Pull it, pull it!' a woman screamed.

Her mother? Her employer? Victor pulled the door himself, spun round because he thought he sensed the policeman make a move. Everyone was still as statues, the woman who had shouted crying, a man holding her. Victor prodded the girl through the doorway, pulled the door shut behind him and turned the key. He said to the girl, 'I need a doctor, I have to see a doctor,' but God knew what sound came out, not that, not what he had said.

She stumbled on, holding her hands up now, like a hostage in a film, an old film, kicked open another door that led into a room full of metal chairs and trays. There was a way from here into a back yard, through french windows, bolted top and bottom, and beyond the yard rain falling, a grey board fence, the tree trunks and gloomy aisles of the wood. Victor said to the girl, 'Open those doors, windows, whatever you call them. You open them.'

He turned her round to him, pointing the gun. She gave a terrified gasp.

'Do it. Didn't you hear me?'

'I can't understand you, I don't know what you're saying!'

'Don't move.'

He could hear sound now, pounding feet, a shaking of the house, the sound of someone running at a door, using powerful shoulders on it. With the gun he motioned her to a stack of chairs. She shrank up against it. Keeping the gun pointed at her, Victor knelt down to undo the bottom bolt on the french window. A muscular spasm, unheralded, convulsed his body, throwing his arms out and arching his back. He cried out through forcibly clenched teeth, tried to get up and was felled to the floor by his own muscles fighting him.

His back leaped, bounded, jack-knifed, and he thrashed about the floor, still keeping hold of the gun until the most powerful spasm he had yet known snatched it from his hands and flung it across the room in a high arc, where it encountered the glass of one of the windows, smashed it and passed through. Victor reached out, grabbing empty air. The girl crept towards him, whispering. His back arched, whipped, coiled like a spring and his limbs danced. The girl knelt beside him, asking him what was wrong, what was happening to him, what could she do, and the tears she was still shedding fell on to his twitching leaping face.

The door opened just as the series of spasms passed and the policeman who came in stood over him, looking in a kind of hushed horror at the man on the floor whose flesh was fighting him to death.

19

The tortoise moved up the garden path at a steady, measured, unvaryingly slow pace, from where it had spent the afternoon under the shade of the rhododendrons. It had seen or smelt or otherwise sensed the small pile of cos lettuce leaves placed for its delectation on the lowest of the stone steps. The little dog watched it but she was used to it now. Patting its shell and seeing head, limbs and tail recede into the horny dome had ceased to amuse her. It might as well be a mobile stone for all she cared. With renewed vigour she applied herself to her marrow bone.

David Fleeetwood reached down over the side of the wheelchair and patted the dog's head. He and Clare were fast accumulating a menagerie: first Sally, then this tortoise that had wandered in from nowhere two days ago, and this morning a neighbour had offered him a kitten. But Clare had put her foot down there. The gnats were bothering him and he lit a cigarette to keep them off as much as anything. The evening was very warm, the air already taking on that dark blue look of a midsummer dusk. A big white moth had spread its wings flat on the house wall, waiting for the outside lights to come on, waiting to burn itself to death on the sizzling glass.

Clare came out of the house by the french windows. He thought she looked pale and rather tired, but you couldn't really tell in this light. She had a glass in her hand containing what looked like a stiff whisky. She drank too much, not much too much but more than she should. Someone had told her that the other day, she had said, but she hadn't said who.

'Do you want one?'

He shook his head, pointed at his half-empty beer glass.

'Are you going to ring the hospital?' he said.

'I already have.'

Her face told him. She sat down at the table very close to him and took his hand. He didn't look at her. He looked at the tortoise nibbling lettuce leaves.

'Victor died this afternoon,' Clare said. 'About three this afternoon, they said. If he'd got through today there might have been some hope. Apparently people with tetanus sometimes recover if they survive the first four days.'

David said rather violently, 'How the hell did he get tetanus?' He lit another cigarette from the stub of the first. 'That was nonsense about my stabbing him with a piece of glass. I never touched him.'

'I know. It's a mystery. Perhaps it was something which happened that night after he left here. He did tell you he'd had a horrendous night and was lucky to be alive, whatever that meant. If he cut himself somehow . . . They say the soil round here is full of tetanus. I looked up tetanus in a book on bacilli at the hospital. The poison itself is one of the deadliest known. It's excreted by the bacterial cells and carried in the bloodstream to the spinal cord . . .'

David shuddered. 'Don't.'

'There is a sort of irony there, isn't there? If you choose to see it that way.'

'I choose not to. It was the merest accident. It has all been accident, Clare. Victor's shooting me, his seeing my photograph in the paper, taking the train to Epping and seeing where I lived, coming here that night when I was away . . .'

She looked beseechingly at him but it was too dark to see her eyes.

'All accidents. For all we know, his killing the old woman was an accident – or started off that way. There's no answer to it, no pattern. If I've been over it once I've been over it a thousand times, the events that took place in that house in Solent Gardens. I even thought of getting Victor to do a reconstruction of it with me, the two of us trying to recreate the situation in a similar set of rooms with other actors . . .'

He peered closely at her, trying to gauge her response. Her face was in repose, wondering, sad, a little lax and vague from the whisky she had drunk. She held his hand in both hers now.

'I'm serious. I meant it as a catharsis for him as well as me. I thought of us getting together with Bridges maybe, wherever he is now, and perhaps finding Rosemary Stanley, and furnishing the place just as it was down to the pictures on the walls.'

'The pictures on the walls?'

'Oh, yes. It was a nicely furnished house, it was pretty. You know I said, Whose blood is that? because I didn't know it was mine then, I thought what a shame to stain that pale cream carpet, what a waste. There were little pictures all the way down the stairs and on the landing walls. Birds and animals mostly, reproductions of famous prints and engravings. Durer's *Praying Hands* and the one of the hare and of cowslips, and Audubon and Edward Lear.'

'I thought he wrote limericks.'

'He did lithographs as well, of animals in menageries. There was that bat of his, I remember, and the turtle.' David glanced at the tortoise that was making its slow way back to shelter beneath the rhododendrons. 'That one was right in the centre with the praying hands just above it. When I fell I had my eyes fixed on those praying hands. I had this elaborate idea of reconstructing all that, only I wanted to wait until I felt I could – trust Victor. And that time never came.' Gently David disengaged his hands. 'Put the lights on, Clare, will you?'

She got up and went inside the dining room and switched on the lights, one on the edge of the terrace, one on the house wall among the honeysuckle leaves. The moth fluttered off the wall and came to the light to burn its tender white feathery wings.